Regency Romance

Regency Ladies In Love

Arietta Richmond

Dreamstone Publishing © 2019 - 2024

www.dreamstonepublishing.com

ISBN-13: 978-1-922735-33-1

Disclaimer

This is a work of fiction. Names, characters, places, organisations, events, and incidents are either products of the author's imagination or used fictitiously.

Dedication

For everyone who had the grace to be patient while this book, and every other book that I have written, was coming into existence, who provided cups of tea, and food, when the writing would not let me go, and endured countless times being asked for opinions.

For the readers who inspire me to continue writing, by buying my books! Especially for those of you who have taken the time to email me, or to leave reviews, and tell me what you love about my books, and what you'd like to see more of – thank you – I'm listening. I hope that you enjoy my newer series (a number of which feature some appearances by old favourite characters from the His Majesty's Hounds series), just as much as my other books.

For my growing team of beta readers and advance reviewers – it's thanks to you that others can enjoy these books in the best presentation possible!

And for all the writers of Regency Historical Romance, whose books I read, who inspired me to write in this fascinating period.

Introduction

This anthology brings you five of my stories in one collection! Each story is a little more focussed on the heroine, although you'll see both hero and heroine's perspectives.

This is your chance to immerse yourself in Regency reading, and sample stories from various of my series while you do. Each story can be read standalone, but each story also has intertwined relationships with others in the series it represents.

All of these stories are clean.

Book	**Series**
An Enchantress for an Earl	The Elbury Bouquet (6)
Lady Augusta's Letters	Standalone
A Maiden for a Marquess	The Elbury Bouquet (7)
Lord of the Betrayed	Regency Gothic (5)
The Marquess Marries a Twin	The Duke of Traithewood's Legacy (1)

I hope that you enjoy reading this collection of Regency stories! (and if you do, please try some of the other books in the various series – I'm sure that you will love them too!)

Arietta Richmond

Table of Contents

Books by Arietta Richmond

His Majesty's Hounds

Claiming the Heart of a Duke
Giving a Heart of Lace
Enchanting the Duke
Finding the Duke's Heir
Healing Lord Barton
Loving the Bitter Baron
Rescuing the Countess
Attracting the Spymaster
Intriguing the Viscount
Being Lady Harriet's Hero
Redeeming the Marquess
Winning the Merchant Earl
Kissing the Duke of Hearts
Falling for the Earl
Betting on a Lady's Heart
Courting a Spinster for Christmas
Restoring the Earl's Honour
A Scandalous Spring (An additional short story)
The Scent of First Love (an additional short story)
From Soldier Spy to Lord (contains the first three books in one volume)
To Love a Determined Lady (Contains Books 4, 5 and 6 in one volume)
Love Heals a Lord (Contains Books 7, 8 and 9 in one volume)
To Love a Dashing Lord (Contains Books 10, 11, 12, and 13 in one volume)
For a Lady's Honour (Contains Books 14, 15, 16, and 17 in one volume)

A Duke's Daughters – The Elbury Bouquet

A Spinster for a Spy (Lily)
A Bluestocking for a Baron (Rose)
A Minx for a Merchant (Primrose)
A Maiden for a Marquess (Iris)
A Vixen for a Viscount (Hyacinth)
A Diamond for a Duke (Camellia)
An Enchantress for an Earl (Violet)
A Heart for an Heir (Thorne)

The Family Sagas Collections

The Barrington Saga
The Morton Saga
The Dartworth Saga
The Edgeworth Saga
The Windemere Saga
The Chester Saga

The Nettlefold Chronicles

The Duke and the Spinster
A Duke in Autumn
To Wed an Earl
To Dance with the Dangerous Duke
A Christmas Bride for the Duke
The Marquess Elopes
The Scandalous Countess

Lady Canterford's Conspirators (The Mayfair Ladies Poetry Society)

A six book series (coming soon)

The Duke of Traithewood's Legacy

The Marquess Marries a Twin
Lady Musette Ruins a Lord (Coming Soon)

The Regency Gothic Series

Lord of the Storm
Lord of the Darkness
Lord of the Shadows
Lord of the Lost
Lord of the Betrayed

The Regency Scandals Series

The Gift of a Christmas Scandal
Lady Mariel's Scandalous Love
Christmas with *That* Duke
Lord of Dragons (written with Kyrii Rayne)

The Derbyshire Set

A Gift of Love (Prequel short story)
A Devil's Bargain (Prequel short story - coming soon)
The Earl's Unexpected Bride
The Captain's Compromised Heiress
The Viscount's Unsuitable Affair
The Count's Impetuous Seduction
The Rake's Unlikely Redemption
The Marquess' Scandalous Mistress
The Marchioness' Second Chance
A Viscount's Reluctant Passion
Lady Theodora's Christmas Wish
A Remembered Face (Bonus short story – coming soon)
The Duke's Improper Love (coming soon)
A Gentleman's Unconventional Courtship (coming soon)
The Derbyshire Set, Omnibus Edition, Volume 1 (the first three books in one volume.)
The Derbyshire Set, Omnibus Edition, Volume 2 (the second three books in one volume.)
The Derbyshire Set, Omnibus Edition, Volume 3 (the third three books in one volume.)

Themed Collections

The Regency Christmas Hearts Collection
The Regency Christmas Love Collection
The Regency Spring and Valentine's Hearts Collection
The Regency Summer Hearts Collection
The Regency Autumn Hearts Collection
The Regency Spring Love Collection
The Regency Summer Love collection
Regency Lords in Love
Regency Ladies in Love

The 'Her Duke' Collection

Her Summer Duke
Her Passionate Duke
Her Absent Duke
Her Determined Duke
Her Generous Duke
Her Christmas Duke

Other Books

The Scottish Governess
The Duke's Christmas Vow
Lady Augusta's Letters
A Gifted Earl
The Crew of the Seadragon's Soul Series, (coming soon - a set of 10 linked novels)

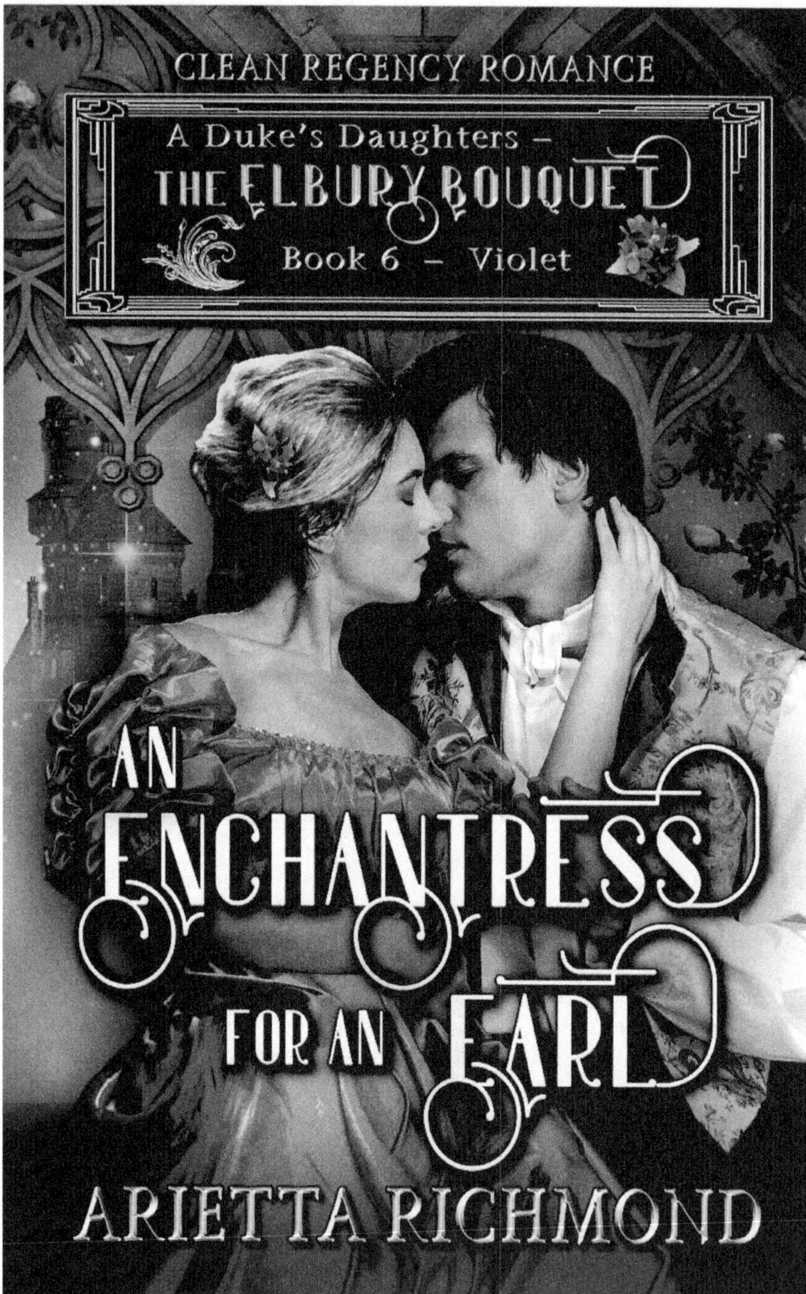
CLEAN REGENCY ROMANCE
A Duke's Daughters –
THE ELBURY BOUQUET
Book 6 – Violet
AN
ENCHANTRESS
FOR AN EARL
ARIETTA RICHMOND

A Duke's Daughters –
The Elbury Bouquet - Book 6 - Violet

Clean Regency Romance

An Enchantress for an Earl

Arietta Richmond

Chapter One

"Did you hear the latest gossip, Violet? Westerhazy's son and heir has been sent down from Oxford. Apparently, he challenged one of his professors in a most inappropriate manner."

Lady Violet Gardenbrook looked up from her book, her expression one of horror. Her sister watched her, expectantly.

"Sent down? How disgusting! Men have no appreciation for the advantages they hold. I simply cannot imagine being given the gift of being able to study, to learn, in a place like Oxford and being so irresponsible and foolish as to throw that chance away, for the sake of what was probably just some childish bad behaviour!"

Iris looked at her, amused.

"You would think that – you would do anything to immerse yourself in a book. Well, perhaps except missing a Ball, although I think that would be a difficult decision for you."

Violet threw a cushion at her sister.

"Just as difficult as if you had to choose between learning a new piece of music, and a Ball."

Iris sipped her tea, and regarded her sister seriously.

"That may be true. But still... apparently, the Marquess of Westerhazy is not at all pleased. I suppose we'll hear more of it at the Jamison Ball tomorrow. I do wonder exactly what he did, though – I am not even sure what subjects he was studying. Perhaps Lady Fotheringhampton will know more, and will be telling everyone."

Violet nodded, and went back to her book, but found that she could not concentrate. The very idea that a man might waste the chance to study, by doing something that got them sent down, offended her deeply. At least men had a chance to study! As a woman, no matter how much she wanted to, she would not be accepted into Oxford or Cambridge, women being deemed, by most men, to be too featherbrained to be capable of deep learning. That kind of thinking maddened her, but she had come to accept that most of the *ton* believed it to be true.

At least her family had a very large library, and her father believed that his daughters should do unconventional things, if that made them happy. He did prefer that they not cause scandal, of course, so Violet kept her penchant for study and her ability to read five languages as a thing discussed only amongst her close family.

She stared at the page, not seeing it, trying to remember if she had ever met the Marquess of Westerhazy's son. After some rumination, she realised that she had – only once, last year at a Ball, when he had been in London close to Easter. He was Arryn Carrington, the Earl of Merryfield. He would be twenty-three, now, so in his last year at Oxford.

And, if her memory served her, he was as handsome as sin.

Which was not, in her opinion, a redeeming feature. Nothing could redeem a man who had thrown away his chance to study at Oxford.

*****

Arryn Carrington, Earl of Merryfield, regarded his father unhappily as the Marquess paced about the room. He had dreaded this moment, from the very minute that he had been handed the notice informing him that he was being sent down.

The Marquess turned, and fixed his son with a steely look.

"Arryn, what on earth did you say to your Professor that so offended him?"

"I told the truth – I told him that he was wrong. I had all of the research, all of the proof, but he insisted on being a blind fool, and ignoring the last thirty years changes in law and due process. I could not simply agree with such blind, wilful ignorance!"

The Marquess groaned, shaking his head.

"Could you not have simply kept your new research to yourself, and pandered to the man long enough to receive your Degree? It wanted but another three months, and you might have been done with the place, honourably. At that point, your new research would have been most useful to me in the House of Lords, backed by the 'evidence' of that Degree."

Arryn felt the frustration rise again – why could no one understand that he could not simply ignore the outright dissemination of incorrect information?

"No, I could not. It is positively criminal that a Professor should remain so ignorant of modern developments, and continue to teach students things which have ceased to be in any way correct."

"Perhaps, my son, before the day when I am no more, it would behove you to learn something far closer to diplomacy. Else you will spend your whole life arguing. And sadly, those who habitually lie tend to be far more successful in life, for they tell people what they want to hear. But for now, we must deal with the results of your actions."

"And how do you suggest that we do that? I refuse to go back to Oxford, and that man's classes!"

The Marquess went to the sideboard, and poured two brandies, then returned to hand one to Arryn.

"I suspected that you would be stubborn, so I have made some enquiries – and some subtly pointed suggestions. The Professor who offends you so will develop the sudden desire to retire at the end of this year, encouraged by a generous stipend from the University, in recognition of his long service. And during the following academic year, the University will see fit to give you one last chance to finish. By then, I trust that you will have prepared yourself to swallow your pride, and simply endure that last few months until you can pass the exams and receive your Degree. But in the immediate term, you will set yourself to charming the *ton*, and giving the gossips no further material to work with."

Arryn took a sizeable swallow of the brandy, feeling the pleasant burn of it fill him with reassuring warmth. He did not like his father's requirement, but he accepted that it was sensible. And he did not envisage too great a difficulty in avoiding providing the gossips with material.

He had little interest in society and the simpering hordes of young women who sought husbands with merciless determination. None of them had the slightest intelligence in their heads. They rarely spoke a second language, let alone more, they did not read, beyond silly novels and the fashion magazines, and they seemed able to discuss nothing but the weather.

The very idea of spending the rest of his life tied to a woman like that, no matter how physically beautiful she might be, revolted him. He would be driven quite, quite mad.

"I see. Much as I do not wish to admit it, that is sensible. I will do my best to do as you wish."

"Good. You can start by attending Viscount Jamison's Ball tomorrow, and letting the gossips see that you are a sensible man, who dances politely with young women, does not drink excessively, and does not gamble. Do not, no matter what, go into the card room."

Arryn sighed, swallowed the rest of the brandy, and gave his father a mocking, flourishing bow.

"As you command."

****

Violet scanned the ballroom, assessing who was present, who she wanted to speak to, and which gentlemen she wanted to avoid. She never had any trouble filling her dance card, and found most Balls entertaining – so long as she did not expect serious conversation. At Balls, she tried very hard to forget whatever she had been studying most recently, and pretend to simply be just another vapid young woman of the *ton*. That way, no one remarked on how strange she was, no one gossiped about her, and no one noticed who and what she listened to.

Which meant that she often overheard some truly fascinating things. Beside her, Iris also looked around.

"Violet, do you think that any of our sisters and their husbands will be here?"

"I don't know for certain – possibly Lily, although now that she is increasing, perhaps not. Hyacinth and Kevin are at Chester Park, and Rose and Evan are visiting them. Camellia and Damien might be here, but Primrose and Gabriel are off in France, I think. We will just have to make do with other conversation."

"That's a pity – Lily and Trent always seem to know everything about everyone, which can be terribly useful."

Violet nodded, her attention on the other side of the room. So far, she knew everyone she had seen – which was not unusual, but was frustrating – she had no interest in any of the men she knew, and if she did not meet any new people, then she was like as not to end as a spinster.

The crowd on the other side of the room shifted as newcomers entered the room, and she studied them, for want of anything better to do. Her eye was caught by the Marquess of Westerhazy – or rather, by the man beside him.

The sinfully handsome man she had only met once, over a year ago.

The man who must be the Earl of Merryfield, the current subject of extensive gossip.

The man who was even more breathtakingly handsome than she remembered him as being.

There were two women with them – one older, who was likely the Marchioness, and a younger one, a woman she had never met, who bore enough likeness to the Earl that it was almost certain that she was his sister. Her hair, like his, was a rich dark brown, with glints of deep red through it.

Iris had apparently noticed where she was looking.

"Oh! Look – that must be him, the Earl. He looks so... respectable... I wonder what he can have done, to offend a Professor so badly as to be sent down? We must arrange an introduction – surely Thorne will know him?"

"Why do you want to be introduced, Iris? Any man who gets himself sent down must be disreputable, and not worth your time."

"Violet, are you blind? The man is unbelievably handsome. I could swoon on the spot, just looking at him. I do not care if he offended some stuffy old Professor – not when he looks like that!"

Violet forced herself not to grind her teeth – sometimes, Iris was just as vapid as most of the young women of the *ton*. No amount of handsome could redeem the Earl in her eyes. The opportunity to study was sacred, and not to be thrown away for anything.

"Then you had best wait to swoon until he is close enough to catch you as you fall."

The sarcasm in her voice was obvious, and her tone sharp. Iris blinked, almost shocked.

"Goodness, Violet, for a moment there, you sounded just like Hyacinth."

"I do believe that I meant to."

With that, she turned away and went to her mother, who stood a short distance away chatting to Lady Fotheringhampton. Even listening to gossip was better than watching her sister melt into a puddle at the sight of a handsome man. But when she reached her mother, it was just in time to hear Lady Fotheringhampton speak, in the lowered tones reserved for passing on something salacious.

"Did you hear about Merryfield? It has been suggested to me, by someone who should know the truth of it, that he offended the Professor by stealing away with the man's mistress! I'm not surprised – a man as handsome as that, in a town with as many... lightskirts... as there are reputed to be in Oxford...."

Violet found her eyes turning to the handsome man across the room. Might what Lady Fotheringhampton said be true? She did not know, but if it was, then all the more reason for her to despise him – to throw away one's chance to study for the sake of a lightskirt...

It was too dreadful a concept to even consider.

Just as she was thinking that she should find a corner to hide in, a cheerful voice spoke from behind her.

"Violet, do come with me – I want to introduce you to someone."

Thorne grinned at her when she turned, and she allowed her brother to lead her away.

Her relief at escaping Lady Fotheringhampton's gossip was short-lived, however, when she realised just where Thorne was leading her.

There was, it appeared, to be no avoiding a certain person.

"Violet, may I make known to you the Earl of Merryfield. Merryfield, my sister, Lady Violet Gardenbrook."

Merryfield took her hand, and she shivered at his touch – there was something about him... he bowed.

"I am delighted to meet you, Lady Violet."

"And I you."

Not really, but I will be polite.

The thought slipped through her mind as years of training took over.

*****

Arryn forced himself to smile, and to keep smiling, as it became obvious that the whole room was whispering about him. A flutter of young women drifted in his direction, but some were drawn back by parents, who obviously were paying heed to some gossip or another. He wondered what he had been described as doing – undoubtedly something far more heinous than arguing with a wilfully ignorant old man.

He stepped forward, and a movement caught his eye. A man he knew, coming towards him – but with a young woman at his side.

Her hair was a rich pale gold, a lighter version of the deeply burnished locks of the man beside her. She moved elegantly, and he found himself caught, watching, instead of looking away. She looked up, and met his eyes. Even from a distance, he could see that hers were a startling blue violet in colour.

They reached him, just as he remembered who the man was - Thorne Gardenbrook, Marquess of Wildenhall.

"Wildenhall – good evening to you."

"Good evening, Merryfield. Violet, may I make known to you the Earl of Merryfield. Merryfield, my sister, Lady Violet Gardenbrook."

Arryn took her hand and bowed.

"I am delighted to meet you, Lady Violet."

"And I you."

He had the strangest feeling that her words were not sincere – which was remarkable – normally any young woman was genuinely delighted to meet an unmarried Earl. But she was beautiful, and showed every external sign of being as feather-brained as all of them were – so perhaps it was just his irritation with the whole evening making him think her statement insincere. Silence extended, and he sought words, a way out of the conversation.

"Lady Violet, might I hope that you have a dance available? This one, if possible?"

What had he done! That was not what he had intended at all. She looked unsure, then gave the tiniest shrug.

"Of course, Lord Merryfield."

Chapter Two

A distressing feeling of being trapped filled Violet.

He had asked her to dance – and his expression said, all too clearly, that he thought her another vapid young woman with little education and even less interest in anything other than fashion. But politeness required that she accept, especially when her brother appeared to regard the man as a friend. She swallowed, made sure that the smile stayed on her face, and responded.

"Of course, Lord Merryfield."

He looked, for a fraction of a second, as if he felt shocked in some way – then his face took on a smile which matched her own – and which she suspected was equally false. That was interesting – why would he react like that? He had asked her to dance, after all, and if he was the sort of man that rumour suggested, then she would have expected him to be genuinely pleased by her acceptance.

Regardless, now she was committed.

He offered his arm, and she placed her hand on it, allowing herself to be led to where the dancers were forming up for the next set. It was to be one of the slower country dances – at least not a waltz! That would limit the amount of conversation she might be expected to make with him, which was a relief. Perhaps, if he were actually the typical sort of young rake that the rumours implied, he would not expect her to truly converse, but simply to smile, and nod, and agree with him in the appropriate places. Most young men, she had found, were far more interested in talking about themselves than in hearing words from a woman.

But... as they took their places, he said nothing, and she felt the silence stretch thin between them. Despite her best intentions, she found herself surreptitiously glancing sideways at him from under lowered lashes. The way that the light from the chandeliers made his handsome profile seem even more chiselled quite took her breath away. Internally, she chastised herself – his handsome appearance mattered not one whit if he was the sort of man who could throw away the chance to study.

The orchestra struck up, and they stepped into position. He met her eyes and smiled, and for a moment, she thought that it was genuine – but no, he looked away quickly, and irritation surfaced – she was used to men finding her good to look at, even if she wasn't as pretty as some of her older sisters! And still, no conversation! She would just have to do something about it herself. The steps of the dance began, and when they came back to being face to face, she spoke softly.

"Lord Merryfield, you seem somewhat preoccupied – what fills your thoughts so?"

It was a rather forward thing to ask, but Violet felt oddly at ease with this man, even though she shouldn't.

She also felt that he did not deserve consideration – for the very idea that he had allowed himself to do something that got him sent down still filled her with anger.

He almost started – she felt it through his fingers, where his hand held hers for a moment as they turned, and she brought her eyes to his, that gaze almost demanding an answer.

"I do apologise, Lady Violet. Before we came out this evening, I was studying some matters of law, and I find that my mind is still pondering some of that – it is nothing which would interest a lady, and I am sorry that I let it intrude on a moment when courtesy demands that I give my attention to you."

It was Violet's turn to almost startle – but she forced herself to simply continue with the pattern of the dance, grateful for the few moments when it moved them apart, so that she could compose her expression to that expected of a young lady. To be told that such things would not interest her! It made her grind her teeth in frustration – why men thought that women had no interest in learning, or in the laws and the workings of government, was something that she simply could not comprehend. She had come to accept that they thought that way, but still, comments like his grated.

The dance turned them back together, and she presented him with her best charming smile.

"I see. I do hope that you are able to let such concerns go, and enjoy yourself a little this evening, Lord Merryfield."

"Of course. I shall set myself to do just that. Let us speak of other things. The weather has been distinctly colder of late, as winter approaches, and I suspect that we will be sadly lacking in opportunities to socialise soon, as many retire to their country estates. Do your family plan to stay in London this winter?"

Violet almost choked, feeling a bubble of near hysterical laughter rise within her. The weather. He had fallen back on talking about the weather! That was beyond dull. But he had given her an opportunity to answer him honestly and politely, yet still, perhaps shake his typical assumption that she cared for nothing more than Balls and fashion. She swallowed the urge to laugh, and waited until the dance brought them around again.

"Why Lord Merryfield, I have good hopes of continuing social engagements this winter, for I believe that Parliament will be in session from November - which means that my father will need to be in London, as will some of my sisters' husbands. Our whole family will stay. I expect that many families will stay in London as a result."

He blinked, and she knew that she had surprised him. The dance turned them apart, and she felt oddly colder without those deep amber eyes regarding her.

*****

Arryn forced himself to smile. Today had been a good day – until the moment when his father had insisted that he leave his research and dress to attend this Ball. Now, he was torn – his mind wanted to continue with the research, but here he was, required to fulfil his promise to his father, and present the appearance of a perfectly charming and well-behaved man of the *ton*.

He was, so far, rather failing at charming, given that Lady Violet had noticed his preoccupation. It really was socially unforgiveable to ask a lady to dance, and then barely converse with her.

Not only had he left it to her to begin the conversation, but he had then, foolishly, actually answered her rather forward question honestly. He should know better – young ladies cared nothing for law, or politics, or anything complicated at all, as far as he could see. But now, as the dance turned them apart again, he discovered himself confounded.

He had turned that conversation to the weather, and the time of year – a perfectly ordinary topic – which she had somehow made not ordinary at all, by her response. She was aware of when Parliament would be sitting – admittedly, her father was a Duke, so she would have some awareness of such things, but still... how should he respond? Perhaps simply by focusing on family, and time together as the Christmas Season approached? They came back together, and he spoke again, his eyes holding hers, finding himself half drowning in their blue-violet depths.

"That should, indeed, provide a situation where more company is available. And to have one's family together throughout the Christmas Season will no doubt be most pleasant."

She smiled, and there was almost a wry edge to it. He wondered if he imagined that expression, for it did not align with his perception of the expressions common on young women.

"Indeed, Lord Merryfield. My family are close, and will appreciate it – but we are just as like to discuss the goings on in Parliament as anything else. One must stay up to date with what is happening in the world."

The music slowed, and they turned through a final set of steps, coming to rest facing each other again. He bowed and offered her his arm, and they stepped away, back towards where her mother and brother waited.

The warmth of her hand on his arm somehow seemed to spread through him, and he discovered that, for the first time in his life, he regretted the dance ending. She confused him, and fascinated him, and, horrifyingly, he wanted to know more of her.

He did not like being confused, did not like having the neat structure of how the world worked tipped awry – which was exactly what she had done, for no other woman he had ever spoken to had presented even the faintest appearance of wishing to understand what was happening in the world, beyond the things with an immediate and direct effect on them. Even his mother and sister conformed to that pattern – and he acknowledged that they were both quite intelligent people.

Perhaps, in future, it would be best if he avoided Lady Violet Gardenbrook, and her very disturbing conversation.

*****

Violet watched him walk away. He had delivered her back to her brother and her mother where they stood on one side of the room, spoken to her brother for a short while, and then left them. She was almost certain that he was glad to escape their company – which offended her a little. But that was silly – she had not wanted his company in the first place, so why she should feel any distress at his removing himself, she did not know.

The evening went on, and she danced with various gentlemen, but she frequently found her eyes drifting, without conscious intent, in the direction of Lord Merryfield. He danced with a selection of young ladies, and appeared in all ways to be an ordinary man of the *ton* – despite the rumours to the contrary. It was a puzzle, one which wore away at the back of Violet's thoughts, until, as she settled into the carriage for the ride home, it struck her – his behaviour made no sense not only because he appeared well behaved and considerate, not paying inappropriate attention to any woman, but also because of what he had said to her.

At the time, she had been so focussed on her annoyance at being informed that ladies had no interest in the matters of the world, that she had not considered his words any further. But now, they came back to her. He had said that he was preoccupied because he had spent the day studying matters of law, and was still considering those matters. He had been studying!

Why would a man so irresponsible as to get himself sent down from Oxford be bothering to study at all, now that it could make no difference to him for a year or more, if indeed, he was ever even considered for readmittance?

It definitely made no sense at all.

And, most annoyingly, it made her want to know why, made her want to understand him.

She pushed that thought aside, and shut her eyes, determined to think no more of him. But despite that intention, he haunted not only her thoughts as they reached home, but her dreams that night as well.

*****

Though it was late, Arryn accepted his father's offer of a brandy in the study, even knowing it likely came with conversation.

Balls, he had concluded, were far more mentally taxing than studying. He took the glass and dropped into a chair as his father took the one opposite him, and stared at the fire in the grate, glad of its warmth. It was October, and the evenings were decidedly cold.

The silence settled between them, not entirely comfortable, and Arryn waited, knowing that his father would have something to say.

No doubt he was considering his choice of words.

At that thought, Arryn almost laughed – for the only reason his father would so consider his words was to ensure that he gave Arryn nothing to argue with him on.

"You did well this evening. Perhaps that will begin to allay the gossip. God knows who invents some of the drivel they whisper – but wherever it comes from, I cannot afford to allow it to continue. We are so close to good progress on the matter of deciding which anti forgery techniques we will require the Bank of England to implement – I cannot risk anything giving the House of Lords, or the Prince Regent, doubts about the decisions of my committee. And whispers about you being a man who is poor of judgement, profligate with money, and enthused by debauchery do not do my credibility any good at all."

Arryn swallowed some brandy in a rather larger gulp than he had intended, his father's words hitting hard.

"I... I am sorry, Father, I care as much as you to see this rampant forgery stopped, and the stability of the country's currency restored. I will do my best, despite loathing everything about occasions like this evening. I would far rather have been here, continuing my research into the different anti tampering methods, so that you might make use of what I learn."

His father sighed, staring into the distance, then spoke almost gently.

"I know that you would. Why, oh why, could you not have simply allowed your professor his outdated opinions? Why could you not have forced yourself to silence for another three months?"

Arryn looked up, meeting the stern gaze of his grandfather from the portrait above the mantel. His grandfather who, he had been told by his great aunt, had been just like him – unable to allow things to pass, when he knew that they were wrong, unable to allow his world to be in any kind of disarray.

"You know that I could not, Father. Professor Whimpferhim is a stubborn old fool. That he was speaking patent untruths is one thing, but that he was teaching those untruths to students was what forced me to speak. He, like so many others, sees the monetary situation that we are now in as a direct result of the decoupling of paper money from gold reserves. He ignores the impact of the wars, the necessity for change, and the changes being made again, now, to restore that balance, that association of scrip to specie, which must happen. He cannot see that paper money has any place in the world, going forward, and rants about that, rather than consider any new options. He ignores every law passed into being since 1797! And when I tried to discuss such matters with him, he decried me as 'speaking sedition, like that devil Cobbett'. The man is irredeemable."

His father met Arryn's eyes, and shook his head.

"I wish you'd just let him ramble, and got that degree, because then you could have helped me prove that, and helped the committee get the forgery prevention methods approved. Now, they wouldn't listen to you, because you've proven yourself to have no respect for the 'authorities' on the matter. The reality of the man's knowledge is irrelevant – he has power and influence – he's a cousin to three Dukes, for God's sake. But we will overcome this – you'll just have to keep being of exemplary behaviour, everywhere."

"I will, as I said, do my best – but please, do not drive me too hard, lest I break, and say what I think to someone. I will do as much research as I can, and you can claim to have done that investigation yourself. I will attend social events, and smile and speak to simpering young women with no thought of anything important, and I will attempt to convince the doyennes of the *ton* that I am not disreputable. It is, I am afraid, the speaking to young ladies which tries me most."

His father eyed him sadly.

"Trying or not, it must be done. And, as I would hope one day to have grandchildren, I must pray that you do find at least one young lady whom you can converse with well enough to marry. For certainly, you marrying would go a long way to convincing the gossips that you are, in truth, respectable."

Arryn nearly dropped the brandy glass. His father couldn't be serious – could he? Marry one of them? The idea sent a shudder of horror down his spine. None of them had a thought in their head.

Except perhaps, Lady Violet Gardenbrook.

Chapter Three

Violet walked into the breakfast room, stifling a yawn. Thorne looked up from his heaped plate and raised an eyebrow.

"Yawning? It's nearly afternoon – I'd have thought that, even after a Ball, you'd have been rested after sleeping this late."

Violet filled a plate at the sideboard, and fixed her brother with a stern gaze as she settled at the table.

"Says he who, from the look of that plate, can only have arrived in this room mere minutes before I did."

"Ah yes, but I am not yawning – that is the important difference."

"I seem to remember that you did not dance as much as I did last night – I do believe that I have, thereby, better excuse to be yawning."

Thorne laughed, and silence fell for a moment as they each attended to the food. Then he lifted his head again, and regarded Violet with an expression which she knew meant a question would follow.

"Dancing... yes, you did, as usual, dance almost every dance. Including one with Merryfield. Who is not exactly known for his love of dancing – or Balls in general, for that matter. What did you think of him?"

"I choose to not think of him. Any man who is so disregarding of the opportunity he has as to get himself sent down is not worthy of my thoughts. He presented no redeeming features – his conversation was lacking, although I will admit that he danced passably well. Why do you ask?"

"My, such intensity! But I should have expected it of you, Violet, given that you would, I suspect, live your entire life in the library given the chance. Still – surely a man is entitled to make a mistake, even if it's one that gets him sent down?"

Violet half choked on her coffee, then set the cup down carefully and fixed Thorne with her best baleful glare.

"No. Getting sent down is a forever unforgiveable sin." She hesitated, but that strange impulse which had taken her last night rose again – she wanted to know more about Merryfield, to understand him. "But... what did he actually do? I heard multiple rumours last night, ranging from 'had an argument' to 'ran off with his Professor's mistress'. Do you know the truth of it?"

"Really, Violet! A young lady should not even know that mistresses exist, let alone ask a question like that!"

"Thorne, you know full well that I am aware of many things in the world that 'a young lady should know nothing of'. So stop avoiding the question – do you know what he did?"

Thorne chewed thoughtfully, intentionally making her wait. She took another mouthful and another sip of coffee – two could play that game.

Then she forced herself to stillness, lest he realise just how badly she wanted to know.

"I am tempted to tell you the most lurid story I can think of, just to watch your reaction, but that would be to do an unfair disservice to Merryfield. I don't know the depth of the detail – but I do know that he had an argument with a professor."

"What argument could possibly be bad enough to get him sent down?"

"I don't know. If you really want to know the truth, why don't you ask him?"

"As if I could! That would be so forward as to destroy my reputation should anyone catch a hint of it. I am not so foolish!"

"Then you will just have to languish in ignorance, won't you?"

"Dear brother, you are impossible! Why did you even introduce me to him in the first place?"

"Ah... that would be because I seem to remember you asking me to find you some gentlemen you had not met before, to be introduced to?"

"Well... admittedly, I may have asked you such a thing – but I did expect that anyone you introduced me to would be reputable. And having been sent down is, by my definition, beyond the pale."

"You know, you could be a good match for him – on some matters, you can be quite as obsessive as he is."

Violet glared, shocked – what did Thorne mean?

"You cannot, simply cannot, mean to compare me in any way to a man who cares so little for the opportunity to study as to get sent down!"

"I can, and I do. He is the most meticulously obsessive person I have ever met." At Violet's horrified gasp, Thorne shook his head, affecting a sorrowful expression. "Really, you are just as ungrateful as the rest of my sisters. I don't know why I bother to try to help. Now that you carry the 'family spinster' title, you seem determined to keep it for as long as possible."

With that, he turned back to his food, and left Violet fuming at him, lost for words, but even more determined than before to avoid Lord Merryfield in future. He did not deserve any more of her attention than she had already wasted on him.

*****

Arryn stepped through the door of Bigglesworth's Books and took a deep breath. There was just something so soothing about the scent of books and the leather of their bindings. Added to that, Bigglesworth's Books was a haven of order. The shelves were arranged with everything in its place, according to its type and topic, so that he could always be assured of finding the thing that he wanted.

Behind the counter, old Mr Bigglesworth looked up from the book he was reading, and gave Arryn a nod of greeting – the old man was perfectly aware that Arryn understood his shelving pattern, and was quite capable of finding the things that he wanted. He worked his way through the narrow spaces between the shelves, until he arrived at the very back of the store. Here, on three groaning shelves, were collected all of the books related to laws, and matters of political opinion.

He had come in search of a rather contentious work, written by a man who had barely evaded being arrested for sedition – yet it was a work worthy of consideration, especially in the face of the matter of paper money and its forgery. Whether he would find a copy of 'Paper Against Gold' by William Cobbett on these shelves, he did not know, but he rather suspected that, if any bookshop in London would have one, Bigglesworth's would. He had heard rumour that Cobbett intended to return to England in the coming months, which made it even more important to understand the radical attitude to these matters, for once the man was on English soil, he would no doubt be outspoken in all ways - through his weekly newspaper, and beyond.

If too many people listened, then no matter what anti forgery methods were put in place, there would be increasing unrest in the country, and all of the efforts of Arryn's father's committee might come to naught.

He sifted through the neatly arranged volumes, and was rather startled to discover not just one, but three copies of the book he sought. Carefully, he examined each one, and selected the one that he determined to be in the best condition. It had been published four years earlier, so any copy to be had might well be assumed to have suffered all manner of mistreatment and annotation. As he went to step back from the shelf, contemplating whether there was anything else here that he might wish to purchase, a hand reached past his shoulder, and grasped one of the other copies of 'Paper Against Gold'.

Startled, he spun around, and found himself face to face with Lady Violet Gardenbrook. He froze, his eyes going to her lips, which parted slightly in the expression of a shock which appeared to mirror his own. Those lips were mere inches from his. He could not look away, could not move, could not, quite, breathe.

She pulled her arm back, clutching the book against her, and for a moment they simply stood. In an impulse unlike any he had ever felt before, there rose in him the desire to lean forward, to close that tiny gap between them, and to bring his lips to hers. It was a shocking thought – almost as shocking as finding her here, selecting a copy of 'Paper Against Gold' from the shelf. He forced himself to look away from those lips, to breathe again, and reached desperately for the practised veneer of appropriate politeness.

"Ah... good day to you, Lady Violet."

"Lord Merryfield."

Silence fell again, as they each regarded the other rather as if they had come upon a viper, sunning itself upon the log they had intended to sit upon. Yet again, she confused him, causing his neatly ordered world to tilt out of any sane alignment. It was unconscionable that she was able to do so, seemingly merely by existing. Then, without any planning on his part, words issued from his mouth.

"Why would a lady read a book by a man nearly charged with sedition? Despite the fact that not all of his ideas are bad...."

It was certainly not the sort of thing one should say to a gently reared lady of the *ton*, was, in fact, unutterably rude. Nonetheless he had said it. He could almost hear his father's voice in his mind, admonishing him. But, rather than appear utterly shocked, or on the verge of an attack of the vapours, she fixed him with a glare almost as harsh as his father's worst, and responded with a question of her own.

"Why would a man so disregarding of the importance of his studies as to get sent down consider reading such a treatise – unless you plan to become a voice for parliamentary reform?"

"Well, actually... I do..."

The words were, again, out before he had any chance to think. Her eyes widened, and a frown creased her brow for a moment, as if she found what he had just said to be nonsensical.

"You... do?"

"I do... eventually."

She almost snorted in disbelief, and he felt a burst of anger. How dare she judge him! How dare any of them judge him – all he had done was stand up for what was right, in the face of unbearable outright falsehoods. Why could people not understand just how intolerable it was, that such things were ever allowed to pass?

"I see. Well, I won't delay you any longer – with aims like that, I am sure that you have a great deal to do."

She spun on her heel, and hurried off towards the front part of the shop, her copy of 'Paper Against Gold' clutched tightly to her. Arryn stayed there, unable to move, simply watching her walk away. As she disappeared from his view, he realised that she had not answered his question – he still had no idea why she would read such a book – and, alarmingly, he discovered that he wanted, very much, to know.

*****

Violet carried the book to the counter, so that Mr Bigglesworth could add it to their family account, and so that she could collect the new sheet music which should have arrived for Iris.

Her heart was beating far faster than normal, and she felt strangely breathless. The way that Lord Merryfield had looked at her face, at her lips, to be precise... the memory of it sent a flush of heat through her. Really, the man was beyond annoying! He was supposed to be quite beneath her consideration, given all that she knew of him... but he kept confusing her, surprising her and, worst of all, making her want to understand him!

She resolved, yet again, to not think about him.

Mr Bigglesworth handed her the parcel of sheet music, made a note of her purchases in his ledger, and smiled as she left, unsurprised by her choice of reading matter. The Gardenbrooks were a somewhat eccentric family, with eclectic taste in books. He approved.

Outside, her footman waited, and soon she was settled in her carriage, and on the way home. She closed her eyes and leant back against the squabs, but the image of Lord Merryfield rose in her mind, his dark amber eyes full of something which had seemed a peculiar compounding of confusion, annoyance, and almost... desire? He was the strangest man she had ever met.

If he had truly meant what he had said, that he intended to work for parliamentary reform, then what, she wondered, did he wish to see reformed? She had asked her father what matters the committees of the House of Lords were currently working on, and he had raised an eyebrow, but answered her honestly. It would not do to have claimed, to Lord Merryfield as they danced, that she was aware of the current matters under consideration by parliament, and to remain ignorant! That conversation was what had led her to seek out this particular book.

It was just her general need to be suitably knowledgeable – it had nothing, she assured herself, to do with the fact that Lord Westerhazy, Lord Merryfield's father, was on the committee looking into anti forgery measures. Nothing at all.

*****

The soft tinkling of the bell on the shop door brought him back to himself. No doubt, that had been a signal of Lady Violet leaving. Determinedly, he turned back to the shelves, and selected another book – a most non-contentious volume on the history of coinage – then took both to the counter.

Mr Bigglesworth greeted him cheerfully.

"Lord Merryfield – still studying, I see."

Arryn almost flinched, for those words implied that even the bookseller had heard of his disgrace.

"Always, Mr Bigglesworth. I am sadly compulsive about such things."

Mr Bigglesworth wrapped the books, raising an eyebrow slightly when he saw 'Paper Against Gold'.

"Not often we sell two of these in one day – they're getting hard to get, and I don't expect there to be a reprint."

"I'm lucky to have come in when you had one, then. It's a work which raises some interesting questions related to my area of study, as it happens."

"So you don't regard Cobbett as seditious?"

"A radical, definitely, but seditious? No, I don't personally see him as quite that."

Mr Bigglesworth nodded, and handed him the parcel.

"I'll let you know if I get in anything new that you might be interested in, Lord Merryfield."

"Thank you. Good day."

When Arryn stepped out onto the pavement, there was, of course, no sign of Lady Violet – indeed, he wondered why he had even looked. She was not a woman he wished to further his acquaintance with, after all.

Even if he had wanted, for that one moment, to kiss her...

Chapter Four

"I heard some disturbing mutterings today, at White's."

Arryn looked up from his book, and raised an enquiring eyebrow at his father.

"Mutterings?"

"Yes. About you. And about me."

"I don't understand what you mean, Father?"

"Even though you've been perfectly behaved ever since you returned to London, there are some who are whispering about what might have got you sent down – and while some of them seem to have at least the core of the story right, there are others drawing a very long bow indeed on the truth – they would appear to have been listening to the gossips, and then exaggerating what they've heard. To make it worse, they are now speculating on exactly where you may have 'learnt such behaviour', and implying that if you are so morally lacking, then you must have become so because I am, too."

"What!"

"Exactly. I don't quite know what they think they gain by so besmirching both our reputations, unless it is to thereby call into question my judgement when it comes to the Committee on the anti-forgery methods."

"But that makes no sense - what would anyone stand to gain from that?"

"I don't know. It seems pointless – but if there is one thing that I have learnt over the years, it's that no matter how illogical a thing seems on the surface, there will be a reason for it, deep down. I just haven't worked out what it is yet. But until I do, it's even more important that you are absolutely perfect in all ways."

Arryn groaned.

"I may be a perfectionist about many things, but I have never believed that I am capable of being perfect! I am not sure that anyone is."

"Just do your best. And make sure that the information you give me, from all this research you are doing, will be enough to convince the House to act, and implement appropriate measures to combat this epidemic of forgery. And, at all times, keep your eyes and ears open – perhaps you will see or hear something at one event or another which might help us discover who is creating these damnable rumours, and why."

"I will, although I don't expect that anyone is likely to say anything in my hearing. Once I refused to gamble with them, most of them decided to ignore me. Lord Villeham positively sneered at me, as if choosing not to gamble made me less of a man. I don't know where that one gets his seemingly bottomless funds – his father never seemed that flush, when he lived."

"You're right there – but mayhap the previous Lord Villeham was just a penny pincher. One never knows – young Lord Harmonton is just the same – spends his time gambling – and worse – with Villeham, and yet I'd not thought his estates capable of supporting that lifestyle. Perhaps they are both deep in hock to the moneylenders. If so, those debts will eventually claim them. I am grateful, Arryn, that you were never tempted by that lifestyle."

"Father, you know me – the whole process of gambling is one where the odds are against you – once I understood enough mathematics to calculate that, I lost all interest in the idea. The idea of trusting my funds to something so disorderly as random chance offends my very soul."

His father laughed, shaking his head a little.

"You are so like your grandfather. I pray that you manage to moderate those traits enough to bring you less argument in your life than he suffered."

"So do I."

*****

Violet leaned back in her chair, allowing the French novel she had been attempting to read to drop into her lap. The novel was good, but she simply could not concentrate on it. Instead, her mind was full of the implications of how the entire British monetary system worked.

She'd had no idea, until she had delved into Cobbett's book, just how complex the matters were – or how important.

It was fascinating – that wealth was determined, in so many cases, by something as simple as a flimsy piece of paper... She could see why the matter of forgery was important enough to have been raised in the House of Lords. But, almost more intriguing than the detail of how it all worked, was the question of exactly what Lord Merryfield was studying, related to this – and why.

Irritated, she pushed that thought aside.

She had resolved to ignore the man, to waste no more time on him in any way, yet here he was, intruding on her mind yet again. She rose, carrying the book, and left the parlour – this evening was to be a soiree at Lady Dartwood's, and she really should set about preparing herself.

Would there be anyone new there, she wondered? Or... would Lord Merryfield be there?

She shook her head, disgusted with herself – of course, she did not care at all whether that man was there, or not.

*****

For so late in the autumn, the soiree at Lady Dartwood's was rather a shocking crush. But then, Parliament would meet again in only a few weeks' time, so perhaps it was simply that so many were in Town for that. The crowd meant that the rooms were overly warm, and that there was really no space for dancing. Instead, people milled about whilst a small orchestra played from a tiny dais set in one corner of the main parlour, and the rumble of conversation nearly drowned out the music.

Beside Violet, Iris appeared to be focused on the musicians.

Violet sighed – one day, Iris would show interest in something other than music and handsome men – but this was obviously not that day. Turning away from her sister, Violet slipped out through the terrace doors they were standing near, suddenly overcome by the need for fresh air and a little space.

There was no-one new here for her to meet, and she had been annoyed to find herself looking for Lord Merryfield – who was not, as far as she could determine, present. A short while in the chill night air should clear her head and allow her to steel herself to appear as if she had no thoughts in her mind beyond the latest fashion.

The terrace was deeply shadowed, with only one lantern at the far end, and the small garden just beyond its railing was equally unlit – it seemed that Lady Dartwood did not expect anyone to wish to venture out into the chill. *She may well be correct in that,* Violet thought, *perhaps only I am fool enough to expose myself to the cold.* She leant on the railing, deep in the shadow against the house wall, and simply appreciated the quiet. The deep thrum of the conversation inside was still detectable, but it was barely so, a background tone, almost more felt than heard.

In counterpoint, there came the quiet call of a bird – perhaps, even here in London, a leafy garden was enough to draw a robin. It was only then, as she stared out into the darkness, that she realised that she could hear another sound. Below her, from around the corner of the building, there came the faint sound of voices. Two voices, she thought, two men. She edged slightly along, until she was hard against the wall where the railing ended, and stood completely still, listening. She should go back inside... but... what might they be talking about, out here in the dark? It was a most strange place to converse... and it did not sound like an amorous assignation...

By some strange trick of the flow of air about the building, when she leant her head against the stone, the sound came clearer.

"...no doubt that, if they do what I've heard rumour of, we'll not be able to continue. Your man may be good, but I doubt he's good enough to match what's suggested. And if we can't continue..."

"...we'll be forced to live in a manner neither of us wants to."

"Exactly. So... what are you going to do?"

"What am I going to do? Why me?"

"It's your... system.... Remember, if it comes to it, and exposure seems likely, I'll save myself, and report my shocking discovery of your activities.... So you'd best find a way to stop them, for both our sakes, and our families."

"Is that a threat?"

"Not a threat, exactly... more a warning... I don't think you want to lose your easy ticket any more than I do, after all. And if I'm to marry your sister, you'll want me to have the money to support her in the way she expects, won't you?"

"You're a hard man, Cater."

"Yes, but you knew that when we made our deal. So I repeat, what are you going to do?"

"Escalate from what we have been doing, and find a way to stop them, I suppose. A way to convince them it's not practical, or possible, or something like that."

"Make sure that you do, and soon."

They fell into silence, and Violet stayed frozen in place, even though the chill of the stone was seeping into her bones. Then they moved.

What if they saw her? She had no idea who they were, but she was utterly certain that she should do everything in her power to prevent them from realising that she had overheard that conversation. The rustle of their movement through the bushes intensified – they seemed to be coming her way. She had only seconds – she spun around and slipped back in through the terrace doors, praying that the sound of their own movement would disguise the sound of hers, and that they would never realise she'd been there.

*****

Arryn reacted instinctively, his hands shooting out to grasp the person before him and prevent her falling, even as he averted an embarrassing collision between them. The door from the terrace had opened, and before he was barely aware of that, the person entering had been upon him.

She gasped and, as he managed to keep both of them on their feet, he realised that he held Lady Violet Gardenbrook, her eyes wide with shock, and her face pale. Her arms, where he held them, were chilled to the touch, and he wondered just how long she had been outside in the cold October night air. A quiver ran through her, and she flicked a glance behind her to where the door had clicked shut.

Then her eyes met his, and everything but the intensity of her blue violet gaze faded away. He was not sure how long they stood like that – probably far too long for propriety – but her soft voice brought him back to himself.

"Thank you, Lord Merryfield. I believe that I am quite able to stand unassisted – you should, perhaps, release me before anyone notices..."

He dropped his hands to his sides, feeling a slight flush colour his cheeks. How was it that, despite his promises to his father, and all of his best intentions, as soon as he came near this woman, nothing went as planned?

"Lady Violet... is all well with you? You seemed rather... hurried, and you look most pale and chilled."

She looked away, as if embarrassed that he had noticed.

"I believe that I stood on the terrace for far too long, contemplating the stars. I am sorry to have startled you so."

He did not, for one moment, believe that there was nothing more to it than that. She had been far too hurried in her entry to the room for it simply to be a return from some time spent in the crisp night air. And that glance behind her... it was almost as if she had expected to be pursued. That thought raised the strangest feeling in him – a desire to protect her from whatever, or whoever, might have caused her to flee. Ridiculous – she was not his responsibility to protect! But... he shook his head, confused, yet again, by her simple presence.

"Let me escort you to your family – perhaps a turn about the room will warm you and put the colour back in your cheeks."

She met his eyes again, and a series of lightning-fast emotions flickered across her face. He did not understand any of them. He offered his arm but, just as she was about to place her hand on it, they were interrupted by a cheerful voice.

"There you are, Violet!"

They both turned.

"Thorne – were you looking for me? I just stepped onto the terrace for a few minutes – it had become quite too warm and stuffy in here."

"I was – Mother asked me to find you, for she is planning to leave early – I suspect for exactly that reason – the close air with this much of a crush is giving her a headache."

"If that is so, then I will be happy to leave with her – I find that this evening has not filled me with any great desire to stay."

Disappointment filled Arryn – he had only just found her, and now she was going to leave? He should not care, but he found that he did.

"Then let me do as I had intended, Lady Violet, and escort you to your mother, that I might at least greet her before she departs."

Wildenhall regarded him with a raised eyebrow, which he ignored, and he offered Lady Violet his arm again. She settled her hand upon it, and they turned, following Wildenhall across the room as he led them to the Duchess. No words were spoken, yet he had the strangest feeling that she was grateful for the support of his arm, despite what she had said earlier.

*****

Violet stood quietly as Lord Merryfield made polite greetings to her mother, father, and sister, watching his devastatingly handsome face, and wondering what he thought of her strange eruption through the terrace doors.

Hopefully nothing untoward. She should have been relieved, but when he eventually bowed and took his leave of her, she found herself watching him walk away, filled with the strangest desire to call him back. Thorne's voice close to her ear pulled her sharply from those thoughts.

"So, you find Merryfield far more interesting than you have admitted…"

"Whatever gives you that impression, my dear brother?"

"Oh… perhaps just that you, the ever steady one, seem flustered. And that your face was very pale, and now has flushed to a deep pink."

"You are mistaken. I'm flushed because, embarrassingly enough, I almost collided with him as I came in through the terrace doors. There is nothing more to it than that."

"Allow me to remain sceptical…"

Violet glared at him, and stepped up to her mother's side.

"I am happy to leave, Mother, whenever you wish."

Chapter Five

As soon as they reached home, Violet claimed tiredness, and took herself to bed. But rest was not easily gained. If truth be told, the evening had left her feeling shaken. First, that most peculiar conversation she had overheard, and then the equally peculiar interaction with Lord Merryfield.

For a moment, when he had caught her as she rushed through the door, fear had filled her – but only for mere seconds, until she realised who it was that held her so firmly. The knowledge that it was Lord Merryfield had made relief rush through her, and for a moment she had wanted nothing more than to crumple against him, and allow his strength to support her.

Which really wouldn't do at all, especially in public!

And him, of all people....

She could not explain that momentary lapse of judgement. The overheard conversation must have shaken her far more than she had realised at the time, for she had needed the support of his arm as they had crossed the room.

And that Thorne had noticed... that was possibly the worst part of it!

Now, as she settled into her bed, a cup of warm chocolate in hand, the memory of that overheard conversation came back to her. It frightened her, with its casual implications of threat and wrongdoing, especially as she did not understand what sort of wrongdoing they might have been discussing – only that it was bad enough that revealing it would lead to some kind of ruin for the men involved and those close to them.

The calmness with which they had discussed it had chilled her more than the stone she had leant against, and left her with a sense that she did not know the people around her at all, despite having been amongst most of the *ton* much of her life. She did not know who those men had been – and the very idea that they could be people she had spoken with, might even have danced with, was terrifying.

One voice had seemed vaguely familiar, but she could not place it, the other, the one that the first man had called 'Cater' had not sounded familiar at all. And that name did not help her, as far as identifying them – she knew of no one whose name was Cater. It had to be a shortening of part of the man's name, one of those casual namings among friends which boys developed at school, before they came into their titles. She sighed, and set the empty cup down on the small table beside her bed. The not knowing would fester inside her, worrying away until she, somehow, discovered the truth of their identities, and the meaning of what she had heard. But tonight, she could do nothing more, unless she wished to go down to the library and scour DeBrett's by faint lamplight, in the hope of finding a name which might reasonably be shortened to Cater.

Which she was not going to do.

She would be sensible, and sleep. Perhaps, in the morning, something helpful would come to her. She blew out the candle, and slid down to curl under the covers, but sleep was slow to come, and filled with strange dreams when it did – dreams in which Lord Merryfield stood between her and some monstrous, nebulous threat.

*****

Trent Weatherton, Marquess of Canterford, leant back in the well-padded chair and sipped the perfect coffee he had just been handed. Opposite him, Cecil Carlisle, Baron Setford, set down his own cup and smiled. It was a rather grim smile, and Trent wondered what that presaged.

"Canterford, I've a more sensitive than usual task for you. You are aware of the ongoing concerns about forgery..."

"Indeed – first we were treated to that rather obnoxiously large report on every small amount of money spent on any imaginable thing for the last few years, then interminable discussion in the House of Lords about the fact that so much forgery was happening that regulation of the country's finances seems impossible. And now Westerhazy's committee are deep in analysing every potential way in which forgery can be prevented. It's taking so long though, that the problem will only get worse, and we may never stop it. And recently, there have been rumours..."

"Yes. Very odd rumours, implying that there is something untoward about Westerhazy – beyond the fact that his son has a low tolerance for pompous old professors."

"I cannot countenance that any of those rumours are true."

"Neither can I, Canterford. But their existence makes the task I have for you more urgent. I will be blunt – I have a more than strong suspicion that someone amongst the *ton* is indulging in forgery. It was only a matter of time, I suppose, given how much debt some of the younger high-flyers are carrying, before one of them decided that forgery might be an easy way to solve their financial woes."

Trent shook his head sadly.

"Some of them have no honour at all. But given the other things we have uncovered at times, I am not truly surprised. Still, forgery of currency is officially treason – who would be mad enough to do such a thing, and risk losing everything, and their family being outcast as well?"

"Someone desperate, with a moneylender hounding them for repayment, perhaps? And if they found a way to do it successfully – for it would require access to a person with the skill to create printing plates of a quality that would pass muster – they would be committed, wouldn't they, after the first note was printed. And greed is such that, once started, they would be unlikely to stop."

"I suppose you are right. Do you have any specific suspects at this point? Or only the hint that it might be happening?"

"So far, only the hint of it. A few men who have previously run perilously close to the wind on their funds have recently been far more flush, and have paid off some debts – not all that they owe, but enough to make me wonder where the blunt came from. I'll give you a list of those, and you can start with observing them. Given that part of my remit in our work for the Crown is to prevent treason, this falls squarely to us to investigate."

"As usual, I'll do nothing obtrusive – I assume you'll have men following them, and other investigations in place, so I'll only need to worry about what they do in the ballrooms and parlours of the nobility?"

"Indeed, exactly that. And I'm sure that your charming and intelligent wife will be able to discover any interesting gossip which might relate, as well."

Trent laughed. Lily was, in his opinion, far better suited to be a spy for the Crown than he was.

"I am sure that she will."

*****

Arryn sat back, allowing the stack of papers to drop to his desk. This research really was turning out to be quite fascinating. The ingenuity displayed by some of the methods which had been developed to potentially make a bank note 'unforgeable' was amazing. The one he had just been reading about, invented by a Mr Ibbetson, seemed to hold the best hope of being effective, without being inordinately expensive to implement.

Before he wrote up his report for his father, he would step back from this for a day, and then read it all again, to be sure that he had understood it correctly. He was certain that he had, but still, it was best to be sure. Then, if his father took that report to the committee, and they agreed, perhaps the forgery problem could be solved, sooner than expected.

It was a pleasing thought, only tarnished by the fact that his name would not be attached to that report.

For the thousandth time, he internally chastised himself for the fact that he simply could not accept the teaching of untruths. Why could he not be like other men, and simply let things like that pass? He did not know, but he had come to accept that he could not, that some inner devil drove him in those moments, forcing him to act, to speak.

Now, however, if he could at least provide his father with the material necessary to move the committee's purpose forward, that might be some reparation for him having been sent down.

He tidied the papers into a meticulous stack, then put that into his desk drawer and locked it. Tomorrow was soon enough to revisit it. Tonight, he had another of those damnable social occasions to attend. As he rose from his chair, his mind went back to the soiree a few days before, when he had literally run into Lady Violet Gardenbrook. Something about her reactions that evening had stayed in his mind, like an object irritatingly placed on the wrong shelf.

She had not been herself, not at all, and he wanted to know why. He did not like things out of place, did not like things not going as they usually did. And Lady Violet was quite confusing enough as her normal self, without confounding him further by behaving so very differently. It was almost as if she had been afraid – but of what?

Perhaps she would be at this evening's musicale?

The thought stopped him, hand on the door – why was he even considering where she might be? He had resolved to avoid her, to make certain that the tidy order of his world was not disturbed by her, yet here he was, wondering if she would be at an event? Almost... hoping... to see her? He was obviously going mad. There was no other explanation.

*****

Lady Ormondston smiled as they entered, and curtsied to her father.

"Your Grace, I am so glad that you, and your family, were able to attend."

The Duke took her hand, always the gentleman, even if he found the woman obnoxious, as Violet knew he did.

"Lady Ormondston, I must apologise for our tardiness..."

"It is nothing, Your Grace. In fact, your timing is perfect, for we are just about to begin – if you will join the others in the large parlour, I will introduce our first performer but minutes from now."

"Of course."

Violet followed her parents through the door of the parlour, in which chairs had been set up facing an area where a magnificent pianoforte and some other instruments awaited. Almost all of the chairs were full, and Thorne tugged her, and Iris, to one side.

"There, there are three seats there – I am sure that Mother and father will find seats as well. Let us be quick."

Unwilling to draw anyone's attention, Violet let herself be guided into the seats. Iris followed Thorne's direction without even looking – her eyes were all on that pianoforte, and a small sigh escaped her – Violet knew that iris was internally praying that whoever was to play might actually be capable of doing so well.

She settled herself, and only once her skirts were neatly ordered in the cramped space did she look to her left.

Dark amber eyes met hers, and a wry smile twisted Lord Merryfield's lips. Had Thorne planned this? Violet half suspected so – she would have words with her brother later! Merryfield's whispered words came softly to her.

"Good evening, Lady Violet."

"Good evening, Lord Merryfield. Do you enjoy musical entertainment?"

She wondered if he did, what manner of music he preferred – it was not something she had imagined him caring for...

"That rather depends on the music, Lady Violet. I have attended some musicales where the... style... of performance was not really to my taste, I must say."

She found herself grinning at him, amused by his attempt at politeness, when she could well imagine what type of performance he might have suffered through. With luck, this evening's would be better.

They said nothing more, for Lady Ormondston called for everyone's attention.

"My dear guests, our first performance this evening will be from my daughter, Lady Anna, who I am pleased to say will be accompanied by Lord Greenleigh. We have not had the pleasure of hearing his playing for over a year, but now that he is past his mourning, we may have that delightful experience again."

She stepped to one side, and Lady Anna and Lord Greenleigh took their places. Beside Violet, Iris shifted in her seat, and whispered close to Violet's ear.

"I have not met Lord Greenleigh, nor even heard of him before now! If he plays half so well as he looks, then he is a man I will wish to meet."

"Shh. That can wait for later."

Thorne's tone, from the other side of Iris, was amused. He understood Iris very well, and knew that anything musical would always intrigue her. There was silence for a moment, and then Lord Greenleigh set his fingers to the keys of the pianoforte.

Violet knew, from the first few rising notes, that the man before her was more skilled than anyone else she had ever heard play – perhaps excepting Iris. If she had held any doubt, the sigh which escaped Iris would have removed it instantly.

If the playing was perfect, however, the singing which accompanied it was not.

Lady Anna had a passable voice, and had chosen a quite difficult piece, from a recently popular Italian opera – but she had chosen to sing it in the English translation. And that choice could be said to have completely destroyed the piece, for the language did not have the lilt and flow that the Italian did, did not entwine itself with the music to provide an extra layer of harmony.

Violet settled herself to endure, and tried her hardest to listen only to the notes of the pianoforte. Beside her, Iris ground her teeth, which forced Violet to stifle a laugh. Lord Merryfield noticed, and raised an eyebrow at her, which she most intentionally ignored.

When the piece was finally finished, and the performers were replaced by a harpist, who was competent but nothing more, it was a relief. That piece was blessedly short, and then Lady Ormondston declared an intermission, suggesting that everyone should move to the ballroom, where refreshment tables had been set out.

Violet made no attempt to move immediately – let everyone crowd out through the doors first, she had no need to hurry.

"What did you think of that first piece, Lady Violet?"

Lord Merryfield's voice made her turn to him. He was, damn the man, so strikingly handsome that he took her breath away, no matter how often she might have seen him. His expression held amusement, and she wondered if he expected her to praise the whole thing, to deliver socially expected platitudes with no thought behind them. If he expected that, then she would surprise him.

"I cannot fault Lord Greenleigh's playing, but as for the singing... It is a difficult piece, admittedly, but I do much prefer it in the original Italian. The Italian language has a fluidity, a lilting pattern which in opera is usually structured so as to enhance and intertwine with the music. I cannot say that the English translation is capable of the same effect."

Even as she said it, she realised that she had broken one of her own rules – she had, by implication, revealed that she could speak Italian, that she thought about things beyond fashion, and complimenting those who society said one should. Would he realise?

*****

Arryn blinked at Lady Violet, momentarily lost for words. She preferred it in the original Italian? Surely that implied... It was almost as if she could speak and understand Italian.... But no, he must be misinterpreting her words. No young lady of the *ton* that he had ever spoken to could actually fluently speak a second language. Disconcerted, he made an agreeing noise, and was saved when they rose, the crowds having thinned enough for them to be able to leave the room.

Chapter Six

"Did you hear me, Violet? You are staring off into the distance in a remarkably improper way."

Violet started, and turned back to Iris. The small ballroom was crowded as the guests partook of the refreshments, and they were tucked into a corner near some potted palms and a decorative drape. Not far away, Thorne stood talking to Merryfield – about the Weights and Measures Bill, and the Bills attempting to limit military training, as far as she could tell.

Merryfield was a puzzle – a deeper and deeper puzzle every time she saw him – for nothing he did or said spoke of a character which would lead to a man getting sent down. Far from it. He seemed studious, and most focussed on matters of importance. All that tempered with a quiet sense of humour, as far as she could see. Which made her even more curious than before about exactly what he had done, to get sent down – what had he argued about?

"I didn't, I'm sorry, I was wool-gathering..."

"About Lord Merryfield?"

"No. I..."

Iris gave a quiet snort of laughter.

"Of course not... that's only where you were looking..."

"If we were at home, right now I would throw a cushion at you, my dear sister."

"I know. I'm taking advantage of the fact that we are in public."

"Really – sometimes you're as bad as Thorne! But what were you saying before?"

"I was telling you that I have discovered that Lord Greenleigh is a Marquess, and unmarried. I think I'm in love. Any man who looks as good as he does, and can play a pianoforte with such consummate skill deserves my attention. I simply must find someone who can introduce us!"

"What! Do you mean to say that Thorne doesn't know him?"

"It appears not... that's rather a first, isn't it?"

"It is. But I'm sure that you'll find a solution. Just don't do anything... improprietous..."

"Violet! Are you suggesting that I might step outside the bounds of good behaviour? I am shocked."

"Iris, where it relates to both music, and a handsome man, I am quite ready to believe you capable of such a thing."

Iris shook her head, but there was a gleam in her eye that made Violet hope that she hadn't just, inadvertently, set her sister on a very unwise course. Interesting men were remarkably dangerous, she concluded, even as her eyes went back to Lord Merryfield.

*****

"Arryn, there's a new round of rumours circulating a White's. And I've no idea where these have come from, any more than the last lot. This time, they are implying that you were involved in some sort of wrongdoing, to finance a life of debauchery in Oxford. And that I probably knew about it, and did nothing."

Arryn looked up, and met his father's concerned gaze.

"That's... that's complete madness. If anyone at Oxford lived less of a life of debauchery than me, I've yet to meet them!"

"I know. I can only assume that someone wants, very badly, to make people question anything that you or I say, or do. What I don't know is why. You haven't received any messages of any kind? Nothing to indicate what these rumourmongers might want?"

"No, nothing. And at social occasions, whilst I can't say that everyone flocks around me, they mostly treat me with an ordinary degree of courtesy. There has been no indication that anyone bears specific animosity to me."

"Then we will just have to continue as we have been, and hope that either the rumours stop, or that at least we receive some indication of why they exist. Without knowing that, I can see no way that we can act to stop them."

"I agree. I've nearly got that report ready for your committee, by the way, and there seems to be a clear leader in the options for anti-forgery methods – so you'll have something to recommend, at least as a trial. I should have it ready tomorrow."

"That's good – I just hope that all of these rumours have not caused too many of the Lords to doubt my capacity to lead the committee. I suppose I will see, when it comes to our next meeting."

"Indeed."

Lord Westerhazy turned, and left the room, but Arryn sat for some time, staring at the door before him, and contemplating his father's words. Guilt weighed on him that, somehow, his actions had brought them to this, to his father's reputation being publicly besmirched. And the worst of it was that he did not know why, or who, held such an enmity for him as to do this.

Somehow, he had to find out, had to make things right. He shook himself out of the daze of thought, and went back to his papers, and the report – at present, that was the only way forward he could see, which would be of any use to anyone. Time passed, and Arryn lost himself in his focus on the work, so much so that he was startled when a tap came at the door.

"Enter."

A footman opened the door and stepped in, carrying the correspondence tray.

"I am sorry to disturb you, my Lord, but this just arrived." He proffered the tray, on which rested a folded and sealed sheet of paper. "It was slipped under the door, my Lord – most irregular."

Arryn regarded it for a moment before reaching out and taking it from the tray. A great sense of foreboding filled him, for here was yet another thing occurring which did not follow the normal tidy order of things. The paper was coarse, the wax which sealed it plain, and not bearing the impression of any crest. The footman bowed, and went out, quietly closing the door behind him.

Arryn studied the hand in which his name had been written on the note, but did not recognise it. It was odd, uneven, like the writing of a child, or a person who did not write often. He broke the seal, and eased the paper open, all the while feeling as if it might contain something venomous and unexpected. The note it bore was written in that same peculiar hand, but it was quite clearly readable. He read it through twice, feeling a chill of worry, almost fear, settle into his core as he did so.

'Merryfield –

by now, you know just how little reputation you have left, and how easily any disgrace of yours can tarnish your family reputation – not just your father, but, unless you do as is required, your sister's as well. I am sure that you will be most helpful, for her sake.

The requirement is simple. Convince your father to have his committee conclude that there is no practical way to make bank notes unforgeable. If that conclusion is not presented to the House in two weeks' time, then it will be obvious that you do not value your sister, and action will be taken.'

He could not do as they asked. But nor could he allow Petrina's reputation to be sullied. His father might weather such a storm – his sister could not – the *ton* would destroy her at the slightest hint of wrongdoing. He folded the paper carefully, and tucked it into his pocket. He would not act precipitately – he would think this through carefully first, before he took any action. But there was one thing he knew, absolutely – he could not lie in his report, could not pretend that a viable option did not exist. He was incapable of that sort of deceit – if he did such a thing, he would be as bad as Professor Whimpferhim, promulgating untruths. Just the thought of doing something like that left him feeling physically ill.

He had a few days – if he delayed giving the report to his father – which he could force himself to do, justifying it as double checking his information – then he could buy himself some time to come up with a plan. The blackmailer – for blackmail is what this was, undoubtedly – was not expecting to see a result for two weeks, and Arryn would need that time if he were to prevent disaster.

As he left his study, the thought came to him – he still did not know why the blackmailer was doing this – and he needed, instinct told him, to work that part of it out, before any solution might be found.

*****

Trent leant against the wall in the card room, simply watching the men playing. The two who were top of Setford's list were there, and playing for fairly high stakes as usual. He did not like their manner, although he could not easily say why. Perhaps it was the fact that they seemed completely unconcerned about losing. No sensible man let money run away from him with no care at all. He almost laughed at that thought – that was the point – these two did not seem to be sensible at all.

He had yet to see anything to justify Setford's suspicions – beyond that casual disregard for losing. Instinct told him that Setford was right – but how he might prove that was something he had no answer for. Perhaps Lily, who was sitting out in the ballroom, talking to her mother and sisters, might hear or see something useful.

*****

Violet looked at Lily, who was definitely starting to visibly show that she was increasing. Her sister was so happy, so certain of her place in the world, in a way that she had not been before her marriage. Violet envied her, wondering if she herself would ever find a man she could care for enough to marry, a man who might actually appreciate her intelligence and interests, rather than regarding them as unladylike.

She shook her head – such thoughts were foolish – it was unlikely that a man of that nature existed amongst the *ton*.

At that moment, Lily turned to her.

"Violet, do come with me – I find that I need to visit the ladies retiring room – this business of being increasing does have some uncomfortable side effects!"

Violet joined her in gentle laughter, and stood.

"Of course – it is so stuffy in here – perhaps it is fresher in the hallways, or there is a terrace off the retiring room."

They passed the card room as they went down the hallway, noting that there was a surge of gentlemen moving about – some leaving the room, some entering, others sitting at the tables, staring fixedly at their cards. Violet did not understand what men saw in gambling – once she had learnt enough to calculate the odds of winning, she had decided that anything other than playing for penny stakes to amuse her great aunts was foolish in the extreme.

The room set aside as the ladies retiring room was a smallish parlour towards the rear of this house, and to their relief, it did have doors that opened onto a small terrace which ran along the side of the building. While Lily attended to her needs, Violet stepped out through those doors, letting them close soundlessly behind her, and walked along the terrace a short distance, glad of the crisp night air.

It was not so cold as that other night when she had stood on a terrace recently… she shivered at the memory. Even as she did so, a sound came to her, closer than the faint strains of music from the distant ballroom.

Voices. Voices which caused her to stop, instantly. The same voices which she had heard that other time, when they had spoken chillingly in a darkened garden.

Her first instinct was to flee. But her second was to creep closer to the partially open door through which those voices issued, and to listen. She wanted, if nothing else, to discover who the men were, that she might most carefully avoid them in future. And if she were to be honest with herself, she wanted to know exactly what wrongdoing it was that they had discussed.

Her flimsy ball slippers made no sound on the paving of the terrace, and she came to rest, yet again, leaning against stone, mere inches from that barely cracked open door.

It was open but an inch or two, and she suspected that the men were not even aware of it being so. But it was enough that, when she eased forward and peered through that opening, she could see the two men who stood beside the fireplace to one side of the room. They were lit only by the flickering flames, but it was enough for Violet to realise that she did, indeed, know one of them, albeit only slightly.

He was Viscount Villeham – a man she had danced with once, and found rather repugnant. The other man she did not recall ever meeting. As she hovered there, watching, Villeham reached into his pockets and produced a thick bundle of something, which he held out to the other man.

"Here, Cater, your share of the latest batch, as agreed. Don't expect more, if you lose it all at the tables tonight."

"And why shouldn't I? You can just produce more..."

"You know that would be foolish – if we seem too flush, too soon, someone is sure to get suspicious, despite the fact that I've put out the story that it appears my grandfather was a penny-pinching hoarder, and in his later years, as his mind went, he hid that hoard about the more obscure parts of Villeham Hall. People believe what they want to believe, and congratulate me on my luck. But you have no such convenient story. "

"I suppose you're right. I'll pay what I owe tonight, and step back from the tables. There's always another night. And I'd prefer that we were not discovered – even if it must be eked out, knowing that there is a limitless supply of blunt available to me is a most reassuring way to approach life. Well, it will be, once we make sure that interfering damned Committee fails to find a solution..."

Villeham smiled – and it was not a pleasant smile.

"Oh I think that we'll have no problem there. So helpful of the son to have got himself sent down, and provided a place for us to start with the rumours and creation of doubt. I've escalated the matter, and I'm sure that he'll do what we want. If not... well then, he won't be the only one to suffer."

With a nod, the man referred to as Cater took the bundle, and shoved it roughly into his own pockets, and they both turned towards the door to the hallway. Violet stood frozen in place, watching them leave.

Watching because, as Cater had pocketed what he had been given, what looked like a piece of paper had fallen from the bundle to the floor, with neither man noticing. It fluttered down, to land close to the fire, and lay there upon the rug.

Only when she was sure that they had gone, and would not return, did she slip through the door and hurry across the room, to scoop that paper up, and tuck it into her reticule. She was shaking with fear, but she knew that she had to see what it was, to be certain that she had understood correctly. And if she had... then Lord Merryfield was in danger – the thought of which sent a shocking twist of pain through her heart.

Back in the ladies retiring room, Lily was tidying her hair, looking much more comfortable. Blessedly, there was no one else in the room. Violet quickly locked the door to the hallway, and pulled the paper from her reticule.

It was, as she had expected, a bank note – or at least it looked like a normal bank note. But from what the men had said, she was almost certain that what she held was actually a forgery.

Chapter Seven

"What is it, Violet?"

Lily came to her, her expression curious. Violet held it out.

"It's a bank note. But... I suspect that it's a forgery."

"A forgery? Why would you suspect that? And where did you get it?"

"That's rather a long story, involving overheard conversations. I think that I need to tell Trent about it."

At that moment, there was a sound from outside the terrace doors, and Violet stopped, her eyes going that way. What if it was Villeham? Or someone else? No one should hear what she was about to say. She shoved the note back into her reticule, took Lily by the arm, and quickly unlocked the door. Lily made no argument to being dragged unceremoniously out into the hallway. She simply gently patted her sister's hand.

"Come to call on us tomorrow, then you can tell Trent and I at the same time."

"I will – that is by far the most sensible idea."

They wound their way back through the halls towards the ballroom, but were stopped near the card room door when Trent stepped out and slipped his arm through Lily's. She lifted her face to his with a smile.

"Excellent timing, my dear. Violet has made a... discovery... and will call on us tomorrow to tell you more."

Trent raised an enquiring eyebrow at Violet, who shook her head, and spoke in a near whisper.

"Not here. Wait until tomorrow. This should not be overheard."

"As you will. Let us return to the ballroom."

*****

In the doorway of the card room, Lord Villeham had come to a sharp halt, not wishing to draw notice to himself by pushing past the people who had stopped in the hall. Which meant that he overheard their words.

Disquiet filled him – it might be a perfectly innocent discussion, about family matters which they wanted to keep private, but still – he could equally interpret those words as meaning that the lady had, somehow, found out something about his dealings with Cater. It seemed unlikely, but nonetheless, a cold shiver ran down his spine.

They would need to be triply careful from now on.

The people turned towards the ballroom, and Cater appeared beside him.

"Why the hesitation in the doorway? There are drinks to be had, and attractive women to dance with."

"There are, but I just overheard something that worries me."

"What?"

"A young woman claiming that she had made a discovery, which should be kept secret, and arranging to tell Canterford about it tomorrow."

"And why does that worry you? It's likely some scandalous affair she's heard about, or the like. Even if she knew anything which might concern us, why would a gentleman believe a silly young woman if she made such a claim, especially a quiet man like Canterford? Relax and enjoy yourself – that's the whole purpose of our... enterprise... after all, isn't it?"

Villeham shrugged, and allowed himself to be convinced, but still, a seed of worry had burrowed into his thoughts, and would not be uprooted. If he saw any evidence to support his concerns, in the next week or two, he would have to act – he was not about to lose everything on the word of a silly chit.

Perhaps he should dance with the girl, and see what she was like...

*****

Arryn had arrived at the Ball later than usual, and been unable to prevent himself from immediately scanning the room, looking for Lady Violet. He saw some members of her family, but not her, and disappointment filled him. Rapidly followed by annoyance with himself.

He had resolved to avoid her – he should be glad that she was not present.

He considered the cluster of quieter young ladies in one corner.

There was always a small group of wallflowers at any event – young women who were not popular, not the prettiest – and he had taken to randomly picking from amongst them to find women to dance with.

They were usually flattered that any man had sought them out, but they did not have high expectations that anything more than one dance might come of it.

Which suited his purposes perfectly.

He chose a young lady he had never danced with before, and led her out for the next set. She seemed so shocked to have been asked to dance that she was barely capable of speech, for which he was grateful. She was also actually capable of dancing quite well, which was a relief. As the dance ended, and he led her back to her chaperone, a movement across the room caught his eye.

Lady Violet was there, just re-joining her family, another woman beside her. Before he had thought about it, he was moving, abandoning, with barely a word spoken, the young lady he had danced with. Behind Lady Violet, just as he reached her, another man turned away, sharply, the sudden and rather jerky movement catching his eye. But there seemed nothing untoward, and he turned his attention back to Lady Violet, who was regarding him curiously.

"Good evening, Lady Violet. Might I hope that you have this next dance free?"

He almost winced – he had been far too blunt, and he knew it as soon as the words were out. Beside her, her sister regarded him uncertainly. But she smiled, as if he had done nothing untoward.

"You might indeed, Lord Merryfield."

He offered her his arm, and turned to lead her to the floor, wondering why the sister now looked shocked. But that was unimportant. Now that he had done this, had, yet again, put himself in close proximity to this woman whom he was supposedly trying to avoid, he did not know what to say.

Silence stretched, and they reached the place where couples were assembling in readiness just as the music began.

A waltz... she had granted him a waltz.

He swallowed, and took her into his arms. She lifted her eyes to his, and smiled again. His heart did a most peculiar thing in his chest, and everything except her blue violet eyes seemed to fade away. The silence no longer felt strained, but somehow, more complicit, as if in the quiet space they shared something secret, known only to them.

They began to move, and it was as if he had never danced before, so different was this moment. No effort was required – they flowed, completely and fluidly in tune with each other, as if they had done this a thousand times before. It was the most extraordinary feeling.

*****

Violet knew that Iris was staring, knew that her sister would have words to say to her later – for she had not had this dance free at all, and now Iris would have to deal with the disappointed Lord Albemarle when he appeared in search of Violet. But she found that she didn't care. She wanted to dance with Lord Merryfield – wanted this particular dance, because it was a waltz.

When he had appeared before her, just now, she had been faced with a shocking realisation – she was happy to see him. No matter her previous resolutions about him, her determination to regard him as utterly beyond the pale because he had been sent down, it seemed that she had come to care for him, to find him attractive. That moment out on the terrace, when she had realised that it was Merryfield, and his family, that Villeham threatened, when her heart had responded with a sharp pang of anguish, had forced her to face her feelings. She had been deluding herself.

The dance began, and the silence between them remained, but now, it felt different. Did he feel the difference in her? Why did she care about him? How could she care for a man who had allowed himself to be sent down? And how could this man – who was studying still, who bought serious books at Bigglesworth's, and who never went near a card room, be the man who was whispered about as a disreputable philanderer?

"Lord Merryfield..." he stiffened slightly, but only for the barest moment, as if words somehow intruded, but then he relaxed again, and smiled. That smile was enough, on his handsome face, to make her feel quite dazzled. She went on, and found herself asking, very forwardly, the question which had plagued her. "Forgive me my impertinence, but I feel compelled to ask you – what did you really do, to get sent down? There are a dozen rumours, but..."

She was sure that she had gone too far, that he would reprimand her and refuse to answer – as he had the right to do, and as she would expect any man of the *ton* to do. They swirled on, and a wry smile crossed his face. Would this be the last time she would ever dance with him like this? Had her curiosity just cost her something which she had only now realised she wanted?

****

Arryn was startled when she spoke, for he had become lost in the dreamlike feeling of dancing with her. He smiled, amused at himself. A flicker of emotion crossed her face, and she went on, her words utterly unexpected. Yet again, she behaved in a manner which he did not expect from young women of the *ton*.

Part of him was tempted to laugh, part to brush the question aside, but the far greater part of him wanted to give her the truth. After a few moments of silence, her expression became worried, as if his response to her very forward question actually mattered to her. Certainly, it wasn't the sort of thing most people would say, to simply make polite conversation.

"Do you know, you are the only one who's had the courage to ask?"

Her expression steadied, and those beautiful eyes brightened.

"I am? I know that it is beyond forward of me, but... I simply have to know. For the way you behave, and the things that you speak of – none of that aligns with the picture painted of you by rumours. And I prefer truth to supposition."

"I must agree with you there. I will give you truth, in return for your courage, although I do not know what you will think of me when I tell you."

"That you are a rare man who speaks more than empty platitudes to women?"

The dance spun them around, and he was not sure in that moment if his dizziness came from that, or the manner in which she had, yet again, utterly destabilised his ordered world.

"An interesting perspective. I do believe that to be interpretable as a compliment. But the answer to your question. To put it bluntly – I told a Professor that he was wrong. I could not bear to hear him teaching things which were outright falsehoods. I had all of the research, all of the information to support my position, yet he would not listen, would not accept that I had any right to question his knowledge. Truth did not matter, only his authority."

Arryn knew, as he said it, that his tone was bitter. What would she think? Probably that he was a fool, and should have respected the pompous old termagant. None but his close family had ever truly grasped just how impossible it was for Arryn to allow things to be incorrect, or out of place.

"But... he was teaching falsehoods? That is horrifying! The opportunity to learn, to study, is a thing to be treasured, and for a man charged with providing that learning to students to so betray its purpose... How can he consider himself a true scholar, if he would not consider your evidence, your reasoning for your position?"

If the world had been spinning before, it was moreso now. What she had just said... such passionate belief in the value of learning – and an implied immediate belief in him as a person – for she had not in any way questioned the idea that he might know more than a professor!

"I do not know. But everyone else seems to think that he had the authority to do as he wished, and that I should just have accepted it."

"Then everyone else is foolish, Lord Merryfield. Wrongs should be righted, even at personal cost."

"Thank you, Lady Violet."

The music slowed, and they spun to a stop. Which did not, at all, slow the spinning of his thoughts.

She smiled at him, and he reluctantly released her from his arms, turning to escort her back to her family. She looked up at him, and her lips curved into a genuine smile. He could not drag his eyes away. He wanted to kiss her – not just because she was a beautiful woman, but because of what she had said. Because she was the first person, outside his family, to unreservedly accept his view on such a matter.

"What will you do?"

Her voice was soft, and the words simple, but he understood the many layers contained in that question.

"What I have been doing. Continue studying. Hope that, within the next two years, I will be permitted to complete my degree. Attempt to turn what I have already learnt to useful purpose where I can. And try, somehow, to find a way to prevent my obsession with things being correct from ruining anything else."

There was that bitter sharpness in his voice again. He swallowed – she was kind, she did not deserve to be faced with his bitterness.

"I do not think that correctness ruins things. Surely it is the unwillingness of others to learn that causes the problem. I do not like lies. In society, there are times when prevarication is necessary, absolutely, but that is a different matter from outright falsehoods."

Kind indeed. Perhaps she did not truly grasp the degree to which his obsessiveness drove him. They were fast approaching her family, and he was startled to realise that he did not wish to leave her.

"It is. Although even prevarication of the socially expected kind is something which I find difficult."

Why was he being so open with her about these matters? He never spoke to anyone of his obsessions, and the difficulty of daily life. Somehow, she felt safe. Perhaps he was an even bigger fool than he had already believed himself to be.

"Perhaps we should set a trend in society, for terrifyingly blunt honesty? Although I admit, given my sister Hyacinth's... experiments... in that approach, I suspect that it would not go well."

"That sounds intriguing – you will have to tell me about that."

She lifted her eyes to his for a moment, and they sparkled, full of laughter.

"I will, for it is a most interesting story – but not one to be told in public..."

Warmth filled him, in the strangest way, for what her words implied – that, one day, they might be in a circumstance which was not in public, where she might gift him family secrets.

Chapter Eight

In a dark old building, not far from the houses of parliament and the wharves, crowded in on both sides by aging warehouses, a man rose from a cramped position, lovingly wiping the last of the old ink from the surface of the machine before him. He stretched, uttering a quiet oath, then limped across to open a door on the other side of the room. Inside, neat stacks of papers waited on benches and tables. Once he was sure that the ink was completely dry, he wrapped each bundle in a sheet of paper, and sealed it closed with plain red wax. That done, he packed all of the bundles into the large safe which was set into one wall. He nodded, satisfied – it was almost enough. His Lordship had promised that, once that safe was full, George would be given one of those bundles, and allowed a month or more to go back to Hamhall village and spend time with his mother and sister, before coming back to do more of this again. Another week or two here, and he could leave, with enough to ensure his family would survive, no matter what.

He locked the safe, and slid the large old noticeboard back across in front of it.

Strange how the skills he'd learned at war, repairing weapons in the field and making bits of jewellery out of the shattered remains of what wasn't repairable, had led him to this life. Once, he would have refused such a choice, but now – it had been better than starving, better than his mother starving. There weren't many jobs for the injured when they returned from war.

And then His Lordship had discovered what he was doing, and made him a devil's bargain. Keep doing it, with better equipment, mostly for His Lordship's benefit, and thereby make sure that his family was safe and could stay on in the cottage on His Lordship's land, or be handed over to the law, and end in prison, or worse.

He had done what any sane man would, and agreed. But he'd known then, as he knew now, that there would never be an end to it. Men were greedy, and what he did made it all too easy to satisfy that greed. The years ahead looked bleak – just as bleak as war had been.

*****

Violet set the somewhat crumpled bank note down on the surface of Trent's desk, and pushed it across to him. She had just repeated for him everything that she could remember of both conversations that she had overheard.

"And you are sure that the voices were the same, for both conversations?"

"Completely sure."

"And that the man you saw was Lord Villeham?"

"Yes. I had only met him once, last year – but I remembered, for I danced with him then and found him rather repugnant."

"I see."

Trent lifted the paper, and scrutinised it intently, holding it close to the candle he had set on the desk for that purpose. After a few moments, he set it down on the desk again.

"Am I correct? Is it a forgery?"

Violet's voice was soft, and she could hear the uncertainty in her own tone. Trent met her eyes.

"You are. It's a very good forgery, but it's definitely a forgery. What gives it away is here." He tapped his finger on one corner of the note. "That text is wrong – the letters are the wrong shape, just slightly."

"So... you will take this to Lord Setford?"

"I will. He is already aware that there seems to be some forgery work happening amongst some of the ton, but this is excellent evidence to allow him to move his investigations forward further."

"Please let me know what happens – it disturbs me greatly that men so casually capable of wrongdoing are accepted amongst us."

"I will. And do be careful – no more listening at doors please! But if you do hear or see anything relevant, tell me immediately."

"I most definitely will. And... do you think that I am correct, in assuming that they threaten Lord Merryfield? I have said nothing to him..."

"I cannot yet be sure – say nothing until I confirm the truth of it."

Violet frowned.

"I... I do not like leaving him unwarned, but... if I am wrong, then I would worry him for nothing."

"Lord Setford will ensure that anyone threatened is guarded, if necessary. Leave I to his to do their job."

"I cannot like it, but I will do as you say."

*****

"They agreed to the demonstration idea."

"That's good. I had best contact Ibbetson again, and get him here as soon as possible."

"Yes – I told the Lords that it would take a week or more to arrange, as the man has to travel – even if it's not all that far, it is near winter, and the roads will not be good."

Arryn took a steadying breath – he needed to ask his father for more detail about exactly what had been discussed when the committee's report had been presented to the House of Lords. But he could not put himself in a position where he appeared interested beyond normal. That threatening note lay locked in one of his desk drawers, and whoever had sent it would hear soon enough, if they hadn't already, that what had been presented in the house was not what they had demanded.

"What did they have to say? Was my report enough to convince them that the committee will produce a result?"

His father gave a short bark of laughter.

"It's enough to have convinced the others on the committee, but many of the Lords seem unwilling to believe that it is possible to create an 'unforgeable' bank note. We'll have to hope that seeing the sample imitation notes and having it explained in more detail at the demonstration, will shift their opinions. A few of them, mostly the younger ones, seemed close to outright mocking of the possibility - almost as if they don't expect anything to come of the committee at all."

"That's... disappointing."

"It is. Some of them just can't believe it's possible – but then, some of them think that we should get rid of paper money completely, and go back to only using coin."

"I doubt that's even a faint possibility."

"You are correct – after the wars and the rather profligate spending of our rulers, we've not enough gold on hand to do so at any time soon. We are working towards it, but I doubt that paper money will ever disappear – it's far too convenient to carry, compared to coin, for a start."

"I'll send a messenger off to Ibbetson today – we'll just have to hope that the demonstration convinces them. Where do you want to hold it?"

"I believe that we will be able to arrange the use of a room in Westminster Hall, for a few hours at least. And more of them are likely to attend if it's there, as they will already be so close by. The parliamentary session will adjourn for the time required."

"Very well – I will leave you to your planning, and write the letter to Ibbetson now."

Arryn rose, sketched his father a bow, and left the room. A deep sense of foreboding had settled into him – he knew that he was doing the right thing, knew that his father's committee needed to present a truly workable solution to the forgery issues, yet he felt certain that whoever had sent that threatening note would not be so easily defied – now that it had been made clear that the committee would not declare its task impossible, it was likely only a matter of time before the blackmailer acted.

Had he just set a course which would bring ruin to his sister?

The afternoon passed, and once the letter was on its way to Ibbetson, Arryn found himself consumed by worry, replaying in his mind everything that he had done, every possible option that he had considered, and ending up still where he was. Regardless of the cost, to himself and his family, he could not outright lie. And he could see no other way forward – he would simply have to be aware of everything, and watch for the blackmailer's next move – although what could be done to combat the insidious nature of such things as rumours he did not know.

*****

"As forgeries go, this is a rather high-quality product."

Lord Setford handed the paper back to Trent with a grim smile, and turned his piercing grey eyes towards the large windows which lined the wall opposite. Outside those windows, the rooftops of London stretched into the distance, blending into the haze of smoke from the fires which warmed almost every building. In winter, the city lived under a pall of soot, as its residents focussed on staying warm enough to survive.

Trent's voice was a little harsh when he responded.

"I agree. Which makes me wonder just how many of these are now in circulation. If what Lady Violet saw is any indication - for Villeham to have handed his co-conspirator a bundle of the things suggests that there could be many."

"Indeed – and tracking them down will be nigh on impossible. Although... perhaps a word in the ears of the right moneylenders will be a good place to start. If they know how to identify the forgeries, then they'll check the notes they are paid with, and perhaps be able to tell my men which of the indebted Lords have been using these to pay off their debts."

"That's a good thought – but it won't directly incriminate Villeham – unless we are very lucky."

"True, but I do believe I have a better idea for that. Did you see his face when Westerhazy announced his committee's progress in the House?"

"He covered it quickly, but what I saw for a few seconds was outright fear and anger – almost as if he had expected Westerhazy to say something different. Which was curious – why might he expect that?"

"I don't know yet – but I will find out. I do believe that we can use this demonstration that Westerhazy has planned to trap the man. I cannot imagine that Villeham won't attend – and we can watch him while he's there. He may do something revealing. But we can also make sure that he has the opportunity to carry off one of the demonstration notes. Because if he does have a man tucked away somewhere doing the engraving and printing for him, then he'll be desperate to show that man what is being proposed, and find out if he thinks he can copy it well enough for the results to pass in use."

"That's a sensible approach – and far better than anything I'd thought of. I'm assuming that you have men watching him now?"

"I do, but they've not been able to dog his steps all the time – that would have made them far too likely to be spotted. But with this..." he indicated the forged note "...all we'll need is for my men to be ready to follow him closely, after the demonstration. If he doesn't lead us to the man who does the work for him, and thus incriminate himself, I will need to come up with another idea – but for now, I am willing to be patient, and hope that nothing more drastic will be required."

"Between that, and letting the moneylenders know what to look for, I am sure that we'll get the evidence needed. I've never been one for drastic action unless it is truly necessary."

"Nor have I. Drastic action is usually far too messy and visible for my liking. And it's part of a spymaster's job to keep his people from being revealed. If at all possible, we get the criminals to expose themselves. Do commend Lady Violet for her quick thinking in obtaining this note, when next you see her. There are times when I've thought that I should recruit that whole family as spies – they all have a talent for noticing the most useful things."

"I am loath to admit it, as my wife is part of that family, but you are correct. Perhaps... we should consider a far more structured approach to what I do for you, in terms of maintaining a watch on what goes on amongst the *ton*?"

Setford laughed.

"Perhaps we should..."

****

Arryn was tidying his papers away, in preparation for going upstairs to ready himself for the evening's Ball, when a tap came at his study door.

"Enter."

The footman who came in was carrying the correspondence tray, and Arryn raised an eyebrow at the sight. This late in the day, the arrival of messages was unusual. He lifted the missive from the tray when it was proffered, and ice ran through his veins at the sight of the writing upon it.

It was the same strange hand as that which had addressed the blackmail note. It seemed that his unknown enemy had wasted no time in expressing his opinion of their non-compliance with his directives.

Arryn waved the footman away, and dropped back into his chair, staring at the letter in his hands as if it were a spider, or some other dangerous beast. It sat there, the plain red wax sealing it, the uneven hand addressing it, and threatened by its mere presence.

He felt shaky, as if his world had, somehow, spun out of his grasp. He did not like this continuous flow of the unexpected, of things which he could not control, or manage in any reasonable way. From the moment that his inability to simply accept the promulgation of untruths had driven him to argue with Professor Whimpferhim, things had become steadily more chaotic.

The odd way in which Lady Violet Gardenbrook destabilised his world was one thing – this horror filled conflict between what was right, and what threatened his family was another entirely.

He stared at the thing, breathing slowly and steadily, and steeled himself to open it. He had no choice – at the very least, he needed to know what the enemy intended, before he ventured into society this evening.

The coarse paper crackled as he broke the seal and unfolded it, flattening it out onto the surface of his desk. It lay there, such a small thing, a scatter of words on a page, and yet it tore him apart. He could not lie, could not encourage his father to lie, yet he could not knowingly allow harm to come to his sister. But the words before him demanded that he do one or the other of those things.

> ***'It is obvious that you are a fool Merryfield. But so be it. Clearly, you do not value your reputation – but let us see if your attitude changes when it is your sister whose reputation suffers. If you want her to ever have any chance at making a decent marriage, then you had best make sure that the committee finds that they have been dealt an impossible task, which must be abandoned.'***

He wanted to crush the thing, to throw it into the fire, and watch it burn, but he did neither. At the moment, the two notes were the only clues he had to the identity of this unknown enemy.

He studied for a while longer, then locked it away in his desk with the previous note. Tonight, he would listen most assiduously to every damned piece of gossip he could detect. He would watch who spoke to whom, and he would, again, attempt to think of any possible reason that any person there might have to hate him.

He needed to uncover who was doing this, and put a stop to it. But he felt, as he had all along, that it was a task at which he was unlikely to succeed.

Chapter Nine

It was some days since she had last seen Lord Merryfield, and even then, that had been at a rather stultifying musicale, where the performances were so bad that almost everyone had appeared to be gritting their teeth in pain, and had mostly left early. There had been little chance for conversation, beyond a polite greeting, and certainly no chance for dancing.

Dancing... the memory of that waltz had stayed with Violet, sending a quiver of warmth through her every time she thought of it. Had she imagined the moment of connection between them? The miraculous sense of effortless flow of their dancing? Surely it had been real. Was she a fool to entertain the possibility that he might find her interesting, now that she had discovered that she found him rather more than that?

Probably.

She pushed the thought aside – there was no point getting herself all-a-dither about something she could not change – especially as she might well see him this evening, and might even dance with him again.

The evening's Ball was to be quite large, and she prayed that he would be in attendance.

And that Lord Villeham would not.

The memory of Villeham and his friend, with their so casual acceptance of carrying out forgery, of treason, chilled her to the bone. Had Trent given the forged note to Lord Setford? Might the Spymaster have discovered anything of use? It was another thing she should not worry about, for she could not influence that any more than she could the whereabouts of Lord Merryfield. She turned her attention to choosing a gown to wear, and then settled to allow her maid to assist her, and to dress her hair into a complex tangle of golden curls with amethyst tipped pins holding them in place.

By the time that they arrived at Lord Cavisham's for the Ball, Violet had only partly succeeded in setting aside her worries – and all of that determined progress was undone in a moment, when, upon entering the ballroom, the first person she saw was Lord Villeham.

She hesitated for a second, making Iris glance at her in confusion, then continued across the room with her family, pretending that she had not seen the man, that he did not exist. They reached the other side of the room and her mother immediately launched into conversation with one of her friends, which allowed Violet to simply stand there, and observe those in attendance.

"Violet – back there, why did you...?"

"Don't ask, Iris. Later, if you must."

Iris regarded her with intense curiosity, but, after a moment, nodded.

Cautiously, Violet glanced around, wondering if Lord Merryfield was there. She could not see him, and disappointment filled her. She looked again, hoping that she just hadn't seen him the first time – but she still saw no sign of him, rather she saw the frightening vision of Lord Villeham coming towards her, an odd expression of determination on his face. She shivered, and looked away, praying that he was not, actually, intending to come to her, to even, oh heavens forbid, ask her to dance!

Unable to help herself, she watched from under her lowered lashes as he came ever closer. What could she do? She had no socially acceptable excuse to refuse him a dance, yet the memory of his voice so coldly discussing threatening Lord Merryfield and his family rang in her mind, and every instinct warned her to flee. Perhaps the ladies retiring room?

"Iris, I..."

Before the rest of the words could leave her mouth, someone stepped in front of her. She looked up, and felt shock run through her. Lord Merryfield stood there, mere inches away, and past his shoulder she could see Lord Villeham turning away, his expression hard. For the second time in as many weeks, she felt the desire to simply step into Lord Merryfield's arms and collapse in relief. How had he come to have such an effect on her?

"Good evening, Lady Violet. Might I hope that you have this dance free?"

"Yes." It came out far too bluntly for politeness, and he considered her with a gently raised eyebrow. She felt her cheeks colour, and hurried to provide a more suitable response. "Thank you, Lord Merryfield – that would be delightful."

He offered her his arm, and led her away towards where the couples were forming up for the dance.

****

Arryn stepped into the ballroom and scanned those present, wondering, as he did so, if his eyes were passing over his unknown enemy. He could not allow himself to make any assumptions, but he also struggled to believe such malfeasance of many of the men he knew. Some however – those who gambled and behaved as if anyone who did not was less than a man – those he could perhaps see in the role of blackmailer.

He shook his head slightly, annoyed yet again at the destruction of the ordered pattern of his life. Across the room, he discovered Lady Violet Gardenbrook, standing with her family. Before conscious thought could intervene, he was moving in that direction. Just as he arrived before her, he realised that he had simply stepped in front of another man who had also been moving her way – Villeham! A surge of strange feeling filled him, protective, and tinged with jealousy, as if he had the right to choose who might approach her.

Madness! She was her own person, and he had no right to such a judgement – nonetheless, he was glad that he had pre-empted Villeham's approach to her.

"Good evening, Lady Violet. Might I hope that you have this dance free?"

"Yes." It came out far too bluntly for politeness, and he considered her with a gently raised eyebrow as her cheeks coloured before she hurriedly went on, "Thank you, Lord Merryfield – that would be delightful."

He wondered what disturbed her so, that she would speak with less than her usual perfect grace. He found that he did not wish her to be discomfited, and the thought came back to him of the expression she had displayed, at that other Ball, when he had collided with her as she rushed in from the terrace. The two together made him pause, and wonder if this discomfort was related to that – but why he should think so, he did not know, for he had nothing to hint at such, beyond a vague feeling.

He offered her his arm, and she placed her hand upon it. For a moment, he was sure that hers shook, but then it steadied. He must have imagined it.

They took their places in the line, and he was glad that the dance was a slower country dance, one with significant periods where the partners were together, and circling about each other. They had not spoken, yet the silence did not feel strained, and, most oddly, given how she had affected him most times they had met, this evening he found her presence almost soothing, steadier and far more predictable than the rest of the world, where an unknown enemy might lie behind every face he saw.

Still, he should speak.

"Have you been well, Lady Violet?"

She looked up, and met his eyes, hers full of emotion of some sort, which left him feeling confused again, and yet not unpleasant. Then she smiled.

"I have. I am not prone to illness, for which I am grateful."

The words were appropriate, yet he felt as if there was something beyond them, something which belied them in some way, which she would not admit. The dance moved them apart for a short while, and he could not help but admire her elegance as she moved.

They came back together, and she raised her face to his. For a moment, the urge was there, as it had been that day in the bookshop, to bend and kiss her. It shocked him, that he should feel so, but he could not deny the fact that he did.

"Lady Violet... do you not find all of this... and the gossip which goes with it... tiring at times?"

How did she cause him to speak such things? Somehow, with her, he uttered what he was thinking, rather than what he should say. He had just asked a question which he could reasonably expect almost any young woman to be horrified by. But no horror showed on her face as they circled. Instead, she tilted her head a little, and gave a soft laugh. That sound warmed him somehow, as if it granted forgiveness for his bluntness.

"Truthfully?" He nodded. "I do find it tiring – if I allow myself to pay attention to it. I have learnt to ignore it, to pretend, at events such as this, that there are no thoughts in my head beyond fashion, and which gentleman is courting which lady. I hear the gossip, but discount the majority of it for foolishness, and regard the rest as likely vastly exaggerated, based on tiny grains of truth. It would never do for the *ton* to discover that I ever think of anything else, now would it?"

There. she had done it again. He felt as if the world spun under him, uneven, unbalanced. He realised, in that moment, that there was only one explanation – she did, actually, think about things other than fashion and gossip. Which opened a vast and intriguing blank space of possibilities – what, exactly, did she think about?

"I... I suppose that it would not. You might shock them, terribly. That is of course, supposing that whatever you do think about includes things which at least some of them would disapprove of?"

There was that soft laugh again.

"Oh it does, I assure you. That is the delightful thing about thinking – unless one chooses to express it in words, no one else knows what you have thought about. It is much the same as reading – unless one lets someone else see the title of the book, they have no idea what you have been reading. One can indulge in quite shocking things in the mind, whilst being primly perfect on the outside."

He blinked, rather startled by the concept, and again, deeply curious about just what sort of shocking things might occur inside her mind.

"I see..."

"Oh dear, have I shocked you? Are you horrified? I really shouldn't have said that, should I? But you ask such delightfully direct questions, that I find myself unable to do anything but answer you, rather than prevaricate."

He laughed, and was stunned to realise that he had rarely laughed since he had returned from Oxford – not until now.

"I am, shall we say, startled. But not shocked, and certainly not horrified. I appreciate honesty, and bluntness. I am honoured that you have placed enough trust in me to tell me such things..."

Those blue violet eyes held his, as they rotated in a stately manner through the figures of the dance, and her fingers tightened on his where the dance required that they touch.

"In truth, I have surprised myself. Originally, when I knew only that you had been sent down, I would not have done so, but now, somehow... things are different. I do hope that you will be faithful to my trust, and not reveal my shocking secrets to the *ton*?"

"I will, indeed, be faithful, and hold what is yours close to my heart."

As he spoke the words, they seemed to have a fateful ring to them, as if he promised far more than the keeping of small secrets. A shiver ran through him, strangely compounded of warmth and uncertainty, and he returned the pressure of her fingers, ever so slightly.

The music slowed, and again, he found that he did not wish the dance to end, that, with this woman, he wanted more – more time, more conversation, more understanding of just what hid inside that beautiful head.

They stopped, bowed and curtsied to each other, and then turned to leave the floor. As he offered her his arm, he glanced across and saw his father looking in his direction, his expression unhappy. Did his father disapprove of Lady Violet? That seemed unlikely. He would have to go straight to his father, once he had delivered Lady Violet to her family.

They were halfway across the floor when he came across his sister, on the arm of Lord Gillieston, who was their uncle, on their mother's side of the family. They stopped, and introductions were made, with Arryn watching closely. He wanted, he discovered, his sister to like Lady Violet...

Lord Gillieston smiled, and spoke to Arryn in an unconvincing 'aside'.

"My wife is an old friend of Lady Violet's mother, you know. I do believe that it's the gossip that bonds them together. I've warned your dear sister here that she should never do anything worth gossiping about, lest her aunt be forced to choose between gossip and family loyalty."

Petrina tapped her uncle lightly with her fan, and turned back to Lady Violet.

"My uncle seems to think that I am doomed to creating gossip at some point in my life. So far, I have proved him wrong."

"I pray, Lady Petrina, that you continue to prove him wrong. Being the subject of gossip is never pleasant."

"Indeed. Although my aunt would have little to do if no-one were ever the subject of gossip!"

They laughed, and then each moved on. Soon after leaving Lady Violet with her family, Arryn was at his father's side, although he had found himself almost unwilling to leave Lady Violet. He was thinking so strangely of late!

His father gave him a somewhat grim smile.

"Step out onto the terrace with me for a moment, Merryfield."

"Of course." They said nothing more until they stood in the chill November air at the far end of the shadowed terrace. But then, Arryn turned to his father, and asked the obvious question. "Just exactly what disturbs you father – for I can tell that you are displeased by something?"

Lord Westerhazy frowned, then spoke softly.

"There is more gossip. But this time, it is not about you or me – it's about Petrina."

Arryn felt chilled to the bone as the words sank in. So, the blackmailer had not wasted any time in acting, as he had feared.

"About Petrina? What are they saying?"

"Nothing definitive, thank God. But there are whispers which imply that she did something scandalous, and we hushed it up. Which means that the gossips are now trying to remember every move she has made in the last two years."

"We know that they won't find anything – because there hasn't been anything!"

"The truth has never been something to stop the spread of rumours, you know that. If they find nothing, it's only a matter of time until someone makes up some imaginary sin, and convinces themselves that they 'remember' seeing it happen. I am at a loss for how we might stop it."

Arryn swallowed, choking back the words which wanted to rush forth. This was his fault! If he had never been sent down, there would have been no seed of wrongdoing for gossip to be built on. If he had found a way to identify the blackmailer, or a way to stop their enemy without also putting his family at risk... But he hadn't. Couldn't. The situation was impossible.

And here he had been, since he arrived here this evening, completely caught up in Lady Violet, and not paying proper attention to what was happening around him. If he had paid attention, would he have heard the same gossip that his father had? Perhaps even have seen something which might give a clue as to its original provenance?

And he still could not tell his father about those notes, despite the impulse to do so, could not bear to see the disappointment which would fill his father's face. He had to fix this, himself, somehow.

"I... I don't know either. But..." The tiniest flutter of hope sprang into being as an idea occurred to him. "...perhaps we can at least try to change things. After all, our aunt, Lady Gillieston, is, not to put too fine a point on it, a leading figure in the gossip circles of the *ton*. Surely she would not believe such things of Petrina? So perhaps, if we enlist her aid in the right way, she can create counter rumours in some manner, to stop others from believing the slander?"

Chapter Ten

In the dimmest corner of the ballroom, tucked away almost behind the small orchestra, and sheltered by some drapes and a few rather sad looking potted plants, Lord Villeham and Lord Harmonton stood together, sipping drinks, and watching the activity in the room. Here, they were unlikely to be overheard, or even noticed – which was exactly as they wished it to be.

"Well Cater, it seems to be working. There are whispers, all suitably vague, but cloaked in the shape of scandal. I look forward to discovering what the old biddies invent to justify their ongoing horrified mutterings."

"It had better work, Villeham. We need Merryfield and Westerhazy to be desperate enough to do our bidding, before we put about anything worse than mere hints of scandal. I assume that you have a fallback plan if this doesn't get the results we want?"

"I... ah... you mean, apart from getting hold of something at their 'demonstration' to show my man?"

"Yes, apart from that. We both know that if they've got anything likely to be effective, then the chances of your man being able to defeat it will be slim."

"Err, no, I don't have another plan, not exactly."

"Well, we'd best come up with one, hadn't we? I've been watching Merryfield, looking for weaknesses. Westerhazy is too hard a direct target, so I think that Merryfield is still our best bet – Westerhazy has always been rather tolerant of his son's idiosyncrasies. Did you notice what Merryfield did this evening?"

Villeham regarded Harmonton with a raised eyebrow.

"What he did?"

"Yes. Almost straight after getting here, he sought out Lady Violet Gardenbrook. Can't say I blame him – she's an attractive enough thing. He led her off to dance, and pretty much ignored everyone else."

"Well, yes, I did notice him approach her – given that I was about to do so myself, and he cut in front of me."

Harmonton laughed, a rather sour sound.

"Well, once you get over your sulk about that, consider what it might indicate."

Villeham glared at Harmonton, but then narrowed his eyes in thought.

"What are you suggesting, Cater? Are you implying that you think Merryfield cares about her enough for her to be leverage?"

"Yes. Exactly that. To my eye, it looks like he cares about her – and I've seen no sign of him giving a damn about any other young woman, apart from protecting his sister. That has to be potentially useful, if the threat to the sister doesn't work."

Villeham nodded thoughtfully.

"Perhaps. But... what would we do?"

"Something rather more drastic than gossip would be required, I suspect. And we'd have to make damned sure that we weren't anywhere near it, or traceable to it, if at all possible."

"Definitely. Let's give it until the demonstration, and see what happens as a result of the gossip about the sister – and more about Merryfield, which will 'shockingly' be discovered in a day or so's time. In the meantime, I'll consider your idea – and exactly what options we have for using it."

"Good. Don't fail me on this Villeham – both of our livelihoods and our families depend on it."

*****

Violet stood with her mother, glad that, for once, she had not committed herself for this next dance. Lord Merryfield had left her rather hurriedly, and she found herself disappointed, after their somewhat intriguing conversation while dancing. Her eyes followed him, but he went out onto the terrace with his father, so she turned her attention back to her mother, just as Lady Fotheringhampton and Lady Gillieston hurried up, their manner one which suggested that they were quite bursting with new gossip to share.

Lady Fotheringhampton was the first to speak.

"My dear Duchess, have you heard the things that are being said this evening? Quite scandalous, and really not what one would expect at all!"

Lady Gillieston fixed her friend with a glare which would have quelled almost anyone else of the *ton*, but had little effect on Lady Fotheringhampton. She raised her chin, and sniffed disparagingly.

"Really my dear, you may be my oldest friend, but I simply cannot forgive you for paying any credence to this at all. My niece would never do anything scandalous!"

Violet watched as her mother blinked in mild confusion before venturing a question.

"Aaah, ladies, might you enlighten me? Which niece, Lady Gillieston? And what scandalous thing is she supposed to have done, Lady Fotheringhampton?"

Lady Fotheringhampton drew herself up, obviously thrilled to pass on whatever the drama was.

"Which niece? Why Lady Petrina Carrington, of course. And as to what scandalous thing – well, that's what makes it so intriguing – no one knows, for certain. There are many things whispered of, but it is supposed to have happened this last spring, and been hushed up by the family. I am determined to discover exactly what it was!

"It was exactly nothing. My niece is a virtuous and well-behaved young woman. This gossip is the worst of slander, spread by some small-minded person who is obviously jealous of her accomplishments."

"But surely... there cannot be whispers like this without there being some grain of truth at the base of it?"

"Balderdash! Petrina would not be party to scandal, ever, and I shall tell everyone I know that fact."

Violet was fascinated. She had never seen the two ladies disagree before.

And, having just met Lady Petrina, she was inclined to agree with Lady Gillieston – she could not imagine Lady Petrina doing anything particularly scandalous at all. But what was strangest about the whole thing was to hear Lady Gillieston decrying someone, anyone, for spreading gossip. Given that the Lady was one of the biggest purveyors of gossip in the *ton*, the counterpoint was comic, extremely.

Violet's mother appeared to be finding the conversation equally strange, and Violet suspected that she was struggling to prevent herself from laughing. The Duchess took what Violet thought was a steadying breath, and spoke again.

"I must agree that gossip can appear, invented out of whole cloth, with no grain of truth needed. But still, this does seem strange, and attempting to find out more about just exactly what she is supposed to have done might then make it easier for you, Lady Gillieston, to disprove the matter. Perhaps you should put your considerable skills for sniffing out what the ton would like to see safely hidden to work again, and try to trace this back to its starting point?"

The two women stopped glaring at each other, and turned to regard the Duchess. Violet was sure that, for a moment, the friendships of decades hung in the balance. Then they both nodded, and said, almost in unison.

"You're right. Let us be about it at once."

And with that, they turned, and set off across the ballroom, two women on a mission.

Violet stifled a giggle. Her mother, not looking at her, spoke under her breath, accompanied by an odd strangling noise.

"Violet! Don't! Or I shall not be able to contain myself."

Violet clenched her teeth, and forcibly prevented herself from laughing. Iris appeared at that moment, returned to them after dancing, and looked at both of them with a face filled with confusion.

"Why do you both look as if you have just swallowed one of Nanny's healing possets? The kind with the close resemblance to green slime?"

The Duchess went quite pink with the effort of holding in her laughter, and Violet managed to utter, in the strangest voice, a command to her sister.

"Iris, I will tell you at home, but please, say nothing more now."

"Well! Now I will die from curiosity, waiting until we get home. You are so cruel sometimes, Violet."

"Yes."

Iris blinked, having expected argument, not agreement, and turned rather huffily away from them as her partner for the next dance set appeared beside her.

Soon, Violet was claimed for that dance too, thankfully by an elderly gentleman who was always kind, and simply liked dancing. But as she moved through the steps of the dance, her mind was elsewhere, and her eyes roamed the room, watching the progress of Lady Fotheringhampton and Lady Gillieston as they worked their way about, talking to absolutely everyone. Iris was not the only one who would die of curiosity – Violet wanted to know what the two ladies were discovering.

*****

Villeham gritted his teeth, even as he danced with Miss Witherspoon. Every conversation he had walked past, this last two hours, had been about Lady Petrina – but not about how scandalous she was – nothing so satisfying – no, they had all been talking about the fact that Lady Gillieston had declared the whole rumour unfounded, and to be ignored.

That woman had influence – far too much influence – and if she kept this up, then the threat to the sister would fail before it had barely begun. Perhaps he would have to take Cater's idea rather more seriously than he had hoped for.

He spent the rest of the evening considering ways in which he might arrange for Lady Violet Gardenbrook to be threatened, and for that to be used against Lord Merryfield. He was, sad to say, discovering that, on this matter, he was not as imaginative as would have been useful.

Still, there was a week or so until the demonstration – surely he could think of something by then.

*****

Arryn gave his father a wry grin as they settled into the carriage after the Ball, but they did not speak until they reached home, and Petrina had gone up to her room. Then, they settled in Arryn's study, with brandy.

"It seems that our aunt feels family loyalty more strongly than even the lure of gossip. We did not need to co-opt her assistance. By the time that we returned to the ballroom, she had already begun her campaign on Petrina's behalf, and even managed to recruit Lady Fotheringhampton to assist."

"Indeed. I am as surprised – and grateful – as you. People will listen to her. So, we can hope that this will blow over with no real harm done to Petrina's reputation. But what worries me is why? Arryn, who could hate this family so much as to continually target us like this? I cannot fathom what any of us might have done for them to believe that we deserve such treatment."

"Neither can I." Arryn swallowed some of his brandy in a rather large gulp. He could not stand it anymore – he could see no way to work out who the blackmail notes had come from – he did not recognise the hand they were written in, and had discovered no other clues. He would have to tell his father about them. "But... I do have something that I have not told you about, which perhaps provides some clues – if only we can understand them."

Westerhazy looked at him, startled.

"Clues?"

Arryn rose, and went to unlock his desk, pulling out the two crumpled notes.

"These. This one came first, two weeks ago. Then this one, a day or so ago. I have looked, and thought, and cannot work out who they might be from, or why, nor could I resolve the conflict between being asked to lie, and needing to protect my family. I am sorry Father – I wanted to solve this, to stop it without you needing to ever see these. But I have failed you, again."

He had dropped the two notes into Westerhazy's hands as he spoke, now he went back to his seat, and settled, waiting as his father examined the notes. Guilt filled him again, and he wished, with all his heart, that he had somehow contained himself, and never told Professor Whimpferhim what he thought.

His father looked up, his expression concerned, but still filled with puzzlement.

"You do not recognise the hand that these are written in?"

"No. No one that I know writes in such a manner. And the seals bore no crest – they were simply sealed with a flattened blob of plain red wax. I have been able to see nothing that gives any clue as to the identity of the person behind these, or their motivation for so harming us. The only slight clue seems to be the fact that they want the committee to decide that creating 'forgery-proof' bank notes is impossible. But I do not understand who might want that, or why."

"Indeed, it is strange, but I think that may be a bigger clue than you realise. What if this person bears no direct enmity for our family at all? What if we are merely a means to an end? For if they want the committee to fail in its quest for a solution to the forgery problem, perhaps they are willing to use whatever leverage they can to force that result."

"Perhaps. But why do they want it to fail?"

"I don't know yet – but we will work that out. Unfortunately for them, we are far more stubborn, as a family, than it seems they expected – especially you. I've no doubt that your inability to perpetrate a falsehood is not something they were aware of, or allowed for. The conflict that this situation induced in you would not be something that most people might reasonably be expected to feel."

"Are you... are you suggesting that my... stubbornness... about order, and matters of truth, might actually be an advantage?"

"I am."

Arryn burst into laughter.

"I never thought to hear you say such a thing."

His father joined the laughter for a moment, then fixed him with a serious gaze.

"Your grandfather would be proud of you, Arryn."

"He... perhaps. But... what should we do?"

"Think on it. Rather than think, as you have been, about who might hold enmity for us, let us both think about what reason any man might have, for wanting to see the committee fail to deliver a solution to the forgery epidemic. Perhaps, that way, we will come to understand better what we are facing. But now, sleep. We can do nothing more tonight, but be grateful that Lady Gillieston wields the amount of influence that she does."

Chapter Eleven

"It all goes back to Lady Hartshorn. Every possible person who had heard anything, heard it from someone who heard it from her."

Lady Gillieston made this declaration with evident satisfaction, then paused to sip her tea, waiting for those around her to obediently ask for more information.

Violet glanced sidelong at Iris, and was met with an expression as amused as her own. Lady Gillieston did rather like making a performance out of things. Had it been a respectable thing to do, Violet was sure that she would have done well on the stage. On the other couch, their mother assumed her best polite smile, and asked the question.

"And where do you believe that Lady Hartshorn heard it from?"

Lady Fotheringhampton took up the tale, setting her teacup down, and lowering her voice to a conspiratorial tone, much to Violet's increased amusement.

"Well, my dear Duchess, that is where the mystery lies! She declares that she cannot remember, precisely, for she overheard two gentlemen speaking of the matter, but that, at the time, there were on the other side of a veritable wall of potted palms in Lady Dartwood's ballroom. She did not see the gentlemen, and cannot be certain, from the voices alone, of their identity. Personally, I suspect that she cannot be sure because, at the time, she had perhaps indulged in an overabundance of Lady Dartwood's port wine punch, which has something of a reputation for potency."

Lady Gillieston tittered at her friend's comment, nodding, then took up the story.

"Indeed. And it is most vexing that she can't provide further information. However, I have come to believe that perhaps, due to the potency of the punch, she may not have heard any of it very well. To the extent that it is most likely that she heard the lady's name incorrectly."

The Duchess sipped her tea, and when it became obvious that the ladies were waiting for her to prompt them, she set her cup down, and did so. Violet was, for the thousandth time, impressed by her mother's patience.

"But... if Lady Hartshorn heard it incorrectly...?"

"Then there is nothing to cast any shadow of scandal upon my dear niece. Which is only what I expected. The only time I can remember that Petrina has done anything at all even slightly less than perfectly appropriate was last year, when she had that unfortunate argument with Miss Felton, about the precise name for the shade of orange she was wearing. That was, to my memory, a truly dreadful gown, but Petrina's main complaint was that Miss Felton had called it the wrong colour. The girl can become rather... obsessive... about some things."

Lady Fotheringhampton nodded at her friend's comment, and spoke to confirm it.

"She can. But then, my dear, you must admit that it seems to be a family trait. Westerhazy is not so much so, but his father.... He had a reputation for arguing about the oddest things. And Merryfield – well, look where that behaviour has left him!"

Lady Gillieston frowned, obviously displeased at the seemingly negative view of her relatives. She gave a sniff of disapproval, and pointedly turned back to the Duchess.

"Well, that's neither here nor there in this matter, is it? I do wish that Lady Hartshorn was not so willing to repeat anything she hears, without at least trying to validate it first!"

At that comment, Violet nearly choked on her lemon cake, for coming from one of the *ton's* biggest gossips, it was a rather outrageous remark. The Duchess managed to respond, although Violet suspected that her mother was also repressing laughter.

"Yes, it would be preferable. But, if you believe that the conversation which Lady Hartshorn overheard was not about Lady Petrina at all, then who do you think those gentlemen were discussing?"

"I have considered that in some detail, quite exhausting myself with dredging through every memory, and have concluded that they can only have been speaking of Lady Petunia Peterwood. The name is similar enough that Lady Hartshorn might have easily misheard it, and there was a small scandal about Lady Petunia, not so long ago – a barely prevented kiss on a darkened terrace, if I remember rightly. At the time, a number of men speculated on what they might... achieve... with the Lady."

The Duchess frowned, with a quick glance at her daughters, who affected the most innocent expressions they could manage, as if they had no understanding whatsoever of what Lady Gillieston had just implied.

"Some men are certainly not gentlemen. So... if that is the case, what is your plan, to clear this besmirching of Lady Petrina's name? I assume that you do have a plan, my dear lady?"

Lady Gillieston preened, presenting a self-congratulatory smile.

"Of course I have a plan! I have already begun to put it into action. I have been speaking to whoever will listen – confidentially, of course – and hinting about the misheard name, without quite directly mentioning Lady Petunia. But they all know who I mean. The word will go around quickly, I am certain, that Lady Petrina has been falsely accused, and that there are far tastier pieces of gossip to be had, by watching other young ladies. Soon, everyone will forget about Petrina's supposed scandal, and go back to remembering her as being overly particular about the colours of gowns, and nothing more."

"I am glad to hear it. Thank you for calling to let me know. I must admit, the whole matter had intrigued me, for I have found Lady Petrina to be unexceptionable in every way."

"As she is. My niece is a perfect model of propriety. But we must be on our way – we have many other calls to make today, to ensure that the word on the truth of this matter spreads through as many parlours as possible. Thank you so much for the tea, and for the lemon cakes – I do so have a weakness for your cook's lemon cakes. It is cruel of you to refuse to share that recipe."

Lady Gillieston sighed, eyeing the last few cakes on the plate as if she might scoop them up and carry them off to fortify her on her calls, then gave the tiniest shake of her head, and rose to depart.

The Duchess simply smiled, and rose as well, to see the ladies out. As they left the room, Iris turned to Violet.

"Do you believe what they said? That Lady Petrina is as perfect as they claim?"

"Iris, what are you suggesting?"

"Well, when I met Lady Petrina, she seemed suitably behaved, by all appearances. But... she had rather a twinkle in her eye, and a sense of humour. Which makes me wonder what secrets she really hides. After all, we both look respectable, but there are things about us that would shock the gossips if they became known – although not so scandalous as kisses on the terrace..."

Violet gave a soft laugh.

"Perhaps. But you might only discover the truth of that assumption if you got to know her better."

Although she didn't say so, Violet rather agreed with Iris. There was something about Lady Petrina which suggested that there was more to her – perhaps, the startling thought came, she was rather better at dissembling than her brother?

"I do believe that I will set out to do just that."

As Iris made that declaration, their mother, rapidly followed by their father, returned to the room. The Duchess dropped back onto her seat, and poured herself another cup of tea. The Duke selected a lemon cake, and bit into it with obvious appreciation. Only when it was gone did he speak.

"I will be away from the house for longer than usual over this next week. I expect the sessions in the House of Lords to be long, and four days from now there is to be a long break in the middle of the day, to allow for the demonstration of some of the anti-forgery techniques that Westerhazy's committee have identified, so when we resume after that, it's likely to go very late into the evening, as the discussion will no doubt be extensive."

Violet regarded her father with curiosity, her attention caught by his words. After her reading of 'Paper Against Gold' and what she had learnt about the issues facing the government with respect to forgery, she was most interested in what might be shown at that demonstration. She sighed – for she was unlikely to find out, being a female. No-one would expect her to care in the least about such things. Her mother also sighed, with a different kind of resignation.

"I know that it is your duty to the country, but sometimes, I really do wish it didn't take up quite so much of your time. It is a pity that parliament is not something that most of your family can join you in."

The Duke laughed.

"It is, indeed, a pity. For most of you would express far more intelligent opinions than many of the Lords. However, on that subject, in this particular case..." He turned to face Violet directly. "...Violet, as you expressed so much interest in how the matter of monetary policy works, I wondered if you would like to attend Westminster Hall, just for the demonstration itself? I am sure that, if you remain quiet and inconspicuous, no one will object, although they'll likely quiz me about it later."

Violet was shocked, the teacup rattling slightly on its saucer the only indication of the quiver which ran through her.

"I... Yes. Thank you, Father."

"I thought so. I'll arrange for William to have the smaller town carriage ready to bring you to Westminster Hall at the right time that day."

As her father gave her a benevolent smile, Iris rose from beside her with a shrug.

"Really Violet, I can't imagine anything more dull. I'll leave you to discuss it – I have new music to play."

As Iris left the room, the Duchess rose also, a frown on her face.

"Are you sure that is wise, Violet? You don't want the gentlemen of the *ton* to decide that you are an irredeemable bluestocking!"

Violet laughed.

"Mother, I am an irredeemable bluestocking. But I promise that I will continue to do my best to hide that fact from them. Which is generally easy to do, given how little expectation they have of intelligence in a woman."

*****

Arryn was at his desk, making sure that everything was in place for the demonstration, every list ticked off, and every item where it should be, when his father, returning from the House of Lords, tapped on the door and came in.

"Still working? It's late, I thought that you might have retired for the night."

"I am about to. Ibbetson's here – our carriage arrived with him late this afternoon. He's brought a miniature printing press, all readied with what will be needed to give a full demonstration. That slowed them down on the road, making sure that nothing was damaged getting here, and it's also meant that I've had to re-arrange what we had planned a little. I sent the man to bed in the guest suite we prepared, but I couldn't go to bed myself until I had updated everything. I won't let anything go wrong with this."

"And I am very grateful that you have that attitude, especially as we haven't heard from the blackmailer again. Given that Lady Gillieston seems to have managed to completely defuse the gossip about Petrina, I've been worrying about what the blackmailer might try next."

"So have I. And I've been doing as you asked, and thinking about what sort of person might want the Committee to fail at its task. I have just one idea. I don't like it, as a conclusion, but I've not been able to think of anything else."

"Oh? What conclusion is that – for I admit I've made no progress at all on that aspect of things – I've been too busy answering inane questions in the House from Lords who don't truly understand what we are trying to achieve."

Arryn set the last of the paperwork aside, stacked it neatly, and slipped it into his desk drawer, before meeting his father's eyes.

"I considered what a person might think they would gain if the committee failed to find a solution. At first, nothing came to me – I could not see why anyone would want to perpetuate a situation where forgery was rife, and there was the risk that any bank note they received might be forged. Then it struck me that I was only considering one group of people."

"One group of people? What do you mean?"

"I was only considering honest people."

"Ah. I can see how you would do that, with your personal insistence on honesty. But... where did that realisation lead you?"

"When I considered who might benefit from forgery continuing, I could only come up with two possibilities. A person who was committing forgery would not want a method set up which would make their task impossible. And a person who was knowingly benefiting from forgery in some way, be that receiving funds or goods, would not want those benefits to stop. Beyond that, the only possibility would be if an extreme radical wanted the country to fail completely, through economic ruin – and I considered that probably too far fetched in this particular case. Radicals usually do things loudly and dramatically, not through quiet threats."

Westerhazy regarded his son consideringly, then smiled.

"That is very sound reasoning. So – which do you think it is?"

"I cannot be sure, but I'm inclined to think it the second – someone who benefits from the forgery. My reasoning for that is that most men with the skills to actually do the engraving and printing of forged notes would be commoners. They would know little of what was going on in the House of Lords, and would mainly be intent upon staying well-hidden. So for them, even if they heard about the committee, which is unlikely, sending notes with threats would be foolish, for it would just risk drawing attention to them. I cannot imagine a man like that trying to blackmail us. But if we have a man of the *ton* who is involved, and benefitting – well then, he would be a far more likely option as our blackmailer, wouldn't he?"

"He would. It seems so obvious now that you say it, yet I had not thought of it. I suppose that I am far too inclined to want to believe that gentlemen of the *ton* are at the core honourable – even the ones who get themselves deep in debt and the like. So the question now becomes – if it is a man of the *ton*, how do we work out who it is?"

"That, I do not know yet. My reasoning stopped there. I can only suggest that you watch closely, when the matters relating to the committee are discussed in the House, and that we both watch everyone closely at the demonstration. We must hope that one way or another, our blackmailer does something which reveals his identity."

Chapter Twelve

It was another musicale – this time one which Violet did not mind attending, for the hostess had prevailed upon Lord Greenleigh to perform. When Iris had heard via the gossips present at an afternoon call, she had insisted that they attend the event.

Apparently, the gossips thought that, whilst his skill at the pianoforte could not be denied, Lord Greenleigh was bordering on scandalous for playing in public with any frequency. Violet was surprised that Iris had not started an argument with them on the spot. Perhaps her sister was developing a greater degree of discretion than she had thought.

Now, as people filed into the parlour where the performance was to take place, Violet cast her eyes about the room for what must have been the tenth time. She was hoping to see Lord Merryfield, she knew it, and though she chastised herself for doing so, she could not stop. She wanted him to be there. Wanted the chance to speak to him again. She was being a silly goose, but there it was, she wanted it.

Iris edged through the crowd of people in a manner bordering upon improper, until she could claim a seat close to the front. Violet let her go, as did their parents, who were well aware of the fact that where music was concerned, Iris would take every opportunity to appreciate skill.

"Do move and take a seat Violet, you are holding everyone back."

Beside her, Thorne's voice jarred her out of her thoughts, and she felt her cheeks flush pink. She did not wish to be the focal point of people's attention! Quickly, she stepped to the side, and slipped along a row of chairs, dropping into a seat close to the end. Moments later, someone settled onto the chair beside her – the last one before that wall of the room. She turned, and stopped, surprise drawing a little gasp from her.

Then a smile overtook her face. It was Lord Merryfield, and his smile matched hers, his eyes sparkling a little with what might have been amusement.

"A gasp, Lady Violet? Is it so startling to see me here?"

"Lord Merryfield. I..." She swallowed, for a moment lost for words, and then the impulse she so often had with him drove her, and she told him the truth, rather than the polite platitude which would normally be expected. "Actually, I was just thinking of you, and was quite startled when you appeared, as if my thoughts had summoned you."

His deep amber eyes regarded her a moment, with that spark of amusement still deep within them.

"I believe that I am flattered. Although, if thoughts truly had the power to summon a person, I suspect that I would be forced to appear in many places which were either inappropriate, or very much not where I wanted to be at that time."

"What an intriguing statement. How shall I interpret it? That people think about you in inappropriate places – my, that has the potential for scandal – or that you have done things which cause others to think of you with displeasure, such that you would not wish to be called before them to face that anger?"

He laughed softly, and an odd expression flitted across his face, as if she somehow pleased and annoyed him at once. Then it was gone, and he spoke again.

"You may interpret it as you wish, My Lady. At one time or another, it is possible that both of those things might be true. For now, if I am to be summoned, I am glad that it is by you, and to a place as perfectly respectable as this."

Violet thought about those words. Lord Merryfield was a most deep and complex man, his conversation never failing to surprise her, one way or another. But she clung to the core of what he had just said, finding her heart beating faster in response to the implication.

"I believe that I am, in turn, flattered."

His eyes heated with a pleasure she had not expected to induce with so simple a statement – could he truly be that pleased to find that she was glad that he was glad to be with her? The hostess stepped up to call for silence, but just before she did, Lord Merryfield whispered, close to her ear.

"Lady Violet, once this performance is done, you must tell me just what you were thinking about me, just before I appeared at your side."

She felt herself blush. That was a request which she could not acquiesce to. Those thoughts were far too close to scandalous to be uttered aloud, especially to him!

The music began, and Violet allowed herself to be swept up by it, to flow with the sound, but throughout, her awareness of the man at her side never dimmed. She watched him, from under lowered lashes, drinking in the strong lines of his face, and the way that he closed his eyes, and actually, fully, listened to the music. He was so... unexpected... in everything he did – but in a good way.

What did he think of her? Was there some hope that he might care for her, even a little?

*****

At the back of the room, just before the performance began, two gentlemen slipped in and moved to the corner, leaning against the wall, as all of the seats were taken. They watched the room, ostensibly looking towards the performers, but actually studying people in the audience quite closely.

They whispered together, so quietly that their words were not distinguishable to anyone but them.

"Look at them, I am sure that I'm right. He cares for her – and she for him, from the look of it. We'll not get better leverage than that."

"That's all very well, Cater, but what will we do to use that leverage?"

"Take her? Or rather, arrange for her to be taken. Make demands in exchange for her return? Through a messenger, so there's no connection?"

"That's rather... extreme... isn't it?"

"Do you have a better idea?"

They were silent for a while, as the pianoforte music dropped to a delicate flowing pattern of notes, before rising to a crescendo again. Then Villeham shook his head.

"I don't. Even with that, if this demonstration shows any real promise, we'll need a campaign against it – something sowing doubt about the technical quality of the suggested methods. We'd best be ready for that too."

"True. I'll do some planning. But we'll know, as soon as we see this demonstration, just how fast, and how hard, we'll need to act. I'm not willing to lose everything."

"Neither am I."

*****

Trent slipped out of the House of Lords leaving others to continue the current discussion, which was on matters of little interest to him. He hurried through the buildings until he stood just outside the large anteroom off Westminster Hall, where the anti-forgery demonstration had been set up. Not long after he arrived there, Lord Setford joined him.

"Canterford – come to see what it looks like, before the crowds?"

"As much as you have Lord Setford. I assume that you have men in place, inside and out?"

"I do. Every second footman is one of mine, and others of the staff in the whole complex, as well as twenty or more scattered through the surrounding streets."

"You are leaving nothing to chance, then? Does Westerhazy, or his son who appears to be organising this for him, know?"

"No. I thought it wiser not to directly involve them. They have enough to concentrate on with making sure that this goes off well and the Lords actually pay attention."

"That makes sense. Still, if I see anything untoward, I do believe that, after telling you, I'll warn Merryfield – just in case our suspects decide to take drastic action."

"That's reasonable – just don't create unnecessary panic. Merryfield is a steady man in most ways, as far as I can see, but he does seem to have an obsession for orderliness. No need to disrupt things for him."

"I won't. Let's just hope that the men we are watching do as we suspect they will, and take a sample note, then leave, so that we can follow them. If there's to be any altercation, I'd rather it was not in these buildings at all."

"That is my preference too. Ideally, none of the other Lords will even know that anything has happened."

They stood quietly for a while, watching as the last things were put in place for the demonstration, waiting for the moment when the Lords would all come bustling down to see what the committee had promised to show them. As they waited, the side door from the street opened, and a footman escorted a woman in. Trent started, and he and Setford moved back a little, into the shadows.

"What on earth is Lady Violet doing here?"

Setford looked amused at Trent's question.

"Indulging her curiosity, I suspect, no doubt with her father's approval."

"Let us hope, then, that nothing dramatic does occur. The need to protect a Lady rather complicates matters, doesn't it?"

"A little, yes. But the men will manage."

Lady Violet was led across to the door of the anteroom, and shown in by the footman as they watched.

*****

Arryn stepped back, for the first time feeling truly confident that the demonstration would go well. Everything was in place, and even Mr Ibbetson, who had been very nervous earlier, was beginning to look more comfortable.

He turned from where the small printing press had been set up, intending to adjust the chairs in the room for a final time, just as the door opened. A footman showed someone in, and closed the door after them. Arryn knew her instantly, even though she was the last person he would have expected to be in that place, at that time.

She lifted her gaze, and her eyes met his across the room. It was as if everything slowed, as if none of his careful planning mattered, as if none of it existed anymore. There was only Lady Violet Gardenbrook. He forced himself to breathe, and stepped forward, wanting to go to her, but she smiled and shook her head gently when she saw his movement, and simply slipped to the side, to locate herself in the dimmest part of the room, beside a large old bookshelf.

With her eyes no longer locked onto his, the world spun back into focus, and he was grateful – grateful that she was wiser than he.

This was not the time to allow himself to be distracted, to be put off balance by her presence. Once the demonstration was done, he could speak to her, could discover how she had come to be there. For now, she was safe where she was, inconspicuous, and unlikely to be questioned by anyone. He turned his attention back to chairs, and squeezing enough into the space, but all the time, subliminally, he was aware of her, as if she were a magnet which drew him, an anchor in the chaos of preparation.

*****

Turning away, allowing her eyes to drop from his, was quite the hardest thing that Violet had ever done. The look on his face in that moment, as he had taken that step towards her, had told her more about his feelings than anything previous. For that few seconds, he had looked at her as if she were the most wonderful thing that he had ever seen, as if he wanted to run to her, to sweep her into his arms.

That look had left her with heated blood, and flushed cheeks, so she was glad of the shadows beside the old bookcase. It was a look which required exploration later, required a conversation in which she would do as she seemed to always do with him, and risk all of her careful management of what others knew of her, by asking him outright what she wanted to know, by revealing that she thought about things seriously, and by telling him the truth.

She stood, and watched as he made certain that everything was in place – neatly laid out, perfectly aligned, and ready for the influx of the Lords, who would, she was certain, put things instantly into disarray.

She found his dedication to precision and order endearing, soothing after a lifetime amongst her rather active family, who, were it not for their loyal and efficient servants, would never have managed to tidy anything. Finally, apparently satisfied, he went to the front of the room, speaking quietly with Lord Westerhazy and the lean man with greying hair and ink-stained fingers, whom she assumed to be the person who would deliver the actual demonstration.

A sound drew her eyes away from him, and she turned to see the door open, and a stream of gentlemen begin to enter. Most she knew, by sight at least, although there were some she had never seen before. Obviously, the demonstration had drawn out many who rarely attended parliament.

Observing them seemed a kind of harmless amusement, until, amongst them, she saw Lord Villeham, and his friend. She froze in place, unable to take her eyes from them, as horror filled her. She should have expected that they would be here, that they would want to see this – for if they were forgers, what was to be demonstrated here today would threaten their livelihood.

They turned, and Lord Villeham's eyes met hers. She did not understand what she saw there, as his cold eyes widened, and then narrowed, hard, his lips twisting into what looked like dark amusement, but it terrified her. He gave a small nod in her direction, and that twist of the lips widened into a wolfish grin, as if he were, for some incomprehensible reason, glad that she was there.

She was not sure how long she stood like that, caught by that frightening gaze, but the relief when he dropped his eyes and turned away to seek a chair was enormous. It was only then that she discovered that she was shaking. Grimly, she clasped her hands tightly together, and stilled the quivering, then steadfastly set her eyes upon the front of the room.

But even as she did, her thoughts were turning upon that look from Lord Villeham – he could not know that she knew of his ill-doing – could he? Why would he look upon her like that? There was no association between them and, as far as she knew, no reason that he might in any way suspect that she was aware of anything about him, except what had publicly been seen at Balls.

Nonetheless, the icy fear remained, for his expression had, somehow, contained threat.

She forced her attention back to the announcement that Lord Westerhazy was now making.

She would watch, and she would hold in her thoughts the look that Lord Merryfield had given her, to warm the ice which had filled her veins when Lord Villeham had regarded her.

Chapter Thirteen

Arryn's attention was only half on the demonstration, on the inane questions that many of the Lords asked, for he was aware at all times of Lady Violet watching from where she stood in the shadows. She had moved away from the bookcase a little, more towards the door, as if she wished to be able to slip out quickly, as if she expected to need to flee. He shook the thought away – it was foolish imagining on his part. Perhaps she simply wanted to be able to make a quiet exit if she found the proceedings so dull as to not be worth her time. Still, he watched her, surreptitiously.

She was obviously attending to the discussion, watching everything intently, as if she understood all of it. Perhaps, the thought came to him, rather shockingly, she did. After all – she had purchased a copy of 'Paper Against Gold'... that odd sensation rolled through him again – the one where she, simply by being herself, shook the very foundations of his perception of the world.

Finally, the questions slowed, all but one.

"Westerhazy, might we take away one of those imitation notes we've just seen printed? I am intrigued by just how difficult that pattern of lines would be to copy, and I must say, until now, I've never that closely examined every tiny letter and mark on the notes that have passed through my hands. I'd like to study this in more detail."

It was Lord Gillieston – and Arryn was oddly pleased that his uncle had chosen to ask such a thing, for he hoped that the man's interest might provoke others to pay more attention to the matter as well. There was a rustle of conversation around the room as the entire audience waited on the answer. Beside him, his father smiled.

"Of course, gentlemen. That was one of our intentions from today – that you might be able to examine these sample notes, and compare the printing accuracy and patterns to other notes you may currently hold. It is also why these are so very clearly marked as 'sample, of no monetary value'. We have printed enough to allow you to each take one, and the ink has dried whilst we have been answering your other questions. If you will come forward in an orderly fashion, we will distribute them to you."

Arryn would not, personally, have described what happened then as 'orderly' but at least it wasn't an all-out scramble. He glanced to the back of the room. Lady Violet had not moved – she still stood deep in shadow beside yet another old cupboard, but her eyes met his, and he saw amusement there, as if she too found the behaviour of the Lords to be reminiscent of schoolboys offered a treat.

He smiled, glad yet again that she was there, for reasons he could not, in any rational way, define. As he watched, a small group of Lords with sample notes in hand hurried towards the door.

*****

Violet had moved closer to the door, driven by that sense of foreboding which had overtaken her in the moment when Lord Villeham had looked at her so oddly. Now, hiding in as much shadow as she could, she watched, frustrated, wanting to see more closely, wanting to gather up one of those sample notes herself, but unwilling to expose herself to more public notice. It was verging on scandalous enough that she was here at all. If her father had not been in the room, it would have been a scandal, absolutely.

While many Lords still pressed forward, reaching for the sample notes, some of the first were already turning away, notes in hand. Among them, two stood out – Lord Villeham and his friend. They paused near the door, barely a yard from where Violet stood, and she held her breath, terrified that they would notice her presence – it seemed that she was destined to, yet again, overhear their conversation.

"I've made sure to get one where the ink is truly dry, and won't smudge. I'll leave you for now, and get this to my man. It's not far – I'll see you at White's later, and we can contemplate our next actions over dinner."

"Very well – I'll be most interested to hear what your man has to say about it, most interested."

"So will I."

Violet's heart was pounding, and the need to breathe was becoming extreme, but her thoughts raced. What Lord Villeham had said... she could only interpret it one way. He was going to take the sample note to his forger – and he had said it was not far.

This was an opportunity she could not allow to slip away. And he was already on his way across the outer Hall towards the street doors – there was no time for her to tell anyone what she was doing – only if she went now would she be able to follow him, to discover the location of the man who carried out the actual work of forging.

She took in a deep ragged breath and slipped through the door into the outer Hall, passing between two rather startled Lords, who had not, until then, noticed her presence.

She quickly flicked the cloak she had been holding over her arm around her shoulders, and sped across the space, weaving between other people, just in time to see Lord Villeham disappear out through the street door.

She moved faster, not quite running, and nearly shoved the footman aside as he opened the door for her. Where had Villeham gone? She paused, looking up and down the street, and barely caught sight of him as he stepped up into a hackney cab. At that sight, she did run, scandalous or not, until she reached her carriage.

"John!" Her coachman spun towards her, startled out of his doze. "John – see that hackney?"

She pointed, and he turned, looking.

"Yes, milady."

"Follow it – as fast as you can, without alerting them to the fact that we follow."

Even as she spoke, she flung herself into the carriage, slamming the door after her as it lurched into motion. Quietly, she thanked God for the fact that her family employed people who were loyal, and did not ask awkward questions. She slid the blind open a little, and peered out, trying to see where they were going.

The street they moved along changed rapidly from a clean thoroughfare between the imposing buildings of Westminster and the Churches, to a narrower road, lined by older houses, craftsmen's shops, warehouses, and the like, with crooked lanes running off it towards the river and the stone wharves. It was not a place a lady should go, alone – she could tell that straight away.

The carriage slowed, and for the first time, she wondered what she would do, when they arrived wherever Villeham was going. But really, there was no question about it – she would slip out of the carriage, and attempt to see or hear what went on, once he entered whatever building he might go into. She could not let this chance to gather more evidence against the man slip by. Perhaps Lord Setford had men watching him – but perhaps not – in the heart of Westminster, might that not have been difficult to arrange?

The carriage slowed even more, and her heart pounded, her palms suddenly damp. She would soon see if she had the courage to do what needed to be done.

*****

Arryn's eyes flicked back to Lady Violet – she was moving, and, going from utter stillness to rapid motion in the blink of any eye, she turned and slipped out through the door, as if pursuing something, or someone. In that moment, certainty settled into Arryn's core – something was wrong. She would not do such a thing, would not draw attention to herself like that, after so carefully staying inconspicuous, unless something important required it, or something threatened her.

She might frequently disconcert him, but he had come to know the pattern of her inconsistencies – and this did not fit.

He looked back to the front of the room. His father and Mr Ibbetson appeared to have everything well in hand with the sample notes, so Arryn spun and, without a word to anyone, hurried to the door, determined to follow Lady Violet, that sense of wrongness nagging at him, filling him with fear for her, however little rational reason there might be for him to feel so.

The outer hall was crowded with Lords standing about discussing the demonstration, and Arryn bit back his frustration as he wove through them, wanting to simply shove them aside, and knowing that he could not allow himself to do so. He scanned the space as he went, desperately trying to discover Lady Violet's whereabouts, and was rewarded with the slightest glimpse of her as she whisked out through the street door, nearly colliding with the footman as she did so.

The man had barely regained his balance when Arryn reached him, and was quick to sidestep when he realised the speed at which Arryn was moving. The street outside was also somewhat crowded, with a line of carriages waiting for those Lords who obviously did not intend to go back in when the session resumed. Arryn waved for his own coachman, and as he reached the carriage, he saw, beyond it, a hackney go past, heading away from the city, and moments later, a carriage following it. A carriage in which he saw, for the tiniest moment, Lady Violet – her face barely visible through a crack in the blind.

He flung himself into his own carriage, and ordered his coachman to follow Lady Violet's carriage. Something was, most definitely, wrong – for no lady, alone, should be travelling in that direction from here. That way lay only narrower streets, and the warehouses surrounding the stone wharves. It was a rough district, even though it lay so close to Westminster, having grown over the years as the continual building and rebuilding in Westminster drove a never-ending need for building materials to be shipped to the area. His coachman finally managed to manoeuvre out of the tangle of waiting vehicles, and Arryn forced himself to be still, to simply look out of the window, and trust that Bill would manage to follow the other carriage successfully.

He had no idea what he would do when Lady Violet reached wherever she was going – he might well come out of this escapade looking a complete fool – but still, that nagging sense of wrongness drove him, increased by the direction they were traveling.

*****

Just outside the room where the demonstration had taken place, Lord Setford stood with Trent, watching the milling crowd. A moment before, Lady Violet had hurried past them, startling Trent, but before he had a chance to comment, or move, a footman came to them, and spoke to Lord Setford, so quietly that it was barely audible to Trent.

"My Lord, Villeham just left – he's taken a hackney. Fred's following him – they seemed to be heading down along the river road, away from the city."

"Thank you."

As the footman turned away, Trent was startled to see Lord Merryfield also rush across the space beside them, as if he were a man pursued.

"Setford..."

"Yes, I saw – both of them. You don't suppose?"

"I do. If Violet is anything like her sister, then she will not hold back if she believes that something needs to be done. But Merryfield... that surprises me a little."

Setford laughed softly.

"Really? I think that one may be obvious. Merryfield is observant, and he has also, of late, shown every indication of being somewhat smitten with Lady Violet. If he saw her rush off like that, I suspect that he would feel compelled to follow – if for no other reason than to discover what caused her precipitous flight."

Trent nodded – he could imagine his own response if it had been Lily rushing off to follow a criminal...

"Then we had best follow them, with alacrity. It is not that I don't trust your men – for I do – but my wife would never forgive me if I allowed harm to come to her sister."

Even as he spoke, he started towards the door, Lord Setford beside him.

Soon, they stepped out into the cold afternoon, to be greeted by another footman, who indicated across the street.

"I took the liberty of asking your coachman to bring the carriage up, my Lord."

"Thank you."

They stepped onto the cobbles of the street, and Trent once again marvelled at how efficient everything about Lord Setford was. The carriage they approached was plain, unremarkable, unadorned by any crest, yet of the highest quality.

It was a carriage which no one would take any note of – which was exactly what Lord Setford wanted.

In front of them, barely avoiding collision, a carriage went by, away from the city – a carriage containing Lord Merryfield, with his family's crest clearly visible on the door. They quickly stepped up into Lord Setford's carriage, and Setford instructed his coachman to follow Merryfield.

Wherever they ended up, Trent thought with wry amusement, there was going to be a queue of carriages by the time they were finished....

*****

Lord Villeham stared out of the window of the hackney, watching the buildings they passed go from imposing stone facades to houses of moderate quality, to warehouses and rundown tenements, all in a matter of a mile. The street narrowed, and the rumble of the cab's wheels on the cobbles echoed back to him.

He frowned. The echoes seemed oddly wrong.

He pushed the window open, and peered out, attempting to see both in front and behind them. It was difficult, but as they turned into the even narrower lane which held his destination, he managed to see behind him – and what he saw left him filled with a combination of anger, fear, and dark amusement.

The echoes had seemed wrong, because another carriage followed him. Another carriage which was even now taking the turn to continue following him. A carriage which most definitely did not belong here.

It was understated, as the carriages of the highest nobility went, but it still bore a crest. The Elbury crest. It seemed that Lady Violet Gardenbrook, for whatever reason, had chosen to follow him here.

That rather removed the question of whether they would act against her, to bring leverage on Westerhazy and Merryfield. If she had so foolishly put herself in his reach, then he would take the opportunity offered, and make sure that he secured her – assuming, of course, that she was not accompanied by anyone else. He suspected that she wasn't, for he had seen no one with her in the demonstration room, and her father had still been in that room when he had left, very much occupied in conversation.

When they drew up in front of the narrow building, where it stood between the two old warehouses, he stepped down, and asked the jarvey to wait for him, suggesting that he take the cab down to the wharf where there was room to easily turn around, and wait there for half an hour before coming back. The man took the coin he was offered, and the promise of more later, and made no argument – it was far more than the fare should normally cost.

Villeham went to the door, and let himself in after tapping to warn his man, all the while pretending not to notice the carriage which had stopped some buildings away. Let her think he hadn't noticed her – let her curiosity bring her to him.

Chapter Fourteen

Violet watched through the barely open blind as Villeham got down from the hackney, spoke to the driver, and sent it on its way, then turned and entered a building. Now, she had to decide what to do.

Fear filled her at the thought of moving from the safety of the carriage, but, at the same time, her conscience urged her to hurry – for she could not, most certainly, gather any evidence whilst sitting in her carriage! She pulled her cloak tightly about her, then eased the door open.

"John, stay here. I will be back as soon as I can."

"Milady..."

"I must do this. If I am not back within the hour, then please go for help."

The coachman looked rather startled at this pronouncement, but nodded, obviously uncertain.

Violet stepped down onto the dirty cobbles.

There was no sound but the soft snuffle of the horses as she walked down the street to the door which Villeham had gone through. The building was narrow, with a tiny passageway down one side of it, between it and the warehouse which loomed above it on that side. The other side, it had a common wall with another warehouse.

To the street, it showed just the door, and one very grimy window, covered by curtains drawn tight. There was no understorey, no servants entrance, just that one door. Violet stood there and listened, her ear close to it. There was no sound, except a faint echo from deep in the building, of another door closing.

She would have to go in, and pray that she might find places to hide herself inside, might manage, yet again, to overhear Villeham incriminate himself. There was no option.

She swallowed her fear, and reached out a careful hand to ease the door open.

*****

From further down the street, Arryn watched in confusion and some horror as Lady Violet approached and entered the near derelict looking building. Why would she do that? Who had been in the cab which she had obviously been following? Had they also gone into that building?

There was nothing rational about this situation, nothing orderly or sensible, and his mind rebelled against the circumstances. Yet… she might be in danger… he could not allow such a thing, not when he might possibly protect her. He left his carriage, and walked calmly past hers, ignoring her coachman.

He could see, as he approached, that the door was shut, and the one window well blocked by curtains. He could not, really, simply walk in, or knock on that door and demand to see her – he had no right to do such a thing. But he had to know what was happening, to know whether she was safe or not.

Which left the only option as that narrow passageway – perhaps there were windows along there, or a back courtyard from which he might determine more of what was occurring. He turned into the passage, moving as quietly as he could, and glad that the sun had not yet set – for even with the faint trace of daylight which reached into the space, it was dim, and hard to see his footing.

But, as he had hoped, there were windows – they were as dirty as the front one, but these were not completely covered by curtains. The first revealed a narrow room – little more than a storage space – which was empty of all but dust, and what looked like bales or… rolls?… of paper. He continued, ignoring that puzzle for now.

The next window had curtains, but they were not completely closed. As Arryn peered through the gap, shock filled him. His instincts had been right. At the very moment that he looked in, Lord Villeham, who stood in the room, wrenched the door open, and Lady Violet came tumbling in. Villeham caught her as she stumbled, spinning her around to pin her with her back against him and her arms trapped by her sides.

It was very, very obvious that this was assault, not a lovers' embrace, and relief coursed through Arryn at the removal of a fear he had not even admitted to himself before. But that feeling was short lived, overtaken by his horror at the sight of Lady Violet struggling to get free – and failing.

He had to get to her, to save her.

He turned from the window, hurrying towards the back of the building, hoping for another entry there.

*****

When Trent and Setford stepped down into the narrow street, five men emerged from various spots, and came to them.

"He's in that building, milord. I've another two men in the back lane. But milord – the Lady went in there too, and now another man – looks like a Lord – went down that side passage towards the back of the place. What do you want us to do?"

"We'll go in – and I want a few of you with me, but leave others to guard all exits. If anyone attempts to leave, detain them. If the Lady or the Lord you just saw come out, ask them politely to wait for me, in the carriages."

They turned, and walked past Lord Merryfield and Lady Violet's carriages, until they stood before the house. Setford sent a man back to speak to the coachmen and explain the situation, all the while regarding the building before him.

"What do you expect to find?"

Trent eyed the place curiously, worried for Violet, and wondering just where Merryfield had got to.

"Hopefully, paper, a small printing press, and the forger's plates. And the forger himself. I wouldn't be surprised to discover that whoever it is has not done this willingly – why would a man print mass money for a Lord, when he might keep it all for himself, unless under duress?"

"A good question."

"Let us go in now – I don't think that this calls for any subtlety in the matter, although I'd suggest that drawing that rather excellent blade from your sword cane is likely a good idea."

Trent did as suggested, and Setford opened the front door. From the other end of the hallway, they heard a cut off half-scream, and thumping. It was, obviously, time to hurry. Setford's men behind them, they ran, and Trent prayed that the men sent to cover the back door were in place.

*****

Violet had been sure that she was being quiet as she crept down the hall of the dusty old building – so dusty that it made her want to sneeze, a desire which she repressed as hard as she could. She had reached the door to a room from which came the sound of quiet voices, and pressed her ear against it, trying to discern what was being said.

"...not sure I could replicate that, my Lord – so many tiny lines and patterns overlaying each other – getting it exactly right would be a work for a more skilled engraver than I am."

"Surely you could manage... I'll give you extra if you can – far more than you've had so far..."

"I'm still not sure, my Lord."

Violet shifted her feet, and the dust which rose tickled her throat, causing her to emit a quickly strangled half-cough. She froze, praying that she hadn't been heard. For a moment, nothing happened, and she almost breathed again.

Almost, because, just as she did, the door was wrenched open, and she tumbled into the room, completely off balance.

Hands caught her, and spun her around until she found herself clamped with her back hard against Lord Villeham, her arms trapped by her side.

"Listening at doors really isn't ladylike, Lady Violet. I'm afraid that I take exception to your presence here. But now that you're here, and you've overheard things you shouldn't have, I'm afraid that I can't let you leave."

"What – what do you mean?"

"Why you'll have to remain my guest, in this delightful establishment, until my requirements are met. And even then, perhaps I'll keep you. For my own... entertainment."

Violet felt positively ill at the implication of his words, but refused to let him see just how much that threat affected her. She stared across the room, wishing that she had not been so foolish as to come here alone. No one knew where she was - except her coachman – that at least was hopeful. The dirty window on the other side of the room reminded her that, perhaps, even if Villeham tried to trap her here, there might be ways of escape.

She studied the window, and for a moment, she saw a face in the narrow gap of the curtains. Hope surged. Was it? Surely it couldn't be – she must be dreaming – but it had looked, to her somewhat fevered brain, like Lord Merryfield. Villeham was speaking again, and she twisted in his grasp, suddenly desperate to avoid his touch.

He tightened his grip, laughing again.

"You'll not get away so easily, Lady Violet. George, bring me some rope."

"I've no rope, milord. There's only the cords the paper bundles come tied with."

"Then bring me those."

"Yes milord."

Violet twisted her head a little, and barely caught a glimpse of a man with ink-stained fingers as he limped from the room, closing the door after himself. Villeham brought his lips close to her ear and she shuddered, unable to prevent it, and spoke rapidly, before he could speak, or worse.

"You won't get away with this – someone will come looking for me."

"Not if I make sure that no one can tell them where you are. I'll deal with that matter once I have you secured."

Guilt filled her – her rashness had just put a loyal servant into danger. But what else could she have done? She stood here, in a building where the evidence of the forgery was clearly present – all she needed to do was escape, and tell Lord Setford exactly what she had seen. Although... she had to admit, if Villeham did bind her with something, escape might be much harder than she had thought.

"Someone will still come looking. My father will not easily accept my disappearance."

"Oh, he will – once he, and others, receive ransom letters. He'll not come looking, because he will know that to do so will put you in danger."

She squirmed again, but his grip was too strong. He simply laughed at her, whilst muttering about George being slow with the bindings. But, as he did, Violet heard another sound, from the hallway – not the uneven tread of the limping George, but a softer footfall.

Her heart pounded – had she truly seen what she thought she had, at the window? Had he, somehow, miraculously, come to save her? It was foolish to hope, foolish to cast him somehow in the role of hero, yet even so, she could not stop herself.

Villeham pulled her around so that they faced the door, just as the door burst open and Lord Merryfield rushed into the room.

"Release her, Villeham, at once!"

Lord Villeham lifted one hand and wrapped it around her throat, causing Violet to struggle a little to breathe – but at least that meant that his grip on her body, and his restraint of her arms, was weakened.

"I don't think so, Merryfield. I do believe that I am glad to see you. Now I can simply deliver my demands at once. I could just choke her now, and cut off her air until she collapses, but I do think that I prefer she see and hear everything. There is something rather enjoyable about anguish. Now, let me make the requirement clear. The committee will find that anti forgery methods are impossible to implement, even after today's demonstration, and will present that conclusion to the House of Lords. Any attempt to implicate me will cause this dear lady to suffer regrettable damage – to her reputation, and to her body. I will hear your words of agreement now, and then it will be necessary for me to ensure that you find yourself elsewhere, and that any return to this building will discover it an empty shell."

Violet watched Lord Merryfield's face, and saw the struggle there, a struggle which she understood, even if many might not. He was being asked to lie, to get his father to lie, and he found that concept almost impossible, even to save her. The integrity in that stance impressed her, even while her fear grew.

And what Villeham had said... none of it guaranteed her release, and at least part of it implied hurt to Lord Merryfield, if he was to 'find himself elsewhere'. She could not permit him to be hurt, not for her. She loved him too much to contemplate such a thing.

The thought stopped her breath in her throat, even more than the grip of Villeham's hand already had.

She loved him. There was no doubt of it. Why had she been so foolish as not to truly see it before now? She had acknowledged liking him, but this, this was far beyond that. He met her eyes, and what she saw there left her filled with an agony of guilt.

"I... yes. I will make it happen, if that is what it takes to ensure that you do not hurt her."

That he would do such a thing, for her...

Behind him, a shadow filled the doorway, and Violet realised, seconds before the man moved, that the forger had returned and was about to attack Lord Merryfield from behind. She twisted, hard, in Villeham's grasp, and with what air she had, she screamed.

"Behind..."

The words were cut off by Villeham's hand moving from her neck to cover her mouth, but they were enough. Lord Merryfield spun in place, and narrowly avoided the forger's roundhouse blow swinging towards his head. The two men closed in on each other, each casting careful blows, and seeking advantage. Violet watched, terrified that Lord Merryfield would be hurt, yet glad that she had saved him from that first blow.

The bindings the forger had been carrying lay on the floor in the hallway, out of Villeham's reach for now – which at least left her partly free. If she waited for just the right moment...

*****

The back door to the building had proven to be locked, but also so old and warped that with a few well-placed shoves it opened. Arryn rushed through the small kitchen, and down the hallway beyond – he had to get to her, to save her from Villeham, whatever the man planned to do with her.

As he moved, a door opened ahead of him, and a man came out, closed it, and turned the other way in the hallway, limping onwards. Arryn froze in place, waiting until the man went into another room, even though he could hear Lady Violet's voice coming through that door. At least, if she was speaking, she had not been badly harmed. But he could not know how long that would be the case.

He moved forward again, until he stood just outside the door. Then, with a sudden surge, he flung the door open and stepped into the room.

"Release her, Villeham, at once!"

Lord Villeham lifted one hand and wrapped it around Lady Violet's throat, causing her to struggle a little to breathe.

"I don't think so, Merryfield. I do believe that I am glad to see you. Now I can simply deliver my demands at once. I could just choke her now, and cut of her air until she collapses, but I do think that I prefer she see and hear everything. There is something rather enjoyable about anguish. Now, let me make the requirement clear. The committee will find that anti forgery methods are impossible to implement, even after today's demonstration, and will present that conclusion to the House of Lords. Any attempt to implicate me will cause this dear lady to suffer regrettable damage – to her reputation, and to her body. I will hear your words of agreement now, and then it will be necessary for me to ensure that you find yourself elsewhere, and that any return to this building will discover it an empty shell."

Arryn watched her face, met her eyes, and understood, in that moment that he loved her.

Utterly.

There was a terrible clarity to the realisation which despite his innate inability to lie, despite every piece of resolve, left him certain of what he would do.

He would lie, and get his father to lie, for Lady Violet was more important to him than anything.

"I... yes. I will make it happen, if that is what it takes to ensure that you do not hurt her."

Villeham smiled at him, a smile which was not in any way pleasant, and went as if to speak, when, suddenly, Lady Violet twisted in his grasp, and screamed a word.

"Behind..."

The words were cut off by Villeham's hand moving from her neck to cover her mouth, but they were enough. Arryn spun in place, and narrowly avoided the forger's roundhouse blow swinging towards his head. The man came at him again, and he found himself in a battle. Whilst the man's limp gave Arryn some advantage, it was small – the fellow fought with a desperation Arryn had rarely seen.

All through it, his heart cried out that he should finish this, that anything could be happening to Lady Violet, even as he fought this madman. He redoubled his efforts, pushing the man back towards the hallway.

Sounds echoed, and for a moment he was disoriented – then he realised – he had just heard the front door being flung open. Reinforcements – but... who for?

Chapter Fifteen

Violet squirmed when Villeham tried to move her, and he tightened his grip, even though his attention was all on the men battling in front of him. If she could keep him unbalanced... he grunted with annoyance, and released her mouth, raising that hand, and she realised with horror that he intended to hit her.

"Stay still, woman. Or I will make certain that you suffer for your disobedience."

Even as he spoke, Lord Merryfield threw another blow at the forger, who stepped back to avoid it, and caught his feet in the bindings which he had dropped in the doorway. Lord Merryfield's blow hit him at the same moment, and he went down, flailing, hitting his head hard against the doorframe. For a moment, he still tried to move, then his eyes closed, and he crumpled completely to the floor, unconscious. As he did, the sound came to her of the front door being flung open. She did not know who it might be, but regardless, when Lord Villeham startled at the sound, and loosened his grip, she took full advantage, spinning towards him fast.

He, having expected her to pull away rather than turn towards him, was taken completely by surprise, and that surprise gave her all the time she needed to bring her knee up hard, just as Thorne had taught her, years before. Lord Villeham's eyes widened, and he emitted the most peculiar sound, half scream, half gasp, and completely released her.

She stepped back with alacrity. And as she did, Lord Merryfield stepped past her, and delivered one very efficient blow to Lord Villeham's jaw, resulting in him, too, dropping completely unconscious.

"Well, that was efficient, I do say, m'boy. Here I am with three men to help, and you've knocked both of them out for us."

Lord Merryfield turned to where Lord Setford and Lord Canterford stood in the doorway, his face clouded with confusion. Setford's men set about tying both Villeham and the forger with the discarded bindings as he spoke.

"Lord Setford?"

Violet stepped up beside Lord Merryfield, and slipped her arm through his, looking up at him with a broad smile.

"Yes, Lord Merryfield. Lord Setford has a rather unusual... role... beyond the responsibilities of his Barony. You may now count yourself amongst the select group of people who know that he is also the Spymaster for the Crown."

"Oh. And... you are here because?"

Merryfield's question was directed at Setford. Violet saw the look on his face – the one that she usually caused him to wear, the one that meant that he was mentally rearranging his perception of the order of the world, and not very happy about it.

"I am here because we suspected Lord Villeham of being involved in forgery, and have been waiting for a chance to catch him with the evidence."

"I... see."

Violet spoke now, rushing in to explain, and to give Lord Merryfield time to assimilate what he had just heard.

"When Villeham left the demonstration, I overheard him whisper to Lord Harmonton that he was going to take the sample note straight to 'his man'. I knew that there was no time to waste – that if I didn't follow him, I could not be sure that you would have a man in place to do so, and we might lose the chance to discover the location of the man who actually did the forgery. But... I do apologise... I ran out after him with no real plan, and I am obviously very poor at sneaking about, for he noticed me, and captured me."

Lord Merryfield brought his other hand around, and patted her arm where it curled through his, as if to reassure her. The touch sent heat through her entire body. Lord Setford regarded her calmly.

"Perhaps, dear lady, telling me, or Canterford here, before you ran after Villeham – or at least on the way past us - would have been wise?"

"It would, I'm sorry."

Lord Merryfield looked down at her, and spoke again, sounding still somewhat puzzled.

"But... Lady Violet, how did you know that Villeham should be followed? How did you know what he meant, when you overheard him?"

Violet felt her cheeks colour.

"Because I... ah... I have previously... overheard... two of his secret conversations with Lord Harmonton, and reported them to Lord Canterford."

"Overheard?"

"At Balls. You may remember that time when I came in from the terrace, rather precipitately, and nearly collided with you? That was after hearing the first of his conversations. You would be surprised what one can overhear at Balls, if gentlemen think you a typical woman with little in her head but frivolous matters."

"I see."

His smile was wry, but his deep amber eyes met hers with a warmth that positively took her breath away again.

"There was a time when I was foolish enough to think that of all young women. Then I met you. I will never be so foolish again."

Lord Setford gave a bark of laughter.

"You've made the first step towards true wisdom, Merryfield. But now, let us search this building, and gather all of the evidence. I'll want a detailed statement from you tomorrow, about everything that happened, but presently, we have other things to deal with."

On the floor, Villeham groaned, and opened his eyes. Setford regarded him with that piercing grey gaze.

"You, Villeham, have been caught – you have been observed in the act of perpetrating forgery, knowingly. And that is treason, my Lord. You will be taken from here and incarcerated until your fate, and the fate of your family, can be decided."

Villeham's eyes widened in horror.

"No..."

"Yes. You knew what you were doing, but your greed was too strong. Now you will pay the price. And your behaviour here, today, has guaranteed that you will be shown no leniency."

Villeham groaned again, and closed his eyes. Near him, the forger regarded Setford, his expression one of despair and resignation. Setford met his gaze, and something passed between them, as if Setford understood more of the man than was obvious.

"You, I will speak to privately, and I ask that you answer me honestly when we speak."

"Yes, my Lord."

Setford waved for his men to carry the two bound men away, and set off with Lord Canterford to examine the rest of the building, leaving Violet standing there, scandalously alone with Lord Merryfield. They looked at each other, turning face to face, and Violet untangled her arm from his, only to lift both arms and slip them about his neck. She pushed up a little on her toes, and shamelessly brought her lips to his. For a moment, he was still, then he softened, his lips moving against hers, his arms encircling her, and his tongue slipping out to delicately trace the line of her mouth. It was wonderful, far more so than she had ever imagined a simple kiss to be, and she melted against him, allowing his warmth and strength to chase away the lingering chill of fear. He deepened the kiss with a soft groan, and pulled her hard against him.

For some minutes, they stayed that way.

When, finally, they drew apart, Violet smiled at him.

"I know this is terribly shocking and forward of me, but I have wanted to do that for quite some time. Have I horrified you?"

He lifted a hand to cup her cheek as he shook his head.

"I do not think that there is anything you could do which would horrify me – well, perhaps apart from intentionally teaching falsehoods, or burning a book..."

She laughed softly, and shuddered.

"Neither of those are things that I could ever bring myself to do. On matters like that, we are in complete accord."

"I am beginning to suspect, Lady Violet, that we may well be in complete accord on many more matters than that. So much so that I believe that I want to explore the truth of that – extensively. Of course, it is also possible that my desire to call upon you, frequently, may equally have been influenced by that kiss we just shared."

She felt quite dizzy. He had just said that he wanted to call on her frequently. Did that mean...?

"Lord Merryfield, are you suggesting... are you suggesting that you wish to court me?"

"Directness. Oh, how I love that about you. Yes, that is exactly what I am suggesting. Are you... are you amenable to that idea?"

In answer, Violet slipped her arms back around his neck, and pulled his lips down to hers.

*****

Lord Setford waited in a small room, in an ordinary building, where many things happened which were not ordinary at all. The door opened, and a man was shown it.

"George, is it? Come and sit down. It's time for that private conversation I promised you. Please, help yourself to coffee."

He gestured to the tray on the small table between them. The man limped forward, and lowered himself into a chair, regarding Lord Setford with an uncertain expression.

"George Martin, my Lord. I... I don't understand. Why am I here, and not in Newgate, waiting the hangman's noose?"

"I'll explain in a moment – but first, I'd like you to tell me about you – and how you came to be making forged bank notes for Lord Villeham."

The man sat for a moment, then reached out and poured himself coffee from the tray.

"I might as well savour this while I can. I've rarely had coffee, let alone quality coffee. I don't know why you want to know about me, but I see no reason not to simply tell you the truth about everything. Under the law, I'm already doomed to die. There's an odd sense of relief in speaking about it, like a confessional, almost, if you take my meaning."

"I do. And I appreciate honesty."

"I was a fool of a boy. As soon as I was old enough, I signed up to go off to fight Napoleon. I was lucky. Lucky because I got injured fairly early in my service. With the limp, I couldn't easily keep up, or fight – but I'd always been good with my hands, and as a child I'd thought maybe I'd be a blacksmith. I could fix things – fix weapons, to be precise – and that skill was worth a lot on the battlefield. So they gave me a spot on the supply wagons, and scavenged me a set of tools."

"And that was lucky?"

"It was. If I'd been with my unit only a few weeks later, I'd be dead, like the rest of them. But the regiment wanted my skills, so people looked after me. In return, I fixed their other things too – cooking pots, anything like that, and bits of harness – whatever needed it. But what I did to entertain myself was make jewellery – out of the metal twisted bits of weapons that couldn't be repaired. I learnt to engrave, and to shape it into delicate things. It was soothing, making something pretty out of something that had wrought destruction. Men paid me for them, so I could afford to live a bit better than just my army pay. And I needed that, when the letter came telling me my father was dead – got caught up in the wheels of one of those new-fangled threshing machines, and crushed. So I sent money back for my mother, so she could pay her rent and stay on in the cottage on Lord Villeham's land."

"Ah, I see. But how did you go from that to forgery?"

"The war ended, didn't it? I had enough money from making things to get home, quicker than most of the men, but once I was here, there was no work, was there? Too many men had come back from war, and me with a limp and all – even the able-bodied ones had trouble getting work, I had no chance. And the money I'd saved only went so far. I could see the end of it coming, and Lord Villeham had warned me that if we couldn't pay rent, he'd toss us out of the cottage. I got desperate, to save my mother and my sister, so I turned to forgery. Making the plates wasn't so hard, not with the skills I'd learnt. The printing machine was harder, but the blacksmith let me use his forge if he wasn't busy – he remembered me as a boy – and never asked what I was making. At first, I printed just enough for us, and I was very careful about where I spent those notes, so I got coin to spend in the village close to home. For a while, it worked."

"And then?"

"Then Villeham got suspicious. Followed me one day, and found the press I'd set up in the old charcoal burner's hut in the woods. He offered me a bargain – the kind a man can't refuse. Either he'd turn me in, and I'd go to Newgate, and my mother and sister would be cast out and destitute, or I could keep making the notes – for him. He'd set me up somewhere safe, and give me enough every few months that I could go home for a while, and that my family wouldn't starve. Of course I agreed – what choice did I have?"

"None. Which is what I thought might be the case."

"So, my Lord – why are we having this conversation?"

"Because I'm going to offer you another bargain you can't refuse. I think that you'll find this one more palatable than the last however."

George had flinched at the start of those words, then relaxed a little.

"And what would this bargain be, my Lord?"

"I'll be blunt, George. I think I can trust you. You've proven that you can keep secrets, and I'll forgive your attack on Merryfield as the act of a desperate man facing the loss of everything. It's simple – apart from my daily life as one of the *ton*, I have another role – I am the King's Spymaster. And part of what I do is attempt to prevent treason."

George had paled rather dramatically at the mention of the King, but now he drank some more of his coffee, obviously thinking.

"And… forgery is officially treason? So you want me to… do something to help stop it?"

"Exactly. I want to recruit you to the King's service. I want you to teach my men how to identify forged notes, and how they are made, and I want you to work with the engravers who make the plates for the real Bank of England bank notes, to implement whichever anti forgery technique the House of Lords decides to adopt. In return, I'll pay you a good wage, and give your mother and sister a decent cottage on my estates. I know that it will be hard for them to leave the place that has always been home, but once Villeham's disgrace comes out, they'll be better away from it. You can spend time there, but I'm afraid you'll need to be in London much of the year. In London, I've a small house you'll live in, sharing it with another of my 'specialists'. There's a cook, a maid, and a footman, so you'll not have to worry about daily chores. Will you accept?"

George regarded Lord Setford with astonishment.

"You'd give me so much, just to teach others about these things? I'd be a fool to say no, wouldn't I? I never meant to do anything but survive, and keep my family alive, despite where I ended up."

"Then you'll do it?"

"Yes."

Chapter Sixteen

Violet sat in the library, books scattered across the desk in front of her. Nothing could hold her attention today. It was three days since her failed attempt to be a spy, three days since she had kissed Lord Merryfield, and he had declared his intentions. Three days in which she had thought of little else. And today, he would call. He had sent a message to say so. From the moment that she had received it, her mind had ceased to function as usual, and had, instead, been consumed by the memory of his lips against hers, by the words he had spoken, by everything about him. She had been sitting here for hours, trying to read, and no matter the subject material or the language, she had singularly failed to get more than two pages into anything. In the distance, she heard the faint sound of the door knocker, echoing through the building. Was it him? She fidgeted, straightening her skirts, pushing all of the pins in her hair firmly into place, and generally panicking inside. She did not know how to do this 'courtship' thing!

Footsteps sounded, coming closer. Her mouth went dry. A tap came at the door, and Marks stepped in.

"Lord Merryfield to see you, Lady Violet. Shall I show him here? Or in the main parlour? I have Annie here ready to chaperone."

Behind him, the maid hovered, a smile on her face. Before Violet could answer, however, Lord Merryfield appeared behind Marks.

"Please forgive my invasion of your home, but... I heard the word 'library'."

He smiled, and Violet forgot, for a moment, how to breathe. He was so utterly handsome, so wonderful. Then Marks cleared his throat and she realised that everyone was waiting for her response. Heat flushed her cheeks.

"Ah, here will be perfect, thank you Marks. Please arrange for a tea tray, with the lemon cakes, of course. Annie, you can sit over near the other window, and catch the sun while there is still a little of it. This close to Christmas, the days are so very cold." She rose, and went forward to greet Lord Merryfield. "Lord Merryfield – do come in, and forgive the mess which I have made of the desk. Today, I have not been able to settle to anything."

He stepped forward as Marks melted away, and Annie discreetly settled in the corner. Their eyes met, and the world slowed down. He reached out, and took her hand, bowing to place a kiss on her bare skin there. She shivered, the memory of his lips on hers resurfacing.

"Neither have I." His smile was full of self-amusement. "May I see what you have been reading?"

She laughed, somehow immediately at ease.

"Trying to read, is rather more the correct phrasing."

He went to the desk, and lifted one book after another, his eyebrows lifting a little further each time. Was that horror at the fact that she read so many languages, that she was so utterly a bluestocking? Would this make him less interested in her? The though sent a pang of pain through her heart. She waited, until he had looked at them all. He turned to her. Her knees felt weak, all of a sudden, and she collapsed onto the couch.

"Please, be seated."

She patted the seat beside her, wanting him close, wanting to touch him, even as she feared that he would not want to be there. But he came to her, and settled there, just as the tea tray was carried in. Only once she had served him tea, and he had eaten one of the famed lemon cakes, did he speak again. By then, she was certain that she would expire if it took any longer.

"Five languages. Do you read and speak them all fluently?"

"I read them all very well – how well I speak them – that is harder to determine, as for some of them, I have no one else to speak them with. But I believe that I would be passably understood by native speakers of each of them."

He lifted her hand and kissed it, sending sparks through her in the strangest way.

"You, Lady Violet Gardenbrook, are a remarkable woman. I begin to think that you are quite terrifyingly intelligent, as well as spectacularly adept at hiding that fact. Which is a skill that I am in awe of, for I am so terribly bad at dissembling myself. And this library – this I envy you, intensely."

"Envy? But surely the library at Westerhazy House is extensive?"

"It is, and the one at Merryfield House is even bigger. But neither match this."

"Then you must spend some time here, and explore these shelves."

As soon as she said it, Violet realised how forward it was, and yet she had meant it sincerely. He smiled, and that twist of his lips made her long to lean forward and kiss him. She forced her eyes away.

"I most certainly hope to do so. Will you show me what is here?"

"I... you... you are not... concerned... by my rather... bluestocking tendencies?"

There, she had done it again – no matter how much she tried for decorum, with this man she somehow always simply blurted out the truth, the blunt question. The smile broadened, and he burst into laughter.

"Concerned? Never – more say, delighted! I had hoped that one day I might meet a woman who had some native intelligence, and used it, but my experience amongst the *ton* had led me to conclude that I never would. Now you have proven me wrong, in the most wonderful way."

"Wonderful...?"

She could hardly believe her ears.

"Yes, wonderful. I take it, from some of those volumes, that you have been studying matters of history and the differences in law and culture of various nations? Is that a common habit, or a temporary whim?"

Violet swallowed – here was the core of it.

"It is a compulsive habit. I am always studying something. The world is endlessly fascinating. I... that is why, when I first spoke with you this year, after you had been sent down, I was so very... shall we say, bordering on rude? I was mortally offended by the idea that a man, with the privilege of being able to study at Oxford, should have done anything which got him sent down. The concept that someone could throw away their chance to study...."

He laughed again, and reached for her hands, pulling her towards him. She went, unsure of why he laughed, or what he wanted, until the moment that his lips met hers. Shock coursed through her, and then she threw caution to the winds and sank into his kiss, despite knowing that Annie watched from the corner.

When they drew apart, she glanced that way for a second, to see Annie carefully looking through a book – an illustrated guide to the birds of Great Britain, Violet thought. She turned her eyes back to his, allowing herself to be drawn into their amber depths. He lifted a hand to trace her lips with his finger, sighing, then smiled again, as if coming to some decision.

"Lady Violet Gardenbrook, I know that it is traditional to spend some time courting a lady before doing what I am about to do – but I find that I cannot bring myself to wait. I already knew, after the moment that I saw you trapped by Villeham, that I love you – at that moment, nothing mattered more than saving you – but now, after this conversation – now I know that you are beyond perfect. Will you marry me, Lady Violet?"

Violet felt as if the world was spinning under her, whirling her about in a maelstrom of thoughts and feelings. She had hoped, had come more and more to want... but this... now...

"Yes. I... I love you too, and knew it in that horrible place as well, so clearly, when I saw that you had come for me. Can we... can we spend most of our time in libraries, studying together? Can we avoid the inanities of the *ton*? I cannot imagine anything better than you, and doing that – well, apart from some kisses too..."

He bent to kiss her again, as an affirmation of what she had said.

"Oh! So, I have another wedding to plan, do I?"

They pulled away from each other, and Violet turned to find her mother standing in the doorway. The Duchess looked amused, rather than annoyed, and Violet relaxed, even as Lord Merryfield twined his fingers with hers before addressing her mother.

"I believe so – Lady Violet has just done me the honour of accepting my rather precipitate proposal."

"Then I'll start doing so now – I'll call upon your mother tomorrow, and we can plan together." She paused, and regarded them fondly for a moment. "And you really should tell your father, Violet – although I suspect that by now he has given up all hope that any of you will do this in the traditionally expected manner."

With that she swept from the room.

For a moment, there was silence, and then Violet burst into giggles.

"Oh dear…. Oh dear… she's right – we have all done the unexpected and precipitate, as far as love, and I rather suspect that Iris and Thorne will be no different in that way – much though Thorne would deny any similarity to his sisters."

Epilogue

For once, Violet felt more beautiful than any of her sisters. The gown she wore was simple – an underlayer of shimmering white silk, with an overlayer of a fine silvery net, upon which tiny amethyst gems glittered, their colour echoing that of her eyes. In her hair, pins tipped with the same gem sparkled, and the necklace she wore bore a single large amethyst set among diamonds. It was, she thought, the simplicity of it which made it so effective. When she had looked in the mirror as Annie set the final pins into her hair, she had felt rather as if someone had performed magic, transforming her, and wondered if it was only conceit, or if others, if Arryn, would think it beautiful too.

Now, as she stepped into the church and her eyes met his, she knew that it was not conceit. His eyes widened, and shone with such love that she could have simply stopped, and stayed in that moment forever. But her father urged her on, and she moved slowly through the scatter of rainbow light cast by the stained-glass windows.

Christmas was but days away, and Violet was glad that they would be married by then, that she might celebrate this year with her family, but as a married woman. They had discussed the idea of a wedding trip, but decided to put such activities aside until spring or summer. Around her, those gathered to see them wed shifted and watched her, a weight of friendly eyes upon her. They reached the front of the church, and she took her place beside the man she loved, more than ready to say the words which would bind her to him forever.

*****

Arryn turned at the whisper of sound which filled the church when those assembled saw Violet step into the church. She was spectacular – almost ethereal, an enchantress, a sparkling picture of white, touched with amethyst fire. All else faded away, and he simply stood, captivated, and watched her walk towards him.

He had never imagined that he would find a woman with whom he was so in tune, so happy – yet here she was, a miraculous gift in his life. His love for her overflowed as, when she reached his side, their eyes met, and he saw his own feelings reflected there. The minister began to speak, and they each spoke the words when required, but Arryn was barely aware of anything but her presence, the delicate scent of her hair – a mixture of lavender and rose water, he thought – and the heat of her, standing so close to him that they almost touched.

Finally, it was done, and they stepped out into the crisp cold air, the touch of the winter sun barely warm at all. Around them, friends and family pressed forward with good wishes for their future, and passers-by paused on the street to watch, smiling at the sight of their happiness. Had anyone asked him, just four months earlier, if he would marry soon, he would have laughed, and declared that a thing for the distant future – yet here he was, married, and overjoyed to be so.

He twined his fingers with hers, and they stepped forward to where their carriage waited to take them to Elbury House for the wedding breakfast. The people all pressed close to them made him feel a desperate desire to escape the crowd, and he held to her steadiness as an anchor, only breathing a sigh of relief once they had settled into the carriage and were moving. Sometimes, the press and the noise of people seemed unbearable, and he longed for a quiet library. Now, he longed for a quiet library with Violet by his side.

She turned to him with a smile.

"It's rather overwhelming, isn't it? And now we have to spend the rest of the day smiling at people, and dancing, and generally being sociable, when all I want to do is hide away with you, and enjoy being together."

That she understood so clearly how he felt still shocked him – and delighted him. It was a relief to be accepted for who he truly was, and not expected to fulfil others wishes.

"It is – but we will get through it together – and escape as soon as we reasonably might. But for now, while we have this short interlude…"

He lifted her face gently, and brought his lips to hers, in a kiss which began softly, yet soon deepened into one full of passion, and the promise of what would come later. She returned that kiss with equal fervour, slipping her hands around his neck and pulling him to her.

All thought of anyone else fled his mind, and he savoured the feel and taste of her, marvelling again that she had willingly chosen him.

*****

The ballroom at Elbury House was full, and people stood in groups, talking as the food was brought out. Violet felt strange – for the scene was familiar, even the wedding breakfast part, after the weddings of her five older sisters, yet this time, it was for her, this time she was the one who was married. The thought that this very evening, once the guests had all departed, so would she, to begin her new life, was exhilarating and frightening at once.

Merryfield House had been opened up and prepared for them. It was part of Lord Westerhazy's estates, but had been simply managed with a minimal staff to maintain it whilst Merryfield still lived with his parents. Now, it would be theirs. The thought was wonderful, yet she suspected that she did not know anywhere near enough about running a household...

She smiled, and spoke to people, pushing aside any worry about how she would cope – she ate, drank, danced, and conversed, allowing the day to slip away with Arryn at her side. She felt as if the entire *ton* were in attendance – and, given her mother, perhaps they were. By late afternoon, the eating and dancing had slowed, and people turned to quieter pursuits. The small orchestra left their dais, and were taken to the kitchens to receive their own well-earned meal, leaving the instruments standing there, beside the pianoforte, looking oddly forlorn.

As Violet watched, to her surprise, she saw Lord Greenleigh approach, and take a seat at the pianoforte – it seemed that he was volunteering to play, and she was grateful. With his skill, she regarded it as a wedding gift of great value. Soon, the delicate sounds drifted through the room – a complex piece, which spoke of love and longing, of joy and doubt, and more. Iris knew it, Violet realised, and had played it at times. It was beautiful, and well suited to the occasion. She looked away, and Arryn slipped an arm about her waist.

"Shall we find a seat? I confess that I am tired of standing."

"Indeed, I would be grateful for the chance to just sit quietly with you, and appreciate the music."

He led her to one corner, where a couch had been placed near urns full of flowers and potted palms (both of which were the result of her father's obsession with horticulture, and the greenhouses attached to Elbury House), and they sank onto the seat. Violet leaned against his shoulder, taking in the unique scent of him, and the muscular strength beneath his coat. She sighed with pleasure in the moment.

Then, as she simply relaxed, the music changed – not to a different piece, but in the character of the playing. Startled, she looked across the room, and gave a soft gasp. Beside Lord Greenleigh on the narrow bench, Iris sat, her fingers also moving over the keys. They played the piece superbly, two threads weaving together to carry the same melody, yet layered, each enhancing the other, adding depth to the piece in a way that Violet had not thought possible. Somehow, their hands moved past and around each other, without tangling, without hesitation, as if they had played together for their whole lives, as if they were meant to be so. That thought sent a shiver through Violet – was it possible? The words Iris had spoken, months ago, at that first musicale when Lord Greenleigh had played – 'I think I'm in love' – had she meant them, truly? Violet wished her sister happiness, but still – she was quite certain that there would be gossip about this, despite them being in a room full of people, for there was no possible way to play so without sitting pressed hard against each other.

What else might Iris do, provoked by her love of music? She pushed that thought aside – she would address it later, would ask Iris about this the next time that she saw her, but for now, Arryn was all that mattered. Violet turned her head into the curve of his neck, and he lifted a hand to delicately stroke her face, tracing its lines with a fingertip, as if exploring every contour.

It made her want more, made her want heated kisses, despite how tired she felt. They stayed that way for some time, then rose and moved amongst the guests again, until the world outside the windows darkened and, at last, the guests began to leave.

"Might we also leave now? I fear that I am quite exhausted by the day!"

He looked at her, and his eyes sparkled with mischief, his lips curving into a wry smile.

"Exhausted? Are you sure?" His fingers trailed down her spine, and her breath caught at the sensation. "I had hoped that you might have some energy left for important matters..."

"Important matters?"

"Like the exploration of a library you have never seen before... and kisses... and..."

Violet felt heat fill her core. She licked her lips, and his eyes followed the movement.

"Are you... suggesting wickedness, husband?"

"Only of the best kind, my love."

"Then perhaps, just perhaps, I will find that I am not so exhausted after all."

Not long after that, they took their leave of her family, and Violet discovered that she felt almost tearful at the thought that she would no longer call Elbury House home. Her mother sniffed slightly, but smiled, embracing her daughter.

"I will make sure that the last of your things are sent to Merryfield House tomorrow – most were sent this afternoon, and Annie has gone with them, to arrange everything as you like it."

"Thank you, Mother, for that, and everything about today. It has been wonderful."

*****

Merryfield House still smelt faintly musty, despite being scrupulously clean, and Arryn wondered why he had not had the place opened up months ago.

But he was here now – here with Violet by his side. The staff assembled in the front foyer when they arrived, and he made the introductions, barely remembering their names himself, he had been here so rarely in recent years.

Violet had that look on her face which he had come to understand was concentration of a particular kind. She was memorising what she heard. He smiled, impressed yet again by the attention she gave to everything in life.

Once they had dismissed the staff, he turned to her.

"Shall I show you where things are, or should that wait for tomorrow?"

She smiled, and it was a smile to heat the blood.

"Most things can wait. But... the library?"

He laughed, amused, yet understanding – he would have given the same answer to such a question. He lifted a candle from the side table, took her hand, and led her up the stairs. They passed along the gallery, and the portraits of the previous Earls peered down at them, as if assessing their acceptability. At the end, he opened the door into the library, and showed her in.

She stood there, her eyes roaming the room, which was lit only by their candle and the flickering light of the fire in the grate.

"This is beautiful. So many windows for light, and the shelves so well arranged to fit as much as possible into the space. And the desk, and the couch by the fire to read on..."

"Or do other things on..."

His voice was a little uneven, and desire surged through him. She turned to regard him as he stepped further into the room and closed the door behind them.

"Other things?"

Her voice was breathy, as uneven as his.

He took her hand and led her to the couch, placing the candlestick carefully on the desk.

"Other things... like kisses, and more..."

He sank down onto the seat, and tugged her down until she landed in his lap. She brought her lips to his, a kiss which was exploratory, a kiss which left him aching for more. She drew back after a moment.

"The kisses, I most definitely like, and the more... that, you will have to teach me, husband."

"Gladly, my darling wife. I do believe that you are an enchantress – for how else could it be that I find myself in a library, and not the least interested in books at this moment?"

She laughed softly, and raised an eyebrow at him.

"Perhaps because, after all, some of those things whispered in supposition about why you were sent down – those things about debauchery and the like – require study, to determine if they have value?"

"You may well be right. And that is a matter which we will have to study most assiduously, together."

He pulled her close, and kissed her again – a kiss which was the beginning of the most delightful studying he had ever done.

The End.

Over the page you'll find an Author's Note, with some information about the real history touched on in this story.

Author' s Note

In this book, as in many of my others, there are a lot of things which were real, things which really happened, although not, perhaps, in exactly the way that I have portrayed them. In this book, the following things are things that really happened / existed:

- The decoupling of paper money from gold, which happened in 1797 and allowed bulk printing of money to fund the wars.
- The presentation in the House of Lords in 1819 of an extensive report into exactly what the government had spent money on, over the previous few years.
- The excessive proliferation of forgery of bank notes, after the end of the Napoleonic wars.
- The decision by the House of Lords to investigate methods by which bank notes might be made 'unforgeable'. (although Westerhazy's committee is my invention)
- The implementation of a plan to start having all paper money underwritten by actual gold again, starting in mid-1820 and completed in 1821 (planned in 1819).
- The invention of a method to make notes hard to forge, which involved very complex lines and patterns, by a Mr Ibbetson (who went on to petition the House of Lords in mid-1820 to stop a Bank in the Midlands from using his method without having paid him the licensing fee to use it).

- The existence of a man named Willian Cobbett, who did write a book called 'Paper Against Gold' decrying the state of the monetary system, and founded a weekly newspaper, in which he expressed, very pointedly, his political views. He was a political radical, and fled to America in 1817, when there was muttering about arresting him for sedition. He returned to England in November 1819. He later was charged with libel, but never sedition, and eventually went on to be involved in horticulture, and the promulgation of better self-sufficiency skills for cottagers. (he wrote a book called 'Cottage Economy' – both it, and 'Paper Against Gold' are available from Amazon).

- The existence of an area just south of Westminster along the river which was characterised by warehouses, and wharves which were referred to as the 'Stone Wharves' as a result of them being used to bring in stone for use in the building works of the grand buildings in the area, including the Cathedral, over decades, if not centuries.

  The whole area burned down in the 1830s (along with much of the Houses of Parliament, which were then rebuilt), and was never rebuilt as warehouses or housing (although the wharves were still used to bring in the materials to rebuild the Houses of Parliament). Instead, the area became parkland, as it remains today.

  The area was a triangle, which came to a point at what was then the Horse Ferry point, but is now one end of Lambeth Bridge. On the next page you'll find an image of a map from 1819, and the same area on Google maps today.

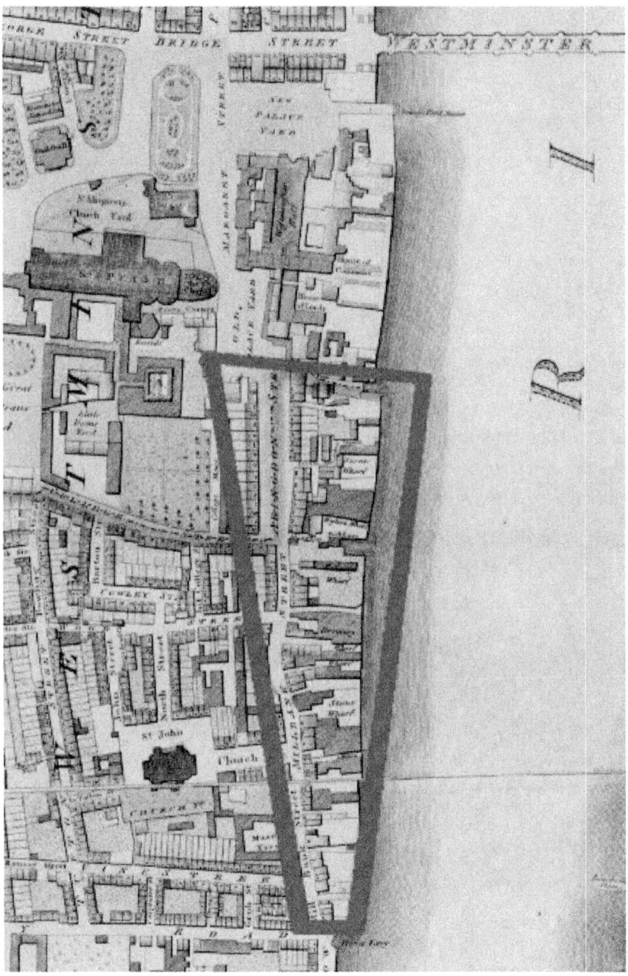

1819

2021

If you look closely, you can see the labels on the 1819 map of 'Stone Wharf' in a number of places.

And here is a picture of what a bank note looked like in 1819. All bank notes were printed as made out to whoever was the Central Manager of the Bank of England at the time, and then, when a person received one, the bank official endorsed it as going to them by signing on the back of it. Every time a note changed hands, it would be endorsed again.

I hope that you enjoyed 'An Enchantress for an Earl'.

Turn the page for another delightful Regency story.

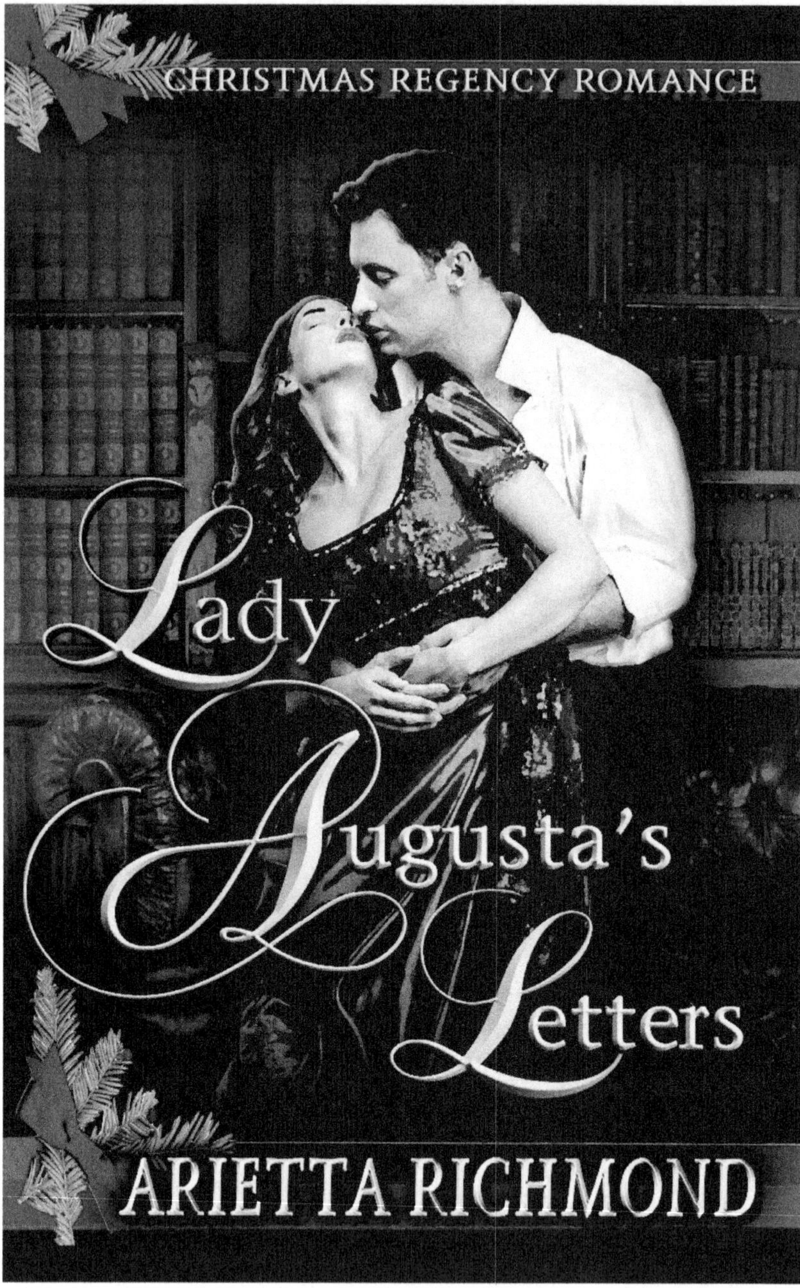
CHRISTMAS REGENCY ROMANCE
Lady
Augusta's
Letters
ARIETTA RICHMOND

CHRISTMAS REGENCY ROMANCE

Lady Augusta's Letters

ARIETTA RICHMOND

Prologue

February 1814

"I know that the times are difficult for travel, my son, but you must go. My health declines – there is no denying it – and if you are to travel, to see our Italian estate where your grandmother was born, you need to go while you still can, before the weight of the title falls onto your shoulders."

Dario Harrison, Marquess of Weatherbrook, regarded his father with something of distress in his face. The Duke of Winterward had not been entirely healthy for some time, that was true, but surely he was not so unwell as to be considering death as something to be expected at any time soon?

"Father, I am sure that you will be with us many a year yet! And the difficulty of travelling, given the war... I would have to take ship, and go the long way, through the Mediterranean. That is a prospect which does not appeal."

"Nonetheless, I think that you should go. Young men usually do the Grand Tour of the continent – with the wars, that option is not easily available to you. But to get to Italy – that is possible. And I know that your grandmother would feel happy when her own time comes, knowing that you have been there, have laid flowers at her father's grave – you bear his name, after all. Surely, a year away is reasonable, and you should see the estate which you will one day own, anyway."

Dario swallowed, a little disturbed by the gravity of his father's tone. The idea of seeing the Italian estate was appealing, even if the prospect of the journey involved in getting there was not. And, if he was truthful, there was nothing, beyond his parents, grandmother, and sister, to keep him in England. Perhaps his father was right, and he should go and see a little of the world while he could.

"Very well, if you think that I should go... But I will leave departure until late this year, I think, for surely it will take some time to organise everything. If we are all lucky, perhaps the war will end before the time when I must leave."

The Duke shook his head sadly.

"I somehow doubt that. But we can hope. I'll get your grandmother to write down everything she knows of the estate, and how to find your great grandfather's grave, as well as asking her to pen some letters of introduction, in Italian, to the estate staff. You may have learnt Italian from her, but perhaps your knowledge will not be enough to deal with the local dialect."

"Thank you, Father."

Chapter One

July 1814

Lady Augusta Carlington slipped along the darkened hallways of Winterward Keep, knowing her way very well by now. With her parents, she had been a guest at the Keep for six weeks now, enjoying a summer idyll away from both London and their northern estate. Her mother, the Marchioness of Shilham, had been a lifelong friend of the Duchess of Winterward, although the two had not seen each other for more than ten years, before this summer.

But it was not the Duke, the Duchess or their daughter Lady Virginia who interested Augusta – it was, instead, their son – Dario, the Marquess of Weatherbrook. Dario, who had captured her heart from the moment that she had seen him in London during the Season, bringing back memories of time spent with him when they were both small children. For two Seasons, Augusta had refused all of the suitors who had begged for her hand – and now, she knew why. Her heart had been waiting for Dario.

She slipped into the library, just as the clocks struck midnight. As she had known he would be, he was waiting for her, silhouetted against the warm glow of the fire which burned low in the grate. He turned at the sound of the door closing behind her.

"Augusta..."

"Dario..."

She went to him, went into his arms joyfully, and lifted her face to his kiss.

Long minutes later, they drew apart and, hands entwined, went to sit on the couch. Augusta felt as if the world was magical, in moments like this. Magical because nothing seemed to exist but the two of them.

She had begun to believe that it might be possible that they would marry... But he had said nothing of that, yet.

He was, in so many ways, the perfect gentleman – he might scandalously meet her at midnight like this, might steal heated kisses in the dark, but he went no further. She rather, sometimes, wished that he would. They sat for some time, just being together, then, in a voice so low that it was barely audible, he spoke.

"Augusta... I've told you about the plan for me to travel to Italy..."

"Yes?"

Her heart fell – surely, he would not leave her? Not without a promise between them?

"It seemed so far away, when we began to care for each other, but... our man of business sent a message today, confirming that my passage is booked, on the Lady Amabella, leaving Portsmouth in the last days of September. So it's real – I will be going. I... I will miss you, so very much, yet I cannot go back on my word – I promised my father, and my grandmother, that I would do this, that I would go to Italy, and see our estate, see my great grandfather's grave."

Augusta choked back a sob. If he had given his word, then she could not expect him to go back on it. But... would he not ask her? She could wait a year, if she knew that he intended to wed her when he returned. In truth, she now realised, she had already waited ten years, since the moment when she had irrevocably fallen for him, as a small child. She would wait anyway, she knew, but it would be better if he asked for her hand, and they were promised....

She lifted a hand to his cheek, her fingers trailing down the curve of his face to his lips. Could he see the faint sheen of tears in her deep blue-green eyes?

"If you must go so soon, then we had best make the most of the time that we have. Especially as my family will return to Shilham Park next week, and I may not see you again before you go..."

He bent to kiss her again, and for some time, they allowed themselves each to forget everything but the touch of the other, to revel in simply being together. Eventually though, they drew apart again, and Augusta asked the question she had hesitated to ask before.

"Will you spend the next few days with me? We can ride, or walk in the grounds, or sit here and read... and we can meet here each night, like this. I do not think that I could bear it if there were no more kisses before you left for such a long journey..."

Dario laughed softly, and kissed her again.

"Yes, my darling Augusta, I will spend as much time as I can with you, and meet you here each night."

*****

Dario watched her slip back out of the library, leaving him feeling cold, and missing her already.

When he had agreed to travel to Italy, he had thought that nothing would make him want to stay in England. And then, in London, his mother had introduced him to her old friend, the Marchioness of Shilham, and her daughter, Lady Augusta. That introduction had jolted his memory – Lady Augusta and her family had moved to a distant one of the Marquess' estates ten years ago, when he and Lady Augusta had been children. In the intervening time, he had forgotten the summers they had spent playing together – but memory came rushing back, and with it the affection he had always felt for her.

An affection which had only grown with knowing her now, as the beautiful woman she had become. Her older sisters were married, he'd been told, but she, although acknowledged a diamond of the first water, had still not wed, even after two Seasons. He had found himself grateful for that fact.

Now, he held her in far more than simple affection. He rather thought that he had come to love her. That was a terrifying concept, as he had not expected to commit himself to any woman for some years yet. But here they were – the weeks of her family being guests in his home had brought them to a point where the thought of being away from her tore at his heart.

Yet what could he do? She, and her family, would return to their home next week, and he, as he had promised his father, would sail away to Italy in six weeks or so from now. He could not, given that, ask her to be his – he did not know when he would return to England.

How could he ask her to commit to him, and wait some indeterminate amount of time which would be at least a year or more? He could not. And there was not time to do anything else – he would not risk her by asking her to become his, and then undertake a journey through war torn waters with him, even if there had been time for such a thing to be arranged.

The taste of her lingered on his lips, and the scent of her filled his nostrils. Somehow, the next few days would have to be enough, enough to last him the year or more until he returned.

*****

August 1814

The week had passed all too rapidly, and even with all of the time that she had spent with Dario, it was not enough. Her heart was breaking more, with every mile that the carriage took them away from Winterward Keep, and towards Shilham Park.

He had not asked her. Had not made things between them formal, as she had hoped – and as she rather suspected that both of their mothers had hoped. He had promised to write to her, to tell her of his travels, and to send her, once he arrived in Italy, the direction to which she might send him letters there.

It was not enough – but it was all she had, and she would cling to it.

Still, doubt wormed its way into her thoughts – did he not love her, as much as she loved him? Was that why he had not proposed to her, as she had hoped and expected?

If he did not love her enough to propose now, even if that meant waiting a year or more to marry, then what might happen in that year? What if he met someone else, in Italy, and married them?

She stared out through the carriage window, watching the seemingly endless fields roll past, and forced herself not to cry. She had to hold tight to the belief that he loved her, and that he would come back for her. No other man would do, now that she had felt his lips on hers.

*****

Late September 1814

The hour was late, and Dario was exhausted. The last few days had been spent in preparation – his waterproofed trunks were now packed with all that a gentleman traveller might need, plus all of the letters and information from his grandmother, and a stack of empty journals which he intended to fill with the tales of his travels.

His valet, Chalmers, had gone to bed some time ago, for he would be up before dawn to get Dario up and ready, as well as himself. Dario felt somewhat guilty about dragging Chalmers off to Italy with him – the man was no longer young.

But Chalmers was dedicated, and had insisted that he could not possibly let his master travel without him. Now, in the quiet room, where the only sound was the settling of the banked fire, Dario lay awake, despite that exhaustion. His mind was turning, rechecking everything, and thinking, as he always did of late, of Lady Augusta.

He had written to her a few times since her family had gone back to Shilham Park, and she had replied. Each letter had made him miss her more, and the thought of an entire year or more away from her made his heart ache unbearably. But he had to go.

Why had he not told her of the depth of his feelings, at least? He had asked himself that, many times, and never found an answer. But now, in the deep dark of the night, in the clarity which comes with exhaustion, he saw the answer sharply.

He had not told her because he was afraid.

Afraid that she might not love him as much as he loved her. Afraid that she would reject him, because he was about to go away. Afraid that his life would change incontrovertibly from the moment that he said the words.

He was a fool. There was no other conclusion to make.

And it was too late to remedy that, in the proper manner – he could not reach her, say the words, and still make his ship in Portsmouth in time. Yet he could not risk failing to ask her, could not risk the possibility of some other man marrying her, whilst he was away.

He pushed himself up from the bed, lit a candle from the embers of the fire, and went to his small escritoire. He would write to her now – would declare his love, and propose to her, would ask that she respond to that proposal by return mail.

Her letter would not reach him before Italy, but at least she would know the truth – and he would know too, as soon as her response arrived. He drew out paper, ink pot and pen, and began to write. The words were simple – they lacked romantic elegance – yet they came from the heart, and he hoped that she would forgive him for that.

It took more than an hour for him to write even the few sentences needed, for writing them drove him to consider himself in detail, and to make a number of promises to himself, about honesty and integrity, and the man he planned to be, when he came back to England. Finally, it was done, and he sanded it, brushed the sand off, and folded it carefully, sealing it with his seal.

He inscribed her name on the outside, and set it down on the surface of the escritoire, alongside the two piles of papers – one the record of his passage paid and all of his travel papers, and the other a copy of those, to be kept here to ensure that no record was lost. In the morning, he would take it down as he went, and drop it on the tray for the footman to send with the next mail.

That done, and feeling far lighter of heart as a result, he went back to the bed, soon falling into a deep sleep, which was filled with dreams of Augusta's kisses.

It was a sleep which seemed to last only minutes, before Chalmers was waking him, the pre-dawn light barely casting a glow into the room.

"Good morning, my Lord. I have a bath and everything ready for you – best to start a long journey feeling as fresh as possible. While you bathe, I will just prepare the final things here, and send the trunks down to the carriage."

"Thank you, Chalmers."

Dario rose, and went into the dressing room where the bathtub sat, steam rising from the water. Chalmers was right – this might be the last decent bath he had, before Italy – best to appreciate it. In the outer room, he could hear footsteps, and the sounds of his trunks being carried out. He lay back for a moment, but then reached for the soap and set about washing, his thoughts all on the travel to come.

When he was done, he rose from the tub and dried himself, then called for Chalmers to come and assist him to dress. Once that was done, he stepped back out into his bedchamber.

"You go down to the breakfast room, my Lord, and break your fast. I'll just tidy up the last of the things here, and then bring the satchel with all of our travel papers down when I come."

Dario nodded, and hurried out, hunger gnawing at him.

Behind him, Chalmers turned to the escritoire.

Into the satchel, he placed one stack of the papers waiting there, then he tidied the other stack of copies and slipped them into the escritoire drawer, before closing the top of the desk. He had checked those stacks of papers multiple times yesterday, so he saw no need to look at each one again.

Which meant that he did not notice the one extra sealed missive which lay on the second stack. It went into the drawer with the rest. Satisfied that all was in order, he lifted the satchel, and went down the stairs, ready to set off with his master on what looked likely to be a grand adventure.

*****

It was only late that night, as he drifted into sleep in the rather uncomfortable bed of an Inn on the way to Portsmouth, that Dario realised that he had not, personally, put the letter for Lady Augusta onto the correspondence tray. That was foolish of him – but in truth, he was not worried, for Chalmers had tidied everything away. The man was meticulous, and would have seen it, would have made sure that it was sent. Best not to think on it – there was no chance that he would see a reply until Italy, after all.

If he was to survive a year or more away from Augusta, it was best that he start, right now, training himself not to think of her, not to yearn for her.

Sleep claimed him, and the morning brought new excitement, as the fact of his journey moved from the imaginary future to current reality. Two more days passed on the road, before they reached Portsmouth, and boarded the ship – days in which he began to record his thoughts in the first of his journals, capturing the detail of the journey, so that he might share it all with family when he returned.

Chapter Two

Late October 1814

Augusta sat curled in the window seat of the bay window at Shilham Park, her book forgotten in her lap. She stared out, her eyes tracing the line of the curving drive with its borders of ancient trees. Their leaves were all shades of gold and red now, and beginning to fall as the year moved inexorably towards winter.

Where was Dario now? Did he think of her at all? He had not written – there had been no letters since the one a week before his departure, and with every day that passed without one, her world became a little colder, her heart broke a little more. Had she imagined it all? Did he not truly love her? She could not believe that it had all been an act, could not believe that he would have chosen to turn away from her. Yet he had not written – that was an incontrovertible fact.

Was he in Italy yet?

Probably not, for a sailing time of five weeks or more might be expected, she had been told, in these uncertain times. She tried to imagine what such a shipboard journey would be like, and could not. Her heart ached for him, and she refused to believe that he would not write. Perhaps he simply had not managed to, before his departure?

Might he have sent a letter from Portsmouth? But no, if he had, it should have reached her by now. She would not give up, would not allow herself to believe that his love had not been true. She would wait. A year was not so long, after all. But she wished that he had written to her, as he had promised to do, just before he had set off on his grand adventure.

*****

Late October 1814

Dario stood on the deck, feeling the rising wind whip his hair about. Ahead, a faint line on the horizon, rose the uneven bumps of land.

Italy. At last.

The journey had been long, for they had sailed out widely away from the land, passing Spain and Portugal at great distance, to make certain to avoid Napoleon's fleets. They had gone as far south as Morrocco, and put in there to resupply, before hugging the North African coast as they slipped up, through the Straits of Gibraltar, and into the Mediterranean. That caution had proven wise, for they had made the journey safely.

Now, with their destination in sight, the wind was rising, the waves rising with it, and the sailors told him that a big storm was coming. It was both good and bad – for it would speed their passage towards Italy, but that speed would come with great risk, especially as they got closer to the coast. They were planning to end their journey in Napoli, which had a good harbour, and easy access to the roads into the countryside, where his family estate lay – but to get there, they would need to pass along a coastline where soaring cliffs and jagged rocks threatened passing ships, even as small bays enticed.

A sailor made his way to Dario, even as the wind blew even harder.

"Time to go below, my Lord. Best ye stay in yer cabin, and out of our way while we ride the storm out."

"I will go now."

The sailor nodded, and went past him, hand over hand along the rail. Darion turned, and in similar fashion, made his way to the small hatch, and down the steep steps to the space where the cabins were jammed together. Chalmers looked up as he stepped into the cramped space.

"I've got it all packed, my Lord – everything but what we're wearing. The trunks are locked, and sealed tight in the oilskins. Beyond that I've a copy of your papers in this oilskin pouch, for you to carry. If we have to go ashore in the rain, everything will survive in good order."

"Thank you, Chalmers."

The movement of the ship had been steadily increasing, and now, a larger than usual swell sent her rolling hard. Dario flung himself onto the narrow bunk, as Chalmers did the same on the other one.

They said nothing more, simply clinging to the bunks and praying, as the storm took hold of the ship and flung it over the waves.

*****

Augusta started awake, to see the cold light of dawn slipping through the crack in her curtains. For a moment, terror filled her, until she realised where she was – it had been a nightmare, then.

She had dreamed of a monstrous storm, of crashing waves and cries of fear. But outside her windows, everything was still. Shivering, she burrowed back under the bedcovers, pushing the sense of deep foreboding away.

Just a dream, she kept telling herself, it was just a dream. But she could not get back to sleep, and the haunting sense of disaster stayed with her all of that day, and beyond.

*****

The storm intensified, tossing the ship about as if it was nothing more than a leaf, and Dario closed his eyes and clung to the bunk, feeling terror seep into him by the minute. Chalmers groaned, and the sound was one of abject fear, barely constrained.

It seemed to go on forever, the wailing of the wind, the crashing of waves, the creak and whine of the stressed timbers all around them, the force of it all building, steadily, to the moment when, with an almighty crash, the ship jerked suddenly, flinging them onto the floor, to be crushed between the trunks. A strange grinding sound followed, and the ship lurched again, heeling over almost onto her side, then righting herself. Shouts came to them, distantly, and screams, as more lurches and crashes followed. They were being, Dario suspected, dashed against the rocks at the base of some cliffs, over and over again. Yet still the ship moved forward – at least he thought that it did, and a tiny hope remained in his heart, that they might somehow survive this. In that moment, his thoughts went to Augusta – with regret that he had not spoken to her when he could, and relief that he had not attempted to bring her with him – at least now, even if he died, she would live.

After an eerie moment of silence, the wind took them again, and flung them against unyielding rocks, so hard that the side of the ship cracked open. Water poured in, and Dario screamed as the trunk closest to him smashed his right leg, and his lower arm, against the bunk. Another crash, and the other trunk slid, hitting his head. Everything went grey, and he fought for consciousness. At some point, as the ship shifted again, Chalmers screamed too, but Dario had not the ability to even look at him.

He stayed in that grey edge of life for what seemed a long time – not quite truly aware, anchored only by the pain in his arm. Vaguely he was aware that the movement of the ship had slowed, but of little else. Finally, as if all effort had become impossible, he slipped into the welcoming blackness, even as the wind outside died away, and the ship settled harder onto the rocks, just past the point of a craggy cape, the relentless shifting of the waves driving those rocks ever deeper into her hull.

*****

There were voices. Voices speaking an odd mixture of Italian and English. He barely understood them, and the effort of opening his eyes to see them was too great.

"There's two in here, Giovanni. Looks like someone important, and his man. And two trunks – lets get them, and their belongings, out before she settles further and breaks apart. If they live, there'll like be a reward, if they don't, there's always whatever's in these waterproofed trunks."

"Si, help me lift the first one." He moaned as rough hands moved him. "Well, this one's still alive then. Not so sure about the other one."

"Haul him out anyway. I'll get the trunks."

Whoever they were, they touched his arm, and he screamed, even as the blackness took him again.

*****

There was pain – more pain than he had ever felt before, he thought, in the few seconds of lucidity before the man standing beside him wrenched his leg sharply, and sent him back into the blessed darkness of unconsciousness again.

*****

November 1814

"Awake, are you?"

Slowly, a dim glow replaced the deep darkness, as he forced crusted eyes to open. Where was he? Who had spoken?

Instinct made him attempt to move, to sit up and look around him – but that proved to be a mistake, as pain swamped him, driving him back into the blackness, even as someone brought a cup to his lips, and made him swallow.

When next he woke, he simply lay there, with just enough memory of the pain to make him unwilling to move. But he must have made some small twitch, nonetheless, for that same voice came again.

"Don't try to move – it will hurt. But if you can open your eyes, we can talk, and see if you can manage a bit of broth."

At those words, a wave of hunger filled him. How long was it since he had eaten? He did not know. In fact, he realised then, with dawning horror, that he could remember very little at all, apart from half waking to pain, multiple times.

He forced his eyes to open.

He was in a small room, in what looked like a fisherman's hut, if the nets and floats hanging on the walls were any indication. The only light came from a small fire in a large fireplace off to one side, and a half-shuttered window on the wall opposite. Beside the bed he lay upon, an old woman sat in a wicker chair, her dark hair greying, but her almost black eyes bright with life and intelligence.

"Where am I?"

His throat hurt, raw from screaming in pain, he supposed, and his voice was hoarse. He did not sound like himself. That thought stopped him, and he felt his own eyes going wide.

Like himself... but... who was he?

He did not know – when he asked that question of himself, no name appeared in his mind, no knowledge at all of any life and identity, before his awakening in this bed.

"In a village two days' travel from Napoli, my Lord."

My Lord?

Was he a Lord, or was that simply a term of respect?

"How... how do I come to be here? And in what manner am I injured, that I feel so much pain?"

"Do you not remember, my Lord?"

Chagrined, he carefully shook his head – even that hurt.

"I do not remember anything."

She laughed.

"Oh but you do, my Lord, for you speak to me now in Italian, not your native English. Your accent is dreadful, but it still tells me that you learnt your Italian from someone who came from near here."

His thoughts spun. He had not, until she said it, considered what language they spoke – he had simply heard and responded. Now, he realised that she was right. So – there was one small piece of his identity – he was English. Not that knowing that changed anything. The rest of his past was a deep black space in his mind.

"I see. But I do not remember what happened to bring me here."

"You were on a ship. She was running before a storm, up along the coast, and misjudged the position of the shoals out around the point. These can be dangerous waters if you don't know them. The ship was wrecked, blown onto the rocks, and dragged by the storm along the cliffs until just past the point, where she settled onto the jagged teeth of the land. When the storm dropped, my man and the others from this village went out to salvage what they could – be that men, or goods. They salvaged you, and your belongings. And your man, but he, sadly, did not live out the night."

He studied her face, finding his confusion deepening. His man? He did not remember. Which, if the fellow had died attending upon him, was dashed unappreciative of him. Why could he not remember?

"I remember nothing of it. A ship, you say? Did... did any but I survive?"

She shook her head.

"None – we thought that your man might, but... he spoke to us once, telling us, with his last breath, to care for you. He told us his name was Chalmers, and so we marked it on his grave. When you are finally strong enough to walk, I will show you."

He shook his head again – that name... it stirred some faint recognition, but not enough for him to grasp.

"I still remember nothing."

"Perhaps what is in your trunks will help you find the memories. My man brought those out of the ship too, risky as it was. But you'll have to break the locks on them, unless you carry the keys?"

"I would not know if I did. But... is it possible for me to sit, and to have some of that broth you mentioned earlier? I find that my body craves food."

"Three days sleep will do that to a man, especially when his body is healing. We managed to get you to take water, and something to dull the pain, but nothing more was possible until you woke. I'll help you sit – but do not try to move your right leg, or your right hand, for both are broken. The apothecary set your leg, and bound it, but it will be weeks, or even months, before you have proper use of it. Your hand – I am not sure how well it will ever heal."

She rose from the chair, and came to slip her arm under his shoulders. Obedient to her instructions, he did not attempt to move his right arm, but instead pushed with his left arm to help as she lifted him to sit. He wobbled, a wave of pain filling him despite his efforts to not move the broken parts, and she hurried to push a pile of pillows, clothes, and old blankets behind him.

"Thank you – I think."

She laughed again.

"You'll mend. And when the men come back from the day's fishing, I'll have help to pull you further up the bed, so you can lean against the wall. For now, this will have to do."

He shifted carefully, leaning into the uneven pile of cloth, and watched as she went across to the fireplace, and the large pot which hung above the flames. At that moment, he was ready to eat anything, no matter how unsavoury – but the scent when she ladled something out into a bowl was wonderful. He would eat, whatever it was – the mystery of his identity could wait.

Chapter Three

November 1814

"Perhaps we should hold a Country Ball here, in the week before Christmas. We have not hosted one for many years. Your sisters and their families would come, of course, and we could invite some friends – perhaps the Duke and Duchess of Winterward, and Lady Virginia, if the Duke is well enough to travel..."

Augusta looked at her mother, and carefully refrained from saying what she actually thought. It would, of course, be pleasant to see her two sisters, and their husbands, especially as each now had two small children – one of which she had not yet met. But the thought of spending the time with the Duke and Duchess, and their daughter, without Dario... that was much less appealing, as every minute would be a reminder of his absence – and of the absence of any correspondence.

"I am sure that would be delightful, Mother. All of the local gentry would be thrilled to have the opportunity to interact with the Duke and Duchess, of a certainty."

"So I thought, indeed. I will set about organising it. Perhaps, if I invite a range of people, a gentleman may take your eye..."

Augusta sighed.

"Mother, no one appeals to me – you know that."

It was her mother's turn to sigh.

"I do know that, and I despair of you. Two Seasons now, and all of those offers – how can you possibly not have accepted any of them? Both of your sisters were married after their first Seasons! The gossips will start to call you Spinster, if you do not choose a man soon." Augusta stared into the fire for a moment, searching for a way to reply, her mind full of kisses in the darkened library at Winterward Keep, and the only man she had ever actually wanted. Her mother went on, after a moment, her voice softer, almost wistful. "Although.... after this last summer.... I had hoped... He seemed so fond of you..."

She sighed, and said no more, but it was enough – enough to make tears start to Augusta's eyes. She forced them back, breathing slowly, staring at the flames. She would believe in him, in his love, despite the lack of any correspondence. She would not let her mother see her doubts.

The silence stretched, and eventually, Augusta felt composed enough to speak.

"Mother, I will marry only the right man – I would be happy, as my sisters are."

"I would wish you happy too – perhaps, this coming Season, you will meet the right man?"

I have already met the right man.

The thought was there, instantly, but she did not voice it. Perhaps a letter would arrive soon, from Italy... Until one did, she would say nothing – over the last two Seasons, she had mastered the art of being polite and kind, without ever truly encouraging any man – she would simply have to continue that way, until she knew, for a certainty, whether Dario loved her, and wished to marry her, or not.

*****

Late November 1814

He gritted his teeth as the somewhat ancient carriage rumbled along the rough country road. The view from the window was spectacular – a huge vista out over the ocean, from where the road ran along the top of the cliffs – but the pain from his leg every time they went over a rut in the road rather distinctly took away from his pleasure in the view. Beside him, stacked on the floor, and partly forming a support for his still splinted and bound leg, were the two trunks which had been retrieved from the ship with him. And tucked into his clothing was the packet of oilskin wrapped papers which had been in that same place when he had been pulled from the wreck. Papers which he had read multiple times, in the hope that their contents might stir his mind to recover memories.

So far, very little had surfaced. But the papers had given him a name, and a place to go.

A name which somehow, even though it seemed familiar, did not quite fit – as if it had belonged to a different man, a man he had known briefly, in some long-ago time. Yet, apparently, it was his name.

Dario Harrison, Marquess of Weatherbrook.

The fisherman and his wife had been impressed, and intrigued – for why would an English Lord bear an Italian name? The papers gave some clue, in that they also contained a letter addressed to the retainers of an estate further north, introducing him as the son of the owner, and the great grandson of a previous local Count. It was a letter he had struggled to read, for his written Italian was not as good as his spoken – and the fisherman and his wife could not read. But he had worked his way through it, to at least basic understanding.

The trunks, once broken open, had provided more – some funds, and clothes, and journals. He had much reading ahead of him, if he was ever to truly understand who he was. Once he had accepted the idea of that identity, he had done what seemed the only logical thing, and sent a copy of that letter, with an additional note, asking that the estate send a carriage of some sort to collect him, and convey him there. Achieving sending that message had been far harder than he'd expected, and had taken weeks – he could not write – his hand was still painful, and somewhat twisted, although he hoped that, by working at it, he might improve his flexibility over time. The fisherman and his wife could not read or write past a few minor things, so he had, of necessity, asked them to find him someone who could – which took time, as the person found came from another village. But eventually, the message was written, the original letter he'd carried copied, and both sent with a messenger. Then there had been more weeks for the message to reach the estate and gain a response. A response had come, borne by a man dressed in faded livery on a somewhat aged horse, but a man who was respectful, and helpful, and assured him that a carriage was following at the best speed it could.

Now, having given the fisherman and his wife more money than he suspected they had ever seen before, in recompense for their care of him, and of poor Chalmers – whom he did not remember, yet who, it seemed, had died trying to save him, he was on his way. The carriage jolted along, and even with the pain, eventually, exhaustion tipped him into a shallow sleep. That sleep was filled with odd dreams – dreams of a young woman with dark hair and deep blue green eyes. Those eyes were like the colour of the sea as the storm approached, and in the dreams, they faded into that sea, as she reached out a pleading hand to him.

Hours later, he started awake as the carriage turned sharply, and for a moment, it was as if those eyes still met his. Then the dream faded, and the reality around him came back into focus. The sharp turn had been made in through an imposing, if somewhat aged, gateway, whose iron gates sat open to the world. A long, gravelled drive stretched out ahead of them, lined with winter bare trees. At the end of that drive rose a very large villa, built of rich golden stone, made to look even more gold by the light of the late afternoon sun which cast long shadows away behind it. If this was to be his home, at least for now, he admitted to himself a sense of quiet relief – something grander than a fisherman's cottage had great appeal, after the last many weeks.

*****

December 1814

The Ball had been a success, and Lady Shilham was happy. Augusta was happy that it was over. She had smiled, and danced, and been everything that was polite, even while feeling empty inside. How different it would have been, had Dario been there!

His parents had been gracious, and thrilled the local gentry with their kindness and cheerful conversation, yet under that cheer, Augusta was sure that she had detected the same gnawing worry which filled her own thoughts. She suspected that they too, had received no letters. Of course, it would have been the height of rudeness to ask...

Now, the Duke and Duchess had taken Lady Virginia, and set off on their long journey home. All of the other guests had already departed, and the house was blessedly quiet. In the parlour, there was no sound beyond the gentle crackle of the fire in the grate, and the clink of her mother's teacup, as she set it down after taking a sip. Bliss. Augusta turned her eyes back to the book she was reading, determined to simply read, and not allow her thoughts to wander to Dario, as they did, so often, every day. She had read precisely two sentences when the door opened, and her father came in, a newspaper clutched in his hand. His face was a little pale. Her mother looked up, and regarded him with concern.

"What is it, George? You look rather disturbed."

"Do you recall the name of the ship that young Weatherbrook sailed on?"

Augusta's heart nearly stopped – why would her father ask that? What was wrong? An icy tendril of fear slipped down her spine. Her mother was looking confused, and thoughtful. The words slipped from Augusta's mouth, instantly, for it was a name branded on her memory.

"The Lady Amabella."

Her father almost flinched.

"I thought so, although I hoped not."

"What has happened?"

At Augusta's question, he simply handed her the somewhat crumpled news sheet. Heart pounding, she set aside her book, and smoothed the sheet out. There, stark on the front page was a large headline.

'English Ship, Lady Amabella, Lost on Italian Coast – No Survivors'

The paper fell from her nerveless fingers, and a wave of faintness almost overcame her. Worried, her mother rose, and hurried to lift the paper from the floor, only, seconds later, to drop it again, her hand going to her mouth to stifle a gasp.

Augusta did not want to believe it – even as tears started to trickle down her cheeks, she snatched up the paper again to read it, needing to know more, to know if there was any hope at all. The report was scant, and did nothing to ease her heartbreak. He could not be dead – she would have known, surely! And then it came back to her, as if from a great distance – that one time, many weeks ago now, when she had woken in the night, from a dream of terrifying waves and wind, and strange crashing noises. Her hand went to her mouth, making her look very much like an echo of her mother, and she sobbed.

"NO! No, it cannot be...."

And with that, unable to bear it, she fled the room, running to her chambers, where she flung herself onto the bed and sobbed inconsolably.

*****

December 1814

The Duke of Winterward gasped, clutching at his chest, his breathing laboured. The Duchess rushed to him, and pulled the news sheet from his grasp, easing him back in his chair, praying as she did so. He'd had these turns before, and recovered, he would do so again. For long minutes, there was no sound but his laboured breathing, and the scurrying of servants' feet.

A footman came into the room, a cup in hand, and brought it to the Duchess, who encouraged the Duke to sip from it. Grandmother's concoction was nasty in taste, but it worked to ease his pains at times like these. Once he was able to take the cup from her, she turned, lifting the paper, wondering whether his turn had been caused by something in that, or by something else. The papers were a few days old, and had been waiting for them when they got home – what on earth might there be in there, to give him a turn like this?

She smoothed it out, and the headline seared itself into her mind. With nary a sound, she crumpled where she stood, fainting for the first time in her life.

*****

Lady Virginia had stepped into the breakfast room at the exact moment that her mother fainted. Shocked, she looked to her father, who had that greyish cast about him which came with one of his bad turns. Fear filled her, and she dashed forward, nearly colliding with the footman who had also leapt towards the Duchess, attempting to catch her as she fell.

"What has happened?"

Her father grimaced, as he swallowed a mouthful of what, from the scent of it, was grandmother's medicine concoction, then spoke.

"Virginia, please help your mother to a seat, then I'll tell you."

Virginia did as she had been asked to, and with the footman's help, roused her mother from her faint, and assisted her to a seat at the table. She settled into the chair beside the Duchess, worry creasing her features.

"Please tell me, now, what has caused this – I do not believe that I have ever seen mother faint before!"

The Duchess' voice came a little weakly from beside her.

"That, my darling daughter, is because I have never fainted before, in my life."

The Duke swallowed more of the medicine, his colour improving, and gestured to the footman.

"Thomas, please give Lady Virginia the news sheet. Virginia, prepare yourself for a shock."

Virginia tensed – what could there be in a news sheet to cause this reaction? The footman placed the sheet in front of her on the table, and smoothed it flat. She looked at it, and for long minutes her mind refused to take in what her eyes saw. Then, as the reality of the headline sank in, she wavered, the world going grey around her for a minute, before she pulled herself together.

"No..."

Virginia barely got the word out. Then, from beside her, came her mother's voice – it was still weak, but it held a core of steel when she spoke.

"I have no doubt, Virginia, that the headline reflects what they believe to be true. But we cannot be certain of it yet. There is no mention of bodies recovered, nor a list of those who were on board at the time. Until we receive confirmation, in detail, I will not give up hope. I will ask our man of business to send urgent enquiries. It may be months before we know, but I will hold to hope, as must you." She turned to where the footman stood, and spoke to him "Thomas, please ask Mrs Hicks to lock up Lord Weatherbrook's rooms – I will have nothing touched, in any way, until we know the truth of this."

The Duke nodded, and added one final dictate.

"Nor will we assume mourning attire, until we know for certain that it is truly required."

*****

Late December 1814

Christmas was a dreary affair at Winterward Keep. No one could bring themselves to be joyous, with the lack of confirmation of Dario's death – or not – hanging over them. The house was decorated as usual, and the gifts and food distributed to the tenant farmers and the staff, yet everything seemed hollow, without Dario there, without the sound of his voice in the halls. He had always loved Christmas as a boy, and it just was not at all the same without him.

But they did not speak of it either.

Grandmother prayed far more than usual, and the Duke knew that she, like he did himself, blamed herself for encouraging Dario to go. Had he been utterly foolish to do so? He had not thought so at the time, but now... now, he worried, not just about what had truly happened to his son, but about the title, and his family. If he died, and Dario was confirmed dead, then the title would go to Dario's cousin, the son of the Duke's younger brother.

And Porter Harrison was a man more interested in gambling and horse racing than in taking responsibility for anything. He did not want everything that he had worked for, on the Winterward estates, to be destroyed by Porter. But if Dario truly was dead... then centuries of responsible stewardship of the land might be brought to nothing. It was not a thought to encourage Christmas cheer.

Chapter Four

Late December 1814

It was a miserable Christmas – quite the worst of Augusta's life.

From the day that they had first seen that terrible headline on the news sheet, she had been unable to sleep properly, tortured by dreams of Dario, in the midst of the shipwreck, reaching out to her, but always being beyond reach. She could not believe that he was gone, dead. Surely, if that had been true, she would have known it, in her heart?

The only thing which gave her the tiniest grain of hope was that there had not yet been a more detailed report of the matter reach England – no list of the dead whose bodies had been recovered, no detail of how matters had actually proceeded at the site of the wreck. Until such a report reached England, she could believe that he was not dead, that he had, somehow, escaped that doom, and reached land.

If he had, surely he would write? To his parents, at least, even if not to Augusta?

Each day seemed grey and unrelentingly sad, especially as the weather at Shilham Park was cold and miserable, characterised by a steady drizzling sleet and ice-cold wind. She huddled by the fire, surrounded by her family, who were all being determinedly cheerful. When small children were placed in her lap, she dutifully cuddled them, but her heart was simply unable to regard the Christmas season with any enthusiasm at all. Her mother watched her, saying little, but Augusta knew that Lady Shilham worried, and would eventually attempt to push Augusta to 'move on'.

How could she do such a thing? Her heart belonged to Dario, even though they had not been formally promised, and the idea that she might so easily turn her attentions to another man was revolting. Each night, before she tried to sleep, she wrote, in her journal, a letter that she would never send – each one a letter to Dario, telling him of her love, and of the events of her life. It was foolish, in the extreme, she knew, yet she could not stop herself. Writing those 'letters' allowed her to feel as if he was still there, somewhere, waiting for the letters to arrive.

*****

His arrival at the Villa D'Oro was met with something resembling a cross between panic and celebration. A veritable flood of rapid Italian overwhelmed him, and he had to beg them to slow down. They laughed, delighted that he could at least manage to get that right, and helped him into the building. Once he was settled in a rather beautiful parlour, he pulled out his precious packet of papers. A man, who, if he had things right, was the estate manager, and a woman who appeared to be the housekeeper, watched him curiously, as others rushed off about things, carrying his trunks away into the Villa, and scurrying around – hopefully bringing him food and drink.

He sifted through the papers, moving his damaged hand carefully, in an attempt not to drop anything, until he found the letter. A letter, which if he understood it correctly, had been written by a woman who was his grandmother – a woman he did not remember. But it was obviously a letter of introduction to the staff here, so he handed it to the man, and waited.

They both read it, with frequent glances up at him as they did, then spoke to each other rapidly. He half understood their words, for how they spoke was not entirely dissimilar from his grandmother... that thought stopped him in sudden shock – he had just remembered something! It was a tiny memory, but he saw quite clearly the smiling old woman, her once black hair now mostly grey, bending over him, and speaking Italian – some childish tale, he thought. Caught, he forgot the room around him in that moment, and clung to that memory, hoping that it would grow – but nothing more came.

"Mio Signore...?"

The man's words brought him back from his reverie.

"Si?"

The man smiled broadly, and then spoke again, slowly enough that it was understandable.

"Your grandmother tells us that you are the great grandson of the man who built this villa, that you are named in his honour, and that, when your father passes, you will own this land, this house."

The thought was strange, unexpected, part of that missing life he sought to recover, yet it was a pleasing thought – this place felt right, somehow. But... he must tell them of his problems with his memory, must explain just how much he did not know – perhaps then, they could help him recover the truth of his life.

"I... believe that to be true. But... at present, ever since the shipwreck from which I was pulled, barely alive, I cannot remember any of my life before. I only know what I have found in my papers, and in the trunks with my possessions, which were retrieved from the ship with me. When I woke, after many days of darkness and pain, I did not even remember my name – that I learnt because my man, who was also pulled from the wreck but did not survive, told it to the fishermen. So, whilst the letters and papers tell me that I came here to see this place, to learn about the estate, and my grandmother's family, I come to you needing to learn about far more than that. I have my whole life to rediscover, and any help you can give me will be appreciated."

Shock coloured their faces, and after a moment the woman muttered something which he rather thought called him a poor lost child.

"Of course we will help as we can, my Lord. But first, I think, we must call the physician, and the apothecary here, and get them to make sure that your broken bones were set properly, and are healing as they should."

"Indeed, I would appreciate that – but to be truthful, right now, more than anything, I would most appreciate some food, then a man to assist me, a bath, some clean clothes, and a bed."

They laughed softly, smiling, and the woman, with a nod, hurried off, apparently to organise all of that. The man went to a heavy carved sideboard, and poured two glasses from the decanter which sat there, then brought one to him.

"The local strong spirit, my Lord – it will fortify you, and help you heal. But it is powerful – do not take too much to start."

He took it, and sniffed the clear liquid. Powerful indeed, if the scent was anything to go by. A cautious sip sent warmth right through him, sharp and smooth at once, like no spirit he had ever tasted before. But it felt good. Despite it all, he decided that he liked this place.

*****

Early January 1815

Dario – for he had come to think of himself as Dario, now, having got used to the fact that so he was named – wobbled across the terrace to the chair which waited for him. Luigi had made him a strange kind of walking stick – very tall, and with a bar across the top of it, so that he could slip it under his right arm, and hold it with his hand – which was barely possible – to assist him with walking, while his right lower leg was still splinted and bound.

Walking with it was difficult, and very slow – but he was determined – even managing the few steps from the chair in the parlour to the chair on the terrace was a victory he relished. When he reached the chair, he dropped into it gratefully, stretching his aching leg out in front of him. On the small table beside the chair, his journals waited, as did a pitcher of water, and a large cup.

Carefully, using his newfound skills with his left hand, he poured the cup full.

Sipping the water, he stared out across the lightly forested land of the estate, reflecting on the last few weeks. It had been a strange Christmas – he had been perpetually dogged by the feeling that there were specific people who should be with him, yet being unable to bring names or faces to mind. Probably, it was his family in England who he half thought of, like that – but the frustrating blankness of his memory left them unknown to him.

He dreamed most nights, and in those dreams, he saw faces – most often a woman with very dark chestnut hair, and deep blue green eyes. Eyes like the stormy sea that had cast him ashore into this half-life. He wanted to know who she was, for he was drawn to her, more strongly than to any of the others present in those dreams. Perhaps the journals would tell him.

Once he had taken a few days to recover from the journey along the coast to this villa, he had, for the first time, explored in detail everything which was in the trunks. Trunks which he had quickly come to realise contained the belongings of the man Chalmers, who had died, as well as Dario's own things. A man who had been, it seemed, his valet. That realisation had brought him a wave of grief, a mourning for a man he could not remember. How much else was currently lost to him, which deserved mourning?

Also in those trunks had been stacks of journals – some written in, and some blank, awaiting use. At first, he had turned away from those, almost afraid of knowing what lay within, and frustrated by how difficult it was to do anything, with limited movement in his right hand. When he had expressed that frustration, an old woman had been brought to see him – a woman whom Luigi explained was the local herb woman, and more skilled in this kind of thing than the physician.

She had taken his hand in hers, and gently prodded and poked, bending and twisting to discover the points at which movement became pain.

Then, she had muttered and shaken her head. He had feared then, that he would never have more use of his hand than he did now, that he would need to learn to write with his left hand, and to do a multitude of other things differently.

But she had turned to him, and spoken slowly, to be sure that he understood, and her words had given him hope.

"If you wish to regain proper use of your hand, there will be pain, then we will strap it, and then, after some weeks, we will need to stretch it every day – which will hurt. But at the end of some months, you should have most use of it."

He had agreed to whatever she would do, desperate to have use of the hand, even if it took time. When she had said that there would be pain, he had not fully understood. The first steps were simple – she produced a small wooden hammer and, holding his hand firmly, tapped it in an assortment of places – he could hear faint cracks from his bones. Then, as the pain of that hit him, she grasped his hand firmly, and pulled and twisted, until, with a snapping sound, his hand lay straight again.

He had blacked out from the pain of that straightening. But when he awoke to see his hand held flat between two carved small boards, and strapped about with bandages so that only the tops of his fingers and his thumb could be seen, he had been overjoyed to realise that, if he commanded his fingers to wiggle, the tips of them did so.

Now, four weeks later, the boards had been removed, and cloth strapping was all that supported his hand. Every day, the old woman came, and gently but determinedly moved each finger, stretching the muscles, then asked him to close and open his hand, and to stretch and fold each finger separately. Progress was slow – he could not fully close his hand, nor could he grasp a pen – but at least he could manage the walking stick device.

Today, for the first time, he was going to read some of those journals. Now, he had enough control of his hand to at least turn a page, while his left hand held the journal steady. He wanted to discover himself, in those pages, wanted to read what he had written, on the long journey which had brought him here.

At the start, it would most likely read like a novel, a tale of someone else's life, but perhaps, as he read it, he would remember those things too, and become more the man he had been. Perhaps, too, he would discover who the woman with the sea green eyes was.

*****

March 1815

The carriage rolled along, getting ever closer to London, and the months of social torture which were the Season. Augusta had begged to be left at home, but her mother had insisted – her father was in Town for Parliament, and they would join him. Augusta was expected to go to all of the Balls, and to do her best to find a man she was willing to marry.

No matter what she had said, her mother had simply persisted – and now, here they were. And a long carriage journey had made her a captive audience for her mother's commentary on the matter.

"Augusta, you really must accept the truth of it, and look forward, look for a man to marry, or you will be a lonely spinster all too soon. I would have been overjoyed if you had married Weatherbrook, but... you must accept that he is dead."

"I cannot. There has been no report of his body or possessions recovered – nothing. Surely, by now, if he was dead, they would have found him. I will not give up hope."

Her mother sighed.

"You say that now, but we will see what happens when handsome gentlemen seek you out. Despite this being your third Season, you are still beautiful – more so, I think, than in your first year - you will be pursued."

"And I will be polite, I will dance with them, I will look kindly upon the flowers that they send, I will take tea with them when they call – but I will refuse them all. My heart is committed, and that is that."

For some time, there was silence, and Augusta watched the world go by, watched the fields become the outskirts of London, and then the centre. She felt oddly detached from it – it was not that she disliked London, but simply that there was nothing to draw her here – the Balls and Soirees of the Season stretched out before her as if they would involve someone else – she could not imagine herself in those settings anymore. Everything in the world was somehow greyer, since the day of that first terrible news sheet headline.

The only thing which was real was her memory of his kisses, in the darkened library at Winterward Keep.

They drew up in front of Shilham House, and with the opening of the carriage door, Augusta's feat of endurance began.

*****

April 1815

Augusta stepped out onto the terrace, wanting to escape the overheated crush of the ballroom. She slipped along to the end, and leant against the cool stone of the wall, standing in deep shadow. But, just as she breathed a sigh of relief, the terrace doors opened, and two gentlemen came out. Thankfully, they did not come towards her, but simply stood there, staring out across the gardens, and talking. However, that meant she was trapped, for to go back in would mean going past them. There was nothing to do but listen.

"Have you decided who to court, Walmsley?"

"I was keen on Lady Augusta Carlington... but she is so aloof – all politeness, but one wonders if there is any capacity for passion there at all."

The other man snorted in laughter, and Augusta bristled where she stood.

"She may be a diamond of the first water, even in her third Season, but there's a reason they've taken to calling her 'the Ice Princess'. I don't think you have any hope of thawing her. It's said that she loved someone and lost them, and isn't willing to ever consider anyone else."

"Which, Chitterford, is exactly why I've decided to court Lady Anna Perkins instead."

They laughed again, and turned to go back inside, leaving Augusta staring at where they had been. 'Ice Princess'? That, she concluded, was good, if it meant that more fops like Walmsley left her alone.

Chapter Five

May 1815

Dario closed the journal, and set it down on the table beside him. The warm spring day was peaceful, and the sound of birds and bees on the flowers surrounded him. Externally, all was calm. Internally, he was far from it.

That was the last of the journals, containing entries from the morning of the storm which had wrecked the Lady Amabella – the ship on which he had been travelling. The further he had read through the journals, the more he had come to feel as if he truly was the man who had written them, rather than just a dissociated reader.

That was, he thought, good. What was not good was the emotional turmoil which had come with reassuming his life. For with the reading had come, as he had hoped, memories. They had risen in his mind in response to the words on the page.

Many had been good, but others... others he did not know what to make of.

He remembered his grandmother, and her desire for him to lay flowers on the grave of the great grandfather he was named for. That was something he was almost mobile enough to do now.

The splints and bandages had been gone from his leg for near three months now, and the muscle which had wasted while he was unable to move about had rebuilt to the point where he could walk moderate distances without pain. There were still aches, of course, but overall, he was extremely grateful – his leg was straight, and he walked without any noticeable limp – it was far better than he might have hoped for, given the circumstances.

He could not be so happy about his hand. Whilst it had improved, after the old woman's ministrations, he still could not hold a pen enough to write, and was beginning to wonder if he ever would be able to. Perhaps, in the end, he would have to learn to write with his left hand.

But not yet – he would be stubborn, and continue to work on his right.

Once he could write, perhaps he would send a letter home. Yet... he found himself reluctant to do so. There had been no letters waiting for him at the Villa D'Oro when he'd arrived, and none had come in the months since – not from his family, and not from Lady Augusta – who he now remembered, as well.

She was the woman with the sea green eyes who had haunted his dreams. And when he had made that connection, between the face in his dreams and the woman mentioned in the journals, a flood of memories had filled his mind, leaving him gasping, with tears running down his cheeks.

He loved her, and had been an unmitigated fool for not telling her so.

There was, of course, the letter he had written the day that he'd left, declaring his love and proposing. The letter to which he had not received an answer. The only conclusion he could draw from that, was that she did not love him, as he'd thought she did. No matter how wonderful his memories were of heated kisses in the library of Winterward Keep, at midnight. Obviously, those kisses had not meant as much to her as they had to him.

Perhaps it was better that his hand gave him an excuse not to write, for now, at least, for he was not sure that he could have managed anything reasonable. That there were no letters from his parents either seemed surprising, if his memories of them were true, but he had to face the fact that no missives had come. He pushed those troubling thoughts aside for now.

He would do as he had intended in coming here – he would learn all he could of the estate, would work with the staff to ensure that all was in good repair, and he would learn about his family history – at least his grandmother's side of the family. And when he was stronger, and had become more accustomed to the idea of who he was, and who he was not, then perhaps he would write. And, eventually, he supposed, he would have to go home to England.

At present, that did not appeal at all. He still did not feel connected enough to the Dario who had written those journals to have any confidence about the idea of walking back into that life. Especially as far as it concerned Lady Augusta – for she still haunted his dreams, and his love for her, newly rediscovered, was intense enough to leave him breathless. If she did not reciprocate that love, if she had married another man while he had lain injured, then his heart would shatter, utterly. For now, it was better not to know.

*****

Late June 1815

They were seated around the breakfast table in Shilham House, a few days before they intended to depart London to spend summer at Shilham Park, when the butler came hurrying into the room, brandishing a news sheet.

"I am sorry to disturb you, my Lord, my Ladies, but there is great news! A magnificent victory! They are saying that this will end the war!"

Augusta watched as her father nearly choked on his food, then quickly swallowed half of his cup of coffee to recover. Once he could breathe, he reached for the paper, and studied it. As he read, a huge smile spread across his face.

"This is good news indeed! Perhaps we will not depart London quite so soon. There will likely be celebrations, but also some meetings of the Lords which I will be required for."

He passed the paper to her mother, who also read it, before handing it to Augusta, who by this stage was fidgeting with impatience.

She read the news – a great victory, with the British having defeated Napoleon at Waterloo. The idea that it might truly end the war seemed most strange – there had been war going on with France for nearly the entirety of Augusta's life, and she could barely imagine the idea of a time when that was not so.

She passed the paper back to her father, and returned her attention to her breakfast. Her parents were obviously ecstatic at this news, but she could not find it in herself to celebrate. It seemed too far removed from reality, as yet. But a small voice in her mind asked her – why could this not have happened a year ago? For if it had, then perhaps Dario would have simply taken ship to France, and then gone overland to Italy, perhaps he would never have been in a situation where his ship could be wrecked, would never have...

She firmly turned that thought aside. She would not believe him dead, no matter what everyone else said. There was no proof of it, no confirmation in the form of a body, or any letters from Italy telling the truth of it. Of course, it was possible that the letters, if sent, had been lost in transit, destroyed in some pointless minor interaction of war.

But she clung to hope, and to the belief that, in her heart, she would have known if he had died. That belief had sustained her though the Season, and had allowed her to remain aloof from all of the gentlemen who pursued her – some of whom apparently found that aloofness attractive, and tried all the harder because of it. And, most irritatingly, her mother had encouraged them!

She would be glad to get back to Shilham Park, and away from them.

There, at least, she could dream of Dario in peace.

*****

July 1815

Things moved slowly in the countryside, but even there, news eventually came.

Dario stared at the news sheet which had been delivered with the mail.

The war was something that he had not thought of much at all – it was so far distant from his life now, and even, in most ways, from his life before, in England. But now, this news... a victory at Waterloo, for the British, which might end the decades of fighting.

He thought about it, reading the somewhat lurid account slowly, making sure that he understood the Italian correctly, and began to see the implications. It would take some time, for war was messy, and damaged vast tracts of countryside, but if this battle really did herald the end of fighting, then over the months which followed, overland travel would resume. It would not necessarily be very safe until after the winter, but it would be possible.

The thought filled him with far more relief than he had expected it to.

It meant that, so long as he waited at least another six to nine months, he might return to England mostly overland, rather than having to face a long sea journey again. For if he was honest with himself, when he thought of a long sea journey, his mind filled with fear. The two to five days to cross the channel he could cope with, but weeks... that he wished to avoid.

And... there was no need for him to rush. There had been no letters. So he must assume that his father still lived, and managed the estates as always, and did not feel the need to write to his son. And Lady Augusta... well, if she had not written to him by now, then he must conclude that she did not love him, did not wish to accept his proposal, and had just as likely married someone else. And if she was not there waiting for him, there was nothing to make him truly wish to return. Here, at least, they seemed to want him.

As he set the paper down on the table, Maria, who was Luigi's wife, and the Housekeeper at Villa D'Oro, came into the room. She gestured towards the news sheet.

"Does this mean that you will leave us, my Lord? For surely travel will be easier now..."

"I am sure that, eventually, travel will be easier – but I do not trust it yet. There has been war for nigh on twenty years, and I am not sure that I can believe it to be ended yet. Mayhap next year, if the fighting truly does stop, I will consider whether I should go back to England. If and when I do, I will go overland – the thought of another long sea journey does not appeal. So for now, I will stay, and continue to enjoy your excellent care of me."

She beamed at him, pleased.

"Bellissimo!"

"Maria... will you tell me more of the history of my family? Of what my grandmother's life here was like, as a child and a young woman? Of what her father was like?"

"Si, I will tell you what I know – but what I know is what my mother told me, and what Luigi's mother told me. I was not yet born when your grandmother left for England, with the Duke who stole her heart."

They spoke for many hours that afternoon, and Maria brought him books from the villa's library, where his ancestors had recorded their family tree, or had written about their lives, as well as sketch journals – some of which, it turned out, had been his grandmother's, when she had been a young girl. He felt, after seeing them, connected with the long dead people who had come before him – more so than he currently did with his family in England.

He supposed that would change, when he saw them again, but for now, they seemed not quite real, like characters in the tales told in his own journals. The only person of those in England who seemed real to him was Lady Augusta...

But the day had moved on to evening, and Maria rose from the chair beside him.

"Tomorrow, my Lord, I will show you the paintings in the upper rooms – for many of your ancestors are represented there. But now, I must make sure that your meal has been prepared – and you should rest, for you still look worn and tired."

"I still feel worn and tired, Maria, although I am far better than I was, when I arrived here – and that is all thanks to you, and Luigi."

She blushed, and dipped her head, before turning and hurrying away.

He leant back in his chair, and closed his eyes – but the image that rose behind his closed lids was Lady Augusta, not any of his ancestors...

*****

July 1815

The Duke of Winterward was not well – even more so than had been the case for the last few years. He could feel his mortality, could feel the cold fingers of death reaching for him. His determination to fight that chill grasp had faded steadily since the day that had brought the news of the shipwreck. Since then, as months passed, and no further news came, the spark of hope he had cherished had been all but extinguished. All he felt now was despairing guilt. A guilt which his mother joined him in. For they had both urged Dario to go, to travel in these dangerous times – and now... it seemed almost certain that he had died as a result of their actions. That was almost more than he could bear.

Today, as the long summer evening wore on, he sat with his wife in the gardens, surrounded by the scent of roses, and stared off across the small lake at the bottom of the hill.

"I miss him. So very much, now that I will never see him again."

"Hush, husband – do not say it. There is still hope – we have no report of a body – no reports at all, in fact. I refuse to give up until there is incontrovertible proof."

"Anne, you may hold to that hope as you wish, but, since the news of Waterloo, I have hoped to hear more from Italy – for surely, with the fighting dying away, travel overland is easier, and also by sea... But there has been nothing, nothing at all. If only Waterloo had been a year ago, Dario might still be with us, might have gone safely across the channel to France, and overland from there, rather than taking ship..."

"True. But it did not happen then, and we must deal with what is."

"And part of what is, my dear, is the fact that I am, undeniably, weakening. Even if, by some great miracle, he lives, I feel in my bones that I will be dead and gone before he could reach us."

"Please... stay with me. I would have your company in this life for as long as possible."

The Duke laughed softly, shaking his head.

"I know that you would. But God will call me to him when he is ready, and nothing I could do will prevent it. At least, if Dario did die in the wreck, then mayhap I will be granted the grace of his company in God's domain."

The Duchess reached out and took his hand, tears sparkling in her eyes, but she said nothing more.

Chapter Six

August 1815

The summer dragged on, and Augusta felt herself slipping ever deeper into an unmitigated sadness. For just a short while, after the news of the victory at Waterloo, she had hoped that now, a letter might come, or at least some news – for surely, with the fighting stopped, the passage of letters and other messages would be easier?

But no letters or reports had come. The dark thought that he might truly be gone intruded frequently, and she pushed it aside, determined never to accept that as truth without proof. But the not knowing sapped her energy, and stole her joy in the world. Summer had been made worse by her memories – for the warm nights brought back those clandestine meetings in the library at Winterward Keep and the kisses which had heated her blood.

She had continued, since the end of the Season, keeping her special journal, in which she wrote letters – letters which would never be sent, letters to Dario, telling him of her love, and her life. When she wrote them, he seemed real, and close to her. Those letters helped her keep hope alive. Perhaps, one day, he would return, and she might show them to him...

But for now, all she had was memories, and dreams.

*****

September 1815

Dario stood beside the impressive marble tomb, which was topped by a stern looking carved angel. He shivered a little, as he read the name engraved on the stone – Dario Russo. It seemed strange to see his own forename on a grave, even though he had known that was what he would see.

Slowly, he reached out, and set the bundle of flowers down at the angel's feet. The bright colours were in stark contrast to the grey swirled white of the marble, and for a moment, an image appeared in his mind, of a tapestry his grandmother had made, full of bright flowers with wide hills behind them. She had told him that it reminded her of where she had grown up. The flood of memory made him almost stagger, so sharp and clear was the image. He rested his hand against the tomb, waiting for the sensation to pass, glad that he had done as his grandmother had wanted, and come to lay flowers on this tomb.

Now that he could walk easily again, he had been venturing farther afield – this was the greatest distance he had yet gone. The sun warmed him, and a bird overhead cried out on the wind. Peace settled into his soul, and he closed his eyes. Here, he had some connection to the world, and the way that felt made him realise that he would, eventually, need to go back to England, even though it was likely that Lady Augusta would not be waiting for him. He suspected that only when he stood on English soil would he find this same peace with that part of his life.

"Mio Signore?"

He opened his eyes, to see Luigi regarding him with concern.

"It is well, Luigi. I am glad that I came. But let us start back to the Villa – I fear that my leg still tires easily, and aches..."

He turned away, leaving the flowers lying there, their petals ruffled by the gentle breeze, and their colours speaking of life in a place dedicated to the dead.

*****

October 1815

The late Autumn wind howled around the walls of Winterward Keep, as if expressing the same sorrow as that felt by those inside the building. The Duke was dying – he was quite certain of that now, and the physician had confirmed it. There was nothing to do, they had been told, but make him as comfortable as possible for his last hours. His mother, who had never thought to outlive her son, sat in the armchair on one side of the bed. On his other side, the Duchess had settled on the bed beside him, and beyond her, in another chair, his daughter watched him with eyes red from crying. He looked at them all, his breathing laboured, his skin a pasty grey shade, and gathered his strength.

"I love each of you well, and I have had a good life. I would wish to stay with you longer, but it seems that is not to be. I have only one regret, and that is that I encouraged my son to travel to Italy, and thus brought about his death – for I can no longer pretend to myself that he lives, not after more than a year. I thought it right, when I did it, but now, I would call it all back if I could, just to see him one more time."

His mother sobbed then, her dark eyes bright with tears, her greying hair dishevelled as she pushed it away from her face.

"That is a regret I share – for I too encouraged him to go, to see my father's grave – I did not think, in asking that of him, that I would be sending him to his own!" Lady Virginia brought her handkerchief to her mouth as tears ran down her cheeks again, but the Duchess was stronger than all of them. "There has still been no proof reach us, despite what the news reports said of the wreck. I will not let go of hope, not yet, and I beg you to hold hope too – do not go to God believing the worst. Do not be miserable now – rather take joy in whatever small time we have left together."

He nodded, but she could see that he struggled to believe that hope was possible. She could not blame him – maintaining her own belief became harder by the day, yet if she gave in to the idea that her son was dead, then despair would overtake her utterly. His mother had already lost all hope, and all strength with it – that she still lived was a miracle. But the Duchess did not think she would last much longer, not once the Duke was gone.

After some time, where the only sound was the Duke's laboured breathing, he spoke again, his voice so soft and weak as to be barely audible.

"Perhaps it is not a bad thing that there is no clear proof of Dario's death, for that means that nothing can be done about the title for many years, unless Dario miraculously returns. So my less than pleasant nephew will not be able to claim it, and you will not be forced from your home. I pray that, in the end, your miracle happens, that your hope is rewarded, and Dario returns – even though I will not be here to see it."

The Duchess bent to kiss him, brought to tears by the fact that, on his deathbed, his thoughts were of her, and her future. They stayed that way, gathered around him, as he dropped into troubled sleep, and the day wore on into night. Each of them drifted into what seemed a waking dream, until that dream was shattered by the one change that they had all dreaded. The sound which had been a constant for days – the Duke's laboured breathing – ceased. An echoingly empty silence settled into the room, and they looked at each other for long minutes as the truth of the matter set in.

When the Duchess bent close to him, there was no brush of breath, no detectable beat of his heart, and she knew that he was gone, this man she had given more than half her life to, gladly. Then she rose, and went to the door, summoning a footman, and directing him to set in motion all that was to be done, to put the house into mourning, and prepare the Duke for his final journey. She did not allow herself to cry again, until she lay in bed that night, cold and alone, with only memories to hold to.

Within the week, he had been laid to rest in the family crypt in the grounds of the ancient church which stood in Winterward Village. Somehow, life had to go on, for the world around her did not stop, even though everything had changed so much. It changed more, two days after his funeral, when the Duke's mother was found, cold in her bed, having passed from this life quietly, in her sleep. The Duchess drew herself up, and dealt with it all again, until another funeral was done. Then, she went home with her daughter, and considered the days ahead. They seemed drear, and bereft of any reason to go on – except for Lady Virginia. Without her daughter, the Duchess might well have allowed herself to simply fade away. But she could not do that – she had a daughter who needed her, and she would not truly rest until Virginia was happily wed.

So she sent all of the required information to their man of business, that he might ensure that everything with respect to the title was in order, so that the rapacious nephew it might eventually fall to did not overstep the legal mark, and also to make arrangements for the reading of both wills, as soon as possible.

*****

Late October 1815

Mr Arthur Sedgewick had been man of business to the Duke of Winterward and his family for twenty years and more, succeeding his own father in that role. He regarded the matter at hand with great sadness, as a result. Concerning the Duke's title, and will, he was faced with a problem. Apart from the assumption that the title and entailed lands would pass to the Duke's son, many other things, unentailed, were left to his son as well. The Duke had not been able to bring himself to change it, while even faint hope existed. So now, whilst the will could be read, much of it could not be enacted until there was proof that Lord Weatherbrook was actually deceased.

Mr Sedgewick spent some hours contemplating his options – for he was not looking forward to the reaction of the Duke's nephew, who would no doubt rudely begin to demand 'his rights'. In the end, he did the only thing which seemed sensible. He wrote a letter. Now that the war had ended, anything sent to Italy had a far better chance of reaching there, and actually receiving a response – and he had to try. If Lord Weatherbrook had somehow, miraculously, survived the shipwreck, surely he would have made his way to the Villa D'Oro eventually, so a letter sent there was the first step in attempting to discern whether he did, in fact, still live. With the letter sent, he set about gathering everything else he would need, to deal with the more mundane bequests in the wills of both the Duke, and his mother, praying that, somehow, the letter reached Italy, and garnered him a response within a few months, rather than longer, or not at all.

*****

November 1815

Dario woke to the bang of a shutter and the howl of the wind.

It was a sound which made him shake, as a flood of memories of the shipwreck crashed into his mind – desperate moments as the storm drove the ship along the rocky cliffs – moments which had, until now, been beyond his recall. At first, he clutched the bed, waiting for the movement, for the crash of waves, and then, when it did not come, his pounding heart slowed, and he came back to the present, to the pleasant room in the Villa D'Oro, and the wind which was only a mild winter storm.

He had been dreaming when the sound woke him – the dream came back to him now. In that dream, he had been in the library at Winterward Keep, kissing Lady Augusta. And now, as he recalled the dream, his mind filled with more memories – detailed memories of that summer before he had come away to Italy, memories of time with Lady Augusta, when he had gone from fondness to love at an alarming rate.

Those memories now made Winterward Keep more real as well, in his mind, but left him filled also with bittersweet sadness – for she had not written, in response to the letter he had sent her, the day that he had left – at least, his journals told him that he had, for he could not yet recall that day.

Had his words in that letter been so poor that she had turned away from him?

He could not imagine it. What he remembered of her said that she loved him, that she was kind and caring, that she would have replied, at least to tell him of her true feelings, whatever they were.

But there had been no letters.

Perhaps there was a reason that she could not write, as there had been reason that he could not, with his damaged hand?

His hand was slowly becoming more useful, and he had, just in the last few weeks, begun to attempt to write. It was not yet any better than the scrawl of a two-year-old child – but it was a start.

And when he could write, would he write to Lady Augusta? Or to his parents?

At this point, he rather suspected that he would not. The fact that no letters had come to him made him less inclined to try. It was a petty reaction, he knew, and he should be above such things, but still, inside, the pain of it was there.

Outside, the wind had dropped, and someone had obviously closed the banging shutter, for there was little sound now. He lay back in the bed, choosing to explore the returned memories of Winterward Keep, and his time with Lady Augusta, rather than allow himself to revisit the terror of the shipwreck.

After some time, as his mental image of the library at Winterward Keep became ever more detailed, with its scent of books, and intertwined with that, inextricably, the scent and taste of Lady Augusta, he drifted from waking into sleep, those memories coming alive as a dream, in which he had not just kissed her, but he had told her that he loved her.

When next he woke, it was morning, and the memories of the night seemed fainter again – all save the touch of Lady Augusta's lips on his.

*****

November 1815

There had been early snow at Shilham Park, and the roads had turned to quagmire. Now, as the weather eased a little, the mail delivery had finally managed to reach them.

Augusta was listless and tired all of the time, for her life stretched ahead of her, empty and lonely, her heart committed to a man who might be dead, or if he was not, might never come back. But she could not stop loving him. She knew that her mother worried about her, and she tried, truly tried, to express interest in some things, if only for her mother's sake.

So, as the rather large collection of correspondence, news sheets, and parcels was brought in, and deposited on the table in the parlour, Augusta stepped forward beside her parents to see what might be there. The news sheets, at least, would perhaps entertain her for a few hours.

She selected one, and sat down, intending to read it, but her attention was drawn by a gasp from her mother, who had just broken the seal on a letter.

"The Duke of Winterward is dead!"

"Dead?"

"Yes, Augusta – the illness finally took him – a few weeks ago now. How sad – dear Anne has no one now except Virginia, for the Duke's mother is also gone from this earth. And Virgina will not have her Season this coming March, for they will still be in mourning. We must visit them, at least, on our way to London."

"Of course."

The sadness of it filled Augusta, and the wayward thought arrived that Dario, if he lived, was now Duke – a difficult situation. For without proof of his death, the title could not be passed on to another. The whole family now lived in a grey space of uncertainty, which might never be resolved. And she had met Dario's cousin, the man who would inherit the title, if Dario was proven to be dead. She had not liked Mr Porter Harrison at all – he had eyed her, as he did all young women it seemed, as if she was a mare on display at Tattersall's, and had assumed that she would find him interesting. He was not the sort of man who would make a good Duke.

Even apart from her own desires, she hoped, for his family's sake, that Dario still lived.

This Christmas, it seemed, would be just as bleak as last Christmas.

Chapter Seven

December 1815

From where he sat on the terrace, Dario could see out across the land at the front of the villa, down the long drive to the gates. It was rare for anyone to traverse that drive – for there were footpaths elsewhere to the nearby village, and there were not often visitors of any kind. But today, as he watched, a figure appeared at the gates. As it got closer, he could see that it was a single man, on an obviously well-bred horse. Curious, he simply studied the man, waiting for his arrival, knowing that one of the staff would greet the visitor. The man passed around the side of the house towards the front door, and out of Dario's view. Minutes later, hurried footsteps heralded the arrival of Luigi, his face pale, and a worn looking letter in his hand.

At that sight, Dario felt a rush of tangled emotion.

A letter! But... who was it from? And what news did it bring? Was it something terrible, something he did not, really wish to know? Or would it bring him joy?

He stared at it, waiting for Luigi to speak, desperately wanting to know, and afraid at the same time.

"My Lord... this letter... it is, it is for you... but the way it is written suggests that they were not sure that you still lived...."

Shock coursed through Dario at those words. Was that why no one had written to him – did they all think him dead? A chill ran down his spine at the thought – he nearly had been dead, and, for so long after the wreck, he had been dead to his past life, whilst it had been lost in the dark mists of his mind. Now that he was recovering his memories, what might the arrival of this letter mean?

He held out his hand – despite the chill of fear, he would not avoid it – he needed to know what the missive contained. Luigi placed the heavy and somewhat stained paper between his fingers, and Dario was pleased that his right hand obeyed him, and grasped the thing firmly. He unfolded it, and frowned as he saw that it had been sent by the family man of business.

That recognition startled him – for, until that moment, he had not remembered that they had a man of business, let alone his name! He pushed the reaction aside, and began to read.

'To the estate staff at Villa D'Oro,

I, Mr Arthur Sedgewick, duly appointed man of business for matters relating to the Duke of Winterward and his family, write to you now to seek information, and your assistance.

I write in the hope that you may know the current location of Dario Harrison, Marquess of Weatherbrook, and that you will be able to pass this letter to him. This is a somewhat faint hope, given that we have had no letters from him since he left England, and no word of him since a single rather dramatized report of the wreck of a ship which we believe to have been the one he travelled on. But, nonetheless, I must try.

The matter at hand is critical – for, if this does reach the Marquess, I must inform him that he bears that title no longer – for he is now Duke of Winterward.

His father passed from this earth during October of 1815, and shortly after his death, the Duke's mother, the Dowager Duchess, also passed. The Duchess and Lady Virginia are left alone to deal with all of the change that this circumstance brings.

If this has reached the new Duke, may I beg him to return to England, post-haste, and to try, before that, to at least write to me, to inform us of his plans? I know that travel on the Continent is currently still difficult (and perhaps this letter will not reach you at all, or will do so after many months) but I beg you, if this has reached you, to attempt travel regardless.

It is imperative that you stand before the House of Lords and have the conferring of the title formalised, such that other possible heirs do not feel tempted to act precipitously.

Yrs. A. Sedgewick.

It gave the direction of the man of business' office, for the purpose of return letters.

Dario felt oddly detached, the words on the page slowly sinking into his mind.

His father was dead and gone, without Dario having had the chance to see him again. His grandmother, who, through the memories triggered by this place, had just begun to feel real to him, was gone also. He was now the Duke of Winterward.

It all seemed impossible, as much a fairy story as his own journals had seemed, when he had first begun to read them. Then, as the simple facts provided in the letter spun through his thoughts, again and again, it was as if another barrier in his mind shattered, and a flood of memory drowned him in an instant. He dropped the letter with a cry, clutching his head, as tears began to pour down his face. Now, now that he was gone, he remembered his father, in a thousand small ways – so many things about his father, so many moments with him, throughout his life. All gone, all hope of ever revisiting any of that, gone.

Why had his father not written? Had they believed him dead, in the shipwreck? He did not know, and now, he never would know what his father had thought.

There was silence, but for his strangled sobs, for some time. Luigi carefully lifted the fallen letter and waited. Once Dario steadied a little, Luigi spoke, his voice quiet and gentle.

"My Lord... will you do as they ask, and go back to England?"

Dario lifted his head, wiping the tears from his face, and tried to think of the future, not the past. He must decide what to do – and when to do it. It seemed that his rather idyllic existence at the Villa D'Oro must end.

"I... eventually, yes – that was always going to happen. As to when... I do not know. For a certainty, I cannot travel now – if this letter has taken two months to reach us, starting before the worst of winter set in, then the roads must be very bad, and will likely get worse as winter deepens. I doubt that travel would be possible before February or March given the already war-torn state of roads and countryside. And I am barely fit enough to contemplate it – a full days travel would leave me exhausted and in pain – many weeks of travel would be nigh on impossible. So I must wait, and get stronger. But next year, in the spring or summer, yes, I will have to go."

"I see. We will miss you, my Lord... Your Grace. But it is duty which calls you. Will you do as the man of business asks, and write to inform them of your plans?"

Dario considered it. He should write, but in part, he did not wish to. If he did so, there was the risk that the letter would never reach England, with winter, bad roads, and the ravaged countryside. But, more than that, there was a part of him which did not yet wish to acknowledge how his world had changed. He wanted the chance to mourn here, in private, without anyone knowing anything of him. They had managed without him until now, and he was certain that they could continue to do so.

His mind went to Lady Augusta, and he flinched away – if he wrote now, if he began a correspondence, then soon enough he would discover the truth of her feelings, and he was not ready for that, was not ready to have it confirmed that she had not written because she did not love him.

Guilt filled him as well – he should go, should be there to support his mother and sister... yet they had already weathered nearly three months of this, without him there, and if he tried to travel now, it would be another three at least before he reached them. He would be better to wait for the spring or summer, to wait for the roads to be in better repair and safer, and for his own strength to have truly been regained. *And that way,* came the insidious thought, *you will not have to deal with the process of mourning in the way that the English nobility expect it to happen.*

That startled him – for it was another memory, appearing whole within his mind – the entire process and ritual around the required year of mourning. He shivered at the thought, almost flinching away from it.

"I will not write yet. For the same reason that travel is likely impractical, so too is the probability of any letter reaching England through the winter. I will leave writing until next year as well – if they have dealt with it all to now, without me, then I am sure that another few months will not change that."

Luigi bowed, acknowledging his choice, handed the letter back to him, and left him there, staring out across the winter sere landscape. Dario did not see what was before him, but rather, his mind provided images of the grounds of Winterward Keep, as many years of memories rose from the darkness in his mind, and filled in more of the blanks of his past life.

*****

Late December 1815

This, his second Christmas at Villa D'Oro, felt strange – he was surrounded by happy people, whilst inside his grief and uncertainty ate at him.

For their sake, he smiled and joined them in feasting and celebrating, but inside, there was little joy to be found. Perhaps, over time, the grief would ease – or perhaps that would not happen until he stood on English soil and laid flowers on his father and grandmother's graves, as he had on his great grandfather's here.

Every day, despite the cold of winter, he went out about the estate and walked. He would strengthen his body, and while he did so, he would do everything he could to prepare the estate for the day when he would leave – when he had arrived, much had been in some disarray – not from lack of care, but from lack of attention, lack of funds. He had put some of what he had carried in his trunks to use, but much more would be needed – he would have to send it from England, once he was back there.

Slowly, as the Christmas season passed, he began to truly think about the future. Some days he despaired of it, other days it beckoned him with its possibilities.

But through it all, there was one constant – he dreamed, almost every night, of Lady Augusta.

*****

Late December 1815

This, the second Christmas since Dario's disappearance, was harder than the first, for everyone expected Augusta to have forgotten her hopes of him, and to be looking forward to the Season to come. Her sisters teased her about her spinster status, and she bore it steadily – but inside, she cried. She would not believe him dead.

Each week, she wrote in her journal, continuing her 'letters to Dario' as a way to hold to his memory. The thought that, now, if he did live, he was Duke – and did not even know that, did not know to grieve for his father, troubled her.

What was Italy like, she wondered, at Christmastime? Was he happy, wherever he was? Her mind was filled with questions, and sadness for Dario's family, for whom this Christmas must be starkly painful.

She pushed her thoughts aside during the day, and allowed herself to be drawn into her mother and sisters' conversations about the coming Season, and what hope there was of Augusta making a match, and what Balls they would go to, and more. Augusta had discovered that, if she smiled enigmatically, and refused to join them in speculation, they simply talked on without her. Doing that made her days more pleasant, even if the coming Season still filled her with dread – how long would it take for her mother to accept that she would stay a spinster - for no man could be to her as Dario had been - and allow her to avoid the Season entirely?

Regardless of all other things, she dreamed of Dario, almost every night.

*****

March 1816

The modiste regarded Augusta with a critical and assessing eye.

"Another year, my Lady? I had thought to see you wed by now... But you have lost none of your beauty – you are always a pleasure to dress. Perhaps, if we make you a gown more stunningly beautiful than any before, a suitable gentleman will fall at your feet, and beg you to marry him – and this time, you will find him acceptable?"

Augusta laughed, shaking her head.

"I am not hopeful, Madame Genet. I find most gentlemen severely lacking."

The modiste shook her head, and went on measuring Augusta, making notes in a small book as she did.

"We shall see. If you do find a suitable man, I hope that I will have the honour of making your wedding gown..."

"Of course, Madame, of course."

*****

March 1816

The Ball was crowded – quite the crush, and Augusta found herself surrounded by attentive gentlemen – some of whom had pursued her the previous year, and some of whom she had never met before. She treated them all with equal distant courtesy.

She suspected that it would not take many Balls before the 'Ice Princess' whispers began again – and she was glad of that. The sooner the better, for when she regarded each of these men, her mind immediately compared them to Dario, and none of them tempted her heart in the least.

"Might I call on you tomorrow, Lady Augusta?"

Lord Hiliard regarded her hopefully, and she forced herself not to sigh.

"If you wish to, Lord Hiliard, I will certainly be at home for callers."

He looked a little crestfallen at her less than enthusiastic agreement to his request – she supposed that he would, eventually, realise that she was not interested in anyone, that this was in no manner a personal slight. He led her out to where people were forming up for the next dance set, and she went willingly, happy to dance, but not willing to grant any one gentleman any kind of specific encouragement.

Her heart was long committed, and none of these men would change that.

Chapter Eight

April 1816

The spring at Villa D'Oro was beautiful, at least compared to the cold of the deep winter, although Luigi and Maria told him that it was far colder still than usual. This year, he could move about enough to at least appreciate it. But with the turning of the seasons, came better weather for travel, as well as reports that, all over France and Spain, roads had begun to be more passable, and the land had begun to recover from the destruction wrought upon it by the war.

Which meant that, within Dario, there was a growing sensation that he should leave Italy, that he should return to England, return to all of the sadness and responsibility which awaited him there. He flinched from the thought – from the arduous travel, from the moment when he would see his mother and sister again, and confront the reality of his father's death, and from the moment when he would discover the truth of Lady Augusta's feelings, once and for all.

Nonetheless, he knew that, eventually, he must go – and that sense suggested that he should do so soon, so that he travelled in the summer and autumn, not the next winter.

But surely, he could stay just a little longer?

Each day, he went out and walked - about the estate, into the village, or to the church, and the graveyard where his great grandfather rested. Each day, it became a little easier, the aches in his bones less. Each day also, more memories returned to him, as if the moment of hearing of his father's death, before Christmas, had broken some barrier, and now, every small thing around him might trigger a memory of part of his earlier life.

More and more, he could bring to mind the places and events of his childhood, and sometimes, as with his memories of Lady Augusta, the events of the last few years, before his departure from England. There were many parts of his life which were still hidden from him, but he now had confidence that those memories would also return to him, as time went by.

As the days passed, however, the weather, rather than becoming warmer, stayed unnaturally cold, with far more rain than might normally be expected. Luigi worried that the crops would fail, if the weather did not improve, and Maria took stock of the food and grain stores which the Villa held.

Dario worried, and knew that, as the owner of the estate, it fell to him to provide funds for extra food, and whatever assistance might be needed.

His walks became more an exercise in studying the estate, and the crops, meeting the tenant farmers, and coming to truly understand the complex web of life that the Villa sustained. Luigi accompanied him on many of those walks, providing introductions, information, and guidance. Increasingly, the rain fell as he walked, but Dario chose to ignore it, finding himself driven, by his sense of duty, to continue.

He suspected, as well, when he was truthful with himself, that he used the need to do the best by the estate as an excuse not to return to England. For, as the weeks passed, the early news of improved roads and some recovery from war was overtaken by worse news – of roads becoming terrible again, due to all of the rain, and of, more and more, food being in short supply. It was not a problem that he could solve directly, yet he longed to be able to. And, for the first time, he found himself thinking about what might be happening to his English estates, and wondering if things were as bad there as they were becoming on the continent.

Perhaps he should, now, try to write that letter?

But what would he say, to excuse his long absence? He turned his thoughts away from that as he trudged back to the Villa one day at the end of April, the rain continuing to drench him, as if punishing him for his failures.

He stepped through the door into the kitchens at the Villa, seeking the warmth of the fires, and sneezed as he did, which caused the cook to turn a worried eye on him, and send a maid off to find Maria. He went to stand before the fire, but somehow, was still just as cold. He sneezed again, just as Maria hurried into the room.

"Your Grace! You are soaked through – come and sit by the fire in the parlour, and I will get blankets to warm you. Cook, please send some tea, and some warm food to the parlour as well."

"Maria, there is no need to treat me like a sick child!"

"Oh but there is- Your Grace, you are quite blue with cold, and shaking – we must get you dry and warm, lest you take a fever."

He allowed himself to be led away, to be fussed over, dried, helped into dry clothes by Marco - the man who had, somehow, moved from being a footman, to being his valet - and given food and drink. He could not deny appreciating it, especially as, contrary to his expectations, even dry, warm, and fed, he still shivered, and his nose had begun to run.

By evening, it was clear that he had a fever, and he took to his bed, praying that by morning, he would feel more himself.

That was, however, not to be. It was a full three weeks before he was well again, and by then, almost all of the gains in strength that he had made over the recent months were lost.

The reports of the road conditions were still bad, as summer approached, and guilt ate at him – here he had been, lying fevered in his bed, unable to even help on the estate, let alone make progress towards his return to England.

Once he could move from his bed, and the physician was satisfied that the fever had truly left him, he set about rebuilding his strength, again. He still walked, as far and as often as he could manage – but no longer did he do so in the rain.

All thought of travelling to England would have to wait at least until July. At this rate, the year of mourning for his father would be over before his feet ever touched England's shores again. By July, he prayed, the roads, and the weather would be better. If they were not, he knew now that he would have no choice – he could not delay longer than that – not given the responsibilities which awaited him in England – he had delayed long enough already.

And, came the heart aching thought, he needed to know what had happened to Lady Augusta, to know why she had not written, to know if the love which still burned within him was returned, had ever been returned...

*****

Late June 1816

Augusta gave a sigh of relief. The last trunk was packed - only the things she would need tonight and to travel in come the morning still remained out. She could leave her maid to check that nothing had been missed. She went down to the parlour, grateful for the chance to simply sit and take tea, after a long day of packing.

When she reached the parlour, however, it was immediately obvious that a quiet moment alone was not available to her. Her mother looked up from pouring the tea, and waved her to a chair.

"I do hope that it isn't raining again tomorrow, or the journey will take us three days rather than two! The roads can become near impassable with too much rain. This year is just so cold – it's as if we're not going to have a summer at all! But sit, Augusta, and have some tea and cakes – at least we can be warm and comfortable today, even if the next few days must be miserable."

Augusta sat, and took the tea her mother had poured.

"Even if it is raining tomorrow, Mother, I will be glad to leave London. This Season has been the most tedious experience of my life."

Lady Shilham looked rather taken aback at this statement.

"But Augusta, surely it has not been that bad? Many gentlemen sought your company – I only wish that you had chosen to accept the affections of one of them."

"Mother, you know my opinion on that by now – none of them are what I want, none of them engage my heart."

"Augusta, you really must accept that Weatherbrook is gone. It has been well over a year now since the report of the shipwreck reached us – surely you cannot still be holding out hope for his return?"

Augusta studied her mother's face.

What she saw was a compound of love, frustration, and a kind of helplessness. Augusta felt rather guilty about the degree of distress which her mother suffered – but she could not change her heart, and she would not marry a man she did not love – that was the recipe for a miserable life.

"Mother, even if I could bring myself to believe that he is dead – which I can't – I still would not wish to marry any of the gentlemen who have offered for me. None of them engage even the slightest bit of feeling within me. I would rather be a spinster than marry any of them. I would very much appreciate it if you would simply accept that. And before you suggest it – no, I am not willing to come to London next year, for a fifth Season. That would make me a laughingstock for the gossips."

"But Augusta..."

"No, Mother. Nothing you say can persuade me."

Augusta lifted her tea and sipped, watching her mother's face. A veritable parade of emotions passed across that face, before Lady Shilham gave a tight nod, and lifted her own tea. Augusta knew that the battle was far from over, but at least this was a beginning. It was a battle that she was determined to win – another Season would be intolerable. For her, no man she had ever met could compare to Dario.

So far, she had filled two large journals with her 'letters' to him, and still, most nights she dreamt of him. He had to live still, he just had to.... But if he did, why had he not yet written...?

*****

Late July 1816

The summer had been barely warmer than the winter, and the rain had rarely stopped. Very little grew successfully, and Dario was grateful for the cautious planning which meant that the Villa D'Oro was well stocked with preserved food. Now, however, he had reached the point where he could delay no longer.

It seemed obvious that, as things were now was the best that they were likely to be, until another year had passed – and he could not, in good conscience, wait that long.

His sense of guilt about not having taken up his responsibilities as Duke, and not having been there to support his mother and sister was great, despite the fact that for a large portion of the time he had been away, he had been physically unable to undertake the journey. At least today, the day that he would leave Villa D'Oro, travelling in his own carriage, it was not actually raining. He had debated whether he should hire a carriage, but in the end, the fact that the funds he had available were rather diminished had swayed him.

It would leave the Villa with a single small carriage, and the heavy cart they used to transport stores, but it was far more sensible for Dario to take his own carriage and coachman. And, as there was no real need for him to hurry, he should be able to travel the entire distance using his own horses – not changing horses would mean covering less distance each day, but he suspected that, physically, he would be glad of the slower pace. He was far stronger than he had been after suffering the fever, but still, he knew that his endurance was not great.

Marco entered the parlour, and gave a small bow.

"Everything is loaded on the carriage Your Grace, including a substantial supply of foods which will last, for we do not know what the conditions will be, in the areas we pass through. We are ready to depart."

"Thank you, Marco. And thank you, Luigi and Maria, for your care of me these many months. I will be certain to send funds and supplies to you, as soon as I reach England, and have access to the rest of the Winterward estates. I will miss Villa D'Oro..."

"As we will miss you, Your Grace."

Dario looked away, almost overcome with emotion. This place had come to feel like home, and was still, even with most of his memory returned, more so than Winterward Keep. But he had to go.

He looked back at them, then went to them and embraced them both.

"I will, most like some years from now, return to see you again – when the world, and the weather, are kinder, I hope."

With that, he went, unable to bear the sadness of parting. He felt as if he stepped into the completely unknown, for how would his barely remembered mother and sister treat him? And would Lady Augusta have married someone else? Or might she still...? He stopped the thought – that way lay madness and heartbreak.

In the end, he had not written – with the weather, any letter would likely reach England no faster than he would himself, and even now, his writing was barely legible. He would go to London, and present himself to the family man of business, and from there everything else could be arranged.

But first, he had to get there – a journey of fifteen hundred miles or so, depending on which roads they took, in conditions where twenty miles a day might be optimistic at times. As the carriage rolled out through the aged gates, and turned north, the prospect of the next three months was beyond daunting. If only he could be sure that Lady Augusta waited for him at the end of the journey, it would all be worth every moment. But he had no certainty at all.

*****

Late August 1816

"Room for two nights, if you please, for myself, my valet, the coachman and the groom. And stabling for the horses and carriage."

Every bone in his body ached, not just his hand and leg, but everything. The carriage seats, although padded, had come to feel as hard as boards, after so many days sitting on them. The Innkeeper looked at him, taking in his rather worn appearance, and obviously balancing that against the fact that he came in his own carriage, with servants.

After a few moments, the man apparently decided that Dario was respectable enough, and likely had money.

"Yes, my Lord. If you will wait here, I will make the arrangements. Your coachman can take the carriage into the yard."

With a nod, Dario dropped onto the bench just outside the Inn door, appreciating the weak sunshine which fought its way through the clouds. They were in Nice, in France, and it had taken them a full four weeks to get there. He was exhausted, and beyond grateful to have Marco with him, to assist.

The idea that he had another four to eight weeks of travel to face before he reached London was enough to make him wish to weep with frustration. But there was nothing else he could do but persist. Everywhere they went, people struggled to survive, for the unseasonably cold summer and the rains had brought illness and near famine. At least he had reasonable comfort, and food.

Marco came out of the Inn yard, carrying one of the trunks, followed by their groom, carrying another, just as the innkeeper opened the door again.

"This way please, my Lord."

They followed him inside, and up the worn steps to a door at the end of the upper hall, beyond which was a tiny private parlour with internal doors leading off it on either side. Marco and the groom set down the trunks, and went back down to collect the rest of their possessions. Dario opened each of the internal doors and checked the size of the bedrooms – small, but quite bearable – then turned to the Innkeeper.

"This will do well. Might I trouble you for a bath? And then a meal for all of us?"

The man frowned.

"My Lord, a bath we can manage, for, this year, there is no shortage of water, although it will take some time to heat enough to fill the tub. I'll have our man bring the tub up immediately. The meal... now that is a different matter – we've some food, but it's plain fare indeed – not what a Lord would be used to. It's all we have, and this year, we're lucky to have even that."

"Plain fare is perfectly acceptable. I am well aware of how little food is available, as we've travelled from south of Napoli."

The Innkeeper's eyes widened at the concept of such a long journey.

"That is a long way indeed, my Lord. Where do you go from here, if I may ask?"

"London, in the end. I must return to my estates in England. With luck, I may reach there before the winter sets in too deeply, but with the roads as they are, travel is damnably slow."

"I wish you well of it, my Lord. Rest now, and I'll be about arranging your bath and your food."

The Innkeeper turned and went, leaving Dario to almost fall into the rather aged armchair which sat by the fireplace. He drifted, nearing sleep, only to be woken again when Marco stepped into the rooms with another trunk, followed by the groom with the final one. Immediately after them, two of the inn staff carried in a huge copper bathing tub – Dario waved them to the bedchamber he had chosen as his.

Two hours later, after they had all bathed – which had required a second filling of the tub – they sat around the small table in their parlour, and contemplated the food they had been provided. There was rough bread, some aged cheese, a sausage so aged that it had hardened almost to inedibility, and a watery soup containing some unidentifiable vegetables and not much else.

Marco rose, and went to their trunks, extracting something from their carefully hoarded food supplies – slivers of meat which had been dried to preserve them. They each dropped some of those into the soup, and ate the bread and cheese whilst the meat soaked up the soup and softened. At least, with that addition, the soup would be moderately nutritious.

Once the food was eaten, they locked the outer door to their rooms and took themselves to bed, even though it was early. The others dropped into sleep quickly, but Dario found himself unable to do so. After some time, he drew out a journal, and a pencil from the trunks, and sat at the tiny desk under the window. There was enough light in the twilight to see what he was doing, and he lifted the pencil, adjusting it in the weak grip of his right hand with care.

He had been practising, a little, for many months, but now, he had become determined to write, to improve his ability, and the flexibility of his hand. As the journey had dragged on, he had gone from writing simple sentences, to writing more of a journal of his travels, and then, in the last week, he had begun to write as if each entry was a letter – a letter to Lady Augusta, written as if she was his, as if she had responded to that first letter, and would be waiting for him in England.

Perhaps he was foolish to do so, but it gave him purpose. She might never read them, but still, he wrote, and his hand became stronger each time that he did.

Chapter Nine

Late August 1816

"No. I completely refuse to accompany you, Mother. I have no interest in going to Bath for the next month. The weather is miserable, travelling would be horrid, and I do not wish to meet any new people. I know that your desire for me to go to Bath is just another ploy to get me to meet gentlemen. I am not interested. Please allow me to fade comfortably into spinsterhood!"

Augusta dropped into a chair near the fire, fully expecting her mother to treat her to a coldly angry lecture, in response to that declaration. What she had not expected was silence. Silence which extended, as she watched her mother stand there, wringing her hands. Finally, Lady Shilham turned away with a sad sigh.

"I cannot say that I am at all happy about you fading into spinsterhood, as you put it, but you give me no choice but to allow it, I see. You are twenty-three, Augusta, and well past your majority. If you wish to live a lonely life, then I cannot force you to do anything different. If only Weatherbrook had never left England, then you might have..."

Her voice trailed off, and Augusta felt her own sadness rise up, bringing her to the edge of tears. If only, indeed.

Determinedly, she lifted her book, and began to read – but the words on the page blurred, and she stared at them unseeing, instead remembering that summer before he had left, and how wonderful the future had seemed to her then. When he had held her, and kissed her, it had felt as if nothing could ever be wrong again, as if they would have forever.

Now, the future looked cold, and as her mother had said, lonely – yet she could not bear the concept of tying herself to a man she did not love, just for the sake of company. Perhaps, after all, she should not be angry with her mother – it was not Lady Shilham's fault that she wanted the best for her daughter.

"Mother," Lady Shilham turned at her voice, looking somewhat startled, "if you promise not the force me into the company of gentlemen, I will go to Bath with you, in the hope that the weather there is a little better than here. At least, if we bathe in the waters, they are warm..."

Lady Shilham laughed, shaking her head.

"That is true. If we go, I will promise not to pointedly introduce you to gentlemen – but I will introduce you to other ladies of my acquaintance. If you insist on not marrying, you will need friends..."

"Thank you, Mother."

*****

Late September 1816

They crested a rise in the road, and there, in the distance, Dario could see a broad blue expanse.

The sea!

Finally, after another month and more of toiling through war devastated countryside, made worse by the incessant rain and cold, they had nearly reached the coast. Below them, on that shore, lay the town of Calais – from which place they would take ship for the last leg of their journey to England.

The thought of boarding another ship still sent a spike of fear through him, but he faced that fear with the knowledge that there was no other way to reach England. He would not flinch from his duty at this late stage. *And,* said the quiet voice in his thoughts, *perhaps Lady Augusta might still be yours, if only you reach England...*

They rolled on down the road, winding off the higher land onto the flatter coastal area, and he lost sight of the sea – but that would not be for long. Opposite him, Marco slept, propped into the corner against the carriage wall and the seat back, but Dario had been unable to sleep for long – the ache in his leg and his hand woke him, every time, for the perpetual bumping of the carriage on the weather worn roads did not agree with his body at all.

An hour later, they drove through the town, seeking an Inn of reasonable quality, not too far from the docks. Eventually they came to one which Dario judged as suitable, based on the quality of the carriages which went in and out of its yard, and the people who were visible. Internally he laughed – their carriage was in far worse order than the ones he was watching, and no doubt looked rather disreputable, after its months of hard travel. The horses were lean, and worn as well, and as the travel had extended, the distance they could be asked to cover each day had reduced steadily.

They turned in at the gates, and Marco, now thoroughly awake, stepped down to organise things. It wouldn't do, he said firmly, for a Duke to be making his own arrangements. Dario flinched at the words – it still felt completely wrong that he was Duke, that his father was gone. He waited, the exhaustion of weeks of travel now washing over him, with the prospect of some rest so close at hand.

A short while later, Marco opened the door, a smile on his face.

"It took a little convincing for them to believe that you are a Duke, but, as ever, money was very persuasive. Perhaps more money that we ideally want to spend, at this point..."

Dario grimaced – funds were, indeed, getting somewhat short. Thank God that he had left England with a range of gems sewn into items of clothing, and tucked away in various places in his trunks. Those had been what had kept him in funds, after the coin and bank scrip he had carried were used. Now, even those were beginning to run out. He would need to find a jeweller here in Calais, and convert a few of the remaining ones to coin. Once they reached London, funds would not be an issue, for the family man of business would arrange whatever was needed.

"We will have enough. We still have some coin, and will have more once I find a jeweller."

"Good – come inside – let us deal with bringing the trunks in while you rest in the rooms."

Dario did not argue – the ache in his leg made him want the softness of a bed, desperately.

"Do I look respectable enough?"

Marco laughed.

"I have told them that we have been on the road for months, and that the first thing you will want is a bath, and then the direction of a decent tailor. So they will understand."

Marco stepped back, and offered Dario a hand to assist him out of the carriage. At least, he thought, it was not raining. The Inn yard was still muddy, but there was enough gravel laid on it that the footing was solid. Inside, they were shown to a suite of rooms on the top floor of the Inn – four bedrooms and a parlour. It was more space than they'd had since leaving Villa D'Oro, but at first, all Dario cared about was the huge copper bathtub waiting for him.

Everything else could be dealt with later.

*****

"Your Grace, I'm sorry, but there'll be no vessel making port here which will be big enough to provide passage for your carriage and horses, as well as you and your men – not for three or four weeks, at least. If you must take the carriage with you, then you'll have to wait. You could, of course, sell it, and then purchase a replacement in England..."

The Harbourmaster regarded Dario curiously, obviously intrigued that a man of wealth would choose to transport something like a carriage, at the heavy cost involved.

Dario had been tempted by the idea of selling the horses and carriage, but, in the end, after their faithful service, the idea had not sat well with him – and he would rather have his own transport to hand, once he landed in England. But another month of waiting… he sighed.

"If I must wait, I must wait. Some weeks of rest will do me good, and the horses too. If you know of a specific ship which might suit…"

"Yes, Your Grace – there's a merchant ship due in a month – she'll be carrying cargo from the Canary Islands, most meant for Paris, but some to travel on to London. So once she's unloaded here, unless she already has other cargo arranged, there should be enough room for her to take you, although it's likely that the carriage will need to be tied down on the deck, and the horses may need to be in temporary stalls on the deck too. But for the short journey across the Channel…"

"Indeed, that sounds reasonable. Please make sure to let the Captain know of my needs as soon as she docks, and send a message to me at the Ship's Bell Inn."

They spoke for a little longer, and Dario made certain to pass the man some coin 'for his trouble', to ensure that what he needed would actually get done. Then, not entirely happy with the delay, but, at the same time, looking forward to a few weeks of simply staying in one place, he went back to the Inn, to tell the others the news.

Perhaps, by the time the ship arrived, his hand would be even stronger, and his leg would no longer ache so much.

*****

October 1816

The few weeks in Bath had been surprisingly pleasant, and Augusta had met a number of ladies whose acquaintance she hoped to pursue in future. To have not been incessantly nagged about finding a suitable gentleman had made all the difference. It had not prevented her from dreaming of Dario, nor from writing her letters to him, in her journal.

She supposed that, if he did not reappear in England, and no proof of his death was ever found, either, then there would come a time when she would have to accept that he was eternally lost to her. But that time was not yet.

Now, back at Shilham Park, with the year closing in and the trees all displaying beautiful golds and reds, Augusta had been forced to admit that she was a little blue-devilled – not just from her ongoing heartbreak, but from the fact that she really did not have a great deal to do. She needed an occupation – if she was not going to marry, then many of the things she might have expected to do with her life would not happen. It was time to contemplate what she might do to fill the hours of her days.

One could not spend every waking moment reading, and embroidery had long lost its interest for her. Painting was rather dull, and the area around Shilham Park did not feature any people or places in dire need of charity work, for her father's care of his tenant farmers and villagers was excellent.

Which left her a little lost.

She was staring out of the parlour window, contemplating possible ideas, when her mother hurried in, a letter in her hand. As happened every time a letter arrived, Augusta caught her breath – could it be...?

Lady Shilham waved the letter at Augusta as she settled onto the couch beside her.

"The Duchess of Winterward has invited us to a pre-Christmas House Party! Just a small affair, but she has chosen to take this first step back into social life, now that the year of mourning for the old Duke is finished. She hopes that we will attend, and that you might consider attending the Season next year to assist Lady Virginia in her coming out."

Augusta's heart sank.

Had her mother planned this?

Had she conspired with the Duchess to put Augusta in a position where to refuse to attend the coming Season would be unforgivably rude? She did not think her mother capable of such a thing... but still...

"I... I do not know Lady Virginia very well, Mother..."

"Then that is all the more reason for us to attend this house party. You can spend time with the poor lonely girl and get to know her well, before next year. You will agree to go to London and help her, won't you?"

There seemed no way out of it, then.

"I will go to the house party with you, if that is what you wish, yes. But I will not decide about the Season, and assisting Lady Virginia, until I have spent some time with her. You know my feelings on the matter of the Season..."

Her mother sighed heavily.

"I do. I wish that you would accept the truth..."

"The truth is unknown at this point Mother. My heart requires proof before being willing to accept such a terrible thing."

"Augusta, it has been nigh on two years..."

"Which matters not at all, with no proof."

Lady Shilham sighed again, shaking her head.

"The house party is to be in the third week of November – you must make sure that you are prepared – we will want to look our best. And we must arrange gifts for the Duchess, and Lady Virginia. Let me think on what might be best suited."

Augusta thought carefully for a moment.

"Perhaps, for Lady Virginia, a piece of jewellery, suited to a girl in her first Season? I think that I have one or two beautiful pieces which never suited me, yet might suit her. I will look through my jewellery box, and see what I find."

"A good idea, indeed. I will think further on what the Duchess might most appreciate, after a year of mourning."

They called for tea, and spoke of other things, but the prospect of the coming house party weighed heavily on Augusta's mind. Not just because of the fact that it would almost certainly lead to her agreeing to attend the Season after all, but also because it would mean going to stay at Winterward Keep.

And for Augusta, the old Duke and his mother would not be the only ghosts to haunt the Keep. It was full of memories for her, of that idyllic summer when the world had seemed perfect, and she could not imagine a future without Dario's kisses. Just thinking of it brought her to the edge of tears, even now – so what would it be like, to step within those walls again?

*****

Early November 1816

After a month in which he had recovered his strength, Dario felt better than he had since before leaving England. His leg barely ached at all, and his hand had regained nearly all of its flexibility. His writing was still rather inelegant, but at least it was now readable. He had put on weight, and, dressed in the new attire which the Calais tailor had made for him, he looked, for the first time in a very long time, the picture of a wealthy nobleman.

He felt like an imposter.

The vast contrast between his life at the Villa D'Oro and the life he was returning to in England was almost incomprehensible. He stood on the dock, the light breeze tugging at his dark hair, and watched the complicated process of the carriage being loaded onto the ship. It had been lifted in a huge sling of ropes, suspended from a crane, and swung across the narrow gap and up onto the deck – now, men scurried about, tying it down securely, so that it could not move during the journey. Beside where it was being tied, two strange looking wooden boxes had been built, and nailed down to the deck – these would act as stalls for the horses, which would be loaded shortly, after the fussing about the carriage was done.

"Efficient, aren't they, Your Grace?"

Marco stood beside him, watching, fascinated, as the sailors went about their business. Nearby, his coachman and groom stood holding the horses – which had benefitted from the month's rest as much as Dario had done.

Their trunks were stacked at Marco's feet, awaiting the moment when they might board.

"They are, indeed. But I am still glad that this is only a journey of a day or two, not longer. A man should not allow fear to rule him, yet I find my previous experience at sea has rather distorted my perception of ships."

"That is understandable, Your Grace."

They dropped into silence, and stayed so as they watched the two horses blindfolded, and led up the rather steep and narrow gangway, and onto the deck.

All went without mishap, and soon, the coachman and groom returned to them. Each man lifted a trunk, and they boarded the ship. The Captain came to them, and welcomed them, but was obviously more focussed on the matter of the ongoing loading, so soon sent them off to their cabins, guided by a sailor.

The cabins were small, but not so small as the cabin Dario had occupied on the journey to Italy, for which he was truly grateful.

*****

Dario had barely moved from the cabin since they had cast off from the Calais docks.

Now, the wind howled in the rigging, and Dario fought to stop himself from being overtaken by panic. The seas were quite gentle – a strong steady swell driven by that wind, and the ship made good progress – the Captain had assured Marco that they would reach the Thames estuary before nightfall, and anchor there until they could go up the river to the London docks on the morning tide.

Carefully, he made his way out of the cabin, and up the steep steps to the deck.

Up there, surprisingly, he found the aspect of the wind and waves less threatening.

He moved to one side, and leant against the side of the carriage, gripping one of the ropes which bound it in place firmly. The wind still howled, yet he could see that the waves were steady, that no rocky cliffs threatened, and that above, a weak wintry sun shone through light clouds – there was no sign of a storm.

Beside him, the upper half doors of the two horse stalls were open, and he could see the horses, unconcerned, eating the hay they had been given, which was hung in huge nets to allow them easy access.

If the horses were calm, then so should he be. Horses were acutely conscious of danger, after all. He breathed out a huge sigh, and loosened his white knuckled grip on the rope. Slowly, he walked across to the rail, and stood there, staring ahead, seeing the line on the horizon that was England, and trying to imagine what might await him there.

His thoughts went, unavoidably, to Lady Augusta, and the letters he had never received.

Chapter Ten

Early November 1816

The Duchess of Winterward studied the list she had made, sitting at the escritoire in her private parlour. After a year shut away in mourning, there were many things which needed to be done before she could welcome guests to Winterward Keep. Most of those things were not difficult – they were just a matter of directing the staff to clean and renew the guest chambers, to order in and to bring up from the cellars the requisite amounts of food, and to ensure that everyone, from herself and Virginia down to the scullery maids, had new clothing to wear, which was not in mourning colours. But there was one thing on the list which she was not at all happy about. It was a task that only she could do, a task that she had put off for far too long now. It should be done before she welcomed any guests, as part of beginning this new phase of her life. And it especially should be done before Lady Augusta stepped through the door.

It was time for her to unlock Dario's rooms, and go through his possessions. She had been hoping for so long, had left everything locked away, just in case, but now, after near two years, she could no longer pretend that her wishes would be answered. She had to accept that he was gone, and act accordingly – for Virginia's sake, if not her own. Tomorrow, she decided, she would unlock those doors, and start the task. Clothing did not matter – that could be disposed of in a number of ways – and much of it would be out of fashion now anyway, but personal effects, jewellery, journals, letters, and whatever else might be there for her to discover – those, she must deal with in private.

It might take a week or more but, she promised herself, it would be done before Lady Augusta walked through the main door of the Keep.

*****

Early November 1816

There was a particular smell to London – a smell he had forgotten, until now. The scent of the docks was different from the scent of the City, yet all of it was quintessentially London. As the carriage moved slowly through the crowded streets, Dario was impressed at how well the horses had adapted – perhaps the near six months on the road had inured them to all manner of strangeness. They had taken up an urchin near the docks as a guide, for the Italian coachman had no way to know the path to take to the building where the Duke of Winterward's man of business had his office. The urchin was enthusiastically helpful – both as a result of the coin he was offered, French though it was, and the chance to ride up on the box beside the coachman.

Finally, they turned a corner into a most respectable street, lined with buildings bearing signs for various businesses, and came to a halt in front of one labelled 'Sedgewick and Son'. Their groom opened the carriage door and let down the steps. Dario stepped out onto the streets of London, feeling beyond strange.

"Wait here with the carriage."

The urchin, wide eyed, nodded. Dario went up the short flight of steps to the door of the building, and rapped the knocker firmly. Moments later, a gentleman with pince nez perched on his nose opened the door. Dario swallowed.

"I am the Duke of Winterward – here to see Mr Arthur Sedgewick, if you please."

The man paled, and lifted the glasses to better peer at Dario.

"The... the Duke of.... Winterward?"

"Yes. Is there a problem?"

The man gulped, wetting his lips, and becoming even paler.

"No, Your Grace. Please come this way."

Dario was taken to a pleasant small parlour, where he waited as the nervous man scurried off deeper into the building. It was not long before he could hear hurried footsteps approaching. An older man almost burst through the door – a man that Dario now remembered meeting a number of times, years ago, when he had come with his father to make arrangements for his access to funds, and the signing over of some property to him. Dario rose.

"Sedgewick – it is good to see you again."

Mr Sedgewick almost staggered, his hand going to the doorframe.

"Your Grace! You are alive!"

Dario blinked in surprise – what a strange way to be greeted.

"Yes Sedgewick, I am most definitely alive. Why would you think otherwise?"

"Your Grace, we have thought you dead for nigh on two years now, since the report of the shipwreck reached London. After that, we heard nothing – no reports of any kind from Italy, and nothing at all from you. Forgive me, but... what were we supposed to think?"

Dario dropped back into his chair, his mind in turmoil. If they had all thought him dead, it was no wonder that his family had not written! And… Lady Augusta… did she think him dead also? Had she married another, not because she did not love him, but because she thought him dead? The horror of that possibility settled deep within him, and for a moment, he was barely aware of the room around him.

"I… see… but… if you thought me dead, why did you write to me, when my father died?"

Sedgewick looked somewhat chagrined.

"I wrote because I wanted an easy answer to the matter of the title and the will. I engaged in somewhat foolish-seeming hopefulness, Your Grace, because without actual proof of your death, part of me believed that there was always a chance, however slight."

"Well, I am glad that you indulged in optimism, or I would never have known, might not have come back for years. But… the fact that all have thought me dead for nigh on two years now - that likely makes things difficult, doesn't it?"

"On the contrary, Your Grace, your reappearance makes things far easier. The title can now clearly and formally be confirmed as passing to you, the final matters of your father's will can be addressed, and your family will have something to be joyful about, after two years of one misery after another."

All of that made sense, and Dario felt a smile curve his lips, as a strange sense of relief filled him. He wanted all of it dealt with, but most of all, he wanted to go home to Winterward Keep.

"Then, Sedgewick, might we get on with it? I am in need of coin, to give the urchin who guided us here, for the coin I carry on me is French, and there is precious little of it left. And I will need some assistance in general – I have three men with me, but they are all Italian, I have a carriage and horses too, but the mews at Winterward House should have ample room for them. But most of all, I will need new attire – this, which you see me in today, is the only vaguely respectable clothing which remains, after six months on the road from Italy. I am sorry that I did not write to you, once your letter informing me of my father's death reached me, but, unfortunately, in the shipwreck, I was injured – and one of those injuries was to my right hand. It is almost returned to normal now, but I still struggle to write legibly."

Sedgewick regarded the hand which Dario held out, studying the obvious scars on its surface, and the way that it did not quite curl into a fist. He nodded once.

"Then we had best set about the arrangements, Your Grace. You will need a week in London, I think, to put everything in place, and have clothing made. Should I write to your family, and inform them of your arrival?"

Dario considered it, turning the idea over in his mind, and trying to imagine how his mother would react. In the end, he decided that a shock delivered in person would be better than a shock delivered by letter.

"I think not. I believe that, so close to being there, it is better if I simply appear. It will be easier for them to believe in my return from the dead if I am there in person when they hear of it."

Sedgewick nodded, then reached into his own pocket to produce a handful of coin. He held it out to Dario.

"For the urchin you mentioned, Your Grace. If you wish to deal with that first, whilst I gather up all of the necessary papers, then I will accompany you to Winterward House, and we can begin to put matters to rights."

*****

Mid November 1816

There had been three days without rain, and the roads, blessedly, had dried out a little – enough that the travel from Shilham Park was bearable. The hardened mud was uneven, and the going was slow, and bumpy enough that Augusta had given up all hope of reading as they went. Instead, she simply stared out of the carriage window, looking at the waterlogged countryside. This was their second day on the road, and the coachman hoped that they would reach Winterward Keep before nightfall. Which was news that Augusta greeted with both happiness – for the sooner this trip ended, the better – and with trepidation. She dreaded the moment when she stepped into Winterward Keep again, the moment when she would be surrounded by memories.

In the two years since Dario had left England, she had dreamed, many times, of returning to the Keep – but in every dream, he had been there, waiting for her. That he would not be there now brought home to her, again, the looming inevitability of his absence, forever. Whether he still lived or not, if she was never to see him again, it made little difference, one way or the other. Her loneliness would be eternal, for her heart still belonged to him.

*****

Mid November 1816

The Duchess of Winterward felt strangely caught between elation and exhaustion. She had spent two sennights now, going through Dario's rooms. Today, she would deal with the final part of it. The part which she had, intentionally, left until last.

Today, she would look through his escritoire. His clothing and small personal items had not been difficult, although she had gone slowly, and looked at every single item, making certain not to miss anything, checking pockets on coats, and opening every hat box and every drawer in his armoire. Now, only the escritoire remained.

What secrets might it hold?

She had never pried into her son's life when he had been here, and now, as she drew the sliding lid of the escritoire up, she felt as if she trespassed. She steeled herself to continue.

The desk surface was clean, with a long dried out inkpot and an aged, ink-stained quill the only things immediately to be seen. Each of the small pigeon-holes above the desk held only writing supplies – some pens, other, still well-sealed, inkpots, and some folded sheets of paper. It was surprisingly impersonal.

Taking a deep breath, she turned her attention to the drawers. There were four. She started at the top. The first one contained only pristine sheets of high-quality paper, and a small bag of sand. The second contained a stack of journals. She reached out a shaking hand to touch them, trailing her fingers over the leather covers, as if by doing so she might touch her son again. After a minute of quiet contemplation, she lifted them from the drawer and, one by one, began to look through them. Some were from his boyhood, and she smiled at the bright and inquisitive character she found between the pages. Some were more recent, and to read them felt like an invasion of his privacy. She skimmed through, just in case there was anything of significance tucked between the pages, but there was nothing. Sighing, she returned the journals to their drawer. She was not entirely sure what she hoped to find – perhaps some new insight into her son that she had previously missed? Regardless, she would treasure all of it, and keep it to look at later, when the memory was not quite so painful.

The third drawer contained various correspondence – letters exchanged with men he had attended Eton and Cambridge with, letters pertaining to the management of those estates which had been his, personally, records of monies spent with tailors and the like. Nothing of significance, just the documentation of the daily life of a gentleman of the nobility. She looked at each one, having made certain that she had removed everything from the drawer, then carefully replaced them all.

One drawer left. Perhaps there was nothing of significance here at all. She pulled it open to discover a somewhat untidy stack of papers. Once she had lifted them all onto the desk surface, and made certain that the drawer was empty, she began to go through them. Immediately that she lifted the first document, she felt tears spring to her eyes. It was a copy of his ticket of passage information on the Lady Amabella. She set it aside, and lifted the next paper – a copy of more of his travel documentation. Perhaps that was all that was here, just copies of the papers relating to his last journey. She set that one aside too, and lifted the next.

The texture of the paper was different, and this one was folded as a letter. It was sealed, with Dario's seal, as Marquess of Weatherbrook. She traced the shape of the wax for a moment, and it cracked under the pressure of her finger, brittle after two years or more in the drawer. She turned it over, puzzled – why would a letter sealed by Dario be here? Surely, if he had sealed it, he had meant it to be sent to someone else? When she regarded the other side of it, she gasped. Clearly inscribed on it was simply a name – Lady Augusta Carlington.

The possible implications filled her thoughts. It seemed obvious to her that this letter had been meant to be sent – but had not been. But why? And how? If he had written it, whatever it said, she could not imagine him changing his mind, and not sending it. Why was it amongst these papers, which were all copies of his travel plans, left here for the records? Had it... had it come to be amongst them by accident, gathered up when they had been put into the drawer, in the hurry of leaving, pre-dawn, two long years ago?

She licked her lips, her fingers still stroking the paper and the cracked seal.

Should she open it? A deep desire to know what he had written to Lady Augusta filled her, even as she told herself that perhaps it should stay private. Or should she give it to Lady Augusta?

To do so might be the right thing... but if she was to do that, then she would read it first. She would wish to be warned of the contents, and thereby Lady Augusta's potential reaction, before she gave it to her. Resolved, she turned it in her hands again, and slowly unfolded it, the paper crackling as she did so.

It was short, and yet the most emotionally intense thing that she had ever read. The tears came then, unavoidable, overwhelming, and she set the letter down on the desk, that her tears might not fall upon it. What might have been different! But he had left it to the last to write this, and it had, somehow, never been sent.

She bent her face into her hands, and cried for all that might have been, for all of them.

*****

Mid November 1816

The sky had gone from dusk into the deep blue of impending night by the time that they turned in through the gates to Winterward Keep. Up ahead, between the winter bare trees, the outline of the Keep was lit by early moonlight. It was beautiful, and yet stark and forbidding at the same time.

To Augusta, it seemed to loom, larger than she remembered it, a place of the best memories in her life, and a threat of days of misery to come. She was beginning to regret agreeing to attend this house party, but firmly told herself that Lady Virginia deserved her kindness.

All too soon, they drew up on the gravelled expanse before the portico, and stepped down from the carriage, glad to stretch their legs and simply stand for a moment, after the two days of travel. The door opened, and footmen rushed down, just as their second carriage, with their maids, her father's valet, and the majority of the luggage, drew up behind them.

They left the footmen and their staff to manage unloading, and made their way to the door. The butler smiled a greeting, and showed them through to the parlour, where the Duchess and Lady Virginia awaited them.

Every step brought memory, and Augusta found herself half expecting Dario to appear at any moment. Sternly, she told herself not to think such things – but the memories flowed around her like ghosts of past joy, and the sense of haunting left her almost shaking. Once they stepped into the parlour it was better, for she could focus on greeting their hosts – but the prospect of the weeks ahead almost terrified her – she was not certain that she would not, eventually, just crumble into tears.

Chapter Eleven

November 1816

"I am so very happy that you could come – I know just how trying travel can be at this time of year, especially after the amount of rain we have suffered this last six months!"

The Duchess had come forward to greet them, and Augusta looked at her, curious – for, whilst her words were of welcome and happiness, in truth, she did not really look happy at all. Her eyes had a look about them of tiredness, and, almost, Augusta thought, of the aftermath of crying. But why would that be so? It made no sense. Beside her, her mother was responding, and Augusta turned her own attention to Lady Virginia, who seemed somewhat hesitant. She stepped towards her.

"Lady Virginia, it is good to see you again. I do believe that you have become far taller in the last two years – and more beautiful. I am certain that your Season will be a success."

Lady Virginia blushed, but looked pleased.

"Thank you, Lady Augusta. I must confess that I am nervous about it. Might I hope for your company to assist me?"

Augusta swallowed – there was no possible way in which she could refuse such a genuinely meant request. It seemed that she must endure the Season yet again.

"I will be delighted to do so, Lady Virginia."

"Thank you! That relieves my mind a great deal."

At that moment, the Duchess called for their attention, and suggested that they should go to their rooms and freshen up after their travel, as dinner would be served in half an hour. The idea greatly appealed to Augusta, for she would be glad to change out of her travel worn gown and then even more glad to eat. She moved to the door, as a maid led her mother away, but the Duchess placed a hand on her arm.

"Lady Augusta, once you have changed, and we have eaten, might I speak with you in private for a few minutes?"

"Of course, Your Grace."

"Thank you."

As the maid led her to her room, Augusta wondered, worriedly, just what the Duchess might want to speak to her about.

*****

Dinner was a rather quiet affair, both because Augusta and her family were tired after travelling, and because the Duchess seemed a little strained. Once the food was finished, they all retired to the parlour, but it was not long before Lord and Lady Shilham made their excuses, and went up to bed. Augusta stayed where she was, slowly sipping her second cup of tea. She would have chosen to retire too, but had held back, remembering the Duchess' request. After a few minutes more, Lady Virginia also chose to retire, and a somewhat strained silence settled onto the room. The Duchess waited until Augusta finished her tea, then set her own cup down.

"Lady Augusta, if you would come with me, I have something to show you – something very personal."

Augusta rose, feeling rather concerned – and puzzled. The Duchess led her from the room, and walking the halls of Winterward Keep in the dark silence of night brought back every precious moment of memory, in a rush that stole her breath.

They went up the stairs, and passed through the long gallery which led to the family wing – *where were they going?* The Duchess stopped at a door, and produced a key from her pockets. The door opened silently once she unlocked it, and Augusta followed her inside. The Duchess closed the door after them, and waved Augusta to one of the chairs which flanked the cold hearth. She sat, shivering a little in the icy room.

"I apologise for the lack of a fire, Lady Augusta, but these rooms have lain unused for two years now." Augusta looked around her, taking in the implication of those words. The Duchess nodded. "Yes, these are my son's rooms. When the word reached us of the shipwreck, I refused to accept that he was gone – I ordered these rooms locked, and all of his things left exactly as they were. It was only a few weeks ago that I managed to bring myself to open the door, and go through his things. I cannot pretend, any more, that he will return – not after so very long. It has taken me many days to look through everything – and I left his escritoire until last, suspecting that perhaps the most personal things might be found there. I was right. And that is why I have asked you to speak to me here, in private, tonight."

Augusta had stifled a gasp at the Duchess' words, her hand going to her mouth.

"What... what is it that you wish to tell me?"

"In truth, it is not so much what I wish to tell you, as what I wish to show you." With that, the Duchess lifted the sliding lid of the escritoire, then opened a drawer, and lifted out what appeared to be a letter. She turned and brought it to Augusta. "As you can see, this is addressed to you. I believe that it was written immediately before my son left to travel to Italy, and was accidentally put away with other papers, rather than being sent as intended, to you. I apologise for opening it – but the seal cracked when I first discovered it, and I did not wish to hand it to you, with no knowledge of what it might contain, and the impact it might have upon you. But please – open it now, and read it."

Augusta reached out and took it, her hand shaking, her mouth dry. A letter which had never been sent? A letter written just before Dario had left? It could be almost anything – it might confirm all of her fears, and destroy the last happiness she held from her memories, or it could just as easily confirm all of her hopes. Hopes which were useless, if Dario truly had perished... She unfolded the paper, the sound of it a soft crackle in the otherwise silent room. The Duchess stood beside her, holding the candle they had brought, so that Augusta could see, clearly on the page, the words that he had written.

My darling Augusta,

I am a fool. There is no other way of saying it. I ask that you forgive me my foolishness, which led me to be so tardy about telling you the true depth of my feelings. The prospect of so long away from you has brought me to my senses.

I love you, Augusta, more than I can describe, more than I ever thought to love anyone.

I would marry you, if you will have me.

I should have asked for your hand many long weeks ago, and I curse myself for ever hesitating. So, I ask you now, knowing that it would be reasonable for you to refuse me, given that I will be away from English shores for at least a year.

But I beg you – do not refuse me! Please, make me the happiest man alive, and say that you will be mine upon my return.

Send your reply to me at our estate in Italy, that I may know peace in my heart, and hurry back to you as best I can, intending never to leave your side again.

Yours,

Dario,

with all my love.

A sob escaped her, and the letter fluttered from her hands, to lie on the worn carpet at her feet. The sob was followed by another, and soon, she was crying with more force than perhaps she had ever cried before.

He did love her! And she would have known that, for all of these long empty months, but for a single accident of fate, which had seen this letter closed away in a drawer, rather than sent to her. She felt guilt for ever doubting him, and joy in equal measure, from knowing the truth of it. But it was a bittersweet moment – for surely, if he felt this way about her, truly loved her as he said, then something terrible must have happened, to prevent him from returning to her.

Could it be that she had been wrong, all this time, to hope? Was he, after all, perished in that shipwreck, torn from her forever?

*****

November 1816

As they pulled into the Inn yard, Dario thought, yet again, about how oblivious he had been... before. The time in Italy, and the privations of his journey back to England had changed his perspective. He slid his fingers over the velvet of the seat beneath him, acutely aware of the luxury of the carriage he rode in. In every way, from the springs which made the ride less bumpy, to the intricate decoration and luxurious fabrics of its interior, it was a masterpiece in comfort and privilege.

He would never take such things for granted again.

The week in London had allowed him to restore his wardrobe, and order more garments to be sent on to him at Winterward Keep, as well as to have his hair trimmed and new boots made which supported his once broken leg. The difference they made to his comfort was remarkable. They had left the Italian carriage in London, to be given long overdue maintenance, but the men, and the horses, from Italy were still with him. The horses would be given a well-deserved partial retirement at Winterward Keep, to be used only for short local journeys hereafter. Marco would remain as his valet, for Dario was accustomed to him now. The groom and the coachman would be given positions at Winterward Keep, but little would be asked of them until they had spent many weeks recovering from the journey.

Now, as he stepped down from the Ducal carriage, to be met by obsequious Inn servants, he felt, yet again, like an imposter. He would, he supposed, get used to it eventually.

"This way, Your Grace."

Marco, who had gone ahead of him into the building, had reappeared, the bowing Innkeeper beside him. He followed, amused in a way, that here, no one asked about money – they knew that he could pay – no one questioned his right to be there, or his title. If he had never left England, he would never have realised what it was like to not be treated like this, would never have known anything else. They went up the stairs, and were shown to an extensive suite of rooms. The Innkeeper had been shocked when Marco informed him that rooms were to be provided in the inn, for the grooms and coachman, as well as for the Duke and his valet. As usual, money had smoothed any doubts.

Soon, his men arrived, carrying the trunks, and two maids brought a large meal, and a decanter of brandy. The evening passed pleasantly enough, and all of them retired to bed rather early, given another long day ahead of them. Once Marco had helped him remove his new boots, and assisted him with preparing for bed, Dario sat in the single chair provided in his bedchamber, a glass of brandy in hand, staring into the flames of the fire which warmed the room. He noticed the chill, after two years in Italy, and was glad of that warmth.

What would he find at Winterward Keep? He had intentionally not sought out anyone of his previous acquaintance whilst in London. He had not wished to know the gossip, to hear the tales of what had been occurring in the *ton*, from anyone but his mother. If he was to hear that Lady Augusta had married another man, then he would much rather do so in the privacy of Winterward Keep.

Why had he been such a fool? Why had he not told her of his feelings when he'd had the chance? And... why had she not replied to his letter? Had news of the shipwreck, and his purported death, reached her before his own letter? But surely not – for his letter had only needed to traverse a relatively small part of England, and news of the wreck had crossed half of the continent.

He closed his eyes, wishing that he had done so many things differently. He did not regret his time in Italy, nor the arduous journey home – he was a better man for all of it. But he did regret the way that he had done almost everything about it, before leaving England, and the foolish way that he had shrunk from telling Lady Augusta of his true feelings. If he were to be granted the chance to see her again... he would do as he should have done, then.

But he was a fool to hope. If she had thought him dead, then she was almost certainly married by now, and lost to him, forever.

*****

Augusta lay in the bed at Winterward Keep, unable to sleep. Her eyes were reddened and sore from crying, and her mind was a turmoil of grief, guilt, and a peculiar happiness.

The clock on the mantel ticked, an inexorable marker of time passing, time lost, time never to be recovered. Her eyes went to it, and even in the dim light from the fire, she could see that it neared midnight. She rose, pulled a wrap about her, lifted the letter from the small table beside the bed, and slipped out into the quiet hallways.

She still knew the way, her heart full of memory, of kisses and the promise of forever in a touch. The library was exactly as she remembered it, a low fire banked in the grate, the scent of books, and something more, something indefinable, which would be part of her, always.

She went to that couch, near the fireplace, where they had sat so often that idyllic summer, and dropped onto it, pulling out the letter to read it again. She cried then, more tears, releasing all of the grief that she had stifled for two long years. When the tears finally slowed, she still sat there, contemplating the letter.

If this had been sent, as had been intended, what would she have done?

Receiving it, would she have simply written an acceptance of his proposal, and sent it off towards Italy? She suspected that she would have. Like all of those 'letters' to Dario which she had written in her journals since, she would have felt compelled to write immediately, to communicate, to tell him how she felt, in return for his honesty about his own feelings.

And what would that letter have looked like?

In her imagination, she pictured him, receiving it, sitting in some sunny Italian villa, and his face lighting up with the joy of knowing that she waited for him. All this time, she had refused to believe him dead – was she, now, after so long, going to give up all hope?

She shook her head, and rose, going to the small escritoire which sat under the window. She lit a candle from the embers of the fire, and set it on the desk. A few minutes was all it took to find a small sheet of paper, an inkpot, and a pen.

Augusta sat before the desk, and contemplated again, what that response to his letter should say.

The words did not come.

There seemed no way in which to address such a thing in a letter. Letters were too formal, too distancing, in some ways, for an answer on a matter of so much emotion.

After all – there was only one answer, and it was a single word – yes.

In the end, that was what she wrote on the paper – a large, calligraphically beautiful, single word. She surrounded it with coiling vines, each bearing flowers, as if the essence of life and growth was held on that page. Once the ink was dry, she folded it carefully, tucking it into his letter for safekeeping, as if, somehow, through the proximity of the two, he might know of it.

In that moment, she stilled, a small gasp escaping her.

That part of her which had hoped for so long still did so. In that moment, the certainty was there again, that he still lived.

She told herself that hope after so long was foolish, yet it rose within her like a growing flame. She suspected that it would never leave her, no matter the years which passed.

So be it then.

Her answer entwined with his question, held tight in her hand, she took herself back up to bed, feeling far better than she had for many months.

Chapter Twelve

November 1816

It had been a long day on the road, and the short winter twilight was fast disappearing as Dario's carriage finally turned through the gates of Winterward Keep. Dario had spent the entire day deep in thought, or staring out at the countryside, taking note of how much the land here, too, seemed to have suffered from the unnaturally cold and wet summer. Beside him, Marco also stared out, fascinated by this new country he found himself in. The closer Dario came to Winterward Keep, the more real everything seemed, and the deeper his grief became. Grief for the father and grandmother he would never see again, grief for his mother, who he had, perforce, left alone to deal with the passing of her husband, grief for his sister, who had lost the year she had expected to be her first Season, as well as her father, and had, most likely, also believed that she had lost her brother. And most of all, grief for himself, and for the love he had almost certainly lost. Lady Augusta was clear in his mind, and with all of his memories now returned, the same questions tortured him – why had she not replied to his letter? Had she loved him, truly, or not at all?

The gravel crunched beneath the carriage wheels, and Dario stared out, seeing the Keep silhouetted against the last of the light. In that moment, he was afraid – he did not know how he would be received, and he feared, most of all, finally hearing what had happened to Lady Augusta.

"Your Grace, it is far more... imposing... than I had expected, even after what you have told me of the place."

Dario laughed at Marco's words.

"It is. It was built to be imposing. The Keep is more than 500 years old, and has been expanded on often in that time. But inside, it always used to be a welcoming place..."

They lapsed into silence again, as it came closer.

A light snow had begun to fall, and he shivered, glad to be arriving before it became heavier. There were lights in the windows – the large parlour, he thought, and he wondered then, why that room, and not the small family parlour? Not that it mattered where his mother and sister were – he would go to them, immediately. When they came to a halt the front door opened, and a footman came running out. No doubt the servants were startled, for they were unlikely to be expecting anyone. He braced himself for what was to come as the carriage door was opened.

*****

Augusta had slept surprisingly well, the entwined letters tucked under her pillow. She had woken to find the day grey, and with the feel that presaged snow. The day had proven difficult, for her mind kept coming back to the letter, to everything it meant, to everything she had lost, and she feared that her conversation was, as a result, sadly lacking. She had spoken with the Duchess and Lady Virginia about the Season, and tried hard not to dampen Lady Virginia's enthusiasm. She was not at all sure that she had succeeded in appearing happy about the idea.

Now, as they gathered in the large parlour before dinner, Augusta felt rather exhausted. Her father had not come down yet, but everyone else was here. Quite how she would manage another week of this, she was not sure. Every corner of the Keep was filled with memories of Dario, and every day would bring more reminders of the fact that come March, she would go to London again, and face the *ton*, as an aging spinster, at least in their eyes. She sat quietly, the entwined letters tucked into her bodice, close to her heart, and simply stared into the fire. If anyone asked, she would simply claim tiredness, after the previous days' travel. Then, unexpectedly, she heard a sound from the main part of the house – the sound, if she had heard it correctly, of the front door opening.

Who could it be? Her eyes turned to the Duchess, but it was immediately obvious that she was equally startled.

*****

The footman who had opened the carriage door froze in place, as the lamp he carried cast light on Dario's face. The man went pale, and wavered on the spot.

"Your... Your Grace?"

"Yes."

The footman stepped back, so that Dario could step down.

"I... We...."

"Thought me deceased?"

"Yes, Your Grace."

"I am, as you can see, rather thoroughly alive. Might we go in? And can you arrange assistance for my valet, coachman and groom?"

"Yes, of course."

The footman turned towards the house, and Dario followed him. At the front door, Harper, who had been butler at Winterward Keep since Dario was born, took one look at him and went even paler than the footman had, staggering back with a hand to his chest. Dario rushed to him, supporting him.

"Harper! Yes, it really is me, and yes, I am real, and alive. Please, steady yourself – I did not mean to give you such a great shock."

"Y... Your Grace! This is wonderful! We thought..."

"That I had perished? Yes, I have only recently discovered that everyone thought that. There is rather a long story behind the circumstances. But now, after a very arduous journey, I think that the first thing I would like to do is see my family."

Harper actually blushed, and drew himself up.

"Of course, they are all in the large parlour."

Harper turned, and Dario followed him through the house, seeing everything through new eyes. He had, he now realised, taken this place for granted, for his entire life. He would do so no longer. Every part of it was familiar, and precious. They reached the well-remembered door, and Harper tapped, opened it, and announced him.

"His Grace, the Duke of Winterward."

Silence greeted Harper's words, as Dario stepped into the room. Before his eyes, a tableau played out, almost as if time had slowed. His mother gasped, and wavered where she stood, starting to fall in a near faint, only to be caught by the woman beside her. His sister, who had been standing, dropped back into her chair with a most peculiar squeak. Beyond his sister, another woman had frozen, halfway through rising from a chair near the fire.

Lady Augusta.

Dario found himself frozen too, as his eyes met hers. Those dark sea green eyes were exactly as he had remembered, as he had dreamed them, thousands of times, all through his time away. The moment extended, and somehow, what was said between them, in that look, would have filled a thousand letters. It was full of love, and pain – such pain that it took his breath away, and made him want to rush to her, to protect her from whatever had caused it. But he did not move – for surely, it was he, himself, who had caused it.

He did not know if she loved him still – perhaps she hated him, for abandoning her as he had – perhaps that was why she had never replied to his letter – and he would not force himself upon her if that was so. But the force of wanting her in his arms made him feel almost like fainting himself. Then, with a movement which was harsh, she turned her head away, the pain in her face so great that he felt it as a knife to the heart.

He did not know what she wanted, and the safest thing seemed to be to allow her to tell him that, in her own time, so he turned, and went to his mother, who was being assisted to a seat by the woman who he now saw to be Lady Shilham. He knelt before his mother, and she lifted a hand to touch his cheek, as if assuring herself that he was real.

"Dario..."

Her voice was broken, her eyes glittered with tears. He pulled her into his embrace, and simply held her as she cried.

*****

Augusta froze in the act of rising from her chair, her eyes turned instantly to the door. The Butler had just announced... It was as if time slowed, as if she existed in a dream – a dream so like many she had dreamed, over the last two years. In the doorway, Dario stood – real, alive, as she had always, somehow, believed.

He seemed as frozen in the moment as she. Then her eyes met his, and everything else ceased to exist. The moment extended, and what was said between them, without a word, was enough to fill a thousand letters. Yet it told her nothing of what she really wanted, needed, to know. Did he love her still? If he lived, why had he not written? Had he.... married someone else? That thought shattered her heart into a million pieces, and she turned her head away, suddenly unable to bear it. As she dropped back into her chair, she heard him move, and a quick glance showed that he had gone to his mother. As was only right, for family, in such a situation, should come first.

She sat quietly, resisting the impulse to go to him, to throw herself into his arms. Surely, if he wanted her, he would let her know, in his own time. She watched as he embraced his mother, then his sister, and his gentleness with them made her love him all the more. Her own mother had stepped back, and intercepted her father as he arrived in the room, explaining the situation in hushed tones. Augusta found herself feeling lost – uncertain of what to do next, yet, by the moment, more determined that, at the earliest opportunity, she would speak to Dario in private, and discover the truth of his feelings, and what had happened to him. Much though she wished to rush to him, and demand answers now, she could not – that would be beyond rude, and she would not intrude on his reunion with his family.

She shifted on her seat, and the slight sound of the crinkling of the letter, where it nestled against her heart, reminded her of what might still be possible – or what she might have lost forever. As she sat there, her heart aching, and her thoughts torn between joy that he lived and had returned to them, and fear that he could never be hers, the butler tapped on the door again, and, rather uncertainly, announced dinner.

There was a small silence following that announcement, as everyone looked at each other, pulled back to the mundane realities of life. Then, after a moment, the Duchess drew back from Dario, wiped the tears from her cheeks, and smiled.

"We should, I think, go in to dinner. No matter how momentous the fact of my son's return, we all still need to eat – and if he has been travelling all day, he most likely needs to do so more than we do."

At her words, there was a murmur of assent, and Dario rose, then offered his mother his arm. They went in to dinner as if this was just another ordinary day, and Augusta found herself on the edge of hysterical laughter, so strange was the situation. The fact that, at a time like this, they all still immediately bowed to the demands of politeness was starkly amusing. Dinner proceeded as if Dario had never been away, to some extent. No one appeared quite brave enough to ask him to tell the tale of what had happened to him, and he did not volunteer the information. Perhaps, she thought, he did not know where to start. As she studied him under lowered lashes, she noticed something, which had only become evident as he ate. He appeared to have some difficulty with his right hand, as if he could not quite grasp his knife with the firmness required. She wondered then, what had happened – had he suffered an injury? She could not ask, of course, could not pry. Once they had eaten, they went back to the parlour, for tea, and brandy for the gentlemen. As they settled into the chairs which were set about the fireplace, Lady Virgina spoke.

"Dario... will you tell us about where you have been, about what happened to you?"

He took a rather large swallow of his brandy, as if even thinking of speaking of it required the bolstering of courage, then met his sister's eyes.

"I will, but not tonight. It is a long tale, and I fear that I do not have the energy to tell it all this evening – not after the journey which was required to get here. But yes, I will tell you, over the next few days. You must be patient with me."

Lady Virginia looked disappointed, but she simply nodded, and answered him quietly.

"Of course – whenever you are ready to tell of it, I will be eager to hear."

An awkward silence fell, and it was not long before Augusta's parents made their goodnights, and went up to bed. Augusta rose, intending to do the same, but then, driven by impulse, she went to Dario, where he sat in the large armchair. He looked up, and their eyes met again. The world stopped. She forced herself to speak, at first quite loudly.

"I am most glad that you are returned to us safe, Your Grace. I too, will be most interested to hear more of your travels."

He had flinched at her use of 'Your Grace', but he still held her gaze.

"Lady Augusta, I am just as glad to be returned safely. I am sorry that I caused such a great shock to everyone."

She swallowed, agonised by the painfully correct and distant form of their conversation. If she was going to change matters, now was the time. She lowered her voice to near a whisper, so that his mother and sister would not easily hear her next words.

"Your Grace... Dario... I would speak with you alone, in private, later tonight if possible."

Something intense flickered in his eyes, and she wondered if she had done the right thing, as moments passed without an answer.

*****

When Lady Augusta approached him, Dario was torn between elation and fear – did she still care for him? What might she say? And... what might he say to her? How did one start such a conversation, without being unutterably rude? When she called him 'Your Grace' he wanted to cry out in pain, to beg her to speak to him as she once had – but he did not – he spoke as formally as she had, though his heart broke to do so. Then, with a quick glance about, she lowered her voice, and made a request which shocked him, and yet thrilled him.

She was so different, and yet so much the same – just as beautiful as always, and yet somehow more self-contained, more reserved, and at the same time displaying a confidence which she had not had, two years ago. That she wished to meet him alone, later tonight, was something filled with possibilities. The very idea of it brought back his hard won recovered memories of that summer they had spent together, of kisses in the library at midnight, and the sense of forever in the air. Whimsical hope drove him, and he spoke before he could reconsider it, his voice just as soft as hers had been.

"The library, at midnight?"

Her eyes flared with understanding, and something else, something compounded of pain and hope, which raised a similar feeling in his own heart.

"Yes." It was another whisper. Then she spoke again, at a more normal volume, as if that whispered exchange had not happened. "I believe that I will also go up to bed – for indeed, you have given us all a great shock, and I find myself more wearied than I expected."

He answered by also returning to their utterly ordinary conversation of moments before, even while he smiled, broadly.

"Then you must rest, Lady Augusta. Now that I am here, we need not hurry about the telling of my tale, and everyone will be the better for a good night's rest."

"You are right, so I will bid you goodnight."

"May you sleep well, Lady Augusta."

She turned and went, pausing to also bid the Duchess and Lady Virginia goodnight. He watched her go, his mind in turmoil again, and full of hope. For a start, no one had corrected him when he had spoken to her as Lady Augusta, which he dared to hope meant that she had not married...

The weariness which had weighed him down moments before had vanished, and now, midnight could not come soon enough. He sipped his brandy, and then also declared himself fatigued, and ready to retire, for he could not face the conversations he should have with his mother, or his sister, yet.

As he left them there in the parlour, he thought, with both grief and guilt, of how much time in the last two years they had spent like that – alone but for each other.

Chapter Thirteen

Augusta went up the stairs to her guest room, her heart pounding and her hands shaking where she held them together.

The library at midnight! Surely, that meant that he still cared? Why else would he choose a place and time so significant to her, to them?

But she must not place too much meaning upon it – what if he had only chosen that time and place to ensure their privacy, so that he could tell her that he did not love her, or, even worse, that he had married in Italy! But surely not that – after all, if he had married, would he not have brought his wife home to England with him?

She reached her rooms, and Mina, her maid, helped her change into her night rail, and a warm wrap.

"Thank you, Mina. You should go to your bed – I will sit here by the fire and read for a while, I think. Today has been wearing, but also so dramatic that my thoughts are spinning."

"Shall I bring you some warm chocolate to drink, my Lady?"

Augusta considered it, but then shook her head.

"No, thank you. I believe that with dinner, and tea afterwards, I have had quite enough for the evening."

Mina curtsied, and left her there. Augusta did not move at all, until she heard the click of the door to Mina's room, which was located on the other side of her dressing room. On the mantel above the fire, a clock ticked, counting the impossibly slow passage of time, yet moving inexorably towards midnight.

She adjusted the position of her candle, and lifted her book, determined to at least try to read. In the end, she failed at that intent. Instead, her mind replayed the scene of his arrival, over and over again, with all of the emotional intensity it had contained. She had swung from the heights of joy to the depths of fear and uncertainty, over and over again.

The fear and despair were feelings she had suffered ever since the news of the shipwreck had reached them – she had thought that she was used to it, to the precarious balance of hope and pain – but apparently, she was not. For tonight, those feelings had overwhelmed her.

When he had not immediately rushed to her, her joy had become doubt – doubt which still burrowed into her thoughts and her heart, making reading impossible. She stood, and paced the room, pausing to pull aside the curtains slightly, and stare out of the window. The world was dressed in purest white, with only the darkness of edges marring it, and a light snow continued to fall.

Moonlight made things silver, black, and white, with no shades of grey. It was beautiful, yet cold.

She shivered, and turned away, pulling the curtains closed again.

The clock ticked on, and she glared at it, then made a decision – far better to go to the library and wait there, than to attempt to occupy herself here. At least, in the library, there were many books, and she could browse through those, enough to occupy herself. She snuffed out the candle – there would be candles to hand in the library, and she could light one from the embers of the banked fire – then slipped out of her robe, and pulled on a simple round gown over her night rail. That, she could get into, and out of, by herself.

She tucked the letters – his, which had been found here, and hers, which she had written in reply, just the previous night – into her bodice, close against her heart, and stepped out into the hallways.

When she reached it, the library was exactly as she remembered it, from that long ago summer, and she stood there, breathing it in, again. Last night, she had come here to think, now, she desperately wished that her thoughts would simply rest, and allow her some peace, before the moment of midnight – the moment when she might discover the truth. She stopped beside the escritoire, where last night she had written that simple response, not truly believing that she would ever have the opportunity to give it to him, and allowed her hand to rest on its surface.

After a moment, she pulled the curtain on the nearby window aside, and simply stood there, staring out at the falling snow, allowing it to capture her eyes, and calm her mind.

*****

Dario approached the library door, feeling more uncertain than he had since the day that he had woken in the fisherman's shack, not even knowing his own name. Would she be there? And... what would he say? He needed to know why she had not written, in answer to his letter, proposing. And he needed to be certain that she had not married...

He opened the door, slipped through it, and closed it quietly. She was standing at the window, staring out at the falling snow, her profile limned in silver by the moonlight reflecting off that snow. The sight took his breath away.

She turned, having detected the quiet click of the door closing, and their eyes met.

The world stopped around them, and for a moment, all thought left him – there was only Augusta, and the swirl of memory of her kisses. What should he do?

Then, the tiniest movement – she lifted her hand, as if to reach out to him, then stopped, uncertainty clear on her face. It was more than he could bear.

He went to her, rushed steps across the room.

"Augusta..."

"Dario..."

"I must ask, before I say anything else. Did you marry?"

"No – Did you?"

"No."

A shudder ran through her, as if she had been holding herself tense, and had just released that tightness, all at once. He reached for her, and she came to him. Dario pulled her into his arms, and bent to kiss her – a kiss which began tentatively, and rapidly became something passionate and deep, something filled with every dream he'd had of her for two long years.

Vaguely, he was aware of a strange sound, as of the crinkling of paper. He pulled back from the kiss a little, raising an eyebrow in question. She laughed, sounding a little shaky.

"The sound? It is this."

She reached into her bodice, and drew out a folded paper. A letter. And, as she unfolded it, he realised that it was his letter, folded with something else as well. That something else slipped from his letter, and fluttered to the floor. He bent to retrieve it.

"What is this?"

"It is for you, but please wait a moment, before you open it. I need to explain – and, to some extent, to apologise."

Dario smiled, a little grimly.

"I have an apology to make to you, as well, if you will hear it."

"Of course I will, although I am puzzled – puzzled about what has happened to you for two years, puzzled about why you did not write – even to your mother, and curious, most of all to know your true feelings now."

"My true feelings? Augusta, I love you, as I always have, as I was too foolish to tell you, to your face, before I left. But the rest, that is more complicated."

"Then shall we sit, and be comfortable as we speak?"

He nodded, and they settled onto the couch, where they had sat with each other so often, that summer. He held her hand, and began to speak.

"It is a long tale, were I to tell all of it, so I will leave that for the morrow, when everyone may hear it. For now, I will tell you the parts that most matter, the parts that answer your questions. First, the simplest explanation of what happened to me. The ship was wrecked, as I gather you know. I, and my valet, were pulled barely alive from the wreckage, with our possessions, by some local fishermen who had gone to examine the wreck once the storm died down. My leg was broken, and my hand crushed. Chalmers was worse off, and did not, in the end, survive – but before he died, he told the fishermen who I was. Which was fortunate, because when I woke, I remembered nothing – not even my own name."

She gasped, and her fingers tightened on his.

"Nothing?"

"Nothing. I would dream of you, but I did not know who you were. I took months to heal, and once I could be moved, it took some time to get a message to Villa D'Oro, for I could not write with my crushed hand, and the fishermen did not know how to. So – I did not write because I physically could not, and at first, I did not remember enough to even know who I should write to. But in my dreams, I kept expecting a letter, as if someone should be writing to me. Why... why did you not write to me, why did you not answer the letter I left for you?"

She lifted his right hand to her lips, and pressed a kiss to it. The touch sent shivers of heat through his entire body.

"I did not write to you, because you were thought to be dead. Although I could not bring myself to actually believe that. But still... and I did not reply to your letter, because I never received it. Not until last night, that is. Somehow, in the hurry of your departure, it ended up amongst your other papers, and tucked away in the drawer of your escritoire. Which is where your mother found it, only yesterday. The wax of the seal had cracked with age. She opened it, and realised all, then gave it to me when we arrived."

He felt the world spin, her words confounding him.

He had put the letter out to be sent... hadn't he?

He could not remember, and he did not know if that meant that he hadn't, or if it was simply a symptom of his still fractured memory.

"It was never sent? Oh! Then I doubly owe you an apology – one for not writing – even if what I could have written would have been near illegible, I should have written some weeks ago, when we reached Calais – but by then, I did not know what to think, and I had assumed that, if you had not responded, then likely, you did not want me. And the other apology, for ever even considering that you did not love me – I should have held more faith in you."

She laughed – a bright sound, full of joy.

"Dario, I will always want you! I loved you regardless, and I owe you an apology for doubting you – in those weeks between when we last saw each other, and when news of the shipwreck reached us, I questioned, over and over again, why you had not written to me, wondering if you loved me at all. Have we not both been foolish? Circumstance conspired to nearly drive us apart, but somehow, we have weathered it, and find ourselves together again."

"We have, indeed, both been filled with doubt, although I do not know if that is foolish, now that I see the whole of it. But… you hold my letter in your hand, now, and I hold whatever it was folded with, when you drew it from your clothes. What is it that I hold?"

"It is my answer to your letter of two years ago – I wrote it last night. I did not know if you lived – indeed, I suspected that you did not, but I wrote it anyway. You may open it."

There was something in her voice, a quiver of deep emotion, even more than that which had been there before. Carefully, he unfolded the paper, and held it up, that the moonlight reflected off the snow might illuminate it enough for him to read it.

There was, on that sheet of paper, a single word.

'YES.'

It was beautifully presented, decorative, and framed with twined vines.

Everything about it spoke of life, of love, and of growth. Amongst the illustrated vines, there were flowers, and it reminded him of that moment in Italy, at his great grandfather's grave, when he had left the bright flowers, speaking so eloquently of life, in the place of remembrance. He set it carefully aside, and pulled her into his arms again, for a kiss so long that it stole their breath, and left them quivering with the intensity of it.

"Yes, you will marry me?"

"Yes, I will marry you. As soon as it can possibly be arranged, if you please. I think that we have waited long enough – even if, for part of that time, you did not remember me."

"Oh, but I did – I did not remember your name, but I remembered you – you were the anchor I came back to, through dreams, when pain and fever might have led me to give up. You were with me, in my mind, every single day that I was away from you."

*****

Augusta could barely contain the happiness which filled her at his words, at the knowledge that her stubbornness, her hope and belief, had been correct, and that, had she allowed herself to be persuaded away from them, she would truly have lost him forever.

Now, she wanted to cling to him, to stay by his side every moment of every day until they were married, and beyond.

Just like that long ago summer, they lapsed into silence – a silence where touch and kisses spoke more than words could, as the world slowly righted itself for both of them, after two long years askew. Much later, as they sat, simply curled around each other, he spoke again, as his fingers traced the curve of her face.

"As soon as possible? I agree. But I also think that we need to give my mother, and yours, the chance to arrange something large, to fulfil their dreams too."

"I suppose that you are right. Can we manage the three weeks for the banns to be read, without going quite mad? And is that enough time for our mothers to arrange things? I think that a wedding just before Christmas will be pleasant..."

He laughed at her words, pressing a kiss to her forehead.

"I am sure that we will think ourselves driven mad, but we will survive – what is three or four weeks, when we have managed two years? And yes, I like the idea of a Christmas wedding. Every year, we will have two things to celebrate."

"Then, in the morning, we should make our mothers happy. I know that they both always hoped for this..."

Epilogue

The week before Christmas 1816.

The conservatory at Winterward Keep was not a place where Dario had ever spent much time – it had been his grandmother's domain. But the flowers she had grown there had always been beautiful, and the warmth of the space had kept things flowering long into winter, especially those plants she had chosen because they flowered late in the year. Now, Dario stepped into the room with a purpose in mind. As he had hoped, everything had been maintained, and some brightly coloured flowers remained, even this close to Christmas. Carefully, he chose a selection, and cut them, to make two small bouquets. Half an hour later, as he stepped out of the carriage in the yard of the Winterward Village church, a sense of rightness filled him. He walked through the graveyard, winding past ancient headstones, until he reached the family crypt. It, like his great grandfather's grave in Italy, was guarded by a stone angel – one of rather gentler visage than the Italian one. Beneath the angel the long list of his ancestors' names had been added to recently - the letters spelling out his father's and grandmother's names were crisp new cuts in the stone.

Carefully, he laid the flowers down at the angel's feet, their brightness startling in the winter sere landscape. As it had seemed to him in Italy, so did it here – the bright flowers spoke eloquently of life and growth, in this place dedicated to the memory of the dead. He hoped that, somehow, his grandmother would know of this. Very quietly, he whispered, his words swirled about him by the rising wind.

"Here grandmother, are flowers for you – like the flowers I left for your father, as you asked me to. And flowers for my own father too. Life goes on, but those of us living do not forget those who have gone before."

The wind lifted the petals a little, as if acknowledging his words, and he smiled, then turned away. It was time to go back to Winterward Keep, to life, and growth, and the future. Tomorrow, he would be married to the woman he loved, and in that moment, all seemed right with his world.

*****

Winterward Keep was decorated for the Christmas Season, and had become a place full of happiness – far more so than it had been for some years. Lord and Lady Shilham had, with Augusta, stayed there for the month of December, at the Duchess' invitation. Now, Augusta's sisters and their families had arrived, overjoyed, and a little shocked, that their youngest sister was finally marrying. It was hectic and wonderful, all at once.

Dario and Augusta had survived the weeks whilst the banns were read, and their mothers conspired on all matters related to the wedding, by spending hours in the library together, every night while others slept. They had kissed, and when that had left them flustered and aching, they had talked, telling each other, in detail, of their lives whilst apart. In one of the earliest conversations, Augusta had admitted to her journal of 'letters' to Dario – and he, in return, had confessed to his journal of 'letters' to her, written once his hand would allow it as they travelled through Italy and France, to return to England. Laughing, he had claimed that the current, almost normal, function of his hand was entirely due to her. As they had each read the other's journals, they been brought, at times, to tears. Now, the night before their wedding, they were curled together on the couch in the library, staring into the glow of the low burning fire, for a moment in silence, each wrapped in their own thoughts. After some time, Augusta gave a soft snort of laughter.

"Augusta? What amuses you so?"

"I have just contemplated my complete failure to plan."

"Oh? And just what have you failed to plan?"

"How to be a Duchess. How to run a large household. How to deal with the *ton*, forever after... When you did not return, when it seemed that you might actually have died, I had no interest in anything but being allowed to retire from society and live a quiet life as a spinster. No other man interested me in the slightest."

"I am heartily glad that is the case. But I am sure that, planning notwithstanding, you will manage all of it perfectly well. Especially as, if, as you have told me, they began to speak of you as 'the Ice Princess'. That implies that you have mastered the art of withering glances and elegant, exquisitely polite put downs of those being inappropriate. Which are excellent skills for a Duchess to have."

It was Augusta's turn to laugh – for now that she considered it, he was right.

"I am sure that your mother will assist me, as well, if I falter."

"She will, undoubtedly, although you may become rather overwhelmed by the endless tales of the history of our family – which she has studied in great detail."

"I think that is more like to be fascinating than dull, actually."

"We shall see."

He pulled her into his arms for another kiss, and she forgot everything but the fact that he was there, alive, and would marry her tomorrow. What had seemed unlikely to ever happen, was about to be her reality.

*****

Dario stood in the church in Winterward Village, acutely aware of the people who had come to see him wed, and the beauty of the church itself. It was almost as old as Winterward Keep, and the simple austerity of its stonework made the beauty of its stained-glass windows all the more evident. Today, it was also decorated with greenery and holly as befitted the Christmas Season, but amongst them were woven winter roses. In simple vases set on two small tables to the sides, there were bouquets of dried flowers, still with some brightness to their papery petals. That brightness, that reminder of summer, even faded, brought to his mind, again, the quiet graveyard in Italy, and the flowers on his great grandfather's grave, as well as the flowers he had placed on his father's grave, the day before. It was a fitting echo, somehow, that this step forward into a new stage of his life should happen amidst a reminder of the past. He hoped that his grandmother would have been happy to see this day, had she still lived.

It could not have been more perfect. There was a whisper of voices, and he turned, to see Augusta entering the church. The flowing gown she wore was of a deep blue green, so like her eyes, so like the stormy sea, and around its hem was a glittering embroidery of small gems, which made it seem almost like sea foam. It felt, then, as if the sea which had nearly stolen his life, and his memories of her, was giving her back to him, lifted on its waves. She met his eyes, and smiled. In that moment, he knew that every difficulty he had endured was worth it, to have this chance at a life with the woman he loved.

She came to him, and the vicar began the ceremony, binding them together, forever. He barely heard the words, for all of his awareness was on the woman by his side. Eventually, it was done, and they turned, hand in hand, and stepped out into the pale winter sun, which had, by some miracle, found its way through the clouds. He suspected that it would snow again tonight, that it might snow for the next few days, to Christmas Day and beyond, but for this one, beautiful moment, the sun blessed them with its touch, after a year of miserable cold. People crowded around, wishing them well, the villagers telling him how glad they were of his safe return, and of their hopes for the future. Finally, they managed to make their way to the carriages, and set off back to Winterward Keep. As the carriage door closed after them, Augusta gave a huge sigh, and leant against him.

"Tired, my love?"

"No, not really, just so very glad that we are wed – I almost did not believe that it could be real, that it would happen. For the last month, I have kept fearing that I dreamed, and would wake to find you still gone. Now, I can release that fear."

Dario felt his heart swell with love.

"I promise you, I will not ever disappear again – I fully intend to have you always by my side, no matter how unfashionable it is for one to demonstrate so clearly that one loves one's wife."

With that, he bent to kiss her, a kiss which spoke of the agonies of the past, of separation, and the passion which the future held. They did not draw apart until the carriage halted outside Winterward Keep. As the footman opened the carriage door, Augusta met his eyes, smiling.

"Be assured that I will hold you to that promise, my love."

The End.

Author's Note

As usual, there are significant things in this book which are historical fact, or based on that.

For this book, the key element like that is the weather.

You may wonder why the weather was so bad in that summer of 1816, that it forced Dario's travel to take so very long – so here is an explanation.

In April of 1815, a huge volcano called Mount Tambora, which is located in what is now called Indonesia, erupted – the largest volcanic eruption for 1300 years. It spewed enormous amounts of ash into the atmosphere, which circled the globe, causing more clouds and blocking sunlight for nearly the next two years.

1815 in Europe was not affected until very late in the year, but from then on, the impacts were huge. The summer temperatures in 1816 were the coldest recorded between 1766 and 2000. There was far more rain than normal, and the cold meant that very little grew. Countryside which had been torn up by the passage of armies could not recover, instead becoming a muddy barren landscape full of starving people.

There were famines – not just in Europe, but in North America and in Asia as well.

There were epidemics in Europe, and in parts of England. Whilst England suffered from the cold, and there were some areas with failed crops, and hence famine, Europe was worse off.

In England and in Europe, there was frost in August, snow discoloured brown and red from the dust in the air (particularly bad in Northern Italy, where it fell throughout the whole year at times – and that is an area that Dario had to travel through), and excessive rainfall everywhere.

The following summer, of 1817, temperatures were still lower than normal, but things had improved substantially.

If you are interested in learning more about this, here are some links:

A Wikipedia article –

https://en.wikipedia.org/wiki/Year_Without_a_Summer

Some interesting videos discussing it on You Tube:

https://www.youtube.com/results?search_query=year+without+a+summer

Many of the thing out there which you will find if you just Google 'Year without a summer' are about what happened in the USA – but if you dig a bit, you'll find more detail on what happened in Europe and England.

The ship that Dario travels on (the Lady Amabella) is entirely imaginary, as is its shipwreck, but there are plenty of places along the Italian coast south of Naples where such a wreck could have happened – think of all of the travel pictures you have seen, with pastel coloured houses perched on cliffs above the sea....

The method used to load his carriage and horses onto the ship in Calais, as he is returning to England, is historically accurate.

I hope that you find this sort of historical information interesting!

Arietta Richmond

I hope that you enjoyed 'Lady Augusta's Letters'.

Turn the page for another great Regency story.

CLEAN REGENCY ROMANCE
A Duke's Daughters –
THE ELBURY BOUQUET
Book 7 – Iris
A MAIDEN FOR A MARQUESS
ARIETTA RICHMOND

A Duke's Daughters –
The Elbury Bouquet - Book 7 - Iris

Clean Regency Romance

A Maiden for a Marquess

Arietta Richmond

Prologue

Lady Iris Gardenbrook was enraptured.

There was no other word for it.

Oh, not by the singing, which was, even if one were to be polite about it, rather painful, but by the skill of the pianist who accompanied it. She ignored the singer, and focussed every part of her mind on the notes of the pianoforte, on the exquisite skill of the man who played.

A man she had never met before. Their hostess had made a passing comment about Lord Greenleigh having recently completed mourning, so it was reasonable that she had neither met him, nor really heard anything of him. But now... she desperately hoped that her brother knew him, and could provide an introduction.

She knew this piece, knew it well, and knew just how difficult it was to play well. Her eyes were locked to Lord Greenleigh – which was not a hardship, for he was a well-made man and more than passingly handsome – and the precise and elegant movements of his hands on the keys. She had long despaired of ever meeting a gentleman who cared for music even half as much as she did, but now, hope flared within her. Surely, he could not have such skill unless he was truly passionate about music?

Beside her, her sister Violet was whispering with Lord Merryfield, but Iris ignored them, ignored everything. Slowly, inexorably, as the piece went on, his exquisite playing seduced her, and by the end of it, she knew that she was in love, that this was the man she wanted.

Which was beyond presumptuous of her, given that she had no idea what his title was, what his family were like, even whether he was already married. She knew it was foolish, but yet her heart cried out, and her soul declared that this was the man. Which meant that she would simply have to discover everything she could about him, and arrange an introduction at the earliest opportunity.

*****

Leon Atherton, Marquess of Greenleigh, wondered, for the thousandth time, if this was wise, even as he settled at the rather beautiful pianoforte in Lady Ormondston's parlour. There had been a flurry of whispers go around the room when it had been announced that he would play, and he knew that many of the *ton* would now consider it inappropriate for him to play in public, now that he bore the title.

Yet he could not have refused. Lady Ormondston was an old friend of his mother's, and his mother would not have forgiven him had he said no. He would not, by any action of his, add further unhappiness to his mother's life.

So, as he always did, he allowed the music to carry him away, to free him from the exigencies of life, and from the knowledge of the spectre that stalked his family, that placed him in an impossible position, every day. Let them whisper if they liked, he would not deny himself this one consolation – and perhaps some of those listening might even enjoy his performance – if they could manage to ignore the somewhat terrible singing of his hostess' daughter, that was.

As the piece drew to a close, he looked up, and allowed his eyes to actually take in the audience. They were quiet, and there was a moment of true silence as the last note died away, the silence of actual appreciation.

Then they offered polite applause.

He rose, turned to leave the performance area, and found his attention caught by a young woman who watched him intently. She was seated beside another who looked quite like her – her sister, he suspected. His eyes met hers, and for a moment, it was as if no one else existed, so intense was her gaze. Her eyes were blue – the blue of the sky on a perfect summer day - and the errant thought came to him then that he was glad they were not green.

He wondered what she saw, why she regarded him so intently. Not that it mattered – he could not, ever, allow himself the luxury of a relationship – well, at least not for many years to come, not until after... He did not complete the thought. He gave the young woman the tiniest nod of acknowledgement, and forced himself to move, to leave the parlour. Perhaps a glass of punch would help him resist the temptation to wish for things he should not desire.

By the time the harpist had finished, and all of Lady Ormondston's guests joined him near the refreshment tables, he was more settled.

Until, across the crowded room, he saw her watching him. His heart ached – if only... but there was nothing he could do but allow time to solve his problem, and pray that it did so soon. For if it did not, if God was cruel, then he might never marry, never have the companionship of anyone, anything, except music.

He should not think like that, should not wish for that resolution, yet he did. It was unchristian to do so, and yet the thought would not leave him, ever.

He refilled his glass, and slipped out onto the terrace, even though the October air was cold – perhaps the chill would shock him back to his senses.

Chapter One

Iris had been hoping for this, from the moment that the pianoforte had been moved into the ballroom, as part of the preparations for her sister Violet's wedding. She stood quietly, hardly daring to breathe as she watched Lord Greenleigh cross the room, and settle onto the bench before the pianoforte. The small orchestra had taken a break from playing and the instruments all sat, waiting for their return. She had not known if this would happen, but she had desperately prayed that it might, that the sight of their beautiful instrument would be enough to tempt him. It was nearly three months since she had first heard him play, had first seen him at Lady Ormondston's musicale, and in that three months, she had managed to achieve an introduction, dance with him once, and have precisely three conversations with him.

She remembered every second of each of those occasions in exquisite, frustrating detail.

When they had conversed, they had spoken only of music.

It was as if nothing else existed in his life – which did not, entirely, worry Iris, for if she had the choice almost nothing but music would exist in her life either. But it was unusual, and it made him all the more intriguing. Even her mother seemed to know little of him, and her mother was close friends with most of the biggest gossips of the *ton*. That did not matter – what mattered was that he was unmarried, willing at least to occasionally talk to her, and he played a pianoforte with masterful skill. She was determined, and stubborn, and capable of patience, much though her sisters and brother might have disputed that claim.

She hoped that she was right in believing that he at least liked her, for occasionally when they had spoken she had seen a warmth in his expression, which seemed to surpass that which might be expected from a mere acquaintance. But perhaps that was only wishful thinking on her part.

He began to play, and her heart flipped over in her chest. She knew this piece, knew it so well that she could play it without needing the sheet music, without needing to even see the keys – it was embedded in her soul as few other pieces of music were. And it was beautifully appropriate as a thing to play at her sister's wedding breakfast.

She moved, slowly and quietly, around the edge of the room, until she stood not all that far from where he played. He was lost in the music she could tell, his gaze unfocussed, seeing something no one else saw as his hands moved fluidly.

The idea came to her then, unbidden, carried on a desire so intense that it took her breath away completely for a moment.

Did she dare? Would he permit it if she tried?

Surely, here, in a room full of people, there could be no impropriety in it? Surely here, even if he thought there was, he would not reject it, for fear of even greater perceived impropriety?

As that thought slid through her mind, she almost laughed – of course there could be impropriety in it, but not so much as to be a scandal. She moved forward, knowing that she was going to do it, to take the risk.

She reached the edge of the narrow bench on which he sat, and he, somehow aware of her presence, glanced up. His eyes met hers, and something passed between them, something inexplicable, yet distinct. She reached out one hand, even as she bent slightly, as if to sit. He understood instantly, a flash of something compounded of alarm and delight crossing his eyes. For one moment, she thought that he would reject her, but then he swallowed, all the while never missing a note as he played through the spiralling, complex piece, and edged across to one end of the bench.

She allowed her movement to complete, until she was sitting beside him, their thighs hard against each other, the scent of him intoxicating around her. Then, she closed her eyes for one moment, and allowed all of her awareness to sink into the music. Anchored in it, sure of her place, she opened her eyes again, and reached out, finding the space around his moving hands, and beginning to play – a second part to the melody, a complex, interwoven strand of the piece, echoing and supporting the main part that he played. As she did, he adjusted his own playing, leaving sections of the pattern which he would have played if playing alone for her to play instead.

It was the most wonderful moment of her life. She did not care what anyone said, what anyone thought – this was worth any price.

If she never had such a chance again, at least she would have this, a memory to hold close.

*****

Leon had considered not attending the wedding breakfast for Lady Violet Gardenbrook – at least in part because it meant that he was likely to see Lady Iris Gardenbrook. But also, as always, because he really had no interest in the social events of the *ton.* Despite his mother's hopes, he had no intention of marrying in the near future – he would not expose a young lady to the home life which he suffered for most of the year.

It was fortunate that his country estates were only a short distance from London, or coming away even for a few days at a time would have been impossible. Or perhaps, he thought wryly, that wasn't fortunate at all – if Greenleigh Park had been further away, then perhaps he might have avoided London altogether, when his presence was not absolutely required in the House of Lords.

But here he was, in a ballroom which currently contained the vast majority of the *ton*, to celebrate the marriage of the daughter of a Duke he barely knew. The first thing that he had noticed, on entering that room, was the pianoforte – it was a magnificent instrument, even if the person playing it, as part of the small orchestra, was of barely adequate skill. It was beautifully made, and perfectly tuned – its mellow tones made his fingers ache to caress its keys.

Perhaps, later in the day, the chance might come for him to do so, and the gossips opinion of that be damned.

He allowed his mother to almost drag him about the room, she using the occasion to introduce him to any young woman she could find whom he had not already met. He smiled when required, and made sure that he appeared as dull and uninteresting as possible, so that none of them developed false hopes. Eventually, she tired of it, and with an irritated admonition to him that he should dance, went to speak with her own group of friends.

Which left him free to take advantage of the fact that the orchestra had just paused in their playing.

Casually, he wandered across the room, and settled onto the padded bench before it. His fingers traced its polished timber surface and the ivory of its keys, for a moment simply appreciating the craftsmanship of its construction, but then, unable to wait any longer, he began to play. The piece came to him instinctively – he knew it so well that it was ingrained in his soul – it was a piece that he played when he needed to be reminded of the beauty in the world, despite all troubles.

Soon, as it always did, the music consumed him, leaving him barely aware of the room around him, and washing away all of the frustrations which normally came with attending any social event. Time passed as he played, until the presence of a shadow beside him made him glance up.

Lady Iris Gardenbrook stood there, her blue eyes fixed upon him, full of an emotion which he had not expected, and did not entirely understand. His fingers continued, uninterrupted, while his mind processed what he saw. She understood – he knew that from their few conversations about music – but what did she want, that she would disturb him now?

And then she shocked him to his core. She reached out a hand towards the keys, and moved slightly as if to sit.

She wanted to join him! This was a piece which could be played as a duet, with the melody splitting into two threads to interweave to make a whole – did she know it, that well? And could he take this risk? If he allowed it, she would need to sit hard up against him, and his mouth went dry at the very thought of it. What would people think? It would be verging on scandalous.

Yet... he wanted it.

Even if she did not have the skill, he still wanted to try.

He'd had no one to play closely with for a very long time...

A kind of madness filled him, and he nodded slightly, shifting himself across to make room for her, even as his hands simply continued playing, completely based on instinct and practice. She smiled – a devastating thing which almost made him falter, and carefully settled to the seat. Her thigh pressed against his, and he could feel her warmth, even with all of those layers of fabric between them. The scent of her wrapped about him, subtle, something not quite floral, mixed with warmer, more exotic elements. His head spun from her nearness.

She stilled completely, and closed her eyes. He could almost sense her allowing her mind to drop into the music, aligning herself with it, and with him. Then she reached out, and her fingers came to the keys, her hands effortlessly interweaving with his, as he shifted his playing to the two-part structure, and she took up the other thread of the melody.

His heart soared – she had far more skill than he might have expected, perhaps more than he had, himself, despite all of the years of practice, and she seamlessly melded her playing into his, until they moved almost as one entity, utterly sure of each other, and every momentary location of each finger.

He had never before experienced anything quite so perfect. No matter what gossip might come of this moment, it was worth it. He wished, in that instant, that it might last forever.

Inevitably, though, the piece came to an end, and they each drew back their hands, allowing the last notes to drift into silence. A silence from which people watched them, he realised. A silence which gave way, after a few moments, to applause – applause which was led by the members of the small orchestra, who had returned, ready to play again. Leon took a deep breath – which only served to make him more acutely aware of the scent of Lady Iris. Their eyes met, and he wanted to speak of what had just happened, to somehow prolong that perfect accord in which they had floated. But here, watched by the entire room, there was nothing he could do but deliver her a seated bow.

"My thanks, Lady Iris, for your skilful accompaniment of my playing."

"And mine for yours." She smiled again, her eyes speaking far more than her words. "I would hope that we might find a chance to do this again, in the future."

"Indeed."

He rose, as did she, and they moved away, to be soon joined by his mother and a number of other people, some of whom were obviously Lady Iris' family. There was no space for anything approaching private conversation, and no words that he might say which would not be, one way or another, inappropriate. He rather thought that she felt the same, from her expression.

The swirling of conversation soon drew them apart, and he felt the loss of her presence acutely, even though he knew that it was for the best. If she knew the truth of his life...

It was best that she never discover the things which his family kept close, the things which prevented him from ever being able to offer her more than conversation, and music, despite his rather terrifying realisation that with her, he was quite capable of wanting more.

*****

Thorne Gardenbrook, Marquess of Wildenhall, looked at his youngest sister and raised an eyebrow.

"Was that wise, Iris?"

Iris met his gaze, her own challenging.

"You know full well that it wasn't, dear brother, and you also know that I could no more have stopped myself from taking that chance than Father could stop himself from obtaining more exotic plants."

"Was it worth the gossip which will result?"

"Yes."

"That certain?"

"Yes."

"Worth it for the music, or worth it for the excuse to be scandalously close to Greenleigh?"

It took the utmost effort for Iris to keep her expression bland.

"Thorne! You know me – the music of course. Whilst I cannot deny that Lord Greenleigh is a well-made man, you know that for me, music is always the most important thing."

"So the fact that he is accounted handsome, as well as being a skilled musician, has nothing to do with it?"

There really was no stopping Thorne when he decided to tease. Iris sighed, for truthfully, it was difficult to contend his point, when she did, very much, want to be close to Lord Greenleigh for more than just his magnificent musical ability. She forced her smile to its best false cheer.

"Perhaps 'nothing' is too strong a word."

Thorne laughed softly.

"Then you will have a challenge ahead of you, if you wish to pursue that possibility. From everything I have heard, Greenleigh looks to consolidate his place amongst the *ton*, and in the House of Lords, but has shown virtually no interest whatsoever in the idea of women and marriage. None of us know him well, nor did anyone know his father very well. The family have been rather reclusive. The gossips were startled that he even spent time in London these last few months."

Iris had already come to that same conclusion, and had, in her attempts to discover more about Lord Greenleigh, found almost nothing. But such things only made her more stubborn in her intentions. Far better a man about whom little was known, than one with a reputation for debauchery and gambling.

"Perhaps. But when have any of us ever allowed a challenge to stop us? And you should be grateful. Unlike all of your other sisters, I have not sought your assistance for introductions to gentlemen. I prefer to do my own choosing of whom I may consider worthwhile – even if that means that achieving introductions is sometimes a convoluted process. I shall not give you grounds to complain about my lack of appreciation."

Thorne laughed again.

"I will just find other things to tease you about, Iris, never fear."

"I am sure that you will. But... if you do hear anything of interest about Lord Greenleigh, you will let me know, won't you?"

Perhaps she was foolish to ask, but her brother was often an excellent source of information, even if the price of it was being teased.

Chapter Two

Leon lifted his hands from the keys, and the last notes died away into the silence, replaced only by the soft snoring of the young woman in the next room. Through the open double door, he could see the figure of his sister Maggie, curled under the coverlet in her bed.

Mrs Withercombe crossed through his line of sight, going to close the bedroom windows for the night. The candles in that room cast it as a scene of night in a forest, the deep green of the wallpaper added to by the shades of green of the bed hangings and the coverlet, echoed by the deep carpet on the floor. Leon shuddered, turning his eyes away.

He had come to hate green, as deeply as Maggie obsessively loved it. In every memory he had of her, in her descent from a healthy laughing child to the faded shell she now was, she was wrapped in green. It was her choice, and his father had indulged her, but over the years, it had become more than a simple liking, had become, instead, something which drove every part of her life.

He rose, and crossed the, blessedly not green, small parlour to close those windows too. Fresh air might be desirable, but this was December, Christmas Eve, and the crispness of the air suggested that there would be snow before morning. He turned back as Mrs Withercombe stepped out of his sister's bedroom, and closed the doors behind her.

"Thank you, my Lord. It's always easier to get her to sleep when you play for her."

"It's the least I can do – for it seems there is little other way I can help. She seems weaker every day, and more... erratic. Was it bad, while we were in London?"

Mrs Withercombe had been with them for twenty-five years now, initially as Nanny to both of them, and then, as Maggie's illnesses began to take hold, as Maggie's companion, and nurse. She would give him an honest answer, he knew, for she truly cared, and felt as much despair as he did at their inability to effect any kind of cure for his sister. She bustled about the room, tidying things, banking the fire, and setting the room to rights for the night. He waited, knowing that she would answer in her own time. When she did, her voice held deep sadness.

"It was... difficult. She wanted you. Wanted the music. And could not remember, from day to day, why you weren't here, nor understand why you could see anything as important enough for you to leave her. I did what I could – I sang to her, and distracted her with reading her simple tales – but she fretted, and sometimes suffered bursts of destructive anger. We will need to buy some more ornaments for her soon, for she has smashed most of the last lot."

"I am so sorry, Mrs Withercombe. I do not know what I can do – I cannot completely avoid my responsibilities in the House of Lords."

"I know it. But my Lord, I am not sure how much longer her strength will last, either. Perhaps, with it being Christmas, and all the pine boughs decorating the rest of the house, it will be green enough for her... and perhaps the good food of the season will tempt her to eat more.... It worries me, though – for if it snows, if it's too cold for her to go out into the gardens, to go into the trees, then she will want to lock herself away here – and we know that she's worse when she does that."

"I will do whatever I can to help, Mrs Withercombe – and thank you, for all of the years you've cared for her – and me, when I was a child. Without you, I am sure that I too, would have descended into a kind of madness by now."

"Whist! Never say it, my Lord. It's a fine man you've grown to be, with a good heart too. You're stronger than you know. Between us, and your mother, we'll find a way to deal with Lady Margaret, until..."

"Yes. Until..."

Neither of them could bring themselves to say it, but each knew what the other meant.

He looked about the room, considering the pianoforte – a small instrument, but beautifully built, he had purchased it for this room, to always be there for Maggie – that was when she would still play, sometimes. It was not an instrument that he ever played for his own pleasure.

He turned, and with a nod to Mrs Withercombe, he left the room. Perhaps, if he went down to the music room, to his own pianoforte, he might play until the music swept away the aching bitter sadness, at least for a while. It would return, of course – but any respite helped him gather the strength to go on. How his mother could conceive that he would marry, when things were like this...

He shook his head as he walked along the gallery where his ancestors' portraits looked down on him, wondering – had any of them suffered so? Was the contamination one of the blood, a madness and physical decline which might appear in future generations too?

He prayed that it was not.

Once he was seated at his pianoforte, it was as if his hands had a will of their own – they began to play the piece he had played just days past, at Lady Violet Gardenbrook's wedding breakfast. It was a piece he often played, to soothe himself, to remind him that there was beauty and peace in the world, that eventually there might be an end to the nightmare he lived with. But this time, it reminded him of something else – inescapably, the memory rose of Lady Iris Gardenbrook seated so close against him, playing with him in perfect synchrony, as if they were two halves of a whole, bound together inescapably by every note that they played.

He wanted to feel that again. To desire it was madness, but he did.

The memory and the desire tangled together in his head with the music as it filled the room, and tortured him, even as it soothed his aching heart.

*****

January dragged on, and once the celebrations of the Christmas season had passed, Iris found herself with little to do. There were still soirees and the like to attend, but with the House of Lords not due to meet again until the end of the month, many families had gone to country estates for those few weeks. When they returned, it would be to prepare for the Season, with all it held. But now, apart from those few thinly attended social occasions, there was nothing to amuse her, beyond, as always, her music. And dreaming of Lord Greenleigh.

The memory of that duet at Violet's wedding breakfast was never far from her thoughts, and the fact that Lord Greenleigh had left London for his estate the day after, and had not been seen in town since, drove her quite to distraction. It meant that she could not even speak to him at soirees, could not seek a chance to discover if he felt, about that duet, as she did. She had continued to seek more information about him, and his family, but with little success – all she had found was a treatise on agricultural methods, penned by his paternal grandfather, which, whilst it showed a most forward-thinking inclination for the gentleman's era, gave no clues as to what values he might otherwise have inculcated in his family.

Even Debrett's was no help, beyond confusing her slightly with mention of him having a sister – but perhaps the sister was long married, or perhaps she had died young, as so many did, and the date simply not yet been recorded when the edition of Debrett's in their library was printed. There was nothing else of note, anywhere. The man was, truly, an enigma.

But that very elusiveness drove her to want him even more, whilst it left her considering a most inconvenient question – how did one pursue a recluse?

She could not flirt with a man who was not there, could not apply inuendo and subtle hints to convince him of her desirability, (excepting, of course those things which might be implied using the discussion of music...), when he did not speak of anything but music.

Hopefully, he would return for the Sessions of the Lords in February, and she would at least have the chance to see him again – perhaps she could convince her mother to invite him, and his mother, to dinner? That would at least give her a chance to see him, but likely not the slightest chance to speak in anything approaching privacy – and she wanted privacy, if she was to speak of that duet.

When she played, she often found herself playing that piece, reliving the moment as she did – but it would never be the same again, without him playing it with her. And at night, as she drifted towards sleep, her deepest desires surfaced, and she imagined what it might be like to kiss him, and more.

Sometimes she even wondered just how far she would be willing to go, if he continued to be stubbornly, excruciatingly 'just a friend', all whilst the warmth in his eyes said that he was interested in more. Would she, ever, be willing to do something she had always despised, and consider... compromise...?

That was a question to which she had not found an answer. In the end, she did not think that she could do such a thing, intentionally, for it would unfairly trap him – and she would have him choose her, without duress, if she could. But in that edge of dream state, there were days when it seemed a deeply tempting thing.

On this day, she had played for hours, and then taken herself to sit in the parlour with a book – the parlour felt odd, empty and cold, now that only Thorne and herself remained at home, of the eight children. After years of noise and constant companionship, it felt strangely lonely. Still, the fire was warm, and the tea and lemon cakes reassuringly familiar. Outside, icy sleet beat against the windows – was it raining where Lord Greenleigh was, she wondered?

That thought was interrupted when Thorne entered the room.

"Remarkable! You are actually in the parlour, rather than the music room! I will mark this day down as one to remember."

"I do spend time in this room, frequently, my dear brother – just not at the times when you do, it seems. Perhaps it is your presence which is remarkable?"

Thorne laughed, dropping into the chair nearest her, and reaching across to scoop up two of the lemon cakes from her tea tray.

"Well, if that is so, you should appreciate my generosity in being here."

Iris pulled a cushion from behind her, and flung it at him. He plucked it from the air, tucked it behind him with ostentatious adjusting for comfort, and grinned at her again. She glared at him.

"You really are impossible!"

He gave her a seated half bow, and went back to savouring the lemon cakes. She opened her book again, and set about actively ignoring him.

Moments later, the parlour door opened again, and they both looked up to see their father.

"Do either of you have clothing suitable for deep mourning?"

Startled, Iris shook her head.

"Last time we needed mourning was some time ago – nothing from then will still fit me – why – who has died?"

"You'd best order some then – deep mourning, ordinary mourning and half mourning – it seems likely that the King will not live much longer."

For once, Thorne was silent, gaping at their father almost as much as Iris was. The King had not been well for many years, it was true, but somehow, this was still shocking news.

"Ah... I see. I had best visit the modiste tomorrow then – hopefully, the weather will clear by then!"

"And I will see my tailor, although I am better placed than Iris, for I have a selection of simple black attire, which can have mourning bands added to it."

The Duke nodded.

"I will keep you informed as things progress – and obviously, this may well change which days I have to be in the House of Lords – there is due process to follow on such a momentous occasion for the Country. Your mother is considering her own wardrobe now. But, beyond the tailor and modiste, do not discuss this anywhere yet – best not to presume upon God's timing."

*****

The messenger rapped on the door of Greenleigh Park in the late evening, when the light had long since faded to night, and the sleet had become a steady light fall of snow. Leon was just coming down the stairs, his hands aching a little in the cold, for he had played for hours, until Maggie had finally drifted into sleep.

The dozing footman startled into alertness, and hurried to open the door, revealing a half-frozen man in the livery of the staff of the House of Lords.

"Come inside man, so that we can shut the door!"

The messenger complied, and the footman closed out the storm with alacrity.

"My Lord..."

The messenger fumbled in the bag he carried, his hands numbed by the cold, then produced a sealed document. Leon took it, then turned to the footman.

"See this man to the kitchens, and make sure that he is warmed and given a decent meal. And ask Mrs Hartford to have a guest room made up for him, and a fire set in its grate – this is no night to be out in the weather."

The messenger bowed, obviously grateful, and was led away, leaving Leon standing there, holding the sealed message. What could be of so much import that a message would be sent, now, when he had planned to be in London within the week anyway, for the next sitting of the Lords?

He turned, and went to his study, where he poured himself a sizeable brandy before settling into the armchair before the fire. Only once the brandy warmed him from the inside, did he break the seal on that ominously official paper. The words inside were formal, yet, for a communication relating to the House of Lords and the monarchy, minimal, stark – yet of a nature which, in an instant, changed the world.

The King was dead, today, the 29th of January 1820. The Prince Regent had acceded to the throne. A coronation would follow in due course.

And he, as all the other Lords, was summoned to London, to the proceedings within the House which would set in motion the formal transition from one King to the next, whilst maintaining order in the Kingdom.

A grim laugh escaped him.

At least he, as the rest of his family, was well supplied with mourning clothes, being but four months out of mourning for his father.

He had best go up and set Belling to packing, before he informed his mother, or attended to dinner for himself. As he hurried up the stairs, he prayed that the morning would bring clear skies, and passable roads, or even the relatively short distance to London would take the full day.

Chapter Three

Greenleigh House was a welcome sight after a day of formal matters – a day in which Leon had felt most strange, for, being dressed in full mourning was rather strange when one was not also in seclusion from society. To go about daily business while dressed that way felt wrong – yet here he was, as was every person of the *ton*, doing just that, in respect for the King's passing. In his home, he could choose to wear something other than unrelieved black – at least when there was no chance of anyone but his mother and the staff seeing him. Not that his wardrobe boasted anything flamboyant, but even small touches of lightness were worthwhile.

He worried, though, about Maggie. She had been terribly distressed by his and Mother's departure, and by their mourning clothes, becoming frantic with the belief that someone else very close to her must have died. In the end, Mrs Withercombe had found it necessary to resort to laudanum to get her to sleep at all the previous night.

They had decided that, whilst he must stay in London for at least the next few weeks, his mother would spend half of each week at Greenleigh Park to attend to Maggie. That decision left Leon wracked with guilt, yet he could see no other option – he needed to be here, needed to be seen in the House, and in society, to do his formal duty, and establish himself as a sober and respectable man in the opinion of those in power.

He settled at the pianoforte after dinner, and allowed his cares to fade away into music – and into the memory of Lady Iris Gardenbrook.

Would he see her at any social events? There were still quiet events held, even with the mourning, and he would attend some of them. Seeing her would not be the same as playing a duet with her... but it would perhaps at least allow them a conversation on the subject of music, even if not the conversation he would like to have with her...

He played that piece again – the one which now seemed barely real without her beside him – and tried his best to forget about everything else. To forget his poor ailing sister, to forget the strain which lived forever on Mrs Withercombe's face, and his mother's, to forget the fact that his life was wrapped in tight bonds by the secrets he must keep.

For the first time, the music failed him – it eased the pain, but he could no longer use it to forget – not now that it was inextricably bound up in his mind with the woman he wanted, yet could not allow himself to have.

*****

Iris sighed, regarding herself in the mirror.

Black did not suit her – it made her pale skin look sallow, and her dark gold hair look tarnished. Eight weeks. So only another six weeks and she could change to less deep mourning colours. And then another four weeks after that before she could shed mourning entirely. Surely she could cope for that long, especially as everyone else had to suffer it too. It would make the latter part of the Season even more bright and colourful than usual, she was sure, once everyone shed the dark shades of visible grief. She fidgeted, wanting to move.

"Do sit still, my Lady, so that I can pin these jet beads into place in your hair." Lina, her maid, sounded only a little annoyed, for she had been maid to Iris for three years now, and knew full well that Iris loathed the drabness of black which deep mourning required. "There. That should stay in place for the evening."

"Thank you, Lina."

Iris rose, and went downstairs, knowing that her mother and Thorne would be waiting. They were to attend a quiet musicale at Lady Wells' home – a musicale at which, no doubt, only the most drear and funereal of pieces would be presented. Even loving music as she did, Iris could not bring herself to enjoy an entire evening of mournful works.

Perhaps, if she were lucky, Lord Greenleigh would be there, and they might manage a conversation about more uplifting music? She had seen him only twice since the King's death, and on neither of those occasions had there been the opportunity for more than a most formal greeting. Their eyes had met, and each time, she had been filled with the sensation that he wanted to say so much more, as she did, that he harboured feelings for her which could not be openly spoken of. But perhaps she was simply deluding herself. If so, it was a delusion she would persist in, until such time as his feelings were proven, one way or the other.

*****

She had smiled at him, and their eyes had met, filled with their shared horror at the painful sounds being presented as music, but there had been no opportunity, yet again, for them to speak beyond a stilted greeting. Now, as he settled into the carriage for the short journey back to Greenleigh House, he wondered if he would ever have more than those stolen glances with her again.

"...possibly suitable to marry? Leon, have you heard anything I've just said?"

He blinked, and brought his eyes to his mother.

"Ah... I have not, I am ashamed to admit. Please, repeat it, and I will give you my full attention."

She shook her head slightly, sighed, and began again.

"I asked you if, amongst the young ladies you have met, you have discovered any yet whom you might consider possibly suitable to marry? Surely, this period of mourning for the King provides an opportunity to see how they comport themselves when they must be sedate and respectable at all times."

"Mother, I have told you before – I cannot see how I can possibly consider marriage, when the situation with Maggie is as it is – and getting worse! Surely you cannot suggest that she is improving?"

For a moment, his mother's face was twisted with grief and pain – then that expression was firmly wiped away.

"Perhaps a little. These last few weeks, as the weather has warmed from the coldest part of winter, she has been stronger – strong enough to go outside, which has made her happier. But... it is most variable. Some days she is wracked with coughing such that she can barely move, sometimes her body rejects all food, sometimes she claws at her skin until it bleeds, declaring there to be an unbearable itching. Every time that I feel some hope, it is dashed again. But no matter Maggie's state, you must marry. You will need an heir, and your wife will simply have to do as you require, and keep Maggie's existence as private as we do. I... I cannot see that it will be necessary for too much longer."

Her voice caught, and Leon reached out to place his hand on her arm.

"I know, though I desperately wish that I could find a way to change that. But can you not see – that is exactly why I cannot marry – I must be patient, and attend on God's will in the matter of my sister. I would not force any woman I married to live with the challenges we do, nor require her silence on the subject – what basis for a marriage would it be, if I did such things?"

"A basis no different from that of most society marriages. And... I would hope that having a wife might bring you some consolation in the face of the difficulties we must deal with every day."

"Mother, no. I will not put a woman in that position – that would be taking my own comfort at the expense of hers. Do not ask it of me."

"I do ask it of you. But I also can be patient. In time, you will come around to my way of seeing things."

"I very much doubt that."

The rest of the carriage journey passed in silence, and they did not speak of the matter again that week, before his mother returned to Greenleigh Park.

The next few weeks brought nothing different – his mother came to town for a few days at a time, bearing slowly worsening news of Maggie, and Leon immersed himself in the matters before the House of Lords, whilst actively avoiding social occasions, and any conversation with Lady Iris Gardenbrook at those events he could not refuse to attend. By mid-March, he felt exhausted by it all, as if he walked in a world of perpetual darkness and misery, where black clad people struggled to ever smile, even though the early spring flowers were beginning to fill the London parks.

The few times he went to Greenleigh Park for a short visit only made it worse, as Maggie clung to him, demanding that he stay with her, that he play for her at every hour of the day. There was not the tiniest trace left of the girl his sister had once been, in this creature who now wore her skin.

*****

"Your grandmother will be attending the soiree this evening, with us. Lady Gillieston is one of her oldest friends, and she has decided that, after months shut away, she really must take this chance to see Lady Gillieston again."

"But... Grandmother has barely spoken to us for two years..."

Leon's mother nodded.

"Which in no way stopped her from demanding that I, as her daughter, ensure that you arranged for us to collect her tonight. I suspect that she will simply pretend that everything is wonderful, or that Maggie doesn't exist. I doubt that she has yet forgiven me for bearing a daughter who suffers so obvious and terrible a weakness, but it is more convenient for her to be able to call on me for assistance than not."

"I see. Then I will be as polite as is required, but do not expect me to greet her with any effusiveness."

"I won't."

They finished their tea in silence after that, and soon Leon went up to dress for the evening, after first giving instructions for the coachman to bring the carriage round a half hour earlier, to allow the extra time for collecting Lady Neelsham.

Two hours later, as he sat in Lady Neelsham's parlour waiting for her to come down, his tea long cold beside him, he wondered if he should have made that an hour earlier. His grandmother appeared to believe that the entire world could wait on her whim, and was now proving that her daughter and grandson would do as she wished, regardless. But perhaps that was uncharitable of him.

Finally, the sound of footsteps on the stairs presaged her arrival. Leon rose, as did his mother, and stepped out into the foyer.

"Let us be on our way then, Greenleigh – no time to tarry."

Leon gritted his teeth, and forced a smile to his lips.

"Of course, Grandmother."

He offered her his arm, and escorted her to the carriage. This evening, he could see, was not likely to be at all enjoyable.

No sooner had the carriage door closed behind them, than Lady Neelsham fixed Leon with a stern gaze, and spoke abruptly.

"Not married yet then? Disgraceful. You need an heir – and pray that whatever child you father is not afflicted with the madness that's taken your sister. A madness which does not run in your mother's side of the family, I remind you... you'd best choose a young lady of the highest possible breeding, and soon."

What could he say to that?

"Grandmother, I am not ready to marry yet."

"Balderdash! Of course you are. Just choose a woman – or are you being affected by this modern whimsy of expecting a love match?"

"Not especially. I am considering ladies, but none have truly appealed to me yet."

The carriage halted outside Lady Gillieston's home.

"Well tonight I'm sure there will be a few suitable ones present – why don't you just pick one of them?"

Leon shook his head, his heart sinking, but was saved from answering by the footman opening the carriage door. They went up the steps in silence, and once through the receiving line, Leon took the chance to escape from his grandmother's proximity on the excuse of greeting gentlemen he knew.

After a few short conversations, he turned to see Lady Iris Gardenbrook entering the room. She was, somehow, more beautiful than ever, even dressed in the stark black of deep mourning. His grandmother's words came back to him – *'just pick one of them'* – and, unbidden, the thought rose – *If I had to choose a woman tonight, it would be Lady Iris.*

That thought shocked him a little, and he turned his gaze away from her. She was temptation incarnate – beautiful, musically gifted and, he was quite certain from their previous encounters, not averse to his company. And if he was to be true to his stated intentions, that meant avoiding her, completely. He would not ever, intentionally, put a woman he cared for as much as he cared for her in the position of having to deal with his family.

Near him, a door opened, showing him a view of a hallway beyond – without further thought, he moved, slipping through the door and down that hall. Perhaps he could find a music room, and distract himself from the social horror that the evening seemed fit to be, and the temptation of Lady Iris' presence.

*****

Iris had been surreptitiously watching Lord Greenleigh from the moment that she had realised he was present. Every time they had seen each other for near two months now, he had been polite, distant, and impossible to talk to. Her patience was wearing thin, even as her determination increased. Perhaps tonight, there would be a chance...

Then, as she sipped at a glass of orgeat whilst her mother spoke with Lady Gillieston, she saw him quietly leave the large parlour by way of a door on the other side of the room – a door which, if she remembered rightly, led to a hallway which ran towards the back of the house. This was her chance!

She tapped her mother on the shoulder and whispered in her ear.

"Mother – I'm going to the necessary."

The Duchess gave a nod, never really pausing in her conversation, and Iris deposited her glass on a side table, and crossed the room, her heart beating hard. Once through that door, she set off down the hallway, wondering where Lord Greenleigh might have gone, and whether there was anywhere in this direction which might provide her with the chance to speak to him privately.

Then it came to her – at the end of this hall, there was a music room.... She almost ran down the empty hall until she reached that door, then paused, peering inside.

Lord Greenleigh was there! He settled onto the pianoforte bench as she watched and Iris took a deep breath, then slipped into the room, quietly closing the door behind her. Now, she was scandalously alone with him, and the small voice of reason urged her to turn back. She pushed it aside – she had waited months for a chance like this, and she wasn't going to waste it!

Chapter Four

Lady Neelsham, whilst to all appearances absolutely fascinated by the gossip which Lady Gillieston was imparting to her, was actually watching her grandson closely.

It had become patently obvious that her daughter was not going to do her duty and see the boy settled with a suitable wife – which meant that she would simply have to take on that task herself.

And now, as she watched, Greenleigh slipped out of the room. Was he actively avoiding the company of young ladies? She rather suspected that he was, and irritation flared – her granddaughter was lost to the ravages of a strange wasting madness, and she wanted to see her grandson wed, and breeding healthy children before she died, to wash that distasteful fact from her mind.

Lady Gillieston droned on, and Lady Neelsham counted the minutes. If he did not reappear within a reasonable time, she would gather up his irresponsible mother and go in search of him.

*****

The click of the door closing alerted him, and he spun around on the bench, annoyed that this sanctuary he had found was already being stolen from him, before he had even played one note. But what he saw shocked him to immobility, his breath caught in his throat.

Lady Iris Gardenbrook pushed herself away from the door she had just closed, her hand falling to her side, and, holding his gaze, she walked across the room until she stood beside him. Her soft footsteps were the only sound, although his heart beat so hard in his chest that he wondered she could not hear it, playing counterpoint to her steps.

For a long moment, neither of them spoke. He simply stared into those sky-blue eyes, watching clouds of some deep emotion flit across them, filled with the desire to reach out and touch her. But he did not. He knew that he should ask her to leave, or leave himself, that this moment was beyond scandalous in all ways. But he did not speak.

The silence stretched, until she smiled, that smile that left him feeling as if he had never been smiled at before, so bright was it, so devastatingly conspiratorial.

"I..." her voice was just a little shaky, "I wanted to speak to you, about... that... that duet... it was..."

Her words trailed away, as if she could find no way to express her feelings. He could understand that – he felt the same.

"It was. I agree."

She smiled again as he spoke, and he felt that somehow, what had just been said was so much more than the words used.

It felt like a declaration.

She swallowed, and her tongue flicked out to nervously trace the line of her lips – lips which, in that instant, he wanted to kiss.

"I want..."

There was that hesitation again, as if she were afraid that he would reject what she was about to say. In that instant, he knew that there was no possible chance of that – he would not, no matter what she said or did, reject her, despite the fact that every moment they stayed here together risked discovery and ruin for her, and the destruction of his carefully kept façade which protected his family's secrets.

"You want?"

His voice was as uneven as hers had been. Suddenly, as if she no longer had the strength to stand, she dropped to sit beside him on the pianoforte bench. There was not enough room, and he quickly caught her about the waist to prevent her from falling, even as he edged across and made space for her to sit properly.

At his touch, she gasped – but it was not a sound of horror or annoyance, more one of pleasure. It was a sound that heated his blood, and made his head spin in a manner that he had never experienced before. She tilted her head up and met his eyes, her face mere inches from his, her lips so close... He bent his head and brushed a kiss across those lips, a madness of the moment making him risk everything to taste her.

That thought made him pull back – madness? What if it lay in his blood too, as it did in Maggie's? She frowned slightly, then spoke at barely a whisper.

"Yes. That is one thing I want. But also, I want..." She moved her hand to trail across the pianoforte keys. "I want to play that duet again, as I would wish to play a thousand duets with you, forever, if each could feel even a tiny part as good as I felt when we played at Violet's wedding breakfast."

He wanted that too, he realised as she said it – a lifetime of magical duets with this woman, whose heart and soul seemed so utterly in tune with his. He could not say that, could not admit how right it felt to hold her, he should run from the room now before he did something unforgiveable, and doomed her to sharing the miseries of his daily life.

Music seemed far safer than words, and he could not bear to leave her, when they had the chance to create that magic again. He reached out a hand to the keys, slowly allowing his other hand to release her waist, sad only that the price of playing with her was no longer cradling her against him. Then, thighs pressed hard together, they began to play, the first notes of the piece filling the room.

It was as if his fingers on the keys declared his feelings, saying all of the dangerous things which he could not permit to exist as words, or even clear thoughts, and a great sense of rightness wrapped him around. It was a remarkable moment, but it lasted barely past the first few bars of the piece, before the sudden opening of the door shattered everything.

*****

Thorne stepped into the hallway of Lady Gillieston's home beside Merryfield, who had suggested that there were actually things in the library here worth seeing – and Merryfield should know, as Lady Gillieston was his aunt. They had taken but a few steps in the direction of that library, when a shriek rang out from further down the hall.

"What on Earth?"

"I've no idea – but I expect we should investigate."

They hurried towards the sound, which had come from an open doorway – a doorway which proved to lead to a music room, in which a drama of epic proportions was playing out. A drama in which his sister, Iris, appeared to be playing a leading role.

Thorne stood there aghast, listening, trying to understand what was happening, despite the sinking feeling which filled him, of a frightening certainty about the matter.

*****

Iris was floating. He had kissed her! And now they were playing. Life was, at that moment, perfect, no matter what might come later. It was a perfection which shattered into a million shards of horror seconds later, as the door opened, crashing back against the wall.

"What is the meaning of this? Greenleigh, what have you done?"

At the voice, they had both turned where they sat, hands dropping from the keys to leave a last, nearly discordant, tangle of notes fading away. Iris recognised one of the two women who stood there – Greenleigh's mother – but not the other, older woman – although from the look of her, Iris would guess that she was Lady Greenleigh's mother – Lord Greenleigh's grandmother. She could feel the tension in the man beside her, where their thighs still lay so close together.

"Grandmother. We are simply playing the pianoforte."

The old woman drew herself up and positively sniffed in disdain.

"Alone in a closed room, with an unmarried young woman. There is nothing simple about that. There is, however, everything scandalous about it. And for this kind of scandal, there is only one remedy. Marriage. You'll have to marry her."

Iris gaped at the woman in shock, then forced herself to compose her expression. She did not like being told what to do, especially by strangers.

But, came the insidious thought, *marrying Lord Greenleigh would not be a bad thing, surely?*

Still, she should protest, should declare the innocence of their actions, for, despite that kiss, it was not at all fair that he should be forced to something because she had sought him out here.

"But we were just playing a duet. Surely there can be no..."

"Of course there can, young woman, and there is. It's utterly scandalous, and now you'll have to marry him. What is your name? I don't believe that we've been introduced."

Iris swallowed, and drew herself up, determined not to be intimidated.

"I am Lady Iris Gardenbrook, daughter of the Duke of Elbury. Might I know your name in return?"

The woman studied her, and Iris thought that there was a spark of amusement in her brown eyes.

"So, you've some courage about you, have you? And a Duke's daughter? Things could be worse, could be worse indeed. Greenleigh, at least you've had the sense to disgrace yourself with a woman suitable to be your wife. I am the Dowager Lady Neelsham, and this reprobate's grandmother."

Even as Lady Neelsham spoke those words, behind her, in the doorway, Iris saw Thorne and Merryfield, and past them, a small crowd of other people.

If there had ever been any hope of keeping this from public knowledge, that hope was gone.

Iris turned her gaze back to Lord Greenleigh, who had sat through that exchange, silent beside her. What was he thinking? What would he do? Would he reject her now? For if he did, that would be even more scandalous.

Not that her father would force her to marry him, should she choose not to, but to not do so now would add a whole extra layer of scandal, and doom her to never finding a good match at all.

He met her eyes, and for a short time they simply sat there, ignoring everyone and everything around them. Emotions chased themselves across his face in rapid succession – some compound of sadness, regret, hope, and almost, desire? Then he smiled at her, a smile which made him seem magnificently handsome, and which steadied her – surely, he would not smile so if he was going to reject her?

He lifted his hand and gently cupped her cheek, as if no one else was present.

"Lady Iris Gardenbrook, if you will have me, I would marry you, and resolve this... difficulty... we find ourselves in. Will you be my wife?"

Across the room, she heard movement, and a flurry of whispering.

She held Lord Greenleigh's eyes, wanting to be sure, and finding certainty there – whatever it was that worried him, it was not her. She had dreamed that there might come a time when she would marry him, but this was certainly not the circumstance in which she had expected it to occur. Why he might have so rapidly acquiesced to his grandmother's demands, when he had been so avoiding of any contact for months, she did not know – but she would not turn aside such a gift as he had just given her, especially as she wanted him.

"Yes. I will marry you, and gladly, my Lord."

"Iris, are you certain?"

It was her father who spoke, and she turned back to discover him, with her mother and Thorne, but a few feet away. He looked deeply worried, as did her mother, and she knew that they were torn between wanting to avoid scandal if they could, and wanting only the best for Iris.

"Yes Father, I am certain. This is what I wish, no matter how... unusual... the circumstances."

Her father studied her, as if trying to see if she told the truth, then nodded.

"So be it then. It would appear that we have an urgent wedding to arrange."

*****

Leon sat there, an odd warmth filling him, a sensation he had never previously felt.

He had been mad enough to do as his grandmother had demanded, and Lady Iris had said yes.

There had been nothing but care for him in her eyes when she had done so, no hesitation. To have someone look at him like that, to want to marry him, filled him with hope.

He had not known just how deeply he needed to be wanted, until now.

Despite what he would face when Lady Iris first met Maggie, despite the challenges which would follow, in the moment, all he cared for was the fact that she had said yes, and he was quite sure that it was not simply to preserve her reputation.

Chapter Five

They had left the soiree rather rapidly after the dramatic events in the music room, surrounded by the scandalised whispers of the guests. Tomorrow, Lord Greenleigh and his mother would call at Elbury House, and arrangements would be made. There would, Iris knew, be a special licence obtained, and the marriage would be quiet, private, and very soon.

Her mother was annoyed with her – not, she suspected, because of the scandalous nature of events, but because the situation, combined with the ongoing mourning for the King, meant that there was not to be a large wedding – and her mother loved arranging large weddings. Now, as the carriage conveyed them home, there was an uncomfortable silence. Iris had never felt uncomfortable with her family before, and found herself quite lost and unsure of everything. Everything, that was, but for the fact that she was to marry Lord Greenleigh. That was something which she was pleased by, and most certain about, no matter what anyone else might think or say.

Once home, they went into the parlour, and called for a tea tray. The Duchess fixed Iris with her sternest expression and sighed.

"What have you done, Iris? I never thought that you might act so! You've always been so well behaved! You must go through with this now – there is no turning back."

"I am aware of that Mother. And... I am quite content with marrying Lord Greenleigh."

"How can you be? You barely know him."

"I know enough to be sure, Mother."

The Duchess shook her head, and turned to her husband.

"Then it seems, husband, that we must discuss many things before the morrow brings Lord Greenleigh to our door. We will leave you here, Iris."

The Duke took the Duchess' arm, and patted her hand reassuringly.

"Let us settle in my study, and plan it all out. Good evening Iris, Thorne."

The Duchess looked back at Iris just as they went out the door.

"Make sure that you rise early tomorrow – there will be much to do."

And then her parents were gone, leaving Iris sitting with her brother in the silent room. The mantel clock ticked loudly, and the fire in the grate crackled, reminding Iris that soon, this would no longer be her home – that this warmth and comfort which had always been hers would not be so, anymore. She would need to find new comfort in a strange place.

For the first time, the prospect of what she was about to do seemed a little frightening.

"Iris..." Thorne's voice was soft, "are you truly sure that this is what you want? There would be scandal, yes, but if you do not wish to marry him, we will find a way to break the betrothal."

She lifted her gaze from the flickering flames of the fire, and met his eyes. That her brother cared enough for her happiness to be willing to brave that sort of scandal, if she wished it, warmed her and reminded her that her family truly loved her.

"I am sure, Thorne. I... I think that I have been half in love with him since the very first time that I saw him, at Lady Ormondston's musicale. It is no hardship to marry him. I am sorry that it has come about in a scandalous manner, and that I have deprived Mother of her chance to organise another extravagant wedding celebration, but I do not regret it for one moment."

"Then I wish you well of it. You know that, should you ever need help, you can always call on me?"

"I do, but I do not expect to need to."

He nodded, but his eyes said that he was not as confident as she.

"Then finish your tea, and go up to bed – if we are to rise early and suffer the entire process of wedding planning compressed into a single day, then you will need as much sleep as you can get."

Iris laughed, for the image of her Mother trying to do absolutely everything in a single day was indeed comic.

"I will sleep well – and tomorrow, I will simply let Mother arrange as she wishes, and if anyone chooses to argue with her, let it be Lady Greenleigh, not me."

*****

The minister regarded Iris sternly as she stepped into the large parlour, but she barely noticed – her eyes went straight to Lord Greenleigh where he waited for her. He was handsome as always, and his dark blue eyes lit with pleasure when he saw her.

That expression sent heat through her entire body, reinforcing for her just how right this was, no matter how they had come to this point.

Her father led her forward, and the people in the room – just her extended family, and Lord Greenleigh's – all watched her, most with broad smiles. She stopped beside Lord Greenleigh, and her father stepped away, the symbolism of that moment not lost on her.

There was silence, and then the minister began to speak, his words binding her to the man beside her, irrevocably. It was exhilarating, and yet also frightening, that so short a timespan and so few words could change so much, forever. Despite that, she was still sure, in her heart and soul, that this was the right thing, that he truly was the right man for her.

And then it was done. She was married. Lord Greenleigh – Leonard, she now knew his forename to be - gently tipped her chin up, and brushed a soft kiss over her lips. She shivered, wishing that they were alone. But then he drew back, and their family gathered around, offering congratulations. Her new husband's grandmother said little – which seemed rather out of character, but Iris put that thought aside for later consideration.

The Duchess swept them all out of the parlour, and along to the ballroom, where tables had been laid out with food and drink. To Iris, it seemed strange – a disconcerting echo of her sister's wedding breakfast, only three months before. A rather ghostly, faded echo, lacking a vast quantity of people and activity. She looked up at the man beside her, to find him looking at her, his eyes full of the same uncertainty she felt.

She smiled, and reached out to place her hand on his arm, suddenly needing to feel his warmth, to know that he was real. He covered her hand with his. She swallowed, emboldened by that touch, and spoke softly, so that only he might hear.

"I admit that I am not sure what we might do to pass the next few hours – with only family present, it is not as if the event will go on as most wedding breakfasts do..."

His lips twisted into a wry smile.

"That is true, although... your family seems vast, compared to mine."

"We can be rather overwhelming, when we are all in the same place, especially now that all of my sisters have husbands too. But I promise you, as a family, we are universally prone to cheerfulness."

Something flickered in his expression, something almost of sadness, and then was gone.

"If that is the case, then I am most grateful. But... rather than us simply standing here, looking uncertain, perhaps we should do something which we know we will both find pleasant?"

He lifted his hand from hers for a moment, and waved to the side, where the pianoforte stood, its golden timbers shining in the morning sun which came through the tall windows. Iris felt her heart beat harder, and her breath catch. Now, no one could disapprove, no one would interrupt them, or try to stop them.

"Yes. I believe that we began a duet at Lady Gillieston's, which we were unfortunately prevented from completing. This seems a most appropriate time to remedy that issue."

His eyes lit with pleasure at her words.

"Then let us waste no time in starting, for if we hesitate, I am quite sure that someone will feel it necessary to come and speak with us."

He led her across the room, and they settled beside each other on the pianoforte bench, the heat of him so close beside her intense, and stimulating all of her senses. But, once they began to play, even that faded away, and there was only the music, and the effortless connection within it, to the man who seemed, when playing, the other half of her soul.

On the opposite side of the room, Lady Greenleigh stood with Lady Neelsham.

"I am so glad that he looks happy. I have worried, for years now, that my son would never have happiness..."

Lady Neelsham snorted almost derisively.

"Happiness? That's not necessary for a successful marriage. But yes, he looks so now, doesn't he? We'll see just how long that lasts once she is told the truth, once she meets your mad daughter. But there's no going back for her now – she's married him, and she'll have to live with it, whether she likes it or not."

*****

Iris released a huge sigh as they settled into the carriage. Opposite her, Lina scrunched into the corner of the carriage seat, eyeing Lord Greenleigh with deep uncertainty. Iris was glad to have her familiar maid with her, but it did mean that she could not yet speak privately with Lord Greenleigh.

His fingers twined with hers, offering silent reassurance, and she allowed herself to lean back, to rest against him, ever so slightly. There would be time enough for talking once they reached Greenleigh House – her new home.

That seemed a very strange concept, but it was now the truth. She would simply have to adapt. At least Lady Greenleigh – oh! The Dowager Lady Greenleigh, for Iris was now Lady Greenleigh! – had been kind enough to go to stay with Lady Neelsham tonight, and they would have the house to themselves, apart from the staff. Staff... staff she did not know, staff who were now hers to direct. It was another thing which felt very odd.

The carriage stopped, and moments later, a footman opened the door, and let down the steps. Lord Greenleigh stepped out, and turned to offer her his hand. She took it, and went down the steps, her eyes on the tall façade of the house before her.

It was of five stories, with a delicate iron edged balcony on one of the upper floors.

Imposing.

She shivered as he led her up the steps and, behind her, the footman helped Lina down, and then set about unloading her luggage. Most of her belongings would be sent over tomorrow - tonight, she had just the minimum necessary.

The door opened, and a line of staff awaited her in the marble floored foyer. Lord Greenleigh nodded to the butler, and led her through the door. For a large house, the number of staff was quite small, but Iris smiled, hoping that they were pleased for their master, rather than regarding her as an interloper.

Lord Greenleigh touched her arm.

"My dear, let me present the staff." He turned towards the staff, who stood in silence. "Ladies and gentlemen, this is my wife, Iris, Lady Greenleigh – your new mistress."

Iris drew herself up, and assumed her best smile.

"I am delighted to meet all of you. Husband, might I know the names of each person?"

"Certainly – this is our butler, Mr Jarrett, and this, our housekeeper, Mrs Earnshaw, and this our Cook, Mrs Harding. These are the footmen, Jones and Fogg, and the maids, Emma, Annie, Jenny, and Abby. You'll meet the stable master and the grooms tomorrow, as well as the kitchen maids."

Iris regarded each of them, trying her best to memorise all of the names.

"Thank you for welcoming me. I will want to spend some time with each of you over the next few days, to come to a good understanding of the running of this household. But for now, if we might have a tea tray in the parlour, and if one of you would show my maid, Lina," Iris indicated Lina, who had just come through the door, followed by a footman with her two trunks, "to my rooms, and the room that will be hers, I would be most grateful."

There was a moment of silence, as if they all assessed her, then Mrs Earnshaw stepped forward.

"Yes, my Lady. Abby, you see to the tea tray once Cook has it ready, and Lina, if you'll come with me, I'll show you the rooms now."

They turned, and the staff scattered about their work. Beside her, Leon released a breath – had he been afraid that the staff would not accept her orders? His hand gently caught her by the elbow.

"The family parlour is just up one floor – it will be far more pleasant than the big parlour down here, and Mrs Earnshaw will have made certain that the fire is laid in there."

"Thank you. Tomorrow, you'll have to show me where everything is. It is the strangest feeling to stand in a house that is now my home, and not have the least idea where anything might be found."

"I will show you everything... tomorrow... but – there is one thing I would like to show you tonight."

Iris looked up at him, suddenly uncertain of everything – what did he mean?

"Yes?"

"The Music Room."

The uncertainty retreated as she nodded, and he led her up the stairs.

*****

Leon had not realised just how worried he was about the staff accepting Iris' new status as the mistress of the house, until the moment when Mrs Earnshaw had paused before accepting her orders. Now, relief filled him as he led his delightful new wife up the stairs. That was one potential hurdle dealt with. Admittedly, those that remained were large, and might yet destroy all hope he had of happiness, but it was at least a beginning.

Telling her about Maggie's existence could come later, once they'd had a few days to get to know each other a little. He frowned, worried again – but this time, about the matter of the marital bed. He would not, he decided, make any move to take what was a husband's by right, until Iris made it obvious that she was receptive to such things.

He desired her, that was unquestionable – he had, almost from the moment that he had first seen her, and the alignment of their musical abilities had intensified that feeling, but he had no knowledge of her feelings on the matter. That she cared for him to some degree was obvious, and he was very glad of it, but he would not presume on the degree of that care. Indeed, perhaps a courtship was in order, now, given that there had been no chance for anything of the kind before their marriage.

How she might react to that choice on his part, he did not know, but he hoped that she would be glad of more time to get to know him, and for them to indulge in music together, before facing things far more emotionally complex.

They went in through the door of the music room, and he turned his thoughts away from doubts and darkness, to focus on her appreciation of the instruments she saw before her.

Chapter Six

"This is a beautiful pianoforte."

The slight echo of the last notes they had played faded away into silence. The room was dark around them, lit only by the single candle they had brought, but it seemed to Iris a comforting darkness, wrapped in the warmth of shared music.

"I commissioned it specifically for this room – music has always been my solace, no matter what else happens in my life."

His voice, as he said those words, seemed to carry a greater depth of meaning, to imply that there had been many things which had driven him to seek solace. A shiver ran through her, as it brought home to her just how little she knew about the man she had married.

"Should we not go to the parlour? If they bring the tea tray and do not find us..."

"They will assume that we are here – or that I am, at least – in that, I am a most predictable man."

He gave a soft laugh, self-deprecating.

Greatly daring, Iris touched his hand, and he curled his fingers through hers.

"Still, I would not like to start out by confusing the staff, who do not yet know anything of me."

He rose, drawing her up with him.

"Then the parlour it is."

The parlour was located closer to the stairs, back past a selection of portraits which seemed to watch them from the walls as the flicker of candlelight momentarily highlighted their eyes. What would those ancestors have thought of her? Did any of those pictured still live? She would have to ask about his family – but tomorrow would do. First, she had to get past the rest of tonight.

And whilst the music had settled her, reinforcing the rightness of her connection with this man, one thing concerned her. Would he expect, tonight, to exercise his right to her body? She was not at all certain how she felt about that, despite quite a few conversations with her married sisters on the subject of what happened in the marital bed.

It was not that she did not find him appealing – he was a very handsome man, and his touch on her hand made her breath come faster, inducing a most unusual warmth in her body – but, somehow, the idea of such intense intimacy, when they knew so little of each other, seemed wrong. She wanted to come to that moment without any uncertainty – in her, or in him.

The tea tray awaited them in the parlour, with the maid Abby, who looked completely uncertain of what to do next. Iris took a steadying breath – now was the time to quietly assert her position, again.

"Thank you, Abby, I don't believe that we will need anything else from you this evening." The girl bobbed a curtsey, looking almost relieved, and scurried from the room. Iris settled onto the couch beside Leon (for he had told her, earlier, that he preferred to be called so, rather than by his full forename), and spoke, as she reached for the teapot to pour. "It's almost as if they expect me to be disagreeable and unkind to them. Do you know why?"

Her husband – oh, how strange it seemed to say that, even in her thoughts – took the offered cup of tea and gave a wry smile.

"Not really. Perhaps because they had so little warning, and I had previously declared that I did not intend to marry at any time soon. Perhaps because my mother, whilst mostly a pleasant woman, can be rather dictatorial when stressed – a characteristic which I believe she inherited from my grandmother, much though she would probably deny it."

He stopped, and sipped his tea. Iris had the strangest feeling that he had intended to say more, but had cut his words short.

"Having seen your grandmother and mother together, I can imagine that to be true."

Silence fell between them, and extended, touched only by the soft clink of the cups on saucers, and the crackle of the fire in the grate. She wanted to speak of the night to come, to discover his thoughts and expectations, but was not brave enough to begin – did he feel the same? It was all very well to have wanted this man, to have been happy to marry him, but now, to her chagrin, she discovered that she did not know how to go on as a married woman, at all.

After some time, he set his cup down, and turned to her. She met his eyes, waiting, caught by the emotion that she saw in their dark blue depths. He lifted a hand to cup her cheek.

"I... Iris..."

He stopped, and for a moment, she saw her own uncertainties reflected in him. Then, with a soft groan, he bent his head and kissed her. It began softly, but soon changed to something deeper as his lips brushed hers, and his tongue teased its way into her mouth, exploring.

Heat flooded her, and she dared to lift her hand in turn, to tangle it in the hair at the back of his neck, even as she returned the kiss.

It was better than she had dreamed it to be, and its warmth eased some of her hesitation about the night – and the days - to come. Then, just when she had begun to melt against him, to want to explore a little further, he drew back, almost sharply.

"Oh!"

"I'm sorry... I should not have presumed..."

They spoke almost at once, then both paused. When Iris simply waited, her heart pounding, and disappointment filling her, he went on.

"Iris – I know that we are married, but... we barely know each other. It is unreasonable of me to presume that you would want my kisses..."

She studied his face – was he being chivalrous?

Did he truly care for her at all?

Had he married her only because of the compromise?

Had that kiss been a test – which she had failed?

Confusion filled her.

"I... I do not object to your kisses. You may remember that, just before the 'moment of compromise', you had kissed me, and I told you then that I wanted it."

She felt heat in her cheeks as she flushed, but they needed to speak of this. His fingers traced the curve of her face.

"I... yes, I remember you saying that. But still, it has all been very sudden, and I would not press you in any way."

A coil of sadness filled her – no matter her own hesitations, she realised that she wanted him to want her – and this felt as if, perhaps, he did not. She must make the best of it, then, until she could discover more of the truth of his feelings.

Surely, they could not be so perfectly aligned in music, and not be so in other ways?

"Tonight. I... will you... will we...?"

Internally, she cursed her inability to speak of such things openly. A small smile twisted his lips, and as she watched it, she ached for those lips to kiss her again. But it seemed that he had understood.

"Only if you wish it. We can spend as long as you like, getting to know each other, before we... Some men would demand it, but given the circumstances of our marriage, perhaps some time would be better for both of us – almost, a period of courtship?"

It was what she had wanted – so why did she suddenly feel disappointed?

"I think that is probably best."

He rose, and held out his hand.

"Then let me show you our suite of rooms, and you can choose the sleeping arrangements which might suit you best."

She took his hand, twining her fingers through his, and allowed him to pull her to her feet. He lifted the candle with his other hand, and led her from the room, through the darkened hallways, and up to the next floor. The door he finally opened let into a small parlour, with doors opening on both sides of it.

The room was beautiful, even though it was small, its walls painted a simple cream, and the chairs upholstered in a blue as dark as his eyes, which was also matched by a fine carpet on the floor.

"This is lovely!"

"I think so – I am glad that you agree. Come," he tugged her gently to the left-hand door, "the rooms on this side are yours – there is a dressing room over there," he had opened the door, and pointed across the room, "and beyond it is your maid's room, which has a separate door into the servants' hallway. And over here," he turned her back the other way, "that door near the window opens directly into my rooms – that is why the little parlour has no window – it thereby allows this piece of wall to exist, and this door. You may, of course, redecorate this room as you wish – but I would ask that you not choose anything green, if you do so."

Iris studied the space, which was also decorated in shades of blue and cream. It was a restful room, with a dresser, a large mirror, an escritoire, and two beautiful armchairs set before the fireplace. On the dresser, her own hairbrush and small personal belongings waited for her. The large window would, she thought, give a view to the back of the house – where there was most likely a garden.

"I have no wish to change it – it is beautiful as it is."

Something very like relief flashed across his face.

"Now let me show you my rooms."

He walked to the connecting door and opened it. The room they stepped into was twin to the one they had just been in, as far as colours and the position of everything, but the few items scattered about were obviously those of a gentleman.

"This room is also beautiful – you have fine taste in furnishings."

"I had these rooms redecorated after my father's death. Mother moved into another suite immediately, unable to face the memories that these rooms contained. Now, she spends the majority of her time at Greenleigh Park, anyway. So I had them redone to be as different as possible, and soothingly plain." He hesitated a moment, then turned, pulling her to face him. "I leave it to you whether you choose to sleep in the bed in the other room, or to join me in this one – for just sleep, until such time as you wish more than that. I... I hope that you might join me, for the simple comfort of warmth, if nothing more."

There was a catch in his voice, and a spark of hope caught within her – did he actually care, after all? Was that a need for her presence that she heard implied in his words? Or was that simply wishful thinking on her part?

The very idea of lying in a bed, right next to a man – and a man who had the intense effect on her that this man did – set her heart pounding. Yet they were married, and this should be an ordinary event – perhaps one day it would seem so, but at present, it seemed some strange admixture of scandalous and deliciously exciting. Could she? Could she actually do that, and... believe that they would do nothing more, at least for now?

And truly, would she actually object, if something more came of it? She was beginning to suspect that she would not...

*****

Leon waited, almost quivering with the uncertainty of the moment. What would she say? And if she agreed to sleep in his bed, would he be able to hold to what he had offered, and do no more than gently kiss her goodnight? He would do his damnedest, for he wanted nothing between them but kindness, and hopefully love. The moment when she was told of Maggie's existence, when she met his sister, would test that enough, without him doing anything to strain the situation first. But, he admitted to himself, he wanted to do more, far more, than kiss her.

That she was now his wife did not make him feel entitled to demand anything of her, even though the law gave him that right – asking her to cope with the existence of his sister, and to keep the family secrets was enough to demand.

She gazed at him with those sky-blue eyes, and expressions slipped across her face in quick succession – expressions which heated and chilled him with equal rapidity. He had to believe that, for a moment, he had seen desire there. She licked her lips, and he wanted to kiss her again, to trace the shape of her mouth with his tongue, to taste her.

"Yes. I... I will join you in your bed. I think that your company will make it easier for me to adjust to a house which is strange to me, yet which is now to be my home."

His heart lifted at her words. Perhaps he was far luckier than he deserved, and she did truly care for him, at least a little, beyond the connection which music had wrought for them. He knew so little of her, but instinct said that she was kind, that she would treat the staff well, and that there was at least a chance that her kindness might be capable of extending to Maggie too.

He would find out soon enough – they were to go to Greenleigh Park in two days' time, once she'd had a little time to adjust.

"Thank you."

Despite his best intentions, he cupped her cheek, and brought his lips to hers. It was the briefest, fleeting kiss, but it contained all he was beginning to feel for her, and all of his hopes for the future. They drew apart again, and her eyes glittered, as if with unshed tears.

"We will find our way, Leon..."

His name on her lips was sweet, and he smiled.

"We will. For now, go through to your room and call for your maid to help you prepare for bed. I will call for my valet, and when you return, I will already be abed."

She gave a nod, and turned to do his bidding. He did not move until the connecting door had closed behind her.

*****

Iris stepped back into Leon's room, her mouth suddenly dry, and a shiver of tension bringing an ache to her bones. True to his word, he lay in the bed, attired, from what she could see, in a simple linen nightshirt. Her thoughts went to the bare skin which lay beneath that fabric, and she wondered what it would feel like to touch him, to touch the parts of a man that were normally hidden from the world by clothes.

She pushed that thought away. She would not be discovering the answer to that question tonight. Tonight, all she was going to do was sleep – for, in truth, she was exhausted, as the stress of the last few days caught up with her.

He met her eyes, and she walked across to the bed, never breaking that connection. What was he thinking? His eyes held warmth, and yet they also held… doubt?

When she reached the bedside, he folded the covers back, inviting her in. She shed her wrap, dropping it on the nearby chair, and stood for a moment, aware of her own bare skin, covered only by the fine linen of her night rail. She felt exposed, vulnerable – but not threatened.

She slipped into the bed, and pulled the covers up.

He reached out, and took her hand, lifting it gently to his lips, and pressed a kiss to the bare skin of her wrist, where the pounding of her heart was made obvious by the pulse in her veins. Then he moved their still twined hands down under the covers.

"Sleep now. Tomorrow, we can begin to find our way as husband and wife, but tonight, just know that I take pleasure in the comfort of your presence."

"Thank you. Good night… Leon."

It was only the second time that she had spoken his name, since the marriage ceremony – she was sure that she would get used to it… in time.

Chapter Seven

Leon stared out of the window as the carriage traversed the familiar roads. Beside him, Iris also watched the London streets give way to countryside, with far more curiosity than he had felt for years. It made him look at it anew, and he had to admit that now, as March moved towards April, it was beautiful. For years, he had regarded the passing scenery only as markers of how close he was coming to renewed pain and sadness – now, the unaffected appreciation of the early spring scenes demonstrated by his wife almost gave him hope for something different.

That was, of course, likely foolish of him. It was not possible that Maggie would have improved. Each time he had seen her over the last six months, she had been worse. There were better days, as well as worse days, but the overall trend led inexorably to her permanent decline. And once Iris saw Maggie... he would not be surprised if she refused to live in the same house. He still had not told his wife about his sister – he had tried, but had not been able to bring himself to ruin the quiet peace of the last few days. In truth, he had lacked the words to explain.

But now, in a few short miles more, the truth would be revealed. His mother would already be there, for she had come back to Greenleigh House only long enough to gather her things before leaving for Greenleigh Park yesterday – and perhaps she would have been able to prepare Maggie for what was to come.

He turned away from the window, filled with a sudden resolve. He had to tell her now – they would be able to see the House from the top of the next rise, he had left it, utterly, to the last possible minute.

"Iris..."

She shifted on the seat, and met his eyes, hers full of concern at his sudden manner.

"Yes?"

"There is something which I have not told you."

Her brow furrowed.

"Something...?"

"Yes. I... I did not know how to tell you. And I apologise, now, for that fact, and for what you are about to face."

At that, a shadow of fear slid across her eyes, and he hated himself, hated the cowardice which had led him to seek his own comfort for the last few days, to pretend, for that short time, that Maggie did not exist, and that he might have a normal marriage. But there was nothing for it. He must tell Iris, and if she turned away from him, so be it.

He wanted her to stay, wanted desperately to have a true marriage with her, this woman that he had, somehow, come to love in a few short days – for that was what had happened, to his own surprise.

"Iris... I have a sister."

She frowned again.

"But... you say that as if it is a bad thing? And... I have never seen her about in society – is she very young?"

"No, she is a few years older than I am. And her existence is not a bad thing, no – but the state of that existence, that is a different, and far more difficult, matter."

She looked confused – as well she might, for he was doing a remarkably bad job of explaining.

"The state of her existence? I do not understand."

He swallowed, wetting his lips, desperately searching for the words which might convey the truth.

"She... she suffers from a malady that nothing has been able to cure. It is in part like a consumption, yet it has far broader effects – the worst of which is that, slowly, over the years, it has stolen her wits in many ways. It has changed how she sees the world – for the worse. She never came out into society, for by the time that would have been appropriate, things were too far advanced, and to do so would have wrought irreparable scandal and pain for all in the family. We have, in the main, kept her very existence a secret, for her own sake. I... must ask you to do the same, no matter what."

*****

Iris stared, aghast, her mind struggling to take in the words Leon had just uttered.

At first, she felt a surge of anger, that he had not told her this, before their marriage – for there had been time, although precious little of it. But then, even though the idea of him keeping secrets from her still rankled, another thought overtook the anger.

To keep such a secret, to live with it every day - it horrified her, for the very concept of seeing a sister suffer so was unimaginable. She had spent her life surrounded by sisters who were hale and healthy, cheerful, and always there to support her – the idea that he, with only a single sister, had then been deprived of that comfort, had, instead, needed to watch his sister suffer so very much was beyond abhorrent.

How could the world be so cruel?

The thought slipped through her mind that this at least explained the strange entry in Debrett's, the mention of a sister whom no-one had ever seen or heard of. That they had succeeded in keeping his sister out of the *ton's* awareness was remarkable – that also explained him, and his father before him, having a reputation for reclusiveness. She could not reasonably refuse the request that he had just made.

"I... of course. But can nothing be done? Physicians?"

"They have all singularly failed to do anything but make it worse. Mrs Withercombe – who was our nanny, and then became Maggie's nurse and companion – does the best she can, and that childhood familiarity means that Maggie will generally let Mrs Withercombe guide her. But it is difficult. I do not know how Maggie will respond to your presence."

"Surely she expected that, eventually, you would marry?"

"I... I do not think that the manner of her thinking is so rational anymore. And she is somewhat... attached... to me. My playing the pianoforte is one of the few things that truly soothes her when she is upset, and she has been used to having much of my attention."

Iris considered those words, and what they might mean. She had never needed to spend much time with a person who was ill, never contemplated what it would be like, or how a person might behave if their illness had damaged their reasoning. What if Maggie took a dislike to her? What would she do?

"I see. I will just have to do my best then, and take things as they come. I do understand, though, that you must help your sister – if one of my sisters were dreadfully ill, I would do everything in my power to help. Perhaps she will accept my help too?"

"I suspect that she won't - but thank you – for understanding my motivation, and for not castigating me for my ill manners in not informing you of her existence sooner."

"In truth, I wish you had told me – but I forgive you that discourtesy. However, in future, might I ask that there be no secrets between us?"

Iris watched his face, and the fleeting passage of emotion – sadness, a deep grief, and something more, something which seemed, for a moment, to be an appreciation of her. But perhaps that was her imagination. The sound of the carriage wheels changed, from the soft muffled rumble of earth below, to the crunch of gravel. Startled, she looked out of the window again, to see, as the drive they travelled down curved, a beautiful old stone house, painted soft gold by the afternoon light, and framed by trees dressed in spring green.

His words brought her back to him, and he smiled, aware of her reaction.

"I will do my utmost to hold to that. I have had enough of secrets in my life. The house is beautiful, isn't it? No matter the sadness I have suffered here, I can still appreciate that beauty."

They drew to a halt, and a footman hurried out to open the door and let down the steps.

"It is beautiful, indeed."

He stepped out, and turned to offer her his hand. Behind them, the second carriage, bearing Belling, Lina, and all of their luggage – which was substantial, as it contained a vast amount of Iris' personal possessions – drew to a halt.

"Belling will see that Lina is shown where everything is, and introduced to the other staff. Come, let me introduce you to the butler, housekeeper, Cook, and Mrs Withercombe. Mother is likely at the Dower House – she has chosen to live there, since father died, but Maggie could not be moved..."

His words left Iris wondering exactly why 'Maggie could not be moved' – was she too frail? Or was it something else?

He slipped his hand through her arm, and led her forward, but they had barely taken three steps when a green whirlwind descended upon them, tearing her away from his side.

"Do not touch him! He is my brother – mine! Who are you to presume so!"

So – not too frail to move, then. Not truly strong though, for the effort which had been exerted to thrust Iris away from Leon had left the girl shaking, breathless, and clinging to Leon for support. She was tall, and very thin – quite gaunt in fact. Her skin was excessively pale, and very smooth where it was not marred with sores, and her hair, whilst thin and limp, was the same rich colour as Leon's. The contrast of its darkness made her skin seem even paler. She was dressed completely in green, with a green bow tying back her hair. Her eyes were blue, but a faded shade, almost grey, like a drab winter sky.

Leon's voice was gentle as he spoke.

"Maggie, this is Iris. Iris is my wife – we were married a few days ago, in London. She will be living here with me, now."

The girl whirled to face him, wobbling on her feet as she did so.

"NO! She cannot! This is our home, and no interlopers are welcome. Send her away!"

Iris swallowed. This was, it seemed, going to be harder than she had thought. At that moment, Lady Greenleigh hurried up to them, closely followed by a grey-haired woman with a kind face who looked, Iris thought, to be exhausted. This must, she deduced, be Mrs Withercombe. Lady Greenleigh went to Maggie and gently took her hand.

"Maggie dear, you mustn't say such things. Iris will be staying – she is Leon's wife – he can't just send her away, and nor should he. You will have to be a good girl, and share your home with her."

Maggie glowered at her mother, and Iris could see that co-operation was unlikely.

"I will not!"

"Maggie, you have no choice – unless you wish to come to live in the Dower House with me?"

Maggie flinched, as if the words had been a physical blow.

"No! I can't... not there... It's... It's not green..."

Iris considered this strange proclamation. Maggie wore only green clothes – was there more to that than just her choice of attire for the day? And what did she mean by those words with respect to the Dower House?

"Then you must cope with Iris being here."

Maggie lifted her chin, looking for all the world like a slightly demented five-year-old who had been denied their favourite treat. It was a shocking thing to see on a woman of twenty-five or so. Mrs Withercombe stepped past Iris, with a quietly whispered, "I'm sorry, my Lady," and went to help Lady Greenleigh lead Maggie into the house.

Silence fell for a moment, then footsteps on the gravel made Iris turn. Lina approached, looking white with shock.

"My Lady... what will you do?"

Iris wanted to run away, to hide from the terrible revelations of the day – but she could not. And, truth to tell, the situation had just invoked her innate stubbornness. She would not be forced away from her rightful place.

"Go on as I had intended to, Lina, and make this my home. Now please continue – make sure that all of the luggage is taken to the right place, and that we have all that we need. I am sure that Belling can help you find the Housekeeper if anything more is needed. I will see you later – when I come up to change."

Lina straightened her back, obviously braced by the fact that Iris appeared unafraid.

"Yes, my Lady."

She turned back to Belling, who stood waiting with a small cluster of footmen near him, each carrying a trunk. Iris released the breath she had been holding.

"That was well done, my dear. And thank you for your forbearance. That was far from the manner in which I had hoped to introduce you to my sister, but now it is done. I apologise for her actions, and her words. She does not truly see the world sensibly anymore."

"I can see that her... condition... is rather worse than I expected from your description. But... why was she out here?"

"In spring and summer, when the leaves on the trees are green, we can get her to come outside, and walk in the gardens. She is better when she does, she seems stronger in the days when she goes outside regularly, even if she cannot walk any great distance."

Iris nodded, her mind catching on the word green, again. Why did green matter? She did not understand, and she had the feeling that the coming days would bring many things which seemed beyond her comprehension, at least at first.

"I see. Where are they taking her?"

"To her rooms – the upper floor of the west wing is all Maggie's domain. They will get her settled, and Mrs Withercombe will see if she can get Maggie to eat. Then, after we have dinner, if Maggie is still awake, I will need to go up and play for her, to lull her into rest. There is a small parlour up there, with a pianoforte just for that purpose."

"So... I will not have your company? Will your mother...?"

"Mother will go back to the Dower House, immediately after dinner. I am afraid that I will need to leave you alone, until we get Maggie to sleep."

Iris took a very deep breath, and for the first time, felt the prick of tears threatening. She would not allow this to affect her so – that would be to let Maggie win. But she had never felt so alone in her life. She could not deny poor crazed Maggie her brother's company, yet she felt abandoned by him, nonetheless. She would manage, and late tonight, perhaps they could talk, and she could learn more of this strange house that was now her home.

"I see. I will retire to our rooms after dinner, then and wait for you."

"Thank you."

He lifted her hand, and pressed a kiss to it, then led her into the house, where a silent footman waited, holding the door for them.

*****

Leon could feel his heart breaking, with every moment. Iris was being determined, and strong, but he could see how much Maggie's words and actions had hurt her. He had been mad to think that this could work, that he could have a true marriage, while Maggie still walked this earth. Now, having been foolish enough to allow Iris to stay in that music room with him, at Lady Gillieston's, foolish enough to allow his musical connection to her to carry him along into marriage, and to this moment, the harsh truth had become obvious – despite the fact that he had come to admire her, to love her, he had to expect that, after today, she would despise him for what he had done to her.

He pressed a kiss to her hand, then led her into the house. Through the introductions to the staff, she carried herself magnificently, as if the scene on the forecourt had never happened - pride rose within him then, and respect for her courage. Dinner was strained, and they spoke little – he suspected that his mother was beginning to wonder if him marrying had really been the right thing, no matter how much she had previously advocated for it.

As he went up to play for Maggie, he wondered if he would ever be allowed untrammelled happiness.

Chapter Eight

The faint distant sound of music had died away some minutes ago, and Iris sat, attired in her nightrail and wrap, her book forgotten in her lap, the candle beside her near guttered out, and the glow of the fire gilding everything around her with a red gold burnish. The small parlour she sat in adjoined their suite of rooms – a different configuration than the rooms in the Townhouse, but with just as much private space and convenience. It was also simply decorated in blue and cream, but this room had a window, and deep burgundy curtains closed out the night. She listened to the sounds of this house, so different from any house she had ever lived in – the soft creaking of floorboards in the hallway the only indication that someone approached. For a moment, fear assailed her, then she pushed that aside. Surely, it was Leon, coming to their rooms now that Maggie slept and he had been released from playing.

But the shiver of disquiet remained.

She turned sharply as the door opened, then sank back in relief. It was Leon. He closed the door behind him, and clipped the lock into place. Curious, she watched. This house had the most modern locks she had ever seen, and she wondered why. And why he locked the door – did he think that someone might attempt to enter, uninvited?

That thought brought another shiver of disquiet.

"I thought that you might have gone to your rest by now. It took far longer than usual to soothe Maggie into sleep tonight."

He walked across to her as he spoke, and settled onto the couch beside her. She set the book down on the small side table, and met his eyes.

"I wanted to talk with you, to understand more of Maggie, and what I can reasonably expect to happen over the coming weeks. I would hope to avoid scenes like that which we suffered on the forecourt today, if I may."

He took her hands in his, and she shivered again, but this time, from pleasure, feeling heat spread through her at his touch. Would he kiss her again?

“I wish that I had spoken to you of this when we were in London. I apologise again for my selfishness in not doing so. I… I just wanted that few days of my life to be separate from all of this…”

“Now that I have met Maggie, I believe that I can understand that desire. But… tell me more – how did she come to be like this? When did it start?”

“Truthfully, none of us are sure. When I was very small, Maggie seemed normal – to me, at least. She was always a little intense, but not irrational. We played together, as children do, and she learnt music with me. But it was never easy for her.”

“Did she play the pianoforte?”

“Only a little, yet she loved to share it with me. For a while, at least. She soon decided that I played so well, she was better just to listen to me. I only really began to see that something was not right when I was about ten years old, and she twelve. Before that, she had clear preferences for things – like the colour of her clothes – but was amenable to variety. At twelve, she became less tractable, and more obsessed with certain things. My father allowed it, spoiling her, for he had always been easily swayed by her smiles. But those obsessions grew, and her health faded away. She became progressively more frail, suffering congestion of the lungs each winter, and being easily prone to sores on her hands and arms. The only thing that settled her, even then, was her own rooms, filled with her own things – which became, over time, utterly dominated by the colour green. I have quite come to hate the colour green.”

“But… the irrationality… the… madness?”

“The madness. Yes, that is the correct word, sadly. That came slowly too. Over a number of years, she was less and less sensible, less and less willing to leave her rooms for any length of time, and more prone to fits of temper. When father spoke of possibly sending me away to school. She became inconsolable – so much so that it was decided to simply arrange tutors for me. When it came the time that we should have been preparing for her coming out, we were, instead, planning how best to keep her away from society, and protect her. By then, her health was very fragile. The times when Father took me to London, to meet my peers and to prepare me for the day when I would inherit, we only ever stayed away a few days before coming back here, or Maggie would become impossible to manage.”

“Then this last week…?”

“Made her quite distraught, and has no doubt left Mrs Withercombe utterly exhausted.”

“Is there no hope of improvement?”

“I do not think so. We have consulted the best physicians, but they all shook their heads and wanted to bleed her – which would only weaken her further. None could offer an explanation of the illness, or any real suggestions which might promote healing. So we have done our best, by observing the times that she is better, and the times that she is worse, and drawing our own conclusions. All we have been able to determine is that, if we can get her to walk outside in the grounds, it is better, and if we can get her to eat more meat, she is strengthened – but she will not walk outside in autumn or winter, and she barely eats, usually refusing all but green vegetables.”

"I have never heard of such a condition before."

"Neither had we, nor have we any reports of others suffering in a manner exactly like this." He tightened his fingers on Iris' hands, and swallowed, pain shining in his eyes. "But the thing that worries me most of all is not the effect of the madness on her, terrible though it is, but the fact that the madness exists at all. I ask myself, over and over again – what if the madness is due to a corruption of the blood, the kind of thing that can pass from one generation to the next? What if a child of mine might be so afflicted?"

He looked stricken, and Iris felt equally so for a moment, before common sense asserted itself.

"Leon... in families where such things have passed from one generation to the next, there has usually been sign of it in multiple people, and in the record books. Unless that is true in your family, it seems very unlikely that it could afflict a child of yours."

"But what if it does? How can we have children, if such a threat hangs over them?"

Iris swallowed, feeling shaken, but still shook her head.

"I do not know what it is that has done this to Maggie, but I cannot believe it a contamination of the blood. There must be another explanation of it. If no other in your family history has suffered so, then I am willing to think it unlikely that another will in the future. At this point, the history of it does not matter – what matters is now – and the fact that Maggie hates me and wants me gone. Yet she is your sister, and I know that you will not abandon her, as I would not abandon a sister of mine. I do not know how those things can be resolved in a manner that can let me live in this house with you."

He looked at her, and for a moment, his feelings were clear on his face – he looked utterly hurt, as if she had thrust a knife into his heart. Then he turned his eyes away from her, and went to release her hands.

"I suspected that you would feel so. I cannot ask you to stay..."

"No! That is not what I meant. I do not want to leave you – far from it. I want to stay, I want to build a life with you – I am simply saying that, at this moment, I do not know how we will manage to do that."

He stopped, mid movement, and she curled her fingers around his, pulling him back towards her. He met her eyes again, and what she saw there took her breath away. There was pure, naked desire, deep relief, and complete confusion, all entangled. It seemed that the desire won, for without another word, he pulled her to him, slipping an arm around her, and lifting the other to cradle the back of her neck as he brought his lips to hers.

She went into the kiss willingly, her heart racing.

She was drowning in that kiss, pleasure flooding her veins as his tongue teased and explored, and she, greatly daring, explored him in return. Minutes passed, and nothing else mattered but the connection between them. This was how it was supposed to be – their bodies cleaving to each other, wanting to meld physically, as they did so easily musically.

When they drew apart a little, both breathing hard, Iris knew that she wanted more – more kisses, and more than kisses. Leon regarded her with something like wonder.

"We will find a way, I promise. I do not yet know what that way might be, but I will not let my sister destroy what we have between us."

"I... I would like to explore more of what we have. More of... the physical..."

She felt her cheeks redden as she said it, but she wanted it said. He drew her closer again, and pressed a kiss to her forehead, then a trail of soft kisses down her face, until he found her lips. She parted them, and his tongue slid through that gap, caressing, exploring. She quivered. His hands caressed her neck, her back, her sides, and every touch was a trail of exquisite fire.

But, like everything where they were concerned, it seemed, the moment was shattered.

A pounding came on the door, accompanied by a high-pitched shouting. They jerked apart, startled to their feet, and for a moment Iris clung to him in fear. Then the words in the shouting became clear to her, and sense regained control of her mind. She pushed away a little, and stood straighter.

"Leon, let me in! Is that witch in there with you? Make her leave. She doesn't belong here. Leon...."

Maggie.

The words tumbled from her, an ever-increasing tirade, damning Iris as a witch and worse. Any desire that Iris had felt left her, as sharply as if she had been doused with freezing water. Even this, a supposed moment of quiet intimacy between them, in their own rooms, had been destroyed by Maggie's madness.

How could they ever risk such moments, when this could happen?

Leon gently lifted his hands from her, and went to the door. He did not open it, or move to unlock it, he simply spoke.

"Maggie, be calm. It is night, and time for you to rest. The whereabouts of my wife is not your concern. I will speak with you in the morning, but now, you must return to your bed."

"I won't – not until I know that she's gone. Throw her out into the night. Do it for me, brother. She does not belong here, she is not family."

"I will not. She is family, for I have married her. Now go to bed."

At that point, hurried footsteps came along the hall, and Mrs Withercombe's voice joined the conversation.

"Maggie dear, he's right – you must come to bed now. Tomorrow is soon enough to talk about how you feel, once you are properly rested."

"I don't want to sleep!"

Maggie sounded, again, like a small child – the tiredness was in her voice, but her words were all denial.

Mrs Withercombe spoke to her for some minutes, and finally convinced her, once Leon had promised to spend some time with her in the morning, to allow herself to be led away to bed.

They stood there in silence, until all sound of footsteps had faded away. Then Leon turned back to face Iris.

"Leon, is that why you locked the door? Because you thought that something like that might happen?"

"Yes. I am sorry. I had hoped..."

"I am beginning to think that hope is unwise. Much though I would like to continue from where we were when the pounding on the door began, I do not think that I could. I am not sure that I will ever be able to relax enough to be intimate when we are in the same house as Maggie."

Leon sighed, and she could see the misery in him, but after a moment he simply nodded.

"You are wiser than I. Let us, then, content ourselves with the solace of music, until such time as we can take a few days in London, alone. And let us try to get Maggie to accept you, at least a little."

Iris went to him then, and rose on her toes to press her lips to his for a moment, then stepped back.

"We had best sleep now, if we are to be fit to deal with the morning."

*****

Days passed, and the time of mourning for the King ended. Outside as Spring moved towards summer, the gardens blossomed, the trees attained full leaf, and the world was generally beautiful.

Had it not been for Maggie, and her impact on the entire household, Iris would have been happy. Wistfully, she thought of her family in London, where no doubt her mother was bringing the force of her expectations to bear on Thorne. With all of the girls married, he would no longer be able to escape their mother's focus on seeing all of her children well matched.

The gardens and greenhouses at Elbury House would also all be in bloom, and perhaps some of the rarer tropical plants might have been coaxed into flower for the first time. But she would not see them. After a long discussion with Leon, they had agreed that before they could go to London, before they could have time to themselves, it was critical that Maggie be convinced to accept Iris.

That was, unfortunately, a project which had so far been almost completely unsuccessful.

Faced with that fact, they found shared solace in music, and persisted, with his mother's, and Mrs Withercombe's, help.

That very morning, when they had come down to break their fast, Maggie had taken a knife from the table, and flung it at Iris, shouting 'go away, witch'. Iris had flinched aside just in time, and the knife had gone on to quiver in the heart of a pheasant in the painting which graced the breakfast room wall. Such moments were becoming more common, not less.

At this moment, she sat in the music room with Leon, the sound of their playing fading away into silence as they both looked out through the floor to ceiling windows at the gardens below. Down there, Maggie could be seen, walking about, a small basket on her arm, as she randomly picked flowers and small branches of greenery. Mrs Withercombe trailed her, watchful as always.

"When she is out there, like that, she looks so quiet, so innocent of all strong emotions."

Leon twined his fingers with hers, and sighed at her words.

"Would that it were so. But it is not. No matter how we try, nothing seems to bring her any closer to accepting you. Although... yesterday, when I left you here, playing, and stepped out to order a tea tray for us, I found her in the hallway. She looked at me as if I must be a ghost, her eyes round, and her gaze flicking back towards the room behind me. I suspect that it was the first time she had realised that you also played the pianoforte. She stood like that for a moment, listening, then turned and hurried away, back up to her rooms. But perhaps that way lies hope..."

Iris considered what he had said, her eyes still following Maggie in the gardens below. Was there hope that way? Was music the path to Maggie?

"Should we... should I...?"

"I think so. I think that, perhaps, you should come up to her rooms with me tonight, and play for her, as I normally do. If she will accept the soothing of music from you, as well as from me, then that will be a very good beginning."

"Let us try that, then, for I confess that I do not know what else we might attempt."

Chapter Nine

Leon felt more trapped than he ever had before. It was his own fault – he had allowed impulse to overrule sense, and brought about the series of events which saw him now married. But, just as he had always feared would happen if he took a wife, Maggie's rejection of Iris was intractable. There seemed nothing he could do to change that, nothing he could do to allow them to have even the faintest shadow of a true marriage – and he wanted a true marriage.

He had discovered that he loved his wife – impossibly, utterly, desperately. And the more that circumstances forced them to behave as little more than friends, the deeper that love became, and the greater his desperation. He had not professed that love to her, not in so many words, for he found himself afraid that, if he did, he would discover that her feelings for him were not of equal strength. He was quite certain that Iris cared for him – but did she love him?

He did not know.

As Maggie's health faded, so the ferocity of her madness seemed to grow – there were more outbursts of temper, more wild imaginings, and wild accusations. Music remained the only thing which could soothe her for any length of time, and he was grateful that he had that ability – and grateful also that he could share music with Iris, for that gave him music which was not tainted by the association with Maggie's illness.

Now, as he walked along the upper hall with Iris by his side, his admiration for her grew yet again. He could tell that she was worried, yet she had chosen to come with him, to play for Maggie. Her quiet courage and determination impressed him at every turn. Her voice, when she spoke, was barely a whisper, and a little shaky.

"I pray that Maggie accepts me, that she allows me to play for her, with you. But after this afternoon... I am doubtful."

Leon wanted to pull Iris into his arms, to kiss her, to somehow protect her from all of this – yet what could he do? Maggie was his sister.

"Mrs Withercombe will be more watchful, after that. I did not expect Maggie to attack you so."

"Did she truly intend me to fall down the stairs, Leon? Or did she simply push at me because I was there, and she wants me to go away?"

"I do not know. But you did not fall, thank the good Lord."

She nodded, and they went on in silence for the last few steps to the door to Maggie's rooms. In his mind, though, he raged at himself, afraid – had Maggie meant it? Would his sister truly try to harm his wife to such a degree? Was Iris' life in danger, if they stayed here? He could not answer the questions, but their very existence terrified him. How could he protect both his wife, and his sister?

They tapped at the door to the small parlour, and Mrs Withercombe admitted them. The doors between the bedchamber and the parlour were closed. Mrs Withercombe leant close and whispered to them.

"I thought it best to leave the doors shut until you start playing, my Lady, that way she'll hear the music before she has a chance to get upset."

"Very wise."

As Mrs Withercombe closed the outer door, Maggie called from the bedchamber.

"Mrs Withercombe, is that Leon? Open the doors!"

Leon led Iris forward and settled her on the bench, standing behind her, with his hand on her shoulder. She began to play, a piece which he had suggested as one that Maggie liked. After a few bars, Mrs Withercombe went and opened the double doors to the bedchamber. Leon met Maggie's eyes, where she sat in her bed, as if daring her to complain. What he saw there was shock, and defiance. Maggie opened her mouth, and Leon shook his head.

"What...?"

He shook his head again, harder, and Maggie actually lapsed back into silence, listening, watching Iris play. Leon prayed more intensely than he ever had before in his life, in that moment, begging God to help Maggie see that Iris was no threat.

Iris tensed ever so slightly under his hand, but kept playing, a smooth, uninterrupted flow of music filling the room. Maggie slumped back onto her pillows, and watched, eyes wide, as if debating whether she should stay there or leap up and push Iris away.

It took two hours, but eventually, Maggie slumped into sleep, not having spoken again. Mrs Withercombe slipped in to close the windows and the drapes, and to make sure that Maggie truly slept, before coming back to them and closing the doors between the bedchamber and the parlour. She gave him a nod, confirming that all was well.

"Iris..." the music flowed on, and he squeezed her shoulder gently, "you can stop playing now."

The notes died away, and she looked up at him, as if waking from a dream. Then her eyes cleared, and she gave him a tremulous smile. He helped her to her feet, nodded to Mrs Withercombe, then led Iris from the room. Neither of them spoke until they stood in their own suite, with the door to the hall locked behind them.

*****

Iris discovered that she was shaking. Whilst she had played, she had allowed the music to claim her, and had intentionally blocked out all awareness of anything else. But now, as the lock of their door clicked home, and Leon came to her, she felt unsteady on her feet. He pulled her into his arms, simply cradling her against him, and pressed a soft kiss to her forehead.

"Thank you, Iris. That went far better than I had any right to expect."

She looked up at him then, and smiled.

"How do you do it? My hands ache, from playing that long with no break at all!"

"I have had rather a lot of practice."

"I suspect that I am about to get a lot of practice too – for that is the only way to take advantage of this beginning, isn't it? For me to play for her on other nights?"

"Yes, I believe so. That is, after all, the first time she has been in the same room with you, without either a verbal or physical attack. And I would prefer that to be the usual way of things, rather than the exception. Her health may be waning, yet when she is agitated, she seems to develop a kind of hysterical strength – I would not have her hurt you, or herself."

Iris shuddered, despite her best effort not to.

"I would also prefer that neither of us be harmed. Leon... that room – the one glance I had into her bedchamber, all I could see was green. I know that you said that she was obsessed with the colour, but truly, until that moment, I had not fully understood the scale of that obsession."

"It is absolute. It is why she spends so little time in the rest of the house – I, and my father before me, refused to make the entire house green for her. Her own chambers are one thing, but the entire house – no. Equally, she will not go to live in the Dower House with Mother, for that is not green either, and Mother refused to make it so. In truth, I think that all of us – the staff included, have seen enough of green to last a lifetime."

Iris shuddered again, unable to imagine what it would be like to be so utterly fixated on one thing.

"I am very glad, then, that I own no green gowns. The colour has never suited me."

"I am also most grateful for that fact. I have no wish to be the kind of husband who is dictatorial, but green might have made me so."

Iris regarded him, wondering what kind of husband he truly wished to be to her – she knew that he cared for her, even that he seemed to desire her – but could he love her? Could they reach that point? She knew that she loved him, that she had from the start, but she had never told him so, was, indeed, afraid to do so, lest his response disappoint her.

She would rather have hope, than know for certain that she would never have love.

Not, she thought with a twist of dark humour, that there was any chance to find out – not whilst they resided in the same house as Maggie. So any internal debate she might have on the matter was rather pointless.

"Then I am doubly glad that it is not an issue. Might... might we sleep now? Today has been very tiring, and I suspect that the days to come will be no better."

"Sadly, I agree – although, in a few weeks' time, I must go to London – I have been away from Parliament for too long, and there are matters which need my attention. Perhaps, if you come with me, we might get a few days respite? I cannot leave Mother and Mrs Withercombe to cope alone for too long, but a few days, perhaps even a week, should be possible."

"Then I will look forward to that time."

Leon bent and kissed her – a soft kiss which quickly became more, but they soon broke apart, neither trusting that there would not come a pounding on the door at any time. They did not say it, but Iris knew it was there – a threat which hung over her, her marriage, and her hope of love – a threat which would not end, until the day that Maggie died – which could be years.

*****

Over the next few weeks, it became obvious to Iris that not only was the approach of having her play to soothe Maggie to sleep doing nothing to improve things at other times, but that Maggie was more cunning than she had at first seemed. When Leon's mother was there, each afternoon and for dinner, Maggie regarded Iris with venomous looks, but did nothing untoward. Lady Greenleigh was, apparently, taken in by this, and believed that the situation was improving. Iris could not bring herself to disabuse her of this notion – the poor woman had enough to bear, with having spent most of her adult life coping with Maggie already.

But when Lady Greenleigh was not there, Maggie took every opportunity she could to disrupt Iris' days, and to cause her physical harm if possible. It might be such simple things as attempting to trip her, or as overwhelming as the day when Maggie leapt upon Iris from the shadows under the stairs, and beat at her with tight fists, all the while screaming her hatred.

The staff assisted where they could, and Mrs Withercombe drove herself to distraction, attempting to prevent such incidents, but nonetheless, Maggie managed to find – or make - opportunities to vent her feelings on Iris almost every day. Some, Leon was aware of, but others, which occurred when he was not present, she could not bring herself to tell him of. He already bore so much, and seemed to feel a weight of guilt for bringing her into this situation in the first place, and she would not make that burden heavier.

The result of it all was that Iris became increasingly tired, increasingly scared, and the house seemed more oppressive every day, as if threat were bound into its very walls. She started at shadows, and flinched at sudden sounds. The only places which felt even slightly safe were their bedchambers, and the downstairs music room which she shared with Leon.

She was afraid – she could no longer deny it. She felt certain that Maggie intended her harm – that if the girl could not drive her away, then she would attempt to hurt her – perhaps even to kill her. There was cunning in that mind, but no rationality, no common human decency remained. Realising that did nothing to help – for she could not ask Leon to abandon his sister, and all she had tried had failed, with respect to changing Maggie's attitude.

Last week, Maggie had surprised Iris in the library, and when Iris stepped back from her in shock, Maggie had snatched up a pen knife which had been left on the escritoire near the window, and lunged at Iris with it. Iris had been frozen, unable to move, and had only been saved by the fact that Maggie's frailty meant that she was unbalanced, which caused her to trip on the edge of the carpet and fall. The knife had spun free from her hand, and slid across the floor to end under a cupboard in one corner.

"Witch! You made me fall. Leave – you do not belong here. Leave, or I will make you leave."

The words had been hissed, cold and sharp, even as Maggie had scrambled back to her feet, and staggered, half-running, from the room. Iris had stayed frozen, shaking, for some minutes, before she had quietly retrieved the knife, and returned it to its place in the escritoire drawer.

Then, this afternoon, Maggie had come upon Iris as Iris went up the stairs, and Maggie came down. At the point where they should pass each other, Maggie had reached out and tugged upon Iris' skirt, hard, so that Iris twisted, and nearly fell down the stairs. Only her proximity to the banister saved her, for she grasped it even as she slipped, and landed sitting on the steps instead. Maggie had wobbled, close to falling herself, but then hurried on, as if nothing had happened.

Iris was sure that, had she truly fallen, Maggie would have done nothing to save or help her.

Leon knew nothing of it, for he was out, riding around the estate to check on the tenant farmers. Now, she waited in the music room, hoping for his rapid return, refusing to allow her fear to send her upstairs to lock herself into their rooms, although that was what she most wished to do.

She could not tell him – could not say 'your sister tries to kill me', despite the terrifying fact that she had come to believe that to be true. What would he think – after all, he would rightly ask why she had not told him sooner. Or, even worse, he would regard her as hysterical – for who would expect a frail invalid of unsound mind to have the ability to attempt to kill?

She shivered, very glad that the promised trip to London was to happen next week. Surely, she could manage to avoid Maggie's attempts on her person until then? Perhaps, safe in London, she might find the courage to tell Leon all of what had happened. Perhaps, in London, they might have the chance to actually be as husband and wife?

She was no longer sure what she wanted, except to be safe.

*****

Leon rode along the lane which would take him back to his stables. In the distance, he could see Maggie's green attired figure in the gardens, with Mrs Withercombe trailing her. That was good – for if Maggie was outside, then she was not making Iris' life a misery.

It was a terrible thing to have to acknowledge, but he could no longer deny it to himself – his sister did not just dislike his wife intensely, she actively sought to harm Iris. He was torn, trapped by his duty twice over, with a need to protect and care for both women. And he did not know how to achieve that.

Maggie became steadily more frail, yet as her body's strength waned, so her determination to have her way in everything grew. He was afraid of what she might do. Afraid that, at the critical juncture, he would not be there to protect Iris, and to protect Maggie from her own actions.

He had not even discussed it with Iris – and he suspected that she had not told him of everything that Maggie had done - but, having avoided the conversation thus far, he did not know how to begin. He could not simply say 'I think that my sister is trying to harm you'.

He passed his horse to a groom when he reached the stables, and set off to the house, glad beyond measure that they were to go to London next week. Perhaps there, with only Iris, he might manage to speak of it, and between them, they might discover a solution.

Chapter Ten

They had been in London for three days now, and it still felt like an impossible dream. Last night, they had gone to a Ball at Merryfield House, and she had, for the first time, danced with Leon simply for the joy of it, surrounded by her friends and family, and secure in the knowledge that Maggie was many miles away at Greenleigh Park.

When they had returned to Greenleigh House, she had been positively intoxicated still, just by the feeling of it all. Exhausted, she had allowed Lina to ready her for bed, but then, with a courage fuelled by the looming threat of their return to Greenleigh Park, she had gone to Leon and reached for him. He had taken her into his arms and kissed her – a heady kiss full of passion and promise, which stirred every part of her. But then, he had gently stepped back.

"Iris, much though I would wish to kiss you – and more – forever, we must sleep – it is near 4 in the morning, and we have promised to visit one of your sisters tomorrow."

Iris had done her best impression of a pouting child, and he had laughed, kissing her again, more softly this time, until she relented and kissed him back.

"Very well. But Leon... I want you to know... you said that we would do nothing more than kisses, until I was ready..."

"Yes?"

His voice was deeper than usual when he said that one word, and what she had seen in his eyes gave her hope for the future.

"I think that I am ready. I want... I want to at least begin to explore what 'more than kisses' would be like, between us – and I want to do so this week, while we are here, and I feel..." she hesitated, unwilling to say the word 'safe' although it almost palpably hung between them, "...sure that we won't be interrupted."

Her heart had pounded in her chest, and she had waited for his response, feeling strange, and wanton, even knowing that such things should be normal between husband and wife.

He had not rejected her request, as she had feared he might, but had, instead, groaned softly before kissing her again, very deeply. The words he had spoken when they finally drew apart, breathing hard, would stay with her forever.

"Iris, if that is what you wish, I will be more than happy to do as you ask – for you are beautiful, and I have desired you from the first moment that I saw you. But, for me at least, once we take that step, every day will be torture, for when we return to Greenleigh Park, I will wish to continue – and to resist that, when you stand before me, temptation incarnate, will be near impossible."

Those words had made her shiver, as fire and ice ran through her veins. To be so desired....

It was more than she had hoped for, that raw honesty in his voice, that heat in his eyes, and she had licked her lips, unsure what to say in response.

He had cupped her cheek, and smiled wryly before speaking again.

"But no matter how much we may both desire it, now is not the right time – your first time should be a thing of joy, a time when you have my full attention – and right now we are both exhausted. Let us hold this intent until tomorrow night, and make sure that we retire early then..."

She had sighed, turning her head to place a kiss into his palm, then nodded.

"You are right, Leon, we should sleep."

Without further words, he had led her to the bed and, once they lay beneath the covers, had curled his body around hers, and held her as they drifted into sleep.

Now, as she regarded him across the breakfast table, the memory of it brought heat to her core. He smiled at her – a conspiratorial smile, as if he knew what she was thinking, and she felt a blush colour her cheeks.

What might the day ahead bring?

*****

Leon looked up from his plate to see Iris watching him. He smiled, remembering her words of the night before, remembering the feel of her, lying beside him in the bed.

She would tempt a saint.

It still astounded him that she was his wife, and his determination to have a true marriage with her had redoubled in the last few days, as they had simply spent time with each other, and with some of her family. He liked her family, unreservedly – which was a relief – one intense dislike was enough to deal with, and Maggie's dislike of Iris was on a scale beyond anything he ever wished to have to deal with again.

"Ah... I know that we have promised to visit your sister Camellia late this afternoon, but our day has just become somewhat more complicated. A message arrived while you were dressing, from my grandmother."

"Lady Neelsham?"

"Yes – she asks that we call on her at two today. And while it is phrased as asking, I know that she will regard it as a summons, and expect our compliance."

Iris paused, her expression uncertain for a moment, then she straightened her shoulders.

"I suppose then, that we must comply. Lady Neelsham is redoubtable, and I would not wish to have her dislike me – any more than she probably already does."

Leon laughed, and Iris looked rather shocked at his response.

"I would not think that, if I were you. I rather suspect that she likes you. I seem to remember her being impressed by your courage in the midst of our 'moment of compromise'. She does an excellent impression of ferocity, but underneath it, I have always found her to be of a far kinder character."

"If that is how she shows her liking, then I would not wish to see her genuinely angry..."

He laughed again.

"You will manage well enough, regardless – for she was correct in her assessment of your courage."

She stilled, setting down her coffee cup carefully, and regarded him, those sky-blue eyes wide.

"You... you think that I have courage?"

"Of course I do, Iris. You stood up to my grandmother from the start, you face Maggie's aggression and dislike with calm determination, and you do not complain. Most women would have fainted away with a fit of the vapours, and then, upon being revived, told me that they were leaving."

She blinked, as if his words startled her.

"Leon! I would never leave you! And I do not faint. Nor do any of my sisters – although we may have been seen to wobble a little, occasionally."

His heart soared – he had not been seeking such a declaration from her, and her instantaneous rebuttal of the idea of leaving him filled him with warmth, with hope. She had said those words in a completely unstudied manner, as simply a declaration of fact. If she felt so strongly... was there hope that she might come to truly love him?

*****

Despite Leon's faith in her courage, the sight of Lady Neelsham's imposing home made her feel quite queasy. It was, of course, in the best neighbourhood.

The nearby homes were equally impressive, and despite having grown up living in just such a street, Iris felt somehow made small. They stepped down from the carriage, and soon stood on the doorstep.

Leon rapped the knocker firmly against the black painted door, and the echo of the sound came back to them, faintly, accompanied by footsteps. Iris stood straighter and made sure that her best socially polite smile graced her face.

The door opened, and a grey-haired butler regarded them seriously for a moment, before breaking into a broad smile.

"Lord Greenleigh! It is a pleasure to see you again. Please, do come in – Lady Neelsham is in the large parlour." He led them up the stairs, and to the door of a room which must, from its position, look out over the square in front of the house. He tapped on the door, and entered when bidden. "Lord and Lady Greenleigh, my Lady."

Then he stepped aside, and Leon led her through that door.

For a moment, she was stunned by the beauty of the room she now stood in. Double glass doors stood open onto a balcony, and she could see the gardens in the Square laid out below. Tall windows either side of those doors let in yet more light, and the entire room was decorated in tones of gold and cream. It was like being in a pool of sunlight.

Then Leon moved her forward, and her eyes came to focus on Lady Neelsham, who had risen from her chair to greet them. In that instant, Iris was acutely aware that she was being studied by the older woman.

"I can see that you like my parlour. Good, I would be worried about your sensibilities if you didn't."

"Grandmother. It's good to see you again."

Lady Neelsham was still watching Iris, who swallowed, and chose to approach this as improperly as Lady Neelsham just had.

"Yes, Lady Neelsham, I very much like your parlour. Thank you for inviting us to call on you."

Beside her, Leon made the strangest small sound, almost as if he had stifled a laugh. Lady Neelsham continued to study her, as if expecting her to look away, or display some sign of nervousness. Iris, provoked to stubbornness by that look, held perfectly still, meeting the Lady's eyes, and waited.

After an interminable silence, Lady Neelsham laughed, looking at Leon for a moment.

"She'll do, Leon." She turned back to Iris. "I did wonder if that flash of courage when we caught you two together at Lady Gillieston's was truly in your character, or an aberration. It would appear that you are consistent. I sent for tea the moment that I saw your carriage approaching around the Square – it should be here in a moment. Please do sit."

Lady Neelsham waved them to the couch which was placed opposite her chair, and Leon led Iris to it. She dropped to sit on it as elegantly as she could, given that her legs were near giving out beneath her from the stress of the moment. As she did, there came a tap at the door, and a maid brought in a large tea tray, which she set down on the table between them and Lady Neelsham. All conversation stopped whilst the maid left and Lady Neelsham poured the tea, as they each selected cakes from the heaped platter before them. Only once tea had been sipped, and Iris had tasted the cakes – flavoured with vanilla and cinnamon, and quite delicious – did Lady Neelsham speak again. This time, it was Leon that she gazed at, and Iris had the feeling that Lady Neelsham expected him to be unhappy with her next words.

"And is your mad sister any better? Or is that too much to hope for?"

Iris felt Leon stiffen, and she knew that he did not like Maggie to be spoken of so disparagingly. Then she felt him sag a little out of that stiffness, as a sigh escaped him.

"That is too much to hope for. She becomes more frail every day, and her mental state varies, but I could not describe any of it as truly 'better' in any way."

Lady Neelsham gave a sharp nod, and turned her eyes to Iris.

"And you, my girl, how do you cope with the mad one? Does she accept you?"

Before she could stop herself, Iris gave a sharp, mirthless laugh.

"She does not accept me, and makes that abundantly clear at every turn. I have tried to encourage her towards at least bare tolerance, but even that seems impossible. I cope, because I am Leon's wife, and she is his sister. If it were one of my sisters so stricken, I would not abandon her – I cannot expect him to abandon his sister. Nor would I abandon him – I knew well what I did when I married him, even if no one warned me of Maggie's plight at the time. But, if we are to be brutally honest, as it seems you desire, then I will most freely admit that it is not easy."

She stopped, wondering if she had just gone entirely too far – at Lady Neelsham's question, all of her frustration with the situation had risen up within her, driving her to speak far more bluntly than she should have. Those sharply intelligent eyes studied her, as if she were some scientific specimen.

"You, my girl, are refreshing. I long ago abandoned all hope of getting honesty from most of the *ton*, but it appears you are an exception. And if the mad sister has not sent you running from Leon's estates to hide with your family, then you're made of sterner stuff than I'd expected. But..." here she paused, and sipped her tea, before continuing in a softer voice, "...if, for whatever reason, you do find yourself in need of... respite... then you may come to me. Sometimes, the safest thing to do is retreat, at least temporarily."

Iris felt her jaw drop, and forced herself to close it, to smile softly, and then to answer. That answer was also honest, and improper – but it was called for.

"Lady Neelsham, I do not know if that offer is a kindness, or a condemnation. If you think that I would so abandon Leon, if things became... difficult, then you underestimate me, and perhaps I should be insulted. On the other hand, if you offer in a genuine wish to help, should true disaster befall – God forbid – then I thank you – for I have gained the impression that there are few people you might make such an offer to."

The older lady froze in place for a moment, her eyebrows rising. Then, after carefully setting down her teacup, she allowed herself to laugh. It was a genuine laugh, unrestrained, and she clapped her hands together once in delight. Leon reached out and twined his fingers with Iris', squeezing gently. When the laughter subsided, Lady Neelsham spoke again.

"I like you. And there are not many young women I like. It was a genuine offer, but the more I hear from you, the more I think that you have the strength to deal with all of this after all. Whatever happens, grant me the favour of always being this honest with me in future. And... make my grandson happy. He does not deserve the difficulties he has been forced to bear."

What could she say to that? Her heart filled with pity for the woman before her, who had seen her loved granddaughter transform into a monster. Lady Neelsham did not deserve that burden, any more than Leon did.

"I... I will do my best, my Lady, and pray that it is enough."

"I begin to believe that it will be. But let me say one more thing – one more thing that politeness says I should not, yet I am beyond tired of it haunting us all and no one speaking of it. My granddaughter is dying – I know that, and you know that. It is a slow painful death, of the body and the mind. I, for one, will be grateful when that agonising process is over. One should not wish anyone dead, yet when the inevitable is plain to see, it is not unreasonable to wish suffering ended. When Maggie dies, my daughter will finally be freed, but I am quite certain that she will also be lost and despairing. Promise me, that when that time comes, you will help her, as well as her son, your husband?"

Iris allowed the words to sink into her mind. They were cold hard words, yet they echoed the thoughts she had considered so often of late. Maggie's death was inevitable, her steady decline obvious, yet no one spoke of it, as if by not saying the words, the truth of them could be avoided. Well, now they were spoken. Leon's hand had clutched hers harder, so hard that it hurt, as his grandmother spoke. Still, she returned that pressure.

"Lady Neelsham, I thank you for saying the words that none of us want to be real. And I promise you that I will do whatever I can to support everyone through the dark days ahead."

Chapter Eleven

"A child, Camellia?"

"Yes, in a few months from now. You will be an aunt, Iris, again."

"I can see by looking at you, that you are well, and happy."

"I am – I have had none of the sickness in the mornings that Lily suffered with hers – and for that I am most grateful! But... perhaps you will soon be increasing as well?"

Camellia regarded her sister with a raised eyebrow, and Iris had to force herself to keep her expression cheerful and undisturbed, despite the fact that Camellia's words made her want to squirm on her seat. She could not admit to her sister that now, even after more than two months of marriage, they had not... She waved a hand as if those words had not just struck straight to her heart.

"I am sure that it will happen when God wills it."

Camellia regarded her closely for a moment, then apparently chose to let the subject drop, much to Iris' relief. Beside her, Leon released a breath, and she realised that he had been holding it, waiting to see where that conversation might take them. At that moment, the servants came to clear that course from the table, and all conversation paused while the dishes were cleared, and the dessert course was brought in.

Once it was served, Damien turned his attention to Leon.

"Tell me a little of your plans for your estates, Greenleigh – are you tied to the traditional approaches to how your land is farmed, or exploring the new ideas?"

Iris almost laughed – that question told her, in an instant, that Damien and Camellia had been visiting Hyacinth and Kevin recently, for they had embarked on a program of modernisation at Chester Park. She realised, as she had that impulse, that she was just as interested in Leon's answer as Damien might be – for she had no idea of his plans. Her life had been so constrained by Maggie, and the difficulty of her days, that they had never spoken of such things.

"I must confess that I am only just beginning to have any plans. During the year of mourning for my father, my attention went to simply coming to know the tenants and the estates properly, and the last few months I have been rather... distracted... from such matters."

Iris froze for a moment – had he just implied that she was the distraction? That was certainly how Damien and Camellia appeared to have taken it. Perhaps that was for the best. She smiled, then took a mouthful of the excellent pudding before her, waiting to see what would be said next.

"Distracted? Well, I suppose that's understandable."

For a moment, Damien and Camellia met each other's eyes, and Iris envied them what she saw in that look. It was full of love – love untrammelled by the need to bow to anyone else's requirements. There was a moment of silence, then Leon spoke again.

"Over the last few weeks, I have concluded that things need to change – some of my lands are less fertile than they used to be, and some are overgrazed. I am looking at what I might do in terms of enclosure, without limiting my tenant farmers', and the villagers', ability to survive well. And perhaps, in one area, there might be benefit to be had from some irrigation. Introducing change will need to be done gently, but I think it can be done."

Iris felt her heart fill with pride for this quiet man she had married – that he thought first of not harming his tenants and the villagers was wonderful, and showed, yet again, how kind a person he was. The conversation flowed on, and for a little, Damien and Leon spoke of the matters which had been discussed in the House of Lords of late. Iris mostly just listened, but she was aware, as she did so, of the way that her sister looked at her own husband. Camellia was so obviously happy, and Iris wondered if she, herself, would ever look like that. She hoped so, but when that chance might come... she did not know, but just thinking of it made her even more determined that, that very evening, once they got back to Greenleigh House, she would pursue the matter of kisses, and more.

And, perhaps, the matter of how they might deal with Maggie. Perchance, that conversation should come before they allowed themselves to be distracted by the physical. Iris felt compelled to tell Leon the truth of everything that Maggie had done, and to explain her own hesitation to speak of it, before now. She wanted no secrets between them – wasn't that what she, herself, had asked for?

After dinner, she went to the parlour with Camellia, as Damien carried Leon off to his study, for port, and for further discussion of estate management. Damien, being Duke of Blackwater, had very extensive estates, and was a man open to new ideas, as well as to preserving history – no doubt they would dive deep into one topic or another, and lose track of time. Once a tea tray had been delivered, and the maid left the room, Camellia fixed Iris with a stern expression – one which bore a remarkable resemblance to their mother's expression, when she wanted to ensure that they did as asked. Iris burst into laughter.

"Camellia! You look just like Mother! Except... I don't for one moment believe that you are actually that stern – you are far too kind-hearted by nature to deliver that look convincingly."

"Oh! Drat! I have been practicing – after all, I will soon have a child who will no doubt warrant such looks at times. Have I failed that badly?"

"No, not really – it's just that I know you too well. But... why are you giving me that look now?"

Iris rather suspected that she actually knew why, but she wasn't about to admit it.

"Because you are hiding something, Iris. You never could do that well – at least not from your sisters. Tell me the truth – are you happy with Greenleigh? Is there a problem of some kind?"

Iris delayed the inevitable by taking a bite out of a small cake.

"Mmmmm, lemon cakes – did you convince the Cook at Elbury house to give your Cook the secret recipe?"

"I did. It took a great deal of persuading, and giving her niece a position as a maid, but I did it."

"Good for you."

Camellia gave her that look again.

"Iris, I do believe that you are prevaricating intentionally."

"I... umm..."

"Just tell me. If there is a problem, perhaps I can help?"

Should she admit any of it? Perhaps, just a little – just enough to get Camellia to stop asking. And perhaps she would plead tiredness, and see if they might go home early – for the conversation she needed to have with Leon was more important than this one.

"I am very happy that I married Leon. We are still finding our way with each other – after all, it was very sudden. And adjusting to his family has taken more out of me than I expected. His grandmother, for one, is redoubtable. But there is nothing at this point that needs your help – although thank you for offering."

No matter how many people offered her an escape, Iris knew that she would not take it – she would solve her problems with Leon's help, and stand by him. Camellia studied her, then gave a little shake of her head.

"I do not know that I entirely believe you, Iris. But I will not pry. It is just that I wish you to be as happy as I am, to have the kind of love that I have with Damien."

"Camellia, I assure you – I fully intend to have that kind of love too."

*****

Leon sat close beside Iris as their carriage took them back to Greenleigh House. By the standards of the *ton*, it was still early – well before midnight – and his heart beat a little harder at the memory of those kisses the previous night – might they...? He twined his fingers through hers, and she looked up at him, smiling. The silence held them, but it was a comfortable silence.

He remembered the question that Blackwater had asked him, earlier in the evening – 'was he happy? Was Iris happy?' – he had said yes, but was that the truth? Not really. How could either of them be truly happy whilst Maggie's actions pushed them apart? He needed to bridge that gap, needed to speak to Iris of the truth of his feelings – he had promised her 'no secrets' yet here he was, not speaking of the truth of his suspicions about Maggie. When they got home, he would tell her – everything. And then, perhaps, they might finally indulge in exploring each other, physically.

The carriage drew to a stop, and they stepped down, going up to their front door as the carriage rolled away behind them, to be taken around to the coachhouse in the mews behind the house. The footman on duty opened the door and, once inside, they asked that a tea tray and a port decanter be sent up to their private parlour. Twenty minutes later, both attired for bed, and sitting with the tea tray beside them, that silence remained. Leon sipped tea, and then set the cup down – he should speak first, and begin this – after all, it was the fact that he had not told her of his sister, before they married, which had brought them here.

"Iris... I.... there are things we should speak about."

"Yes. I agree. But after we talk..."

She set her cup down also, and leant to him, bringing her lips softly to his, for the veriest brush of a kiss.

It was enough to send heat through him with an intensity that took his breath away.

"Iris, I promised you 'no secrets' - but I have not told you everything of late. Not everything of my feelings, nor everything of what I believe is happening with Maggie. I apologise for that – I want what is between us to be honest. And the very first thing that I must tell you is how I feel about you."

She did not move from where she sat, nor do anything at all, yet he could see the tension in her – she was afraid of what he might say. In that moment, he cursed himself – he should have spoken to her of his feelings from the first point that he had truly come to recognise the scope of them.

"And... how do you feel about me?"

Her voice was low, a little shaky. He bent forward and brushed his lips over hers, as softly as she had kissed him just minutes before.

"I love you."

The words were baldly stated. Were not such declarations supposed to be flowery, and full of poetic language? Yet he had no words like that, only the bare truth. Her sky-blue eyes widened, and her lips opened on a soft gasp.

"You...love me? I... I had hoped..."

"I love you. I think that I began to love you the very first time that we played together. It was as if that opened a door in my soul, and once opened, it could not be shut. And the more time I have spent with you, the deeper that love has become."

"Leon... I... I love you, also. From the very first moment that I saw you play at Lady Ormondston's musicale, I knew that I loved you."

His heart raced, and a bubble of joyous laughter rose within him.

"I am doubly a fool then, for not telling you my feelings sooner – but I was afraid – afraid that you might not be able to love me, that you had only chosen to marry me to avoid scandal."

"Then we are fools together Leon, for I was afraid to tell you, lest you had offered for me just to do the honourable thing. I knew that you at least cared for me, but I was afraid that I might discover that that caring did not extend to the point of love."

He studied her for long moments, allowing the meaning of her words to sink in, allowing his heart to expand, and the fear that he had carried for so long to drain away.

Then he kissed her.

Properly. Deeply. With every ounce of his being.

When they drew apart, he was dizzy with it still. But he could not allow this happiness to prevent the rest of the conversation, for to do so would leave this tarnished by secrets.

"Iris... before we go any further, I must speak to you of Maggie. I did not wish to believe her capable of it, but I have come to the painful conclusion that she has genuinely been trying to cause you actual physical harm, intentionally. I must beg your forgiveness for my failure to prevent that from happening. It is a man's responsibility to protect and care for his wife, and I feel that I have failed you. Equally, I have failed my sister, by not protecting her from herself."

"Leon, I do not judge it that way. I know that you cannot abandon your sister! But... I agree that something must be done, for I do not know that I can go on as it has been. For I have not told you all of what has happened. I did not intend it as secrets between us – I simply could not bear to burden you further. Nonetheless, it has become as if a secret."

"What has she done, that I don't know of?"

Pain and dread twisted within him – he had suspected that Maggie had done more than he had been aware of, but now, to have it confirmed.... Iris looked away for a moment, taking a sip of the cooling tea. Then she turned back to him.

"She waits until neither you, nor your mother, are there and she slips away from Mrs Withercombe to wander the house until she 'accidentally' comes across me, when no one else will see. Then she trips me, or tries to make me fall on the stairs, or attacks me with whatever sharp object may be to hand. She has even flung herself upon me, and beaten at me with her fists, until the footmen had to physically remove her, and take her back to Mrs Withercombe. If she were stronger... then I might have suffered true damage. It has come close, a number of times. I am sorry that I did not tell you sooner, but I kept hoping that it might change. It has not, and lately, I have begun to fear that she wishes to kill me."

Shock coursed through Leon at her words.

"Kill you? That is... utterly beyond the pale. I know that she is no longer a rational being, and I had concluded that she wished to harm you, but to kill..."

"I denied it to myself until shortly before we came to London, but then, I could no longer pretend. Here I feel safe. There, I do not."

He stared into the fire for some time, his heart shattering within him. There was only one conclusion to draw from her words. His sister no longer existed. Her body still walked and talked but the person within it, the sister he had loved, was gone, irrevocably stolen from him by the disease which ravaged her body and mind. That recognition simplified things, in an odd way, made it easier to see what he must do.

"Iris, I can see only one solution for this. If we cannot get her to see that what she does is wrong, then I will lock her away -not in the rooms she now has – that would be too difficult, but in the East wing of that floor, which connects to the rest of the house by just one door – there are not even servants' stairs or corridors into that floor of the East wing. If she is truly that completely no longer my sister, then she must be locked away to protect both you, and her, from the consequences of her madness."

Chapter Twelve

Iris looked out of their breakfast room window at the garden, full of flowers. It was a perfect May day, after a perfect night... in bed with her husband – who loved her, as she loved him. Now, she understood that look on Camellia's face in a whole new way. The only thing about the day which was not perfect was the fact that it was the day before they would have to return to Greenleigh Park. The thought of Maggie, and the conversation which Leon intended to have with her, stole the brightness from the day in an instant.

Whilst the fact that Leon was willing to lock Maggie away if that was what it took to protect Iris made her feel a little safer, it also made her feel deeply guilty. She could not shake the feeling that, somehow, she should have been able to avoid this situation, should have been able to discover a solution which did not force Leon to choose between his wife, and his sister. For that was what he was doing, and it broke her heart to see him make that choice, no matter how much Maggie intended her harm.

She could not imagine it – what if it had been one of her own siblings who threatened Leon? What choice would she have made?

She moved away from the window with a sigh, and went to fill her plate at the sideboard, just as Leon entered the room. She turned, and smiled at the sight of him, her heart racing and her breath coming short as memories of the night before rushed through her mind.

He returned the smile and settled into a chair, accepting a cup of coffee from the footman. Iris joined him at the table.

"Have you eaten, Leon?"

"I have – some time ago. I left you sleeping, for you looked so very peaceful, but I've been up for an hour or more, dealing with all that must be organised for our return to Greenleigh Park."

The food seemed to turn to dust in her mouth, and she reached for her cup of tea to wash that sensation away.

"Truthfully, I dread the moment when we arrive at Greenleigh Park. Not because I dislike the estate itself, but because I cannot imagine a way in which the next few weeks or more will not be distressing for all of us. And with the Season ending, and Summer ahead, there will be no reason for us to return to London for many months..."

Leon set down his cup, and met her eyes.

"We will deal with it – together. No matter what it takes. I am not willing to allow things to continue as they have been, with you in danger. If we can help Maggie, I will be happier, but if the only solution is to lock her away, and have her cared for in isolation, then so be it. As grandmother said, her decline seems to lead to only one inevitable conclusion, and we must face that."

"Yes... but I would not have her suffer that alone."

"Neither would I – but my first aim is to keep you from harm, as I minimise any harm to Maggie."

"I pray that is possible..."

Iris watched, and saw the flicker of grief which passed across Leon's face. Would that she could somehow make things better...

*****

The countryside was green, as Spring moved inexorably towards Summer, but Leon took no joy in it. Green had become the colour of death in his mind, the marker of Maggie's descent into madness. Still, he could not deny that Greenleigh Park looked beautiful, with the well-tended garden beds a riot of colour, and the sunlight bringing a soft golden tone to the walls. The carriage drew to a stop on the forecourt, and he stepped down, looking around carefully before assisting Iris out as well. There was no sign of Maggie. Perhaps they could get into the house without a scene, this time.

The gravel crunched beneath their feet, and behind them, the second carriage rolled up the drive, bearing Lina, Belling, and a large amount of luggage, for more of Iris' possessions had been sent from Elbury House to Greenleigh House while they had been out of London, previously. Leon looped his arm through Iris' and led her up the steps to where Waring stood, holding the door open.

"My Lord, my Lady, it is good to have you home."

Those words, so innocuous sounding in their basic meaning, were ominous to Leon's ears, for they suggested that he was needed here, to help deal with difficulties.

"Thank you, Waring. Is my mother here? Or at the Dower House?"

"At the Dower House, my Lord. I believe that she will be coming back here for dinner, as usual."

"And my sister?"

Waring's normally impassive face showed a hint of emotion for a moment, before it was ruthlessly suppressed.

"Lady Margaret was out in the gardens for most of the morning. Mrs Withercombe is trying to get her to take a nap."

"I see. Then I will not disturb anyone. Please have a tray with a light meal for both of us sent up to our private parlour. We will likely remain up there until dinner is called, unless my mother wishes to speak with us sooner. Belling and Lina will need food as well, and there is quite a quantity of luggage to deal with. Please make sure that they are fed."

"Of course, my Lord."

Waring bowed, and turned away to deal with their requests. Iris spoke, very softly, as they began to ascend the stairs.

"Is it wrong of me to be relieved? For I am."

"Not wrong. It is perfectly understandable."

They went on, and had almost reached the door to their rooms when a sound made him turn. Maggie was running down the hallway towards them, her movements uneven, and her face contorted. He realised, just before she reached them, that she was not seeing him at all – her entire attention was on Iris.

"Evil witch!"

The words came out as a shrill gasp, and Maggie lashed out at Iris, her hand curled - like a cat clawing at a mouse. Leon caught that hand, just as it passed his own face, and pulled, hard. Maggie lost her balance completely, and crumpled against him.

"Maggie, sister... you must not do such things."

"Why not? She doesn't belong here. Send her away, or I will make her go away, one way or another."

Leon felt the sharp chill of fear run through him – there seemed little doubt as to what Maggie meant by those words. He caught Maggie's face in his hands, and held her, making her meet his eyes.

"Maggie, she does belong here. She is my wife. I married her, and I want her here. You must accept that."

"I won't. I won't share you with anyone but Mother. We are family, and that's all we need. She's making you turn away from me, making you hate me. She's a witch."

"Maggie, I do not hate you. You are my sister, and I love you, but I can't let you hurt other people. It simply isn't right. You have already tried far too often – don't imagine that I don't know of it! If you cannot accept that, if you can't behave, then I will have no choice but to lock you away in the second floor of the East Wing."

He waited, watching her face as she processed his words, seeing the rebellion shift to sheer horror as she thought about it. Beside them, Iris stood frozen, silent, barely breathing as the drama played out.

"Noooooo! Not the East Wing! You can't, you wouldn't.... It's.... it's not green!"

"I can, and I will, if you do not promise to behave."

For just a moment, there was a look in her eyes which suggested rational thought, and hope flared within him.

"I'll promise. I beg you, don't lock me away in there."

"Promise - and actually fulfil that promise – hold fast to it, regardless. You must not attempt to harm Iris in any way, is that clear?"

Maggie tried to look away, but he held her in place, even though his heart broke at the need to do so. After long minutes, she gave a small jerky nod.

"I promise not to try to harm Iris in any way. Are you satisfied? Will you leave me with my freedom?"

"I will – but this is your one last chance. If you fail to hold by that promise, then you will be locked away, despite any protest you may make – and I will not redecorate that wing in green, no matter how often you ask. Now go back to your rooms, and rest, and think on this, to make sure that you remember."

He released Maggie, and she stepped back, turning to face Iris, and hissed like an angry cat.

"That promise holds me not to hurt you – but that doesn't mean I can't hate you, witch. Never forget how I feel about you."

With that, she spun, a motion spoiled in its drama by the wobble which resulted, and hurried off towards her own rooms.

*****

The lock clicked on their door as Iris dropped onto the couch, her breath ragged. Leon came to her and gathered her into his arms. She wanted to cry, to run away, to pretend that none of this existed. But she refused to allow the tears to fall. She looked up at her husband's face, and forced a tremulous smile.

"I had not thought that you would be having that conversation this soon after our return. Will she truly hold to that promise, do you think?"

"I can but hope so. I do not want to have to lock her away, but what I saw out there... the look on her face as she flung herself at you... She was not even aware of my existence. There was nothing rational in that, nothing but the intent to harm. And I will not allow her to harm you."

"Leon... what will happen if you do lock her away, in rooms that are not all green? Will that break what little grasp she has on reality completely, do you think?"

Iris waited as a cascade of emotions crossed Leon's face. He swallowed.

"I... I do not know. Perhaps it will. Or perhaps it might change things for the better, might make her look at the world differently. I have often thought that for her to be in other rooms, which are brighter, fresh, might be better for her. I find the deep green walls in her rooms oppressive, and then, there is a scent to those rooms – an odd scent, like rodents, or illness, and I cannot but wonder if being immersed in it makes her worse. But no physician has ever suggested that a change would help, so perhaps that is my own wishful thinking."

"I suppose that we will find out. Either she will hold to that promise, or she won't, and we will know that within weeks, I suspect. But... please stay near me, until we are sure of her choices. I am ashamed to admit that I fear her."

Iris felt her cheeks flush at the admission, but they had promised no secrets between them, and she would tell him only the truth. He bent to kiss her, a soft kiss, full of longing, and heartache. She melted into it, only for it to be interrupted by a tap at the door. They drew apart, and Leon rose, even as the voice came to them.

"Your meal, my Lord."

He opened the door, and a maid brought in a large tray, laden with food and drink. She set it down on the table, curtsied, and left. Leon locked the door behind her.

"Iris, for now, eat, and then rest – we will see what behaviour dinner brings, with Mother present as well. I will hope for the best."

*****

Two weeks passed, as May became June, and Spring gave way to Summer. Outside, the world was beautiful, bountiful. Iris wanted to be happy, wanted to share that with Leon, but every day brought more misery.

Despite the fact that Iris played for Maggie, always with Leon at her side, Maggie's hatred of her never waned. Every time they were in the same room, Maggie would hiss at her, or speak up, telling her to leave, calling her a witch, or worse. After each encounter, Iris was left shaking, the fear that Maggie would shift from words back to physical actions never far away. And towards the end of the second week, that fear began to seem more justified.

A number of times, Maggie stopped beside her, and reached out a hand, only to pull it back with a hiss of frustration. Iris suspected that, without the promise, Maggie would have attempted to pull her into a fall, or to trip her, or to hit her. At the dinner table, Maggie would meet Iris' eyes, then rather violently stab her meat with her table knife. The message was abundantly clear.

How long would it be, Iris wondered, before Maggie's desire to harm her overrode the thin strand of rationality which kept Maggie bound by that promise?

Iris went about her days with care, in Leon's company as much as possible. She rode out with him to meet their tenant farmers, sat with him as he met with his estate manager, and began to learn as much as she could about this place which was her home. It made her feel stronger to be more connected to it, to understand more of the workings of the house.

She spent more time with the Housekeeper and Cook, until they relaxed enough in her company to occasionally tell her stories of the past, of how Maggie had been, before the madness began to take her. Hearing those stories, her heart broke for Leon, all over again.

One evening, as they sat down to dinner, a knock came at the front door. Everyone looked up, startled. No one ever came to visit, and the messengers who brought mail or supplies generally only ever arrived in the early part of the day. Maggie flinched back in her chair, as if afraid, and Iris wondered what she was thinking, what monsters her mind had populated the world with, behind that knock on the door.

A footman soon came into the dining room, the correspondence tray in his hand.

"A messenger has brought this, my Lord. I have sent him to the kitchens to be fed."

Iris looked on as Leon picked up the sealed missive, and opened it, the flakes of red wax dropping from it onto the table. He read in silence for a moment, as everyone else watched him, then looked up.

"Grandmother is coming to visit us, next week, Mother."

"My mother? How peculiar. She hasn't been here for three years."

Maggie was frowning, and Iris got the impression that she was attempting to remember who her grandmother was. Then her expression tightened, and she hissed.

"Grandmother? I don't like her. She hates me." Maggie's eyes turned to Iris. "I like her even less than I like you, witch. Leon, tell her not to come."

"Maggie, I will not. She is our grandmother, and if she wants to visit us, she can."

Maggie hissed again, but with a glance at her mother, left it at that. Iris firmly repressed the bubble of hysterical laughter which rose in her throat. It seemed that Lady Neelsham was going to provide her some respite after all – just not in the way that either of them had considered, at the time of their conversation in London.

Chapter Thirteen

Preparations were made for Lady Neelsham's arrival, and Leon watched with some horror as Maggie teetered ever closer to complete madness, and to breaking her promise.

Her health was fading faster every day, her skin marked by lesions, and her body racked by coughing, but she still wandered about the house, with poor Mrs Withercombe trailing after her, doing her best to protect her from harm.

In his darkest moments, he considered the fact that death was coming for her, and coming fast, but he pushed those thoughts away – there would be time enough to deal with that when it happened.

Twice, as they set about the business of the house, Maggie followed them, and almost reached out to hit at Iris – each time, Leon spoke her name, clearly and firmly, and she jerked back, as if she had not been aware of what she was doing. He had the sickening feeling that it was only a matter of time – a short time – until his voice would not stop her.

He would simply have to stay vigilant.

On the day that Lady Neelsham was expected, in mid-afternoon he stood in the hallway, near the landing of the main stairs. He, with Iris by his side, had just finished inspecting the rooms prepared for Lady Neelsham, accompanied by the Housekeeper. Maggie had trailed after them, muttering to herself all the while, and Mrs Withercombe had trailed after her, looking more worn and exhausted than Leon had ever seen her. It was, he thought, a rather comical sight, that procession – at least it would have been had Maggie's state not been so terrible.

"Everything appears to be in order Mrs Jermyn. I will trust that you can adapt, if Lady Neelsham brings more staff with her than we expected."

"Yes, my Lord, I've planned for the possibility."

"Thank you."

Mrs Jermyn bobbed a curtsey, and turned to the servants' stairs.

As she did so, Maggie hissed, then stepped up beside Iris, and grabbed her arm, shaking her. Mrs Jermyn stopped and looked back, obviously concerned, as Leon firmly took hold of Maggie.

"Maggie, no! You promised."

Maggie struggled, and hit at Leon, as well as at Iris, the strength of hysteria allowing her to pull from his grasp.

"I don't care! As if she wasn't bad enough, now there will be grandmother – and even more people! You didn't tell me that she would bring anyone with her!" She spun to face Iris again, and slapped her across the face. "You, it's all your fault, all of it!"

Iris staggered back, and Leon took hold of Maggie, far harder this time.

"Maggie, that's it. You promised, and you knew the consequences of breaking that promise. You are banished to the second floor of the East Wing, now, and forever."

Maggie stilled in his grasp, and then flung herself about desperately, even as Mrs Withercombe hurried forward. Iris stepped back in horror, until the corner of the banister and balustrade at the top of the steps stopped her.

"Noooooo. It's not green.... No Leon, no." Maggie lurched, twisting, and pulled free from Leon again, evading Mrs Withercombe as well, and flung herself at Iris, her arms flailing, her fingers clawed. "You! You should have left! I hate you, you ruined everything when you came here, everything!"

Downstairs, the front door opened, but no one on the landing heard it.

Maggie reached Iris, and crashed into her, screeching, unbalanced, and completely out of control. Time slowed as Leon watched, and his heart filled with terror. They were at the top of the stairs, and Maggie's momentum was carrying both women to the very edge. Iris was about to fall. He could not lose her, could not have his love snatched from him, now that he had found her.

He threw himself forward, just managing to grasp Iris' skirts as she began to tumble, and tipped himself backwards to the landing floor, desperately pulling Iris with him. The fabric of her skirts tore a little, near giving way, but, after teetering, she fell back, directly into his arms.

Past her shoulder, he saw, as if impossibly slowed, the moment when Maggie, without Iris to even slightly stabilise her, was carried over the edge by her own ferocity of motion, and tumbled, her screeches becoming a scream of fear, down the steps. He pushed to his feet, his arms still cradling Iris to him, and looked down.

Maggie reached the bottom, tumbling awkwardly, and came to rest with a sickening crack, her head at a very odd angle on the marble floor.

Standing not three feet away from where Maggie lay, the front door still open behind them, were Lady Neelsham, his mother, and Waring, all with matching expressions of horror. Behind him, a rather solid thump sounded, and he turned to see that Mrs Withercombe had fainted. Mrs Jermyn rushed forward to tend to her.

Iris stirred in his arms.

"Leon... is she.... Is she...?"

He swallowed, breathing deeply, trying to steady himself, as a torrent of grief filled him, closely followed by a flood of relief – a relief of which he was ashamed.

"Yes, I believe so. We had best go down. Can you manage the stairs? I could not bear it if you fell now...."

He could hear the edge of hysteria in his own voice. Iris stepped out of his arms, back away from the stairs for a moment, as if assessing her own stability, then nodded.

"I can, but I will keep a firm grip on the banister."

Leon turned back to where Mrs Jermyn was fanning Mrs Withercombe.

"Mrs Jermyn, I'll send one of the maids up with some smelling salts, and leave you to assist Mrs Withercombe."

Mrs Jermyn looked up.

"Yes, my Lord. And... I'm sorry. We had all hoped that one day, she might get better."

He nodded, the grief surging through him again, then followed Iris down the stairs. There was nothing he could do for Maggie anymore – but he was certain that, right now, his mother needed him.

*****

Iris reached the bottom of the stairs, and stepped carefully around poor Maggie. But then, she stopped, unsure what to do. Moments later, Leon went past her and went to his mother, folding her into his arms. Lady Neelsham seemed frozen, shocked into silence. Waring stood near them, his face filled with a great sadness.

Iris realised, in that moment, that it was up to her to act.

She was Lady Greenleigh, it was her responsibility to deal with things which happened in this house. And the best way that she could help Leon and his mother was to do the things which were necessary.

"Waring... the door, if you please. Then summon two footmen to take urgent messages. We must arrange for the physician and the undertaker to come, so that her death will be correctly recorded. While we wait for them, she must be decently covered where she lies, and the small parlour prepared for her to be laid out in. Oh, and send some smelling salts up for Mrs Withercombe."

Waring started, as if coming out of a daze, and bowed.

"Yes, my Lady."

He turned, closed the front door, then hurried away to summon the footmen and send them on their way.

His movement seemed to bring Lady Neelsham out of her shock, and she met Iris' eyes for a moment, before speaking.

"You there," she waved her hand at one of the maids, who was peeking out of a door down the hallway, "Bring some coverings – a large sheet, or the like."

The maid nodded and scurried away.

"Thank you."

Iris was grateful for the older woman's assistance, for her own sense of shock was beginning to take hold.

"You're shaking, my girl. Take a steadying breath now."

Iris did, just as Waring reappeared, followed by two footmen and two of the maids – who promptly gave squeaks of horror at the sight of the body. Lady Neelsham fixed them with a stern glare.

"None of that fuss. Cover her with that sheet you're carrying, and then prepare the small parlour for her laying out. And ask the cook to send a tea tray to the main parlour – we will all need some sustenance to get through this."

Iris left Lady Neelsham to deal with the maids, and turned to the footmen.

"I must assume that you know where to find the physician, and the undertaker?"

"Yes, my Lady. But the physician is a distance away..."

"Then you must hurry. Each go for one of them, now, and ensure that they come immediately."

"Yes, my Lady."

They bowed, and with sidelong looks at the maids covering Maggie's body, turned, and left. Iris assumed that suitable horses were available to them in the stables – they had said nothing, so she had to trust that all would happen as she needed it to.

The maids had finished laying out the sheet over Maggie, and Lady Neelsham spoke again.

"You – stay here and make sure that nothing is disturbed. You, go and arrange a tea tray, and then set things up in the small parlour."

The maids curtsied, and set about doing as instructed. Iris was quietly impressed by the fact that they had not become hysterical.

She went to where Leon stood, his mother sobbing into his shoulder, and gently touched his arm.

"Come into the parlour. Nothing is served by us standing here. The physician and the undertaker have been sent for."

He looked at her, as if waking from some nightmare, only to find that the horror was real. Then he sighed.

"Mother, come to the parlour. Some tea will help settle you."

The Dowager Lady Greenleigh gave a barely perceptible nod, tears still running down her face, and allowed herself to be led away from the stairs, and the silent, sheet-draped bundle which had once been her daughter.

Without anything else being said, Iris and Lady Neelsham followed them to the parlour. Inside, Iris was a riot of emotion – grief, that it had ended so, and that Leon and his mother were so deeply affected. Shock, that she had come so close, herself, to meeting Maggie's fate. Relief, that the threat which had hung over her from shortly after her marriage was gone. Guilt, that she felt that relief. And a different kind of fear – that there might be things which she should do now, of which she was unaware.

But she would manage. And the presence of Lady Neelsham beside her was, unexpectedly, deeply reassuring.

*****

Late that evening, they finally stepped into their rooms, both exhausted and overwhelmed by the events of the day. Automatically, Leon went as if to lock the door, then stopped, his hand upon it, and gave a bark of half bitter laughter.

"I suppose I need not do that, anymore."

He turned away from it, and went to Iris, who leant against him and spoke softly.

"It seems still like a nightmare I will wake from, even though I know it is real. Part of my mind wants you to lock the door still, for it is as if she cannot be gone, as if she might come and pound on that door at any moment."

Her words echoed his own feelings precisely.

"I agree – it does seem impossible, even though I know it is real. It is hard to countenance, I think more from the manner of it than the fact. After all, despite my dearest wishes to the contrary, we have known for some time that her death was inevitable – but I did not expect it like this. That it came as a result of her trying to harm you makes it worse. Iris – when I saw you teetering, about to fall as she flailed at you, my heart near stopped – all I could think of was saving you, that I could not bear to lose you. But... in saving you, I made her fall a certainty, even though that was not my intent. That weighs heavily upon me."

Iris slid her arms around him, holding him tightly, and turned her face up to his.

"You must not blame yourself in any way, Leon. She made her own choices, however irrational they were at the end. Had she not thrown herself at me like that, neither of us would have been at risk. You could not have predicted her actions. And... I am very grateful that you saved me."

He bent and kissed her, the terrible emotional intensity of the day suddenly demanding release in a most physical demonstration of his feelings. After a few minutes, they drew apart.

"Come to bed, Iris, and let us make better memories."

Chapter Fourteen

The graveyard was full of small summer flowers – daisies determinedly pushing their way up beside age-old headstones, to accompany those flowers left by relatives of the deceased. Overhead, the sky was a clear blue, with a light drift of clouds, and birds circled, singing. It was altogether too beautiful a day for the sadness of the occasion.

There were few mourners at the graveside as Maggie's coffin was lowered into the ground - a simple coffin, draped with a plain green cloth. The coffin was lined with green, also – let her go to God surrounded by the colour she had loved so well. Leon stood with his family, Mrs Withercombe, and most of the staff from Greenleigh Park, and held back the impulse to weep. If he did so, his mother would lose all composure, and she had fought hard to get through the day so far. That the bright sister he remembered from his childhood had come to this was a travesty, an unreasonable cruelness which made him, at times, doubt God's plan. But all he could do now was go on, help his mother go on, and make a life with Iris. And perhaps they would be blessed with children, which would give his mother something to step back into life for, after the long years of Maggie's illness draining her vitality too.

The vicar's voice was sonorous, steady, sending Maggie on her way, underlaid by the percussion of the soil landing on the coffin, as the gravediggers shovelled it in, closing her off from the light forever. And then it was done. Silence surrounded them, broken only by the cry of a bird. Lady Neelsham was the first to move, gently herding everyone towards the carriages which stood waiting in front of the old village church. For three centuries the Atherton family, the Marquesses and Marchionesses of Greenleigh, had been buried here – perhaps half of the gravestones marked the memory of those Leon could count as relatives and ancestors. At least, the thought came, Maggie went to her maker in company of family. The servants bundled into carriages, and set off up the road, even as he, his mother, Iris, Lady Neelsham and Mrs Withercombe stepped up into their own conveyance. As they rolled away from the church, Lady Neelsham spoke, her voice soft, and pensive.

"I loved her once, when she was a child. I wish I could have truly maintained that love as the madness took her. I regret that failing on my part. Perhaps, if she has, in heaven, regained her sanity, she will hear me, and forgive me."

Lady Greenleigh shattered at those words, sobs of grief racking her, and Leon slipped his arm around his mother to comfort her, as Iris reached out to place her hand on Lady Neelsham's.

"I am sure that she forgives you, Lady Neelsham."

They lapsed into silence, Mrs Withercombe sniffling into a handkerchief, and Lady Greenleigh's sobs dying away after a while. Soon, the house came into sight, and then Lady Greenleigh spoke.

"Leon, can we remove every trace of green from the house? I have already done so at the Dower House – I had to do so for my own sanity – but now, I would ask you to do that in the main house as well. I would keep the memories of her childhood, not the ones after the madness began."

"Mother, I am more than happy to do so. Indeed, I had intended that very thing. I will arrange for the work to begin tomorrow. Of a certainty, the house will feel lighter and brighter, with that oppressive colour gone. The more Maggie became obsessed with it, the more I came to hate it, for it was as if the colour had stolen her from me."

Mrs Withercombe looked up at that point, and for a moment, Leon wondered if she would object, but then she smiled.

"I am so very happy to hear that. I have seen enough of green to last a lifetime, and over the last few years, since that wallpaper was last replaced, I have not felt at my best – indeed, I worried at times that my own mind was suffering by some contagion. And it was so hard to keep the rooms clean – that paper seemed to shed a dusting of green on everything, at least at first."

Leon nodded, for he had noticed that issue too.

"I thank you, Mrs Withercombe, for your devoted care of Maggie. Will you help us redecorate those rooms, and others in the house? Will you stay with us?"

A tension which he had not noticed until now left Mrs Withercombe's frame.

"I will, and gladly. I had wondered if I would still have a place, now..."

Opposite him, Iris met his eyes, then spoke.

"Mrs Withercombe, of course you have a place. And... if Leon and I are blessed with children, will you be nanny to them, as you were to Leon?"

Mrs Withercombe burst into tears again, but these were happy tears, and Leon felt his heart swell at Iris' words. Children... he had thought that perhaps he would never have children, and now... how much everything had changed in just a few days.

*****

Iris stood at the window of the room which had been Maggie's and watched the first cart rumble away down the lane, past the stables and off towards the village, and beyond. That cart contained the last of the furniture and furnishings which had been in this room, and the second cart held the last of the rubble – the stripped wallpaper, the torn away green painted wainscotting – every last trace of what had been, every last touch of green.

Around her, the room was clean, fresh, the walls cleaned back to bare timber and plaster and simply whitewashed, the floor newly ground back and polished. No green dust remained to tarnish it, no strange scent of rodents and illness. The only scent was the floor polish, and that was a pleasant smell. Tomorrow, the men would come to install new wainscotting, in the palest of timbers, to reinforce the lightness of the room. After that, there would be furniture, and drapes – all pale, all soft colours – nothing bright or harsh. They had decided that these rooms would become a guest suite – rarely used, but pleasant to be in. There were too many memories here, even with the green gone, for anyone in the household to wish to live in these rooms.

Down the hall, not far from the rooms she shared with Leon, was another newly redecorated room – a room designed to be a nursery, when that time came. She was happy – happier than she had ever been in her life, and she felt clearer of mind than she had since she first came to Greenleigh Park, as if all that had happened was a distant dark dream. Everyone seemed happier – and healthier – Mrs Withercombe, now well rested, and without the stress of daily dealing with Maggie, seemed ten years younger, and declared herself healthier than she had been for years. Iris couldn't help but wonder if that was at least in part due to no longer having to go into that green miasma for part of each day.

The carts disappeared from sight, and Iris turned away from the window. She would go down to the music room, and play, would let the music speak of her happiness in ways that words could not. Perhaps Leon would join her, once he was back from his weekly check on the tenant farmers.

*****

As Leon strode from the stables to the house, the sound of music drifted to him on the summer air. Iris was in the music room, playing. He smiled, and looked down at himself – was he too dusty from his riding to go straight to her? He thought not, as he brushed away what dust he could see. A few minutes later, he slipped quietly into the music room, and went to sit beside her on the pianoforte bench. She kept playing, but turned her head to grant him a smile. Effortlessly, as he moved his hands to the keys, she changed the pattern of her playing to allow him to take up the second strand of melody in the piece.

Peace filled him, and a sense of wholeness, as the music wrapped around them, binding them ever tighter together, soul to soul. They played for some time, until the light through the windows changed to the gold of late afternoon, then, reluctantly, he drew his hands back. Iris played the last poignant notes of the pieces, and stopped also. She turned her sky-blue eyes to him as the sound faded away, and he bent to kiss her, happier than he had ever been in his life. She returned the kiss with passion, and he contemplated the idea of simply carrying her off upstairs, but then he stopped – that, desirable as it was, could wait – he had things to tell her.

"Iris... I have something to ask you."

His tone was light, almost teasing.

"Oh? And what would that be?"

"Would you like to join me on a journey? For it occurred to me that we did not have a wedding trip, as so many do."

"A journey... that could be pleasant – but where would we go?"

He lifted his hand to stroke her cheek gently.

"I thought that, whatever we might do, it should involve music. Does the idea of a few weeks in Bath, and a visit to Mr Loder's Music Warehouse appeal to you?"

Her smile was as bright as the summer sun.

"I should very much enjoy that. But... what would we buy when there? For surely we couldn't visit such a place without buying something...."

He laughed softly, amused at her expression.

"I agree – we couldn't. Which is why I thought that we might order a new pianoforte, of the latest design, and perhaps a harp to accompany it?"

She clapped her hands together in delight, then pulled him to her for another kiss, before declaring that delight.

"You, Leon, are truly the most wonderful man."

"And you, the most wonderful woman. I must thank you, as I think I have never done so before, for slipping into the music room at Lady Gillieston's that day, so long ago – for had you not done so, I would not have ever had you as wife, and had the happiness I now have."

She laughed, an infectious giggle of delight, before finally managing to stop it long enough to speak again.

"Oh dear – that is so very funny – that after all of those years of being taught to be proper, and always behave with propriety, the thing which has brought most happiness into my life was the one time that I did everything I shouldn't have."

He joined her in the laughter at that, then pulled her to her feet to twirl her around the room in a waltz to silent music. Soon, dizzy, they stopped, and simply stood, holding each other. He grinned at her again.

"Shall we leave tomorrow? Grandmother is here, and she can keep Mother company, as well as Mrs Withercombe – there is no need for us."

"Yes. Tomorrow would be wonderful – although perhaps Belling and Lina will not be very happy, to have to pack everything for us, so fast."

"I am sure that they will cope – after all, they are very efficient. And I simply can't wait to run away with you, to have a holiday from all responsibility, with nothing to do but love you, and think about music."

Epilogue

"I absolutely refuse to get into a carriage until late enough in the day that I have ceased to feel disgustingly ill. So we will depart Bath after midday tomorrow. I do not care that it means we will have to stay in an Inn overnight, halfway home."

Iris, prepared to defend her demands, had found herself laughing instead, when Leon simply shrugged, and bowed in a very theatrical manner.

"As my Lady commands."

They had stayed in Bath far longer than they had intended, both for sheer enjoyment, despite their need to wear mourning clothes still, and because they had met the Earl of Westmoreland who, it turned out, had grand plans for creating a National Academy of Music. That meeting had led to many more, and many long discussions, which would likely change the path of their lives forever, should his plans come to fruition.

Every day had been a joy, and she was quite certain that she was increasing. The sickness in the mornings was a rather tell-tale sign.

Now, in the early afternoon of the next day, she settled into the carriage, glad that the queasiness had passed. On the seat opposite them, their new harp was settled, wrapped in cloths and tied into place. It was, she thought with amusement, even more fragile than she was.

Soon, they were moving, and she allowed herself to lean against Leon, who slipped his arm around her and held her as she drifted into sleep. She woke as they slowed, turning into an Innyard, just as the last late gold of the dusk turned to the rich blue-violet that presages night.

The Innkeeper greeted them with enthusiasm, and provided a large suite of rooms, with enough space for Belling and Lina too and, after an excellent meal, she gratefully fell into the surprisingly comfortable bed with Leon. She fell asleep soon after, with his hand resting gently on the curve of her stomach.

*****

Leon woke to the sound of Iris retching. The light through the edge of the shutters suggested that it was early still, but he could hear the sound of activity in the innyard below. He pushed himself up out of the bed, pulled a banyan around him, and took a glass of water to Iris as she sat back from retching.

"I will be so glad when this stage of the process is over! Why am I not as lucky as Camellia? She was barely ill at all!"

"I am told that it is different for each woman, my love, but that it rarely lasts past the first few months."

"This retching cannot end soon enough!"

"I agree. Shall I send for some simple food? Will that help, or make it worse?"

"I do not know, but it is worth doing, in case it does help."

The food was duly sent for, and Lina roused to help her dress and restore herself to a semblance of normal. Leon left them to it, allowing Belling to dress him, even while the valet muttered about the impossibility of keeping garments uncrushed when travelling.

The food, it turned out, did not help. So they sat in their private parlour and read, until the point in the day when Iris declared movement a safe possibility. In truth, Leon did not mind – to travel slowly like this was a new experience, and rather pleasant.

Once they were on the road, his mind went to what would be waiting for them at home. The echoes of the old dread still rose in his mind, and he had to remind himself that Maggie was gone, that there would be no scenes, no dragging grief of watching her suffer. He was not glad to have lost a sister, but he was beyond glad that she no longer suffered.

Greenleigh Park would be welcoming, and calm. That thought was, all by itself, exciting. He imagined the harp in the music room, imagined how the new pianoforte, of the very latest design, would look when it arrived, and he imagined how the nursery would look, once it was completed.

Mrs Withercombe would be so in alt at the idea of a baby to care for soon. That made him smile – she deserved the chance to be happy again too, and she had always been happiest when caring for young children.

He leant back into the corner of the seat and the carriage wall, with Iris leaning against him, and allowed himself to drift into sleep, lulled by the rumble of the carriage wheels on the earth of the road.

*****

Home.

Iris savoured the word as it rose in her mind.

She was home.

Greenleigh Park glowed with the lamplight from its windows, a welcoming beacon in the last of the summer twilight.

No trace of fear remained within her at the sight of it – only a deep-seated happiness, and the certainty that this was where she was supposed to be.

She pushed herself up to sit straight, leaving Leon still dozing, leaning against the wall, and watched the house as they approached. The scent of roses came to her as they turned onto the gravel of the forecourt, and she breathed deeply of the still warm summer air.

The carriage slowed, and Leon woke, sitting up and reaching for her hand. She twined her fingers with his, and they simply sat, watching. Of course, as soon as they stopped, that peacefulness was shattered by the bustle of getting down from the carriage, of the harp and their other luggage being unloaded, and of the staff all finding reasons to be in a position to welcome them home.

Once inside, they were met by Lady Greenleigh, Lady Neelsham, and Mrs Withercombe, all fussing about and overjoyed to see them. The house felt different, Iris realised, as if any lingering echoes of the pain of the past were gone.

The three women all looked bright and healthy too. It was as if the shadows had been brushed away from everything.

Lady Neelsham regarded her quietly as Leon greeted his mother. Those sharp, intelligent eyes missed nothing, and a small, pleased smile curved the old woman's lips.

"Well then girl, increasing, are you? About time. This house needs new children to brighten it up."

Mrs Withercombe and Lady Greenleigh spun to face her, their expressions hopeful, and she laughed at the sight.

"Yes, I am increasing, I believe. Lady Neelsham, you are as astute as ever. But I strictly forbid any coordinated fussing over me, or I shall go quite spare." Everyone laughed, but she could see that Mrs Withercombe struggled to prevent herself from dragging Iris directly to the nursery. "Mrs Withercombe, I promise that tomorrow, after I have finished retching for the morning, we can set to work on preparing the nursery."

Mrs Withercombe smiled broadly, and they managed to move forward out of the foyer, and into the parlour. They ate the food that was pressed upon them, and drank the tea gratefully, but then, claiming tiredness after travelling, chose to retire.

When they neared their door, Iris took Leon's hand, and tugged him on, towards the rooms which had once been Maggie's. He allowed himself to be led, and soon they stood in those rooms, which were lit only by the rising moon.

"Leon, does it feel right to you? Now that we have changed it?"

"It does, but..." he walked around what had been her bedchamber, his fingers trailing over the new pale wood wainscotting, then back into the little parlour where the smaller pianoforte still stood. The sheets which had covered it while the work had been done had been removed, and the inlaid wood of its surface gleamed in the moonlight. He sat on the bench, raised the lid, and traced his fingers over the keys. "...play with me?"

Iris went to him, and settled beside him as she had done so often before. Yet this time was different. As she sat, she felt watched – it was not a threatening feeling, more one of curiosity.

Leon began to play – one of the pieces that Maggie had most loved – and she meshed her movements with his, and joined him playing a gentle melodic counterpoint to his rendition of the main piece.

The music filled her, and joined them as it always did.

But there was something more.

It was as if fingers brushed her cheek gently, then trailed down her arm to her hand. She kept playing, but turned startled eyes to Leon.

"Did you..."

"I felt it too."

"Do you think...?"

"Perhaps. Perhaps it's a blessing. Or a goodbye."

"Then I will speak as if it is, despite that some might think me unhinged for doing so. Maggie, if what I feel is you, know that I bear no ill-will towards you. Go in peace to whatever is next. I am glad that your pain is over. I wish that I had known you, before..."

They kept playing, both so well practiced that they could separate the act of doing so from what they thought or said. The sensation of being touched came again, and Leon spoke, as softly as Iris had.

"Farewell sister. I did the best that I knew how, and it was not enough. Forgive me."

There was no sound but the pianoforte, but somehow, they each heard words in their minds – only later would they, speaking of it, discover that they had both heard 'I forgive you'.

The piece they were playing came to an end, and silence filled the room.

Then, ever so gently, the keys of the pianoforte moved, a light glissando of barely-there sound. Then the sense of presence was gone, and the rooms around them were truly empty of all but moonlight.

Outside, an owl called, and the sound shattered the peculiar stillness. Leon took her hand, and stood, pulling her to her feet, and into his arms. The kiss was deep, and full of so many things unspoken, full of life, and love, and the possibilities of the future. They drew apart in the end, slightly breathless.

He released her, and twined his fingers with hers.

"Come, my love, we should go to bed. That was a necessary ending, but now, it is our time for a new beginning."

"I love you Leon, I always have."

The End.

I hope that you enjoyed 'A Maiden for a Marquess'.

Over the page you'll find an Author's Note about the science behind what happened to Maggie.

Author's Note

In this book, as in many of my others, there are things which were real, things which really happened, although not, perhaps, in exactly the way that I have portrayed them.

In this book, the following things are things that really happened / existed:

- **Copper arsenite poisoning.** That is what Maggie is suffering from, although in 1820, it was only just being identified by a small number of doctors. Arsenic compounds were used in all sorts of things, from 'health tonics' to makeup, even in food colouring (!!!) all through the centuries.

  People therefore, whilst they were aware that ingesting a large quantity of arsenic would kill you, regarded small quantities, and its use in non-food items, as harmless.

  The use of arsenic in the colours used for clothing, wallpaper, carpet, paint and the like resulted from the fact that it made the colours brighter, and made them last longer. In the 1770s a colouring agent made using copper and white arsenic (Scheele's green) became popular, and was soon used extensively.

  Despite the fact that people who worked with it were suffering terribly and dying, that was ignored – the wealthy wanted their bright colours (green was the main culprit, although arsenic was used in other bright colours too). In around 1814, an enhanced version of that green colouring, which was even more permanent, was invented (called Paris green) and it was, accordingly, even more poisonous.

  The stuff came off flocked and patterned wallpaper as dust, it 'gassed off' as arsenic gas out of garments and wallpaper, as oxidation occurred over time (it was said to smell like a mouse nest) and it could be absorbed through the skin, as well as breathed in or eaten.

  Which meant that pretty much everything coloured was poisonous.

There were many deaths, especially in the poor who worked in the factories which produced coloured things, and amongst the older or very young members of wealthier families who could afford the wallpapers and brightly coloured cloth. (those deaths were slow and agonising, with impacts on the gut, the ability to breath, the skin and more, as well as the mind in the end)

What confused matters a lot was that, it turns out, the more protein you eat, the better equipped your body is to process arsenic out of the system – so the healthier, wealthy adults, with larger body mass, and a higher protein diet, either didn't get sick, or didn't get as sick – and they were the ones making decisions about what was happening.

It took until the 1850s for the truth to be recognised, and even longer for laws to be passed in various countries banning the use of arsenic in almost everything. (so, if you ever decide to buy a genuine mansion which dates from the early to mid-1800s, and has green wallpaper or paint anywhere... Get it tested as soon as you go near the place).

As this story is set in 1820, no one understood what was happening to Maggie.

Mrs Withercombe was minimally affected, because she was only in that room when helping Maggie a few times a day – but Maggie slept in there, which vastly increased her exposure to the poison. The others' refusal to decorate any of the rest of the house in green saved their lives.

- **King George III dying and the Prince Regent acceding to the throne** – This really happened – King George the third, who had been ill for a long time (that's why the Prince Regent was Regent) died on the 29th of January 1820.

- **The timing of mourning for the King** - There was a strict official protocol for how long mourning should be for a member of royalty. The different degrees of mourning determined how 'severely dark' the clothing was which could be worn, as well as activities which were allowed. Here is the table with the details.

	Deep mourning	Mourning	Half mourning	Total
For the King and Queen	8 weeks	2 weeks	2 weeks	12 weeks
Son or Daughter of the Sovereign:	4 weeks	1 weeks	1 weeks	6 weeks
Brother or Sister of the king or queen:	2 weeks	4 days	3 days	3 weeks
Nephew or Niece, Uncle, Aunt		1 week	1 week	2 weeks
Cousin German		7 days	3 days	10 days
Distant Relations		4 days	3 days	1 week

- **The calling of the House of Lords to manage the formal bits of the transition from one King to the next –** This is part of the process – for the Lords of the land must make sure that the transition is smooth, undisputed, and that no lawlessness occurs while it happens.

- **The existence of the Loder Music Warehouse in Bath** – Bath was, from the early 1700s on, filled with 'toy-shops' which also sold instruments, music, and pretty much any complex mechanical gadget, as well as small children's toys.

  There were different ones which were there at any one time, and different ones which became pre-eminent in their era.

  In 1820, John David Loder's Music Warehouse (he was the third generation Loder to run it) was the pre-eminent musical everything shop in Bath.

- **The Earl of Westmoreland wanting to start a National Academy of Music** – this really happened (and he succeeded, some years later.)

So there you have it – a scatter of real history rolled into your fiction. Maggie, of course, also shows some signs of being mildly autistic – hence the OCD like obsession with green – an obsession which doomed her, one day at a time. The only reason that she lived as long as she did, was that she left the house to walk amongst the 'green of the gardens and trees' which gave her some time away from the fumes and dust in her chambers.

I hope that you find this sort of historical information interesting!

Arietta Richmond

I hope that you enjoyed 'A Maiden for a Marquess!

Turn the page for another great Regency story.

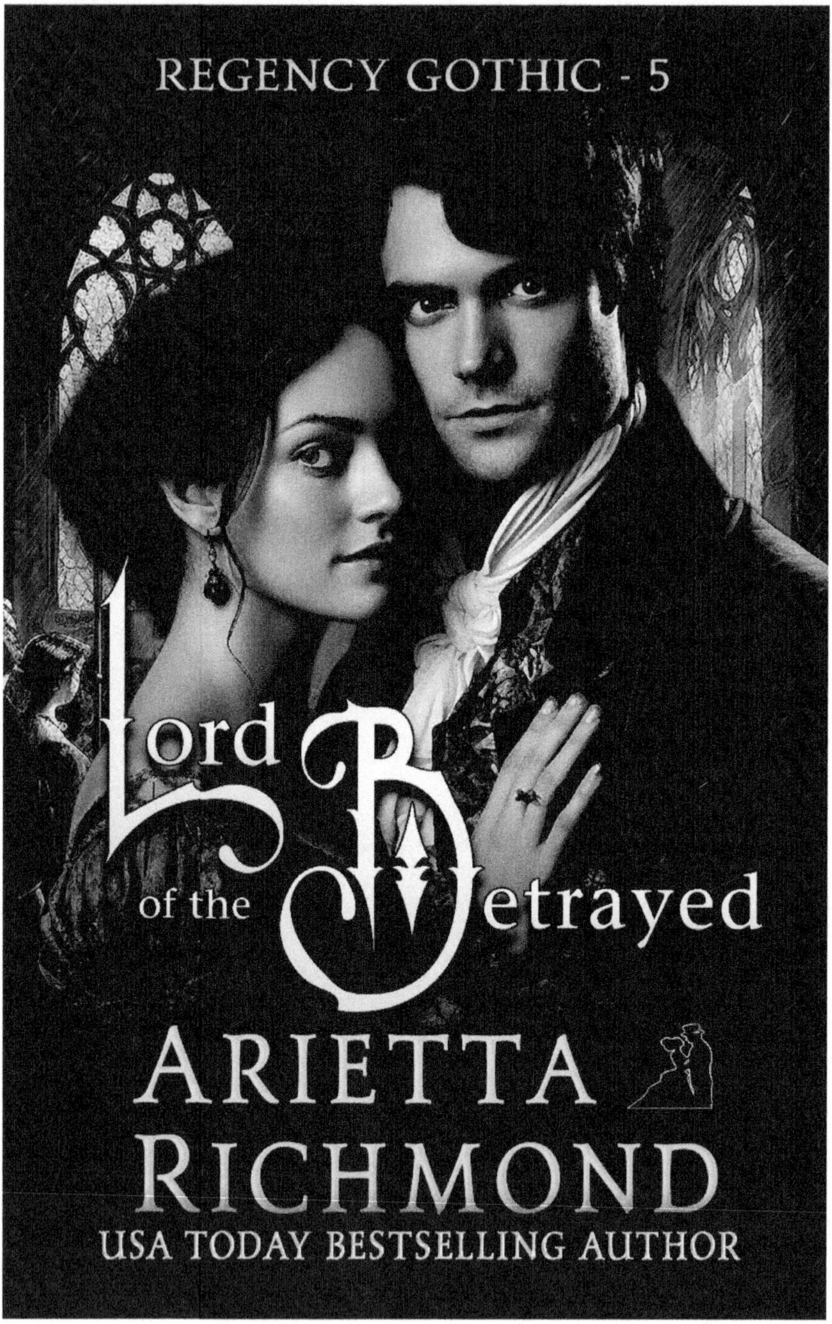
REGENCY GOTHIC - 5
Lord of the Betrayed
ARIETTA RICHMOND
USA TODAY BESTSELLING AUTHOR

Regency Gothic - 5

Lord of the Betrayed

Regency Romance

Arietta Richmond

Prologue

1808, near Grimstoke Village

The late afternoon sun gilded the meadow to a rich dark gold, scattered with the brightly coloured gems of wildflowers. Two children ran through the grasses, laughing, until, eventually, the girl flung herself down in the shade of a large tree.

"I can't run any more. I'm just going to lie here for a while."

The boy tilted his head, looking at her, then gave a nod.

"Aye, if ye wish it. I've summat else to do. I'll be not long, then I'll be back to ye."

She waved him away, as if any further movement was far too much effort, and closed her eyes, simply lying there, feeling the warmth where dappled sunlight reached her through the leaves above. She might have drifted into sleep, or only into dreams – dreams where a handsome knight – who bore, if she were to admit it, a strong resemblance to the somewhat scruffy blond boy she had been running with – cast himself down before her, protested undying love, and asked her to marry him.

It was a dream she'd indulged in often, a dream similar to dreams held dear by most young girls approaching thirteen years of age, as she was.

She had no idea, really, what should happen in the dream after that – there was simply a romantic declaration of love, a proposal, and the giving of a keepsake of some kind to seal the pact. Everything afterwards was simply not as important as that part...

Something touched her cheek, and she started, sitting up suddenly, her eyes blinking open as soft laughter faded away. Before her was a picture which made her wonder if she was still dreaming. The boy, looking surprisingly serious, and somehow older – and more handsome – knelt beside her, his hand held out towards her, almost imploringly. The silence stretched, the faint echoes of that soft laughter disappearing, and she swallowed, uncertain.

Then he spoke, and the sense of still being in the dream intensified.

"Will you marry me?"

She giggled, caught up in the moment, and put her hand in his, words tumbling forth as she nodded, delighted by the extension of the dream into the waking world.

"Of course, of course!"

The boy lifted his other hand, and slipped something onto her finger – the finger that people wore wedding bands on. She looked at it closely. It was a carefully woven twist of the finest stems that hold new rose leaves. She looked up and met his eyes, the feel of the makeshift ring on her finger conveying its meaning clearly. It was, in its way, a wedding band; a seal, a promise that one day a true ring would replace this makeshift one.

His voice was breathy, shaking a little now.

"Do you mean it? Do you promise?"

"I do! I do!"

When she gave that commitment, he leant forward and brought his lips to gently brush her cheek, close to her own lips, but not quite there.

"And I promise, also."

His voice carried more intensity of meaning than she had ever heard before.

Chapter One

1817

It still seemed improbable that she had accepted his suit. The banns would be read for the first time tomorrow.

Roland Shelton, Earl of Eldwood, sat in the garden of Crooked Hill Manor, surrounded by the scents and sights of spring flowers. It made him think of the times he had spent in the garden at Grimstoke Castle, sitting with Lady Gabrielle Vickery. Gabrielle, who he was to marry in a few short weeks' time.

She was beautiful, the daughter of a Duke – she could have any man she wanted, and yet, somehow, miraculously, she had chosen him. A shiver ran through him, despite the warmth of the sun. Did she truly love him? Might she, one day, realise that she could do far better than Roland, and abandon him? Might she call it off at the last minute, and leave him in misery?

He shook his head – he was being foolish. He chastised others when they indulged in maudlin thoughts, so why was he allowing himself to do so?

Still, no matter what he told himself, the doubts ran riot through his mind. He had tried, so hard, for the last few months especially, to behave as a courtly suitor was expected to, with effusive expressions of his love, with poetry and more. Lady Gabrielle had appeared to like it – but that wasn't him, not really, for such effusive words felt false, and he felt artificial, like an actor on the stage, saying them.

Had it been the wrong choice to behave so?

Did she truly love him, as he loved her, or was she enamoured of the façade he had been presenting?

But she had agreed to marry him...

Perhaps he should be more dignified, less effusive, more truly himself... In the past, she had still seemed to like him, before he had tried too hard to court her as he thought was necessary...

The bees buzzed around the flowers, and the serenity of the scene was utterly in conflict with the churning uncertainty inside him. Nothing in his life had felt certain, not since his father's death and the moment when the title, and all of its responsibilities, had fallen heavily upon his shoulders. Responsibilities which he had, from that first day, feared he would fail to fulfil.

And beside that fear, there was, always, another – that he might trust too much, and that those he leaned on for assistance might betray him, might fail him in turn, might see him as unworthy, and turn away. His fears with respect to Lady Gabrielle ran in parallel with those, and he perpetually argued with himself, determined not to give in to those fears, not to fail his father's expectations of the legacy left in Roland's hands. Those fears of betrayal were not entirely unreasonable, for, in his years at Eton, he had been often betrayed. Whilst quite athletic, he had still been the thin, studious, quiet boy, the one in his year who was the easy target. And to begin with, he had given his trust freely – and it had taken a great deal of pain for him to learn that trusting was not safe, that it led to betrayal. He did not, in many ways, trust himself, any more than he trusted others.

But soon, he would have no choice. Soon, he would be married, and he refused to consider a life with someone to whom he did not give the courtesy of his trust. But what if she betrayed it? He had not, he must admit, really shown her all of the truth of him. With his family, he could have a devilish sense of humour, a sharp wit – but he rarely showed that side of him to anyone else – what if she disliked that aspect of him?

He sighed, and stood. Time to go back inside. Lady Gabrielle's mother was closeted with his own, discussing their plans for the wedding, and the Wedding Breakfast, which would be held here, at Crooked Hill Manor.

He had no choice but to go forward – he had made his commitment, now he must follow through on it, and believe that he could trust both himself, and Gabrielle.

He had to believe that a happy future was possible.

*****

When the Vicar, Mr Wardle, read the banns the following day, a flurry of pleased whispers ran around the church. Everyone in Grimstoke Village and surrounds knew the Earl and Lady Gabrielle, and for them to marry had a pleasing symmetry, for Lady Gabrielle's brother had married Lord Eldwood's sister just last year.

At the back of the church, a sharp-eyed older woman pursed her lips at the news. She would have to write to her son – he would want to know.

Not that he would reply, she suspected, for he thought himself too important now to bother with his old mother. Still, she wrote to him regularly, and told him all the news of the district – it was only right that he know, and since her husband had been taken from her three years ago, when the horse he was shoeing had kicked him in the head, she had no other family.

She'd only discovered where her son was, recently, for he had disappeared from Grimstoke years ago. She'd thought him lost to her, until a letter had arrived, telling her what he had achieved. Just telling her, mind you – not a speck of money, nor a parcel of goods to help her, even though he was, according to the letter, well off.

Still, she mustn't complain – better that she knew he lived, and had a good life, than that even knowledge of him be lost to her. She rose when the banns were completed for that reading, and went out into the morning sun with her neighbours, to indulge in gossip for a pleasant hour or two.

*****

Lady Gabrielle Vickery smiled to herself as the carriage conveyed them back up the hill to Grimstoke Castle. Hearing the banns read had finally made it seem real. She had dreamed of marrying Roland for years, since they were both little more than children, if truth be told, and long before he had become the Earl of Eldwood but, even after he had proposed, and she had accepted, it had felt rather like those dreams – until now.

For the last few months, he had been so very attentive, so demonstrative of his love for her, that she had become quite overwhelmed. She hadn't expected that expressiveness from him - for he had always been a little reserved, even during the last year, since his sister had married her brother – but she had delighted in it. She couldn't wait to marry him, to have the freedom to be with him, all of the time.

When the Vicar had spoken the banns, she had glanced sidelong at Roland hoping to catch him looking at her, but he hadn't been – he'd been looking fixedly forward, his face a bit stern, almost as if he disapproved of something. Which worried her, for a moment, until she pushed that concern away. He loved her, and she loved him, she was quite sure of it.

She only had to wait another few weeks, another two readings of the banns, on the next two Sundays, and then another three weeks after that, to the day set down for her wedding. In that latter three weeks, she would have the excitement of going to London, to an exclusive modiste, to have new gowns made for her new life. Sadly, her mother would not be going with her, for the Dowager Duchess suffered horrible travel sickness. Instead, a maid would travel with her, to the home of Margaret, Lady Charrington, one of the few close friends that Gabrielle's mother had. Lady Charrington would come to collect her, and would chaperone her in London, and see that she obtained everything that she needed.

It was all very exciting – quite the most exciting thing that had ever happened in her life – well, apart from the moment when Roland had proposed, of course!

*****

Two weeks later

The carriage trundled down the hill towards Grimstoke Village, and Gabrielle's mind trundled with it.

Opposite her Devlin - the Duke and her brother - and his wife Desdemona, the Duchess, laughed and smiled and made merry. Her mother, Emilie Vickery, the Dowager Duchess, who sat beside her, looked at them fondly, her smile broad, even though she was in a dreaded carriage. She could stand the terrible motion sensations for such a short distance as this.

Gabrielle should also have been making merry. Oh, yes, she should have been the merriest of them all, for they were on their way to church, and on this day, the banns would be read for the third and final time. But Gabrielle was not at all merry – she felt something more akin to a mockery of that emotion. How had it come to this?

Put on a hat, m'lady, it's time to become a jester!

She would have giggled at the ridiculous thought, if life were as simple as all that. But it wasn't. Slowly, and unexpectedly, over the last two weeks, everything had changed. She had thought that finding a husband she loved, and who loved her was simple, and once done, would stay that way, forever. But it seemed that finding a husband was not simple, and that the heart's desires were stricter and more complicated than one might at first think.

"Does something trouble you, Gabrielle?"

Desdemona, who was usually called Mona by the family, was a beautiful woman, with a grand aura about her. One could have thought her a queen. Whenever she spoke to you, you felt as though the Earth turned on a pivot, regarded *you*, and smiled upon *you*. But even Mona's intense attention could not dislodge the worry which had settled itself in Gabrielle's mind. Beside her, Gabrielle's mother watched, curiously, waiting for her to answer Mona's question.

"Oh, I do not know," Gabrielle said noncommittally. "The sun is awfully hot for April!"

She was fully aware that it was an inane thing to say. But a Lady must fill silences.

Mona raised an eyebrow, looking at her, making it quite clear that she expected a better answer than that. The Dowager Duchess gave a little smile, knowing her daughter far too well to believe that her words were anything other than avoidance. Her brother, wisely, chose not to say a word, and did not even smile – he simply met her eyes, and she was the one who looked away. Her eyes slid down his face, and then to her own hands in her lap. Her thoughts sought distraction from Mona's question.

Devlin's beard had been smoothed over his scar, but it was still visible: a testament to his service in the war. Gabrielle found herself, oddly, envying Devlin that scar.

There was a certainty about it.

No ambiguity there, she thought. *He knows that he has a scar. He knows why and how it came to be. Oh, what if ailments of the mind were as clear as ailments of the body? Does Roland love me? Or is he only happy to be marrying ever-so-slightly above his station?*

"Gabrielle," Mona said, stroking Gabrielle's hand. "We are friends, are we not? I have seen you blossom into a woman. Look at you! Regard yourself, I beseech you!"

Mona laughed musically, shaking her head. She and Devlin had become much less serious since their marriage. Where once there had been brooding, now there was laughter – which was wonderful.

"Of course we are friends, Mona," Gabrielle laughed. "Of course we are the best of friends." Gabrielle sighed. "We are the best of friends," she went on, as the carriage rolled closer and closer to Grimstoke Village, and the church. "I daresay that we are the friendliest friends who have ever —"

"Sweet sister, I fear that with your rambling and repetitions, you are attempting to effect a shield to my inquiries. You are normally quite forthright - could it be that you don't want to answer my initial question?"

Gabrielle blushed.

"Am I so transparent?"

Mona smiled and gave a little nod, much to Gabrielle's embarrassment. The Dowager Duchess emitted a very small sound, which Gabrielle rather suspected was strangled laughter.

Mona's eyes sparkled, and she spoke again, her tone reassuring.

"To say that you are transparent is not an insult. It simply means that you are not cunning. There is nothing amiss about that. Now, Gabrielle, tell me. What troubles you?"

Did she really need to explain? Could not Mona see, instantly, what it was that concerned her? Apparently not.

Gabrielle realised then that she was in that peculiar state of mind where one assumes that everybody else can sense one's problems. She was so consumed by them, she reasoned, that surely the arrangement of her features, the length of her pauses, and the monosyllabic bluntness her discourse of late would show clearly to any observer what lay beneath. Most assuredly, her logic ran, any person expending a small amount of energy could read her features, in all their drama, as plainly as a penny dreadful novel. But Gabrielle discovered then that she, like so many ladies in the clutches of a problem of the heart, of the mind... *can I say of the soul...* had overestimated the abilities of those around her to discern information which they had not been made privy to.

She took a deep breath, readying herself for battle. Mona would not allow her to avoid answering, so it was best that she simply admit, at least in part, to the thoughts which tormented her.

"Oh, Mona, this will be the third week of the banns being read," she said, speaking quickly to lessen the discomfort of admitting her worries. "For the past two weeks we have sat in the church and listened to the banns spoken, and I have — I have been positively sure that Roland does not love me as much as I love him. Before the proposal, Mona, we were so in love! I was certain of it, for his words and his manner of declaring his love for me was intense, near overwhelming. And yet now all appears to have changed – now I am a mere annoyance to him, I fear, a pest. Like a mouse, squeaking, discovered where it should not be, requiring attention at the most inconvenient times. Tell me, Mona, how does a mouse find love?"

Devlin gave a snort of laughter then.

"I disagree with your premise, sister. Nothing I have observed has led me to believe that you are a mouse. On the contrary, I believe that you are a fiery, frightening, outright dangerous woman. Although there are times when you are annoying..."

He smiled playfully.

"Oh, husband, do be serious. Can't you see that she is distressed?"

Mona tapped him on the hand, chastising him, even as she smiled.

"Roland is a lucky man, to be marrying a Duke's sister," Devlin said. "If his wooing of you has waned, remind him of *that*."

"Oh, I could not do that," Gabrielle spoke hurriedly, wanting to defend him. "He is so kind, so handsome, so dashing." She blushed when she realised that she had spoken so freely. "And of course, he is an Earl. It is not as though he is a Viscount. Or worse, a Baron."

Her cheeks felt hot, and she felt rather foolish – oh, if only Mona had not asked the question in the first place!

"If he was a Baron or a Viscount, sweet sister," Devlin said, "your courtship would not have begun. A man courting you had to be worthy of that honour."

"Devlin!" Mona cried. "Do you forget that he is my brother?"

Devlin had the kind of smile which instantly dispelled all negativity levelled towards him. He aimed it at his wife now and her fury softened.

"I do not," Devlin said. "But that does not change the way that things are."

Before Mona could respond, they came to a halt. The four of them had soon stepped down from the carriage and gathered outside the church, where other people greeted them. Not long after their arrival, Roland Shelton, the Earl of Eldwood, and his mother Wilhelmina Shelton, Lady Eldwood, arrived and came to join Gabrielle's party. It was a pleasant surprise to see Lady Eldwood, as the woman had been ill for the past several weeks and had looked far older than her actual years.

Now, though, she seemed sprightly and wide-awake.

Perhaps the impending marriage is as exciting to her as it is to me! Gabrielle thought.

Everybody greeted them in turn, and soon the throng of people – mostly merchants and artisans and working folk, who were all respectful in the extreme – began to move into the church. Their group moved to the front pew, which had long been set aside for the two aristocratic families, and sat. Gabrielle found herself wedged between Lady Eldwood on the one side and Roland on the other. From one she received an enthusiastic smile, from the other she met with cold indifference. Roland kept his face turned forward. His sharp, dashing looks could be enthralling. But they also lent his appearance a sharp aspect when he wished, the air of an eagle in flight, uncaring for its surroundings, for anything but itself.

Gabrielle wished to reach out, to touch him, but of course that was madness. She folded her hands into her lap and kept her eyes on the front as the Vicar came to the pulpit, ready to give the sermon.

He was a tall, pot-bellied man with sharp bright eyes which one could truly believe had access to heaven. When he looked out over the congregation, he appeared like a shepherd looking over his flock.

*****

When Roland stepped out of the carriage, and saw Gabrielle, where she stood with her brother, his heart twisted within him. She was so very beautiful – he did not deserve her, he was certain. How could she possibly be satisfied with him? And yet, today, they would hear the Banns read for the third time.

It still seemed improbable, yet he was, cautiously, allowing a joyfulness about it to fill him. He had been so uncertain for the last few weeks – he had been less effusive in his expressions of his care for Gabrielle, had tried, instead, to be dignified. He was still not certain that he had made the right choice...

Gabrielle turned, then, as he escorted his mother towards the group, and as she saw him, a wonderful smile spread across her face. It warmed him to his core, and he tried desperately to maintain his dignity, to not grin like a lovesick fool. Perhaps he was too successful, as her smile dimmed a little.

They all went into the church, then, and he found himself sitting beside her on the family pews, his thigh hard against hers, his mother seated on her other side. The heat of her body reached him, and the sensation took his breath away. He forced himself not to look at her, to simply hold his attention on the Vicar, for if he had turned to her, he would have wanted to pull her into his arms – which would be beyond improper.

The sermon was blessedly short, and as it came to an end, as the moment approached when the banns would be read, he felt Gabrielle's hand slip into his, where it lay on his leg, so close to her. His breath hitched, and her fingers squeezed his. It was almost more than he could bear – the need to remain calm and proper, with the whole district looking on, was overwhelming. He held himself frozen in place and, after a short while, as the Vicar made the call for any with objections to declare them, her hand released him. He felt the lack of that touch acutely.

He had expected a few moments of silence, rapidly followed by the Vicar closing the service for the day, but that expectation was not met – instead, an unexpected sound filled the silence – the sound of movement, of someone rising from their seat.

It was a sound that was rapidly followed by the sound of the entire church full of people moving, turning to see who had risen, to see if, truly, someone was about to object to their joining.

That was a thought which struck him like a blow to the stomach, stealing his breath, crushing his growing joy in an instant.

Had he been betrayed?

Had Gabrielle seen someone else, and found them of more interest? Had she dallied with another? Were all of his dreams of love illusions?

He turned, slowly, unable to stop himself, to see what form the destroyer of his hopes took.

Chapter Two

"Let us read..."

As the Vicar began his sermon, Gabrielle was intensely aware of Roland beside her, of the warmth where his leg lay close beside hers. A Lady often finds herself guilty of small sins in church - Gabrielle knew that her mind should have been utterly transfixed by what the Vicar was saying, but, again and again, she found herself wondering what Roland was thinking. Once, she snuck a look at him. In her mind – the foolishness of love – she had imagined that he, too, would be sneaking a look at her. But when she examined him, he was doing no such thing. His gaze was firmly set forward. This was a two-pronged rebuff - it served to remind her of his recent coldness, and it made her the guilty party for allowing her attention to stray. So the service passed, and then came the reading of the banns.

A gentleman, of course, could quite easily obtain a common license or even, if he was resourceful and could afford it, a special license, and thus expedite the path to marriage, but it had been Gabrielle's idea to have the banns read in place of a license.

She'd had images in her mind of Roland smiling warmly at her as Vicar Wardle read the words. Fancies, in truth, had invaded her mind, and moulded all of her imaginings to a romantic shape. It is so often, Gabrielle was discovering, that a Lady's romantic ideals are proven just that — ideals, imagined, not real.

"I call the banns of marriage between Roland Shelton, Lord Eldwood, of Crooked Hill Manor, and Lady Gabrielle Vickery of Grimstoke Castle." There were no trumpets, no cheering, no open expressions of love. *Oh, a Lady's plight! A Lady's struggle! Must I accept that his face is carved of stone? Will he let no emotion pass it?* "This is the third time of asking," the vicar went on. "If any of you know cause or just impediment why these two persons should not be joined together in Holy Matrimony, ye are to declare it now."

As was her habit, she squeezed Roland's hand in secret when this portion was read, in the hope of some loving response. But he only stared ahead with a countenance which had turned from stone to ice.

Of course, there was nobody in England – nay, the world – who could find any reason that she and Roland should not be joined in marriage. It was ludicrous, in fact, to even entertain such an idea.

She and Roland were above all such nonsense. They were immune to this brand of foolishness. They had led unimpeachable existences. They had always been honourable—

A rustling sounded at the back of the church - the rustling of clothes as someone stood. At once, every head turned to regard the source of the sound. Gabrielle was the last to move, her heart pounding, her mind screaming with disbelief. This could not be happening! She saw the Vicar heave a sigh and look to the back of the church.

Finally, Gabrielle turned.

A man of around her and Roland's age, two-and-twenty, stood there. He was well-dressed, but not in the mode of a Lord - he wore clean, but quality fabrics which a higher-class merchant might wear, though his were not stained as some merchants' so often were. He held a hat to his chest. His short brown hair was cropped close to his head. His eyebrows were soft, his eyes wide, his lips full, giving him an amiable, welcoming appearance.

So at odds with Roland, Gabrielle thought, before she could stop herself.

Roland, who was right there beside her, his shoulder against hers as they both looked to the back of the church. She felt disloyal, and ashamed of herself for the thought.

Her heart beat rapidly, torturously, pounding in her chest.

What did this man – this stranger – have to do with them?

It was most unusual. It was most frightening.

"I am afraid," the man said, with the tone of voice of a man who has learnt enunciation rather than been born to it, "that I object."

The church was immediately seized by an uproar. Lady Gabrielle and the Earl were favourites of the people of Grimstoke Village and the surrounding districts. In such a small settlement, with so few Lords and Ladies, the higher orders who lived there were held close to the bosom of the villagers. That this man, who seemed to be a stranger to Grimstoke Village, should cause a commotion was most unwelcome.

It was unwelcome, too, to Gabrielle. Her frantic heartbeat became quicker, heavier, until she could barely hear the calls of the congregation over its thumping in her ears. Around her, whispers began. The congregation looked scandalised – this was the most dramatic thing to occur in the district for a year or more. Even the Vicar looked bothered. His mouth fell agape, as though he – a man well skilled in belief – was unable to believe what his eyes reported to him.

"Come here," he said finally, waving a hand at the gentleman. "We shall discuss your claims in private."

"There is no need," the man said.

Several people called out then, as the initial shock wore off.

"Liar!"

"Sit down!"

"Don't you talk nonsense about m'lord and m'lady!"

"Off with him!"

"Stranger! Leave!"

The man withstood these barbs bravely.

"I will tell you why I object!" he shouted over the noise. "I object because the lady is promised to me!"

At that, a horrid aching silence ensued.

Gabrielle looked desperately at Roland, but Roland did not look at her.

She was tempted, for a moment, to swoon.

*****

At the man's words, it was as if the ground tilted beneath him. Roland gripped the edge of the pew with a shaking hand, his mind awhirl with questions – and with a deep, sinking certainty that he had been a fool to think that he might be able to succeed in this, that he might be able to find happiness, that someone other than his mother and sister might truly love him.

Had Gabrielle actually done as this man said? Had she pledged herself to him, and then, deceitfully, to Roland also?

It seemed impossible – yet if it was not true, why would the man have come here, to claim that it was? What could the man hope to gain?

Roland did not know, but he realised then that he could not permit this to happen, could not permit this man to steal Gabrielle away from him, not without a fight. Just how he could fight such a thing, he did not know, but he had to try.

Still, even as he turned towards Gabrielle, to meet her eyes, to see what truth might be writ upon her face, the dreadful thought still echoed in his mind.

What if she really did betray me? What if she does not wish me to fight for her?

*****

After a long moment, Roland turned to her.

His gaze was of such intensity that Gabrielle shrank back.

"I — I do not know him," she stammered. "I have never seen him before!"

Even as she spoke, the Vicar's fury rang out across the church.

"If you have business to discuss regarding the banns, sir, come with me!" A pessimistic person would say that the Vicar's protective instincts regarding the Sheltons and Vickerys originated with the substantial generosity both families displayed when the collection plate was circulated, as well as in the living paid to him by the Duke, on whose grounds the church stood, but whatever the reason, Gabrielle was glad of it. The Vicar's red face trembled; his bright eyes darted across the church like daggers. He repeated his demand, encapsulated in one sharp word. "Sir!"

The man moved into the aisle and towards the Vicar, who had stepped down from the pulpit to await him. As he passed, people muttered near obscenities, even expletives, which caused Lady Eldwood to flinch a little. Finally, the man reached the front. He did not spare a look towards those he had recently distressed. Instead, he approached the Vicar and was led to a door to one side.

Roland's gaze bit into Gabrielle.

"What! What... what is the truth of this???"

He seemed completely unable to form any further words for a moment. Into the space left by the fact that Gabrielle was equally struck dumb by the situation, Lady Eldwood spoke, her voice a little querulous as she frowned at Gabrielle.

"This *is* strange, indeed," she said. "This is very, *very* strange. Is one to expect a spectacle every time one ventures forth from the sickbed?"

"No," Roland said stiffly. "No, Mother, one is not. You are correct. This is most unusual."

"Most unusual," Devlin echoed Roland's words, his fingers tracing his scar absently. "Sister, who is this creature? From whence come his absurd claims?"

Gabrielle felt a fierce blush rise in her cheeks.

She was aware that all eyes in the church were surreptitiously locked upon her. She had never before realised how mouse-like she was. This must be how a mouse felt, when trapped by a cat. Being the centre of attention – negative and possibly judgemental attention - like this was not agreeable to her in the least. *It is as if I am a sideshow*, she thought, the blush deepening. *Like a freak!*

"I do not know, brother," Gabrielle managed to say. "I assure you, I have never before set eyes on this man. He is an utter stranger to me."

"Most unusual!"

Lady Eldwood muttered again, her expression troubled, and a little confused. Gabrielle swallowed her fear, forcing herself to stay calm, for there was nothing for them to do but wait as the mysterious stranger and the Vicar discussed his slanderous claims. Roland looked thunderously angry, and icily calm – was he angry with the stranger? Or with her? Gabrielle could only wonder, and shiver with dread. Nothing good could come of this.

Around them, people were looking about, surreptitiously, or not so surreptitiously, looking at each other's reactions, and looking at Gabrielle and Roland, and their families.

And why should they not? Gabrielle thought. *This is quite the show. Oh, people will be discussing this for years to come. I am sure that Lords and Ladies across England will hear about it. That's how it happens, is it not? A travelling merchant hears it, and he passes it along, and so on and so on, until the Lords and Ladies in London are expressing deliciously titillated horror at it.*

She sighed and interlocked her fingers in an attempt to stop her hands from shaking. She failed in that endeavour.

At length, the door of the side room opened, and the Vicar approached them, whilst the stranger stood in the doorway, waiting.

"I am sorry, Your Grace, my Lord." He bowed stiffly to Roland and Devlin. "I am afraid that I cannot proceed, in light of the man's claims."

"What, precisely, are his claims?"

Roland's tone was frosty, filled with ice to match his expression.

"He wishes to introduce himself and his claims in his own words, if you will permit..."

Devlin waved a hand.

"Bring him forth."

The Vicar approached the lectern, nodded to the congregation, and then made an announcement.

"Here we adjourn our worship. Please, leave in an orderly, godly fashion!"

His red cheeks, his talon-like grip of the lectern, brooked no argument. The congregation filed out of the church, many grumbling at being denied the next act of the drama unfolding, and the Vicar, after waving the stranger forward, disappeared to the back room. Roland, Gabrielle, Lady Eldwood, the Dowager Duchess, and Devlin and Mona were left alone with the man who had so mysteriously appeared to disrupt their lives.

The man approached them calmly, obviously not intending to rush his explanation, nor to draw things out and prolong the inevitable. He seemed perfectly at ease. Upon reaching the group, he bowed deeply to Devlin.

"Devlin Vickery, Duke of Grimstoke, Brigadier, and hero of Waterloo, it is an honour to make your acquaintance. I wish to express my condolences for the passing of your father. He was a most respected man." Devlin tilted his head at the man. The surprise he felt at this official, proper introduction was writ plain on his features. The man turned to Roland. "Roland Shelton, Earl of Eldwood, my Lord, it is a pleasure to make your acquaintance." He bowed deeply once more, and then turned back to Devlin. "I apologise for the grandiosity of my display, but I have felt the need desperately to see Gabrielle again, and I am ashamed that the moment bested me."

"I do not know you!" Gabrielle suddenly snapped. "I have never seen you before! If I passed you on the street, I would not stop to converse!"

"Quiet," Devlin said. "Let the man explain himself."

"Thank you, Your Grace," the man said, though his lips twitched, and his nostrils flared at Gabrielle's words. "My name," the man said, "is Nicholas Hodge. You may remember me, Your Grace, as the scruffy blacksmith's son with whom your younger sister started a – if I may be so bold as to name it so – a friendship. Your sister and I were friends from our third to thirteenth years when, as I gather, you, or your father, instructed her to cease her unsuitable association with a boy of my station."

An invisible hand struck Gabrielle in the chest.

As the man had approached, everybody had risen. Now Gabrielle fell back onto the pew. Her head felt heavy, her eyelids weighted.

Nicholas! Could it be true? Had the scruffy, mop-haired boy with whom she had shared such joyous times become this groomed, well-spoken man before her? Had he changed so drastically? A score of memories fluttered into her mind like hummingbirds, each one vying for space. She saw Nicholas carrying her, a slight girl, across a stream to protect her fine clothes by making his dirty boots even dirtier. She saw a young boy, grinning and shaggy-haired, steal a kiss to the cheek of a young, grinning girl. And she saw – yes, and she could not deny it, no matter how much she wanted to – a young boy kneel in the summer grass with a looped, shaved rose stem as a makeshift ring, and ask, quite sincerely: 'Will you marry me?'

And she saw the young girl giggle and reply: 'Of course, of course!'

In the memory, the boy slipped the stem onto the girl's finger - a wedding band, a seal, a promise that one day a true ring would replace the makeshift stem.

'Do you mean it? Do you promise?'

'I do! I do!'

The memory slipped from her, and Gabrielle swallowed something sickly.

These were poisonous memories indeed!

The man had continued to speak, and Gabrielle was only faintly aware that, as she had been seeing that memory in her mind, so had he been speaking it to those gathered around them – but he told it in a manner that cast it as shining and wonderful...

"Gabrielle!" Mona cried, and sat beside her. "Gabrielle, come, tell me, tell your mother, that this man is a wicked liar!"

"I cannot," Gabrielle whispered, and Mona's face dropped.

Beside her, the Dowager Duchess put her hands to her face, unable to meet her daughter's eyes.

Guilt filled Gabrielle.

"I ran away when you told her, Your Grace, that she was no longer to associate with me. I was too poor and too uncouth to be a proper associate for a young lady. I see that now. I went to London, a young boy, and I learnt the trade of acquiring and selling fine cloth and wool. I worked as an apprentice for many years in Saville Row. From an apprentice I became an expert. And from an expert I became a business owner. All through those long years of struggle, Your Grace, it was your sister's face which I saw. I returned to Grimstoke Village to request a meeting – only last night, I returned – for my mother had sent me a letter, of all the news from the Village, and mentioned that today would be the third reading of the banns. I felt I would be going against my personal integrity if I did not say something."

Gabrielle had recovered somewhat and managed to climb to her feet. She looked the man in the face, and wondered at how he had grown. Here was little Nicholas Hodge, the boy with whom she had shared so many happy, carefree moments. She searched her heart and found that the spark which had existed for him was not completely extinguished. Looking at him, she saw through his exterior into the kindness, the joyfulness beneath. If it is common for one to see in a man the boy he once was, Gabrielle had never seen it as clearly as this. His struggles were plain in the hardness of his hands, but in his face was no sign of low qualities. Somehow, it seemed, he had retained his appreciation of life.

Gabrielle felt as though she should say something, as if all around her were waiting for her words.

The problem was that she did not have a clear idea of what to say.

She knew that she, the Lady, had to refute this man, had to beat him back — humiliate him, perhaps. But the idea of hurting little Nicholas was abhorrent to her.

To insult or not to insult, that is the question!

She cleared her throat; the group turned to her. Her moment was before her. She would have to make her position clear. Words began to form.

But then Roland stepped forth, shoulders wide, and stood opposite Nicholas.

"Let me tell you, sir," Roland said, his words hard, "that your childhood fancy was exactly that - a fancy. Playful words spoken as a child do not constitute a vow which one might hold a person to. What of the countless children who make believe that they are knights? Are we to dress each and every one in a suit of armour? Ha! You will find, sir, that Gabrielle and I shall be married. It is official, and it is proper. What you have seen fit to do is certainly *not* official and certainly *not* proper. What you have seen fit to do is, in fact, improper in the extreme. I would ask you to retract your absurd claim and save what little honour you have managed to retain."

Gabrielle gasped – did Roland love her? Or was he simply defending what he saw as his own? Nicholas did not reply to this assault – he turned away from Roland and faced Devlin.

"Your Grace, would it be possible for me to speak to Lady Gabrielle privately?"

Roland stepped forward again.

"I forbid it!" he growled. "I forbid it! Your Grace, do not allow this man to treat us in such a dreadful manner!"

This sudden possessiveness, coming as it did out of nothing, shocked Gabrielle. She had never heard in Roland's voice such angry force. During their courtship, he had been kind, respectful and loving. This new side of him was not pleasing to Gabrielle's ear. She did not wish to be treated as a possession!

"Brother!" she touched Devlin's sleeve. "I am not yet Roland's to command. It is only you who can decide whether or not I and this man meet for private discourse. I appeal to you, brother, to allow this meeting." She had not planned on saying this, but Roland's words had pushed her. "We were friends for ten years, brother. Ten years! I beg you, dear brother, do not forbid me this. Oh, it will make me wretched if you do. What harm can a single meeting cause? What wicked events do you imagine will transpire from entertaining this man – this man who has been most courteous and proper – for one meeting?"

Devlin sighed, and Gabrielle knew that she had won. Devlin had been beaten, in so many ways, by the war. Now he despised conflict, Gabrielle knew, and was perpetually seeking peace and happiness.

"One meeting," he said, "and one only."

Chapter Three

"Devlin!" Roland hissed. "You cannot mean it! You will insult me – us – by allowing this man... *this man...*" His words left him, and he took a step back, as though seeing afresh the scene which lay before him, seeing it with new eyes which probed depths never before interesting to him. "This is an insult. Would you not agree, Mother, Your Grace?"

The Dowager Duchess merely nodded, still seeming overwhelmed entirely, but Lady Eldwood, who had been hitherto largely ignored, flinched when she was addressed. She closed her eyes for a few moments and then nodded shortly.

"Perhaps it is an insult, my son," she said. "But I do not imagine that it is our place to dictate what His Grace decides. And I would caution against opening a rift between yourself and His Grace, for it would serve no purpose."

Everybody nodded at these words, even Mr Hodge. Lady Eldwood's voice had penetrated her son's shield of anger. His face changed from one of total darkness to one merely pained. He swallowed the fear which prompted the anger – fear of losing Gabrielle, fear of her truly betraying him, with Nicholas Hodge. But the fear simply simmered, ready to engulf him again. He did not, in that instant, know what to do, but he felt his future slipping away from him, by the second. Devlin approached and looked down at him.

"Return to your estate, I will take care of this situation. There is no reason for you to trouble yourself. I promise you, Roland, you will be kept abreast of all developments. I will not leave you in the dark."

"That is for the best," Lady Eldwood said, close at Roland's ear. "*I* believe that is for the best. We must not behave uncivilly, simply because we do not agree with a person. That is not our family's way."

"Father would not have behaved like this," Mona reminded him. "You know that he would have been civil. Go home and take care of Mother." Mona smiled at Lady Eldwood. "You know how she has been worried of late."

"I fear that this will trouble you further, Mother."

Roland watched as his mother's face crumpled a little, as if comprehending all of it was almost too much, and another fear filled him – would poor health steal her from him too?

"I want sleep," Lady Eldwood said simply.

Roland nodded.

"Come, Mother. Your Grace, I will hold you to your promise."

Roland and Lady Eldwood shuffled out of the church, their steps slow due to her apparent weakness.

*****

Gabrielle watched as Devlin turned back to Nicholas, who had, to his credit, stood silent through the previous exchange. Devlin's face was impassive, but Gabrielle knew him well – he was seething within. His words, when they came, were cold, excruciatingly polite, and quite clearly underlaid with disgust.

"You may visit this afternoon."

As Devlin turned away from him, Nicholas shot Gabrielle a look. Shameful feelings seized her at that look. It was as though the look did not simply reach across the short space between them, but instead across the vast expanse of time. His eyes gazed out of her childhood, and reminded her that once upon a time she had been carefree and reckless.

"My Lady," Nicholas said, and bowed.

Gabrielle nodded, saying nothing, and joined the others as they made their way out of the church.

"You never told me about this, sister!" Devlin huffed as the carriage rolled back towards Grimstoke Castle. "I asked you, at the time – and I distinctly remember this – if there was anything I should know. And you told me *no*!"

"Oh, Devlin, do no berate her," Mona said. "Do you not recall how you were as a child? I seem to remember a ragged little boy walking all the way to the coast and trying to become a fisherman."

The Dowager Duchess nodded.

"Indeed, Devlin did that, foolish as it was, and survived it, due to the kindness of others."

"Unfortunately, Mother, dear wife, the rules are not the same for a man and a woman. Perhaps that is a sad state of affairs, but it is the state of affairs we have." Devlin sighed and clasped his hands. "Do you truly wish to speak with this man, Gabrielle?"

"I truly do," Gabrielle replied. "He is my friend. For the longest time, he was my dearest friend. I do not think that I should be grudged a single meeting with him."

Devlin unclasped his hands and then clasped them again, as though unsure of what to do with them. Gabrielle felt oddly guilty for distressing him, even though this mess was really none of her doing. He spoke softly, tension in every word.

"This has created problems. Conflicts. You know how a Duke despises conflicts!"

"Oh, and a Brigadier?"

Mona's question came with a wicked, rather cynical, grin. Devlin smiled then, his normal good humour coming to the fore.

"Oh, Mona, you do love to put a man down!"

*****

Roland saw his mother to the care of her maid, who readied her for bed, then he went and shut himself in his study. His mother's health worried him, yet she had the best of care – there was nothing else he could do, but hope that she slowly became stronger again, now that it was spring, and the days were warmer. But more than his mother, right at that moment, he worried most about his own future. Had he been betrayed, again? Was he somehow not adequate, no matter how he tried? Had all of his worst fears just been proven true? Did Gabrielle desire another man? She had not denied what Mr Hodge had said...

He shook his head. They had been children, not quite thirteen – a promise made then could mean nothing now – it had been all part of a game, not an official arrangement, and Roland was quite certain that the old Duke would never have agreed to promising his daughter to a blacksmith's son! The very concept was ludicrous! No matter how good a man a blacksmith's son might be, he was not of the same social status as the daughter of a Duke! And a father would always choose the match which did best for his daughter. Surely no one could believe that the man had any true claim to Gabrielle!

He shuddered. None of his own thoughts mattered – what mattered was Gabrielle, and what she wanted – for if she did not want him, the love he felt for her would make no difference... He went to the sideboard and got himself a glass of brandy, even though it was early in the day for such things – he needed the bracing warmth of it. He saw no option but to put on a determined face, to believe that Gabrielle would not betray him, to believe that she cared for him, and to believe that neither Devlin, not the Vicar would put any support behind the outrageous claim made by Mr Hodge. Fear might eat away at him internally, but he would put on a brave face, and bluster his way through the next few days.

*****

A footman led Nicholas into the large parlour, where Gabrielle waited for him.

She had contrived to be sitting by the window in a calm pose, the light behind her making her seem to glow, so that when Nicholas entered he was met with the sight of an almost angelic figure.

But this final pose had come after many discarded attempts: she had stood by the bookshelf with a novel open, pretending to read; she had reclined on the divan coquettishly; she had stood near the door, waiting; all before settling on this tactic. In the furthest corner of the room, seated on a chair tucked away between a bookshelf and a sideboard, Gabrielle's maid, Abby, concentrated on some sewing. She was there to ensure that propriety was served, and was tasked with being as unobtrusive as possible. Gabrielle did not turn when Nicholas entered. Part of this was because she knew that her expression of aristocratic distance, and her carefully fabricated defence against the pull of memories, would crumble if she looked deeply into his eyes. Part of it was because she was aware that her position was a precarious one. She was walking the tightrope of etiquette and propriety, and one slip could see her fall into disrepute.

"My Lady, may I sit?"

"You may."

There was a silence that Gabrielle did not care to break. She was distressed, and felt almost trapped – for her horror and annoyance at what he had done to her, before the entire congregation, fought with a softening towards him, born of her memories of golden days in the sun, when they were children. *He has chased me, in this dreadfully improper manner, so let* him *explain himself.*

"My Lady, I assure you that I did not mean to cause you any offence."

"Then you are extraordinarily talented," Gabrielle said, her bitterness surprising even herself.

"How so, my Lady?"

"Because you have caused me offence without trying."

She had never in her life been so sure that somebody was blushing without looking at them to check. It took all of her strength to simply stand there, and say no more.

"I wish to tell you the story of my life since we parted, so long ago, my Lady. I wish to tell it to you because I am sure that it will explain my conduct and will win me your sympathy. If I am wrong in this belief, then you must castigate me as a fool, because if that is the case, I am wrong about our entire friendship; and that is something which I cannot believe to be the case. My Lady, may I tell you my tale?"

Gabrielle felt as though she was a disinterested queen listening to the pleadings of one of her people, for she did not want to hear this. *An awful thing to think, you naughty woman!* But Ladies are naughtier than they ever show, are they not? It felt as if Nicholas had come to pay homage to her – homage she did not wish for, and had no concept of how to deal with.

"Yes," she said, with a queenly wave of her hand. "You may."

She heard him adjust his sitting position. His eyes burnt into the back of her head. She could feel them. He wanted her to turn, but she would not turn, not yet.

She was not sure if he was aware of the power his return to Grimstoke had over her, but she knew that his awareness would be awakened if she allowed him to look upon her face.

"I left my home when we were parted, because I knew then, for the first time, that I was too poor, too uncultured, and too rough for you, my Lady. I left because I knew that there was something inherently wrong with me which did not allow us – great friends, full of love – to be together. Of course, at the time I did not think in those terms, but that is how I felt. That was the driving force which led me to flee across England to London. I will not lie. For a time, I scavenged, and I begged, barely surviving."

"Oh...."

An image of Nicholas picking through the leavings of others, where things cast aside lay piled on dirty streets, filled Gabrielle's mind. She had almost gasped when she saw him in her mind, her young friend, covered in mud and dirt, his hands holding a half-eaten apple which would be his supper. She wanted to go to him now, to hold him, to somehow provide comfort in reparation for what he had endured, all those years ago, as a result of words spoken by her father, but she did not dare. She did not look at him. She remained statuesque, unmoving. Nicholas sighed.

"It was humiliating," he went on, "but it was necessary. For two years I lived as a mouse or a bird might, scavenging and only striving to fill my belly for that day, each day. All through it, I was miserable. I fear that I would have gone mad if not for the perpetual image of your face which stayed in my thoughts. If not for your countenance, my Lady, I would have lost my mind. I happened upon Saville Row one wretched morning, when I had wandered far out of the areas I might normally have frequented, and that was when I saw him for the first time - Mr. Wilkins. One would think there was nothing special about him, if one were simply to glance at him. He was a small, pinched man with pained features and a crook in his back, making him appear even smaller. Even then, he was old. I mean to say, he appeared old. I did not think much of him, but then a fine, fine Lady approached him. At the time, I took her for an angel. Now that I have seen you again, my Lady, I admit that I was mistaken. You are the only true angel I have laid eyes upon."

Despite herself, Gabrielle blushed. She did not know what to say, so she said nothing. Constantly, her gaze was tempted to turn to him. As though some otherworldly force was pushing her – some pesky love-filled Cherub, or some other creature indulging in matchmaking – Gabrielle felt compelled to open her heart to him. *But I will not give in to the pesky Cherub!* she told herself.

"The fine Lady approached this ugly man, who was in the process of unlocking the door to a shop, with something approaching diffidence. I, hiding in a nearby alleyway, watched the whole exchange. 'Good sir, do you have any...' 'Yes, yes!' the man interrupted. 'Come, Lady Crosswold, and we shall see to your every need.' I was not sure what they spoke of, not truly, but as the Lady passed, I heard her purse rattling with coins!" He paused. "Do you wish to hear the rest?" he asked tentatively.

"Go on!" Gabrielle urged him, a little too forcefully. She had to remind herself that she was supposed to be indifferent to this man. Roland was her betrothed. Yet Nicholas' story intrigued her. She had to keep a proper distance. "If you will," she added, with the hope of dampening some of her enthusiasm.

"When the Lady left, I knocked on that man's door. He made to kick me away from his doorstep – I suppose he took me for a beggar – but I leapt out of the way. 'Sir,' I pled. 'I wish to learn your trade. I will work as an apprentice without pay for as long as you deem fit, sir. I will become a slave for you!' As you can see, my Lady, I was desperate. The man's pinched eyes regarded me for a moment. 'For free, you say?' For Wilkins was the kind of man for whom money was the most important thing, no matter what. 'For free,' I said. He grabbed me by my collar and pulled me into the shop. Oh, the silk! The cloth! It was like a treasure cave of fine material, all laid out for Ladies' and Lords' perusal. 'No pay,' the man said. 'Two bowls of soup a day, and don't you ask what's in it!' I nodded, and I set to work the next day."

"Ah..."

She couldn't help it, that small gasp of astonishment which escaped her, at the thought of surviving on such meagre fare. She simply could not imagine a life like that. Nicholas went on, as if she had made no sound at all.

"Every second, I thought of you. I cared not about the state of my body, or the callouses growing on my hands. All I cared for, my Lady, was you. I saw your face in every one of my labours. I suffered greatly in those first years. I turned from a boy to a man. But I did not forget you. Even when low women approached me, I did not forget you. 'I am promised to another', I told them, and left them, with your visage burning bright in my mind's eye. And over the years, I learnt the trade, until I could talk to any Lord and Lady as expertly as Wilkins. Now, Wilkins is dead, and I am the owner of the business. I have striven for one goal my entire life, and that is to become worthy of you and your family. And I am – I am good enough, I hope you can see that. I am not highborn – we can never pretend that – but I am wealthy, and I have manners, and I love you. Yes, I love you!"

The passion of these words, combined with the imagery which assailed Gabrielle's mind, caused her great consternation. She tried to keep her gaze focused away from him, but at length she turned. He was every bit the boy who had been her great friend. His soft, friendly features regarded her gently. She felt a maternal urge to smooth a crease from his forehead. For a moment doubt assailed her – was this all truth? Or was it a false façade? Did he really care so much? Surely he did, for why else might he do this, and declare himself so? It must be truth.

"That is the most romantic thing I have ever heard!" she exclaimed, and then quieted her voice, lest somebody should overhear. "But..."

"But?"

"But I am promised to somebody else." These words, which should have brought her great pride, were like spears to her heart. Had Roland striven to win her? Had Roland striven to prove himself to her? But Roland was an Earl, and this man was not a Lord at all, not even by a courtesy title. He was a merchant, albeit a quite wealthy one, it seemed. "I can't—"

"Oh, do not speak in haste!" Nicholas jumped to his feet, reached into his pocket, and approached her, a card in his fingers. He thrust it into her hand. For a moment their hands touched, and Gabrielle felt a warm shiver. "This is my address in Saville Row. If you ever find yourself in London—"

"I will be there, one week hence," Gabrielle muttered, knowing it was wrong to admit as much to him, but unable to stop herself. "I am collecting items for my trousseau."

"Then come to me, my—"

There was a sudden rap on the door, then it opened, and Devlin walked in. Gabrielle quickly slipped the card into the pockets of her dress.

"That is quite enough," Devlin said. "Mr. Hodge, I believe it is time for you to leave."

"Of course, Your Grace."

Nicholas bowed and left them. Gabrielle smiled at her brother, all the while the card feeling as if it pressed through her dress and into her skin.

Chapter Four

It was late afternoon, and the view from the family parlour windows at Grimstoke Castle was quite breathtaking, with the newly redone gardens in the foreground, and the rolling hills visible beyond the riot of flowers. They sat comfortably, the remains of a sumptuous afternoon repast scattered on the small tables amongst them. The ladies held cups of tea, the gentlemen glasses of brandy. The conversation, as it had all afternoon, centred on the events at the church, and Mr Hodge's impertinent claim. A claim which there was, as yet, no decision about how to deal with. Gabrielle sipped her tea and watched him as Roland laughed bitterly, and then spoke in a rather arrogant tone.

"Whoever heard of a blacksmith's son hoping to win a Lady from an Earl?"

She held her tongue. Gabrielle did not like the tone in which Roland talked about Nicholas, but if she voiced this concern there would be an argument of most unpleasant proportions, she knew. She could almost hear the reproving words which would result: *You cannot be defending somebody as impudent as him! You are fighting for an upstart!* A clever Lady must know when to hold back her words, and this was one such occasion - Gabrielle's words were well and truly repressed. Mona shook her head at her younger brother – Roland had always been prone to bluster when uncertain, and she could feel the concern in him now. Devlin sat beside Mona in silence.

"Brother," Mona said. "Let us not forget that this Nicholas was a quite handsome fellow, with manners rivalling even yours. Where you can afford to be brash and abrupt, this Nicholas fellow must be proper in the extreme to overcome his low beginning in life. The effect is quite striking."

Devlin smiled indulgently as he sipped his brandy. He set his glass down.

"Ignore her, Roland, she is teasing you. My wife has become an expert at teasing, of late."

"Teasing!" Roland laughed, but there was no humour in the laugh. "Generations of Earls, and this blacksmith's son has the *gall* to dance in here and interfere with the banns. She was a child, Devlin, a child! I admit that once, as a child, I made a vow, but—"

"Oh, do stop," Mona said. "We all know that you are the finer man, brother. There is no need for this tirade. Have some self-assurance."

"My wife is right, dear fellow," Devlin said. "It would be a strange world, indeed, where a blacksmith's son, a merchant, could claim the sister of a Duke to wed."

Gabrielle stayed silent throughout this, feeling more and more troubled by it all. She was glad when the door swung open and her mother, the Dowager Duchess, walked into the room. She settled onto the couch beside Gabrielle and looked about the room.

"What, may I ask, is the topic of conversation?"

"The absurd confidence of this blacksmith fellow," Roland said.

Gabrielle risked a look at him and saw that his jaw was clenched. The distance in his manner had grown worse since the arrival of Nicholas, and his expression had been hard and almost cold each time she had seen him. Or angry... She felt as if he blamed her for what had happened, although what she might have done to prevent it escaped her. Oh, how she longed for days past, when he would rain loving attention upon her!

"Who is this blacksmith?" the Dowager Duchess whispered.

Mona hurriedly explained, no doubt wishing to prevent Roland from exploding with further frustrated commentary.

"Mother, you heard what he said at the church – we know little more than that, even after he spoke to Gabrielle – we have no more to tell you than what you already know. He is the son of the blacksmith who lived in Grimstoke Village – the one who died three years ago. This man apparently left here nine years ago, and has done well for himself, as a prosperous merchant. What I do not know is why he should think that the games of children might bind him, and Gabrielle, as adults – but it appears that he thinks exactly that."

Her mother's cheeks quivered. It would appear that the older woman had been desperately hoping that some new information might have emerged, to alter the situation.

"Gabrielle! You cannot think of marrying this — this — impudent commoner! That would kill your poor old mother!"

"Of course not, Mother," Gabrielle said. What else could she say in the face of the poor woman? She could certainly not point out that she did not think her resilient mother could ever be so easily killed.... "Of course not."

But even as she said those words, her heart betrayed her. She could not view Nicholas with the utter distaste which came so easily to those around her. They had not spent ten of their formative years in his company. They had not roamed across the hills and played at kissing and holding hands with him as children. They had not made sweet childish promises to him. She no longer knew what she wanted, unless it was to magically turn back the days, and choose to marry by license, rather than banns. That would have prevented all of this confusion and pain.

"If your father was here, Devlin, if your father was here, do you think he would have allowed this?"

Devlin sighed. Gabrielle winced internally, on his behalf, for she knew well that such a question would cut to his heart, and his own doubts about how well he lived up to his father's memory.

"What can I do, Mother? Mr Hodge was quite proper. He did not give any cause for offence – beyond the fact that he has made this claim at all. We would have been wicked to turn him away. *We* would have been the low and improper parties."

Devlin's words were correct, but it was obvious to Gabrielle that he disliked having to say them.

"Oh, if your father was here..."

There was a moment of silence, as if everyone was uncomfortable, and no one knew how to change the mood. Gabrielle's eyes were on Roland, and she wondered what he was thinking, what he might do or say – never before had they been so uncertain of each other. Then he took a sip of his brandy, set the glass aside, took an obvious deep breath, and spoke, his tone dry and rather sardonic.

"An Earl or a blacksmith's son, what a difficult decision! Just as one might agonise over which to choose, a peacock or a slug!"

The whole room erupted into laughter, even the Dowager Duchess, who was usually most proper – it broke the tension, yet it left Gabrielle feeling more distressed than ever. She felt a strong urge to stand up and announce to them - 'You will *not* mock him!' But as a Lady must do a multitude of times in her lifetime, she suppressed the urge. She nibbled on the last lemon cake on her plate, though her appetite had quite gone, so that she would not voice her unexpected pain. The damnable memories... the dreadful things that he had told her of his experiences... a flood of images flowed through her mind. She saw Nicholas in a thousand dire situations, suffering the most abhorrent pain by his own choice, and all for her. Her romantic sensibilities had never been so deeply touched. Mona's voice broke through that tangle of thought.

"Now Roland, I hardly think that a fair analogy! You are certainly not a peacock – and I thank God that you are not so much a fop as that. And you must admit that Mr Hodge has significantly more visual appeal than a slug. Perhaps the comparison of eagle to pigeon is better?"

Roland glared at his sister, and Gabrielle wondered, again, where the kind and loving man she'd thought she knew had gone. Mona's words were well chosen, Gabrielle though – Roland, especially when taken by anger like this, had the sharp look of an eagle. But his voice when he spoke was no kinder than before, although perhaps less bitter.

"Let me tell you something then! A blacksmith's son – a blacksmith's son! –will never steal my betrothed from me! I will not permit it. What a worm! What a snake! What a snivelling excuse — My poor mother abed with illness, and now this man...! Ah...!"

Something in Gabrielle snapped. Did he think that she had no say in this? She rose, body trembling.

"I fear that I am completely exhausted — yes, quite exhausted."

Ignoring everybody's caring words of inquiry, she walked from the room, her head suddenly pounding with a megrim.

*****

Roland no longer felt sure of anything. The appearance of Nicholas Hodge had left him feeling as if his life had been upended, just when he had started to have some confidence in things going well. As they sat and talked, that uncertainty, and his fury at being put in that position, had made him say things in a manner rather more aggressive than he usually might. He did not, as he heard himself speak, really like the man he sounded to be. And he had the most horrible suspicion that Gabrielle did not like that man either. He did not know what to do – it seemed that all choices, at this point, could lead to him losing the woman he loved. Yet he could not just quietly wait, could not let this man come out of nowhere, with nothing to recommend him, and carry Gabrielle off – not without at least fighting, somehow, to retain her affection.

When she swept from the room, he watched her go with a sense of almost despair. Not long after that, he made his farewells and took himself back to Crooked Hill Manor, hoping that his mother might be feeling better, that she might come down for dinner – otherwise, he would be alone, and worried about her, as well as everything else. He was fortunate, in one thing at least, it seemed, for Lady Eldwood was in the parlour when he arrived, happily reading a book, with a cup of tea close to hand. A layer of tension which he had not realised he was holding fell away at the sight of her.

"Good afternoon, Mother, it is wonderful to see you feeling better!"

She turned to him, setting the book down, and smiled.

"It is wonderful to be feeling better. The warmer spring weather most definitely helps. But Roland, you are frowning – are... are things not yet resolved about... that man?"

Roland sighed and dropped to sit on the couch beside her.

"They are not. And in truth, I do not know how we may resolve them. The Vicar does not wish to perform our marriage, unless Mr Hodge steps back from his claim – and I do not see him being likely to do that. Gabrielle also seems most disturbed by this, and I think that her memories of him as a pleasant childhood friend cloud her ability to assess him clearly, as an adult. I must let her make her own decisions, yet, at the same time, I will not lose her without a fight – I will not simply give up the woman I love."

Lady Eldwood studied him for a short while, then spoke softly.

"Then perhaps you had best focus on making Gabrielle happy, on courting her all over again, so that she can have no doubt that you love her, and is reminded of her love for you. Mayhap a gift that emphasises the strength of your love?"

"A gift? But what? What would speak to the depth of my feelings?"

In truth, the thought of assiduous courting made Roland a little queasy, for he might well end up back in a situation where he did not feel that he was acting truly as himself. And presenting a false face to Gabrielle was the last thing he wanted to do! But a gift was something he could see his way to doing. Lady Eldwood had lifted a finger to her lips, tapping it gently as she considered. Then a brilliant smile lit her features.

"Perhaps jewellery – something beautiful, that she might wear on your wedding day. But not just something bought in a hurry. I have a great deal of jewellery in my care, even after gifting much of it to your sister – pieces which were your grandmothers' on both sides. The pieces which never took my fancy, or which didn't suit me are simply packed away. If you think some of them might suit Gabrielle, then you should take them to London when you go next week, and have them cleaned, repaired or remade just for her. That would be a gift which speaks of family history, and of the place you see her holding in this family's future."

He contemplated her words, imagining how such a thing might be received. It was a good idea, and he was almost certain that Gabrielle would appreciate such a gift. He nodded slowly, feeling lighter at heart immediately, simply for having something he could do, which might help the situation.

"I believe that is an excellent idea. Please, do show me the pieces, before we have dinner, so that I can make a choice. And then, before I go to London for Lady Charrington's soiree in our honour, I will also speak to the Vicar again, and see if I can convince him to see that a promise given during a childhood game cannot possibly be treated as binding, no matter what Mr Hodge suggests. I would most definitely prefer to have this resolved before I mingle in London society as a betrothed, and soon to be married, man. I want no scandal to touch our union, beyond that which has already been caused."

*****

Margaret, Viscountess Charrington, dropped into a chair in the parlour of Grimstoke Castle, smiling broadly. Gabrielle, who had been rather doubtful, found herself immediately taken with the woman. Which was fortunate, for she was to stay with Lady Charrington in London. Lady Charrington was one of the few true friends that the Dowager Duchess had, for during the wars, the fact that Gabrielle's mother had been born in France had made many people turn away from her. Lady Charrington had not, and they had corresponded regularly. Now, when the Dowager Duchess had contemplated the idea of the two-day journey to London, she had not been able to face the degree of travel sickness which it would cause her, and had thereby written and begged her oldest friend to assist with Gabrielle's visit, so that Gabrielle might obtain all of the new gowns and the like that she should have.

So the day after tomorrow, once Lady Charrington had rested, they would settle into her carriage, and travel back to London, to Lady Charrington's Mayfair townhome. Gabrielle was excited at the prospect of the time in London, but also worried, for the whole matter of Nicholas, and his claim that she was promised to him, was as yet unresolved. Nicholas had gone back to London, apparently, to his business, with the Vicar's assurance that he would send a letter to Nicholas once a conclusion had been reached.

The fact that Nicholas was in London, and that she was going there left Gabrielle tempted, and confused. Could she resolve the matter, once and for all, somehow? And what did Roland think, really? She had seen him a little more often over the last few days, but he seemed distracted, still rather distant, even when he expressed his affection for her. She knew that Lady Charrington had planned a Soiree for a week or more's time, and that she expected to introduce Gabrielle and Roland, who would come to London for the event, to Society – which was a rather terrifying idea, from Gabrielle's point of view. And especially so, if, at that point, the matter of Nicholas was still unresolved. Which meant that somehow, Gabrielle had to find a way to resolve it, without scandal, and rapidly.

She shook her head, and turned her attention back to Lady Charrington. Lady Charrington was a somewhat plump, strong-looking woman with wide hips and powerful hands. Everything she said had a booming, dominant quality. Indeed, one was hardly sure if she was angry or thrilled when she spoke. Her husband was, Gabrielle had been told, a much thinner and quieter man.

"How you have grown!" Lady Charrington exclaimed. "Oh, how you have grown! But of course, it must be fifteen years since I've seen you!"

Gabrielle nodded.

"Yes, we do tend to do that, don't we?"

"Oh, and the wit! The wit!"

Gabrielle wondered then, if time with Lady Charrington might not become somewhat wearing... The conversation shifted to Gabrielle's mother and Lady Charrington catching up on the last many years, and Gabrielle slipped away after dinner and went to her room, to make sure that she was all organised with everything that she wanted to take with her. Her maid, Abby, quickly assured her that all was ready, and she chose to go to bed early, suddenly feeling unable to face more of Lady Charrington's brightly cheerful company that evening.

*****

Except for the frequent exclamations about one thing or another on Lady Charrington's part, the journey was uneventful. They stayed overnight at a respectable Coaching Inn, where the noise of so many people coming and going kept Gabrielle awake, but she still felt only moderately tired when they finally arrived at Lady Charrington's house.

As footmen scurried to unload their luggage, Gabrielle followed Lady Charrington up the steps to the front door, which opened as they reached it, presenting a view of an immaculately attired butler, who bowed and stepped back.

"Good evening Lady Charrington."

"Barham, this is Lady Gabrielle. Please have her, and her maid, shown to her guest suite. We will freshen up and change before dinner."

"Of course, Lady Charrington."

Abby hurried in behind them, and a footman led them up two flights of stairs, and along to a door.

"Your rooms are in here, my Lady. Your trunks will be brought up momentarily, and someone will come to guide you down to the family parlour once you've had a chance to change."

With that, he opened the door, bowed, and left them.

Chapter Five

Gabrielle changed out of her travelling clothes, after washing herself with the bowl of blessedly warm water that a maid brought up. There came a knock at her door just as she had finished her toilette, while Abby was putting the finishing touches to her hair. A footman informed her that dinner would be served in an hour, but that Lord and Lady Charrington were having a pre-dinner drink in the family parlour, and invited Gabrielle to join them.

She followed the footman down the stairs and to a pleasant small parlour at the rear of the house. It was decorated in rich burgundys, with cream and gold accents – a colour scheme which suited Lady Charrington perfectly.

Once Gabrielle was seated, with a glass of sherry in hand, Lord Charrington cleared his throat.

"My dear, do you have anything planned for two days from now?"

He regarded his wife as he asked her, with an expression which Gabrielle thought indicated that he knew full well that she had plans. Lady Charrington gave a dramatic sigh.

"I do indeed, Roderick – I am sure that I told you, before I set off to collect Lady Gabrielle, that on that day I had arranged fittings at the modiste's for her. And I must be there to chaperone her, you know that. It is difficult to get appointments with Madame Odette – she is most exclusive – and I can't simply change things at the last minute."

Lord Charrington looked somewhat put out. He sipped his brandy while his wife watched, as if needing an excuse to think before saying anything more. Eventually, he spoke.

"But my dear, we are holding a large soiree in little more than a week." He turned to Gabrielle. "As you know, my Lady, it is a soiree for your benefit, and that of Lord Eldwood. We will introduce you to Society as the Earl and his soon to be Countess, and all shall know of the excellent match you have made!" He smiled, and Gabrielle forced a smile onto her face. "There are certain particular... challenges... with the arrangements which evade my ability to resolve, dear wife. I wish you to be here on that day to see to these difficulties, for I have arranged for the relevant merchants to call."

"Husband," Lady Charrington said gently, "I have promised Gabrielle that I will stay with her for the duration of her fitting and, as I have told you, the appointment cannot be moved."

Lord Charrington thought over this for a few seconds, sipping his brandy again.

"This is a difficulty," he said, setting the glass down. "Yes, this is a distinct difficulty. I would hate, of course, to be the cause of any distress for you, Lady Gabrielle."

He cast an almost fearful glance at his wife, and Gabrielle thought 'poor man'!

"I do not wish to be the cause of any distress," Gabrielle said. "Might I suggest that Lady Charrington accompanies me to the modiste's, but returns here whilst I am choosing fabrics and being fitted? My maid, of course, can stay there with me. Then, Lady Charrington can come back to the modiste's when it is all completed?"

Lord Charrington nodded.

"That is most sensible. Yes, a fine solution!"

It was agreed upon, then.

Late that night, alone in her bedroom before she went to bed, Gabrielle sat before her mirror and brushed her hair, her mind filled with thoughts of the two weeks ahead, and especially the grand Soiree at Charrington House.

Lords and Ladies from London and beyond would come to see them, as the Earl and his soon-to-be Countess. It was an accepted thing amongst high society that, being betrothed, Gabrielle and Roland were all but married. Some of them, of course, might know about the problem with the banns. But it was also understood that a man of Roland's means and status could quite easily obtain a common or even a special license. The affair had not yet passed into scandal status, she hoped, please God!

She felt as if her life was proceeding at a precipitous speed. One moment she had simply been a young woman, unsure of her place in the world. Conceptually, she had always known that one day she would marry, and marry a man of status, given that she was a Duke's daughter, but none of it had seemed quite real – until now. Or at least, until that moment in the church when Nicholas had challenged the banns.

Now, she felt unsure – what if the Vicar refused to proceed? What if Nicholas did something else, to try to force her hand? She shuddered.

Though Lord Charrington was a Viscount, he was considered by all to be a man of significant societal prestige and influence and, in theory, as Gabrielle was to be Roland's wife, his Countess, she would appear amongst the *ton* under his patronage. She did not wish to reflect poorly on him, after his kindness.

Gabrielle was conscious that she and Roland were entering into a situation from which they could not retreat – not with their reputations intact, that was. They must appear perfectly correct, and without any shadow of scandal. After they appeared at this Soiree, they would forever be linked in the minds of the attendees. In many ways, this appearance was more solid than the reading of the banns had been.

This should have filled Gabrielle with overwhelming joy. Her mind should have been wholly occupied with imagining the regard in which she and Roland would be held. She should have focused solely on how wonderful it would be to stand beside Roland as his future wife. But her thoughts, again and again, turned to Nicholas. She opened a drawer and removed her reticule, and from it, his card. His shop was only around the corner from the modiste's, if she had correctly understood the map she had seen.

It was one of those coincidences which make a lady consider the possibility that providence has contrived a particular series of events, that providence has some plan for her, of which she is not aware.

Gabrielle fingered the card as her mind settled on Nicholas. He had fought hard for her. He had fought like a warrior for her. He had fought ceaselessly for her. Her chest filled with warmth when she thought about how hard and for how long he had fought for her. There was no comparison in her mind to the struggle he had endured. It was truly like something out of one of her mother's French romances.

An idea rose in her mind. She needed to know, with certainty, how she felt about Nicholas, and how he felt about her. She needed to make a decision, and ensure that it was acted on with great speed, for if she hesitated, she suspected that the result would be a very large scandal, no matter what decision she later made. She stared at the card, her fingers rubbing the texture of its high-quality paper.

What if, she pondered, she was to somehow sneak from the modiste's to Nicholas' shop? What if...?

But no, a Lady must not think like that.

Her thoughts, however, did not wish to be ladylike...

****

Two days later, it all happened as Gabrielle had suggested. That intervening time had allowed Gabrielle to build up a feverish anticipation of what she might do, despite those being very unwise thoughts indeed. Lady Charrington's house was mostly quiet, and the rest after the two days in the carriage was welcome, even if Lady Charrington chattered incessantly about the Soiree and other events to come. On the day of the modiste's visit, excitement filled her, and it was only enhanced when they arrived at the modiste's. The shop was wonderful and, not far away at all, was Nicholas' shop... and temptation.

After helping her select the fabrics, and the styles, Lady Charrington left Gabrielle alone with the modiste and her assistant, and Abby. Gabrielle smiled sweetly as Lady Charrington left, though behind the smile lurked a snake-like twist of the lips. Something which had never before captivated Gabrielle captivated her now: the idea of being cunning. She had never been a creature of cunning, but it whirred through her mind now in an oddly fascinating manner.

"I shall be back in no more than two hours," Lady Charrington said.

Gabrielle nodded, pleased with the situation, although still unsure whether she would have the courage to follow through with the idea which had taken hold of her thoughts.

"There is no rush," Gabrielle said. "I know that you have *so* many responsibilities."

Lady Charrington nodded, and left.

The fact that Abby was with Gabrielle might, if Gabrielle was to follow through on her thoughts, have been a difficulty, but then, as if the hand of providence moved again, after a short while, Abby begged Gabrielle's leave to go to the shop next door – a book shop – for the maid had become a voracious reader after Gabrielle's mother had introduced her to the delights of romance novels. Gabrielle granted her leave to do so, gladly, saying that she would come to find Abby once the fitting was done, or perhaps she would send the modiste's assistant to get her.

The modiste – a deferential older woman with a solid, professional look about her – proceeded to fit Gabrielle for her gowns, with the assistant's help. There were four fittings in total to be completed, but after the third one Gabrielle began to feel a strong urge to leave the shop and find Nicholas. It was an urge most unlike her, and totally against her best interests, an urge which she resisted, arguing with herself in her thoughts, but it stayed with her all the same, becoming steadily more insistent.

She began to breathe rapidly, to feel almost light headed. Even she did not know if this was by design, as an attempt to make an excuse, or a genuine response. Was she captivated by her own performance? Then, yet another circumstance aligned, when the modiste sent her assistant to another nearby shop, to fetch something she had run out of. It was too much – she gave in to the temptation, for everything had aligned to make it possible...

"I apologise," Gabrielle said, as she stepped out of the carefully pinned fabric in the changing room. Moments later, she emerged in her own dress, a simple gown she had worn because it was easy to get in and out of. "I fear that I feel rather heated - I need a moment of air."

The modiste bit her lip. Gabrielle knew that she was putting the woman in an awkward situation. What was she to do, refuse a Lady? But then again, she was a Lady... if something happened to her, she would be in an even *more* awkward situation. After a moment, the modiste settled for bravery.

"My Lady," she said, facing her with a somewhat stern expression. "I fear that would be most unwise. Lady Charrington asked me, specifically, to watch over you whilst she was gone. This is not a downtrodden area of London, it is true, but one can never be too safe. I ask you, with the utmost awareness of my inferior position, if you would wait for Lady Charrington's return."

This speech was given with such calmness and self-control that it would have defeated Gabrielle, but then the bell rang at the door, and an imperious looking older woman walked in. Gabrielle gathered, by the modiste's stricken expression, that this elderly woman was a customer of some importance. This assessment was confirmed when the modiste turned from Gabrielle and addressed the woman. Gabrielle recognised the name when the modiste greeted her with a deep curtsey - the woman was a distant relative of the royal family, and could, under no circumstances, be ignored.

Gabrielle could not neglect this opportunity. This was it, now — or never. She doubted that she would ever have a chance like this again.

She backed away to the shop door, keeping her eyes on the modiste and the customer. After a moment of conversation, the modiste was forced to enter the back of the shop to collect something for the woman. This was her chance - the shop bell rang once again as she slipped out the door, and Gabrielle was in the street, alone, without a chaperone.

*****

Roland settled the box containing the jewellery he had chosen into the lockable compartment under the seat in his carriage, confident that it would be safe there for the journey to London. He had chosen to go some days earlier than his original plan, and had sent a message ahead so that his rarely used town house could be opened, ready for his use.

He intended to see a jeweller immediately upon arrival in London, so that there might be a chance for the jewels to be ready before the planned Soiree at Lady Charrington's home.

He settled into the carriage, accompanied by his valet, and leant back, hoping to sleep for some of the journey – for two days on the road was never appealing. He had suggested that Lady Eldwood come with him, but the very thought of travelling that distance had made her wish to retire to bed on the instant. He took advantage of her not being there to sprawl along the seat, and was drifting into a doze when an unexpected sound brought him back to complete awareness.

It was still early in his journey – so early that they were still traversing the more distant parts of his estate, when a pitiful wail from the verge caused his coachman to stop with some alacrity.

What followed would, had Gabrielle been able to see it, have demonstrated to her, quite clearly, that any impression Roland gave of coldness was false...

Roland looked out through the window, just as the footman jumped down and came to open the door.

"It sounds as though somebody is hurt?"

"It's a child, my Lord."

The footman let down the steps, and waved towards the front of the carriage. Roland got out, then walked to where the footman had indicated.

The lead horse sniffed at a crumpled pile on the edge of the road, and as Roland got closer, he could see that it was a small girl, around four or five years of age. She had bloodied knees and a torn dress. How she had come to be like that, on this quiet country road, he could not imagine, but he felt a pang at the sight – no small child should be alone and hurting!

Without a word, he pulled out his fine linen handkerchiefs and ran to her. Kneeling in the dirt beside her, he gently wrapped his handkerchiefs around her knees as she stared at him with huge eyes, the tracks of tears clearly visible on her face.

Another carriage passed them then, carefully, and slowly, for the road was narrow, but Roland was focussed on the girl, who looked at him with wide eyes.

"What is your name?"

Her voice was quiet, frightened, as she spoke.

"Janie Carter, m'lord."

"And how did you come to be here, in such a pickle as this?"

In fragments, with much stopping and starting, the story was coaxed from her.

She had been playing in the fields with boys from the closest village, when a mean older boy had thrown stones at her legs, tearing her dress, and cutting her knees, then chased her until she was exhausted. She'd hidden in the hedge until the boys had gone away, then scrambled out, tearing her dress even more, to find herself on the road, rather than in the fields.

She was afraid to go home, because her father had told her not to go into the fields with the boys any longer, and she was sure that he would be angry.

But if she was not to go home, she didn't know what to do, so she had just collapsed here, and waited.

"For God or somethin'," she concluded.

Roland bit his lip, thinking, and then nodded to his coachman.

"Simms."

"Yes, m'lord?"

"Do you know where to find this girl's father?"

"Yes, m'lord. He's a small farm at the edge of the next village."

Roland nodded, pleased.

"Then we must take Janie to him. You can tell him that we witnessed her fall over on the road and scrape her knees. Why was she out here? Quite simple, at that - she was out here to see if the blackberries in these hedges were ripe yet. You see, she wanted to make a pie for him. Tell him that Lord Eldwood, his Earl, vows to the truth of this. Tell him, also, that if his Earl discovers that any harm has come to the girl, there will be severe consequences. Impress upon him the seriousness of it, mind."

"Yes, yes, m'lord," Simms said eagerly.

Roland hooked one arm under the girl's head and the other under her knees.

"I was wantin' to be pickin' berries for pie," she told him as he carried her to the carriage.

"Yes, you were. Well done."

Roland carefully passed her to his valet, who settled her on the seat in the carriage, and then he climbed in to sit beside her.

Ten minutes later, the carriage halted at the end of a very narrow lane, the footman jumped down to hold the horses, and Simms lifted the now somewhat recovered child, and set off down the lane towards the farmhouse which was just visible through the hedges.

In the quiet of the countryside, sound carries, and Simms could be heard giving the father a firm speech.

As they left the village, a few minutes later, Roland knew that the girl would be safe.

"Begging your pardon, my Lord, but that was very kind of you," his valet said, as the carriage rolled away. "Why did you do it? Many a Lord wouldn't have cared about a farmer's child."

"Sometimes, Chilton, it is pleasant to do kind things. That is all."

But it was more than that, Roland knew, if he was honest with himself.

The sight of the child had made him think of the children he and Gabrielle might have, God willing, and how he would wish them to be helped and cherished, of how much he wanted to have a child of his own, to cherish.

Of course, for that to happen, he must trust that Gabrielle had not betrayed him...

****

Her heart beat like a criminal's, in fear of discovery. The day was tolerably warm, and the sun shone through London's somewhat grimy air. In every shadow this weak sunlight created, Gabrielle saw phantoms. Each person she passed became the modiste, or Devlin, or Roland. Neither of whom were in London, but still, her mind imagined them.

But she walked on. Thankfully, the walk was short. Presently she was at the address of Nicholas' business. She stood before the storefront and gazed up at it, struggling to believe that this shop was owned by the playful boy with whom she had spent so many years in her childhood. He truly had made something of himself, despite all the odds.

It is time for me to turn back, Gabrielle told herself. *It is time for me to flee this place. I have tarried here too long – I should not be on the street alone. I am a fool to stay here one moment longer than I have already. What madness grips me? Madness!*

But even as the logical internal monologue went on, Gabrielle found herself stepping towards the door, on shaky legs. A bell rang as she pushed the door open, and then she was in the shop.

It was empty apart from her childhood friend, who turned at the sound of the bell. His face was that of a typical shop owner – filled with false kindness and deference – but it changed utterly once he saw that it was Gabrielle who had entered. Wordlessly, he walked to the door and bolted it, drew the curtain, and then faced her.

The click of the door locking alarmed her, and she swallowed.

"You came!"

He went to step towards her, as though he was the happiest man alive. His face was beaming, his cheeks immediately ruddy.

Gabrielle took a step back, the chill of what felt to almost be fear slipping through her.

Chapter Six

"I am your friend," she said, not wanting to offend him, but having to set limits. "Your friend, Nicholas!"

Her voice sounded strained, even to her own ears.

He nodded and kept at a distance.

"I am glad that you have come, my Lady." There was something different in his bearing. It was less restrained, but not monstrously so. It was as though nobody had ever told him how to behave in a Lady's presence. At intervals he would lean in, far too close, and then back away as though momentarily uncertain. Though Gabrielle knew that he acted without self-awareness, it still discomfited her. "Oh, how glad I am!" Nicholas laughed, and clapped his hands together loudly. "How I have dreamt of you, my Lady! How I have dreamt of the look which would be on your face when you saw what I have made of myself! And now, I can see that, at this very moment!"

"Yes," Gabrielle said, nodding, and waving her hand to indicate the room around them. "It is wonderful."

She was not lying; the fabrics were magnificent.

Although she wished that she was not seeing them this way, with the door locked behind her...

The utter impropriety of it overwhelmed her, and she wished, desperately, that she had not come.

Nicholas seemed unaware of her reactions, and kept speaking, his voice full of almost obsessive enthusiasm, with a very strong edge of pride.

"Yes, yes!" Nicholas laughed, crossing the room and hurriedly pulling a piece of fabric towards him. He did so with injudicious energy and a lack of care - several rolls of fabric fell and thumped to the floor.

He shrugged, lifted the bolt of fabric, and approached her. "This alone —" His eyes watered as though he could not believe the words which were about to pass his lips. "This single piece alone would have been enough for me to pay my way for a year, as a child! Now, I have hundreds of these! I have made something of myself, my Lady! And all for *you*!"

Gabrielle nodded as calmly as she could. She knew that she had to steer the conversation into less turbulent waters.

The differences in their class, and their upbringing, were becoming clear, and Gabrielle resented that. She wanted to view him as she had viewed him as a child, but now... shockingly, she found herself thinking... *Class is class, after all...* for his manner was rather... crass? Or perhaps it was simply that this was not the manner of a good man, who cared for others' comfort, more than his own?

For it was increasingly clear to Gabrielle that Nicholas' focus was entirely on his own desires.

"Do you plan on returning to the country, now that you have made your fortune? London is such a loud place."

She said this calmly, to try to instil the same calmness in him. It had almost the opposite effect.

"Return? Ha!" He clapped his hands again. There was something uncouth about that gesture, the loudness of it, the brashness of it, that Gabrielle did not appreciate. He seemed so different now, from the way that he had presented himself when he had called on her at Grimstoke Castle, almost as if that had been a carefully constructed façade... "London is the only place in England worth living. There is so much going on here. Grimstoke Village... what a boring, mundane place! What a predictable place! If it were any farther west, it would be in the ocean, I say! A place full of mundane people. Oh, Lords and Ladies excepted, of course."

He spoke without apparent thought, words tumbling from his lips as though he had no control over them.

"How is it that you have not yet found a wife?" Gabrielle said.

"I have been waiting for you, dear, sweet lady!" he laughed. He clapped his hands *for a third time*. The sound was like the tolling of an unseemly bell. "Yes, waiting for you. And such dreams I have had of our marriage! You see, my Lady, I travel for nine months out of twelve, with my wares. I travel all over England, while my assistant, who is out on errands at present, runs the shop. I have had dreams of returning from these travels to a warm fire and a beautiful, loving wife and many children! You will greet me with a smile that I have worked for years to attain! It warms my heart to think of it. It warms me greatly. We will be the happiest family alive! We will laugh and make merry for the rest of our days. Oh, Lady Gabrielle, I am so, *so* glad that you came here to see me! You have made the right choice."

"Choice?" Gabrielle said. "I have made no choice."

Something changed in his face.

It was as though all of the hope and optimism which had been filling him suddenly dissipated, leaving his face drooping, deflated. He tilted his head at her.

Her words, she sensed, were unintelligible to him. He had worked for years for her - his prize. How could she choose anybody but him? At least that seemed to be the thought which animated him.

But she had misjudged him, and herself. She had taken his carefully constructed façade of manners for the real thing; and she had thought herself capable of ignoring class – or perhaps it wasn't class which mattered, but simply the truth of the person behind the gloss of manners. And she was beginning to see that the person he had become, the person behind that façade, was self-centred, greedy, and acquisitive – and she, herself, was just another acquisition to him, it seemed.

She had made a very large mistake.

"I am afraid," Gabrielle said, suddenly all too aware, again, of these improper circumstances – she was, after all, completely alone with him, in a locked and curtained shop! - "that I must return to the modiste's. I have been away too long as it is."

"Return?" he muttered, his eyes glittering wetly. "My Lady, why on earth would you return so soon? Let us stay together all day. I will close the shop!"

"That is a most improper suggestion!"

"Ah! Propriety! Ah!"

Gabrielle felt as though insects had just crawled over her skin. His words triggered guilt within her, and regret that she had ever come here. He had done nothing dreadful, but his manner, his obvious disregard for propriety and the possible consequences for her, was distasteful to her, and she did not want to be in his presence any longer.

She wished, more than anything, that she had not ever accepted that card from his hand, that she had not shattered her untarnished memory of him, that she had not had to discover this inability in herself to accept him as he was, without expecting the social niceties which came with having been raised in a different stratum of society.

She took a step back, feeling a strong need to escape the situation.

"I must go."

"But, but, my Lady, you have broken off your betrothal to Lord Eldwood, have you not? Is that not why you are here? Please, tell me that is the meaning of your presence." He flinched when she did not confirm his assumption, but instead slowly shook her head. "But he has not worked for you as I have! He does not deserve you! He is a rotten fellow!"

Gabrielle gasped. This was beyond the limit of what she was willing to hear. He had, quite simply and clearly, gone too far. No one ever spoke of an Earl like that! *He was a blacksmith's son, and he was impudent*, Gabrielle thought, unable to stop herself, despite disliking herself for that class-based judgement. But she did not voice this thought. Her fear was too strong.

Why am I afraid? He is my friend, my dear friend.

Nonetheless, fear touched her.

"I am afraid I really must go."

She spun, and fumbling, managed to turn the lock quickly and dart out into the street. She could not bear to see his face as she left him like that.

But she had barely set a foot upon the paving outside when she felt a hand upon her arm. She was jerked back into the shop and Nicholas stood before the open doorway, blocking her escape. More than anything, he looked surprised by what he was doing. He looked down at the hand which had touched her with shock, but that expression quickly fled.

"Nicholas!" Gabrielle wept, unsure of when the tears had started. "You have hurt me!"

"*I* have hurt *you*?" he murmured, like a man a thousand miles away. "*I* have hurt *you*? How long have I worked for you?" He was speaking more to himself than to Gabrielle. "I have — yes — I have earned you! I have *earned* you! You have no right to deny me. My Lady! Please! Look at the fabrics! Look at them!"

In that instant she knew that he had somehow become so obsessed with her that he had stopped being rational, at least for that moment. Which thought utterly terrified her.

"Please, let me pass," Gabrielle said, the tears flowing freely down her cheeks. What an awful mistake she had made in coming here! "Just let me pass, I beg you."

"Beg?" Nicholas said, shaking his head. "No, no, my Lady. I will not hurt you. You do not need to beg me. I love you, my Lady. I have always loved you!" Gabrielle went to step around him, but he blocked her way again. She took a step back, and then walked directly at him, praying that he would move out of the way. But he did not. Instead, he gripped both of her shoulders in clamp-like hands. "I have waited a lifetime to do this."

Desperation shone in his eyes, and his lips trembled, as emotion overwhelmed him. Gabrielle tried to move away, but his grip was iron. He bent and pressed his lips forcefully against hers.

She tried to keep her mouth closed, but his tongue probed her. She screamed, but it was muffled. Revulsion filled her.

Finally, he released her.

Gabrielle was already distraught, but what she saw next made everything worse.

Looking over Nicholas' shoulder, her eyes fell upon Lord and Lady Tayleigh, a Baron and Baroness whom Gabrielle recognised – for Lady Charrington had pointed them out just that day, as she had escorted Gabrielle into the modiste's, as they passed on the other side of the street.

They would be attending Lord and Lady Charrington's soiree and would soon be witness to Roland and Gabrielle's entrance into society as a betrothed couple. But now they had seen her with another man, alone, being kissed, in public... They looked quite surprised, quite unable to speak.

Catching Nicholas by surprise, Gabrielle fled the shop, fled the accusing eyes of Lord and Lady Tayleigh, and ran back towards the modiste's. Tears flowed from her eyes and her whole body shook with the horridness of it.

He defiled me, she thought, anger and shame washing over her. *He defiled me. Oh, Roland, forgive me! Oh, Roland, please forgive me! I was wrong to meet with him! I was wrong!*

Once she was certain that Nicholas did not pursue her, she slowed, and pulled a handkerchief out of her reticule. She was quite certain that her frantic drying of her tears would not entirely wipe away the evidence of their presence, but she had to try. She was sure that Abby would still be deeply absorbed in books, so she should, if she could look convincing, be able to pretend... enough, at least.

By the time she reached the modiste's, she was calm, and she walked back in, as if nothing untoward had happened. The modiste eyed her dubiously, and Gabrielle put on her best smile.

"I am so sorry for how long I took! The flowers in that small park across the road are beautiful, but I fear that they have quite set my nose and eyes to running – I should know better than to go near such things in spring time!"

The modiste smiled at that.

"Indeed, spring can be trying. My own granddaughter suffers from the same. But let us hurry and get your final fitting done – we have everything ready, and I am not expecting any other customers in the next hour."

"Of course."

Obediently, she went through the process again, of having fabric folded around her, and pinned into place, but all the while she was filled with thoughts of despair – thoughts of just how certain it was that she was ruined, and all by her own foolish actions.

The thought that she would almost certainly lose Roland as a result brought home to her just how much she loved him, no matter how distant he might have been of late.

Any sniffles she did not manage to repress were taken as signs of the spring fever, and all went well, so that she even had time to step into the bookshop and retrieve Abby, before Lady Charrington arrived to take her home.

*****

Any romantic fancy Gabrielle had held for Nicholas was as thoroughly shattered as a fine china vase dropped onto a flagstone floor – into tiny fragments, which could not, ever, be put back together.

Her mind – and her heart, her heart most of all – had been completely altered. She no longer entertained, with any seriousness, the concept of Nicholas' affections. They were, she had seen, low and callow; and he was as low and as callow as his supposed affections. He had shown that quite clearly.

He did not love her – he loved the idea of her, of having her, of treating her as a reward for his effort, in the same way that having the successful business gave him status.

But she could not hold this new knowledge with any happiness or contentment. She had learnt it too late. She had allowed herself to be drawn too far into this maelstrom of confusion and conflicted emotions.

She cursed the day that Nicholas had interrupted the banns, cursed it with a viciousness which was quite unlike her.

Sitting on the edge of her bed, face buried in her hands, tears squeezing between her fingers, she cursed him completely. Lord and Lady Tayleigh had not only seen that Gabrielle was in the company of a merchant, but that he had kissed her.

It was a disaster unlike anything she had ever experienced before in her life. A disaster she had not the slightest idea how to deal with.

And now I will be a ruined woman!

She sobbed violently, all of the stress and drama of the day suddenly overwhelming her again. She abandoned herself to tears.

And now all of it will end in misery! I have ruined myself! I have ruined it all! Oh, what will become of me? What will become of my family?

Roland would undoubtedly cast her aside. There was no avoiding that. That was, unequivocally, what would happen. By society's rules, that is what he would be expected to do. So she would be one of those ladies who grow old alone, and eventually grow as malicious and hateful as the circumstances which secured their loneliness. It had always been a supreme fear of Gabrielle's that she would become like that, but that was the road which was now laid before her.

So she wept. Violently, with sobs which racked her body, she wept. She wept, and wept, for she knew not how long — time passed — and then a knock came at her door. Gabrielle was forced to lift her face from her hands. Her skin stung with dried tears. She wiped her cheeks and cleared her throat.

"Yes?"

Her voice was shaky and high-pitched.

"It is me."

Lady Charrington's voice was so full of kindness that it set Gabrielle to weeping again. She bit down on her lip to stop any sounds from escaping her. After a long pause, she wiped her eyes and managed to speak again.

"Yes?"

"May I enter? I have brought tea."

It would have been inexcusably rude for Gabrielle to refuse this simple, kind request.

"Of course."

Quickly she grabbed a handkerchief and wiped her cheeks and her eyes yet again.

Catching sight of herself in the looking glass, she knew that this would not fool Lady Charrington. Her cheeks were bright red, and her eyes were puffy and pink. Lady Charrington smiled kindly as she entered the room with the tea. She set the tray down on the dressing table, poured two cups, and then handed one to Gabrielle. Gabrielle drank, trying to be as delicate about it as she should, but truly wishing to simply gulp it down in a hurry. It seemed that hours of crying had made her quite thirsty. Drinking the tea also served the purpose in delaying speech, which Gabrielle wished she could delay indefinitely. The calm kindness in Lady Charrington's countenance was too much. Finally, she stopped sipping the tea. Fresh tears rose in her eyes. She blinked them away and forced herself not to sob, which she only managed by biting her lip again.

"Something, dear girl, is clearly wrong," Lady Charrington said. "I cannot believe that these tears have appeared for no reason, that these tears are – what? – miraculous happenings. No, no, these tears have a source. You have looked quite unlike yourself, quite distraught, from the moment that I arrived back at the modiste's. Please, child, tell me what it is that troubles you so. We would be poor hosts indeed if we allowed a woman so dear to us to weep alone in our house. Please, Gabrielle, tell me what ails you. I will do everything in my power to help you."

Gabrielle almost told her the truth. It danced on her tongue.

I have been ruined by a blacksmith's son! I snuck out of the modiste's and met him secretly! I have been utterly ruined, my dear friend!

But though she had lost her future, she had not yet lost her faculties. It was clear to her that she had to say something, that she could not push this tenacious woman away. Lady Charrington had the attitude of a woman determined to do some good - Gabrielle had to give her some answer, or she would simply keep pushing – kindly, but relentlessly. So she settled on something which was true, despite not being the source of her tears. Something which she had used to deflect enquiry before...

"I fear that Roland does not love me," she said. This way, she did not have to lie, only to tell a truth which was not the relevant truth. "I fear that he does not love me, Lady Charrington. I fear — yes, and it is a horrid fear... I fear that he wants me because of my position, my dowry, or because I am convenient for him. Of late his affections seem to have waned. He is not the loving man he once was!"

You cannot be in earnest! a voice whispered viciously. *You have betrayed him and now you weep because you fear that he does not love you! What about you, hypocrite? What about you? You must see the absurdity in what you are saying! You must!*

Indeed, she did. But if a Lady is capable of anything, it is of holding two opposing ideas in her mind at once.

"Oh, Gabrielle," Lady Charrington said, setting her hand upon Gabrielle's wrist. "You must understand that some men do not express their affections in an open, forthright way. Some men are not comfortable with it. It is my belief, too, that some men think that a request for marriage is the best declaration of love which exists in this world. It would make sense, then, for that type of man to cease excessive displays of affection if – in his eyes – he has already declared his love in the loudest possible terms."

During this speech Gabrielle had jumped to her feet. Now she laid the cup of tea down and paced about the room, wringing her hands with much consternation. What had started as an excuse to distract Lady Charrington from the truth had turned into something important. Whether or not she would come through this ordeal did depend, in the main, upon whether or not Roland had any serious feelings for her. More generally, it depended upon whether or not Roland was *capable* of serious feelings. She had seen it before. Or was that mimicry?

Chapter Seven

Roland's visit to the jewellers had gone well, and he was to receive the finished pieces in a few days' time.

Of course, that left him to worry about Gabrielle – and whether she loved him, or whether she was fickle enough to turn away from him for Mr Hodge. He wanted to believe in her, wanted to believe that she would not betray him, yet it was beyond difficult to do so.

He went to few places in London, content to sit in his misery of uncertainty and hope, and contemplate what he might do.

For he had, as he'd promised his mother, gone to see the Vicar before leaving Grimstoke Village. The Vicar had been serious, and kind, but very resolute. He had stated quite clearly that he found himself faced with a crisis of conscience, where he could not simply make a decision based on his own opinion, for he knew those involved too well.

The final conclusion they had come to did not please Roland, although he understood it well enough. The Vicar felt that he could not proceed with marrying them unless he received a written statement, from Mr Hodge, to the effect that Mr Hodge was withdrawing his claim that Gabrielle was promised to him.

Roland had given him an undertaking that he would obtain exactly that, and within the month.

He fully intended to achieve that – what he didn't know yet was exactly how he would manage to do so.

*****

Gabrielle had paced for some minutes, whilst Lady Charrington simply sat, sipped her own tea, and watched. Gabrielle was thankful for the courtesy of time – for she needed to think, very hard.

Was Roland capable of deep feeling?

She had always thought so, even though he hid it, much of the time, behind brashness or quiet. She was quite certain that he loved his sister and his mother, which would indicate that he was just as capable of truly loving her as well.

Once some time had passed, and Lady Charrington had finished her tea, she rose and put out a gentle hand to halt Gabrielle in her pacing. Then, arms outstretched, Lady Charrington enveloped her in a motherly embrace, gently patting her back.

"Has he ever given you cause to doubt his noble intentions? Has he ever given you reason to suspect that he will not protect you, that he does not respect you?"

He had been cold at times, yes, but had he ever disrespected her?

She searched her mind and found nothing. His coldness was not disrespect, merely inattentiveness. He was never rude to her; he never behaved as if he considered her worthless, or beneath respect.

"He has not," Gabrielle admitted. This realisation should have gladdened her, but it did the opposite. The increase in her respect for Roland only served to highlight her own failings. "He has, in every respect, been quite proper."

Yes, it is I who has trodden the path of the improper! I walked blindly into the worst situation, foolishly fearing no evil. Why, pray tell? How could I think myself immune from risk?

But I did, and now I pay the price – impropriety has condemned me! Ruin is undoubtedly mine!

"And has he," Lady Charrington went on, unaware of her internal monologue, her hand smoothing down Gabrielle's hair, which had become disorderly in her distress, "ever shown attention to another lady in front of you? Has he ever betrayed you in that way?"

Lady Charrington could not have aimed a truer strike at Gabrielle's resolve if she had been trying. Immediately at the mention of betrayal with another, Gabrielle crumbled. Tears poured from her eyes, and she collapsed upon the Lady before her, wrapping her arms around her neck like a child. Lady Charrington led Gabrielle to the bed, muttering banalities which were comforting despite their meaninglessness.

"It will be all right, sweet girl. There is nothing to worry about, sweet girl. Please, please, do not weep. You have so much happiness ahead of you."

Perhaps that was true. Perhaps she truly would come through this, somehow, unscathed. But to Gabrielle it seemed much more likely that she would fall into the whirlpool of ruin and degradation which was always hungry for more naïve, wayward Ladies, and be swept away.

She could feel the furious waves of this whirlpool, swirling beneath her, hungry for her company, growing larger in proportion with her tears.

*****

Roland knew that he was being cowardly. He had not been able to bring himself to call upon Gabrielle at Lady Charrington's since his arrival in London. His mind had been too full of what he needed to achieve, and too desperate to keep an image of Gabrielle in his mind, as she had been before Mr Hodge had shattered everything.

He feared, he knew, that if he called, and she did not wish to see him, he would entirely lose his way in life.

For no matter what, he loved her.

He had more strength than that, he was sure, yet he still hesitated. Finally, two days before the Soiree was due to occur, he decided to call – he must know where he stood, before that event, so that, if everything was as his worst fears suggested, he could convince them to call the Soiree off...

He could not face society as a rejected man, he simply could not bear the thought, let alone what such a situation might do to his family, and Gabrielle's.

So he steeled himself, and went – earlier in the day than it was perhaps ordinarily polite to call, but he needed to act. He was shocked, therefore, to find other callers on the doorstep at the same time. They were admitted, and shown into a large parlour where, moments later, Lord and Lady Charrington joined them.

The conversation of the next few minutes was, perhaps, the most unpleasant of Roland's life.

It ripped his heart out, and effectively tore it up before him.

It displayed just how thoroughly he had been betrayed, and how foolish he had been to ever believe that he might be allowed lasting happiness. And he had to sit there, through that, maintaining a calm façade, and then, on top of it all, face Gabrielle...

*****

Gabrielle woke to the sound of visitors arriving.

At first she was not sure who it might be, so early in the day.

Then she heard Roland's voice — her Roland!

She jumped out of bed and hastened with her morning toilette, paying extra attention to the colour of her face. She applied a little rouge to disguise the worn look which the recent crying had caused.

When she was finished, she hoped that she looked young and beautiful. She knew that she would have to rely heavily upon her beauty in the coming meeting with her betrothed.

Her beauty (physical and otherwise), she was aware, was what had brought Roland to the courtship in the first place.

Now it would be her refuge and her main weapon. It would be her sword and shield both.

As she descended the stairs, she overheard Lady Charrington speaking to her husband.

"He stopped for a little girl, as Lady Drydale tells it. The girl was in a fright before Lord Eldwood saw to her. He soothed her – even gave her his fancy handkerchiefs – and thoroughly calmed the situation, then took her to her home in his carriage. Is that not wonderful?"

Gabrielle hurried on, not wanting to be caught eavesdropping. Her regard for Roland soared at overhearing this. If ever she had needed proof that he was kinder than she had hitherto given him credit for, it was here. She wished that she had seen it.

It was difficult for her to imagine Roland – who had been so stony-faced of late – being so kind. But he had been kind to her in the past. And had he truly been unkind to her? Or had she, like so many ladies, let her romantic desires get the better of her?

More and more, she was sure it was the latter.

She walked down the stairs and to the small parlour, but it was empty. Perhaps they were in the large parlour?

Suddenly afraid to see him, she went to the enclosed garden and sat for a time amidst the pleasant-smelling blooms. She wished that she could take strength from these scents, but the longer she sat, the more nervous she grew.

After around fifteen minutes had passed, she went back in to the house, and to the large parlour.

Roland was there. She glimpsed him through the doorway, as the door was ajar, and it was as though she was seeing him for the first time. He was slightly reclined in his chair and, though his features were sharp, there was an openness and an amiability to them which was quite refreshing.

In that instant, she saw her betrothed with completely new eyes.

For a blissful few moments, she forgot the nastiness with Nicholas. A genuine smile spread across her face as she entered the parlour —

And died when she saw that Roland was not alone.

Lord and Lady Tayleigh, the Baron and Baroness who had seen Nicholas kiss her, also sat in the room. What she had taken for amiability on Roland's face, she now saw, was his effort to mask his pain. His lips twitched, wanting to grimace rather than keep the forced smile.

The room was full, in fact, and Gabrielle had only seen Roland because her focus had finally settled in its rightful place — just at the time when the object of her focus would be taken from her!

Lord and Lady Charrington, Lord and Lady Tayleigh, and Roland all turned and stared silently at her. Lady Charrington's expression was both understanding and betrayed, as one who has been taken into confidence only to find that the confidence was incomplete, and nigh on under false pretences. Lord Charrington was astonished that something like this could happen to a young lady under his care. The Baron and Baroness, strangers to Gabrielle, were more difficult to read. All she could discern was simple disgust and confusion. Roland's face left no room for interpretation.

He looked up at her arrival, his façade vanishing. A look so full of pain that it stabbed directly to Gabrielle's heart took hold of his face.

"I have just been told," he said simply. "There are many emotions which might take hold of a man at a time like this, I fancy. But what currently fills my breast is not disgust or hatred. It is not repulsion. It is not even resentment. No, what fills my breast is numbness. You have numbed me, Gabrielle, to all that I have previously felt for you." He sighed. "You see," everybody, including Gabrielle, listened to his words raptly. A peep into a man such as Roland's mind would have been difficult to resist at the most placid of times. In the present circumstances, it was irresistible, "you see, I had a great amount of love for you. *Had*, I say. Perhaps I still do. But I cannot feel it right now, Gabrielle, because you have betrayed me. Yes, yes! You have betrayed me in a most wicked manner! How can I look at you, Gabrielle, when you have done this? How can I be near you? What do you expect of me? To submit to this man's usurpation of my place? Is that what you wish? Do you want to make this man your husband?"

"No!" Gabrielle broke out. Tears slid down her cheeks and ruined her rouge. "I can explain, Roland, if you will give me but a moment!"

"Most improper!" Lord Tayleigh snarled. Lord Charrington, the small, scared-looking man, nodded in agreement like a squirrel who has just spied a nut. "Most improper!" Lord Tayleigh went on. His wife's head bobbed beside him.

So that's two squirrels.

The thought was ridiculous, and utterly out of place, yet her mind insisted on throwing it out, as if the mere idea of looking at things seriously would lead her to collapse.

Lady Charrington did not nod. But three had taken against her and Gabrielle had little in the way of resistance. All she could do, she did, and desperately.

"Roland, Roland," she pleaded. "I beg you, listen to me. I can explain. It is not what you think. I promise you that. It is not what you think!" With tears flowing, she cried on: "If you will but come with me, and let me have a word with you in private, I can make this all quite clear! I promise you, I can! Oh, Roland, please, do listen to me! I can make it all clear!"

"I am afraid, Gabrielle," Roland said, "that I cannot believe you at this present time."

Slowly, he rose to his feet, walked past her out of the parlour, and left the house. Gabrielle was left standing like a jester before them all — a jester who has run out of jokes. It was as if she was an actress in a tragedy which had no hope of a happy ending. She wiped the tears from her cheeks, but more tears replaced them instantly.

I can't let him go! I can't!

She left the parlour and went towards the front door. She would have made a frightful spectacle on the streets of London, but from this embarrassment she was saved.

Lady Charrington followed her to the front door and took her arm.

"You cannot," she said, in a tone of voice which left no room for argument. "You cannot follow him, Gabrielle. It would be extremely improper. I implore you, do not make your situation worse than it already is. Child, child, listen to me, I who have your best interests at heart."

She nodded, accepting the truth of Lady Charrington's words.

The tears were so fierce now that every sob threatened to tear her asunder. She was afraid that her body would collapse in upon itself if she allowed it. With a great effort, she managed to stumble up the stairs and into her bedroom. She all but fell into the chair at the desk.

Taking paper and a pen, she wrote rapidly, pouring out her feelings, her thoughts, and her pain, her writing so hasty that it would be illegible to anyone but herself.

> *I have pushed away the only man whom I ever loved, and I am a blasted fool and I do not know what to do and — ah! Life is cruel for Ladies, is it not? I would like to find the man who created the concept of correct behaviour for upper-class Ladies and give him a stern talking to, yes, yes, I would! Mayhap I could be a milkmaid and milk cows all day long and think of nothing but the cows and their milk! Yes, that would be a sweeter life! And if a milkmaid kisses somebody, is there a tribunal? Ah, the shackles of privilege!*

She took deep breaths and went on, more steadily:

> *It is quite clear to me now that Roland is easily the better choice. I love Roland and I have no feeling at all for Nicholas except disgust. When one reads 'steal a kiss', one does not know how objectionable it can be! I did not want his lips upon mine! I did not ask for them! And now the world is set against me and the man I wish to marry turns from me, too. What can I do? Tell me, somebody, tell me what I can do! I want to be Roland's wife. I want it with every shred of my being. And now it is impossible. I have ruined it all and if I was a braver woman I would—*

What would she do?

She set the pen down, picked up the paper, and savagely tore it to pieces, then tossed it into the fire.

She knew now what constituted the fundamental difference between Roland and Nicholas.

She knew now the true source of her earlier foolishness.

Where Roland gave loving attention to her and wanted her because he wanted her, the person that she was, Nicholas only cared about impressing her with his altered status in society, and impressing others with having a Duke's daughter as his.

Roland had paid attention to her for the pleasure of her company, and for the suitability of the marriage, for both of them. Nicholas, on the other hand — Nicholas had wanted only to wave the physical evidence of his new wealth and position before her, in an attempt to bedazzle and mesmerize her.

As though I am some kind of kitten, to grasp at shiny things!

Nicholas saw her as a reward for his efforts, another thing which he could show off to the world – no matter what she might personally want.

The scene which now filled her mind was one of Roland's earliest visits to her, at Grimstoke Castle. It was summer. She and Roland sat in a garden in the Grimstoke Castle grounds, the flowers blooming, the atmosphere exceedingly pleasant. For a long while they had not said a thing, but somehow that had not been discomfiting.

Even then, they had been very comfortable in each other's presence.

After the silence, Roland had spoken.

"It pleases me to simply sit here with you, my Lady. I hope that you do not think that I am overly forward, but I would like to see you again. I would like to frame myself by your regard; I would like to spend enough time in your company that we come to know each other's thoughts without recourse to speech. Is that something which interests you, my Lady?"

"It interests me greatly, my Lord," Gabrielle had replied truthfully. "I, too, would like us to grow used to each other's company."

And that was what had damned her. She had strayed because they had become *too* used to each other's company. Gabrielle had taken that intimacy for which they had both striven, and achieved, as coldness and disinterest. But looking back, his apparent coldness had always turned out to be quiet affection – an affection which did not need excessive representations, but simply the joy of being with each other.

I have damned myself by not appreciating what we both strove for! I have damned myself by being too weak to see the value in the prize for which we both worked!

Gabrielle was too close to the situation to truly appreciate the irony of it.

*****

Roland walked out of Lady Charrington's house, and, barely aware of where he went, kept walking until, some hours later, he came back to himself in the midst of Hyde Park, in a quiet glade amongst the trees. There was a fallen log, so he dropped to sit on it, and began to sort through his thoughts and feelings, consciously.

The image of Gabrielle's face, so full of distress, of her voice, desperately pleading with him, filled his mind. Should he have stayed, and listened to whatever she wanted to say?

But what could she have said to change anything? She had betrayed him, had been seen in public, kissing... *that* man.... Surely nothing could excuse such a thing?

He should simply walk away from the betrothal, should ignore her – that is what society would expect... yet he found that he couldn't so easily let go of the dreams he had held for years. He wanted to know what she would have said. Wanted to know if there was any possible way in which what Lord and Lady Tayleigh had reported might not be complete and utter betrayal.

The bald truth was that yes, he was a fool – a fool who still loved her, regardless of all else.

Chapter Eight

The day after the scene in the parlour, Gabrielle's weeping was interrupted by a knock at her door. Though she felt wretched, she knew that she should respond.

"Enter."

Lady Charrington came quietly into the room. The plump lady looked down, with a sad grimace of pity, at the pitiful creature that Gabrielle had become. Roland had returned the previous night, only long enough to assure Lord and Lady Charrington that he was well, and to tell them that he was going to his own Townhouse. He had not accepted Gabrielle's request for an audience. He had not wanted to talk to her at all, he had said. Lady Charrington was not so sure that those words were entirely truthful, but she had held her counsel. Meanwhile, Gabrielle had given herself over to hopelessness. Now she managed to sit up and prepare herself to take the next blow – for surely Lady Charrington had come to tell her something – and she could not imagine it to be anything good. Lady Charrington sat on a chair beside the bed. Her expression was quite unlike her normal demeanour, seeming far more serious, and almost uncertain. She took a deep breath, as one who is about to dive under water, and then spoke quickly.

"We have decided to cancel the Soiree, Gabrielle. The Soiree's purpose, of course, was to present you and Roland as a betrothed couple, but with the objection at the banns, and this current scandal... how can we do that, Gabrielle? It is quite uncertain – I do not mean to hurt you, but this is the truth as I understand it – it is quite uncertain that Roland will — will go through with the proceedings. So you see—"

"Oh, I see!" Gabrielle growled. "I see quite well! Yes! Now, if you will please leave me."

Ignoring Lady Charrington's stunned look, even though she knew that she had been unconscionably rude to the woman who had tried to help her, Gabrielle lay back down and turned over, buried her face in a pillow, and threw herself into crying. Sobbing had become her natural state now. When Lady Charrington sighed and left the room, the door's closing was like a trigger for more sobs.

After an hour or two – time had become fluid – Gabrielle began to formulate a plan in her tempestuous mind. Undoubtedly, it was a plan conceived in desperation, but it was a plan which became, to her perception, more and more necessary the more she cried - it was the only solution she could see to her problems. There was nothing else which would save her she was sure. She wanted Roland, and this, she thought, was the only way to make it happen - Nicholas had to retract his objection. Nicholas had to quell this scandal which he had caused. Nicholas had to make it right. After all, it was his fault it was wrong. Her plan was solidified when she realised that she had nothing to lose. It was this or spinsterhood — or worse.

She waited until late afternoon, when Lady Charrington had gone to make calls, and Lord Charrington had gone to his club. It was the time of day when the servants were less active as well, except those in the kitchen preparing for dinner. She wiped her tears away, dressed in a plain gown, - she did not call for Abby, for she had demanded that the maid leave her entirely alone, earlier in the day - then crept from her room, down the stairs, and out of the front door at a moment when the footman on duty had stepped away for a few minutes. Gabrielle had never walked faster in her life than she did in that short space between the front door and the small gate which led into the street. When she closed the gate behind her, she let out a long breath and turned towards the lane which would take her to the shortest route to Saville Row, and her confrontation with Nicholas.

As she went, she clenched her fists so hard that her nails bit into her palms, determined that nothing would stop her from demanding what was right.

*****

Roland had spent the night, and the morning, in mental turmoil. There was only one possible way forward – he had to speak to Gabrielle, and hear what she had to say, to understand whether she truly had betrayed him, or if there was some other explanation, however implausible that seemed. And if there was... then the next thing he needed to do was wring a written retraction of his claim out of Nicholas Hodge. If there wasn't... he refused to contemplate that possibility. It was late afternoon when he knocked on Lady Charrington's door, to be admitted into a flurry of activity which centred around Lady Charrington moaning and wailing and wringing her hands.

"My dear Lady, whatever is the problem?"

She spun towards him, and wrung her hands harder.

"Oh! Lord Eldwood! She has disappeared! Whatever shall we do? What if something terrible happens to her?"

Roland felt a dreadful sinking sensation in his stomach.

"Who has disappeared, Lady Charrington?"

"Lady Gabrielle! I went out on calls, and Rodrick went to his club. When I got back, just now, I went to see how she was, as she has been so very distraught, and she wasn't there! Just gone, not even her maid with her!"

Roland swallowed, and forced himself to stay still.

"Had she said anything which might indicate....?"

Lady Charrington half shook her head, then paused.

"Not really – she had been weeping, and she said some things about it all being Mr Hodge's fault, that she should demand that he put it right, something like that..."

Roland swallowed, hard. 'That she should demand that he put it right...' – he could take those words one of two ways. The first, and the one which tore at his heart, was that Hodge should marry her, having publicly ruined her. The second, which he desperately hoped might be what Gabrielle had meant, was that Hodge should disclaim any interest in her, and admit to having touched her against her will – for surely that was the only possible cause for what Lord and Lady Tayleigh had seen, if Gabrielle did not want Hodge?

The latter would still be a rather shocking scandal, but it would, at least, mean that she had not willingly betrayed him. There was only one way to discover the truth – speak to her. And if Lady Charrington's report of what she had been saying was correct, then he suspected that he knew where she might have gone...

"Thank you, Lady Charrington. You've been most helpful. I fear that I know where she has gone. If I find her, I will send her back here, in my carriage. You are to pack her belongings, and ready her to travel back to Grimstoke Castle, as soon as possible."

With that, he spun, and hurried out into the street, leaving the Lady staring after him with a bemused look on her face.

*****

Gabrielle barged into Nicholas' shop without heed of who might be in there. She hardly cared, as long as she could dig her claws into the man who had sent her into this spiral of wickedness, and extract whatever was needed to fix things. The shop was empty apart from Nicholas, who turned at her entry. She was so ready for combat that his smile unbalanced her for a moment.

"I am so glad that you came back," he said, as though he had never been unreasonable. *As though he were not* the *devil incarnate!* "I have prayed for your return, my sweet friend, and here you are. It warms my heart. It makes me happier than you can imagine. Oh, how you have pleased me, sweet child!"

"Don't!" Gabrielle snapped. "I will not listen to one moment of sophistry! You are a trickster, sir, and have naught to do with the boy I once knew. I am here with one purpose." She took a step forward, fists clenched, and would have flown at him had her breeding and long education in proper behaviour (not to mention her cumbersome dress) not made it impractical. "I am here to tell you to withdraw your pathetic objection to my marriage to Roland. You cannot truly think that an oath made as children – when we were too young to know what oaths were – means anything now. You cannot truly believe that I would fall into your arms because once, before we were old enough to know better, we made a silly promise. No, you cannot truly believe *that*!"

"I do believe it," Nicholas said, shrugging. "If you have changed since that time, I have not."

"You are wrong," Gabrielle countered. "You have changed considerably. The boy I knew never would have caused me this pain. The boy I knew never would have forced himself upon me!"

"Is that what you call our kiss?" Nicholas said, bringing a hand to his chest at the blow. "Is that what you call our beautiful kiss?"

"You are deluded, sir," Gabrielle said slowly. "You are thoroughly deluded. I ask you, please, withdraw your objection. It is groundless. We live in a poor state indeed when a child's promise can dictate a Lady's actions, but it is as it is, and there is little I can do about it. Withdraw your claim — withdraw what you should never have been allowed!"

"Look at this." Nicholas waved a hand at the fine silk and cloth. "I have buyers who are Dukes, just like your brother. I have prestigious buyers. Do not let my simple attire fool you. I have no pretensions, but I am wealthy, most likely beyond the scope of your imagination. I could go anywhere, Gabrielle."

"I do not want to go anywhere with you," Gabrielle retorted. "I am happy for you, truly, but my only wish is to marry Roland. I do not even know if that is still possible, but it is my wish, and you are in the way of it. I ask you again, withdraw."

"From what am I supposed to withdraw? Shall I withdraw from the Lady who I love more than life itself? Shall I withdraw from her who blesses my very soul? You underestimate me, Gabrielle. I am tethered to you. There is no other way to say it. I am tethered to you — completely. Yes, yes! You are mine and I am yours. It is, I think you will find, as simple as that. So you can make your objections, you can cry, you can scream, but it will not change the fact that I adore you. I have travelled; I will bring you things from all over the world! I will go to Egypt and Paris and — and to the moon! Yes, to the moon I shall venture for my sweet beloved."

If it had not hitherto been clear to Gabrielle that this man was a pathetic figure, it was now. His words were as empty as the wind. His bold declarations were as meaningless as the melodramatic gestures with which he embellished them. He was pathetically obsessed with the world as he had imagined it – including her – and no longer saw reality at all. He was a man, Gabrielle now realised, who could gesticulate and bellow, but who lacked the subtlety of a man like Roland. She felt a strong urge to slap Nicholas across the face. What a sight that would have made! But she restrained herself and instead focused upon him as calmly as she was able.

"I am sorry, sir," she said, in the calmest voice she could command, "that you view me as a Lady who can be bought as cheaply and easily as that. I am sorry, moreover, that you think so little of yourself... it is a poor man indeed who must use riches to win the heart of a Lady. I must make this clear to you, for I see that you are having trouble comprehending my words. I will not, under any circumstances, marry you. My heart belongs to Roland, and with Roland it shall remain. You have hurt me, monstrously, brutally. Withdraw your claim!"

With these last words Gabrielle waved her hands frantically, as though she could mesmerise him into submission. Nicholas only turned his nose up with contempt. Now, for the first time, the true Nicholas peered at her through his transformed face. Where he had been kind and open, now he was wicked. A shadow had overtaken his countenance, and Gabrielle shrank back from it.

"You are a romantic, Gabrielle," he said. "That is why I love you so. But we must beat this overzealous strain out of you. Really, now, please, one almost thinks that you are hysterical. Must you speak to your future husband in such low tones? Do not forget that I am a *lordly man* now."

"Ha!" Gabrielle coughed out the laugh. "Ha!" she repeated, and was satisfied to see him flinch. "You will never be lordly. Had you all the fineries in England, had the King himself knelt at your feet and proclaimed you a god, you would still not be lordly. A Lord is what he believes and does, more so that what he owns. You cannot clean what is inside you, Nicholas. A man who would knowingly and vindictively harm a Lady, as you are doing, will never – never – be lordly."

With a flash, Nicholas darted forward so that he was within inches of her. A scent suspiciously like liquor flowed from his mouth. *I should not have come here,* Gabrielle thought, her body beginning to shake. Whatever courage she had felt, moments ago, fled. She looked up at this looming stranger and felt a prick of fear more intense than any she had ever felt before. She was aware of the door behind her, but she was also aware that her back was pressed against it, closing her in with him. She feared that he would touch her, but for the moment he only leaned over her, staring down at her. Looming, threatening. A quiver ran through her, and it was obvious that he saw it.

"You are right to fear me," he said, his pretensions scattered like dead leaves. "You should not forget that I lived as a savage for a time. It is only natural that one who lives as a savage should do savage things. Do not imagine that my time of suffering was noble or empowering in any way at all. It was not. Let me tell you quite clearly — it was not! I was a mean, brutish boy. I did things which would make a Lady such as yourself squeal in fear. I stabbed a boy two years my senior —"

"I will not hear it!" Gabrielle protested, bile rising in her throat. "I will not hear it! I will not hear it!"

He gave a half-strangled laugh. Her stupidity in coming here willingly was laid plain before her. Ghastly images of obituaries filled her mind, for she felt that, in that moment, he was quite mad, and might do almost anything – including kill her if she resisted him too much. Yet she could not just tamely allow him what he wanted – she could not! She backed further into the door, the wood pressing hard against her body. She looked around the room for something which could be refashioned as a weapon, but nothing presented itself.

She was trapped. She thought about applying her knee to him, precisely where it would hurt most – or so she had been told. Of course, a Lady does not knee people. But a Lady must also be adaptable. Perhaps it was possible that this Lady could adapt her knee to this ruffian's private parts? But her thoughts were cut short when he seized her arms and pinned her leg with his knee, pressing her into the door even harder. Gabrielle struggled, which only resulted in Nicholas twirling her around to the counter, as though in some sickening dance.

"You will give me what's mine! You will give me what I have earned!"

"You are delusional," Gabrielle breathed, struggling to form words under the immense weight of him. "You are quite delusional, sir!"

He moved his face towards hers. Time seemed to slow as Gabrielle waited for those repulsive lips to reach hers. She moved her head from side to side, but he advanced, his face looming ever closer.

"No, no," she said. "No! No! *No!*"

A crash — a release— Gabrielle found herself on the floor, panting.

At length she looked up and saw Roland, fists clenched, standing at the now open door. Nicholas stood above her, a shocked look on his face – it seemed that Roland's forced entry had startled Nicholas, causing him to release her.

"What," Roland said through gritted teeth, "is the meaning of this?"

Gabrielle let out a cry as Nicholas grabbed for her, dragging her to her feet again.

*****

Roland had hurried from Lady Charrington's, his carriage arriving in the street just in time to see Gabrielle thrust the door of the shop open, and charge inside. The way that she moved, the way that her hands were clenched into fists at her sides, did not suggest a woman rushing into the arms of her lover, and some of his fear left him. He flung himself forward, and came to a stop outside the door. Should he go in? Even as he considered the question, the sound of their voices came to him. He stepped closer, and placed his ear to the door, engaging in the most ungentlemanly practice of eavesdropping. What he heard stole his breath.

Gabrielle was declaring her love for him, Roland! And Hodge was demanding that she love him instead, in a manner suggestive of madness. He realised, quite quickly, that Gabrielle was standing against the door – which left him in some difficulty, for opening it would almost certainly hurt her, or at the least push her harshly aside. So he stayed there, listening, his horror growing, until it reached a point where the door shuddered as Hodge thrust her against it. She fought him, and Roland's heart nearly broke to imagine what she faced. Just as he considered battering the door in, even with her against it, he heard the scuffle of feet, and her protests – Hodge had swung her away from the door. Without hesitation, Roland flung it open, and stepped in, ready to plant Hodge a facer if necessary, to get him to release her. But the shock and surprise of his entry had removed the need for that – Hodge had released her, dropped her, basically, and now faced Roland with a countenance full of fury.

Gabrielle scrambled, attempting to rise, and without breaking his eye contact with Roland, Hodge reached for her, grasping her harshly and pulling her up, his face purpling, his expression one of mixed horror and despair, greed and obsession. Roland forced the words out through his near clenched teeth, holding himself back only because Gabrielle was far too close to danger.

"What is the meaning of this?"

Hodge sneered at him, not deigning to answer, and instead pulled her closer to him. Gabrielle, he was proud to see, was shifting her feet, slowly resisting that pull, looking for a moment when she might remove herself from Hodge's grasp.

He shifted himself – he would try talking the man into releasing her, into sense, but he was prepared for fisticuffs if it came to it.

"You will let her go..."

Chapter Nine

Nicholas held Gabrielle roughly by the arm as he faced Roland. She knew, then, that this was no longer about her. Nicholas would have snapped her arm if it had meant winning a victory over the man who now challenged him.

"You will let her go," Roland said. "You will let her go or you will spend the rest of your short life in custody, at the end of which the onlookers at Newgate will have a pretty show indeed."

Roland spoke with utter control, the kind of control which few men find themselves able to match. Nicholas was not one of them. After regarding Roland for a few seconds to gauge his earnestness, he released Gabrielle. It was clear to her that fear for his own safety overrode any of the affection he professed to hold for her. She nearly staggered, even though she had been preparing for that moment, for the chance to escape. She fled to Roland, expecting an embrace, a shred of affection. What she got instead was a dismissive wave of the hand, and a very hard look.

"Roland..."

"Get to the carriage, tell the coachman that I order him to take you back to Mayfair, immediately."

"But—"

"Tell the coachman - I will hear no more about it. Do you have no shame? Your only thought now should be of returning to Lord and Lady Charrington's house. That is all I want from you."

Though he spoke with sternness, he did not look at her. This, incongruously, gave Gabrielle reason to hope. *He will not look at me because he feels too deeply,* she reasoned. *He will not look at me because the pain is too much for him to bear. Because he loves me.* But how to tell if that was truth or only her wishful thinking?

Left with no choice, Gabrielle went into the street, passed Roland's message to his coachman, and climbed into the carriage. As the carriage drove away, she wondered fitfully what was transpiring between Roland and Nicholas. She feared violence, firstly.

But secondly and thirdly and fourthly she feared innumerable social ruins. If they did not kill each other, it was possible that they would somehow conspire to harm her, although she could not really think that of Roland, no matter how angry he was. Or that others would see their altercation, and that gossip would spread, utterly removing any hope that she had left. *None of which could harm me more than I have already harmed myself.*

*****

Coldly sending Gabrielle off like that was one of the hardest things he had ever done – but it was necessary. She needed to understand how serious the situation was, and Hodge needed to see no weakness on his part at all, or who knew what mad action the man might try to take. He stood there, saying nothing, simply glaring at Hodge, until he heard the sound of the carriage wheels on the cobbles, as it turned and carried Gabrielle away. Then he carefully closed the door.

"Sit." He pointed at the chair behind the counter. Hodge hesitated, then sat. Roland smiled, a rather wolfish smile, and went forward to lean casually on that counter. "We have, Hodge, rather a lot to talk about. I take it from your reaction just now that you have come to the sensible realisation that you value your life, and your prosperity, more than your obsession with Lady Gabrielle?"

Hodge ground his teeth, then gave a surly nod.

"I do, although it pains me to say it, for I have desired her for so long. But still... no woman is worth giving up my life for."

"I am glad that you see it that way. Now let me describe some possibilities for you, about how your life might go, from this day forward. Then you can make a choice. And, let me make one other thing clear before I tell you that – if you should attempt to do me harm, here and now, your business and your reputation will be destroyed, completely. I have made certain that there are those in power who know rather more about you than you would wish spread about, and who will ensure that any foolishness on your part meets with swift retribution. So... shall I begin with the least pleasant possibility for your future, or the most?"

*****

When Gabrielle arrived at the house, she was met by Lady Charrington, who led her to her bedroom. Gabrielle found her trunks stacked there, already packed.

"I do not understand," Gabrielle said. "My dear friend, I do not understand. Is it that you wish to be rid of me?"

"Not I! Not I, never think it!" Lady Charrington took her friend's hands and together they sat upon the bed. "You see, Gabrielle, Roland noticed your absence and he went looking for you. 'I fear that I know where she is', he told us, and marched from the house. There was nothing we could do to stop him. He was like a force of nature as he stormed out! He told us that when you returned, you were to be sent back to Grimstoke Castle. You are to leave now, Gabrielle. Oh, please, don't hate me, for I am your dear friend, who has tried to be like an older sister to you!"

The strangeness of the situation was highlighted by Lady Charrington's pleading. She rarely pleaded, but Gabrielle could not deny that it was happening in front of her eyes. For a moment, she was tempted to lash out at the woman, which would be a shameful thing to do, but the impulse dies as quickly as it had come. To do such a thing would take more energy than was left in her body – the events of the day had drained her, leaving exhaustion and despair. She felt immensely tired, that was all, as though she could sleep for a thousand years, and not be rested. She would sleep for eternity if the phantoms of her mistakes would only leave her be.

Tears poured down her face, but they were the type of tears which a Lady cries when crying can be of no use - quiet, reserved. There was no point in wailing loudly or pleadingly. The time for that had long passed... She did not know what Roland would do, did not know if he would ever even speak to her again, and that tore at her like a knife to the heart. She did not want to go, did not want to accept the truth of the utter ruin of all of her hopes... *But I cannot fight it any longer!* She would go.

*****

Sitting in the carriage, with naught but a very quiet Abby for company, Gabrielle criticised herself, internally, examining everything which had happened, and finding a thousand wrongs on her own part. She also made excuses for herself. Self-criticism and the prodigious production of excuses are not mutually exclusive within a certain stratum of English society, for the *ton* had long ago mastered that strange contradiction as a near art form. Gabrielle had, growing up, learned how to be part of this not so noble tradition. So, whilst she thought with pure self-hatred of how she had destroyed all of the good things in her life which had been given to her, she also reasoned that she had been at a disadvantage from the start. She truly did not know how to be completely honest with herself, to completely accept all of her failings, and to attempt no words in her own defence. So she stared out of the carriage window, sitting in silence, and the thoughts flowed, a continuous series of contradictions.

How could she, who had never involved herself in events of this kind, have foreseen the quagmires which would so captivate her? How could she, who had never been tricked, know that she was being tricked? But she was a fool. She had made a dreadful mistake. She was beyond redemption. But was a Lady ever, truly, beyond redemption? She had not committed the worst sin. She had been sinned against. Her sins were unforgivable. Her sins were perhaps forgivable. She had merely been foolish. Nay, she had been as an animal. She was not fit for company. She was fitter now than she had ever been before, heightened by life. It was not her fault; it was her fault.

Thus, her thoughts ran. If she had taken the time to pick through the details of those thoughts, she would have concluded that her kind nature and her desire for clear, demonstrative affection had led her down this path. She had wanted Roland to sweep her up as he had done in the early stages of their courtship. And she had been too kind to turn an old friend away. These were her sins. Were they so bad? Did these desires and these quirks of character damn her evermore? The night at the Coaching Inn passed peacefully, and she went about eating and resting in something of a daze, caught between a dread of having to explain things to others and a desperate desire for her home, and things familiar.

The next day, they were away early, and she stayed quiet, Abby not daring to disturb her reflections. It made the time seem to pass interminably slowly, and so quickly as not to have been there at all. Soon she was being jostled down the familiar road through Grimstoke Village and up to the Castle, whence awaited her a brother and a sister-in-law she could hardly stand to face. She wondered then, idly, how many Ladies had jumped from carriages and run across the fields to escape judgment, and she knew that, if she gave in to her basest desires, then the count would be at least one.

*****

Her arrival at Grimstoke Castle was greeted with some shock and bewilderment and, confronted by her mother's concerned face, Gabrielle lost all courage, pled exhaustion from travelling, and fled to her rooms. For the next three days, she would not leave those rooms, as the very idea of venturing out into a world which had caused her such distress was repulsive to her. She thought that she might be content to stay in this room forever, if it meant that she did not have to face those she had wronged, and those who had wronged her. Maids brought her food, which she rarely touched, water, which rarely passed her lips. She was constantly astonished at her capacity for tears. Where did these tears come from? Her lips were cracked, and her mouth was dry, but she wept. She wept for the path of pain which she would now eternally walk. There was no way out, as far as she could see. Roland had not called, at least to her knowledge – he was most likely, she realised, still in London. But perhaps worst of all, Devlin had not even tried to talk to her. Eventually, late on the third day, the tears eased, and she simply lay there, exhausted. She could not live the rest of her life like this, she knew – but what else could she do? The true scale of the disaster which she had brought upon herself sank in now, and the tears were replaced with a fretting, exhausted inability to sleep, or to do anything but think repetitive doom-laden thoughts, with no possible good outcome from anything.

*****

Mona sat in the breakfast room of Grimstoke Castle, facing her mother-in-law, who was barely eating, simply pushing the food about her plate.

"But Mona, why will my daughter not speak to me? How can I help her – whatever it is that is wrong – if she won't even tell me?"

Mona set down her tea cup.

"Do not fret so, Mother. She will get past it, no matter how impossible that might seem at this moment. Whatever has happened, she is here, she is not ill, and amongst her trunks are the extra ones with, no doubt, the gowns and the like which she went to London to obtain. It does seem strange, however, that the Soiree which Lady Charrington had intended to hold was cancelled – the letter she sent, which arrived only hours before we would have been due to leave to go to London to attend it, did not explain why, at all. Can it be that something dreadful has gone wrong, between Gabrielle and Roland?"

The Dowager Duchess looked horrified at the thought.

"I do so hope that is not the case! But I confess that I cannot imagine what else might have caused this much distress."

"Indeed. But we will help her through it, whatever the difficulty is – and if I need to influence my brother, I will do my best on her behalf. But for now, let us leave it. Later today, I will try to talk to her, to discover exactly what occurred in London."

"Thank you, Mona – perhaps she will talk to you, more easily than to me, for she no doubt thinks that I, as her mother, will be more likely to criticise her – about whatever it is...."

*****

On the fourth day – In the afternoon, Gabrielle thought, although she wasn't sure as, having drawn the curtains, she truly knew not if it was day or night – Mona pushed into the room holding a tray, after only the tiniest tap at the door.

"Gabrielle."

Gabrielle turned over and faced the wall. Mona could not know how that one word, spoken in a loving tone, tore at Gabrielle. She felt as though, at the hint of kindness in the word, the world would collapse upon her, and crush her. She closed her eyes tightly, but tears still escaped. She had ruined a betrothal to a fine man, and for what?

"Gabrielle," Mona repeated, closer now. Gabrielle heard the sound of the tray being set down, and felt the impression on the bed when Mona sat upon the mattress beside her. "You cannot give yourself to despair like this. Please, talk to me. Please."

Mona laid her cool hand upon Gabrielle's shoulder. It was like balm to a wound.

"What is there to say?" Gabrielle muttered at length. "What is there that I can say which could change any of this? I have ruined it all."

"Tell me."

If her sister-in-law had spoken further, if she had implored with more insistence, Gabrielle's natural response would have been to refuse to speak, to withdraw further into herself. But somehow the simplicity of the request spoke to her state of mind. She found herself turning over and facing the kind woman, who was only a few years older than her, yet seemed so much wiser. In low tones, she recounted the entire tale, ending with the scene in the shop and her return to Grimstoke Castle. All through this, Mona nodded attentively.

"There are some who would refuse to speak to you after what you have told me," Mona said. "But I am not one of those. Do not forget that my circumstances were not so much nobler than yours. And do not forget, either, that Devlin's circumstances were even less so. Let me tell you a truth which will help you in whatever you decide to do in this world. In the game of etiquette, Ladies are at a distinct disadvantage. One can wish until one is inconsolable that it were different, but it is not and, despite what certain people sometimes profess, I hardly see that changing in our lifetimes. So, what can we do? Let me tell you. We persist. That is what we can do. We persist until we find joy."

"Joy," Gabrielle echoed, as though she had quite forgotten the meaning of the word.

"Joy," Mona confirmed. "A lady's lot is to stay sane long enough that, one day, she no longer needs to stay sane with such vigilance. That is what I have learnt in my time upon this Earth. You have been – how shall I say it? – more sheltered, more innocent, than I was. But let me ask you, do you love Roland?"

At this question some life infused Gabrielle's limbs. She sat up in the bed and no longer felt quite so half-dead. She nodded vigorously.

"I do," she said. "I do, and I rue the day that I ever allowed that — that *merchant* to come between us. I regret with every shred of my being that I allowed him to poison my mind with doubt, to trick me with his false demeanour. I let him in, sister, and in the dark of my thoughts he betrayed me."

"You love Roland. You are all the more certain of that now. That is what matters." Mona smiled. "Do not doubt that love is a powerful force. Take me and Devlin, for instance. Over a decade of war did little to dampen our love. A decade of war only heightened it. It was dark to begin with, when we were reunited – too dark – but the light came, with persistence, and we solved the problems which plagued us. I do not think it is unreasonable to say that the light will come for you and Roland, as it came for me and Devlin. Hopefully, sooner than you think. It does pain me to see you in this state!"

"I do not wish to pain you," Gabrielle said. "But it is so difficult not to distress others when all you feel is pain, so much so that hiding it is impossible. What can I do? If it is as you say, if Ladies truly are at a disadvantage in the game of etiquette, what am I to do? I can hardly make the initial move for reconciliation, can I? That would only worsen matters. So I must remain here, alone, fostering my grief, nurturing my regret, tending to my self-loathing. And the longer I stay here, the worse it becomes. Until... until what, I ask you? What will become of me, now that all I ever wanted has been taken from me? No, that is not right. It was not taken from me. I gave it away!"

"Hush, my dear girl." Mona patted her hand. "You must not let your thoughts take this course. You will recover. You will recover, and one day you will shine so brightly that you will not be able to believe that it was once so dark."

After that, Mona left her to think about what they had said.

Gabrielle tried to take solace in the words, but she was horribly aware that they related only theoretically to her current position. Nice words they were, but they did not have the power to bring Roland back to her.

Only *he* had that power.

But would he come?

Or was it too late?

Chapter Ten

There had been much to do in London, once his conversation with Mr Nicholas Hodge was complete, and Roland had found every moment of the near five days a quiet torture. He wanted to go to Gabrielle, wanted to tell her that he loved her, that she need no longer fear, that all would be well. But to ensure the truth of that, he had to stay in London, and make certain of it, in every way. No matter how distasteful the last week had been, no matter how many whispers were circulating in society about Gabrielle, and him, there was nothing confirmed – he had managed to prevent outright scandal, and Lady Charrington had put about that the Soiree had been cancelled due to illness, nothing more.

But no matter what resulted in Society, he was happy – for those moments outside the door of Hodge's shop had torn from him the darkness of his own doubts, forever. Hearing Gabrielle's voice declaring so bluntly that it was he that she loved, hearing her defend him so stoutly from Hodge's nastiness, had warmed him through, especially when he realised that she was doing so knowing that she risked harm to her person in the process. She had not betrayed him – far from it. Her bravery had lent him strength, and made his interaction with Hodge far easier.

And he must have projected that confidence well, for Hodge had not once doubted his words – which was all to the good, given that he had not, in fact, informed anyone of where he was going, or of Hodge's misdemeanours – he had simply claimed to have done so, as a method of dissuading the man from physically accosting him.

He should emulate her courage, now, and declare his feelings clearly, no matter how uncomfortable that made him feel at times. Just how he might best do that, he did not yet know, but he had some ideas. Ideas which drifted into dreams as the carriage finally bore him back towards Grimstoke Village, and the woman who would be his much beloved wife.

*****

It was three days after her conversation with Mona that Gabrielle awoke to a minor commotion in the house. Rising from her bed, she crept to the door and pressed her ear against it. If she were able to see as well as hear through the door, she would have seen Roland, smiling, his features as sharp as ever, as he was greeted by Devlin.

"Am I to assume that the situation has been dealt with, then?" Devlin said, returning the younger man's smile.

"Yes, it has been," Roland's smile grew wider. "This ghastly business is behind me, at last!"

But Gabrielle could not see the smiles of the men and the tones of their voices were neutral. And because a sufferer will constantly twist the good into the bad, at the phrase 'ghastly business' Gabrielle became more distraught even than she had already been. There was little doubt in her mind that the 'ghastly business' which Roland referred to was their betrothal.

"Good."

Did Devlin wish it ended too? Had she ruined herself so much that her brother no longer wished her happy?

"I should tell her myself."

Roland was still smiling, but how was she to know! Gabrielle felt fresh tears sting her cheeks, and would have given herself over to utter despair had she had the strength for it. As it was, all she could do was rest her head against the door and pray that the inevitable moment would not come. A shaft of sunlight slipped past the curtains and the darkness to rest upon her face. It was as though the heavens were mocking her. When the knock came upon the door, she quailed.

"Yes?"

Her voice sounded more like a whimper than anything else.

"His Grace requests your presence in the parlour," a footman informed her.

"I will be half an hour!"

Gabrielle knew that it was almost impudently rude to delay that long – yet it would take her that long to make herself look reasonable – and she would not let Roland see her looking so utterly dishevelled as she was now. Hastily, she rang for Abby, and together they made herself presentable, or as presentable as it was possible to make her at this time. She had no delusions as to her current state of beauty. She knew full well that days of crying and neglecting food did little to heighten one's more attractive features. But there are few problems in a Lady's life which a small amount of rouge cannot assist, at least to some degree. She applied it, and brought some life to her cheeks, then donned a becoming gown and a simple-yet-alluring necklace, before regarding herself in the mirror. She was not the beauty she had been, but she was still remarkably beautiful. She hoped, most likely in vain, that she was beautiful enough to fight fate.

But has there ever lived a person beautiful enough to cast off the bindings of fate? I doubt it, and certainly not you, my girl!

She descended the stairs as one who descended into a dirty pit, her steps tentative, wishing with every step that she could retreat. But retreat was not an option.

If he chose to discard her, at least she could look upon him once more. She would always have that memory, even if it was a painful one. Whatever happened past this point, she would always be able to bring his face to her mind. After all that had happened, that was the most she could hope for.

*****

Roland felt as nervous as he had the first few times he had called upon Gabrielle, at the beginning of their courtship. It was ridiculous, yet it was there. And a new fear had replaced his old doubts – the fear that he had treated her too coldly in Hodge's shop, and in much of the preceding weeks, and that she might, now, still choose to reject him. It would be understandable if she did. But he desperately prayed that she wouldn't – surely, her words in the shop meant that she might forgive him?

He was alone in the parlour – Devlin had retreated to the hall, having declared that Roland should have some privacy to speak to Gabrielle at first. The time passed, and he paced the room, pausing to stare out of the window, unseeing, his mind churning. What if he was wrong? What if she did turn away? He was so disturbed from his usual routine that he had forgotten the rather important box which he had brought back from London, and had needed to send one of Devlin's footmen over to Crooked Hill Manor to ask his valet to bring it to him here. Hopefully the man would arrive in time... In time, that is, if Gabrielle did not reject him...

*****

She started when she entered the parlour. Roland was alone, and rose from his chair as she entered the room. Behind her, Devlin quietly closed the door, and stepped away into the hallway, making certain that their conversation would be private. Simply setting eyes upon him again was almost more than she could cope with. He appeared unchanged, and that was strange to her. She had changed so drastically that somehow she had convinced herself that he, too, must be likewise altered. But he was much the same as he had been when he had saved her from Nicholas' violence. He smiled at her. This discomfited her. In her state, she was sure that the smile was one of mockery.

He wants to draw this out, she thought, pained. *He wants to make this hurt*. She struggled to keep her countenance impassive - she failed miserably.

"My Lord," she said.

Roland inclined his head.

"My Lady."

Gabrielle could feel the force of the events which had compelled them to this moment as though they were physical entities, pressing in the air around them. She seated herself opposite him and he resumed his chair. For a long while neither spoke, thus it seemed, confirming Gabrielle's suspicion. Her thoughts ran wildly.

He is enjoying this. This series of events has ruined him as much as it has ruined me. He wants to see me squirm. He wants to exact every piece of misery from me that he can. He wants to thoroughly humiliate me. He wants to hold me up as an example. See this Lady. Do not do as she did! Do not make her mistake!

She felt tears starting in her eyes and cursed her wretchedness. She wished that she could be like Mona. Mona would never have given herself over to misery like this, but Mona had an essence of strength which Gabrielle lacked. Mona was a strong, unflinching creature. Gabrielle was, in her own mind, quite the opposite.

"It is good to see you," Roland said, breaking the intolerable silence. Gabrielle, not wanting to indulge his malicious games, did not reply. Roland sighed. *He is sighing as a man does before he inflicts a cruel blow*, Gabrielle's traitorous mind whispered. *He is sighing as one does before immense pain is caused.* "I have been in London these past days, seeing to certain arrangements," he said, and Gabrielle knew full well what these arrangements must have been. Of the particulars she was unaware, but the effect was laid bare in the thought of the coming countless tear-filled nights. "I confess that I am struggling to find the words. Here, this will make things much simpler, I think."

He reached into his pocket and brought out a folded piece of paper. When he extended it to her, Gabrielle took it with a trembling hand. What curse did this paper contain? What abject misery would unfold along with the crease of the page? But unfold it she must, because nothing would be gained by delaying. The hounds which dogged her could not be outrun this time. It was a dissolution of their betrothal, she was sure. She knew that without looking at it. She needn't look at it. She could have read it with her eyes closed. But she unfolded it all the same, trying to steel herself against its message. Her eyes traversed the page, uncomprehending, and then followed that path again. She only knew that she had started to cry because the words blurred in her vision. She wiped her eyes and focused on the ink which would seal her fate. Without truly reading the main part of the paper, her gaze was immediately drawn to the bottom of the page, where there was a signature - *Nicholas Hodge*. She knew not why *he* would have written her a note. To add to the humiliation, perhaps? She read.

"Is this true?" she ventured, fearing a trick. "Roland, is this true? Can it be true?"

"Are you not happy?"

"Is this true?" she repeated. "Please, do not treat me cruelly. Tell me, is this the truth?"

"Treat you cruelly?" Roland leaned forward and placed his hands upon Gabrielle's, which trembled dreadfully. "Cruelly?" he went on. "I love you. It is true. He has renounced his claim. It was an absurd claim to begin with, but he has formally renounced it all the same. You and I are to be married, if you will still have me. I desire nothing more in this world. I will say it again. I love you!"

Gabrielle could not stay steady at these words.

She dropped the note and gave herself wholly to tears. Roland tightened his grip upon her hands. For ten minutes or more they stayed like that, the Lady weeping and the Lord quietly tending to her. He moved his hands over hers as a physician over a patient, soothing, soothing.

"I have to tell you," Gabrielle said. "I have to tell you why I was there, Roland. I cannot let you think that my intentions were impure. I could not stand that. I must tell you the truth. Yes, the truth, for once and for all! I must —"

Roland pressed his forefinger against her lips. His touch was warm, and sent shivers through her whole body.

"You do not need to," he said. "I have heard it all. I was there, outside that shop door, as you spoke with him – I could not come in to help you, until he moved you away from the door, lest I hurt you by forcing it open – but I heard every word... You are in the right, my love, and I do not care what this or that Lady will whisper. I know that your intentions were pure. *I* know that you never strayed from your affections for me. I know that you love me. Most of all, I know that I love you."

Gabrielle broke into a fresh bout of tears at these kind words. Roland touched her cheek.

"I did not realise that it would distress you so to learn that you are to be my wife."

His tone was playful, reminding her of the early days of their courtship, and she smiled, the tears slowing.

"What... happened? How did you achieve this?"

"I talked to the man, for a long time," Roland said. "I made him see the foolishness of his position. He has apologised, as you can see in the letter, and he even congratulated me for winning your heart."

"He is a brute," Gabrielle said. "We should not believe a word he says."

"Oh, I don't. But we have it in writing, signed with his known signature. It would be disastrous for his reputation – and his business – if he were to make trouble now. I would make sure of that. He could not afford to lose the business of the *ton* – or of the modistes who make for them."

Gabrielle took some solace from this, for he was right – the threat to his business would keep Nicholas silent, more than any other threat possibly could, she thought. Roland bent down, picked up the letter, and tucked it back into his pocket. Gabrielle's future, minutes ago so bleak, suddenly beamed brighter than sunlight. She regarded Roland with wide eyes, regarded her very existence with wide eyes, seeing everything anew. Then Roland glanced at the closed door and leaned close to her.

"My Lady," he said, with a wicked, alluring glint in his eyes, "since everyone believes that you were giving kisses out so freely, do you think that I could steal one?"

Gabrielle felt the blush rise in her cheeks, but far from begrudging it, she welcomed it. She had thought about kissing Roland many times, of course, but she never would have admitted it. And this was the first time that he had ever made the request.

She glanced at the door and saw that it was still closed. The room suddenly felt smaller, but in a way that made her feel closer to Roland.

"One kiss?" she asked.

"One kiss," Roland confirmed.

"You may."

She lifted her face to his. Slowly, he leaned down, and his lips brushed hers. His lips were soft, loving, and awoke a world of pleasures within Gabrielle. She gave a soft whimper, and he a low moan. Then, as quickly as it had started, the kiss was over. Roland bent away, blushing fiercely, and Gabrielle offered him a timid smile.

"Was it worth it, my Lord?"

"You are worth anything and everything, my soon-to-be wife!"

"Wife!" Gabrielle laughed. "Oh, do say it again!"

"Wife! Wife! Wife!"

The two began laughing like children. Even as they did, Gabrielle thought about the time after their wedding, when the kisses would come frequently, when the pleasure would rarely stop. Today had turned out to be a truly wonderful day.

*****

Seeing her face transform to joy was worth all of the difficulties he had faced. And the feel of her lips beneath his had left him aching for more. But most remarkable of all, on this remarkable day, was that he felt not at all uncomfortable expressing his feelings. Somehow, his uncertainties on that matter had disappeared as well. He would sing her praises, to her and to others, with no hesitation. And again, he was in awe of her courage, for, even in the face of her obvious despair, she had attempted to look her best, had been polite to him, even when she had suspected that he was being cruel – which was, he rather thought, simply a reflection of her own fears, after the cruel way that Hodge had manipulated her. That she could maintain that calm in the face of it impressed him. Even if she had spent the past week weeping, she had not bowed to that despair, nor, it appeared, had she ever truly lost hope. Nor had she stopped loving him, any more than he had stopped loving her. He pulled her to her feet, and swung her around, just like children playing will do, until, laughing, they collapsed onto the couch together.

"Gabrielle, I will have a copy of Hodge's letter made, and in the morning, I will take it to the Vicar. With that in hand, I am sure that we can have a new reading of the banns this Sunday, and marry as soon as we may wish after that."

"Yes – although I know that I, for one, will sit through that new reading of the banns in utter terror, lest some other person bring forth an unexpected obstacle!"

"There will be no such thing – do not even contemplate the possibility!" he shook his head, smiling at her. "But now, I think that we had best open the door, and call Devlin and Mona in to hear of the happy conclusion to all of this drama."

She nodded, and went to open the door.

Chapter Eleven

Mona and Devlin joined them, and the four of them sat together, discussing topics so beautifully mundane and ordinary that Gabrielle thought she might break into tears once more from the sheer relief of it. Even when Mona or Devlin was talking, Gabrielle could not tear her eyes away from Roland. She appraised him with eyes made more discerning by suffering. She was to be his wife! Joy moved through her every fibre. They were discussing flowers or theatre or some such lovely, comfortingly ordinary topic when there came a knock at the door.

"Lord Eldwood, your valet has brought your package. Do you want me to bring him through, or—"

"I will come out."

Roland smiled broadly, rising to his feet, and disappearing through the door into the hallway.

"Oh, I am so happy for you!" Mona whispered.

"I am too, sister," Devlin said, smiling at her. "You and Roland will make an excellent—"

But his sentence was interrupted when Roland walked back into the room, holding a carefully wrapped object in his hand. Without a word, he walked to the small table near Gabrielle and undid the wrapping as they watched. Curious, Gabrielle leaned forward to see. The wrapping revealed an inlaid timber case, shorter in height than it was wide or long, but of considerable size overall. Whatever could be in it? When he opened it, folding the lid back to lie flat, her breath caught. Magnificent jewellery was revealed – diamonds and deep blue sapphires forming a large and elegant parure set, comprised of a necklace, accompanied by sapphire drop earrings, hair pins, a small and elegant tiara, and a bracelet.

She lifted her eyes to Roland's face.

"For you, my love. These were my grandmother's – they had been tucked away for many, many years, as they needed some repair. I thought that the sapphires would look magnificent on you, for they match your eyes, so I had them cleaned, repaired, and remade into a more modern styling for you. They have been in our family for generations, and now you will wear them - let them be a symbol of the enduring nature of our love."

Gabrielle gasped, and tears started in her eyes again – happy tears, this time.

She realised instantly that Roland must have arranged this, even whilst the entire drama with Nicholas had been happening – he had trusted in her love enough to do this... In that moment she wished that Mona and Devlin were not there, for she found that she wanted to kiss her husband-to-be again! She saved that desire for later, determinedly swallowed the tears, and smiled.

"They are absolutely the most beautiful thing I have ever seen. I will wear them with pride. Thank you!"

And then, quite taking her breath away, Roland bent to her, and softly brushed his lips over hers. The touch was fleeting, but it filled her with heat, as nothing else ever had.

*****

The silence in the church was profound. No one moved. The Vicar had just said the words of the new official third reading of the banns, and it was as if every person there held their breath. Seconds passed, feeling like hours, until the Vicar gently cleared his throat.

"I believe that means that there are no objections. This marriage will proceed, on a date to be set. And that concludes our service for today."

Gabrielle allowed herself to breathe again. Her pounding heart slowed as the fear subsided, and she clung to Roland's hand tightly. Around her, the church slowly filled with the sound of people moving, speaking quietly, going about their normal lives. She turned and looked into Roland's eyes.

"I feel so much better now. It is almost as if, if I try hard enough, I can pretend that Nicholas never walked through that door."

Roland regarded her with a serious expression, and she wondered what he was thinking. After some time, he spoke quietly.

"You know, Gabrielle, I don't think that I would want to pretend that it never happened. For his intervention has made us stronger – it has made both of us face our doubts, and has brought us a true understanding of the depth of our love. I would not wish those things away."

He smiled, and his words resounded in her thoughts. He was so very right.

"When you put it that way, I cannot wish it away, either. But we must move – I do believe that the Vicar is waiting to speak to us."

They stood, and went to Mr Wardle, hand in hand, happiness radiating from them.

*****

Devlin and Mona left the church, each with their mother beside them. The two older women looked happier than they had for months, and Devlin sighed in relief. Lady Eldwood patted Mona's arm.

"I knew that your brother would sort things out – no matter how much he doubts himself sometimes, he's a very capable man. I'm glad that he's happy, and I'll be glad also to have another woman in the house again – it's been very quiet since you married Devlin."

Mona shook her head in some amusement.

"Perhaps you should appreciate the quiet while you can, Mother, for I fully suspect that we shall both be presenting you with grandchildren very soon – which will certainly deal with any excess of quiet in each of our houses..."

Lady Eldwood beamed, and the Dowager Duchess, overhearing this exchange, laughed softly, a brilliant smile on her face.

Epilogue

It was a perfect spring day, and Gabrielle could hardly believe that it had finally arrived – today, she would marry. She rose very early, unable to sleep any longer, and was ready well before time, standing in her rooms, the rooms which after today would no longer be her home, in front of the mirror, stunned at how she looked.

The gown was simple, and elegant, a rich pale blue, overlaid with near translucent silvery lace, embroidered with tiny sapphire gems scattered across it. She wore the jewellery which Roland had given her, as well as another sapphire bracelet which had been her own maternal grandmother's. She looked, and felt, more beautiful than she ever had before.

She just hoped that Roland liked it.

Her mother came to tell her that the carriage was waiting, and her eyes sparkled with tears at the sight of her daughter. Gabrielle could have joined her in that, for she felt most emotional – but she'd had enough of weeping...

She stepped down from the carriage in front of the church, and was shocked to see that not only was the church full, but people crowded around outside – it seemed that the entire district had come to see her wed. Devlin led her to the doors, and as she stepped out of the bright sunlight, for a moment all she could see was Roland, picked out in the dimness by a beam of multi coloured light, cast from the stained glass rose window high on the church wall.

It made him seem more than real, as if he was a painting of a great hero, or the like. He turned then, as the sound of her feet on the stone floor reached him, and she saw, in his face, just how much he liked what he saw. It was an expression of love, and more, and it made her heart swell with joy.

He held her eyes as she walked to him, and once she stood beside him, Devlin having stepped to one side, his fingers entwined with hers.

The ceremony passed in a blur, all but that one dreadful moment, when the Vicar was required, once again, to ask 'If anyone knows a reason why these two should not be wed...'.

She did not breath for the moments that followed, her knees weak, and her heart fluttering, but nothing untoward happened, and the Vicar went on with the service as required. That moment, as he began to speak again, she had the most dreadful urge to giggle hysterically. Roland knew, for he clasped her hand even tighter, as if to hold the laughter in for her, but the corner of his lips twitched up, regardless.

*****

Roland could feel the laughter within Gabrielle, could see it in the quivering of her lips, and knew that it was born of inexpressible relief. He clasped her hand tightly, and willed her to maintain a semblance of proper calm and seriousness.

She succeeded, and the time came for them to walk back out of the church as man and wife. It seemed almost impossible, after all that they had been through, that they had finally reached this point – but he was overwhelmingly happy that they had, that she was his wife, that they could now start their life together, with nothing of difficulty hanging over them.

Outside they were greeted by cheers, and a shower of thrown flower petals. As if in a dream, he led Gabrielle to the carriage, and settled in beside her for the short drive up to Crooked Hill Manor. His home, and now her home too.

It was a pleasing thought, for the house had been quieter, more empty, since Mona had married Devlin, and he would welcome the change in so many ways.

But first, they had to get through the rest of the day – the Wedding Breakfast, and the enthusiastic congratulations of so many people. He had been surprised to learn just how many people would attend the Breakfast – even Lord and Lady Charrington had come from London, with the Lady declaring loudly that, after all that had gone on, how could she possibly miss it?

"Roland... I am not sure that I can cope with the next few hours.... I feel utterly overwhelmed already – delighted to be your wife, and glad that we are finally wed, but... all of these people...."

He bent and pressed a soft kiss to her brow.

"You will manage, as will I. Just remember that they are all here because they care for us. We need only manage until late afternoon, and then we can leave them all to entertain each other, and lock ourselves away in our rooms. I am quite certain that the moment we close that door behind us will be more than worth waiting for..."

Heat flushed through him at the thought of finally being alone with her, of taking her into his arms, and kissing her properly. She looked at him then, with mischief in her eyes.

"Oh! Well, when you put it that way... I am sure that it will be... very, very sure."

*****

The carriage turned the last tight curve in the steep drive up to Crooked Hill Manor, and Gabrielle saw it through new eyes. Her home. It seemed strange, and wonderful at the same time. She could explore it, and discover all of those parts that one never sees from the public rooms of a house, discover its history, and its secrets.

The carriage stopped, and once the door had been opened, Roland stepped out and helped her down. He offered her his arm.

"Welcome home, Lady Eldwood. Come, your staff are waiting to meet you." Then he bent until he brought his lips close to her ear, and whispered. "And I am waiting for the end of today, and the moment when I can kiss you until you swoon in my arms from the pleasure."

She was sure that her cheeks flushed, and she felt a sharp desire to either kiss him right then and there, or to run into the house, to get this part over with. She did neither, but her fingers on his arm curved, and traced delicate patterns, and she felt his breath hitch in response.

"Of course, my Lord. Now please, do introduce me to the staff..."

THE END

I hope that you enjoyed 'Lord of the Betrayed'.

Turn the page for another delightful Regency story.

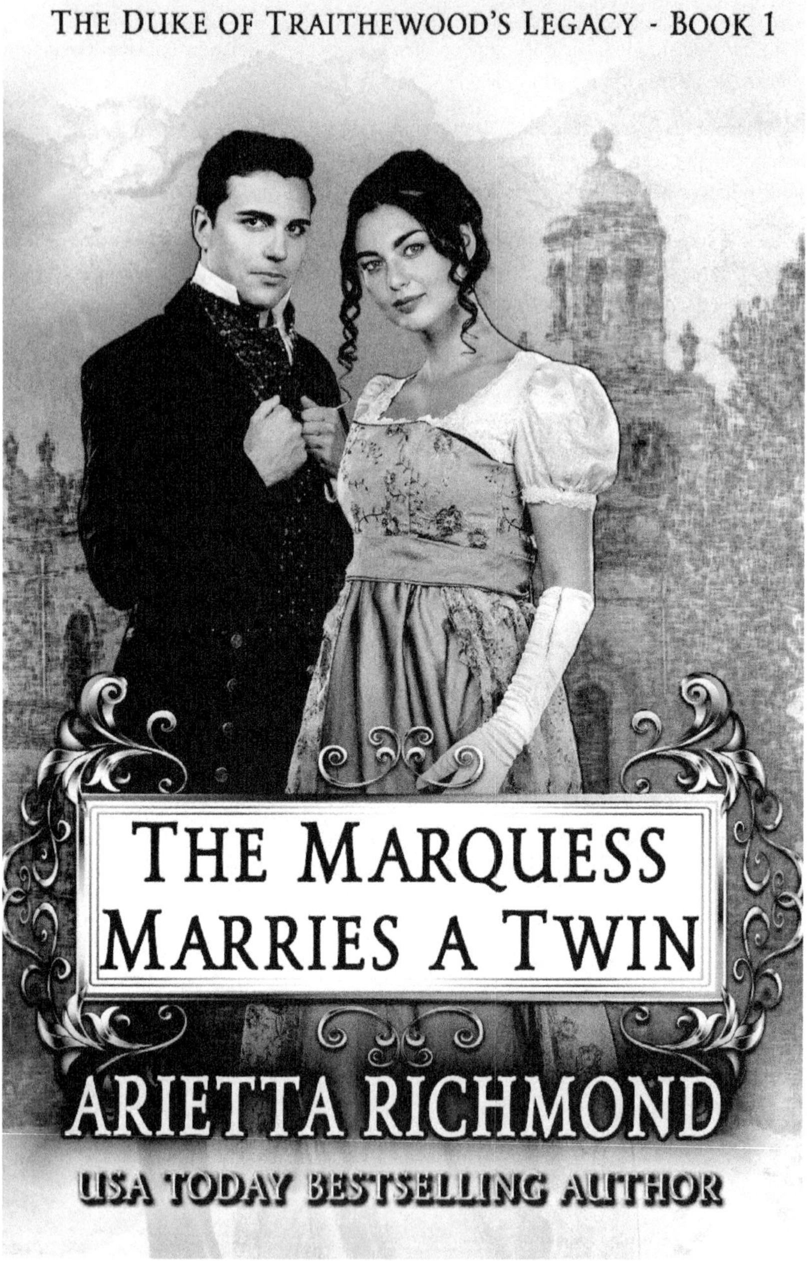
THE DUKE OF TRAITHEWOOD'S LEGACY - BOOK 1
THE MARQUESS MARRIES A TWIN
ARIETTA RICHMOND
USA TODAY BESTSELLING AUTHOR

THE DUKE OF TRAITHEWOOD'S LEGACY

The Marquess Marries a Twin

A Christmas Clean Regency Romance

Arietta Richmond

Prologue

1814

"Have you, Your Grace, been party to this treasonous plot?"

The words hung in the over-scented air of the Prince Regent's most private meeting room, redolent with the threat of death, and the potential for the destruction of everything that Albert Darley, Duke of Traithewood, and his ancestors, had worked to build.

"No, Your Highness, I have not. I have been your father's friend, always, and now yours. I would not betray your trust."

The Prince Regent sighed, shaking his head.

"Yet you do not deny being involved in various business dealings with men who have been proven, quite unequivocally, to have been part of this mess. Given that, how can I trust you? I do not want to suspect you, for you have, as you say, always been a true friend to the Crown, yet if I am to value my father's life, and my own, I must consider the concept that you might lie. Especially as what we know, so far, indicates that there are likely many others involved, beyond those we have already uncovered – others it may take my men years to reveal."

"Your Highness, a business venture is just that – nothing more. A vehicle for investment. I have no other ties to these men you have named to me, beyond those two investments – investments which have not delivered the expected returns, I might add. I do not know how I might prove my loyalty – certainly, you are welcome to inspect every part of my records – I place my man of business at the disposal of whoever you may choose to send to investigate. But I beg you to consider my long years of loyal service, and not condemn me without due evidence. I am old – I do not care so much for myself, but I would hope that my son, and my grandson, would have the chance to come into the title, and to inherit what I have built, to carry on the legacy of our family."

There was silence for some time and the Duke waited, knowing that, whilst the Prince Regent could be capricious and indulgent, he was, at heart, inclined to be a fair man. All Traithewood could do now was hope. For if the Prince Regent decided that he was guilty without evidence, then he would hang, and his family would be stripped of lands and titles, and left in penury.

In those moments of ominous quiet, images of his life flowed through his mind – his wife, some years in her grave now. His son, hale and hearty, but with a wife who was frail. His grandchildren, boy and girl – twins, twelve years old now, who were so alike, and yet so very different. He wished, for the thousandth time, that his wife had lived to see them born, for she was a twin herself, and would have understood them far better than he did. But the past could not be changed, and all his life's work might disappear in a wave of the Prince Regent's hand.

"I find myself inclined to treat you with clemency, Traithewood. I hope that I do not live to regret this moment, but I believe I will take the risk. Of course, should any true proof come to light which shows that you were aware of the plot, then you will suffer the consequences. But until then, should that time ever come, I make these requirements of you. You will cede to the Crown your two smaller entailed estates, although you may keep the unentailed ones. You will sell your London townhouse, and you will retire to Traithewood Grange, and your son and his family to Holmdale Abbey, and stay there. You, and your family, will not actively engage in society."

The Duke released his held breath, saddened, yet relieved. To deprive his family of social contact was cruel – yet it was better than death, or penury.

"Thank you, Your Highness. We shall do as you command."

The Prince Regent smiled then, but there was some sadness in his expression too.

"And Traithewood – should you find, in any of your papers, information which might help us track down any of the men who are guilty of treason, then I would be most appreciative. Especially if you can find anything which also makes it clear that you are innocent. Should you find that, I would be delighted to release you from these constraints."

The Duke bowed deeply, finding that a small flame of hope remained in his heart – he did not know how he might prove his innocence, but he certainly intended to try.

"I thank you again. Rest assured, that, should I be able to discover anything, I will report it to you. And – how might I best do that, Your Highness?"

The Prince Regent turned considering eyes upon the Duke, then smiled.

"I find it in my heart to allow you some small social interaction. You will be visited, occasionally, by Baron Setford. I am certain that you will find him convivial company – and you may speak to him on any matter pertaining to this. He has my utmost confidence. He may, in fact, choose to make this easier for you, by supplying you with a... ah... recommended servant for you to employ. A footman, or a groom, perhaps..."

The Duke was somewhat startled – he had met Setford but once - the man was unremarkable in appearance, and was a person gossip never touched. But the Prince Regent's words had just made him see that in a whole new light.

"I see, Your Highness. I will, then, welcome him to my home, and be sure to take his advice in matters of staffing, should he offer it."

"Good, good, I see that you understand the situation, Traithewood. Now, take yourself off – you have a lot to organise – I will grant you two months to get everything arranged, and while you do, I expect you to not attend any events at all."

The Duke bowed deeply again, and left the room, his mind in turmoil, although his face was impassive.

*****

Four months later – Holmdale Abbey

Barely a week after Christmas 1814, Charlotte Darley, Marchioness of Holmdale, breathed her last gasping breath, as the consumption which had progressively stolen her strength finally overwhelmed her. Her body was transported, with all due ceremony, to be interred in the Traithewood family crypt at the church next to Traithewood Grange, as was fitting for the wife of the heir to the Traithewood title.

By the end of January, it had become obvious to the Marquess that, with his wife gone, he could not provide the education which his daughter deserved. His son was another matter – the boy needed to learn all he could about the estates and their management, even if they could not go about in society – and Lord Holmdale felt up to the task of providing that education – it gave him something to do, for there was little else to occupy him during this damnable isolation, and it distracted him from grief. But his daughter should be educated by a woman, and should learn all that was required of a lady of the *ton*, and eventually of a wife to a man of good breeding, although God only knew how she might meet such a man, if they were to remain isolated. Then, as he sorted through his late wife's room, finally looking at her papers to decide what should be kept, and what should be disposed of, and to where, he found something which might solve the problem of his daughter's education for him. She would miss her brother, of a certainty, but it was the only viable possibility he had found.

*****

Late June 1815

The Duke of Traithewood had received the news of the victory at Waterloo by the medium of the London papers, which made their way, albeit slowly, into the countryside, and to his door. He was pleased for his country, glad that they had, finally, won the war which had raged for near a third of his lifetime, on and off. But he was also rather bitter. Now, if they were no longer at war, there was no reason for treasonous plots – the men whose traitorous natures had caused Traithewood and his family to be shut away from society had failed in every way, and the cause they had supported was lost.

Nothing had ever been found to prove that Traithewood had been a part of it – because he hadn't. But equally, there was nothing he could find which might, in any way, conclusively prove that he was innocent – traitors do not write, in their notes of their meetings 'Traithewood wasn't there because we didn't invite him, and he had no idea what we were doing'.

Still, perhaps, one day, the Prince Regent might see fit to trust him again, and towards that day, he would keep every single record related to the time period when those damnable traitors had been plotting – and milking the businesses which Traithewood had invested in to fund their nefarious aims. He had asked that his man of business send all of it to him, here at Traithewood Grange, and now, he had packed it away into a largish iron banded chest, re-reading each document as he did, hoping that he had missed something useful.

He hadn't.

So now, he closed the lid of the chest, and locked it, the large brass lock looking rather excessive against the dark timber. He would put it away, and one day, perhaps, if his family were still bound to the countryside, it would go to his son or his grandson, so that they might continue to argue for their freedom.

He would spend his days walking his estate, or riding out to talk to his tenants. He would read, and perhaps even write some of the dreadful poetry he had been fond of composing as a young man. It would still be written for his wife, who, though gone to God some years ago, lived in his memory, regardless. Perhaps his grandson would visit him at times, but he suspected that he might never see his granddaughter again.

That thought almost brought tears to his eyes. Now that his son's wife was dead, Chester had sent Jenneta away, to some distant relative of her mother's. He knew it had been done for all of the best reasons, but still, it tore at his heart, for Jenneta looked so very like his own dear Amelia had, when he had first married her.

Chapter One

December 1820

"I have decided that we must go to London. You must have a chance to find a husband, amongst those of the right status."

"But Aunt... what of the King's demands of my family? If I am obedient to those requirements, then I cannot possibly go to London. And... it is a very long journey – are you... are you well enough for that?"

Dona Esperanza de Leon drew herself up and regarded her great-great-niece sternly.

"Jenneta, I am sixty-eight years old – that is a good age, yes, but not so old that I am incapable! A few weeks on a ship will not harm me, and I would like to see some relatives and friends of mine that I have not seen for many tens of years. As far as the requirements of the King – they were made seven years ago now, when he was still Prince Regent – surely he will not object to your seeking a husband?"

Jenneta shook her head, rather terrified by the idea. She was not sure that she wanted to go to London, to the Season – she wasn't even sure that she wanted a husband. Although, she did want to see her twin brother again...

"But the King's requirements – what if he hears that I am there, and does something terrible to our family as a result?"

Dona Esperanza smiled.

"Lady Jenneta Darley has not been seen in England for seven years. If anyone remembers that she exists, they may also remember that she was sent abroad to a relative of her mother. They will not know what she looks like – for you were twelve when you came here, and now, at nineteen, you are vastly different from the way you were then."

"Still – if we give my name, many of them will look me up in Debrett's – won't they? – and then the gossip will run wild."

Dona Esperanza laughed.

"They might – if we gave them your name as Lady Jenneta. But we will introduce you as Lady Marisela De Leon, my niece. It is not so far from the truth, as Marisela is one of your names, and De Leon was one of your mother's names. But it is not a name that any of them can look up. And given that you have been here with me on Gran Canaria for seven years, your English has a decidedly Spanish lilt to it. You can move in society freely, and allow the men to court you. If you find one you want to marry, you can choose whether you ever tell him the truth or not."

Jenneta was shocked, but not entirely surprised – her aunt was a cunning woman, who usually got her own way.

"But... men will expect me to have a dowry – and I am not sure that I like the idea of hiding the truth of me from a man I might marry."

"You do have a dowry, even as Lady Marisela – I have put that aside for you, and it is quite large enough to tempt any man. What you do with the truth, if you do find a man you wish to marry, will be your choice..."

"Perhaps... perhaps that could work. And if we go to England, I could see my brother, and Father..."

Dona Esperanza shook her head sadly, and Jenneta's heart fell at the sight. Jenson had occasionally sent her letters, which came wrapped in letters that her Father had sent to Dona Esperanza, but she missed him every day. Being twins, they had been inseparable as children, and when Jenneta had been sent to the Canary Islands to live with Dona Esperanza, she had felt as if she was only half of herself, without him there.

"Jenneta, if you are there as Lady Marisela, then you will not be able to go to see your father and brother, for that would give your identity away. You will have to be strong, and keep the secret. I had hoped that your father might find something, anything, which the King would accept as proof of your grandfather's innocence, so that you might return freely – but that has not happened, so, if you are to have a life and a family of your own, where you belong, we must indulge in subterfuge. I would not see you end as a spinster, nor married to one of the few lesser nobility who live here, pleasant though the Island is."

Jenneta spun away, sudden tears filling her eyes, and a soft sob escaped her. Moments later, Dona Esperanza wrapped her in her arms, and rocked her gently. A handkerchief was pushed into her hand, and she brushed her tears away.

"I miss him so much..."

"I know – but you must be strong. If you go to London, and you find a good man to marry, then at least you will be in England, and after that, at the right time, you might be able to see him. It is all the hope that I can offer you."

Jenneta swallowed, considering Dona Esperanza's words. Outside the door of the room where they sat, the small fountain in their courtyard bubbled softly, and everything about her seemed suddenly crisp, distinct, and oddly perfect. She knew, then, that she would go, and that she would miss this place, once she left it. But no matter how much she liked the Islands, England, with a chance at some point in the future to see her brother, was a better option than eternity here, missing him.

"What must we do to prepare? And when will we leave here?"

Dona Esperanza laughed again, and hugged Jenneta to her for a moment.

"I knew that you would have the courage for this. I have booked us passage in March. Now you must let me continue to arrange things – it is nearly Christmas, and you should enjoy the festive season, and your birthday, for, if all goes well, this may be your last Christmas in Las Palmas."

*****

February 1821

Lancelot Williams, Marquess of Bainbrook, regarded the note which he had just been handed with a doubtful expression. He did not recognise the seal.

"Open it Lance. It's genuine, and you will want to pursue the opportunity it offers."

Lance lifted his head and met the eyes of the man who had spoken, the man who had personally delivered the note to him, minutes ago.

"How do you know what it contains? Not that I question your truthfulness, Lord Geoffrey, but..."

Lord Geoffrey Clarence laughed.

"You are wise to be cautious, and to question everything – but that trait is exactly why you are receiving that letter. Your sister has often spoken to my wife of your... tenacity... in the face of any challenge."

It was Lance's turn to laugh.

"My absolute stubbornness, you mean? I will admit that the only person I know who is more stubborn than I am, if he wants to be, is my brother Kenric."

A languid voice cut into the conversation.

"My dear brother, I am wounded – how can you possibly claim that I am more stubborn than you? That would require far too much energy!"

Both Lance and Lord Geoffrey ignored the remark, and Geoffrey went on, as if the interruption had not occurred.

"Perhaps – but I believe that she actually had complimentary things to say about your ability to solve problems..."

"Ysolde actually said complimentary things about me?"

"Yes – or at least, so Harriet tells me..."

Lance shook his head, half amazed and half amused. He looked back at the letter in his hand, wondering what was in it – and why he felt almost afraid to open it. From across the room, his twin brother's voice came again.

"Well Lance, are you going to open it? Or just stare at it as if it might bite?"

How Kenric managed to sound so completely nonchalantly uninterested, even when Lance knew him to actually wish to know something, Lance wasn't sure. But it went with Kenric's almost foppish, wastrel image – an image which was rather thoroughly misleading. Lance repressed his annoyance, dropped into a chair, and broke the seal.

Bainbrook,

It has come to my attention that you are possessed of skills which might be extremely useful in inconspicuous service to the Crown. I would appreciate meeting with you, to discuss this possibility further. Please attend me at Bigglesworth's Books, at 3 tomorrow afternoon. Upon arrival, simply say that you have come for a meeting.

My best regards

S

Lance looked up at Lord Geoffrey, raising an eyebrow.

"This is... ah... rather unusual, and mysterious."

"Which is why I have delivered it to you, rather than some footman. I assure you, it is genuine, and I believe that you should go to that meeting. Afterwards, depending on the choice you make, I may be at liberty to reveal more to you. But do go."

"Oooh, mystery! Excellent – perhaps this may even be interesting enough to rouse me from my ennui."

Lance sighed at Kenric's reaction, and was amused when Lord Geoffrey turned and spoke to his brother.

"Lord Kenric, I fear that your ennui will have to remain, for I suspect that you will likely not be told any of the detail, no matter what your brother decides."

Kenric frowned so darkly that Lance had to stifle laughter. When Lord Geoffrey turned back to meet Lance's eyes, his expression held equal amusement.

"Well, Lord Geoffrey, I do believe that I will go – at least as much to drive my brother to distraction as because of your recommendation."

Kenric emitted a snort of indignation, which Lance utterly ignored. Already, his mind was worrying at the possible implications hidden behind the simple wording of the letter, and he knew that, in truth, he would have gone regardless, just to discover what was meant.

*****

The bookshop was small, on an unexceptional street not far off Bond Street.

Now that he stood before it, Lance could faintly remember having been there before, a few years earlier, when he had been seeking a particular reference book. He pushed the door open, and a small bell tinkled. To one side, rows of high shelving groaned under the weight of an eclectic assortment of books, and ahead of him, he could see a counter near the back of the shop, where a somewhat elderly man had just looked up from the books he was wrapping for a customer. Lance felt, right then, remarkably like a goose. Was this an elaborate prank? He certainly wasn't about to go and speak to the man until the customer was gone! So he turned to the shelves beside him and browsed through the travelogues he found there, until the customer finally departed the premises. Then, setting the rather dull study of the peculiar animals and plants of South America back on the shelf, he went to the counter.

"Good afternoon. I... ah... I am here for a meeting."

For a moment, nothing happened, and Lance felt like simply running from the shop, so foolish did it all seem. Then the old man's face split into a broad smile and he nodded.

"Here t'see himself, eh? This way then." He pulled aside the somewhat dusty looking curtain behind him. "Through there, into the back corridor, along to the end, up the steps – they're not as rickety as they look, mind – and knock on the door at the top."

Lance swallowed, and did as he'd been commanded. The curtain dropped closed after him, and the scent of age-old books, dust, and oft-polished timber wainscotting surrounded him. A few steps took him through a creaky door and into a dim corridor, where his footsteps echoed lightly as he walked. At the end, there was a sharp turn, and stairs ran up, hard against the wall, back in the direction he had come from. He went up, alarmed by the creaks and shifting of some steps under him, until he stood at the top, before a worn-looking door. He reached out, wondering yet again if he had been wise to come here, and knocked on the surprisingly substantial surface of the door. From inside came a hint of the sound of footsteps. Then the door opened.

The man who stood there was dressed in the best quality tailoring, yet was somehow ordinary. In a crowd, one might walk past him and not notice. The only remarkable thing about him was his piercing grey eyes. Those eyes quickly scanned Lance from head to toe, a small smile gracing the man's lips as he made his inspection.

"Do come in, m'boy."

He stepped back, and Lance did as he'd been bid, and stepped into the room. It was a startling space, rather unexpected after the dingy corridor downstairs, and the rickety seeming steps. Light flooded in through two big glass windows (glass! here!), which were actually clean, a desk sat under the windows to one side, and a workbench to the other. Opposite the desk, a table with chairs and two couches with side tables were arranged near a carved and polished fireplace. Quality carpets, which would not have been out of place in his own study, graced the floor. The scent of perfectly prepared coffee filled the space, obviously emanating from a tray set on one of the side tables.

The man shut the door behind him. For a moment, Lance was at a complete loss for how to proceed – after all, he didn't even know who the man was! Had he been foolish to trust Lord Geoffrey's word? Lance turned, and watched as the man approached him, ever more intrigued by the moment.

"I... ah... I believe that you invited me here?"

"I did indeed. Do take a seat. Coffee?"

Lance sat, glad of the warmth from the fire.

"Yes, thank you."

There was silence, apart from the clink of a cup on its saucer. As soon as the coffee had been handed to Lance, the other man sat. Who was he, Lance wondered? After all, there were no servants in sight, and yet the man obviously had influence, and presumably importance... They both sipped their coffee, and Lance was startled at the quality of it – it was, quite simply, perfect. Then, with a sigh, the gentleman set his cup down, and brought those piercing grey eyes to bear on Lance once again.

"You are curious, no doubt – but I see that you are wise enough to wait and observe before saying anything."

Lance stifled the urge to laugh.

"Wise... I am more often accused of being too serious, too dull. To see my quietness as wisdom is a new perspective."

The man nodded, as if pleased with that answer.

"Allow me to introduce myself. I am Cecil Carlisle, Baron Setford. I have some... unusual... duties in service of the Crown. And I believe that you can assist me. Your family has a long history of loyalty, and you are reputed to be intelligent, far more clever than you permit people to see, and prone to persisting in the face of complex problems. Would you agree with that assessment?"

"I... I suppose that I would. Although, such things could also be said of my brother, much though he works to hide the slightest indication of it."

Lord Setford laughed, shaking his head slightly.

"In future, that may be useful – but Lord Kenric is a little too noticeable for what I have in mind, at present."

"And... exactly what would it be, that you have in mind?"

It was a blunt question, bordering on rude, yet Lance instinctively felt that this man would prefer his directness.

"I have a complex puzzle, most of which has been solved over the last four years. I need new eyes, and a new perspective brought to it, to find the last pieces that I, and those who assist me, are obviously missing. But this is a problem on which lives hinge, including, perhaps, that of our King."

Setford's words struck deep into Lance, and he felt the compulsion to know more, to solve this problem, rise up within him. Had Setford known that would happen? Had he engineered the path of this conversation specifically to ensure that Lance would be drawn into his plans?

"I see. And if I may be so bold as to ask – why does this problem rest with you?"

"It does because I fulfil an important role for Crown and Country, a role which it is not commonly known that I hold. Whilst I am working to pass that role on to a worthy successor, it is still a deeply significant part of my life."

"I am afraid that I don't entirely understand, my Lord."

"It's very simple, Bainbrook – I am the King's spymaster. And whilst the end of the wars has reduced the workload associated with that role, there are still those who are enemies of the Crown, who must be dealt with. Treasonous plots still occur, and they can reach deeply into society, in the most innocuous guise."

Lance was, despite the whole mystery of the process which had brought him to this moment, rather shocked. Talk of treason, and of spying, went rather beyond 'a puzzle to solve'.

"I see. What place in all of that do you see for me, my Lord?"

"M'boy, it's a simple matter of skills – I need a man who is tenacious, who is good at noticing things that others don't see, who questions rather than assumes, and who can move about amongst the *ton* comfortably. I will be blunt – I want to recruit you. There is at least one man whose innocence needs to be proved, and others whose guilt needs to be confirmed. I believe that you are the man for the job."

Chapter Two

"So, what was this mysterious meeting about, Lance?"

Lance regarded Kenric, his expression serious. Just how much could he risk telling his brother? He was used to sharing his thoughts with Kenric freely, but he had sworn an oath on this, to protect the information he would be privy to. Yet... his brother could be a very useful assistant in the matter, for his rather eccentric style and his manner of appearing not to give a damn about most things made people careless in his presence... which could be useful here – and that meant, for Lance, likely a later conversation with Setford.

"Something that I can't tell you about, in detail."

Kenric snorted, waving a hand as if dismissing that 'excuse'.

"What can possibly require such secrecy? It's not as if you were on the trail of someone plotting against the King, or the like, now is it?" Lance froze where he sat, his brandy glass halfway to his mouth. Kenric was damnably good at somehow honing in on the most accurate perceptions, without ever starting out with that intention. Kenric eyed him, waiting for an answer, and Lance watched his expression change as he took in Lance's stillness. "Lance... you look rather... pale... Do I take it that, in fact, the mystery meeting was about just such a thing?"

Lance rediscovered breathing, and movement. He brought the brandy to his lips, and took a sizeable swallow, appreciating the burn as it warmed him.

"I am not at liberty to tell you any details. But you, dammit, have the instinct of a bloodhound on the trail."

"I'll take that as a compliment, brother. And I won't ask just how or why someone chose you for something which seems to me to be a rather unusual occupation for a Marquess. But I will ask you how I can help – even if you can't tell me what you are doing, or what you seek to discover. I always rather liked those stories about dashing spies...."

There it was – the word that Lance had been avoiding, mentally, as well as outwardly.

Spy.

It was not a role he'd ever harboured any ambitions towards, but it seemed that he had become just that, regardless. He looked at Kenric with a wry smile.

"Well, you have always done flamboyantly dashing far better than I..."

Kenric fanned himself extravagantly.

"Two compliments in as many minutes! I declare, I shall faint away from the shock of it..."

Lance shook his head, and sipped his brandy, wondering just how he could use Kenric's offer of help, without telling him everything – at least until he got Lord Setford's permission to do so.

*****

Late February 1821

Lance sighed, and set his pen down, then simply sat, staring at the portrait which hung on the wall opposite him, as his mind went round and round in familiar circles, considering what he had learnt so far. He was not really seeing the portrait – a rendering of his father some thirty years ago, before Lance was born, when his father had still been Bainbrook, rather than Duke of Cairnmoor, and had lived here, not at Cairnmoor House – but it was as good a place for his eyes to rest as any. Lord Setford had sent him an alarmingly large chest full of papers – original documents going back many years, plus the notes about what those documents held, as put together by multiple of Setford's men over the last four years and more. He had spent the time since that had arrived in his possession working his way through them, making sure that he understood the size and shape of the problem which had faced Setford and his men, and attempting to see anything which they might not have addressed, or explored deeply enough.

They had been thorough. To date, very little had leapt out at him as worthy of further exploration. In that four-year period, they had uncovered many who had been party to the treasonous plotting, and brought them to justice. There were just a few loose ends, and one conundrum. Setford had explicitly pointed out to him the issue relating to the Duke of Traithewood – a gentleman of the highest reputation, who, it appeared, had suffered the great misfortune of having invested in some of the same companies as had the traitors. This fact had made him suspect, in the Prince Regent's eyes at the time, of potentially being party to the plot. It was not something for which there had been any direct evidence, and it was not something which His Royal Highness had wanted to be true – but it had been, apparently, impossible to prove to be untrue.

It was testament to Traithewood's previous service to the Crown that he had not been arraigned as a traitor regardless, but had simply been forced, with his entire family, to retire from all public life. Lord Setford had suggested that, if Lance could uncover anything which could unequivocally prove Traithewood's innocence, then the King, and Setford, would be grateful. It was clear to Lance that Setford believed the man innocent, but could not act on that without proof, for that would destroy the spymaster's credibility, apart from anything else. The painted eyes stared blankly back at him as he mentally went over all of it again. He was quite sure that there had been nothing missed, in following up on all of the evidence that the papers in the chest provided.

Which meant that he had to look beyond that, to things, businesses and people which were associated, in less obvious ways, with the identified traitors, and their business activities, meeting places etc, hoping to discover new documents, or new areas to explore, new people to investigate in detail. Not that some degree of that hadn't already been done – it had – but it had stopped perhaps too close to the known plotters. Then, as he considered where to start, an idea came to Lance, a flash of insight, a moment where he almost saw a map of the possibilities in his mind. A map which was as important for the absences and blank spaces upon it, as for the known and detailed elements.

Decisively, he lifted his pen again, pulled a new journal from the collection which waited in his desk drawer, and began to make notes, occasionally checking things on other documents as he went. Those notes all centred around one person – the Duke of Traithewood. He would look deeply into the Duke's family – all those he could identify who were alive, or had been so seven years ago, when the whole thing had first come to light. He would also look deeply at those businesses where the Duke's investments had coincided with those of known traitors. Surely, whilst doing so, if there was any connection between the Duke and the traitors, beyond the accident of an investment choice, Lance would find it.

And if he did not? Then he would be looking for that which had been impossible for anyone to find, for seven years now – a document, somewhere, which categorically proved that Traithewood was not involved.

*****

Early March 1821

The early morning sun painted Las Palmas in delicate shades of pink and gold, which washed over its stark white walls, and darker stone buildings, all topped by the spire of the cathedral. Jenneta stood by the stern rail of the ship, and watched the city retreat, becoming ever smaller, until it looked like a painting of an imaginary place, and then vanished from sight entirely. It was somehow foreboding, as if a chapter of her life was closing, with no hope of ever going back. No matter how much she had missed her brother, she had come to love Gran Canaria, and was sad to leave. The wind lifted, filling the sails, sending them speeding across the waves, whipping Jenneta's hair loose from its pins.

"Come Marisela, let us go below, and put our possessions to rights in our cabin. Then perhaps we may seek out some food – if, that is, your stomach does not betray you?"

Jenneta turned, still startled to be called Marisela, to see Dona Esperanza smiling at her. She would get used to the new name – she must, for the maid they had hired to travel with them, and attend them in London, knew her as nothing else – Dona Esperanza had deemed that wisest, for then no accident of speech between servants could reveal her true identity. It was interesting that her aunt looked remarkably happy, and not the least daunted by the idea of setting out on this adventure.

"Of course. The cabin is so small, it will be a challenge to put things where we can reach what we need, without unpacking and packing everything, every day. And no, my stomach does not betray me – I feel quite well, even invigorated by the sea air. If I remember correctly, I did not suffer from seasickness on my way to you from England, although Mrs Elverham did so, dreadfully."

Dona Esperanza waved a dismissive hand.

"That woman... she did her best for you, teaching you, but she has no courage. To simply declare that she would never set foot on a ship again... But at least she seems happy teaching other children now, as governess to various of the wealthy families on Gran Canaria."

Jenneta looped her arm through Dona Esperanza's, and they made their way to their cabin with care, adjusting to the steady roll of the ship as she made good time away from the island.

*****

Mid-March 1821

Multiple volumes of Debrett's Peerage were piled on a chair beside Lance, with one open on his desk before him. On a page of his journal, a rather inelegantly drawn family tree had taken shape, as he looked at the Duke of Traithewood's family. Like most of the aristocracy, that tree was a tangled web, and if he allowed himself to delve too far, for the sake of completeness, it would become an impossible mess. So he forced himself to ignore the compulsion for detail, at least as far as older generations were concerned, and focused entirely on those who still lived, or who had been alive in 1814, even if they were not now. Discovering anything about them was surprisingly difficult. It seemed that they had obeyed the Prince Regent's command with startling efficiency, and completely disappeared from the view of society. Seven years of not being visible meant that only a few of the most determined gossips still remembered anything about them, and given that Lance could not be seen to be prying and asking pointed questions, the flow of information was almost non-existent.

Even Kenric, who he had told some of it after Lord Setford had given his agreement to that, had been unable to uncover much at all, and Kenric normally did rather well at eliciting information from a range of unusual sources. Lance looked at his diagram again, his eye caught, as it had been each time, by the fact that Traithewood's grandchildren – a girl and a boy – were twins, as he and Kenric were twins. That fact left him with an odd feeling of connection with them, these people he had never met. What would it be like to have a twin who was not of the same sex as you? Perhaps, one day, he would meet them, and might be able to ask that question, just to satisfy his curiosity.

He shook his head. This was not about his curiosity, this was about protecting his King, and perhaps clearing the name of an innocent man. He brought his mind back to the purpose of documenting the family tree – what was there here that might be relevant? Had any of Traithewood's relatives invested in the same companies as he had? Had any of them any known social association with any of the men who had been proven to be traitors? Was there anything which might indicate an opportunity for a clandestine association? Did any of the men belong to the same clubs as had the traitors? Lance turned the page of his journal, and wrote that list of questions, and more. He would work through discovering the answers to each of these, methodically, and hope that he discovered something. Once that list was written, he set that journal aside, and rang for tea. A maid brought it to the door, and handed the tray to him, knowing that he preferred that no one but himself and Kenric enter his study. As he sipped the fragrant mixture, he realised that there was another question he needed to address, one he had not considered until now.

What if the papers which Setford's men had collected about the plot were not the whole of it? Despite the volume of documents, there was nothing to say that, somewhere out there, there might not still be more, which a conspirator had carefully hidden away, so well that Setford's men had not uncovered them. And if that was the case, how was Lance to go about finding such documents? The fact that Lord Setford, as astute as he was, had set Lance this task and still believed that there was more to discover, was enough for Lance to feel driven to prove it, one way or the other. He set the tea down, and began another journal, another list. This list detailed all of the places where documents had been found in the past, and which of the plotters residences or other properties they had been found in. Once that was finished – which would take some time, as he would have to go back through all of it again, he would look for what wasn't there – which known plotters residences had not yielded any documents at all?

Once he knew that, he would know where to start looking.

*****

Late March 1821

Jenneta shivered, huddled in a carriage blanket, as the carriage conveyed her, Dona Esperanza, their maid, and their trunks through London. To her perceptions, after seven years living in the Islands, the air was cold – miserably so. She knew that it was early spring, and not really that cold, but still, her senses had become adapted to far different weather. More than ever, she was impressed by Dona Esperanza's planning, and by how wide her great-great-aunt's circle of acquaintances was. It was apparent that Dona Esperanza had been corresponding with distant relatives, and with friends she had long been apart from, such that, upon the arrival of their ship, a carriage had been waiting – a most impressive carriage. Jenneta was grateful for the comfort, after the long days aboard ship – and would be even more grateful for a warm bath and clean clothes, once they reached their accommodations.

As if the thought had summoned the moment, she felt the carriage slow, and leant forward to peer out at the street. They were in a large square, with a central park which was fenced by an iron railing. On all sides stood tall houses, perfectly cared for, and obviously owned by some of the most wealthy of London's inhabitants. It was more than she had expected. Not quite at the level of exclusivity that her family's townhouse had been, when she was a child, but wonderful, nonetheless.

The carriage stopped, and the door was opened by a footman, who let down the steps then assisted them as they stepped out. Embarrassingly, Jenneta found that her mind still perceived the ground as moving, as the ship had. She stumbled, then righted herself as their Spanish maid hurried to her side. Stepping past her, Dona Esperanza appeared to have no difficulty, and led the way up the steps with an assurance that Jenneta envied.

"Come, Marisela, let us get settled in as soon as possible. I would wash the sea salt from my skin, and taste tea which has not been thrice brewed!"

"Yes Aunt, I can only agree with that desire."

The door was impressive, topped by a fanlight, and with a carved panel above that which declared this to be 'Fairway House'. The door opened as they reached the top of the steps, and a serious looking butler bowed. It seemed that Dona Esperanza had managed to not only arrange the lease of this townhouse, but the employing of a full staff, all by correspondence – did she, perhaps, have a man-of-business in London? It was not something that Jenneta had ever thought about, before now.

"Welcome my Lady. Do you wish refreshments immediately? Or would you prefer to take some time to recover from the journey first?"

Dona Esperanza regarded him as if judging his suitability, then smiled.

"We will go to our rooms first. We will require a warm bath, and some time to change into attire which is not travel stained. But please also send up a tea tray whilst we do that. What is your name? I must be able to address you appropriately."

The butler bowed.

"Fortnum, my Lady, at your service."

"Thank you, Fortnum. Please also arrange to have the staff all attend us in the parlour, once we come down, so that you can introduce them."

The butler bowed again, and waved forward the maid who had been lingering near the stairs.

"Meg – please show the ladies and their maid to their rooms."

The maid curtsied, and led them up the stairs, just as two footmen began to carry their trunks in. A few minutes after that, Jenneta was finally able to collapse into a chair, as the tiredness of weeks of travel overwhelmed her. Meg, and Beatriz, the maid they had brought with them, hurried about, unpacking trunks, tidying things away, and soon directing the footmen who brought a large copper bath tub, set it in the dressing room, and then went back and forth with buckets of heated water to fill it.

It took until she had bathed and dressed in fresh clothing, before Jenneta felt capable of doing anything at all.

Chapter Three

Late March 1821

"I swear, brother, it's a wonder that you can still see well enough to read a word! You have spent so much time going through those documents, I am surprised that you haven't gone quite mad."

Lance looked up to see Kenric standing in the doorway of his study. For a moment, his brother looked blurry, until Lance's eyes managed to shift focus. Perhaps Kenric was right, and it was a wonder that he could still see. But it might be worth it – for finally, he had found something odd, a place to start, to explore possibilities that Setford's men had not yet looked at.

"I haven't gone mad – I'm afraid I have deprived you of that entertainment. But I have found something – or rather, I have found a lack of something."

Kenric frowned, and his usual look of casual ennui was suddenly replaced by a sharp concentration.

"You have found... a lack... of something?"

"Yes, finally."

"I think you'd best explain how a lack of something can be useful."

Kenric came into the room fully, closing the door after himself, and settled into the chair opposite Lance. Lance waved at the chest of papers, where it sat to one side.

"You know that I've been through those multiple times, as have a number of Setford's men before me. I found nothing new amongst those documents, so I decided to take a different approach. I looked at where those documents were found, as well as at identifying all possible people who had some association with the known plotters – however slight that association might have been."

"I see – and what, exactly, did that provide, as far as useful information?"

"A list of names of all even slightly associated people. And a list of which names were quoted in the incriminating documents, and which names represented people in whose possession, or homes, those documents were found. Once I subtracted the latter two from the first, I was left with a list of people – a blessedly fairly short list – who were closely associated, but who were not named in any documents, or found to have been in possession of any documents."

"Aah... I begin to see how the lack of something is useful..."

"Yes. I now have somewhere to start – tomorrow, once I have slept, and my mind is clearer. But I do have one question for you."

"For me? Do you suggest that I have deep dark secrets?"

Kenric's words might have been taken as serious, if not for the exaggerated expression on his face, and the glint of mischief in his eyes. Lance laughed.

"Not at all... but I do suggest that you might have... accidentally of course... uncovered other people's deep dark secrets..."

"Oooh! And whose secrets do you hope I might betray?"

"Bertram, Lord Diddington.

Kenric regarded Lance with another frown.

"The name is faintly familiar, but I can't say that I recall who he is. Care to explain to me why you think I might know anything of him?"

"I thought you might have heard things, amidst the drunken conversation found in the disreputable gambling hells you have been known to frequent... The man is some kind of cousin to Hellmont's father, I believe, although closer in age to Hellmont himself. Diddington seems to have invested in at least four of the same companies as most of the conspirators."

Kenric sighed, and gave an expressive little shudder.

"Hells which I no longer frequent, and company I now most assiduously avoid. Hellmont and his friends play far too deep for my liking, and treat their servants with far too little care. But for you, dear brother, I will push aside my qualms, and make some enquiries. Perhaps those mistreated servants could be a good place to start – I know where Hellmont's coachman drinks, for a start."

A thread of relief ran through Lance – he had not, quite, been sure that his brother could, or would, help with this part of it.

"Then I shall trust your ingenuity – and your curiosity – to discover anything that might be of use. This, Kenric, is where you get to be the dashing disguised spy you declared an admiration for..."

At that Kenric rose and delivered a flourishing, dramatic, and outrageously overdone bow to his brother.

"But of course – although I shall be as inconspicuous as a mouse, so that no one realises I am watching them..."

Lance shook his head, groaned, and rose also.

"I think, after that, I need a brandy..."

*****

Early April 1821

"So many invitations!"

Jenneta looked at the pile on the correspondence tray which Fortnum held out towards Dona Esperanza and struggled to comprehend how it had all been arranged. They had been in London but a few weeks, and yet so many people knew of them, and were inviting them to events!

"But of course, Marisela – it is as I intended. Just because I have lived in Las Palmas for many years, it does not mean that I have lost contact with the friends I made here in London, all those years ago, or with a scatter of my distant cousins. But I will sort these," Dona Esperanza lifted the pile from the tray, and Fortnum left with a bow, "and we will see how many we will accept – it is best to be selective, for I want your presence to be sought after by all."

Jenneta shook her head, overwhelmed, and allowed the force of Dona Esperanza's will to drive her along, like a leaf before the wind.

"Who are these people – the ones who have sent these invitations?"

Dona Esperanza smiled, even as her fingers opened each missive and sorted them into three piles.

"They are of the *ton,* although only a few are of the highest ranks. Most are lesser nobility – with enough influence to be useful, and much more likely to welcome a new face to enliven their days. If you do well, then we may begin to see more invitations from the high sticklers – but as Lady Marisela, a cousin of mixed Spanish and English heritage, you are not as easily accepted as the granddaughter of a Duke might be... But that is not a problem, for with your rich dark hair and dark violet eyes, they will think you exotic, and more appealing for it."

Jenneta half choked on her mouthful of tea, as laughter took her. Perhaps this strange masquerade might even be entertaining at times – once she stopped being afraid of discovery. It was darkly funny that a simple adjustment to her name might magically make people perceive her appearance so differently.

In her childhood here in England, no one had ever considered her anything vaguely approaching exotic!

"What are the three piles?"

"This one," Dona Esperanza indicated the smallest pile, "is the invitations which we will decline. They come from people who are beneath the level of society which we wish to move in, and in some cases from families which have been touched by scandal – and scandal is a thing which we will, for certain most obvious reasons, avoid at all costs."

"And the others?"

Dona Esperanza waved at the pile which was only a little larger than the first.

"These, we will accept, unquestionably, and first. These are from people of higher social standing, of higher titles, and who have great influence – whether that be for their title, or by the fact that they are inveterate gossips. They must take precedence, for their interest in you will cause others to wish your acquaintance." She moved her hand to the third pile, which was significantly larger than the first two. "And these, we may accept, if they do not conflict with one of the important ones, and if we have the capacity to fit them in, without quite exhausting ourselves."

"I see. I begin to think that this whole enterprise will require far more stamina than I had expected."

Dona Esperanza laughed – a full rich sound, which invited others to share her amusement.

"You will find yourself more than able to cope, I assure you. But be glad that we have already arranged your new wardrobe – for we would have little time to do such a thing, now that the invitations have begun. The last of your new gowns, as well as the shoes, bonnets, and gloves, will be delivered tomorrow, and then you will be ready to conquer the ballrooms of London."

Jenneta closed her eyes, for a moment imagining what this would have been like, if her family had never been touched by scandal. For a start, Jenson would have been with her... the familiar surge of sadness caught at her heart – London seemed so close to him, and Papa, yet so impossibly far away! She was brought back to her surroundings by Dona Esperanza's muttering, as she further sorted the largest pile.

"Aunt... when is the first event we will attend?"

"Tomorrow night, Marisela – a Ball at the Earl of Merringway's residence. He is not a man of great influence, nor is he disregarded – he is very much a man of good family, and reputed to be reasonably wealthy. The Ball will be a good place to start – not too overwhelming."

Jenneta swallowed, and reached for her tea again, suddenly unsure. What her aunt perceived as 'not too overwhelming' she suspected would be more than challenge enough!

*****

"A-ha!"

Kenric swept the sealed missive up off the correspondence tray and examined it closely. Lance lifted his head from his notes as Kenric walked into the study, brandishing the object in his hand.

"And what is it, brother, that you sound so pleased about?"

Kenric broke the seal, unfolded the heavy paper, and then, after a moment, passed it to Lance.

"It is an invitation – which we will be accepting."

Lance scanned it, and frowned.

"Merringway? Why would he invite us – unless he perceives that we might provide some cachet to his event, for some reason?"

Kenric grinned – the kind of grin which Lance knew meant that there had been mischief involved, somewhere, in this invitation.

"He invited us because I had a word in the right ear – the ear of his secretary's mistress, to be precise."

"And you did this because...?"

"I did this because you asked me to."

"I what?"

"You wanted to discover more about Diddington – and it was you who told me he was related to Hellmont's father. Well, Merringway is Hellmont's father, and I have it on good authority that Diddington is also likely to be at this Ball. So, oh great spy, I have provided you an opportunity. What you do with it is up to you. But at the least you should go, and dance with the ever-hopeful young ladies, even while you attempt to discover more. I, of course, will be there with you, looking as fashionable and rakish as usual, and being, undoubtedly, tempted by the card room. The card room, where gentlemen have those conversations which they insist are not gossip..."

Lance laughed – Kenric was, as usual, right.

"Then I shall do as you say, and charm all of the young ladies into false hopes, whilst you eavesdrop on private conversations. But I will be watching every move that Diddington makes, if he's there."

*****

"Lady Esperanza De Leon, and Lady Marisela De Leon."

The announcement of their names brought a sudden hush to the ballroom, as people turned to look. Jenneta hesitated for a moment, nervousness running through her.

She had never been the centre of this much attention before in her life!

Then Dona Esperanza's hand was at her elbow, gently urging her forward.

She took a deep breath, and moved, all of her attention on the process of walking down the stairs into the room below, looking as calm and elegant as possible.

It was as if the act of her moving had released the occupants of the room from that momentary hush, and the susurrus of conversation returned. She risked a look up, her eyes scanning the room as she reached the bottom of the stairs. Very few people were looking at them now, and she felt the tension leave her shoulders a little.

Then, as they moved to one side, Dona Esperanza leading her towards a group of older women near the wall, the crowd of people shifted, and for mere moments Jenneta had a clear view right to the other side of the room, to where a long row of doors led out onto a terrace. In front of one of those doors, a man stood, perfectly still, his gaze trained on her.

Their eyes met, and everything else seemed to fade away.

He was tall, older than her, but not so very old, with dark brown hair through which streaks of almost dark red glinted in the light. His clothing was elegant, simple, almost severe, and yet obviously of the highest quality. And he was the most handsome man she had ever seen.

The crowd moved again, and she lost sight of him, her focus snapping back to the noise and the crush around her, as she released the breath she had not realised she'd been holding. Who, she wondered, was he?

They reached the women who seemed to be Dona Esperanza's destination, and stopped. Curious eyes came to rest on Jenneta, then turned to her aunt. For a moment there was silence, then one of the women reached out a hand, and spoke.

"Esperanza? Is it truly you, after all of these years?"

Dona Esperanza laughed, apparently delighted.

"Si, Luisa, I am here, after all these years. And this is my great niece, twice removed, Lady Marisela De Leon, come to steal the hearts of London's finest gentlemen. Marisela, this is my friend, Luisa, Lady Hermitage."

Jenneta curtsied. Lady Hermitage regarded Jenneta with assessing eyes for a moment. Then the woman gave a small sharp nod.

"You will do well, Lady Marisela. You have something of the same look as your aunt had, when she first came to London."

"Thank you."

As if that assessment of her had opened the floodgates, the other ladies clustered around them, introductions were made, and Jenneta wondered how she would ever remember all of the names. From there the evening passed in a blur, with the ladies sharing reminiscences with Dona Esperanza, and bit by bit introducing Jenneta to a positive horde of other people. None of whom was the man whose eyes she had met, across the room – much to her disappointment.

She danced with a number of the gentlemen, and was pleased to discover that she had not forgotten any of the steps. She even managed to converse with those gentlemen, about such inanities as the weather.

But each time, it was a relief when they returned her to Dona Esperanza's side.

One of the gentlemen she danced with, a Lord Alphonse Hellmont, seemed rather arrogant, and held her hand for just a little too long as the moves of the dance brought them together. She was especially glad to be free of him, but politeness required that she not show it, for Dona Esperanza had whispered that he was the son of their host.

It was not until just before their departure at the end of the evening that she again saw the gentleman whose eyes she had met. She leant close to Dona Esperanza, and whispered, so that none might overhear her.

"Aunt... over there, near those potted palms – the gentleman who is so plainly yet elegantly dressed – do you know who he is?"

Dona Esperanza looked, casually, as if simply scanning the entire room one more time, then brought her fan up to her face, and whispered in return.

"I do not. He is a fine figure of a man, is he not? I will discover his name – but not tonight."

*****

Lance and Kenric had arrived almost unfashionably early, much to Kenric's disgust.

As promised, after circulating a little, and watching with amusement as mothers warned their daughters away from him in whispers concealed behind fans, Kenric drifted off to the card room.

Lance stayed in the ballroom, circulating, greeting everyone he knew, however minimally, always mentally ticking those names off the lists of possible associates of the plotters. There were only a few who warranted further attention – including Diddington. He also, as he circulated, dutifully allowed himself to be cozened into signing the dance cards of a selection of the young ladies present, creating, as he had known it would, a wave of false hopes.

Once he had done that, he paused near the terrace doors to catch his breath, strongly tempted to slip out into the cool evening air, away from the heated mixture of perfumes and colognes which filled the ballroom. He stayed, however, and simply watched. After a moment, some more new arrivals were announced, and Lance turned his gaze to the entryway, startled, for the names which had just been announced were ones he had never heard before. And after his recent in-depth perusals of Debrett's, he had thought that he knew of every person who might be in London for the Season. It appeared that he had been wrong in that assumption.

The names were Spanish, and the women both had the dark hair and slightly exotic cast to them that went with that provenance – but the younger one drew his eyes most. She was unquestionably beautiful – breathtakingly so, even from this distance, and something shifted within him, as a strange urge to go towards her surfaced. He repressed it, and as he did, his eyes still on her, the crowds parted a little, and she lifted her gaze, meeting his eyes from the other side of the room.

He ceased to breathe, ceased to notice anything else, until the movements of the crowd stole the view of her from him again.

Chapter Four

Lord Alphonse Hellmont regarded the small ledger in front of him balefully. His debts were mounting, and his father had, so far, refused to increase his allowance. And yet he was sure that his father was beyond wealthy enough to do so, despite Lord Merringway's claims to the contrary. He closed the ledger, and dropped it back into his desk drawer, locking it away. Above the fireplace, there hung a painting – a supposed record of his parents' wedding – a record which he rather thought had been 'enhanced' – making his mother more beautiful, his father more handsome, and the setting more attractive than they likely actually had been. Nonetheless, the one part of it that he did not think had been exaggerated was the rather excessive collection of jewels which his mother wore in the image. Not for the first time, he wondered where the wealth for those jewels had come from, and where that wealth was now. Especially as his father denied that they had any great amount set aside in bank deposits or possessions. It was galling not to know – after all, he was his father's heir, he was well past his majority, and at this point, he had rather expected to have been shown all there was to know about how their estates and fortunes were managed. But that had not happened – yet.

Was his father hiding something?

It was a disconcerting thought, but it popped into his mind, nonetheless. Perhaps it required investigation... but that would take time, and he did not have all that much time, right now. He needed some funds soon, or at least the visible promise of them, to stave off his creditors. And the only thing he could imagine which might serve to do that, short of his father falling ill enough to appear to face imminent death, was if Alphonse became betrothed to a lady reputed to have a substantial dowry. Given his father's rather ruddy health, the latter looked like the best option.

He cast his mind back over the last few events he had attended, those which were respectable enough to be attended by women he might conceivably marry, mentally cataloguing possible candidates. Sadly, there were not many. Not that there were no young ladies – no, far from it – but there were not many who had an appearance and manner he could stomach, and were of suitably superior breeding, in combination with a reputedly large enough dowry to be worth selling his freedom for.

He concluded, after a few moments thought, that possibly the only one who might serve his purposes was that Lady Marisela De Leon who had attended his father's Ball. She was attractive enough, had behaved quietly and appropriately, and was reputed to have a startlingly large dowry – at least according to the old tabbies he had overheard gossiping on the night. There was just one small problem – he knew almost nothing about her family. That she was some three times removed niece of Dona Esperanza De Leon gave him little to go on. Dona Esperanza was respected enough, at least according to the old gossips, but that did not really say much about Lady Marisela. And he couldn't exactly look up members of the Spanish aristocracy in DeBrett's! Still, he would pursue her acquaintance, even whilst he attempted to discover more about her family. At worst, she would provide him some entertainment, at best, depending on what he might find, she could be the solution to all of his problems...

*****

The hour was late, even by London standards, and Jenneta had gone up to bed, exhausted by yet another evening of dancing. Dona Esperanza sat in the parlour for some time, staring into the flames of the fire, and thinking – about the past, and about the present, and about her hopes for Jenneta's future. Then, she rose, and went up through the now quiet house and settled herself at the elegant desk in the tiny private parlour which adjoined her bedchamber. She drew out paper, uncapped her inkwell, and set about writing a most difficult letter, yet one which she felt compelled to write, now that she was sure that Jenneta was being accepted into society. It took her three tries before she was satisfied with the result, and she sanded that final version, setting it aside to dry as she carefully burned the first two attempts in her fireplace, watching them curl, flare with that odd blue green flame for a moment, and then crumble completely into the dust of white ash. That done, she turned back, folded and sealed the missive, and addressed it. Then, filled with a strange sense of relief, she set it on her bedside table, and rang for Beatriz to ready her for bed. The maid came quickly, and efficient as always, soon had her in her nightrail, with her long hair plaited up and coiled lightly on her head.

"Thank you, Beatriz."

The maid curtsied.

"Will there be anything else, my Lady?"

Dona Esperanza smiled.

"Just one more thing." She lifted the sealed letter, and held it out to Beatriz. "Please see that this is sent with the morning mail."

The maid accepted the letter from her hand, and curtsied again.

"Yes, my Lady."

With that, she turned and left the room. Dona Esperanza settled into the bed with a sigh, and blew out the candle in the small lantern which sat on the side table.

She was still not, entirely, sure that she had done the right thing – but it was done now, and could not be called back, so she pushed all thought of it away, and allowed herself to sleep.

*****

It was late afternoon when Jenneta rose, the megrim which had kept her abed earlier finally relenting. She dressed, and was seated at her mirror with Beatriz pinning the final coils of her hair into place, when Dona Esperanza came into the room. Beatriz stepped back, curtsied, and left them there.

"I see, Marisela, that you are feeling somewhat better?"

"I am – my head no longer hurts abominably – now I just feel a little weak, and perhaps even hungry."

"It is well, then, that I asked Fortnum to have a tray sent up, and a tea service."

Even as she said those words, there was a tap at the door, and Meg came in bearing one tray, followed by a footman with another. They set the food down on the small sideboard, and, at Dona Esperanza's wave, left the room. Dona Esperanza shed her bonnet and gloves, and dropped her elegant shawl atop them, then poured the tea. They said nothing more between them, until they both had food and tea, and had at least tasted it. Then, Dona Esperanza turned to Jenneta with a smile, setting down her tea.

"I made some calls on various ladies this afternoon. The kind of ladies who simply love to talk, and to prove that they know absolutely everything, about everyone. So I encouraged their garrulousness with little leading questions and exclamations..."

Jenneta regarded her, raising an eyebrow.

"And what dread secrets did you learn?"

Dona Esperanza laughed, waving her hand dismissively, before taking a bite of a lemon cake. Jenneta waited.

"I do not believe that 'dread' is the appropriate word, dear girl. 'Interesting' is perhaps better – and not exactly a secret, either..." Jenneta gave a little huff of frustration, wishing just to know what this was about, and Dona Esperanza smiled broadly before continuing. "I believe that I have discovered the identity of the gentleman who caught your interest at Merringway's Ball – the one you asked me about."

Jenneta set her tea cup down, and focused her attention on Dona Esperanza, finding herself feeling unaccountably flushed.

"Yes, that qualifies as 'interesting'. So, please tell me – who is he?"

Silence stretched as Dona Esperanza ate more of the lemon cake, and Jenneta knew that her aunt was teasing her intentionally, so she stilled herself, forcing patience. Eventually, she was rewarded.

"His name is Lancelot Williams, Marquess of Bainbrook. His father is the Duke of Cairnmoor, and Bainbrook is accounted one of the most eligible men in London this Season. But he's a reputation for avoiding social activity, much of the time – and the gossips tell me that he is, therefore, a great disappointment to the matchmaking mothers of this Season's crop of newly come-out young ladies. They despair because he is so reserved, and seems to have little interest in finding a bride – but then, they all paused and went on to say, in that hushed voice which so often betokens the edge of scandal 'but better reserved than like his brother...'"

"What could they possibly mean by that?"

Dona Esperanza's expression showed, quite clearly, just how much she was enjoying making Jenneta wait. More tea and lemon cake was consumed, as Jenneta's mind considered the words, unable to find clear meaning in them. Frustrated, she sipped her own tea. From outside, she could faintly hear the sounds of carriages passing through the square, but all else was quiet.

"It seems, Marisela, that Bainbrook has a twin brother – Bainbrook being the elder by a mere five minutes – and that brother is a complete contrast to him – a little foppish, a little wild, a bit of a rake and sometimes a gambler, but attractive, nonetheless. Exactly the kind of man no mother wants her daughter to marry..."

"A twin...?"

"Yes."

For a moment, it was as if the world spun. Jenneta had met very few other twins in her life, and the thought of what it would be like to have a twin of the same sex intrigued her. Surely it made things easier, even if their personalities were so different?

"I think that I would like to meet Lord Bainbrook... and his supposedly disreputable brother."

Dona Esperanza smiled, well pleased, for now.

*****

Lord Jenson Darley came down to breakfast at the usual time – quite early – thinking about the tasks ahead of him for the day. It was Spring, so there was much to do on the estate, with the planting, and the preparations for the growing season ahead. His thoughts were so caught up with that, that he would never have noticed the letter which lay on the correspondence tray, were it not for the beam of morning sun which came through the fanlight above the front door of Holmdale Abbey, and picked it out, such that the rich red of the sealing wax which closed it seemed to positively glow. He stopped sharply, his train of thought broken.

What could it be? They never received letters – at least, not from anyone but Mr Chatterfield, of Broadmoor and Partners, the family man of business, and he used a dark blue wax on his letters. Anyone else they might correspond with was either a supplier of goods, or a tenant, and their notes were far less formal, and not sealed.

Markham appeared, obviously having heard his footsteps. The butler lifted the correspondence tray, and proffered it. For a few moments, Jenson looked at the letter, half afraid that it would disappear if he tried to touch it, and filled with what was almost foreboding. Then he shook off those feelings, and lifted it from the tray. It was addressed to his father.

"Markham, is Father at breakfast?"

"Yes, my Lord – he came down but a few minutes ago."

Jenson nodded.

"I'll take this in to him then, and we can look at it once we've broken our fast."

Markham bowed, and Jenson turned, his mind now full of the mysterious letter – which showed no note of who the sender was – with all consideration of the spring planting gone from his thoughts, and went into the breakfast room. His father looked up from the plate he had only just settled on the table before him.

"Good Morning, Jenson. What's that you've got there?"

Lord Holmdale's eyebrow had risen, and his face was full of curiosity – Jenson suspected that he was equally shocked by the presence of an unexpected letter. After seven years isolated from society, the arrival of such a thing really was quite extraordinary.

"A... a letter. It's addressed to you, and there is nothing to identify the sender – on the outside, at least. The seal is uneven, and I can't quite make out whatever the symbol impressed in it is."

He set it on the table beside his father, and went to fill himself a plate. When he turned back, the plate heaped, it was to find that his father had not moved, but was simply staring at the thing, almost fearfully. The sound of Jenson pulling back a chair seemed to snap his father from that almost trancelike state, and Lord Holmdale reached out and lifted the letter, turning it to examine the seal in better light. After a moment a look of surprise crossed his face, and he examined it again, as if not quite trusting what he saw.

"I recognise the seal, I think. You are right – its rather blurred, as if it moved when it was impressed. But... if that's who it's from, I would have expected it to look different..."

Jenson took a mouthful of his food, contemplating his father's words as he chewed. He washed the food down with coffee.

"Different? Why? And who is it from?"

"I'll just confirm that..." Lord Holmdale broke the seal, and unfolded the thick paper, flattening it out onto the table beside him. He gave a sharp nod. "I am correct – it's from Dona Esperanza – and I expected it to be different, because her letters are usually larger, and sealed in oilcloth pouches to keep them safe on their journey here from the Islands. This is smaller, and simply folded, as a letter sent from close by would be."

As he spoke, his eyes were tracing down the page. Jenson ate some more of his breakfast, allowing his father the time to read it, before asking more. But when he next looked up, it was to see that his father had gone almost alarmingly pale.

"Father?"

Lord Holmdale looked up, shaking his head.

"I never thought..."

Then, seemingly lost for the words required, he simply pushed the letter across the table to Jenson. Jenson turned it, and flattened it out beside him, where the light from the window fell upon it making it easier to read the somewhat flourishing hand.

'Holmdale,

This is but a short missive to let you know that J###a and I are in London. If she is ever to have the life she deserves, then she must come to know how society works in England.

Do not fear, I have made sure that there is no risk to your family. But to maintain that assurance, I ask that you make no attempt to contact us, in any way. Separation is critical, for very obvious reasons.

Still, I felt myself honour bound to let you know. And obviously, should anything change, we would be delighted to be in your company again. J###a still, and always, misses J###n dreadfully.

Yours, E De L

Jenson felt, for a moment, rather faint, the morning light too bright, the scent of coffee too strong, the chair somehow wobbly beneath him.

"Jenson...?"

His father's voice pulled him back from it, and the world snapped into sharp focus again.

"Yes. What does she mean, 'not contact them'? Of course we must! I would see my sister again, after all these years!"

Lord Holmdale shook his head sadly.

"Of course we must not! Whatever she has done to keep this quiet enough not to threaten our family, we must not destroy that. To do so would risk revealing that one of us has, effectively, broken the requirements set upon Traithewood by the King. And to make such a thing visible could utterly destroy all that we have left."

"But I must see Jenneta!"

"No, you must not! I absolutely forbid it. I know that you were both distraught when I sent her to Esperanza, but that was seven years ago – surely you are capable of coping without her continuous presence now?"

Jenson regarded his father with anger – why could no one understand what it was like to be a twin? The bond he had with his sister was not something one 'recovered from'!

"But I must see her..."

"NO. And that is my final word on the matter."

With that, his father reached across the table and captured the letter, folded it, and tucked it into his pocket, then rose and left the room. Jenson stared after him, a coil of rebellion rising within him. He had always been dutiful, had accepted the need to do as the King had asked, and had turned his attentions to the management of Holmdale Abbey and the two other small, unentailed estates they still held, always hoping that, at some point, they would be freed from their isolation. But this... this was too much to ask.

And... surely, if there was a way that Jenneta could be in London, then it should be possible for him to find a way to do the same? Regardless of the fact that his father had forbidden it... In that instant something shifted within him. He would do it, somehow, no matter what it took. He would go to London, to his sister, without also betraying his family – there had to be a way, and he would find it.

Chapter Five

Lance walked into Bigglesworth's Books, and was greeted cheerfully by Mr Bigglesworth, who waved him though the curtained doorway to the back room. Lance gave him a bow, but said nothing, and was soon in that dusty corridor where the few beams of light which managed to reach through the small number of dirty windows only served to make the dust more obvious, as it spiralled in the light, sparkling, disturbed by his passing. At the top of the creaking stairs, he knocked on the door, which opened nearly immediately. Lord Setford stepped to one side, and Lance went in, yet again startled by just how large, clean, and light-filled the room was. The door clicked closed behind him.

"Do be seated, m'boy. Will you join me in coffee?"

"If it's as good as the coffee you gave me last time, I will, of a certainty."

Setford chuckled, and turned to the side table, pouring from the pot which sat there. The scent was wonderful, and Lance dropped into a chair, reaching out to take the cup that Setford passed him. He was fascinated, in a small way – for here was a man of the aristocracy, serving himself, and not a servant in sight. One day, he might ask Setford why.

"You've done well, m'boy. I sent men to those three properties you suggested we search, and two of them turned up most useful caches of hidden documents. We've two gentlemen in custody as a result – quietly – house arrest for now, with my men to guard them, and we are going through those documents. The third we found nothing – but I'm thinking to search it again – for now, I've a man in there as a footman, and others watching closely all our suspect does. So – at this point, do you have any more suspects for me? Or any other... ah... useful information?"

Lance shook his head, savouring the coffee for a moment.

"There are a few more I am looking into, but I am not yet convinced that you should close in on them. One in particular I suspect – he and perhaps his close relatives – but I've not enough to go on yet. And before you ask directly – no, I have not yet found anything which incriminates Traithewood in any way, nor, sadly, anything which incontrovertibly clears his name."

Setford sighed, and lifted his own cup to sip at his coffee.

Lance felt, for a moment, like a child who had disappointed his parent, given the sadness in Setford's face. He shook off that strange whimsy, and waited.

"Keep looking, if you will. I've the feeling that there will be something to find – though God knows why, after all this time. But my instincts are rarely wrong. And – another question, while you are here, away from all possibility of being overheard. What does your brother intend to do with his life?"

Lance near spilled his coffee at the question.

"My brother? Kenric? Why...?"

Setford laughed at his expression.

"Don't look so shocked, m'boy. You're the one who told me he'd be an asset to this investigation, no matter what face he presents to the world. And you were right – I've been impressed so far. I'd even go so far as to say that the boy has a talent for this covert business of ours – and a nicely deceptive level of strength and fitness, too. I'm of a mind to offer him a situation of ongoing... entertainment... to relieve his ennui."

That brought Lance to laughter.

"If you do, I suspect that he'll accept your offer – be in alt about it, actually. He likes to have some purpose to what he does – likes to make things – either make useful things happen, or physically make things, and struggles with the fact that society really doesn't see such things as suitable for a gentleman."

"Oh? What sort of things?"

"Truth to tell, I think that, if we weren't born into high society, he would've gone and apprenticed himself to a blacksmith, and been happy at it. But in the absence of that being an acceptable thing for a gentleman to do, I am almost certain that he could find satisfaction in thwarting those who seek to harm Crown and Country."

Setford's piercing grey eyes met Lance's deep brown ones, and something approaching conspiratorial mischief passed between them.

"I see. I shall have to invite him to view some interesting books... perhaps Bigglesworth has a few on the history of blacksmithing.... and we'll just have a chat about Lord Kenric's unique... skills."

*****

Lance stared at the pile of notebooks on his desk – he'd been through them all again, and was still faced by the same conundrum. Every instinct said that Traithewood was innocent, that he had been the unfortunate victim of coincidence, in the matter of the two businesses he had chosen to invest in. But logic said that, surely, given the tangled web of associations between the large number of traitorous men who had been involved in the plot, to have been that close to them should surely have meant that Traithewood was involved, somehow. Every other man who had invested in those two businesses had been party to the plot.

And there was no evidence available, to tip the balance either way.

He sighed, frustrated by the fact that Traithewood's family had been removed from society – for that meant that he could not observe them, could not seek hints in their demeanour, or interactions with others. Perhaps there might be hope in the documents that Setford's men had recently retrieved, based on Lance's investigations so far? Lord Setford had promised Lance that those documents would be sent to him, as soon as Setford himself had examined them. It was the only hope he had, of getting further clarity around the truth of the Duke of Traithewood's potential involvement.

Until then, he would continue to attend social events, watching everyone – especially Lord Diddington, for everything about that man felt wrong, and Lance was certain that it was only a matter of time until he found the clue which would prove his culpability. At the thought of more social events, however, it was not Lord Diddington's image which manifested in his mind – it was, instead, the image of Lady Marisela De Leon, a woman who had intrigued him from the moment that he had first seen her. He wanted to know more about her, wanted, if he was honest about it, to make her acquaintance, to dance with her. And that was the strangest thought – he had never actually wanted to dance with the young ladies who swarmed about at Balls, never once, until now.

*****

The Ball was crowded, and Jenneta, even though she was becoming accustomed to these events, still felt rather like a leaf tossed on the wind as the crush of people swirled about. She was grateful when Dona Esperanza guided her through the press of the *ton* to a relatively quiet spot near one wall, where Lady Hermitage and her friends were gathered beside some potted palms which flanked the doors to the terrace.

"Luisa! It is such a crush! I fear I shall become quite faint from the heat of all these people."

Lady Hermitage turned to Dona Esperanza.

"Esperanza my dear, I am sure that you are made of sterner stuff than that – you never were one to swoon."

Jenneta stood there, allowing the conversation of the ladies to wash over her, even as she scanned the room, assessing who was present. Most of the young ladies, and the eligible young men, she now knew by sight, and she mentally catalogued the men according to her opinion of them – those she found unpleasant, those she found bearable but not appealing, those she found at least reasonably pleasant, and those – well, just one, really – that she actually found appealing.

Would he be here? Her eyes roved the room again, and she gave a sigh of displeasure when she saw Lord Alphonse Hellmont – she would try to avoid him, but if he asked her to dance, she would have little choice but to accept. Her gaze moved on, and, as she looked towards the entry, a new arrival was announced. Her breath caught – it was him – the Marquess of Bainbrook. He looked across the room, and as had happened the very first time she had seen him, their eyes met. She felt the strangest compulsion to move forward, to go towards him, and it took a great deal of effort for her to hold herself still. But then the moment was gone, he had turned away, and she castigated herself, internally, for being a silly goose. The evening moved on, and Jenneta danced with a number of gentlemen – all unexceptionable, and all rather dull.

Even as she did, she could not prevent her eyes from following Lord Bainbrook, watching as he danced with other young ladies, and finding herself envious of them. How, she wondered, might she contrive an introduction? She intended to speak to Dona Esperanza about it, but when her current partner delivered her back to the older ladies, Lord Alphonse Hellmont swooped in, almost immediately. He bowed before her, and she repressed her wish to step back a little.

"Lady Marisela – I am delighted to see you – will you honour me with this dance?"

Beside her, Dona Esperanza paused in her conversation for a moment, glancing at Jenneta, but saying nothing. Jenneta swallowed, curtsied, and pasted a smile onto her face.

"Of course, Lord Alphonse."

He offered his arm, and perforce, she placed her hand on it, and allowed herself to be led towards where people were forming up for the next set. As they went, Jenneta realised that, quite close to where she had stood, Lord Bainbrook had come to a halt, and was watching her. She flushed, quickly looking away. Had he been coming to her, seeking an introduction? She shook her head – that was most likely foolish wishful thinking on her part. They joined the line of dance just as the music began, and Jenneta concentrated on the steps, glad that it was a fairly vigorous country dance, so that conversation was most limited – as was physical contact. Nonetheless, she could feel Lord Alphonse's gaze upon her at all times, and it contained a warmth that she did not feel for him in return.

"You dance very well, Lady Marisela. You are as elegant and skilled as you are beautiful."

"Thank you for the compliment, Lord Alphonse."

He smiled at her then, as if he had, of course, given her a great gift, which it was only to be expected she would be grateful for. It was an arrogant, almost predatory smile, and far from warming her heart, it left her feeling quite chilled. Their conversation faltered there, and she suspected that he had thought that she would compliment him in turn – which she truly could not bring herself to do. They finished the dance in silence, and he led her back to Dona Esperanza still in that silence. Only once there did he bow and take his leave of her.

"My thanks for your company, Lady Marisela."

Jenneta curtsied, and smiled rather stiffly, saying nothing. The annoying man left, and she turned to Dona Esperanza, only to find the lady reaching for her hand.

"Marisela my dear, Lady Hermitage wishes to make an introduction."

Dona Esperanza drew her forward, and Jenneta found herself facing Lord Bainbrook, who stood beside Lady Hermitage. Suddenly, she felt quite faint. His dark brown eyes met hers, and she wet her lips, her mouth quite dreadfully dry. His eyes followed the movement, resting on her lips for a moment, then he smiled, and it transformed his already handsome face, such that it quite took her breath away. Lady Hermitage was speaking.

"Lady Marisela, might I present Lancelot Williams, Marquess of Bainbrook? Bainbrook, this is Lady Marisela De Leon, great niece of my oldest friend, Dona Esperanza De Leon."

Bainbrook took her hand, and bowed over it, causing Jenneta's heart to beat rather frantically for a moment.

"Enchanted, Lady Marisela."

Lady Hermitage smiled indulgently as Jenneta managed to curtsey.

"Bainbrook is the son of another of my long-standing friends. It is good to see him in town this Season, for in previous years he has been quite the recluse..."

Bainbrook turned that stunning smile on Lady Hermitage, releasing Jenneta's hand, and somehow, she managed to breathe again.

"Not entirely a recluse, Lady Hermitage... although I will admit to having far less enthusiasm for the Season than my brother..." Lady Hermitage laughed, and Jenneta wondered what that was about, even as Lord Bainbrook turned back to her. "But Lady Marisela, this moment should be about you, not reminiscences of the attitudes of my family! Might I hope that you have a dance remaining free, my Lady?"

Jenneta shook herself out of her half-stunned state, and smiled again.

"I do indeed have this next dance free, my Lord, and would be delighted to grant it to you."

He smiled at her again, that smile which so overwhelmed her senses.

"Thank you."

At that moment, the music began, and he bowed, offering his arm. She placed her hand on it, acutely aware of the palpable warmth of him, feelable through the superfine of his coat. He led her away and she went happily, unaware of Dona Esperanza watching her with a speculative expression.

*****

Lance had been circulating about the ballroom, having escaped from the rather insipid young woman he'd just danced with, when he had come across Lady Hermitage. He had almost not moved in her direction, for he'd seen Lord Alphonse Hellmont nearby, leading a young lady out to dance. Hellmont grated on him, just by existing, and more so in that instant when Lance realised that the woman he was leading out to dance with was Lady Marisela. A surge of something close to jealousy had filled him, and he had forced himself to turn away, seeking to greet Lady Hermitage to distract himself from that odd reaction. She, being a friend of his mother, had greeted him immediately, and proceeded to ask him about his mother's health, his sister's health, and more, until he wished he had not begun the conversation. When the music slowed and the set came to an end, he made as if to escape, worried that he was not fulfilling his duty to Lord Setford, but, rather than Lady Hermitage allowing him to withdraw, she had reached out and taken his arm, gently pulling him closer, insisting that there was someone he should meet. His first response had been, as usual, a desire to run away, to escape the need for more social niceties, but he had drawn himself up and forced himself to behave as if yet another introduction was exactly what he wanted. Moments later, as the people beside her turned, he realised that this introduction was, in fact, truly one he wanted.

There before him was Lady Marisela de Leon – and she was even more breath-taking close up than she had been when seen across the room. For a moment, all else faded away, and his eyes took her in, almost hungrily. She looked nearly as stunned as he felt, and she licked her lips, moistening them.

The movement caught his attention, drawing his gaze inexorably to those lips – lips which were lush, and somehow begged to be kissed. That thought shocked him – it was not the sort of thing he thought, ever! Especially about young women of the *ton.* He gathered himself, paying attention to Lady Hermitage's introduction, and her gentle teasing. But then he did something he had not intended – something he did not realise he was going to do, until it was done – he asked Lady Marisela to dance. A frisson of pleasure ran through him when she accepted, and he led her away as the music began, acutely aware of the scent of her beside him.

They swept into the figures of the dance, finding their place in the line, and for that short while, he allowed himself the luxury of simple enjoyment. Their eyes met, and somehow held to each other, even as they turned and moved through the steps. Each time that the dance required him to take her hand, it was as if a small burst of heat ran from her fingers to fill his whole body. There was no sense of a need to converse, although he knew that manners called for at least some conversation with his dance partner. Still, the silence between them was warm, comfortable, and he rested in it, enjoying just being with her. When the music ended, he bowed deeply, then gathered her hand on his arm, and led her back towards Lady Hermitage.

"Thank you, Lady Marisela – that was quite delightful, although I must apologise for the sparsity of my conversation. I do hope that you can forgive me?"

Her fingers tightened on his arm, and for a moment his breath came unevenly. She looked up at him, smiling gently, then replied, her voice soft.

"Indeed, Lord Bainbrook, there is nothing to apologise for. After the rather... uninspiring... conversation of most others I have danced with, your companionable quietness was rather refreshing."

Her words surprised a slight laugh from him – he had never been thanked for silence before!

"I am glad that I have pleased you, my Lady – might I hope to dance with you again, at other events?"

He had startled himself again with that request, but he found that he desperately hoped she would say yes. She tilted her head a little, her eyes bright, then answered with that same soft tone.

"I do believe that I should like that, my Lord."

They reached Lady Hermitage, and Lady De Leon, where Lance, perforce, released Lady Marisela, and took his leave of them. As he turned away, he saw, not far along the side of the room, Lord Alphonse Hellmont – who was watching Lady Marisela, if he was not mistaken. That sight drove a surge of irritation through him, and the sensation made him pause, then turn out through the terrace doors, to stand in the warm evening air, and consider his own reactions. It was as if he wanted to protect Lady Marisela from Hellmont – which was a little ridiculous – he had no right to want to protect Lady Marisela – he had only just met her! Yet that urge was there. He contemplated it, carefully, and realised at least part of where it stemmed from. From what he knew of Hellmont via Kenric's past adventures, there was every reason to feel concern for any woman that the rake turned his attention to – but an even greater concern arose from his investigations for Lord Setford. For if Lord Diddington did turn out to be involved in the plot, then so might be Hellmont and his father....

And what that could imply for any woman Hellmont focussed on, was not to be borne – it might utterly destroy reputations, and lives.

Chapter Six

Lord Alphonse Hellmont had chosen not to dance this set, and instead had secured a drink, and settled near the terrace doors. He was considering Lady Marisela, and what his next steps might be in that direction, when he saw her step out onto the floor with Bainbrook. He paused, his hand tightening on his glass. Damn Bainbrook! The man was regarded as the catch of the Season, and had the wealth and breeding which might turn any young woman's head. Bainbrook was the last person Alphonse wanted paying attention to the woman he had decided would be his best choice as a wealthy bride! Obviously, Alphonse would need to make a concerted effort to charm her. And to discover more about her – he needed to know her provenance, to know more of her family – he could not afford to take on a woman who might have scandals in her family history! And so far, in what little checking he had done, he'd discovered precisely nothing. He swallowed the entire glass of wine in a single gulp, and set off across the ballroom, towards the card room – not that he could easily afford to play tonight, but perhaps someone might know something about her – for men gossiped just as much as women, he had found...

*****

Early May 1821

The weeks passed in a blur of social engagements, and Lance began to feel as if he would never find the last pieces of the puzzle to reveal the final plotters, and, hopefully, to prove Traithewood's innocence. The only thing which made it all bearable was Lady Marisela. He had danced with her at every event, and found himself looking for her as soon as he arrived anywhere. He felt foolish, and yet he could not stop himself from seeking her out, or from watching which other men paid her attention. He attempted to tell himself that what he felt was not jealousy – but he rather suspected that he was failing to convince himself... Today, he had volumes of Debrett's spread out across his desk again, with all of his diagrams of family trees beside them.

What frustrated him most, of course, was that none of that was any use to him in discovering more about Lady Marisela. Oddly, the only place he had found any trace of the De Leon name was in Traithewood's family – his daughter in law had De Leon as a middle name, and had been born in Spain, apparently. Could there be a connection? It would be most strange if there were. He would keep digging for information, but today, he needed to turn his attention away from the enigma that was Lady Marisela, and focus on the boxes of documents which Setford's men had delivered to him this morning. Those boxes contained everything recovered from the properties which had been searched as result of Lance's work so far, and now he needed to read every one of them carefully, and discover where the information they contained fitted into the broad pattern of everything they knew from the earlier documents.

It was a daunting task, but one which he attacked with some enthusiasm – perhaps here he might find something to more directly incriminate Diddington, or to exonerate Traithewood? Six hours later, when he stopped and locked them away, before going upstairs to ready himself for the soiree he was to attend that evening, that enthusiasm was waning. The documents he had been through so far had reinforced the guilt of those already taken, but had not, as yet, given him anything further to work from, with respect to Diddington, or any other possible conspirator who was not yet known. Still, he would persist – he had not come this far with it to give up.

There was one more box to look through – perhaps it held a clue...

*****

Lord Alphonse Hellmont was not feeling his best. The previous night, he had allowed himself to be drawn into an extended drinking session with a few of his less reputable friends, and despite a decent amount of sleep, he was still suffering the effects. It was well after midday, and Alphonse had just, grudgingly, allowed his valet to near drag him from his bed, and assist him in becoming at least vaguely respectable. Now he was making his way down through the house towards the breakfast room – although the idea of food was not, at present, at all appealing. As he walked along the corridor which led to his study, his father's study, and a number of parlours, an unexpected sound caught his attention. Was that... a raised voice? He stopped, listening, rather puzzled, for it was a man's voice, he thought – and there was no other man to be expected here, beyond his father, himself, and the servants. It seemed to be coming from his father's study. Alphonse moved again, keeping his steps quiet, until he came to a halt right beside his father's study door. The voice was slightly muffled by the closed door, but it definitely came from within the study, and, with a little concentration, Alphonse could understand most of what was being said.

"...I'm certain, Merringway – both Sharrow and Gelford are under house arrest. The authorities are being quiet about it, but they can't stop servants from gossiping. Apparently men came in some numbers, blocked all accesses to their houses, searched and took away boxes of papers, and left men behind to guard them."

Alphonse frowned, wondering what on earth the conversation was about. He was almost sure that the man speaking was his father's cousin, Lord Diddington – but what did he mean by what he'd said?

Sharrow and Gelford were two men who Alphonse had only ever vaguely heard of – Baronets, he thought, men who had some investments in common with his father, perhaps? His thoughts were brought back to the conversation he was blatantly eavesdropping on when his father began to speak.

"Do you think...?"

"I do – we're almost certainly doomed to a bad end. That we haven't been swept up in all this so far has been a miracle – but now – we're the only ones left free, I think, and what are the chances that we won't be incriminated by the papers that Sharrow and Gelford had?"

"Shhh, Diddy. Don't even say such things – what if someone heard you? Besides, there's still one other, apart from us. And if we go, so will he, for I've all of the papers..."

There was a gasp from Diddington, and Alphonse struggled to understand the implications of what he was hearing.

"Merringway! – is that wise? Wouldn't those papers be better off burnt?"

There was a moment of silence, then Alphonse heard his father speak again, in a tone that was chillingly cold.

"No. Those papers are my insurance. With those, perhaps, if it comes to it, I can bargain my way out. But perhaps we'd be wiser just to leave England for a time. There's the chateau in southern France..."

"We'd best decide soon, then, if we want to leave without looking suspiciously hurried."

"Yes – give me a few days, and I will see what I can discover – but I'll start to make some travel plans regardless. Annabelle will be annoyed with me if we miss the King's coronation – but so be it."

"True. I will call on you again in two days' time."

Alphonse moved, suddenly aware that the study door might open at any time, and reveal him – which seemed, at that moment, like a very bad idea indeed. He had the distinct impression that, should it be known that he had overheard that conversation, there would be very unpleasant repercussions. He hurried down the corridor, keeping his steps quiet, then down the stairs, all vestiges of the aftereffects of the previous night's drinking now gone from his system, replaced by a startling clarity of thought which was tinged by true fear. He was opening the breakfast room door as he heard the study door open on the floor above him. Forcing himself to be calm, he went to the sideboard to fill himself a plate, then settled at the table, accepting the coffee which the footman brought him.

He ate and drank, but his mind was not on the food at all – instead, he turned over all that he had heard through the study door, examining it in his thoughts, looking for any way in which it might be interpreted as nothing to worry about. But there was no possible way in which that was true. It seemed that he had been right, and his father was hiding something – something big, and dangerous – but... exactly what? And... what chateau in southern France?

*****

Jenson had spent some time planning, despite a desire to simply drop everything and rush off to London to find Jenneta. He would, after all, need money, accommodation, suitable clothing, and a good reason to be away from Holmdale Abbey. The latter was the easy part – for the last three years, he had been managing their small estate, Rosedeen Manor, which was far closer to London than Holmdale Abbey. He regularly went there for many weeks on end, and his father was pleased by that, for it meant that Jenson had developed all the skills needed to manage an estate.

But to then go on to London would take rather more organisation... Money was not too difficult, although Jenson's budget would be slim, for, mostly, he had no need of ready cash – their dealings with suppliers in the country were generally run on account. But over the years of isolation, he had built up a supply of coin and notes, handy for those times when he went into the village near Rosedeen to get things for himself. And if that failed, perhaps he would take the risk of going to the family man of business, and swearing the man to client confidentiality... There were other matters, with respect to suitable clothing – for much of what he had was somewhat out of date, although, thankfully, his tendency to wear plain clothing helped there. He went about his normal days, all the while planning, until, not all that long after Dona Esperanza's letter had arrived at Holmdale Abbey, he was ready. He had packed a sizeable trunk, planning to be away for a month or more, as he had done often in the past – but this time, the contents of the trunk were rather different.

He drove himself in his small chaise, and took no servant with him – there were staff at Rosedeen, although very few, and he was quite able to do for himself. Perhaps, once he was in London, he would have to change that – but that was a problem for the future. By the time he left Rosedeen again, a few days later, his plan had solidified. All at Rosedeen though he was going back to Holmdale Abbey, and indeed, at first he went in that direction. But soon he turned off, going back towards London, but first going to a large town which was on the way there. A town where he stayed at an Inn as Lord Albert Carlton (those being his two middle names), and where he had some new clothes made by the tailor, to suit a man stepping into London society for the first time. Two days after that, he drove into London. He had sent ahead to reserve a small suite of rooms at a most respectable, yet affordable hotel, on the edge of the more fashionable part of London – a hotel which still boasted some stables and room to store his chaise, although the expense for that was huge. Now, with all of that achieved, it was time to insinuate himself into society, explaining himself as a fourth son of a Marquess whose entire family had chosen to retire to their Scottish estates. The less detail he provided anyone, the better.

*****

The Ball was quite crowded – far more so than the ones earlier in the Season had been, and Jenneta stayed close to Dona Esperanza's side as they moved through the throng towards her friends. Now, Jenneta was beginning to have friends of her own, and quite a few young ladies greeted her as she passed them – it was a strange feeling, after the years in Las Palmas, where they had socialised with so few people. As she always did now, she watched the gentlemen they passed, studying them from under lowered lashes, looking for the one man she truly wished to see. Since the evening of their first introduction, he had danced with her at every Ball where they had both been in attendance, and it was those dances which made all of the socialising worthwhile. Would it ever come to more than dances? She did not know, but she hoped...

She did not see him, and her heart fell a little as a result. But perhaps he would arrive later... They stopped, Dona Esperanza having found her friends, and a rapid flow of conversation swallowed Jenneta up. People came and went, and a number of gentlemen asked a dance of her. Just as she was beginning to think that the evening might be quite bearable, if not as good as if Lord Bainbrook had been present, Lord Alphonse Hellmont appeared before her. She gritted her teeth and forced a smile.

"Good evening, Lady Marisela. I hope that you are in fine health? Might I claim a dance?"

For a moment, Jenneta was tempted to refuse, for she found Lord Alphonse remarkably unpleasant. But to do so, having accepted dances with other gentlemen, would cause rather a scene, a scandal, almost – and being noticed for scandalous behaviour was the one thing that she must avoid.

"Good evening, Lord Alphonse. Yes, I do still have a dance free – the Quadrille."

His eyes lit up with almost predatory delight, and internally she shivered.

"Wonderful! I shall attend upon you promptly when the Quadrille is called."

He took her hand and bowed over it, in a manner almost proprietary, and she barely stopped herself from pulling her hand away. He held it for just a fraction too long, then released her and walked off. Jenneta swallowed, trying to steady herself – how on earth was she going to get through dancing with him?

"Marisela? Are you well?"

Dona Esperanza spoke quietly, close beside her. Jenneta looked around, making sure that no one would overhear, before answering.

"I am – although I cannot manage to truly like Lord Alphonse. He has done nothing inappropriate, yet..."

Dona Esperanza nodded.

"I understand. You have no... affinity... for him. But you must tolerate, must be all that is polite."

"Yes."

They said nothing more, as the orchestra began, and the gentleman who had claimed her for the next set appeared to lead her away. He was an older gentleman, a kind man, who was always polite if rather dull, and Jenneta was glad of it, for he would expect little of her but to dance. The evening flowed on, quite tolerably all in all, and Jenneta managed to remain polite even to Lord Alphonse – which was made easier by the fact that she saw, just as Lord Alphonse led her towards the floor, Lord Bainbrook arrive. As she had fervently hoped, all the while that she danced with Lord Alphonse, Lord Bainbrook was waiting with Dona Esperanza when Jenneta was returned to her. Lord Alphonse gave Bainbrook an arrogant glare, and removed himself with a barely courteous leave-taking. Jenneta almost sagged with relief that he was gone.

"Lady Marisela, I do hope that you are well?"

The words were ordinary, but Lord Bainbrook's eyes had followed Lord Alphonse for a moment, then returned to Jenneta with true concern in their depths. That concern warmed Jenneta through.

"Indeed I am, Lord Bainbrook. I trust that you are also well?"

He looked, Jenneta thought, rather tired, and she wondered in passing what a man such as he might do with his time.

"I am – might I hope that you still have a dance free?"

"You are in luck, my Lord, for I do have one dance remaining – the waltz before supper."

Because I made sure to keep it free, in the hope that you would attend.

She did not say those words, but they ran through her mind, nonetheless. His face lit with a smile, and warmth spread through her.

"Wonderful!"

There was no artifice in his manner – she was sure that he meant it, that he was as pleased by the situation as she was. It was such a relief to deal with Bainbrook, compared to almost everyone else. He stayed and spoke with them a little longer, charming Dona Esperanza and the other older ladies, until it was time for the next set, and another gentleman came to lead Jenneta away.

The waltz, she thought, even as she began to dance a country dance, could not come soon enough.

*****

Lance had stepped into the ballroom, his mind still turning over the possibilities inherent in the documents he had been reviewing that afternoon – but his attention was immediately pulled away from that by the sight of Hellmont leading Lady Marisela out to dance.

His first thought was to rush to her, to somehow prevent Hellmont from touching her – which was rather ridiculous – he had no right to think so, for she could dance with whoever she wished, he had no claim on her. But... did she actually wish to dance with Hellmont? Or was she just being polite, because there was really no easy way to escape it?

In that moment, he desperately wanted to know the answers to those questions. He forced himself to steadiness, making his way slowly about the room, greeting acquaintances as he went, until he reached the cluster of older ladies where Dona Esperanza De Leon stood. There he engaged in genteel conversation, until Lady Marisela returned. Hellmont glared at him, and took himself off rapidly, for which Lance was most grateful. The conversation which followed soothed his tension, and resulted in Lady Marisela granting him the waltz.

Now, as they danced it, he felt better than he had for days, allowing himself to forget all about traitors and hidden documents, and think of nothing but the feel of her in his arms, the slightly exotic scent she wore, the warmth in her deep violet eyes when she regarded him, and the fact that, as far as he could tell, she'd intentionally kept the waltz before supper for him, in a room full of men who wished to dance with her. Their eyes held as they danced, and he felt the strongest urge to bend and kiss her as they moved, no matter how shocking such an action would be.

Chapter Seven

The dining room was full, with gentlemen who were resident in the apartments that the hotel rented out, and with those who came to visit them, and some who, it seemed, were tempted by the decent food the place offered. Jenson sat at a corner table, slowly working through the large meal he'd been served, whilst listening to and observing the others in the room. He felt remarkably unsophisticated in the face of these men – the impact of not having been about in society since he was 12 years old was substantial. So he studied their manners, noting those who appeared to put on affectations, and those who were quieter, considering how they spoke, and what they discussed. Almost every seat in the room was full when the door opened again, and a man came in who caught Jenson's attention. He was fairly tall, with dark hair which showed flashes of almost dark red tones in the lamplight, dark eyes, a manner which was flamboyant and genial, and clothes which ran the edge between being dramatically stylish, and outright foppish. He stopped just inside, and scanned the room – a few men called out a greeting, which the newcomer acknowledged with a wave of his hand. Then, his eyes alighting on the empty seat opposite Jenson at his corner table, he turned and came straight to him, waving at the man who managed the dining room as he did. Jenson wasn't sure how he felt about it, but before he could do or say anything, the fellow had dropped into the seat opposite.

"Good evening to you! I do hope you'll take pity on a famished man, and not object to me joining you, given that all other seats in this room appear to be taken. It's the curse of London – any place that serves good food is always overfull – but at least this place is rarely too raucous."

Jenson set down his utensils and met the fellow's eyes. There was something genuinely friendly there, and in that instant, Jenson found himself tempted to be rash – he could do with a friend, could do with something of a guide, as he sorted out how to insinuate himself into society, and this man felt, for no discernable reason that Jenson could see, oddly safe.

"Be welcome to the seat. If we are to be tablefellows, perhaps an introduction is in order? I'm Lord Albert Carlton."

The flamboyant man grinned.

"Well met then, Lord Albert. I'm Lord Kenric Williams. I've not seen you about before – what brings you to London?"

Jenson paused to take a draught of his ale, and as he did, one of the kitchen maids hurried up, and dropped a tankard and a plate in front of Lord Kenric – it seemed obvious that the man was a regular here. Once the maid had hurried off, Jenson answered that difficult question.

"I'm the fourth son of a Marquess who is so reclusive that everyone has forgotten the family exists. Neither the idea of the church, or the army, nor law appeals to me, so I decided to come and see what society is actually like, for I've concluded that my father's view of it is probably rather biased..."

Lord Kenric laughed.

"I can see why you'd do that. Being 'not the heir' and 'not destined for anything else in particular' leaves you in a rather empty place in life, doesn't it?"

"It does. But now I'm here, I begin to see that I've no idea where to start, how to get introduced to anyone vaguely significant – and I'll get no taste of society without introductions, will I?"

"You've the right of it there. But perhaps I can help, if you've an open mind."

"An open mind?"

"Yes. My circle of friends is rather... eclectic... shall we say. Everything from the quite exhaustingly proper to the scandalously improper. So I'd be happy to introduce you around a bit, and you can then decide for yourself where you want to 'settle' in society."

Jenson ate, using that to give him a moment to think, and Lord Kenric set to his own food as well. After a few minutes of companionable silence, Jenson spoke again.

"I'd appreciate those introductions. I'm not one for the extremes at either end – I can't afford to gamble to excess, or the like, and I'm not significant enough in the scheme of things for the high-sticklers to do anything but look down their noses at me, but everything between those two – yes, that's helpful, if you'll do it."

Lord Kenric lifted his tankard in salute.

"Drink to it then – we're agreed – I'll introduce you about a bit, and you can entertain me by telling me your private opinions of the people you meet – confidentially, of course."

Jenson gave a half snort of laughter, and raised his tankard too.

"We're agreed. I am staying here at present, so I'm easy to find. Just let me know where I need to be, when, and we'll go from there."

*****

By late May, Jenson, as Lord Albert, had met an alarmingly large number of people, mostly men, from all aspects of society, with Lord Kenric's help. Help he was glad of, especially where that involved warning him of which men to avoid, and why. That he was beginning to achieve his aim was confirmed when the first invitation to a Ball arrived. Jenson worried, a little, that things were taking as long as they were, for soon, he would have to go back to Holmdale Abbey, via Rosedeen, at least for a short while, if his subterfuge was to continue to work. He pushed that worry aside for now, and instead focussed on the invitation.

The Ball was to be held at the home of a Viscount Petershaw – a man of moderate importance with a few useful connections – or at least that was how Lord Kenric described him. What would it be like? Jenson worried, a little, that he would make some social mistake – but he had to try – what if Jenneta was there – what would he do? That, he would decide if it happened. For now, he had to simply keep practising being Albert.

*****

So far, the Ball was interesting, if rather painful in the matter of excessive politeness and propriety. Jenson began to understand why, perhaps, Lord Kenric had acquaintances of a less respectable nature, too. He had been introduced to a positively head spinning number of people, and found that young ladies regarded him with interest, until they discovered that he was a fourth son – what would they be like if he had been there as his true self? It was an interesting thing to consider. Now, as he paused near the side of the room, studying those around him, his eye was caught by a woman near the small dais where the orchestra sat. He stilled, his wine glass halfway to his mouth, his heart suddenly pounding.

Could it be...? She was of moderate height, with rich dark hair, and a good figure. But it was her face which had captured him. He was almost certain, in that moment, that the woman was his sister. He had not seen her for seven years, yet somehow he knew – perhaps because she looked so like the portrait of his grandmother, which hung at Traithewood Grange, and perhaps because the lines of her face were, in some ways, rather like the lines of his own. His first impulse was to go to her, but he forced himself to be still, forced himself to finish lifting the glass to his mouth.

"Striking, isn't she?"

Lord Kenric's voice surprised him – he had not thought the man close by at all. Jenson turned to meet Kenric's eyes.

"The dark-haired woman over there? Yes, very striking. Who is she?"

It seemed the simplest way to discover more. It had become apparent to him that Lord Kenric, despite his foppish and rakish surface, was remarkably astute – and knew everyone. Kenric was also, apparently, the son of a Duke.

"Her name is Lady Marisela De Leon, and you, Carlton, are not the only one who finds her striking – my brother is, not to put too fine a point on it, smitten – although he denies it. Many others are smitten too, although some hesitate as so little is known of her family – one can't look the Spanish aristocracy up in Debrett's after all."

Jenson's head spun. Was it Jenneta? Or not? Surely it was... But why the subterfuge of the different name? That question lasted but a few seconds in his thoughts, before the obvious answer arrived to supplant it – the subterfuge on her part was undoubtedly for the same reason that he, himself, was here using a name not exactly his own. Still, it was disturbing, to see his sister carrying out such a deception – if it was, in truth, his sister.... Internally, he mocked himself for a hypocrite, for being disturbed by her deception, whilst carrying out his own – but the discomfort remained.

He continued to watch her, and the older woman beside her – who certainly looked the part of a Spanish great aunt! And... De Leon... that was the aunt's name, and, he realised, Marisela was one of Jenneta's middle names, as Albert and Carlton were his own. That thought made him almost choke on his drink again, amused at how alike their thinking apparently was. He had to be sure, or he would go mad – which meant that he had to achieve an introduction, somehow. Beside him, Lord Kenric watched, those astute dark eyes missing nothing.

*****

Jenneta scanned the room, as always, looking for Lord Bainbrook. She could not see him. She did, however, discover his brother, Lord Kenric, who was standing with another man, near the terrace doors. A man who turned at that moment, and looked directly at her. Her heart near stopped, and breathing became suddenly difficult. That was... it could not be... but surely it was... her brother?

When she was still for too long, Dona Esperanza gently took her arm, and drew her forward. The spell was broken, and she looked away, maddening doubt filling her. She wanted to rush across the ballroom to that man, to demand, outright, that he tell her the truth – but what if she was wrong? If she asked, and she was wrong, her own subterfuge would be revealed, and all would be lost. Thinking frantically, she continued with the evening – all the time watching that man, even when Lord Bainbrook finally arrived. But by the time that she had danced with Bainbrook, she was no further ahead – had not developed a plan to discover the truth – had not, at that point, even had anyone mention the man's name. The evening was close to an end, and Jenneta felt filled with desperation, yet she could do nothing. The remainder of the evening was possibly the most difficult of her life.

*****

Lady Marisela was distracted, and Lance felt a shaft of worry fill him – could it be that she was tiring of his company? But surely not, for she spoke as she always did, she met his gaze with her deep violet eyes and smiled in that way which took his breath away, it was just that... she seemed to be watching other people, far more than usual. After their dance, when he went to join Kenric, the dissonance of it stayed with him. Kenric was standing with another man – someone Lance had not met before, and the two turned to Lance as he approached.

"Ah, brother, let me introduce a new friend of mine. Lord Albert Carlton, this is my brother Lance, Marquess of Bainbrook. Lance, Carlton here is new to town, a younger son from a family who have been rusticating in the north for generations. He was rash enough to accept my offer of some introductions and assistance in finding his way into society."

"Glad to meet you, Carlton. Despite what others may say, trusting my brother is actually a wise decision – just don't tell the fast set he runs with that I said so."

Lord Albert, who had been looking down a little, gave a small bow, then raised his head to meet Lance's eyes.

For a moment, Lance felt utterly unbalanced. Carlton's eyes were a deep violet, they reminded him of someone else's eyes – didn't they? Then Carlton broke the connection, and Lance pushed that whimsy aside – why should he think this man had eyes like someone else? Eyes were not something that Lance usually studied very closely, anyway. Carlton laughed softly.

"I have detected that Lord Kenric has rather... greater depths... than he projects, at times. I am most grateful for his help. And I am pleased to meet you, Lord Bainbrook, as well – London society seems rather like a battlefield set with many traps, rather than a setting for genteel conversation, most of the time."

That made Lance laugh, for he agreed with Carlton – and he also appreciated the man's forthright honesty in saying it. They continued to talk, and a number of other acquaintances of Kenric's joined them. Lance observed as the introductions were made, all the while also watching the others present in the ballroom - the act of doing Setford's work had become habit, completely. When he turned back from a scan of the room, he noticed that Carlton was focusing his attention across the room, rather than on the conversation. Across the room at Lady Marisela, specifically. Tension twisted in him, shockingly hard, and his hands balled into fists. He did not wish, he realised quite clearly, for any other man to look at Lady Marisela with that degree of obvious interest. That fact shocked him – was he... being jealous... of another man simply *looking* at her? That was patently ridiculous... but also patently true. To overcome the feeling, and to distract Carlton as well as himself, Lance engaged the man in conversation again, discovering, to his pleasure, that Carlton had an excellent understanding of estate management, and of some of the newer agricultural techniques which were being tried. It wasn't exactly the usual ballroom conversation, but it was, in the end, refreshing.

*****

Another two weeks passed, for one of which Jenson perforce, left London and returned to Holmdale Abbey, via Rosedeen, only to leave again. His father was a little surprised, but shrugged – Jenson was old enough to do as he chose, so long as he stayed to the family properties, to fulfil the King's requirements. The second week, when Jenson returned to London, was filled with multiple Balls and soirees – despite it now being June, more of the *ton* than usual were staying in London, for with the King's coronation set to happen in mid-July there was no point in retreating to the country yet. At every one of those events, Jenson watched 'Lady Marisela' – the woman he was increasingly convinced was his sister – and he was quite sure that she watched him as closely. It was driving him quite mad. Especially as he watched Lord Kenric's brother dance with her, and lavish attention on her.

Was he good enough for his sister? How did Jenson feel about her having a suitor – if it was her, of course? And he was beginning to realise that Lord Bainbrook was aware of Jenson watching Lady Marisela, and that he wasn't happy about it – did Bainbrook think Jenson a competitor for her attentions? That idea had brought him to near hysterical laughter, once he was safely ensconced in his rooms at the hotel. By the next morning, after some reflection on the matter, Jenson had determined that he must ask Kenric to arrange an introduction to 'Lady Marisela' – surely, if he spoke with her, he would know? So that evening, as he stepped into yet another ballroom, it was with great determination that he would not leave without that introduction occurring. He asked about it, as soon as he came upon Lord Kenric.

"You ask a lot, Carlton. I know that my brother will not be happy, should I introduce you." Kenric looked away for a moment, and Jenson felt his heart sink. But then Kenric chuckled softly, and spoke again. "However, my sister is a force unto herself, and Bainbrook knows quite well that she will do as she wishes, regardless. Therefore, do come this way."

A little confused by his words, Jenson followed him, and was led to a cluster of young ladies in one corner of the room. As soon as Jenson saw them, he knew which was Kenric and Bainbrook's sister – she had hair like theirs – dark and lustrous, with rich red undertones, and her face shape echoed theirs, just with softer edges.

"Why Kenric, what could possibly cause you to seek me out at a Ball?"

Lord Kenric smiled, his best casual, devil may care look, and half the other young ladies sighed at the sight.

"My dear Ysolde, what do you think might cause such an aberration? I want something, and you are the one person who can provide it."

She blinked, obviously curious.

"You want something... that ***I*** can provide? My, that is... unusual..."

Her eyes flicked to Jenson, and back to Kenric. Kenric fanned himself as if worn down by the need to ask her, and Jenson stifled a laugh.

"Yes, isn't it. But first, let me introduce my companion. Lady Ysolde Williams, this is Lord Albert Carlton. He is new to London, and is attempting to meet... everyone..."

Jenson bowed.

"I am delighted to meet you, Lady Ysolde."

She met his eyes as he rose from the bow, and gave him a small curtsey.

"I am pleased to make your acquaintance. Do I detect that what Kenric wants of me has something to do with you?"

It was a bold question, but Jenson found it charming, rather than rude. It was Kenric who answered her, before Jenson could, with an exaggerated sigh.

"Ah sister, you have seen through my wiles, yet again. Indeed, poor Lord Albert here is the subject of my request. I would like you to introduce him to all of your young lady friends, and, perhaps, to Lady Marisela? I simply do not know everyone, although..." at this his voice dropped to a whisper, "...I will, of course, deny having ever admitted that."

Jenson waited with his heart pounding, and his mouth dry as she considered the request. She studied him carefully, and he found himself wondering if his cravat was crooked or crushed, so intense was that examination. Then she smiled.

"Of course, I can assist with that, as can my friends. If you would come this way, Lord Albert."

Chapter Eight

Half an hour and dozens of introductions later, Jenson found himself face to face with Lady Marisela. She went pale as he approached, but managed to stand steadily, and go through the motions of introduction, even as her great aunt watched from nearby. When she spoke, Jenson was even more sure it was Jenneta, but still...

He gathered his courage, and asked her to dance. She agreed, and he was shocked at the relief which filled him – part of him had been truly terrified that she might refuse. After that, Lady Ysolde and her friends carried him off for more introductions, and somehow, he managed to remain polite and friendly through it all. Finally, they released him – just in time for him to go to 'Lady Marisela' for their dance.

As she placed her hand on his arm, he could almost feel Bainbrook's eyes upon them – Kenric was right, it seemed, Bainbrook was smitten....

They stepped into the line of dancers, just as the music began – this was a slow dance, with a lot of turning around each other – a good opportunity for conversation, if he could in any way work out how to begin. They bowed and curtsied, then began, turning about each other, then stepping close before stepping back.

As they were at their closest, she whispered, startling him.

At least, it seemed, she had the courage to begin.

"I do believe... Lord Albert... that perhaps we have met before..."

It admitted nothing, but left the opportunity open – very wise and cautious of her. He considered his words, waiting until the dance brought them back to that close position.

"I do believe, Lady Marisela, that you are correct. And that it was in settings far less... formal... than this."

They rotated again, their eyes meeting, two pools of matching deep violet, filled with secrets and uncertainties.

"Happier days, perhaps, long cut short by doubt and duty?"

That stole his breath – she had to be referring to the King's doubt of their grandfather, and the family's adherence to the duty he had laid upon them.

"Indeed, days before bereavement and separation."

Her breathing was uneven as they turned through the next figures, and for a moment he thought that he saw the glitter of unshed tears in her eyes.

"An aching wound that never heals, a presence missed every day."

He could not have put it better. It was time to take a risk.

"Jenneta?"

It was barely more than a breath with no substance, a whisper of thought made real, yet it was enough to make her nearly stumble.

"Yes. Jenson?"

His heart soared, even as utter frustration filled him. Here he was, having found his sister, after seven long years, and he could not speak to her more, not here, in front of the entire *ton*!

"Yes. Somehow, we must talk – alone, without anyone knowing."

"Yes. But I do not know how."

"Neither do I, yet."

"We will find a way."

The music slowed, the dance completed, and they bowed and curtsied again, before he led her back to Dona Esperanza, whose sharp black eyes considered them, before she gave a wry smile.

"Marisela, you must introduce this young man."

"Dona Esperanza, this is Lord Albert Carlton."

She held out her hand, and Jenson took it, bowing deeply over it.

"I am pleased to meet you, young man." There was nothing in her words but the ordinary, but in her hand, under her slightly curled fingers, there was something – a card, which she dropped into his palm, as he released her hand. Shock filled him, and he was hard pressed to prevent it from showing on his face. He curled his own fingers around the card as she continued speaking. "I am sure that we will see you again, and soon."

"Of course, my Lady."

He bowed again, and left them, slipping the card into his pocket as he did so. He would look at it later. Walking away was quite the most difficult thing he had done, since coming to London.

*****

Jenneta watched him walk away, her heart crying out to run after him, even as she held herself still, her face impassive. She could not make a scene, could not risk giving everything away, no matter how much she wanted more time with her brother. Then, to make matters all the more difficult, Lord Alphonse appeared in front of her, reaching out to take her arm in a most annoyingly proprietary way.

"I believe that we are promised for this dance, Lady Marisela?"

With a sinking heart, she realised that it was true, and allowed him to lead her to the floor. That dance was quite the most miserable experience of her life, as he held her too close, for too long, at every opportunity.

She barely managed to mumble inanities in response to whatever he said, but it seemed not to matter – all he cared for was to speak, and have her appear to be interested. As they turned in the dance, her eyes went to the other side of the room, where Jenson now stood with Lord Bainbrook, and his brother, all of them apparently watching the dancing – it felt as if they watched her, specifically – but surely that was her imagination?

They also, occasionally, cast sideways glances at each other – Jenson and Bainbrook with some asperity to the look, and Lord Kenric with what she rather thought was amusement. None of that made any sense – but at least by looking at them she could avoid looking at Lord Alphonse.

*****

Jenson somehow reached the other side of the room where, to his surprise, he found Lord Kenric – he had thought that Kenric would have retreated to the card room, but instead, here he stood, watching the dancers, his face a study in ennui – except for the astute brightness of his dark eyes. He nodded at Jenson, and Jenson turned to stand beside him, also watching the dancers.

Moments later, his breath caught. Jenneta was dancing with Lord Alphonse Hellmont – hadn't Kenric said...

"Lord Kenric... am I correct in saying that Lady Marisela is dancing with Lord Alphonse Hellmont?"

"You are."

"If I remember rightly, you warned me away from any interaction with Hellmont – 'an unsavoury wastrel' I believe your words were?"

Kenric gave a sharp snort of laughter, even though his expression never wavered.

"Yes, you have that correct. Why do you ask now?"

"I... ah... found the young lady rather pleasant, and unaffected – Hellmont is not the sort of man I would see as suiting a woman like that."

It was as close as he could go to expressing his feelings, without giving away his interest in 'Lady Marisela'. He hoped that Jenneta did not find Hellmont appealing – he was not the sort of man he wanted his sister associated with! Kenric turned his head to him, just a little, and gave the smallest of nods.

"He is not a man suitable for a decent young woman, no. Much though he tries to present himself as such. I do believe that it's likely he is looking for a wife – no, let me correct that – he is looking for an easily accessible dowry, attached to a woman who is not too objectionable. But I'm not sure I'd worry in this case. Lady Marisela doesn't exactly look enamoured of him, and I suspect that my brother has intentions – whether he admits them to himself yet or not – in Lady Marisela's direction. He is perfectly capable of dealing with the likes of Hellmont..."

Jenson said nothing more, allowing his eyes to still follow Jenneta – Kenric was right, she did not look very enthusiastic about dancing with Hellmont. As he watched, he contemplated the other part of what Kenric had said – about Bainbrook having intentions. Just how did he feel about that? Would he be happy to see Bainbrook courting his sister? Disconcertingly, he found that he did not really know how he felt about it – beyond it being a vast improvement on a man like Hellmont.

*****

Lance had managed to keep these last few dances free, despite the best efforts of some young ladies to get him to ask them. Instead, he had circulated a bit, talking to various gentlemen, his mind half on the papers Setford had most recently sent him, and on the elusive connection he was still missing. He felt as if it should be obvious, as if something was right in front of him, and he simply wasn't seeing it. Reinforcing that feeling, he caught sight of Hellmont, dancing with Lady Marisela.

It was enough to make him grind his teeth. Perhaps he would go back to looking at the Traithewood family, and any possible slight associations there. He moved across the room to where Kenric stood with Carlton, watching the dance floor. That Kenric was out here, not in the card room, was interesting – Lance wondered why, wondered what he was looking for...

As he went that way, he couldn't help but notice that Carlton watched the dancers with some intensity – and his eyes appeared to be fixed upon Lady Marisela. A sharp flash of jealousy ran through him – it was bad enough that Hellmont appeared determined to pay her his attentions, but if Carlton was interested too...

Lance discovered that he wanted to simply rush across the room, disrupt the dancing, and drag Lady Marisela from Hellmont's grasp. Which was ridiculous, and so far out of character for him as to be beyond shocking. She appeared to be coping with Hellmont perfectly well, and there was no sign at all of her needing 'rescuing' no matter how much he felt the desire to act.

Kenric greeted him with a nod, his dark eyes assessing, and Lance was certain that Kenric knew exactly what he'd been thinking. Which was damnably embarrassing.

"Have you tired of social conversation, Bainbrook?"

"As much as you have apparently tired of the card room, Kenric."

Kenric waved a languid hand.

"There is no point playing with some men… there's just no challenge in winning against a man with no skill…"

"No skill, and nothing interesting to talk about?"

"Indeed."

Carlton had half turned to listen to their conversation.

"Good evening, Bainbrook. I can't say that I see either of you as likely to be obsessed by the cards – but perhaps I am wrong?"

Carlton frowned, and his eyes slid back to the dancers for a moment. Lance shook his head, but it was Kenric who spoke.

"Hush, Carlton, you'll ruin my carefully crafted reputation as a wastrel. My brother, however, is the respectable one in our family – barely touches a card, ever. Bainbrook is quite the opposite of men like…" here Kenric inclined his head towards the dance floor, his eyes alight with mischief, "…Hellmont there."

Lance clenched his jaw, knowing that Kenric did it to madden him, to see what he would do. Years of training kept him steady, but he would make sure that his brother paid for this later.

"My dear brother, being a better man than Hellmont hardly requires any great effort – Hellmont is only accepted in society because of his father, and even that, I begin to think, will not be enough soon. Rumour has it that he is thoroughly pockets-to-let, with the creditors closing in."

Carlton's face darkened a little at those words, and his eyes went back to where Lady Marisela danced with Hellmont – was that simply concern Lance saw in his expression, or self-interest? Jealousy tightened in his stomach again, a strange, twisted mixture of protectiveness, possessiveness, and desire. Kenric's voice broke him out of those thoughts.

"His father should let him fail – at least long enough to thoroughly scare him for life. What man would want an heir whose approach to life would bankrupt his estate?"

Lance had to agree, although he did not put that into words. The music ended, and he watched as the dancers stopped, and Hellmont bowed to Lady Marisela, before leading her back to her aunt. It was not until Hellmont had released her and turned away that Lance found himself able to breathe easily again. He would, he thought, perhaps actually take the step of calling on Lady Marisela, even though that would be tantamount to a declaration of his intentions. But… the gossips would produce a positive banquet of speculation if he did such a thing!

*****

"What will I do if he calls on me?"

"He hasn't yet, Marisela, and may never do so. So you might not ever need to discover the answer to that question."

Jenneta shuddered.

"I hope you are right. There are many men I find uninteresting, but those, at least, are not objectionable – if they call, I can be distantly polite, and they will realise that calling on me is wasted effort. But Lord Alphonse Hellmont... he is persistent, and somehow makes my skin crawl, even while not quite doing anything that I can say is beyond propriety. And no matter how disinterested I appear, he acts as if I desire his attentions. How does one dissuade a man like that?"

Dona Esperanza gave a slight shrug.

"By being persistently, coldly polite, and not allowing him any opportunity to believe you offer more."

Jenneta shivered at the thought of what 'offer more' could be taken to mean.

"I can certainly treat him like that."

"Good. But Jenneta, the year is passing, and you are no closer to finding a husband – only three men have shown any definite interest in you – Hellmont, Bainbrook, and Sir George Wilton – who is old enough to be your father. What will you do, if that is still the situation, once the King's Coronation is over, and the last of the *ton* leave London for the summer?"

At her words, Jenneta's thoughts went to Bainbrook – was he truly interested in her? He seemed so, at Balls and soirees, yet he had not called on her...

Did she only imagine his interest?

For, if she was honest with herself, she was interested in him – so perhaps her thinking that he might be interested was just wishfulness?

"Perhaps we will go back to Las Palmas?"

She did not, entirely, mean it, she realised, yet what else could she suggest? The thought of that, of leaving Jenson again, when she had only just found him, hurt, yet she did not like the idea of languishing in London, with little to do, either.

Dona Esperanza drew herself up and pinned Jenneta with a stern glare.

"We will do nothing of the sort. If you are to have a future, we must find it here. That is my last word on the matter."

"But how will we do that! I cannot even see Je..."

Dona Esperanza cut her off before she could say the name, obviously afraid that a servant might overhear.

"Do not say that! You will find a man whom you wish to marry, I am sure of it. But to do so, we must be here. Perhaps you should encourage Lord Bainbrook more?"

"And just how will I do that? I freely admit that I welcome his presence, but he seems not inclined to take things further than dancing at Balls..."

"Then you must encourage him."

Jenneta, in a fit of complete frustration, almost threw her book down onto the seat beside her.

"I would, if I only knew how!"

*****

Lance brushed the dust from the cover of the book which Mr Bigglesworth had just extracted from the back of a dark shelf, at the back of a narrow aisle in his shop, and opened it to the title page.

He regarded the book with tentative hope.

The title page declared it, rather grandiosely, to be 'An Accounting of the Entire British Aristocracy, Their Families and Relations, as Recorded by Mr Simpson, in This Year 1813'. It was the only book he had found, published within the time frame he needed, which addressed the aristocracy – apart from DeBrett's, of course, and what DeBrett's had to tell him, he had already thoroughly plumbed.

He handed it to Mr Bigglesworth, pleased.

"I will take this one, thank you. If you would send the account?"

"Of course, milord. Just come over here and I'll wrap it up for you."

Lance followed him to the counter, and waited as he wrapped the book. But before Bigglesworth handed him the wrapped book, he bent, and pulled out another package from below the counter.

"If you could do me the honour, milord, of delivering this on behalf of himself?"

Bigglesworth handed over both parcels, and Lance, startled, read the direction which was written on the wrapping of the second parcel – Lord Kenric Williams.

"I... oh." The memory of a previous conversation came to him. "This parcel... it wouldn't happen to contain some books on the subject of blacksmithing, would it?"

Bigglesworth grinned, and gave him a nod.

"You're a right clever one, there's no doubt. Himself told me you'd know."

"Well... I'll deliver it then, and thank you."

"There's a letter in there – himself said that you'd know what that was about too."

"I do, indeed I do."

Chapter Nine

Jenson drove away from Holmdale Abbey again, anxious to be back in London. He felt uncomfortable with telling so many lies to his father, yet he could not stop – he still had not gathered the courage to call at the address which had been on the card given to him by Dona Esperanza, and he still had not had the opportunity to speak to Jenneta in any kind of privacy. At least, having been here for two weeks, he could now be away for a month or more without his father worrying. The miles rolled by, and he allowed himself to remember each and every conversation he'd had in London, and to wonder, yet again, if he would ever be able to be in society as himself, if ever anything could be found, which would clearly exonerate his grandfather. Part of him had hoped that in London, he would uncover something useful – but the more time he spent there, the more he understood just how unlikely that was.

Still, he could hope. His thoughts turned then to perhaps his biggest concern – was Bainbrook truly interested in Jenneta? And if he was, and he set about courting her seriously, would Jenneta ever tell him the truth of it all, and risk disaster for their family? It was a frightening thought, yet, in a way, he would wish her to tell him – for to marry a man without him knowing the truth... He would deal with all of that, if and when it happened. He pushed aside the thought which followed it.

What would he do, if he, himself, found a woman he could come to care for?

*****

Lance had settled himself into his study, the book he had brought home from Bigglesworth's on the desk before him. It might turn out to be a dry accounting of the families of the aristocracy, or it might turn out to be little more than a gossip sheet – but at least it was a new source of information. Off to one side lay his journals – the ones with the Traithewood genealogy and his notes about the family, just in case he found something useful.

Perhaps he was deluded to expect anything, but still...

The door opened, and Kenric stepped in.

"Hard at work already? I've barely risen! I don't know why you can't keep decently late hours like the rest of the *ton,* brother!"

Lance shook his head, amused, as Kenric dropped into a chair opposite. Then he opened a drawer, extracted a parcel, and pushed it across the desk.

"This is for you. I suspect it may even have the power to wake you up properly."

Kenric eyed it warily, and Lance went back to the book in front of him, leaving his brother to decide what to do. After some time, during which Lance discovered that 'Mr Simpson', author of the book, had a dry wit about his words which rendered his commentary on the aristocracy sharp and amusing, very close to gossip, without quite being so, Kenric finally reached out and lifted his parcel.

"OOF! That's heavier than I expected."

"I see – and why were you expecting anything at all?"

"In truth, I wasn't – it just looked... not heavy?" Lance laughed as Kenric undid the string and pulled the paper away. Three books were revealed, with a sealed letter sitting on top of them. Kenric put the letter to one side, and examined the books. "A Detailed History of the Art of British Blacksmithing?"

Lance smiled.

"Interesting?"

"Yes." He lifted the other two books, to discover more in the same vein. "But... why would someone send me these? No one but you, and Ysolde, would know that I have the slightest interest in such matters."

His expression was so confused that Lance struggled not to laugh uproariously.

"Perhaps you had best open the letter and find out?"

Kenric glared at him for stating the obvious, but did as he had suggested, lifting the letter and breaking the seal. Lance turned his attention back to the foibles of the aristocracy, as recorded 8 years ago, while Kenric read. Lance was scanning the index of illustrations – prints of paintings of various aristocratic families were included, it seemed – when Kenric made a slightly strangled exclamation.

"S? Does that mean this is from who I think it is?"

"Yes. He is apparently impressed with your ability to look languid in card rooms whilst remembering everything that everyone says."

Kenric spluttered for a moment, apparently caught between laughter and outrage. He settled closer to laughter, giving a broad wave of his hand.

"I am delighted to be appreciated then. But... why the books? Why *these* books, in particular?"

"He asked me about you – about what you might do, if the exigencies of society didn't constrain you... It seems that he appreciates skills in a man – a very broad range of skills..."

Kenric lifted the letter again, his eyes running down the page.

"Damnation! His suggested meeting is today – in but an hour, no less! I suppose I should go..."

"Of course you should..."

At that, Kenric gave a sharp nod, scooped up the books and the letter, and left the room. Lance sat for a moment after the door closed, wondering what, in the end, might come of the conversation that Kenric was about to have. Then, he turned back to the book in front of him, looking for any and all possible references to Traithewood's family and close associates. At first, he was sure that there was nothing new, but then something caught his eye, when he glanced back over the family tree he had drawn. There was something there, some name he had just seen on the page... he studied it, then went back to the book, reviewing the list of illustrations and the list of chapters again.

Ah! There it was – in the illustrations. 'a family portrait, painted 1812, Mq Holmdale'. The Marquess of Holmdale was the Duke of Traithewood's son and heir. Lance flipped through the book to the correct page and studied the print he found there. It seemed a good rendering of the painting, with the colouring well done, and likely true to the original. The Marquess stood in front of a large marble fireplace, above which part of a huge mirror in a gilded frame could be seen. In front of him sat his wife, a woman with dark hair, and a distinctly continental look to the lines of her face – a face which was extremely pale, in that almost translucent way which came with consumption. Beside her, looking a little stiff, as children so often did in portraits, stood a boy and a girl, both with abundant near black hair, violet eyes, and a face shape which echoed, to some extent, their mother's, as well as each other.

The twins, he realised. He studied them, deeply curious – what would they be like now? For by now, they would have to be around nineteen or twenty. An age at which, under other conditions, they would be out in society. There was something about them... as if they resembled someone he knew... but that was beyond unlikely, given their age when isolated from society, and his age then... he shook his head, pushing that thought aside, and found the section in the book where the text talked about Traithewood, and Holmdale, hoping for clues about other close relations.

*****

The June heat felt good to Jenneta, like a memory of Las Palmas – but that only made her less certain of what she should do, as time wore on and Bainbrook made no move to call on her, even though he danced with her at each event. That fact caused her to be irritable, and this morning she had argued with Dona Esperanza again, on the matter of what they should do, once the King's Coronation was over, and most of the *ton* began to retire to their country estates. Dona Esperanza was adamant that they should remain in London, making no attempt to slip into the country to see her Papa and Jenson. Jenneta had declared that, if she could not see her family, what was the point of remaining here? Could they not go back to Las Palmas, and return next year? Dona Esperanza had waved aside everything she said, and refused to consider anything but staying here. So, tonight, as she entered the ballroom, she looked for Bainbrook as always, but also, perhaps more urgently, for Jenson. He had been absent from events for the last week or more – having gone back to Holmdale Abbey she supposed, to maintain the fiction of him not having come to London at all. She wanted to discuss the whole matter with him, for they had always, as children, solved problems together.

Neither of them appeared to be present, and that just made her even more irritable, but she forced herself to keep a pleasant expression on her face, and be polite to everyone, as usual. At least she hadn't seen any sign of Lord Alphonse, either. Half way through the evening, just as Jenneta began to despair, Jenson arrived, and she breathed a sigh of relief. Soon, he came to greet them, being Lord Albert perfectly – did she look as comfortable as Lady Marisela as he did as Lord Albert, she wondered?

"Good evening Lady Marisela, Dona Esperanza. I trust that all is well with you?"

"It is, Lord Albert."

There was an edge to her tone, for that answer was not really truthful. Jenson regarded her steadily for a moment, and she knew, of a certainty, that he was quite aware of her lie.

"Am I lucky enough to be able to claim a dance, even though my arrival has been most tardy?"

"Of course. I still have the waltz free, and I do believe that it is next."

She'd been keeping it for Bainbrook, but he wasn't here, and she needed to talk to Jenson. He raised an eyebrow at her, even as he bowed and made exclamations of gratitude. He stayed with them for the short while before the current set ended, and the orchestra prepared for the waltz, discussing nothing of importance – the heat, the scale of the planned festivities for the coronation and the like. But as soon as it was proper, he offered her his arm and led her to the floor. The dance began, and, taking advantage of being able to hold her relatively close, he wasted no time in whispering to her.

"It is patently obvious to me, Jenneta, that everything is not at all well with you. What troubles you?"

She said nothing for a short while, suddenly unsure how to start, then she took a deep breath, and said the first thing which rose to her mind.

"Everything! I was supposed, according to Dona Esperanza, to find a man I might care to marry – that was why we came to London! Yet here we are, in June, and I seem no closer to achieving that than I was in March. I suggested that we should, therefore, go back to Las Palmas, and return here next year."

"I take it that your suggestion was not well received?"

"It was not. She insisted that we should stay in London, until such time as we find me a husband, no matter how long it takes. And that we could not possibly go to Holmdale Abbey…."

She could hear the edge of tears in her own voice, and she stopped speaking, concentrating, instead, on dancing. He said nothing for some time, and eventually she met his eyes again.

"Jenneta – she is right, you know…"

She gasped.

"Jenson, how could you!"

"Easily – for I would protect us all. Is there no man who appeals to you?"

Jenneta felt herself flush, as the image of Bainbrook immediately came to her mind. She was tempted to lie, yet… this was her brother… she had never lied to him… She sighed.

"There is one. But he has not called upon me, has shown no sign of interest in anything more than dancing with me…"

"Ah. Do I know him?"

"Yes."

Jenson grinned at her, and she was completely sure that he knew who she meant, on the instant.

"Then if I have it right, I approve."

"Good, though much use that is, if he never does anything about it..."

"You, sister, have always lacked patience."

She regarded him with a glare.

"As if you could cast aspersions about that..."

"True. But you must wait, must try to encourage him."

"I will, even if only because, if we are to stay in London, I shall be utterly without anything to entertain me, if I don't."

*****

June moved into July, and the soirees and Balls continued, a never-ending round of dull politeness, dancing with men she had no interest in, trying to avoid Lord Alphonse whenever she could, and alternating between hope and despair where Bainbrook was concerned. To her shock, Jenson called upon them at home one day, telling her in a whisper that Dona Esperanza had passed him their direction, surreptitiously, but that he had, until then, not had the confidence to carry out the deception in her home. And indeed, it was difficult – but there were servants who might overhear. So they sat, and took tea, and spoke of other people, and of the King's Coronation to come – and of nothing which they truly wished to discuss at all.

The previous night, she had waltzed with Bainbrook again, and felt sure that the connection between them had become stronger, that perhaps he might say something... but he had not. Now, she contemplated the evening to come, which would be the last Ball to be held before the coronation, the last of this extended Season – would he be there? And if he was, what might she do to encourage him? She wasn't sure, at all, but she was determined to do something.

*****

Lord Alphonse was beyond worried. He had received a rather pointed letter from his creditors, and it had been enough to make him stay at home and worry at the challenge of obtaining more funds. He was sitting in the library at Merringway House, his mind running in ever more desperate circles.

This afternoon, he'd heard Diddington talking to his father again, both of them agitated, but he'd not been able to get close enough to actually hear what they said..

But just the visit was enough to remind him of the conversation he had overheard, weeks earlier – the conversation he still did not really understand. He'd not had any chance to get into his father's study, or investigate his papers at all – but he rather desperately wanted to, wanted to discover what the man was hiding, that had Diddington in such a lather too. It had to be bad, for the other two men they'd mentioned – Sharrow and Gelford – had not been seen about in society at all in the intervening weeks.

And there was still that remark about southern France...

If he couldn't get into his father's study, where else might he find something useful, perhaps? His father tended to keep things – as he'd said in that overheard conversation – so where might he put things? Alphonse was gazing blindly before him as he thought, but after a few moments, he realised that his eyes were resting on the bank of cupboards which ran along one part of the library wall, beside some of the bookshelves. Cupboards which he generally completely ignored, so much a part of the scenery were they.

Cupboards which had been there most of his life, and which his father sometimes put things in.

What things?

A very good question indeed.

It was time he had a look – if nothing else, he might gain some entertainment from it, and at best, he might discover something useful.

He stood, and went to them, starting at one end, and opening the first. Stacked papers faced him – papers of all kinds, from ledgers to news sheets from years ago. The volume was daunting, but the contents might actually be genuinely interesting.

He settled in to read.

Many hours later, he looked up, shocked to see that the long summer twilight was beginning to fade to true darkness. Had he truly spent that long reading old gossip sheets and news?

It seemed that he had.

He looked back to the news sheet in his hand, deciding to finish that one, and then seek out some food, and a brandy. It was dated May 1801, and the page he was looking at was a gossip column.

One name caught his eye, amongst the columns of text – De Leon.

Well... he had begun this in an attempt to learn more about his father's activities, but perhaps, here, he held something which might help with his other problem – discovering more about the family provenance of Lady Marisela De Leon...

He dropped back into a chair, as close to the window as possible, and used the last of the fading light to read it.

Chapter Ten

July 1821

Lance pushed the papers aside. He had just finished reading the last of the documents which had been found in the two conspirator's houses, as a result of his work so far. There was something there – not something direct and clear, but something, nonetheless. Those two had primarily associated with three other men – Diddington, and Merringway, who Lance had already come to suspect, plus Mr Charles Harrington, the third man that Lance had suggested to Setford. Lance let his mind run over what he had just read, again, and suddenly, the connection came clear – he pulled the stacked papers to him again and dug through them urgently, looking for the name he was sure he had seen. Two thirds of the way through the stack he found it. Harrington, who had, for the last seven years, been proprietor of his own business, as solicitor for various gentlemen, had previously been a junior partner in 'Broadmoor and Partners'. And Broadmoor and Partners were Traithewood's men of business. It was an unquestionable link – but was it evidence of culpability on Traithewood's part, or simply evidence of how Traithewood and various of the plotters had come to invest in the same companies?

Lance did not know – but at least it gave him a new place to start – whilst Harrington's residence had not turned up any documents on Setford's initial investigation, carried out whilst Harrington was not at home, Lance now felt convinced that such documents would exist – potentially locked away in a safe in Harrington's business premises. First, Lance needed to discover more about Harrington's client list, especially at the time that he had started his independent business, for if that list closely matched the list of known conspirators.... For the first time in the last few months, Lance felt an enthusiasm for the task, and a hope that the last missing pieces of the puzzle might be uncovered soon.

*****

That evening, there was to be a Ball – the last event of any significant size before the King's coronation. Lance was distracted as he dressed, his mind still caught by the discoveries of the afternoon, and the potential they had brought to solving the last parts of the puzzle of the conspiracy. But, at the same time, he looked forward to the evening, to seeing Lady Marisela, to dancing with her. More and more, she held his attention, and if he were to be honest with himself, he must admit that he was coming to care for her. And that was a concern, for it drew his attention away from his work for Lord Setford, and it also left him more and more concerned that he knew so little of her family, and her history before she had appeared in London for this Season. Especially given his work for Setford, he could not afford an association with a family who were touched by scandal in any way – and yet he knew nothing of her – the risk was great.... His valet finished attending to the perfect folds of his cravat, and Lance gathered up his hat and cane, and went down to the foyer, to discover that Kenric was already there.

"So, brother, what provokes you to such early readiness? Has your conversation with Lord Setford given you a new enthusiasm for delving into the secrets of the *ton*?"

Kenric waved a hand languidly.

"Perhaps. Or perhaps I am simply finding the entertainment available here so dull that I am driven to seek out society to amuse myself."

Lance laughed, shaking his head.

"And did you send for the carriage, knowing that I would be punctual as usual?"

"I did indeed. Let us set off – we can discuss your plans for the evening as we go. Do you expect me to pay attention to the activities of any specific gentlemen?"

They went out, and down the steps just as the carriage drew up, and were soon settled inside it, with the chance to speak in private as they went. Lance quickly informed Kenric of his discovery of the afternoon, and they mulled over how they might discover more of Harrington – for a man of business, no matter how successful, would not be present at a society event. The distance was short, and soon, they were stepping down before the large townhouse where the Ball was to be held. They joined the receiving line, and made their way in, Lance studying those around him as they went.

As always, he looked first for Lady Marisela, but, by the time they had reached the ballroom, he still had not found any indication that she was there. What if she did not attend? That thought drove an alarming spike of disappointment through him – once the King's coronation was done, Lance would need to go to his father's estates for at least a week or two – his mother would demand it, if nothing else, and the idea that, if he did not see Lady Marisela tonight, he might not see her for a month, was nigh on unbearable. He pushed those thoughts aside, and concentrated on circulating, greeting people whilst looking to see if Merringway, Diddington, or anyone else of interest was present. Kenric faded off to the card room, and Lance almost envied him the ability to do so, without anyone taking particular note of it.

An hour or more later, Lance had nearly given up hope of Lady Marisela appearing, and was contemplating the fact that he now had a number of young ladies he had promised to dance with, and absolutely no indication of anything which might help his work for Setford. The only person present who had any association with Merringway or Diddington was Hellmont, and that was not an acquaintance Lance wished to put any effort into at all.

Seeing the man did, however, make him wonder – if Merringway was implicated in the plot, did his son know of it? Was Hellmont a conspirator too? Somehow, Hellmont had always seemed too foolish to be a person anyone would involve in a secret... Still contemplating those possibilities, Lance finished the dance set, and delivered the young lady back to her mother, then stepped to one side, tempted to simply slip out through the terrace doors and escape the oppressive heat of the ballroom. But even as his hand touched the door, some new arrivals were announced, and he looked up to discover that Lady Marisela and her aunt were amongst them.

His heart pounded, and his mouth was suddenly dry. He wanted to push through the crowd and go to her. Instead, he stood quietly, and simply watched, not moving until she had greeted various people, and had come to a halt with her aunt's group of friends. Once they were still, he moved quietly to them, greeting the older ladies first, as always. When he came to Lady Marisela, he allowed his eyes to meet hers, and in that instant, the sounds of the ballroom seemed to fade away – there was only her.

"Good evening, Lady Marisela, might I hope for a dance?"

She smiled and nodded.

"Of course, Lord Bainbrook."

A sense of relief filled him, and when she handed him her card, he chose the waltz before supper, knowing that to do so was bold, and almost a declaration of intent, but utterly unable to stop himself from doing so. She accepted the card back, and flushed as she glanced at it.

"I look forward to it."

After bowing again, he stepped back as others came to speak to her, despite the fact that he would have preferred to stay by her side. He moved away, locating himself near the terrace doors again, and contented himself with watching her, when he was not compelled by earlier promises, to dance with other young ladies. As usual, after a short time, Hellmont sought out Lady Marisela, and Lance had to force himself not to step forward, not to step between them. It was irrational of him to wish to intervene in such a manner, yet the desire to do so was strong. He was greatly relieved when Hellmont returned her to Dona Esperanza without anything untoward having happened.

Finally, the time for the waltz arrived, and Lance went to Lady Marisela, anxious to have her in his arms. The evening might not have provided any opportunity to move forward with his work for Lord Setford, but at least he would have this chance to be close to Lady Marisela, to speak to her. The thought came to him then, as it had more frequently of late, that he could call upon her, that he could claim time with her that way, but again, he shied away from the fact that to do so would be a declaration of sorts. He offered her his arm, and led her to the floor. Neither of them spoke, as was so often the case, and yet it felt comfortable, right, somehow. They swept into the movements of the dance, and he found himself wanting to pull her closer than was proper, wanting to bend his head and kiss her, to say physically all of the things he could not bring himself to admit in words. But he did none of that – propriety held him, and he behaved exactly as he should, no matter his desires. When the dance moved towards a close, however, he swallowed, and spoke before thinking could prevent it.

"Will you walk with me on the terrace, Lady Marisela?"

She looked at him, a little startled, then gave a decisive nod.

"I will, Lord Bainbrook."

They came to a halt as the music stopped, and he offered his arm, then led her to the terrace doors. As he did, he glanced across and saw Dona Esperanza watching them. The old woman, smiled, and gave him a small nod, which both shocked and pleased him. It seemed that she had decided that he was trustworthy. The terrace was near empty – there were some people walking in the garden below, and another couple simply standing on the terrace, but after the crowded ballroom it was most pleasant. Lance led her along to a point where they were distant from others, and not entirely in the full glare of any lantern, then simply stopped, suddenly uncertain. She looked up at him with a smile, and heat filled him, accompanied by a return of the desire to kiss her. He pushed that aside, and sought acceptable conversation.

"Lady Marisela, once the King's coronation is over, what will you do? Will you be staying in London? Or returning to your home? Or perhaps visiting friends in the country? With the coronation, it is such a strange year – no one is doing quite what they might normally be expected to do."

Her eyes met his, and for a moment, he thought that he saw something there – something peculiarly akin to fear – but why would she have such a reaction to his rather banal questions? He must have imagined it. She looked away then, and the light from the nearby lantern caught the side of her face, limning it in soft gold, highlighting her beauty. His breath caught – as did his mind, for in that instant, she reminded him of someone – he just wasn't quite certain who.

"In truth, we have not decided yet. It seems most likely that we will stay in London, for home is... a long way away... and Dona Esperanza thinks it best that I ensure the maximum opportunity to meet gentlemen, to perhaps find a match."

Her words were like a knife to his heart – the mere concept of her marrying... anyone... anyone but him... was unbearable. And in that moment he knew that he was coming to love her, that he could no longer hide that fact from himself. His voice, once he managed to bring himself to speak, was ragged, almost harsh, and she turned back to him a little, as if surprised.

"And... has any particular gentleman caught your attention?"

It was, perhaps, a rude thing to ask a young lady, but he could not prevent the words slipping out. He watched her lamplit face, barely breathing. Her lips twisted into a wry half smile, and he wondered why.

"Lord Bainbrook, how do you expect me to answer that? If I say yes, you will wish to know who. If I say no, then you will still be curious... and perhaps... disappointed..."

His breath caught again – did she mean...? Did she hope? Should he? There were no answers, but in that moment, he was deeply tempted to declare his interest. His mouth began to open, rash words rising within him, and then she shifted a little, the light catching in those deep violet eyes, and he stopped, as a wave of shocking possibility ran through his thoughts. His previous concept, that she resembled someone he knew, or had met or seen, came back to him full force. It was true, but the person she resembled was nothing he might have expected.

She looked, in that moment, terrifyingly like the twelve-year-old girl in the portrait of the Marquess of Holmdale's family, in Mr Simpson's book on the aristocracy. Was it possible? Could Lady Marisela de Leon actually be Lady Jenneta Darley, granddaughter of a suspected traitor?

*****

When Lord Bainbrook asked her to walk on the terrace with him, Jenneta's heart raced – could it be that he was interested? That he might say, or do, something more than simply dance with her? The thought filled her with a mixture of fear and hope. But when he asked her about what she would be doing once the coronation was over, it was fear which overwhelmed her. How could she possibly answer, without saying something which might hint at the truth of her family? In the end, she chose an answer which was true, and yet really gave away nothing. But when she mentioned the concept of finding a man to marry, he seemed to stiffen.

Was that because he cared for her? Or for some other unknowable reason? And then he asked her an even more difficult question, which left her breathless and feeling trapped. Part of her wanted to simply turn to him, and state, outright, that he was the only man she was interested in – but to do such a thing was simply beyond the pale – ladies did not make such declarations!

Somehow, she found words which perhaps hinted, yet which admitted nothing, and for a moment, she thought that he was about to speak, to perhaps say that he cared for her, but then, as if something had changed on the moment, he stopped, staring at her, his expression aghast, as if she had transformed before his eyes into a monster.

It was beyond mortifying!

Minutes ticked by, and they stood there frozen in awkwardness, until Jenneta could bear it no longer – she had hoped, had been deeply tempted to tell him the truth, but now... she shuddered.

"Lord Bainbrook, supper will be starting. Perhaps we should go back in?"

He gave a little start, as if his thoughts had been completely elsewhere, and then bowed.

"Of course, my Lady."

He offered his arm, and she took it, relieved, and crying inside at the same time. What had she done? What had he seen in her, to make him react as he had? She might never know, but at that moment, she felt all of her hopes crumble to dust.

But moments later, he surprised her, and confused her utterly. He spoke again, his words quiet, but none the less impactful for it.

"Lady Marisela – I will be out of town for some weeks after the coronation, but, when I return, might I call upon you?"

"I... Yes, of course, Lord Bainbrook – I would welcome it."

*****

Lance had not been able to bear the expression on her face – it was compounded of disappointment, hurt, and something which seemed almost fear or despair. So he had spoken, hoping to change that, to undo something of what he had done by his reactions out on the terrace.

And now, he had made a promise to call upon her, against all of his best intentions – what if his suspicions were correct? What if she was Traithewood's granddaughter? What would he do?

Find something that proves Traithewood innocent…

The thought rose in his mind – he had already spent months trying to do exactly that, yet what other solution might there be, which would not hurt both of them? He would try. Still, the insidious thought remained – what if Traithewood was guilty?

They reached the supper room, where they obtained plates of food, and glasses of a rather dreadful punch, before settling at a small table where Kenric and Lord Albert were already sitting. Dona Esperanza was nearby, and again just watched and nodded. Her apparent trust made Lance feel guilty, given his dreadful suspicions.

The supper conversation would have lagged terribly if not for Kenric, and Lance felt more off balance than he ever had before in his life. He was glad when supper ended, and an older, unexceptionable gentleman came to claim Lady Marisela for the dance which followed.

But his relief was short lived, for, as he followed Kenric and Lord Albert out of the supper room to find a spot on the side of the ballroom to talk, the light caught Lord Albert's profile in sharp relief, and that dreadful sense of recognition accosted Lance anew. His breath stopped – surely not?

They reached a spot with potted palms and a few chairs, and stopped. Lord Albert turned to face Lance, and asked Kenric a question about someone – Lance had no idea who, for his attention had been caught – by Lord Albert's eyes.

Which were the same deep violet shade as Lady Marisela's.

A terrible conviction filled him.

Surely, the man before him was Lord Jenson Darley, twin brother of Lady Jenneta Darley. For both of them to be here, deceptively presented under names other than their own, had to mean something.

But was it a sign of guilt, of complicity in the treasonous plot, of them using these other identities to move between other conspirators unnoticed? Or was it a sign of innocence, of a desperate desire, after seven years of isolation, to circumvent the King's orders, and move about, just a little, in society?

And how was Lance to determine the truth?

Chapter Eleven

Lord Alphonse had, in the end, taken the 1801 gossip sheet up to his chambers, and, after appearing at dinner as usual, gone back up to read through it again, to make certain that he had fully understood its implications. The article was short – part of a selection of gossip snippets about who was in town for the 1801 Season, and the matches which had been made that year so far.

> *'Lady Charlotte Carlton, daughter of the Earl of Welwood, presented this year under the auspices of her great aunt, Lady Esperanza De Leon, due to the sad demise of her parents in recent years, has done well for herself, securing a match with the Marquess of Holmdale.'*

It seemed unlikely that there would be two persons by the name of 'Lady Esperanza de Leon' who were in a position to move in London society. It was time to look up the other names given in that gossip snippet – for they were English names, and likely to be in Debrett's. And if this was the same 'Lady Esperanza' who currently chaperoned Lady Marisela, then perhaps there was much to be learned here. He slipped back down to the library, found the editions of Debrett's most likely to cover the relevant people, and dug through the cupboards for gossip sheets dated between 1801 and the current year, then took them back up to his chambers. Two hours later, he had come to more than one rather startling conclusion. One about his father, and one about Lady Marisela De Leon, and her family. Both of which left him in somewhat difficult spots.

If he was right, she was certainly of good enough family for his purposes, but that family was, at this point, tainted by scandal – which did not suit him at all. He did not wish to marry into scandal! Especially given the alarming conclusion he had come to about his father... He paced about the room, considering his options. Then it struck him – perhaps he would not need to marry her. After all, what he needed was money, and, if what he had uncovered here was as he thought it to be, then he could obtain money without the need to marry her.

This was a situation, he rather thought, which would lend itself nicely to blackmail...

*****

Lance had spent the last two days worrying, the shocking conclusions he had come to at the end of the Ball whirling through his thoughts, giving him no rest. Proving the truth of those conclusions, one way or another, was critical to his work for Lord Setford – but also for his own peace of mind – and possibly for his future. He had also spent those two days going through documents again, cross referencing the list of clients of 'Harrington Solicitors', as at 1814, which Lord Setford had obtained for him, against all of the other documents they had. That list contained every single one of the known conspirators, plus Merringway and Diddington.

What it did not contain was the Duke of Traithewood or his son.

Given that, the next logical step was to obtain a list of the clients of Broadmoor and Partners, during the year that Harrington had worked there, as a junior partner, before starting his own firm. Lance sent off a letterlocked message to Setford, asking him to obtain such a list. Depending on what that might reveal, Lance held cautious hope that the Duke of Traithewood might be provably innocent – and he had come to desire that outcome intensely – not just because Lord Setford hoped for it, but because Lance was not sure what he would do, should it be proven that the woman he was coming to care for deeply was a traitor's granddaughter. He had just locked all of the papers away again when Kenric slipped into the room.

"And have the latest lot of documents produced any new clues, brother?"

Kenric dropped into a chair, and watched Lance's face. Lance shook his head.

"Not quite. I feel like I am close, but I have just sent off another request to Setford – I still don't have all of the pieces. It's infuriating – this has quite taken over my life! Now I look at everyone with some degree of suspicion."

Kenric laughed, waving his hand.

"Perhaps because we are all guilty of transgressions – some just more minor than others?"

"Perhaps. I truly wish this puzzle to be solved, so that I might view the world differently again. But... after your conversation with Setford, have you been tasked with anything interesting?"

"Not really, at this point, although I am learning a great deal about the business of spying. That part is quite interesting. But as yet, I have nothing to hone my information gathering skills on, beyond assisting you where I can."

Lance sat in silence for a few minutes, his worries of the last few days running through his mind again, then met Kenric's eyes.

"Then let me challenge you, and test the skills you've been developing."

Kenric raised an eyebrow.

"By all means."

"On the assumption that any person might be of interest, who has even the slightest of connections to the *ton*, I must also assume that you have been ferreting information out about everyone you know or meet. So – tell me – how did you meet Lord Albert Carlton, and what do you know about him?"

Kenric frowned.

"Why him?"

"Because he seems the most innocuous and inoffensive of men – which if he was a conspirator in anything, would be a perfect disguise."

"True, it would. Well, let me think – as to where I met him, that was pure chance. I went into the Hartford Hotel one evening, in search of a meal, for they actually produce decent food. The place was a complete crush, and there was but one seat left – at a table where Albert already sat. He was kind enough to allow me to join him, and we struck up a conversation."

Lance frowned, a frisson of disquiet running through him.

"And how did that lead to you introducing him about town?"

"He seemed unsure, and I was curious – I asked him about his life, and he freely admitted to not being au fait with society, due to his father's reclusive nature. I pitied him that life of isolation, and the mammoth task which faced him, of somehow, as a fourth son, getting any introductions at all. So I offered to help."

"Was that not rather precipitate of you?"

"It was – but I liked him."

Lance closed his eyes for a moment, distressed by what he was hearing.

"You liked him? That's a rather... minimal thing to make a decision on, isn't it?"

Kenric laughed.

"Well yes – but it's how I have always done things, and my judgement is generally good."

"That's true, but still... what do you know of his family? Did you look them up?"

"I didn't – if it had happened now, perhaps I might have, but then – I wasn't thinking that way. And I've seen no sign of him being anything other than a decent man."

"Neither have I – yet still, perhaps looking him up would be sensible. What do you know of him?"

"He's the fourth son of the Marquess of Birchwind, who has an estate on the Scottish border, where he has stayed for the last 40 years, having eschewed society entirely. Albert has no sisters, and he had no interest in the army or the clergy."

Lance frowned.

"That's not much to go on – but I'll look him up nonetheless – I began this for a bit of fun about your spying skills, but now I'm intrigued."

"If it keeps you entertained, rather than frowning grumpily at the chests full of documents, then certainly, indulge your investigative skills."

With that, Kenric left Lance sitting there. The silence settled on him, and for some time Lance didn't move, then, with a sense of trepidation, he reached for the now ever-present volumes of Debrett's.

*****

The coronation was over, and London was settling into a period of quiet. Most of the *ton* had retreated to the countryside, to their estates, or had gone to Brighton, or Bath, or the like. Jenneta had dreaded this point in time, expecting to find herself filled with ennui, and yet, in the end, the opposite had been true. She enjoyed walking in the Park, which was far, far less crowded than in the Season, she enjoyed the summer heat, which reminded her of Gran Canaria, and she most enjoyed the fact that, most evenings, there were no events to attend – she could simply curl up and read. The only truly frustrating thing was her regular conversations with Dona Esperanza about her lack of a potential husband. It was now mid-August, and, apart from those discussions, everything had settled into a peaceful routine. Jenneta missed Jenson – even what little she had been able to see of him at society events - but knew that it was necessary for him to stay away, for it was harvest time, and he had responsibilities.

Jenneta was curled in the bay window seat of the parlour, a book in hand, when Dona Esperanza came into the room.

“Ah, Marisela, I’ve had a message from Lady Hermitage – she is back in London for a few days, while Lord Hermitage deals with some matters of business, and has invited us to dinner this evening. Of course, we will go. I shall write our acceptance immediately.”

Jenneta thought that a quiet dinner might even be pleasant, and simply nodded. But as Dona Esperanza turned to leave the room again, there came a most unexpected sound. A knocking at the front door. They met each other’s eyes, startled, frozen in place as they heard Fortnum’s footsteps in the foyer, going towards the door. Moments later, Fortnum tapped on the parlour door, and announced, in a voice which seemed a little tinged with disapproval:

“Lord Alphonse Hellmont, calling on Lady Marisela.”

Jenneta dropped her book in shock, suddenly feeling quite ill, and Dona Esperanza straightened to her tallest, looking displeased.

“What shall we do?”

Jenneta’s voice was barely a whisper.

“We shall graciously receive him, and be as coldly polite as possible – there really is little other choice.”

“If we must.”

At that, Dona Esperanza turned to where Fortnum waited.

“Please show him in Fortnum, and send up a... simple... tea service.”

Fortnum bowed, and left. Jenneta forced herself to rise from the window seat, and went to sit in one of the armchairs near the fireplace – she certainly would not sit on a couch, where he might dare to sit beside her! Dona Esperanza sat in the chair closest to Jenneta.

Moments later, Lord Alphonse was shown in.

They both rose as he bowed his greeting, but gave him a barely polite reception before dropping back into their seats. He ignored their coldness of manner, and came forward, looking irritated when he realised that there was no possibility of sitting beside Jenneta. He took the seat opposite her instead.

"It is a delight to see you again, Lady Marisela – and you also, of course Dona Esperanza. I have missed the pleasure of your company over the last few weeks."

Jenneta wanted to simply say nothing, but she forced words out.

"How kind of you to say so, Lord Alphonse. I must, however, personally admit to having found a few weeks without any intensive social activity rather peaceful and pleasant."

Lord Alphonse looked somewhat startled by her words, as if he had expected her to declare that she had missed him – the man's conceit was insufferable. Before he could respond, there was a tap at the door, and the tea tray was brought in, and set down before Dona Esperanza. Blessed silence reigned whilst she poured the tea, and passed cups to Lord Alphonse and Jenneta. They sipped their tea, and nibbled on the rather unappetising biscuits which Cook had managed to find – a master stroke in discouraging unwanted guests, Jenneta thought. After some time, Lord Alphonse set his cup and plate down, and cleared his throat.

"Ah... Lady Marisela, I was hoping that you might allow me to take you for a drive in Hyde Park this afternoon?"

Jenneta's heart sank – how could she escape this? For she most certainly did not want to be alone with Lord Alphonse, even if it was in an open carriage in a public place! She cast her eyes towards Dona Esperanza, and was relieved to see that Lady smile gently at her, before she spoke.

"I am afraid, Lord Alphonse, that such a thing is not possible today – we are committed to a rather early dinner party this evening, and will soon need to prepare ourselves. So thank you for your kind offer, but I fear that Marisela must decline."

Lord Alphonse's face fell, and Jenneta tried very hard to prevent herself from looking relieved. The man took another sip of tea, then rose, and bowed to them, his expression showing barely concealed irritation.

"I see – then I will not impose myself upon you any longer. I will, however, call again in the near future, and hope that my timing is better..."

Jenneta swallowed – what would it take to truly discourage this man? She and Dona Esperanza rose also, and bid Lord Alphonse farewell. They said nothing, and did not take their seats again until they heard the front door close behind him. Once it had, Jenneta near collapsed onto her chair, her head in her hands.

"I truly cannot like that man, not even a little! I do not want him to call again!"

"Neither do I, Marisela – but we cannot simply turn him away – gossip would result. We shall have to endure, and make certain that you are never in a position to drive out with him."

*****

By late September, the harvest at all of the Traithewood and Holmdale estates was complete, and Jenson found himself relieved, yet frustrated. Now, it would be harder to sneak away to London. Whilst the harvest had been in progress, he had managed to go to London twice, each time for a very short visit, and had called upon Jenneta and Dona Esperanza.

It had been horrible – a taste of what they could not have, so close to his sister, and yet unable to speak of anything but trivialities. They looked at each other miserably, and the sense of desperation it caused drove Jenson to thinking of new ways that he might change things. Perhaps he should try to convince grandfather to allow him to go through all of the papers, to see if he could discover anything which might help – for in the end, what they truly needed was something which would clear grandfather's name.

Jenson was not so resigned to simply hoping that someone else might find such a thing as his grandfather and father apparently were.

He resolved to visit Traithewood, and speak to his grandfather on the matter, as soon as he could.

****

It was nearly the end of September, and the rest of the year stretched out ahead of Jenneta, seeming hopelessly empty and purposeless. She had not seen Lord Bainbrook since that Ball just before the King's coronation, despite his promise to call once he was back in town, and she had begun to believe that he had no interest in her, that she had been holding on to foolish daydreams where he was concerned. Still, her night time dreams were full of him, making her wake, as she had today, feeling bereft and abandoned. She rose from her bed, and allowed Beatriz to dress her, and deal with her hair, hoping that her mood would improve.

Breakfast helped, but she still moved through the day listlessly, lacking hope for the future.

Early afternoon found her disconsolate, reading a book she had read many times before, and at a loss for anything else to do.

Until her mood was shattered by a knock on the front door.

At first, she winced, assuming that it was likely Lord Alphonse yet again, and contemplating what excuse she might use to escape his company. But then she heard, faintly, the voice of a man speaking to Fortnum – a voice which was most definitely not that of Lord Alphonse.

She rose from her chair, and went to the parlour door, opening it a little to listen. The voice came again, and she half staggered, catching herself on the door frame. Surely she was wrong…? But no, there it was again – unmistakably the voice of Lord Bainbrook!

Chapter Twelve

As he stepped into the foyer of the elegant house, Lance wondered if he had made a mistake. He wanted to see Lady Marisela – rather desperately after the many weeks which had passed, but his doubts of her identity still haunted him, especially after what he had found – or rather, not found, when he had looked up 'Lord Albert Carlton' and 'the Marquess of Birchwind'.

He had put off this call, unsure how to deal with it all, until, somehow, it had reached late September, and he had realised that he must act.

For he had promised her that he would call.

The very proper butler took his hat and cane, and asked him to wait a moment. Lance watched as the man went up the stairs, obviously to notify Lady Marisela and Dona Esperanza that they had a guest.

Ten minutes later, the butler returned.

"If you would follow me, my Lord."

The man turned, and Lance followed him up the stairs, and along a corridor to an imposing set of doors, where the butler tapped.

"Enter."

The butler opened the door and stepped in.

"Lord Bainbrook."

The butler stepped aside, and Lance went in, to find Lady Marisela and Dona Esperanza stepping towards him. The sight of Lady Marisela took his breath away. She was, if anything, more beautiful than he had remembered her to be. She met his eyes, and he was lost, drowning in those deep violet pools, all of his concerns about her identity suddenly seeming meaningless in the face of her presence.

Dona Esperanza spoke, shattering the stillness of the moment.

"Welcome, Lord Bainbrook, I am most happy to see you again. Please do be seated, and I shall send for tea."

Lady Marisela stepped closer, and also spoke.

"I too am glad to see you again, Lord Bainbrook – I confess that I had wondered if you would call, now that most of the *ton* are not in London."

It was a gentle reprimand, which he deserved, and he swallowed, seeking the right words.

"I do apologise for my tardiness in calling. My mother demanded my presence at Cairnmoor Park, and I have only recently managed to return to London."

That was at least mostly the truth.

She seemed to accept it, and moved to take a seat on a couch near the unlit fireplace. Greatly daring, he went to sit beside her. At that moment, Dona Esperanza returned to the room from speaking with the butler, and settled into a large chair opposite them.

Lady Marisela shifted on her seat, so close to him that he wanted to reach out and touch her...

"I see – I can imagine that one could not refuse one's mother's requests."

There was wistfulness in Lady Marisela's words, and he wondered at it – if she was who he suspected her to be, then it made sense, for her mother was long gone to God if that was true. He smiled wryly.

"I will admit that my mother is most talented at getting her own way, whatever she may want. But enough of me – what have you found to fill your days in London, whilst society has been elsewhere?"

She shifted again, as if unsure how to answer, and he considered what might trouble her in such a question. Just as she opened her mouth to speak, two maids appeared with the tea service, and a large plate of most delicious looking small cakes. Perforce, the conversation halted whilst tea was poured, and food offered.

Some minutes later, Lady Marisela set her cup down, and turned towards Lance again.

"To answer your question, my Lord, I have done very little – and rather enjoyed that. We have walked in the Park, and spent time in peaceful activities at home. It has been quite refreshing after the demands of the social whirl of the Season. I am sure that sounds very dull to you, but I have enjoyed it."

Dona Esperanza chose that moment to speak as well.

"Indeed, it has been pleasant. Whilst I have enjoyed spending time with friends I have not seen for so very many years, the Season was hectic, and this chance to rest for a few months has been good."

Lance regarded them, feeling awkward, and rather lost for words. What else could he talk about? Again, the sense that this call was a mistake filled him, even though he had so strongly wanted to be in Lady Marisela's presence.

"I am pleased to hear that your summer has been relaxing. The next few months will probably be more active, I fear, for many of the *ton* are returning to London, now that the worst of the heat is over, and there will undoubtedly be social events."

Dona Esperanza nodded.

"There will, and I hold out some hope that Marisela may yet attract a suitor."

At those words, Lady Marisela flushed, and Lance felt himself tense, hating the idea that another man might court her. He forced himself to stillness.

"I cannot imagine that no gentlemen have expressed interest!"

Dona Esperanza shook her head with a mournful look.

"Few gentlemen have, and the one who is most persistent is not… entirely the sort of man one would hope for…"

Lance felt ill at those words – the idea that Lady Marisela might end up with an undesirable gentleman was unbearable. In his mind, the thought appeared.

You could court her – you already care for her….

But what if she was who he suspected her to be? Did he care for her enough to risk the difficulties that would bring?

*****

His call on Lady Marisela had been awkward, and Lance had departed Fairway House feeling out of sorts. Now, he sat in his study, with his notes before him, and confronted his suspicions, and the evidence that he had gathered.

He needed to make a decision. In his investigation of 'Lord Albert Carlton', he had been forced to conclude that no such man existed. Nor did the Marquess of Birchwind exist.

Lord Albert resembled Lady Marisela quite strongly, once one looked – the lines of their faces were similar, and their deep violet eyes near identical. And they both resembled the children in that family portrait of the Marquess of Holmdale.

Lance could no longer deny the fact that they were most likely Lady Jenneta and Lord Jenson Darley, grandchildren of the Duke of Traithewood.

So the decision which Lance must make was simple, and terrible at once – were they innocent of any association with the plot, and simply defying the King's requirements to seek a better life for themselves, or were they complicit in the plot, and hiding behind false identities to allow them to carry messages between their grandfather and the other remaining plotters?

Logic said the latter was likely true, but Lance could not, in his heart, find it in himself to believe her guilty.

After some thought, he concluded that he would give himself one month more of observing and investigating, hoping for clarity, and then force himself to a final decision.

For the idea that he might lose Lady Marisela forever was utterly unbearable.

*****

Lord Alphonse sat in his study, contemplating yet another demand from his creditors. He needed to do more – the concept that he might manage to speak to Lady Marisela alone, and see how she reacted to statements implying that he knew her secret, had proven to be a difficult one to action. So far, whenever he was in her presence, Dona Esperanza was also there. He had not managed any drives in the Park, nor even a semi private walk anywhere.

Which meant that he would need to change his tactics. Perhaps, if he was officially courting her, then he would be allowed more leeway, more chances to be alone, or nearly alone, with her. He need not actually proceed to marrying her, unless he wanted to – but to blackmail her would require private conversations... he would call on her again, and ask to officially court her – the girl had no other suitors that he knew of, so surely the old woman would be glad to accept his courting her.

*****

Jenneta and Dona Esperanza had just returned to the house after a walk in the park – where more of the *ton* were visible, now, as the autumn moved on, when a knock came at the door. They turned, still in the foyer, as one, and regarded the door with concern – who might it be?

Fortnum hurried forward, and opened it, to reveal, unfortunately, Lord Alphonse Hellmont. Jenneta sighed inwardly – there was no possible excuse she might give at this point for not allowing him to sit with them, for at least a short while.

Lord Alphonse stepped into the house, and bowed to them, rather floridly.

"Good day to you ladies – I am so glad to have found you at home!"

Jenneta forced herself to smile.

"Good day Lord Alphonse. I trust that you are well?"

"I am, dear lady, and all the better for seeing you."

Dona Esperanza had been speaking quietly to Fortnum, and now turned back to Lord Alphonse.

"Do come up to the parlour, Lord Alphonse. I have sent for tea."

Jenneta smiled to herself – when Lord Alphonse called, the tea which Dona Esperanza sent for was not of the highest quality, and the biscuits which Cook sent with it were quite dreadful. Lord Alphonse never seemed to notice, which did not speak well for his taste.

They went up the stairs, and were soon settled in the parlour. Once the tea had been served, Lord Alphonse began to talk – a steady flow of inanities, as usual, about the weather, and about the important things which he apparently had to do. After a while, however, his conversation slowed, and he looked strangely nervous.

"Ah... Dona Esperanza, there is something I would like to ask you..."

Dona Esperanza raised an eyebrow, but simply encouraged him to go on. Jenneta felt, strangely, worried.

"Yes? And what is that you wish to ask, Lord Alphonse?"

He drew himself up, and appeared to take a steadying breath.

"Dona Esperanza, I would ask you, officially, for your approval for me to court Lady Marisela."

Jenneta felt a rush of pure horror fill her. She knew that it showed on her face for a moment, before she managed to stifle the reaction, and prayed that Lord Alphonse had not noticed. For a moment, Dona Esperanza met her eyes, and Jenneta knew that she, at least, had seen that reaction.

Silence fell, as Lord Alphonse looked expectant, and then a little confused. It was clear to Jenneta in that moment that the insufferable man had expected them to be delighted by his offer! Dona Esperanza folded her hands in her lap, and fixed Lord Alphonse with a rather harsh glare.

"Lord Alphonse, I will not give you an answer now. I must take this under careful consideration – for I must take into account your place amongst society, and your ability to support a wife in appropriate conditions. I will give you an answer in two weeks' time."

Lord Alphonse gaped at Dona Esperanza, his expression stunned, then puffed up into an annoyed fuss, which reminded Jenneta of nothing so much as an irritated rooster. She forced herself not to laugh at the image in her mind.

"I... I will call upon you then, if that is your requirement."

"Thank you."

He did not stay long after that, to Jenneta's great relief, and the sound of the front door closing behind him released her to laugh – a shaky laugh, but at least a laugh. Moments later, Fortnum appeared at the door, bearing a tea service with their best tea, and Cook's lemon biscuits.

"I thought, ladies, that this might be more to your taste."

"Thank you, Fortnum."

He set the tray down, and Jenneta took a lemon biscuit, feeling the need to fortify herself.

She looked at Dona Esperanza.

"Please, tell me that we have a way to deny him this! I could not bear to be courted by such a man. He would be certain to try to take liberties!"

"Hush child. Of course I will refuse him – but then he will most likely be difficult, and we must be ready to deal with whatever he does at that time."

"I will be – For surely, nothing he might do could be worse than being courted by him!"

*****

Using the excuse of ensuring that all had been completed as it should be for the harvest at Traithewood Grange, Jenson went to see his grandfather. The Duke was pleased to sit with him, and talk of the harvest and such things, but when Jenson tentatively turned the conversation to society, and their ongoing isolation, the Duke became irritable.

"Do not think on it – there is nothing we can do. If there had been something, I would have done it long ago."

"How can I not think on it? The London papers reach us, and I read about the Season, and the activities of the *ton*, and I cannot help but wonder what it would be like to be amongst them, as I would have been if not for the King's requirements. I look at my future, and I see no way in which I might ever find a bride, no way in which my life might change. I find myself wanting to try, although I know that you have done all that you could find to do, many years ago. But my foolish heart hopes that if I look, I might find something new, something to prove you innocent, something to release us from this stultifying isolation!"

The Duke shook his head sadly.

"Do not start – it is hopeless. I kept every paper from those years, I have those, and other things, locked away. But they were no help. When I die, you and your father will have them, and can do as you wish, but for now, I want only the peace of this estate – everything else is too difficult."

"Would you not give me the papers now? At least allow me the chance to look?"

The Duke sighed, sipping his brandy.

"No. That way lies only disappointment and frustration. Accept the life you have, my boy – for we might have been far worse off."

Jenson gritted his teeth for a moment, then forced himself to let the matter drop. Perhaps another time, his grandfather might be more willing to allow him to look into it.

*****

Jenneta stepped into the ballroom feeling most uncertain. This was the first large event she had attended since before the King's coronation, and the first since the day that Dona Esperanza had refused Lord Alphonse permission to court her. What if he was there? What would she do? What might he do?

That last question weighed heavily on her. Still she smiled, and greeted Lady Hermitage and others as if all was well. And all was well, until about half way through the evening. But then, Lord Alphonse arrived, and immediately sought her out.

"Good evening, my dear Lady Marisela. Please tell me that you have a dance available for me?"

Beside her, Dona Esperanza stiffened. But there was little she could do – her dance card was not full, and to refuse Lord Alphonse would likely cause a scene. She swallowed her fear, and nodded.

"I do have a dance available, Lord Alphonse. This next dance, in fact."

It was best, she thought, to get this over quickly. He smiled at her – a smile which was more predatory than pleasant, and offered her his arm.

"The current set is just finishing, so let us make our way to the floor."

She set her hand on his arm, and allowed herself to be led away. Ten minutes later, as they moved through the steps of the dance, he leant close to her and whispered.

"You really should accept my courtship, Lady Marisela. If you do not, I fear that I will find it necessary to reveal the... unfortunate... truth that you are hiding. And that would cause a scandal – and have more far-reaching consequences as well, now wouldn't it?"

Jenneta's blood turned to ice. He couldn't mean... he surely couldn't know who she truly was – could he? And yet what else could he be referring to? She was terrified – the idea of being courted by him, or marrying him, was abhorrent, yet the idea of having her identity revealed was almost as frightening – what would happen to her family, if he should do such a thing.

They moved through the dance, and he smiled that predatory smile, watching her, waiting for her to say something.

In the end, she took a deep breath, and answered him – an answer which still left her terrified, but which was true to her heart – even for her family, she could not condemn herself to a life with this man.

"No. I will not accept your courtship."

"Then you are a fool – do you not understand what would happen, if I reveal the truth?"

"I do, but I still will not accept you."

He snarled, fury for a moment transforming his face.

"We will speak of this again, soon – I will give you one last opportunity then, before I act to expose your perfidy to the *ton*."

Jenneta stayed silent, and returned to Dona Esperanza shaken. She said nothing to her of the matter, wanting to think it through overnight, wanting to be sure that there was no other meaning to be taken from Lord Alphonse's words. But she did claim a megrim, and ask to go home early.

Chapter Thirteen

It was past mid-October, and social activity in London had resumed, somewhat, with people beginning to talk of their plans for the coming Christmas season. Lance had resigned himself to attending more social events, again, still searching for what might be the final clues in solving the puzzle that Setford had set him. At least the information about who had been Broadmoor and Partners' clients, before and after Harrington having split off his own business, appeared to corroborate all of Lance's suspicions. And that corroboration had eased, to some extent, his suspicions with respect to the Duke of Traithewood's family, and thereby of the two he was almost certain were Lady Jenneta and Lord Jenson. But that might just be his heart speaking – he must focus on logic, and not let emotion lead him astray.

Tonight, there was to be a Ball, and he would attend, would dance with various young women, and would watch the gentlemen as usual – but now with a very narrow focus on Merringway, Diddington, and their close family and associates. And, of course, he hoped that Lady Marisela would be there, would dance with him... He stared into the mirror as his valet made final adjustments to his cravat, and prayed that the whole matter of treasonous plots would soon be done with. Tonight, he had decided, if circumstances allowed it, he would ask 'Lord Albert' for the truth of his identity – for knowing that, for a certainty, would change everything, would allow him to approach the final parts of his investigation very differently. He settled into the carriage beside Kenric as they set off to the Ball, and, after a few minutes Kenric spoke.

"What troubles you, Lance? You are far too quiet, and you look as if your attention is on other things, far from here."

Lance turned to meet his brother's eyes.

"Indeed, you are correct – my attention is on other things. But they are things where this evening may bring a change. If that is to be so, I will need your help. If Lord Albert Carlton is in attendance, I wish to find an opportunity to speak to him, very privately – do you think that you might be able to conspire to facilitate that?"

Kenric raised an eyebrow.

Lance was shocked, and yet elated – for she had just, effectively, told him that she cared for him. That moment of elation faded fast, however, as he realised that this made the uncertainty of all of his suspicions as far as her identity, and the relationship of those to her grandfather's potential treason, far, far worse. So he bowed, and offered her his arm.

"Then I will treasure the moment, my Lady, even if we must pretend that it did not happen. But now, perhaps we should go back inside."

*****

Jenneta's heart pounded as Lord Bainbrook led her back into the ballroom. He cared! All of her hopes and dreams burst into her thoughts again, even as her mind replayed the kiss for her, over and over. It had been wonderful – better than she had imagined a kiss might be. She barely noticed the people around her as he took her back to Dona Esperanza, and then took his leave of them. Part of her wanted to be able to talk about her feelings – which in her younger years would have meant 'talk to Jenson' but now... she realised that she had no one to confide in, in the way that she wanted. She had thought that she'd glimpsed Jenson earlier, as Lord Albert, of course, but when she looked around now, he was nowhere to be seen. This evening, so far, was one of contradictions and confusion – the horror of dancing with Lord Alphonse, and him making insinuating comments again, contrasted wildly to the joy of the kiss she had just shared.

Perhaps she could talk to Dona Esperanza about it, tonight when they went home? But no, that didn't feel right, either. She sighed, and decided that she would think about it tomorrow, when she was well rested, and clearer of mind.

*****

The group around Kenric was far smaller when Lance joined him again, with only a few remaining, most having been drawn into dancing, or off to the card room. Kenric was speaking quietly to Lord Albert, and turned to Lance with a grin when he came to a halt beside them.

"Good, I'm glad you are back. Given the earlier conversation, there is something I've realised I would like to show both of you."

Lance raised an eyebrow.

"There is?"

"Yes – I've remembered that our host has quite the collection of books on the new agricultural techniques tucked away in his library. The sort of thing that only the two of you showed any real interest in. So come, do, and let's escape the ballroom for a while."

Lance exchanged a glance with Lord Albert, who shrugged.

"As you wish – lead on Kenric."

They followed him from the ballroom, and through a tangle of corridors, until he opened a door into a library which was lit only by a few candles set on tables, and the fire in the hearth. Kenric went forward with confidence, lifting a candlestick to aid him, and turned in amongst the shelves, soon returning with a small stack of books, which he placed on a table, along with the candlestick. Lance wondered just how Kenric had come to know what books were here, and exactly where, but decided that, perhaps, he did not wish to know.

"There you are – I'll leave you to it – enjoy your escape from the stuffiness of the ballroom."

And with that, Kenric slipped out of the room, leaving them standing there, with no sound but the tick of a clock on the mantel. Lance moved to the books, and looked at the titles, before turning his eyes to Lord Albert, who met his gaze with what looked to be a mixture of curiosity and trepidation. There was no easy way to begin a conversation such as this, so, in the end, Lance chose to be utterly blunt.

"Lord Albert, whilst it is true that we share an interest in the subject matter of these books, and I would normally be keen to discuss them, today, I wished a chance to speak to you privately, on another matter entirely."

At his words, Lord Albert became very still, his expression cautious, and concerned.

"I see. And what matter might that be?"

"Your true identity." Lord Albert near flinched as he said it, and Lance became, in that instant, fully convinced that he was right. "I believe that you are Lord Jenson Darley. I have no intention at this time of exposing that fact, but I would ask you to confirm the truth of it for me, and of your reasons for this subterfuge."

The silence extended, full of the weight of the risk that hung on the next words which would be spoken.

"Lord Bainbrook, I have come to respect you, and your brother. When you say that you have no intention of exposing this, at this time, I must trust that you are being truthful. I must also assume that you understand the risk inherent in this situation."

"I do – lives and reputations hang on the truths we are addressing."

Lord Albert nodded.

"Then I will take the risk of trusting you. Yes, I am Lord Jenson Darley."

"Thank you. Will you explain to me the reasons for your subterfuge?"

"I will, although they are not anything noble or dramatic. In the simplest sense, I am here as Lord Albert because I am rebellious, and beyond the easy acceptance of a life of isolation. But it took a catalyst to make me act."

"A catalyst? Your sister, perhaps?"

At that, Lord Albert / Jenson gasped, shock evident on his face.

"How do you...?"

He stopped, obviously concerned about what he was revealing. Lance gave a wry half laugh.

"I worked out her identity in much the same way I did yours. Your faces are quite similar, you know, and your eyes are identical. There was a family portrait, painted when you were twelve... So, if the reason for your being here is the fact that she was here – what is the reason for her being here?"

Lord Albert (Lance had decided that it was best to continue to think of this man in that way, for now) laughed.

"The stubbornness of an old woman, and her determination that Jenneta and I should have a future beyond isolation. Nothing more than that. We have nothing to do with whatever suspicions may still hang unfairly over our family, although I, and my father, have tried at times to find a way to prove grandfather's innocence. It is a great risk that we take, this subterfuge, but if Jenneta had the courage for it, how could I not have the same? And I have learnt a great deal this year, no small part in thanks to your brother, things which, should we ever find the key to our release, will see me well in my future life."

Lance met his eyes, finding that he trusted this man's word, that he believed in his innocence, as he believed in Lady Marisela's.

"The other reason that I discovered your identities is that I was looking – looking at your family, and looking at every possible remaining connection to that treason, because I was asked to do so in service to the Crown. I believe that you speak the truth, when you say that you, and your family, are innocent – but belief is not enough – we need proof. Will you, still as Lord Albert, work with me to find that proof? For I believe that I am close to discovering it."

"Of course I will – I would do almost anything to clear my family name."

"Thank you – there is one more thing I must ask of you – your sister must not know that I know her identity, or that you are working with me on this matter."

"I... I am not happy about hiding anything from her, but if that is necessary, then yes, I will agree to that condition."

*****

Lance studied the lists on his desk. There was no doubt in his mind now – every client of Broadmoor and Partners who had moved to the new Harrington Solicitors firm on its creation was a member of the conspiracy. And all but Merringway and Diddington had already been swept up. It was time to close the trap on the last two, as well as Harrington himself. And perhaps, in the papers that Merringway and Diddington might hold, there would be something, which combined with the fact that Traithewood had not moved firms, might exonerate Traithewood, finally.

Of course, to sweep up Merringway and Diddington would result, sooner or later, in Hellmont being investigated in more detail, and potentially being indicted as a traitor at worst, or simply impoverished at best. Which meant that Hellmont's association with Lady Marisela had to be prevented, completely, as soon as possible.

Chapter Fourteen

November 1821

The footman deposited the sixth large trunk onto the floor of Lance's study, bowed, and left. Lance sighed, and set about dragging the things into more convenient places. These trunks contained every document which had been found in the premises of Harrington Solicitors, and anything found in Harrington's home. Harrington himself was in custody – held in house arrest by Setford's men. Now, it was up to Lance to sift through all of this, and find any papers related to the conspirators, their investments, and their plans. It would likely take him near a month, from the look of it, and until he'd been through this, he did not want to tell Setford that it was time to pull in Merringway and Diddington, although both were being watched closely, in case they tried to leave the country, or the like.

Once he'd heard that Setford had these, and would be sending them soon, Lance had invited Lord Albert to stay at Bainbrook House for a week or two, which would allow Jenson to assist with going through the papers – Lance was of the opinion that no one had more motivation to study these well, and hopefully find things than 'Lord Albert' did. A week later, they had made far more progress than Lance had expected, for it seemed that Harrington was methodical, and had created and stored his records in good order. What they had found utterly confirmed that Merringway and Diddington had been part of the conspiracy, but beyond that, there was one note about a meeting held with all of the 'investors', which contained wording that had sent a flame of hope through both Lance and Jenson. The notes, attached to some commentary on decisions made at the meeting – commentary which Lance strongly suspected was code with respect to their plot – were simple. They said

> *'After discussion, the members of the investors' committee decided not to invite the other they had considered, after all, feeling that his attitudes and family history made him too great a risk. Therefore, he will not be presented with an invitation to move his business to Harrington's Solicitors, and will no longer be considered in any way related to these investments.'*

The implication, when looked at in the light of the client lists of those who had moved to Harrington's, and those who had stayed with Broadmoor and Partners, seemed obvious – the note referred to the Duke of Traithewood.

"Can we be right? Or are we making assumptions, because that is what we wish to find?"

Lance heard the slight shake in his own voice as he spoke.

"I do not know – but to me, it seems obvious – there is no one else I can see in the Broadmoor and Partners list, who would meet that description. The others are either conspirators who moved to Harrington's, or merchants and City men – people not of high rank or importance, despite their wealth."

"But will what seems obvious to us be enough to convince the King?"

"I do not know – we can but hope. I will, now, take what we have found here to Setford, and suggest that he sets things in process to take custody of Merringway and Diddington – perhaps in their papers, we will find the final evidence we need..."

*****

It had been more than two weeks since Hellmont had whispered his threats to Jenneta, and the fear had not left her. She had, as much as possible, tried to avoid going out in society, terrified that he would force an opportunity to speak to her alone, that he might do more than threaten obliquely. Dona Esperanza was annoyed with her, more and more so, demanding that Jenneta tell her just how she might expect to find a husband, if she never went anywhere that gentlemen might be met. Jenneta would not explain, beyond the fact that she felt uncomfortable meeting Lord Alphonse, since Dona Esperanza had refused his request to court her.

"Faugh! You are too sensitive – you have more courage than this, Marisela! We will go to the Ball tonight, and you will not argue. Think only of the possibility that Lord Bainbrook might be there, rather than that Lord Alphonse might, and I am sure that you will do well."

"I... if you insist, Aunt, but I am not happy."

"Do not fuss – all will be well."

And to Jenneta's surprise, for that evening at least, all was well. Many men asked her to dance, near filling her dance card quickly, and as Lord Alphonse came towards her, Lord Bainbrook appeared as if by magic, and stepped in front of him, claiming her last available dance. The relief she felt was enormous, especially when she then had to refuse Lord Alphonse, and see the nasty sneer which flashed across his face.

"I see, Lady Marisela. Do not think that by avoiding my company you will avoid me pressing you – If you do not take the sensible path soon, I will be forced to make some... unpleasant... revelations."

With that, he turned and left, as Jenneta stood there, shaking. Later, when she danced with Lord Bainbrook, Jenneta could not help but remember that kiss, and hope for another – but his manner was perfectly respectable at all times, much to her disappointment.

What would it be like, if she could tell him the truth? She cared for him – far more than she had wanted to admit – and she hated lying to him, hated every day of subterfuge more.

*****

Lance observed Lady Marisela's interaction with Hellmont, and was, more than ever, sure that something was very wrong there. She seemed afraid, rather than simply uninterested in the man, and he struggled to understand why. He was not sure when Setford would act on taking in Merringway, but now, he found himself fervently hoping that it would be soon, that Hellmont would be swept up too, under suspicion of being involved in the plot - which he very well might be. The contrast of Lady Marisela's warm reception of himself, to her coldness to Hellmont pleased him – the last few weeks, he had come to wonder if she was avoiding him, after that delightful but inappropriate kiss, when she had not been present at many events. Perhaps it was not him, but Hellmont that she had been avoiding?

Each time he saw her now, he found himself wanting to ask her for the truth, to tell her the truth of what he knew, and of what he was trying to achieve, with her brother's help. But he held back, wanting to be sure, hoping to have true evidence of Traithewood's innocence. He had come to care for her – rather intensely, and with every day that passed, he hated keeping secrets from her more. They danced, and spoke for some time afterwards, but the conversation was awkward, as the need for polite ordinariness battled with his intensifying desire to pull her into his arms and kiss her. By the end of the evening, he felt exhausted by it all. Somehow, most of the year had gone by, and he had not managed to resolve the puzzle that Setford had set him – although he was at least pleased that he had made significant progress – when would Setford act on Merringway and Diddington, and allow that part to be finalised?

*****

December 1821

Lord Alphonse stared at the blatantly threatening letter from his creditors, and paled. He had been too gentle with Lady Marisela, obviously. He had allowed her to avoid him, to make it difficult for him to make clear to her just what he threatened. It was time for serious action, or he would be doomed – either to debtors prison, if his father would not save him, or to physical violence from the moneylenders' enforcers. He shuddered at the thought, and tucked the letter away.

There was to be a Ball – an early celebration of Christmas, in a little over a week's time. At that Ball, he would somehow take Lady Marisela aside, and very directly either demand money, or her agreement to marriage. And if she tried to refuse – well then, he would simply ensure that he forcibly trapped her in a compromising position at that very Ball. Ruined, caught in such a position by one *ton* gossip or another, she would have to marry him – and with that would come her dowry.

It was not the plan he would have preferred, but it was the only plan he had, and it would have to do – he could not allow himself to fail, for the penalty for that was simply unacceptable!

*****

"We will go to this Christmas Ball at Lord Heatherington's. Everyone of significance will be there, and you must be seen. You must encourage Lord Bainbrook – given that he has called on you a number of times now, surely he is truly interested? I had so hoped that you would be married by now, that this Christmas we would be celebrating that, as well as your birthday, and the festive season."

Jenneta sighed. She knew that tone in Dona Esperanza's voice – there would be no escaping this Ball. In part, she did not wish to escape it, for to dance with Lord Bainbrook, and perhaps walk with him on a terrace... that would be pleasant. But it was a certainty that Lord Alphonse would be there, and that he would attempt to threaten her again. That made her shiver with fear, for she had no concept of how she might deflect his intent – and what if he truly did know her identity, and revealed it to all? But Dona Esperanza was implacable...

"Yes, Aunt. But I do not know that I can magically make any man wish to marry me before Christmas."

Dona Esperanza laughed.

"Just do your best, Marisela, that is all I can ask."

Jenneta nodded, but her thoughts went to Christmas, and the fact that she would see it here, as Marisela, unable to be with her family – which was enough to make her wish to cry, an impulse she fought, for if she did, Dona Esperanza would wish to know why...

*****

Lance read the letter again, making sure that he had grasped everything he needed to know about Setford's plans. The wording was simple, and would make little sense to someone who did not have the rest of the information, but it left him with a feeling of relief, that they were so close to this finally being concluded.

B,

We will act to take the last two, as advised by you, on the evening of H's Ball. The houses may be secured while the occupants are out, and the occupants secured upon their return. Those houses will undoubtedly yield another trove of things to be studied, so expect a delivery after that day. With thanks for your work on these matters.

S

It would be strange to see Merringway and Diddington (and Hellmont, he wondered?) at the Ball, and know what awaited them, but he was sure that he would be able to keep his knowledge behind an expression of polite disinterest.

The thought of yet more trunks full of papers did not inspire him – except for the fact that such might contain the final piece to clear Traithewood's name – at least he hoped so. For that, he would slog through them carefully, contemplating every word. He turned back to the study, where Lord Albert and Kenric were sifting through the very last of the papers which had arrived in those six trunks, and showed them the letter. Kenric spoke first, his voice filled with satisfaction.

"I will be glad to see them taken, to see the end of this tangled mess. Although I am sure that Setford will have other things just as tangled for us to look into in the future."

Lord Albert sighed, dropping the last paper on his stack into the trunk beside him.

"You, perhaps, but not I – after all, I am not really supposed to be here and involved at all. It is only the gift of your trust that has allowed me to help, and I doubt that Lord Setford would be happy to know of my involvement."

Lance regarded him, wondering what the man might do, if they did manage to free his family from isolation.

"I would not be so sure, Albert. If we do find what we hope for, you will be free to do many things – and Lord Setford may find your situation useful, if you agree..."

"Do you think so? I must admit, I have given little thought to what I will do once we are free, should that time ever come..."

"Perhaps you should begin to consider such things, now?"

"Perhaps I should."

*****

Jenneta had spent the day of the Ball sitting in the parlour, thinking about her life. By this time, she had hoped to be married, or back in Las Palmas – although there, she would not have been able to see anyone of her family, even surreptitiously. Instead, here she was, not married, still in London, and afraid, because of one very obnoxious gentleman. That thought stilled her where she sat. Why should she allow the greed and arrogance of Lord Alphonse to ruin everything? She had come here knowing that there would be a risk of her identity being revealed, and she had accepted that risk – so why did Lord Alphonse's threat make her so much more afraid? It should not, she decided. She did not want to live in fear – if he did reveal the truth, he might not even be believed! She would go to this Ball with courage, not cringing, and deal with whatever happened at the time. For surely, if Lord Bainbrook, and perhaps Jenson, were there, then she would be safe?

That decision made, she had gone about the rest of the day more happily, and now, in the carriage on their way to the Ball, she felt anticipation as she thought about Lord Bainbrook. It was anticipation which was to initially be disappointed.

When they arrived, she saw no sign of Lord Bainbrook, nor of his brother, or her own. But Lord Alphonse was very much in evidence, dancing with a young lady who looked no more happy about it than Jenneta would have been.

Jenneta turned her eyes away from the sight, and followed Dona Esperanza across the room to Lady Hermitage and the others of her set. Perhaps, if she simply stood with them, Lord Alphonse would not notice her? The ballroom was decorated for the Christmas season, with branches of pine and holly, and large swathes of red and green cloth draped along the walls, and around the urns in which more greenery was displayed. It was beautiful, and the sight lifted Jenneta's spirits. For some time, all was well, until a voice came from behind her.

"Good evening Lady Marisela. I am beyond glad to see you here tonight. I look forward to dancing with you at the earliest opportunity."

Jenneta swallowed, turning slowly, to meet Lord Alphonse's self-satisfied smile. She shuddered, and he saw it, his smile becoming broader. There was nothing for it, she would have to accept. Perhaps if she granted him this next dance, then it would be done, and she might escape his attentions thereafter? Beside her, Dona Esperanza turned slightly, to watch what would happen.

"Good evening Lord Alphonse, I trust that you are well?"

Lord Alphonse looked irritated, but he continued to smile.

"I am indeed. Ah... the dance?"

It was so blunt as to be rude, and Jenneta took a shocked breath.

"I do have the next dance free, Lord Alphonse."

"Excellent."

There was no escape. The orchestra was just starting up again in preparation, and he offered his arm, his expression expectant. She placed her hand on it, revulsion filling her, and he led her to the floor. The dance was a slow one, with much circling close to one's partner, and Lord Alphonse made sure to be far closer to her than propriety suggested was proper. As soon as they were close, he whispered, his voice soft, but threatening.

"Have you reconsidered, and come to your senses, Lady Marisela? It really would be best if you accepted my suit, and let the world see that we will soon marry. Surely you do not wish to face the consequences of rejecting me? Those consequences would, of course, go far beyond you, personally, and touch the entirety of your family..."

Jenneta almost stumbled, and Lord Alphonse grinned at her, rather like a wolf considering its prey.

"I do not know what you imply, Lord Alphonse."

It was unlikely that he would believe her, but she needed to at least delay until she could think what to do.

"Oh, I am sure that you do, Lady... Marisela... is it?"

Icy fear filled her. There was no mistaking what he meant. At that moment, they came to the end of the line of dance, and instead of turning back to the other end, he simply took her elbow, and led her out through the terrace doors into the cold evening air, as if that was the most natural thing in the world.

Chapter Fifteen

Lance had arrived just in time to see Hellmont leading Lady Marisela onto the dance floor. His fists clenched, and his jaw tightened, frustration filling him. Lady Marisela's expression and movements indicated, quite clearly – at least to Lance's perception - that she wished to be anywhere else but with Hellmont in that moment. But there was nothing he could do – nothing inappropriate was happening.

So he went across the room, leaving Kenric and Lord Albert to do whatever they wished, and stepped out onto the terrace. Perhaps the cold December evening air would cool his anger, and allow him to simply ignore Hellmont. Once the dance had finished, then Lance could seek out Lady Marisela, to dance or to talk, to hopefully make her look far happier than she had looked, just now.

He went to the far end of the terrace, standing in the deep shadow where a large pine tree grew beside the railing. Below, the gardens were in near complete darkness, Lord Heatherington having apparently assumed that the night would be too cold for anyone to wish to walk outside, even though this house was large, with very extensive gardens for something this close to the centre of London. It was peaceful, but Lance found himself troubled, regardless. He wanted to be with Lady Marisela, wanted to tell her the truth.

For he had reached the stage of trusting her, and her brother, completely – with all that had been discovered, he could no longer countenance any possibility that their grandfather had been involved in the treason.

Inside, the music continued, and the thought that Hellmont still held Lady Marisela, still danced with her, filled him with jealousy. He forced himself to simply stand there, silent, utterly still, and wait.

Moments later, one of the terrace doors opened, and two people stepped out. The light from inside caught their faces, and Lance felt his breath near stop. It was Hellmont, and Lady Marisela – and she looked, he thought, afraid. He did not move, unsure of what was happening, and simply watched, ready to step in should his assistance be needed.

Hellmont was speaking in a low voice, nearly a growl, which seemed full of anger and threat – certainly not the way a gentleman should speak to a Lady. He caught only some of the words, but what he did hear shocked him.

"...are a fool girl. Take what I offer, or I will reveal.... And your family will be destroyed."

"No. I will not allow you..."

Hellmont laughed, pulling Lady Marisela towards the steps which went down into the dark gardens.

"Allow? There is no question of you having any choice. If you are determined to be a fool, there are other, more expedient ways. I have been patient, but my patience is at an end."

And with that, Hellmont dragged Lady Marisela down the steps, catching her as she stumbled, and dragging her off into the darkness.

For a moment, Lance did not move, his mind in shock, trying to understand what he had heard. There was only one way he could interpret it, and that thought drove him into movement, along the terrace, and down those stairs, going as fast as he could in the direction that Hellmont had taken. Ahead of him, he could hear the scuff of footsteps on gravel, and Lady Marisela's voice, remonstrating – quietly, so perhaps she feared scandal?

*****

Kenric and Jenson had watched Lance go straight to the terrace doors and outside, then turned to each other with furrowed brows.

"That's not like him – Bainbrook doesn't like socialising, but he's dutiful about it..."

"It does seem out of character, from what I've seen before."

Jenson's eyes had found his sister as they spoke, and he was alarmed to see that she was dancing with Hellmont, and didn't look at all happy about it. Kenric said nothing for a few minutes, as they made their way across the room, greeting others occasionally.

When they stopped, Kenric began to speak.

"I wonder what's disturbed..."

Jenson, at that moment, gasped, and cut across Kenric's words.

"Look – Hellmont has just summarily dragged Lady Marisela out onto the terrace, in the middle of the dance set! I can't think that's good."

Kenric paled, then met Jenson's eyes.

"I believe we'd best spend some time on the terrace ourselves, don't you?"

"I do, indeed."

"But, I think, you'd best get Dona Esperanza – propriety may need to be seen to be followed, if you understand my thinking?"

Jenson felt positively ill, but gave a nod, and sped across the room, even as Kenric near ran out through the terrace doors.

*****

Jenneta was startled at how ferocious Lord Alphonse had become, his threatening words making little sense to her, until he dragged her down the steps into the dark garden. As he caught her when she stumbled, and set off pulling her along the path deep into the darkness, it all suddenly came clear.

He meant to ruin her.

To take her against her will, right here in Lord Heatherington's gardens!

"No, you can't, I won't..."

Her voice was weak, and shaky – what if someone heard her, and came – she might be forced to marry Lord Alphonse anyway, just by having been found with him, alone, here! He laughed at her protests, his laughter cruel.

"Oh I can, most definitely, and I will. You will learn – I'll have the money I need, either by you paying the blackmail I've demanded..."

"No!"

"Or, as you refuse, by way of you marrying me, and me obtaining your dowry. You're less than I'd prefer as a wife, given your family is touched by scandal, but I need the money."

"No!"

"Well, if you won't sensibly agree to that either, then I'll just have to ruin you, now. You're appealing enough to look at, so I won't find that any hardship."

He laughed again, and Jenneta felt true fear take her at the ruthlessness of his words. She stopped trying to speak, struggling just to stay on her feet as he pulled her along the path, past the end of a hedge, and into what seemed to be a folly of some sort, with a stone bench set within it.

He pushed her down onto the bench, lowering his body over hers, his weight pinning her there, no matter how she squirmed. She opened her mouth to scream, but barely a squeak escaped her before his mouth was upon hers in a rough and ravaging kiss which made her feel so ill that she near retched. Even as he did that, she felt his hand slipping under the edge of her skirts on one side, pulling them up, inexorably.

Moments later, as his hand slid along her upper thigh, the sound of feet on gravel came to her, and seconds after that, Lord Alphonse was physically lifted off her.

He gave a roar of displeasure, but Jenneta took advantage of the moment, and lifted her knee firmly as he was pulled away, apparently landing it where she had hoped to, given the sound that he made. She could not tell what was happening, until she heard the distinctive sound of a fist colliding with a jaw, and saw Lord Alphonse fall backwards, staggering.

"Are you well, Lady Marisela? Has he hurt you?"

It was Lord Bainbrook's voice! He had come to save her! Even as she opened her mouth to answer, she saw Lord Alphonse drag himself to his feet, turning to run.

"I... yes – but... he's escaping!"

Even as Lord Bainbrook turned at her words, another shadow stepped past the hedge, and delivered a solid roundhouse blow to Lord Alphonse, who fell to his knees for a moment.

"Kenric?"

"Yes."

After receiving that reply, Lord Bainbrook ignored Lord Alphonse, and turned back to Jenneta, helping her to her feet, then pulling her into his arms. She went willingly, finding that she was shaking, and appreciating his support. All else seemed to fade away, and Jenneta looked up into her saviour's eyes, uncertain. At which point he kissed her, gently, and her heart exploded with joy. The sound of more feet on the gravelled paths made them step apart. As they did so, Lord Bainbrook leant close to her again for a moment, and whispered in her ear.

"I must be truthful with you – I know your true identity, and that of your brother. But I will not reveal that, and unlike Hellmont, I have no intention of using it against you – I love you too much to ever consider such a thing."

Jenneta staggered, sitting down on the bench suddenly with the shock of it. He knew...? But he had said... he loved her...?

He reached out and gently traced her jaw, just as Jenson and Dona Esperanza – bearing a small lantern, obviously purloined from the terrace – stepped around the end of the hedge.

Their arrival was distraction enough that Lord Alphonse, now obviously a little recovered, wrenched himself from Kenric's grasp and ran. Moments later, they heard the click of the back garden gate, and the sound of uneven footsteps receding down the mews. Kenric stepped into the lantern light.

"Good riddance to him. If he goes home to Merringway House, he will be captured, and held under suspicion of worse things than he has attempted here. And I am sure that he will go home, for I don't think he has the slightest concept of what awaits him."

Lord Bainbrook and Jenson nodded, whilst Jenneta and Dona Esperanza regarded them curiously. After a moment, Dona Esperanza took the lantern from Jenson, and came to Jenneta.

"Do stand please my girl, and let me look at you. I hope the blackguard didn't manage to tear your gown?"

Jenneta stood, her head spinning, but soothed by Dona Esperanza's practicality.

In the end, they determined that her gown was intact, although with a few small stains on the back of it, and that her hair, whilst somewhat disarrayed, was rapidly fixable by the appropriate reapplication of pins.

Once all were sure that there were no major repairs needed, Lord Bainbrook bowed to her.

"We three gentlemen will now disappear back into the Ball, and leave you two ladies to return at your leisure, having taken the air out here to escape the stuffiness of the crowded ballroom. Lady Marisela, I will call upon you tomorrow, if you will permit it?"

Dona Esperanza nodded, seemingly completely serene amidst the madness of the evening, and Jenneta flushed, remembering the kiss, and what he had said.

"I should be most glad indeed to have you call upon me, Lord Bainbrook."

*****

When Jenneta woke the next morning, memory of the previous evening came rushing back, all of it seeming beyond improbable. But as soon as she sat up, she was reminded of its truth by the small graze on her elbow, and the aches in her body.

She rang for Beatriz, who hurried in, and helped her to dress for the day.

"Dona Esperanza asks that you break your fast with her, my Lady."

"Of course."

Jenneta considered the light from the window, and concluded that it was already quite late in the day, for the pale winter sun was well risen. Perhaps Dona Esperanza had slept late as well.

Once she was ready, she went down to the breakfast room, finding that, now she was moving, the aches retreated. Dona Esperanza was sitting at the table, a well filled plate before her, sipping coffee. Her dark eyes measured Jenneta carefully, and she nodded with satisfaction.

"Good morning, my dear. You are well rested, I hope?"

A footman brought Jenneta a plate of food, and then, at Dona Esperanza's wave, left the room, shutting the door after him.

"I am, although I ache a little, and there is this..."

She lifted her arm, indicating the mark on her elbow. Dona Esperanza made a tutting noise of displeasure.

"We must be glad that it is nothing more! The arrogance of that man! I did not like him, but I did not think that he would stoop to such behaviour! You were right to worry, and I apologise for not taking your concerns seriously, dear girl."

Jenneta sipped some coffee, finding it steadying, the day beginning to feel almost normal.

Her memories of the night before were tangled, the horror of Lord Alphonse's attack upon her person mixed with the warmth of the memory of Lord Bainbrook kissing her, of him saying...

She stilled a little, her face flushing.

He had said that he loved her!

It seemed impossible, but he had said it, just after he had said... that he knew her true identity.

The shock of that memory stilled her completely. Did he truly know? And had he meant it, when he had declared that he would not use it against her? She shivered, confused, and a little afraid.

She forced herself to eat, to sip the coffee, while Dona Esperanza watched her. Eventually she spoke, her words hesitant.

"Thank you. Do you think... do you think that Lord Bainbrook meant it, when he said that he would call on me today?"

"I am certain that he did. He is not a man to not be true to his word, from all I have seen. We should expect him in a few hours' time, when the day is suitably advanced for calling to be appropriate."

Jenneta nodded, and went on eating, her thoughts in turmoil.

*****

Lance stood before the door of Fairway House, feeling most peculiar. He knew what he wished to say, wished to do, but he was not at all certain of the reception those words and actions would receive.

After all, he had not been honest with her, for these many months now.

He squared his shoulders, and rapped the door knocker. Footsteps sounded inside, and the door was opened by the very proper butler, who smiled, and stepped back to allow him entry.

"Good day, Lord Bainbrook, may I take your coat?" Lance passed over his outer coat, his hat, and his cane. "If you would wait here a moment, my Lord, I will inform the ladies that you have arrived."

Lance nodded, and watched the man move away.

Ten minutes later, he was shown into the parlour.

Lady Marisela and Dona Esperanza came forward to greet him, and not long after that, he found himself seated on a couch beside Lady Marisela, with tea being served as Dona Esperanza sat opposite them.

Once that was done, and no servants remained in the room, Lady Marisela spoke.

"I must thank you for your very timely assistance last night, Lord Bainbrook. I fear to even think of what might have transpired, if you had not reached me when you did."

A little shudder wracked her frame, and Lance wanted to pull her into his arms, to protect her even from the memory of it.

"It was fortuitous that I was standing on the terrace when the blackguard brought you out of the ballroom. I could not, of course, allow him to do what he obviously intended to do. Especially not to you, my dear Lady." Her eyes met his, and the warmth that he saw there encouraged him. He flicked his gaze to Dona Esperanza for a moment, and, further encouraged by what he saw, he went on. "I will be blunt, and hope that you, and you, Dona Esperanza, will forgive me for it. As I said last night, my Lady, I have come to love you. I would have declared my interest long since, had it not been for some work I do, for the Crown."

Lady Marisela gasped a little, looking confused.

"For the Crown?"

"Yes. It was through that work that I became aware of your... subterfuge... which left me torn with respect to what I should believe of you. But now, things have moved along in those matters, and I am convinced of the innocence of your family, and of you, yourself."

She was staring at him with wide eyes.

"Convinced? But... can you prove it?"

He shook his head sadly.

"Not yet, although I believe that I am very close."

She sighed, and turned away for a moment, sadness in every line of her body. Into the silence Dona Esperanza spoke.

"Then if you cannot yet prove it, you must not speak of identities, not here, where a servant might overhear, nor anywhere else. Proof is the only way to find safety."

Lance smiled, a little grimly.

"I had come to that conclusion. I am pursuing that proof. But I will say that I do not care, in the end, what happens there – I wish to court, and marry, you, Lady Marisela, and I would do that, whether the proof is ever found or not."

Her hand went to her heart, and she looked away for a moment. Then she turned back, her expression stern.

"But Lord Bainbrook, without that proof, you should not... associate with me, for what if you doing so incurs the King's displeasure? For I have come to love you too, and I would not have my family's tarnished history harm you..."

At that, despite the presence of Dona Esperanza, he reached for her, pulling her into his arms for a moment, and pressing a gentle kiss to her brow. He gave a soft laugh, at which she looked most startled.

"My darling, I do not care what others may think, and, in fact, as a result of my work for the Crown, I have a few... connections... who may be able to help ease our path – if you will have me?"

Her eyes filled with the sheen of tears, and she nodded then, lost for words.

Chapter Sixteen

Lord Alphonse did not attempt to call for the family carriage, for his father was still inside Lord Heatherington's Ball. Instead, he simply ran, aching in multiple places where blows had landed, along the mews, and out into the nearby streets. Then he paused, straightened his attire, and flagged down a passing hackney cab. He would go home, and drown his frustrations in brandy. Decisions about the future could wait until tomorrow. The cab rolled through the streets, and his mind replayed the events of the evening, making him grind his teeth – it had all seemed such a simple and effective plan – how had it gone so wrong? When they reached Merringway House, he stepped down, handed the jarvey the requisite coins, and went up the steps to the door. Above him, lights showed in the windows, and he wondered why – what were the servants doing? He rapped the knocker, and, after a moment, the door opened. But rather than their butler, he was confronted by a tall, dark man of threatening visage, who simply smiled, gripped Lord Alphonse's arm, and pulled him into the house.

"How helpful of you Hellmont, to return early. I am sure that you can provide information which will speed up our search considerably."

"Search?"

"Search. Your father, his cousin, and you, by association, are to be held in custody on suspicion of conspiracy to committee treason. We are the King's men, sent to take you under house arrest, and to gather all papers from this house which may, in any way, relate to that treason. You can help us, or, if you refuse, that will be seen as a probable admission of guilt, and you will be locked away to await the King's pleasure."

Lord Alphonse sagged in the man's grasp, horror filling him – he had known that his father and Diddington were involved in something bad, but he had never suspected something on quite this scale.

"I... see."

"So – will you be sensible? Where does your father keep most of his papers?"

Lord Alphonse laughed, on the edge of hysteria, and the man looked at him oddly. He forced himself to stop laughing.

"My father keeps almost every damned paper that ever crosses his path. I wish you well of sifting through it all. You will find the largest collection in the library."

The man nodded.

"Show me."

*****

Two days after the Christmas Ball, a note had come to Lance, from Setford. Merringway, Diddington, and Hellmont had all been taken, and were being held under house arrest, whilst their houses were searched and cleared of papers. Lance was to expect a very large collection of documents within days. So – the time between now and Christmas would be spent reading endless papers. Lance sighed, shaking his head – would those papers hold what he hoped for? Three days after that, Setford's men delivered the papers. This time, there were twelve trunks full of the damned things. Lance called Kenric to help him, and they rearranged everything, somehow managing to squeeze all of it into the study. Once it was in, they collapsed onto chairs, eyeing the trunks balefully.

"Trust the last to be the biggest of the lot!"

Kenric nodded, obviously sharing his annoyance at it all, but then, in a manner typical of Kenric, he simply pushed himself to his feet.

"Well then, lets at least see what we've got, and if it's in any sort of order or not."

He went to the closest chest and opened it, groaning when he saw the tumbled state of its contents. Lance went to another chest, and opened that, expecting to find the same sort of mess, but was startled to see that this one contained more ordered stacks of papers, tied together with string, and in some cases labelled. On the top of the papers inside it, there lay a large leather folder. Lance lifted it, and went to his desk, laying it out open on the desktop. It contained a letter from Setford, explaining where the contents of each chest had been found, and the conclusions his men had so far drawn from it all, based on their quick look through it. Lance settled to read the letter carefully, hoping that the information might suggest a plan of action. After some time, he looked up at Kenric, who had opened each of the other newly delivered chests, and was standing there, with a look of exasperation, trying to decide where to start.

"At this point, I really wish that Lord Albert was still in London – but he was right to say that he really did not have an excuse to stay here. His help would have been useful indeed."

"It would. There is so much here! It looks like Merringway kept every single piece of paper he ever touched!"

"Which is why this note from Setford is useful. Start with Chest number 4 – apparently they have numbers painted on them – what's in that is described as coming from Merringway's personal study."

Kenric poked about, finding the correct chest, then hauled it to beside a chair near the desk.

"Which one will you go through?"

Lance stood, closing the folder to clear desk space, and stepped to the chest he'd found the folder in.

"This one. The content is more orderly, and apparently it came from Hellmont's study – so it's less likely to be relevant, and perhaps I can get through it and classify it as unimportant, rapidly."

He pulled the chest to beside his chair, and lifted the first stack of papers up onto the desk. Hours later, he lifted the last pile out of that chest. Most of what had been in there had been evidence of Hellmont's profligate ways – gambling vowels, a ledger recording a rather horrific amount of debt, unpaid bills from his tailor and other vendors, occasional letters from an acquaintance, and the like. Lance did not expect this last bundle to be much different, although it did appear to include a number of rather aged newssheets, which was curious. He untied the string, and spread the papers out. They didn't seem to be in any order, so he chose to look at the newssheets first. He found the one with the earliest date – 1801- and began to read. It was dull, until he came to the gossip column, at which point his breath stalled.

> *'Lady Charlotte Carlton, daughter of the Earl of Welwood, presented this year under the auspices of her great aunt, Lady Esperanza De Leon, due to the sad demise of her parents in recent years, has done well for herself, securing a match with the Marquess of Holmdale.'*

He stared at it, stunned. In all his researching of the Duke of Traithewood's family, he had found nothing like this, and it occurred to him now that not seeking old gossip this way had been foolish of him. Eager now, he read on, meticulously examining each newssheet in the bundle. Every one of them had some reference to Traithewood's family, to Lady Marisela / Jenneta's family. He stopped to consider it – why had Hellmont had these in his study? Unless... was that what Hellmont had been threatening her about, as he dragged her into the gardens? Had Hellmont also discovered her true identity? It was a sickening thought.

He turned back to the papers, setting aside the newssheets, and looking at the rest of the bundle. Those documents were an odd mixture, most of them appearing to be notes about meetings of some 'investors' club'. The names referenced in those notes rapidly made Lance realise that the 'investors' club' was actually the group of treasonous conspirators – especially when he found one note which referred to 'moving business matters to Harrington'. It seemed obvious then, that Merringway's habit of keeping everything had ensured his downfall, and given them all the corroborating evidence they might wish for about the others, including Diddington. Lance wondered then why these had been in Hellmont's study – had he been part of it? Lance had not thought him intelligent and cautious enough that men plotting would include him. Then, an idea came to him.

Had Hellmont suspected his father? Was this evidence of Hellmont trying to understand just what his father might be involved in? Would... would Hellmont have blackmailed his own father? It was possible, if rather horrifying. Lance lifted the last paper from the bundle, at first glance just another note about a meeting, his eyes running down the page quickly. Until he stopped, giving forth a gasp so loud that Kenric looked up, startled, raising an enquiring eyebrow.

There, on the page, was the name he had looked for, through thousands of documents.

Traithewood. Lance set it down, his hands shaking, and studied it, reading each word again carefully, praying that it would absolve, rather than condemn.

The initial page was labelled 'investors' club meeting' with a date in 1814.

Then, after some rather cryptic notes, which, if Lance remembered correctly, were similar to some of the code used in Harrington's notes, there was a single sentence.

> *'After discussion, it was decided not to invite Traithewood to join. Too much risk. He will remain unaware, and will not be invited to move to Harrington's, or invest in further ventures. His accidental inclusion in two previous company investments is an annoyance created by Broadmoor.'*

Lance read it again, a bubble of joy beginning to rise within him. Here it was, the clear exoneration they had needed. Kenric had been watching his face, obviously, for he now reached out a hand to touch Lance lightly on the arm.

"What have you found?"

"The treasure we've been looking for!"

*****

Bigglesworth's Books was as it always was – a book scented peaceful oasis full of fascinating things that could draw one in for days on end. Mr Bigglesworth greeted Lance cheerfully, looking at the folio he carried with open curiosity.

"Ah... good day Mr Bigglesworth. Would... himself... happen to be here today?"

The old man met his eyes, as if weighing his answer, then gave a nod.

"Aye, he's in the usual place. I've no idea if he expects anyone, but take yourself up, and ask if he'll see you."

"Thank you."

Lance sighed with relief as he went through the curtain, out into the corridor, which was icy cold this late in the year, and up the stairs to that unprepossessing door. It opened to his knock, and Lord Setford simply raised an eyebrow, and waved him in. Only once he was seated, with the usual – and very welcome – cup of utterly perfect coffee, did either of them say anything.

"Thank you for seeing me with no warning of my calling."

Setford waved a hand.

"I make the assumption that, if you thought it necessary to come here, there is a matter of urgency to discuss."

"There is indeed."

They sipped their coffee for a moment, Lord Setford's sharp eyes going to the folio that Lance had set down on the couch beside him.

"You have found something important?"

It was a reasonable assumption, and Lance nodded.

"I have. In fact, I have found that which we believed might not exist at all."

Setford's eyes snapped to meet Lance's.

"Do you mean to say, m'boy, that you've found proof...?"

Lance reached out, and pulled a small side table to place it between them, then opened the folio, and set two pieces of paper on it – one, the cryptic note they had found in Harrington's papers, and the other the very clear note he had found in Merringway and Hellmont's papers. He waited as Setford examined them, seeing a tension in Setford release, as if the man had been part holding his breath for all these years since Traithewood had been banished to the countryside.

When Setford then lifted his eyes to Lance again, for a moment Lance would have sworn that the piercing grey orbs swam with unshed tears.

"I think this should be proof enough, my Lord."

"Indeed. You have performed a miracle here, m'boy. My faith in you was not wasted. Do you believe that with this, we are finally done with everything associated with that damnable conspiracy?"

"I do. And... I have a very personal request to make, if you will hear it?"

"I will, of course. What is it that you wish to ask?"

Lance shifted on the seat, suddenly nervous.

"I ah... I have, in the course of this investigation, discovered rather more than history written in various papers. I have uncovered a current subterfuge, one somewhat unwise, although one perpetrated for the best of reasons."

At that, Setford's eyebrows rose.

"I see. And what subterfuge might this be? It is related to all of this mess of treasonous plotting in some way, I assume?"

"It is. I will be blunt, but before I tell you the core of it, I will admit my own deep personal interest in the matter. What began as something which risked other people's futures has become something which also risks my own future happiness, for my heart is irretrievably engaged."

"Your heart, m'boy? Well, that is a most important matter, all by itself. Do tell me the rest."

"I have discovered that Traithewood's grandchildren have been here in London for much of the past year, each going by another name, and carefully concealing their actual family relationships. They came to the decision to do this independently of each other, and did so only in the hope that they might find a way to escape the prison of permanent isolation, a way to have a decent future themselves. For in isolation, how might they have ever found suitable people to marry? They were aware of the risk, and also hoped, rather naively, that they might perhaps find some way to prove their grandfather's innocence. For a long time, I was doubtful, suspecting them, as I did not have proof of Traithewood's innocence, but the further things went, the more I came to see that they too were innocent. And the more I investigated to prove that, the more my affections became engaged. You see, I have come to love Traithewood's granddaughter."

Setford gave a great guffaw of laughter.

"A dramatic tale indeed. So – who have they been passing for, in society? And what would you have me do – what is this request you wish to make?"

Lance sipped some coffee, searching for the right words, then gave up, and simply asked.

"I want to marry Lady Jenneta Darley, who has been in London this year as Lady Marisela De Leon. Her twin brother has been here as Lord Albert Carlton – in fact, in the end, I recruited him to help go through the last of the papers – that is how deep my trust has become. So – given that we now have this proof, is there a possibility that you could... intercede... with the King, such that at least the younger generation might be released from isolation? So that I might marry her, sooner rather than later?"

Lord Setford regarded him consideringly, for quite a long time, and Lance wondered if he had overstepped the mark, but eventually, Setford spoke.

"I will see what I can do. Obviously, I must take this proof to the King, regardless – and I know that he will be pleased to see it, for he was never happy with the idea that Traithewood might be a traitor. But what will happen then... that will take planning, for the King will need, if he is to fairly release Traithewood and his family from the constraints put upon them, to make it a very formal process. I expect that he will also grant them some lands and other advantages, as a kind of compensation. But perhaps I can persuade him to allow you a quiet marriage, at Holmdale Abbey or Traithewood Grange, by Special Licence, well before the main formalities are dealt with."

Relief filled Lance, and a bubble of happiness seemed grow within him.

"That is all I could ask for, my Lord. Thank you."

"I will send a message, asking you here to speak with me, as soon as I have any news. For now, rest, and know that I, and the King, hold you in high esteem for the work you have done."

*****

The following days seemed long, and Lance felt trapped, for while he could call upon Lady Jenneta, all was still, of a necessity, being kept quiet. In Society, there were murmurs, the beginnings of gossip, about the fate of Merringway, Diddington and Hellmont, although the whispers had no true information behind them. He went through his days feeling odd, as if he should still be digging through huge chests of papers – but those were gone, collected by Setford's men, and Lance found his days, as a result, surprisingly empty.

Then, but five days before Christmas, a message came from Lord Setford, summoning Lance to Bigglesworth's Books. Praying that it meant what he hoped for, Lance went, almost rushing out the door.

Chapter Seventeen

Jenneta was in the parlour, curled in the window seat with a book, yet again. Outside, a light snow was falling, making the square look like one of those idealised illustrations of Christmas settings which the periodicals insisted on publishing at this time of year. A chill radiated off the window, despite the thick drapes, and Jenneta shivered, thinking longingly of Las Palmas and its warmth. There was nothing particularly joyous about this Christmas, for she could not see her family. It was her birthday today, and that left her feeling empty, for it was Jenson's birthday too, yet they could not see each other. She had barely seen Lord Bainbrook since the drama at the Ball, and his call the next day, and part of her wondered if she had imagined it all. Had he really declared his love, declared his wish to marry her? The further in time she got from that day, the more improbable it seemed.

She shook her head, and turned back to the book, determinedly trying to convince herself that she was interested in the story. From downstairs, there came the faint sound of someone knocking on the door. Jenneta dropped the book, startled. Who would be calling? It was quite late in the day, and with the snow, she would not have thought that anyone would choose to go out on calls!

Jenneta reached down, and lifted the book from the floor, then set it beside her, before standing, and smoothing her skirts. Footsteps sounded outside the parlour, and Dona Esperanza hurried in.

"It's Lord Bainbrook, Marisela – are you respectable?"

"I am, although this gown is very plain..."

"It will do."

At that moment, Fortnum appeared at the door, and announced Lord Bainbrook. He stepped into the room, and Jenneta went forward to greet him. He took her hand, and bowed over it, pressing a kiss to the tips of her fingers as he did. Heat rushed through her from that touch, and she felt her cheeks flush.

Beside her, Dona Esperanza smiled.

"Lord Bainbrook, it is so good to see you again, please do be seated."

He did not release her hand, but led her to the couch, and settled beside her. Hope filled her – perhaps it had been real, after all? Lord Bainbrook cleared his throat.

"Lady Marisela... or rather, Lady Jenneta... I will ask again, as you did not, exactly, give me an answer, the day after that dreadful Ball. Will you marry me?"

Jenneta gasped, her eyes going to Dona Esperanza, who merely smiled and nodded, as if this was what she had expected all along.

"I... are you sure? And what of the King? I..."

Lord Bainbrook gave a soft laugh, and withdrew some folded documents from his pockets.

"What of the King? Here, signed and notarised as is appropriate, is his approval." He set one document down on the side table and unfolded the other. "And as to whether I am sure, here is a Special Licence..." he set that document down as well.

Jenneta's head spun as she leant forward to look at the pieces of paper which, by their simple existence, changed her life.

The missive from the King made note that evidence had been provided to him, which changed his opinion on the matter of the Duke of Traithewood's family – the results of which would be dealt with in good time – and which situation made him inclined to release Lady Jenneta and Lord Jenson from some constraints immediately – to whit, by allowing them to marry, should they so wish, so long as the marriage, should it take place before the greater scope of these matters was dealt with, happened at either Holmdale Abbey or Traithewood Grange, with no great public attention involved.

Jenneta sat back, stunned, and Lord Bainbrook took her hand again.

"Will you marry me, my darling? At Traithewood Grange, perhaps, in the next few days before Christmas?"

She lifted her hand, and discovered, to her shock, that tears were sliding down her face. He bent and softly kissed them away, as she struggled to find words. In the end, only the most important word managed to escape her.

"Yes."

*****

Jenson looked at the letter in his hand, hardly daring to believe that it was real. He read it again, the truth of it slowly sinking in, then he gave a whoop of joy which made his father look up from the newspaper with an expression of confusion.

"What is it, Jenson?"

"All we have wished for, and more. You'd best pack, for we need to be at Traithewood Grange in two days!"

With that, Jenson cast the letter to the table beside his father's plate, and near ran from the room, hurrying upstairs. The Marquess of Holmdale lifted the three sheets of paper and read, his expression going from confusion, to hope, and then to a joy as great as his son's.

He had given up all hope of this ever happening, after the long years of isolation, and now, to know that it had happened, and that, in addition, his daughter was to marry the heir to a Duke... It seemed impossible, and yet, here it was, quite clearly spelled out, in her letter, and in the copy of the document from the King. The third sheet was a shorter missive – an apology from Lord Bainbrook, regretting that he had not been in a position to ask Lord Holmdale for permission to marry his daughter, before he had asked Jenneta herself, and hoping that he might be forgiven.

Holmdale laughed, truly laughed joyfully, for the first time in near eight years, and went upstairs to speak to his valet, and set the household completely into panic at needing to pack and plan everything, and get to Traithewood Grange in just two short days.

*****

The church next to Traithewood Grange had not seen so many people since before the family had been consigned to isolation. Today, it was near full, with boughs of Christmas greenery and swathes of soft ivory cloth making it beautiful. The snow had stopped falling the previous night, and a pale winter sun sent beams of light through the stained-glass windows, rendering the interior of the church into a multicoloured painting, like something from an ancient hymnal.

The Duke of Traithewood sat proudly near the front, with Jenson beside him, and behind them many of the Grange staff, and the villagers, but on the other side of the church, there were people new to this place. The Duke and Duchess of Cairnmoor, Lord Kenric Williams, and Lady Ysolde Williams, and a number of the servants they had brought with them. To see people other than those of her family, and those who lived here, in this place made Jenneta catch her breath as she reached the door of the church on her father's arm.

This moment made it real – that they might have a life again.

Then her eyes went to Lance, where he stood, waiting for her, and everything save thought of him and their future together left her mind. He met her eyes and smiled – a smile that filled her with happiness, and she felt as if she floated to him, through the rainbow tinted interior of the church, her simple ivory gown, embroidered with deep violet flowers which matched her eyes, catching all of the colours as well.

The Vicar spoke the words, and Jenneta and Lance responded as required, both so caught up in each other as to be barely aware that anyone else existed.

When it was done, they turned, and went out into the sunlight, seeing the world as if it was entirely new. People came and spoke to them, and they responded, but Jenneta could not, later, remember a word of anything that was said.

In the carriage on the short drive back to Traithewood Grange, she simply rested her head on Lance's shoulder as he cradled her to him, and savoured the joy of the day. But once they reached the Grange, the day seemed to descend into chaos, with the staff attempting to utterly outdo themselves with the provision of food and drink, and a flurry of very odd seeming conversations, as the two families talked, attempting to get to know each other completely in a matter of a few short hours.

Jenneta watched it all with a rather wry smile on her face, until Lance asked her, quietly, what it was that amused her.

"Simple – so far, they all seem to like each other – that is a small miracle to be thankful for!"

He laughed, and they settled into some chairs in the parlour, thankful for a more quiet space. Soon, Jenson joined them, and Jenneta fixed him with a stern expression.

"Soon, brother, you must tell me all about what happened for you, in London – all of the things I couldn't see, and that you couldn't tell me at the time."

He gave a flourishing little bow, and she rather thought he'd learned that from Kenric.

"I will – so long as you do the same, and tell me all of what happened for you."

They laughed, and something in Jenneta which had been drawn tight for eight years loosened, the world feeling somehow realigned as it should be. She sighed, and Lance looked at her, then lifted her hand to kiss it, as if he had understood just what she was thinking.

Perhaps he had...

Epilogue

January 1822

Twelfth night had been and gone, and the activities of the Christmas season were at an end. Most had returned to their homes, leaving only Jenneta, Lance and Jenson at Traithewood Grange. Soon, Jenneta and Lance would remove to Cairnmoor Park for a visit, but for now, Jenneta was glad of the chance to sit and talk to her grandfather.

"But Grandfather, was there nothing you could do at the time?"

The Duke shook his head.

"Nothing at all. I tried. I have every paper related to that year and more locked away, and we went through it all, over and over again, but there was nothing solid."

"How did you bear it – to be so accused?"

The Duke turned his head away for a moment, and Jenneta wondered if she had gone too far with the question, but then he looked back, his eyes sad.

"In truth, I nearly didn't. At the time, I think I might have welcomed death – if it were not for the two of you."

Jenneta was shocked, and her next words were vehement.

"I am very glad that you are still here!"

The Duke laughed, shaking his head.

"Perhaps not for that much longer, for I am old. But still, I am most grateful for what you have done, Bainbrook. I will be able to die happy, now, knowing that my son and my grandchildren will be free in society again – although no doubt it may take the King some time to formally make that so."

Jenson spoke then, firmly.

"Do not speak of death, grandfather – I am sure it is a long way off for you still. But I agree, I will be most happy when the King does whatever he will, and we are all free again, as it should always have been. I will admit that, through this year, I have become curious about all that happened, about how you came to be suspected of association with those indulging in treason."

The Duke sat quietly for a few minutes after that, staring out of the window, then nodded, as if to himself. Without turning back, he spoke.

"If you are truly interested, Jenson, then you may have the boxes of papers I have kept. If nothing else, going through those may teach you how small the margin is between innocence and suspicion, and help you know what to avoid in your own life. Of course, we will wait until the King has done whatever he will, before you take them away – I am a most cautious man, after all."

"Thank you, grandfather."

Jenneta watched her brother, seeing so much change in him – not just from when she had left England, but even from when she had first seen him in London nine months ago. What did he hope to discover, she wondered? And did it matter?

She didn't know, but she suspected that she would find out, as the next year went by. The next year – the first of her marriage to the man she loved.

The Duke watched them all, then smiled, waving a hand.

"I tire – go and amuse yourselves, and leave me to rest."

They rose, obedient, and left him there.

Jenson went to the library, intent upon finding some specific books, but, as Jenneta hesitated, Lance turned to her with a grin.

"So, my darling wife, do you know the secrets of this house? Did you find them all as a child?"

She laughed.

"I did, or I thought I had at least, although I can't guarantee it. Shall I show you? After a year of hiding the truth of me from you, perhaps sneaking away and hiding with you will be much more fun..."

He pulled her to him, and pressed a kiss to her lips, which left her breathless, then stepped back.

"Lead on, then, and show me your secrets..."

The End

I hope that you enjoyed

'The Marquess Marries a Twin'!

You'll find a preview of the next book in this series,

'Lady Musette Ruins a Lord',

Which will be released in the first half of 2024,

after the 'About the Author' section of this book.

About the Author

USA Today Bestselling author Arietta Richmond has been a compulsive reader and writer all her life. Whilst her reading has covered an enormous range of topics, history has always fascinated her, and historical novels have been amongst her favourite reading. She has worked in many diverse industries and written a wide range of work, from business articles and other non-fiction works (published under a pen name) to various other genres of fiction, but regency fiction has always been a major part of her life.

Now, her main focus is Regency Historical Romance, and she has written more than 60 Regency books so far. These are in a number of series, with a few standalone novels as well, and she has multiple new series planned. The Derbyshire Set is comprised of 11 novels (9 released so far). The 'His Majesty's Hounds' series is comprised of 17 novels, all released. The Elbury Bouquet series is 8 novels, all released. The Nettlefold Chronicles series is seven novels, all released, the Regency Scandals series is four books so far, the Regency Gothic series is five books, and the Her Duke Collection is six books. She also has a number of standalone novels released, and four new series of novels at various stages of planning.

She lives in Australia, and when not reading or writing, likes to travel, and to see in person the places where history happened.

Be the first to know about it when Arietta's next book is released! Her website is not entirely up to date, as writing keeps distracting her from updating the website – but you can sign up to Arietta's newsletter there, at:

http://www.ariettarichmond.com

When you do, you will receive two free subscriber exclusive books - **'A Gift of Love',** which is a prequel to the Derbyshire Set series, and ends on the day that 'The Earl's Unexpected Bride' begins, and **'Madame's Christmas Marquis'** which is an additional story in the His Majesty's Hounds series.

These stories are not for sale anywhere – they are absolutely exclusive to newsletter subscribers!

Connect with Arietta:

Donate and support her on Kofi.com
https://ko-fi.com/ariettarichmondauthor

Follow her on Amazon –

https://www.amazon.com/Arietta-Richmond/e/B016GG1KJ6/

Like her Facebook Page –

https://www.facebook.com/AriettaRichmondAuthor

Follow her on Twitter –

https://twitter.com/AriettaRichmond

Follow her on TikTok –

https://www.tiktok.com/@ariettarichmond

Follow her on Instagram –

https://www.instagram.com/AriettaRichmond/

Follow her on Bookbub –

https://www.bookbub.com/authors/arietta-richmond

Follow her on Goodreads –

https://www.goodreads.com/author/show/14508806.Arietta_Richmond

Here is your preview of
Lady Musette Ruins a Lord

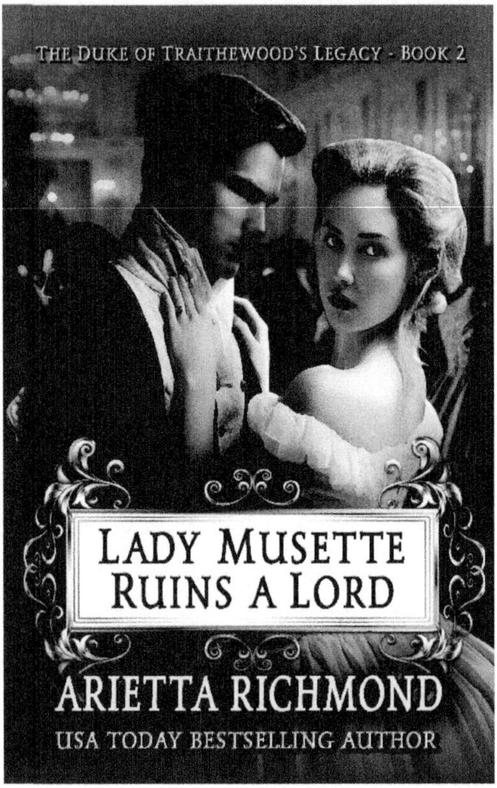

The Duke of Traithewood's Legacy - Book 2
Sweet and Clean Regency Romance

Arietta Richmond

Prologue

Her stomach turned over at the taste of him as he forced his lips down onto hers, but that taste was enough to break her out of the frozen stillness which her terror had caused.

She fought him then, frantic desperation driving her as she clawed at his face. He lifted his mouth from hers, cursing her, and she spun away from him as his hands on her shoulders lessened their grip a little.

For a moment, he still held her, but then, with a sharp sound, the flimsy cloth of her tiny sleeves tore away from her bodice, and his fingers slipped.

She was free.

She ran, utterly unaware of anything except the need to get away, although, deep in her mind, a little voice suggested that perhaps she should scream? Or at least gain some awareness of where she was going? That little voice was ignored, and she simply fled, heart pounding.

Fled until, that was, she collided with something – someone.

She staggered, nearly falling, nearly causing whoever she had collided with to fall as well, until strong hands caught her, gently, and with remarkable skill turned them both around such that they landed against a wall, rather than in a tangle on the floor.

As some semblance of sensibility returned to her, she lifted her eyes to examine the face of the man who held her. She should, after what she had just experienced, have been terrified by any man touching her – but somehow, she wasn't afraid of this man. He held her calmly, his astonishing violet eyes fixed on her face, and waited as she steadied.

It was only then that she became aware of where she was, and of the sounds around her.

They were in the ballroom, just beside the door to a corridor. And they were surrounded by the cream of the *ton*, all of whom, it seemed, were utterly engrossed by the spectacle of the sight of her, in her torn gown, shamelessly pressed against the body of a gentleman who cradled her in his arms.

If she had thought to run from ruination, she had failed. Instead, she had run straight into it.

Chapter One

Late March 1822

Lord Jenson Darley felt some degree of relief as he approached the far side of the ballroom. It had taken him near an hour to cross the room, for so many people had wanted to speak to him.

Yet again, he was stunned at the rate at which gossip traversed the *ton* – it was only yesterday afternoon that the King had finally issued the proclamation, freeing his family from isolation, and restoring all lands and funds to them and there was much work still to be done, putting everything in order. Yet this morning an invitation had arrived at the townhouse of his sister and her husband, where he was staying, asking his presence at this ball.

He had thought it wise to attend, to be seen, and accepted into society again properly. He had certainly not expected to be treated almost as the entertainment of the evening. He felt, already, rather exhausted by it all. He hesitated for a moment, but, at the sight of a number of young ladies and their mothers coming towards him, decided that perhaps he would go straight to the card room – where he would, hopefully, find Lord Kenric Williams.

Kenric, twin brother to Jenson's sister's husband, would have his finger on the pulse of the gossip, and the card room would allow Jenson to escape the ladies for at least a short while. That decision made, he moved again, taking the few remaining steps to the wall and reaching out, ready to push the door aside and slip into the corridor which led to the card room, as well as other parts of the house.

But his hand never touched the door – before it could, the door was flung open, and someone charged through, running, and collided with Jenson, rather forcefully. Instinctively, his reaching hand grasped them, catching them and spinning with the impact of their headlong flight, so that his back slammed into the wall beside the door, and the person – the woman, he now realised – fetched up hard against his body, enclosed in his arms.

The force of that sudden halt to her movement stole the breath from him, and for a moment, his head spun. Then, shaking the shock of it off, he eased his hands out to her shoulders, steadying her as she moved back a little, and caught her own breath. At first, she seemed unaware of him, of where she was, of anything, then, as he watched, her eyes cleared, and she focussed on his face.

She was, he realised then, quite stunningly beautiful. Her eyes were the colour of young spring leaves, and her hair – her rather disarranged hair, he noted, was a rich dark burnished gold. She was breathing hard, and she shook under his fingers – her expression, at first, was one of great distress, but that eased as she finally met his eyes. Once he took in more of her than just her face, he saw that the sleeves of her pale green gown were torn – near completely detached from the bodice, which was slipping in a manner likely to become, imminently, shockingly revealing.

Whatever had happened to set her running blindly was no doubt related to the torn sleeves – and it did not take much to guess that the unwanted attentions of a man may have been involved. He kept his hands on her gentle, even though part of him wanted to clench them into fists, and go in search of whoever had caused her this distress. He forced himself to stillness, to outer calm, and waited, not wishing to frighten her any further. She was still staring at his face, still apparently unaware of the people around them – people who were, en masse, staring at them with the sickeningly titillated delight which went with witnessing gossip worthy events as they happened. He rather thought that, no matter what else happened, he and this young woman were now doomed. If he had thought to re-enter society without scandal, she had just utterly removed that possibility.

Her breathing steadied, and she seemed, only then, to become aware of where she was, of the gathered mass of the *ton* around them, and of the fact that she was held in his arms. Carefully, he allowed his hands to drop away. Which movement must have made her aware of her shoulders, for she glanced down, and gasped, becoming, it seemed, only then conscious of the state of her gown. Her hands lifted, desperately holding the torn muslin in place, and she then turned her gaze to the room around them. At which point she stiffened, and swallowed, the reality of their circumstance obviously coming home to her immediately. Her eyes came back to him. All he could do was shrug slightly.

"I believe, my Lady, that we are past the point of waiting for someone else to introduce us. I am Lord Jenson Darley – and you are?"

He spoke as softly as he could, not wishing to add to the gossip any more than was unavoidable, and she gave him a shaky smile – he suspected that, in that moment, she was close to hysterical laughter.

"I am Lady Musette Farnham. I... I must apologise for my rather precipitate entry into the ballroom. I was...."

She appeared lost for a way to explain, and Jenson felt his heart go out to her, for surely maintaining her dignity at such a time was near impossible.

"...escaping from an untenable situation, which had been forced upon you by a man who had just proved that he was no gentleman?"

Her startled green eyes met his again.

"Yes, that is an accurate summation."

"Sadly, I fear that in escaping one bad situation, you have inadvertently cast both of us into a rather difficult circumstance."

"Indeed – In running from one type of certain ruination, I appear to have run directly into another, and one in which I have, without any intent, inextricably entangled you, Lord Jenson."

His eyes flicked around the room, and he noted the growing sound of whispers as news of what was occurring spread. The worst gossips of the ton were all nearby, indeed, the very worst, Lady Fotheringhampton, was, he now realised, right beside them, accompanied by her friends. It was a miracle that he had not crushed her when he had caught Lady Musette, and spun them against the wall. Her eyes were alight with a devilish pleasure. Had she heard their conversation? At that moment, she stepped forward, fixed her bright gaze on them, and spoke, in a rather loud voice.

"Dear me, what have we here? I do believe that I see scandalous and improper behaviour right before me. Behaviour deserving of nothing less than a betrothal..."

An icy chill ran through Jenson's veins – from the moment that Lady Musette had run into his arms, he had known that this was a possibility – it did not matter that he was not the one responsible for her flight, or her torn gown – he was the one who had been seen, in a very public place, embracing her in her obviously dishevelled state. And it had all happened so quickly that he suspected no one had truly seen what had occurred. He turned his eyes to hers, and saw the same realisation fill her. She took a slow, deep breath, and quivered where she stood. In that moment, Jenson wanted to reach out and pull her to him, to shield her from the vicious pack of gossips that surrounded them, to comfort her. Instead, he simply stood there, hesitating, knowing what he must do, yet unable to believe that there was no other option.

As he hesitated, a man pushed through the crowd, and came to stand beside them, glaring at them both. Lady Musette lifted her eyes to him, going pale.

"Father.... I...."

Well, that simplified matters.

"My Lord, I believe that, in the circumstances, I must ask you for your daughter's hand in marriage."

*****

Musette stood before her father's desk, the painted eyes of her ancestors staring at her from the pictures on the walls. She shivered, still struggling to believe all that had happened. They had just returned from the ball – which they had, perforce, left rather early – and he had called her in here to discuss just exactly what had happened to result in her becoming shockingly, scandalously betrothed in the midst of the ballroom. He looked up at her from his chair, seeming more frustrated than angry, for which she was glad.

"So, daughter, I would understand exactly what happened tonight, before I must discuss it all with your now betrothed on the day after tomorrow. I must say, I am disappointed – I told you, I explicitly asked you, to avoid all scandal. After what my fool of a cousin did last year, getting himself involved in that treasonous plot, we are lucky to still have a place in society. Be glad that he is my cousin through my mother's side, rather than my father's, or most likely we would already be paupers. But society suspects us, and will examine everything we do. Yet somehow, the importance of this appears to have escaped you, and you have brought us to society's attention in the most scandalous way possible, and with a man whose family were suspected of involvement too, and exiled from society for eight years as a result. If you had set out to make our lives difficult, you could not have done a more efficient job of it."

"I... I'm sorry Father. I didn't intend... It was all an accident."

"An accident? How does an accident produce a gown torn as yours is?"

He indicated the offending garment, which she still wore, the torn cloth pinned in place temporarily.

"It was not torn by Lord Jenson, Father."

"It wasn't? Well, I suppose that makes me feel a little better about the man. But if it wasn't him, who did tear it, and... how did you come to be in Lord Jenson's arms in the ballroom?"

Musette wrung her fingers together, and a little half sob escaped her. Her father frowned. Swallowing, she forced herself to speak.

"I was foolish Father." Another sob escaped her, but she worked herself to go on. "I allowed Lord Perchman to convince me to walk with him – I was flattered, and silly. But he quickly took me to a private room off the corridor – I did not resist as I didn't want to create a scandalous scene." At hearing her own words, she gave a half-strangled laugh. "But once in the room, he took hold of me, and... and... he forced his kisses upon me. After a moment's shock, I fought him, trying to escape – I clawed at his face, and he eased his grip, which allowed me to pull away, at the expense of my sleeves. Then I fled – I was not aware of where I was going, or of anything at all, except fleeing, until I collided with Lord Jenson, who, luckily, had the balance and skill to catch me, and turn us to land against the wall, rather than in an inelegant tangle on the floor. It was only unfortunate that where I collided with him was in the doorway into the ballroom..."

With that, she broke down into true sobs. Her father rose from his chair and came to take her gently in his arms.

"My poor dear girl! I hope that you've left Perchman with some very obvious scars on his face – he deserves it! But... if all that Lord Jenson did was to be unfortunate enough to be in the wrong place, and have you run straight into him, causing him to catch you, why did he offer for you? Many men would have loudly disclaimed all responsibility."

Musette forced her sobs to slow, and lifted her head to meet her father's eyes.

"I don't know why he did it, but I am utterly grateful that he did."

"You are truly willing to marry him? For if you are not, I am sure that..."

Musette shook her head.

"No – that would cause an even bigger scandal. I am willing to marry him. He... he was gentle and kind, when he had no reason to be. I am not afraid of him, like I was of Lord Perchman."

"Then marry him you will. And the day after tomorrow, when I speak with him, to begin the arrangements, I will thank him for his kindness. I just hope that both our families previous proximity to that treasonous plot does not cause us problems in the future..."

*****

Kenric had insisted that Jenson not go to his own new – and currently very empty - townhouse, but instead that he should accompany Kenric to Jenneta and Lance's home, where Kenric had been staying. He put it inarguably, in his usual style.

"As you have failed me, Jenson, by allowing yourself to be trapped by a young Lady, I insist that I be given the chance to ensure that you get the next bit right. Really, when I was teaching you, as Lord Albert, how to go about in society, I thought that I had made 'how to avoid being compromised into marriage' the first, and most important lesson! You need to talk this though, and have a solid plan in place before anything else can occur."

Having a solid plan appealed to him at that moment, and, if he were honest, going home to a totally empty house did not seem like a pleasant concept. So he had allowed himself to be bundled into Kenric's carriage. Now, here he was, standing beside Kenric as Jenneta's butler opened the door. The poor man's expression was near comical as he took them in, having obviously not expected to see Kenric for many hours yet, and Jenson not at all.

"M... my Lord? Is all well? I did not expect...."

Kenric waved a languid hand.

"Certainly, all is well, Wherring. The ball simply became too dull for us to remain, once the excitement we had created died away." Then Kenric leaned close to the butler and lowered his voice to whisper. "But do be a good chap and don't tell anyone about this – if the *ton* knew I'd left a ball early and just come home, it simply wouldn't do – it'd ruin my reputation amongst the high flyers."

And with that he winked at the proper looking butler, and led Jenson into the house. The door closed behind them, and the butler's voice followed them towards the stairs.

"Lord and Lady Bainbrook are in the family parlour, my Lord – should I send up some refreshments?"

Kenric paused and turned to speak over his shoulder.

"That a capital idea, Wherring. I suspect we'll need them."

"Very good, my Lord."

They shed their outer coats and hats, handing them to the footman who watched, curious, then set off up to the parlour. All of a sudden, Jenson felt like turning and running from the house – how was he to explain what had happened to his sister and brother by marriage?

"Umm, Kenric... what are we going to say?"

Kenric laughed, which did nothing to soothe Jenson's nerves.

"Simple. We're going to tell them the salient points first, then, once they're over the shock, we will sit down and discuss the detail. Leave it all to me."

They stepped into the parlour, and Jenneta and Lance turned surprised faces to them. Kenric grinned.

"We are home early because Jenson has managed to get himself ruined by a Lady, and agreed to marry her, all before the eyes of the *ton*."

Jenneta near dropped her teacup.

Read the rest as soon as its released – go to

https://www.ariettarichmond.com

Other Books from Arietta Richmond

Books in The Duke of Traithewood's Legacy Series

Books in the Regency Gothic Series

Books in the A Duke's Daughters – the Elbury Bouquet Series

Books in the His Majesty's Hounds Series

Claiming the Heart of a Duke

Intriguing the Viscount

Giving a Heart of Lace

Being Lady Harriet's Hero

Enchanting the Duke

Redeeming the Marquess

Finding the Duke's Heir

Winning the Merchant Earl

Healing Lord Barton

Kissing the Duke of Hearts

Loving the Bitter Baron

Falling for the Earl

Rescuing the Countess

Betting on a Lady's Heart

Attracting the Spymaster

Courting a Spinster for Christmas

Restoring the Earl's Honour

From Soldier Spy to Lord (Books 1 to 3 as a set)

To Love a Determined Lady (Books 4 to 6 as a set)

Love Heals a Lord (Books 7 to 9 as a set)

To Love a Dashing Lord (Books 10 to thirteen as a set)

For a Lady's Honour (Books 14 to 17 as a set)

The Barrington Saga (all books related to the Barrington Family)

Books in The Derbyshire Set

The Earl's Unexpected Bride

The Captain's Compromised Heiress

The Viscount's Unsuitable Affair

The Count's Impetuous Seduction

The Rake's Unlikely Redemption

The Marquess' Scandalous Mistress

The Marchioness' Second Chance

A Viscount's Reluctant Passion

Lady Theodora's Christmas Wish

The Derbyshire Set Omnibus Edition Vol. 1 (the first three books all in one)

The Derbyshire Set Omnibus Edition Vol. 2 (the second three books all in one)

The Derbyshire Set Omnibus Edition Vol. 3 (the third three books all in one)

Books in the Regency Scandals Series

Books in the Nettlefold Chronicles

Regency Collections with Other Authors

Love in Autumn

Regency Christmas Proposal

Love, One Regency Christmas

Love, One Spring Season

A Regency Romance Summer Collection
Regency Summer

A Regency Romance Summer Anthology
Regency Summer Secrets and Soirées

A Regency Christmas Together

Regency Christmas Delight

A Regency Romance Summer Anthology
Regency Mid-Summer Mischief

A Regency Romance Christmas Anthology
Regency Missives and Mischief

A Regency Romance Summer Anthology
A Regency Summer Garden

A Regency Romance Christmas Anthology
A Regency Christmas Doubled

A Regency Romance Summer Anthology
Regency Summer Scandals

A Regency Romance Christmas Anthology
An Earl for Christmas

The Her Duke Collection

Themed Regency Collections

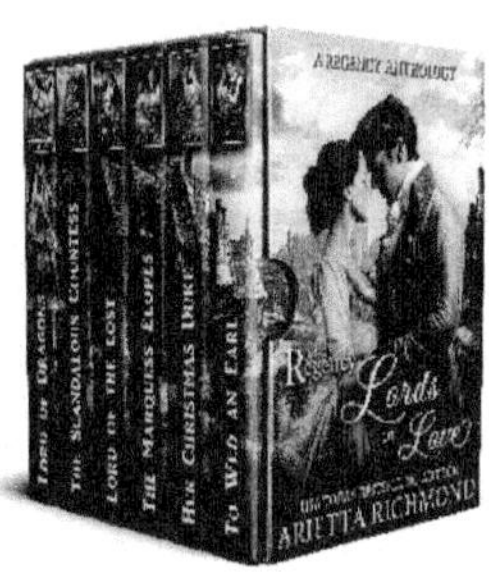

Other Books from Arietta

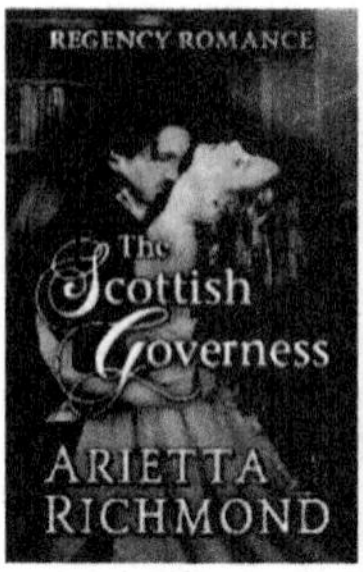

Regency Colouring Books

More coming soon!

Other Books from Dreamstone Publishing

Dreamstone publishes books in a wide variety of categories ranging from Clean Romance to Erotica, to Kids Books, Books on Writing, Business Books, Photography, Cook Books, Diaries, Colouring books and much more. New books are released each month.

Be the first to know when our next books are coming out

Be first to get all the news – sign up for our newsletter at

http://www.dreamstonepublishing.com

Printed in Great Britain
by Amazon

40632530R00304

THOSE WHO LISTEN, CHANGE THE WORLD

•

The Little Book on Dialogue
from the Nobel Peace Center

PREFACE

Good dialogue can resolve conflicts; poor dialogue can create them. At the Nobel Peace Center, we are inspired by the Nobel Peace Prize laureates. Many of them have achieved the near impossible in their struggles for peace, fundamental human rights, freedom of expression and disarmament. They have used a wide range of methods and tools. Nevertheless, there is little doubt that dialogue and listening to the opinions of others has been crucial in their work to create change.

Most of us can remember deep conversations that have had a profound impact on us. Often such conversations are encounters with unfamiliar views that provide new perspectives on ourselves or our surroundings. Conversely, quarrels and conflicts can be experienced as very unpleasant. For many of us, they are so challenging that we prefer to avoid them. In a survey the Nobel Peace Center conducted in 2021, six out of ten said that they have refrained from addressing difficult topics with close relations because this makes them uncomfortable. As many as 46 percent said that they have lost friends or family due to poor dialogue.

The Nobel Peace Center wants to put dialogue on the agenda. We want to contribute to a culture where the public dialogue includes different points of view and allows a diversity of expressions. Dialogue has an important precondition – a belief that we all have something in common. Therefore, dialogue can help us relate to one another and interact in a more peaceful way.

"As many as 46 percent said that they have lost friends or family due to poor dialogue."

This little book on dialogue provides knowledge, tips and examples, and illustrates how a number of Peace Prize laureates have used dialogue in their work. Dialogue expert Chro Borhan is responsible for the content. She has developed the principles based on dialogue theory and linked them to the Peace Prize laureates work. For more information, visit our website.

We hope to inspire you to use dialogue theory methods in your meetings with other people, in order to create enriching, safe and peaceful relationships.

Kjersti Fløgstad
Executive Director
Nobel Peace Center

Chro Borhan has written this
text about dialogue, with support from:
Kristine Fallet, Johanna Foss, Kim Reksten Grønneberg,
Bjørn Helge Vangen and Kjersti Fløgstad.

Thanks to our supporters

Design: Vivi Holtfodt
Translation from Norwegian: Kevin Reeder
Printing and binding: Rolf Ottesen AS - ottesen.no
Year: 2023

ISBN 978-82-92703-12-0

CONTENT

WHAT IS DIALOGUE?

In everyday speech, dialogue is often used to refer to any conversation. But our exploration of dialogue as a method of communication and conflict resolution shows that it is far more than a normal conversation, debate, negotiation or discussion. Dialogue requires something more and therefore also leads to something more.

Dialogue is used as a method to improve communication between people, to resolve conflicts and to shed light on an issue from different points of view. An inclusive process, it can help us find new solutions. You cannot win a dialogue, and there should preferably be no losers.

In today's world of polarization, echo chambers and entrenched views, we believe that the work of the Peace Prize laureates can play a role in inspiring better dialogue. With more knowledge about dialogue methods, we can use them to enrich our interactions with other people and the situations we find ourselves in. If we use dialogue as a principle, we will reduce echo chambers, hate speech and hostile expressions of opinions. Dialogue will help to increase understanding and respect in the public discourse, and in both work-related and private contexts.

We have defined eight principles that together create good dialogue:

1. Dialogue should be a basic attitude
2. Create safe spaces
3. Include all relevant parties
4. In a dialogue, you must listen
5. Let everyone share their experiences
6. Ask questions
7. Talk about the difficult topics
8. Contribute to forgiveness and reconciliation

Knowledge of these principles and an ability to apply them, or just a few of them, can make a big difference in discussions and debates. This book presents knowledge, tips and examples, and illustrates how a number of Peace Prize laureates have used the principles in their work.

Inspired by Mandela and other Nobel Peace Prize laureates who have worked to promote dialogue, the peace bench is designed specifically to bring people together.

"The best weapon is to sit down and talk"

- Nelson Mandela

Nelson Mandela and Frederik Willem de Klerk received the Nobel Peace Prize in 1993. Among other things, Mandela was praised for entering into dialogue with his former enemy without letting bitterness and hatred prevail.

Nelson Mandela has inspired our work with dialogue. With him as an example, the Nobel Peace Center has had a peace bench designed and placed outside our building. The bench is called "The Best Weapon" to reflect the historic Mandela quote, "The best weapon is to sit down and talk".

Designed by Snøhetta on behalf of the Nobel Peace Center, the bench was constructed by Vestre in aluminium made by Hydro.

Sit down with someone you want to talk to – see what happens!

NOBEL PEACE PRIZE LAUREATES AND DIALOGUE

They are role models and heroic figures for millions of people around the world. Most of us think that it is impossible to be like them, but we can all learn something from them.

Many Peace Prize laureates have been branded liars by their opponents, or have been accused of being traitors by the authorities for promoting alternative political solutions. Many of them have been threatened with death and several have been subjected to serious violence. Nelson Mandela was imprisoned for 26 years. Shirin Ebadi eventually had to leave Iran, even though she was actually trying to enter into dialogue with the authorities to create positive change in her country. Martin Luther King Jr. was killed at the age of 39. He believed in dialogue and said that one of the main causes of structural racism was a lack of understanding of Black peoples' lives caused by segregation.

Peace Prize laureates have often been barred from making important decisions. Dialogue, on the other hand, aims to include all relevant parties. Inclusion is such an important principle that it cannot be overlooked. By including people, dialogue incorporates different perspectives and creates a better basis for making decisions. Collective wisdom is the key word. Juan Manuel Santos, who received the Nobel Peace Prize in 2016, understood this. During the peace process in Colombia, he facilitated dialogue meetings between the parties involved in the long-running, armed conflict. Everyone was to be heard. Even the peace agreement was the subject of a referendum.

The Tunisian National Dialogue Quartet received the Peace Prize in 2015. They quickly understood that to avoid civil war in Tunisia after the Arab Spring, they would have to create dialogue between all the political parties. It was essential to find a common starting point for a political agreement. The process was initiated and led by organizations that believed in dialogue, and not by the politicians themselves. Everyone participated voluntarily to find a peaceful solution for the country, using dialogue as a working method.

Women are often excluded from important decisions. Leymah Gbowee, Ellen Johnson Sirleaf and Tawakkol Karman, who received the Peace Prize in 2011, promoted women's participation in decision-making processes.
They all had non-violence as a starting point and were convinced that all conflicts could be resolved without the use of violence or war. Jane Addams, who received the Nobel Peace Prize in 1931, helped establish the Women's International League for Peace and Freedom to prevent conflicts by initiating international dialogue between nations.

"Collective wisdom is the key word"

The results of the work of Peace Prize laureates are sometimes difficult to understand, and it is certainly difficult to do them justice in a short text. In this book, we have selected eight Peace Prize laureates who have all worked to create dialogue. Although we could definitely refer to many more, we have tried to select laureates who embody the eight principles of good dialogue. Common to the laureates' work is that they make visible both the complexity and the humanity in a good dialogue process.

THE EIGHT PRINCIPLES OF DIALOGUE

1. Dialogue should be a basic attitude
2. Create safe spaces
3. Include all relevant parties
4. In a dialogue, you must listen
5. Let everyone share their experiences
6. Ask questions
7. Talk about the difficult topics
8. Contribute to forgiveness and reconciliation

Principle 1

DIALOGUE SHOULD BE A BASIC ATTITUDE

Dialogue is something more than just communication skills. It is about aiming to treat people with respect, equality, openness and curiosity.

Dialogue as a basic attitude allows you to gain better insight into other people's thoughts. It lets you share your own experiences and opinions in an effective way, improves your communication skills and makes relationship building easier. By actively choosing dialogue, you can gradually change your own behaviour, exercise greater influence in your relationships and contribute to positive change in your neighbourhood.

With dialogue as your basic attitude, you have decided to live life in an open, curious and reflective way. Even when you find yourself in difficult situations that are challenging on a professional, personal or private level, you dare to meet other people as equals, show respect and try to listen with empathy. Dialogue should be an attitude that you embody wherever you are and constantly influences how you approach life.

WHAT TO CONSIDER:

1. Treat everyone with respect and equality, no matter what
2. Be open, curious and reflective
3. Decide to apply the principles of dialogue in encounters with others

Nobel Peace Prize laureates and the dialogue approach

It takes courage to enter into dialogue. You risk not getting the same basic attitude and respect back. Nevertheless, many people try to have dialogue as a basic attitude, and several of the Peace Prize laureates have promoted peace and justice through persistent attempts to create dialogue.

The 14th Dalai Lama

– Inner peace, non-violent philosophy and ecological sustainability

The 14th Dalai Lama was awarded the Nobel Peace Prize in 1989 for his peaceful attempts to use tolerance and mutual respect to uphold the historical and cultural heritage of the Tibetan people. This created an opportunity for him to present a plan for peace and human rights in Tibet. The goal was to start serious negotiations on the country's future status, but the Chinese government rejected this.

Despite brutal mistreatment of the Tibetan people, the Dalai Lama continues to uphold his belief in non-violent resistance and wants dialogue with the Chinese authorities to find a solution based on compromise and reconciliation. His Buddhist philosophy of peace is based on the idea of a universal responsibility for all living things, both people and nature itself.

The Dalai Lama's perspective is characterized by respect, equality, openness and curiosity. Actively seeking kinship with both people we deeply disagree with and with the nature that surrounds us – a continuous dialogue process – is his most important practice.

"In human societies there will always be differences of views and interests. But the reality today is that we are all interdependent and have to co-exist on this small planet. Therefore, the only sensible and intelligent way of resolving differences and clashes of interests, whether between individuals or nations, is through dialogue."[1]

The 14th Dalai Lama
Photo: Håkon Mosvold Larsen/Nobel Peace Center

Principle 2

CREATE SAFE SPACES

In our busy everyday life, it can be difficult to find good opportunities for dialogue. It is important to seek out the safe spaces and opportunities, both physical and mental in nature. Dialogue can take place wherever people are treated as equals and with respect, openness and curiosity.

Safe spaces are essential if participants are to engage in the dialogue by expressing themselves openly and honestly. To ensure safe spaces, you should consider the following: Will everyone be able to see and hear each other? How can you ensure physical distance without losing human contact? Where should the various parties sit? Where and when should they meet? You must set aside enough time to allow for dialogue, be aware of the balance of power in the room and ensure the absence of all forms of violence.

If the dialogue is conflict-based and heated, you can use an external dialogue facilitator, who can either be a professional (for example a therapist), a friend or a colleague. The facilitator must not act as a judge or lawyer, but rather help to create a physical and mental safe space. The facilitator helps participants to achieve a constructive dialogue.

TO FUNCTION AS A FACILITATOR, YOU MUST:

1. Remain an impartial third party and support all relevant parties in the dialogue.
2. Ensure that everyone is listened to and that it is safe to ask open and exploratory questions.
3. Conduct conversations with all parties prior to the dialogue to get enough information to facilitate a safe space; what is confidentially shared with you in these conversations must not be shared with others in the group
4. Plan what to say when the parties first meet, including explaining the framework for the dialogue, your own role and any ground rules.
5. Make sure to keep the space safe and be ready to end the dialogue if something unexpected comes up that makes it dangerous or impractical to continue.

Although this advice may seem quite technical and for "professional" use, some of the principles can still be useful in more everyday situations.

Nobel Peace Prize laureates and their attempts to create safe spaces

Several Peace Prize laureates have tried to create safe spaces for dialogue. Some of them have wanted to resolve disagreements in a dialogical and non-violent way, but have been met with violence and threats. Thus, not enough safe space has been established for dialogue.

Betty Williams & Mairead Corrigan

– Non-violent philosophy and local peacekeepers in Northern Ireland

For Betty Williams and Mairead Corrigan, dialogue became much more than just conversation. They were both awarded the Nobel Peace Prize in 1976 for their efforts to establish a non-violent grassroots movement that aimed to create interaction and trust between Catholics and Protestants during the conflict in Northern Ireland.

The road to peace was paved with personal meetings. Williams and Corrigan organized joint peace marches, peace groups, and voluntary activities for Catholics and Protestants. Within a safe framework shielded from imminent threats of violence, it became possible to build trust between the parties through cooperation. Williams and Corrigan found that opponents who met in person showed greater motivation for peace and aversion to violence. People who previously stood on opposite sides of a violent conflict now had the opportunity to see, hear and get to know each other.

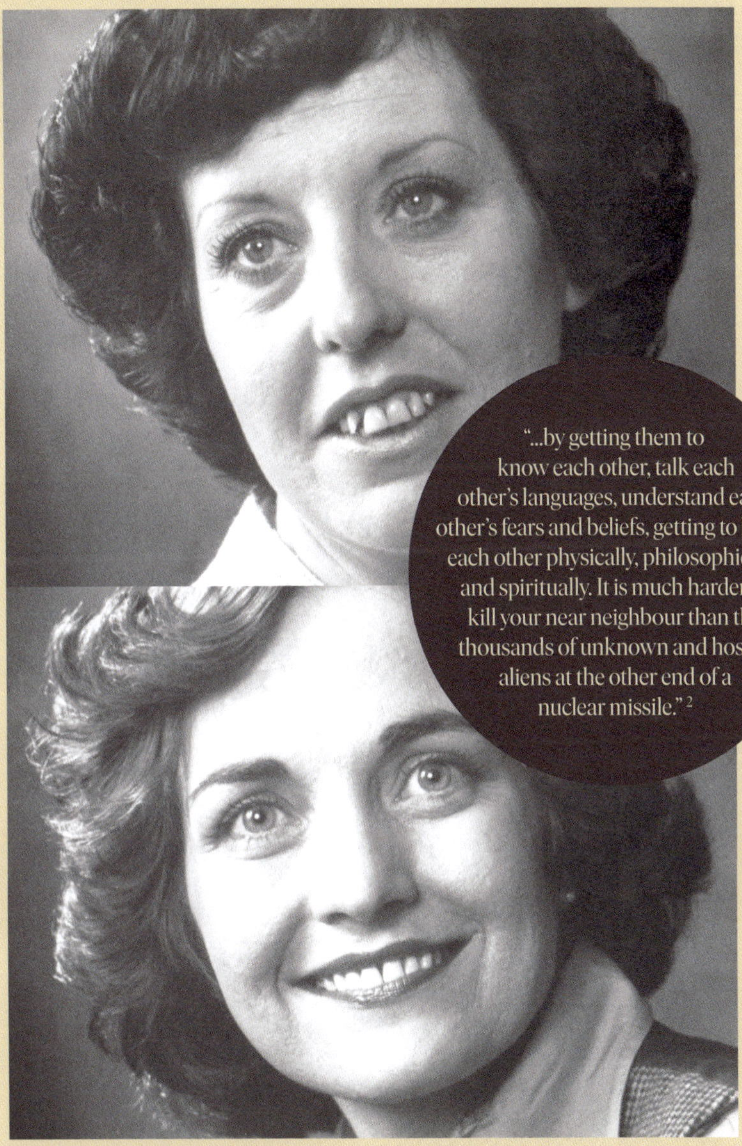

"...by getting them to know each other, talk each other's languages, understand each other's fears and beliefs, getting to know each other physically, philosophically and spiritually. It is much harder to kill your near neighbour than the thousands of unknown and hostile aliens at the other end of a nuclear missile."[2]

Betty Williams (over) Mairead Corrigan (under)
Photos from the Nobel Foundation Archive

Principle 3

INCLUDE ALL RELEVANT PARTIES

Who decides who should be invited into a dialogue? An experience of omission and exclusion can contribute to creating divisions and obstruct participation.

Inclusion is a method that brings more people into a dialogue, holds more people accountable and gives more people a sense of belonging to the process itself. Active participation increases the possibilities of finding collective solutions.

By inviting and including people with different backgrounds in a dialogue, you will gain a more diverse perspective on your life at home and in the workplace, as well as a more diverse public debate. This will provide a broader basis for making decisions. A collective collaboration begins when you include people. This creates a stronger commitment to and increased participation in the building of democracy and in the creation of important institutions. Conflicts are resolved more effectively by inviting everyone to the table.

AN INCLUSIVE PROCESS:

1. Invite all the relevant parties.
2. Ask the question:
   Who needs to talk to whom about what, where and when?
3. Ensure a transparent and open process about who should participate in the dialogue.
4. Try to include everyone who should talk to each other. There may be vested interests in not inviting relevant parties to the dialogue.
5. Find out if a party wants to set the agenda themselves, and will not give others access to important arenas where topics are raised and decisions are made.
6. Sometimes someone refuses to join a dialogue.
   Respect that this is their right.

Nobel Peace Prize laureates and inclusion

Many Peace Prize laureates have worked to create inclusive decision-making arenas. Several have experienced being prevented from speaking and being barred from important negotiations. In many cases, minorities, women and children have been left out of decisions that concern them. It is crucial that we allow a larger part of the population to have a say. To create lasting change, we must open up the conversation to people with different backgrounds, roles and perspectives. Many Peace Prize laureates have understood and done just that.

The Tunisian National Dialogue Quartet

– Democracy and national dialogue

Following the Jasmine Revolution (the beginning of the Arab Spring), Tunisia was on the brink of civil war. Just when everything could have collapsed, 21 parties managed to agree on how to create a national constitution. Today, it is considered the most egalitarian and democratic constitution in the Arab world. One of the success factors in this turnaround operation was the Tunisian National Dialogue Quartet, which received the Nobel Peace Prize in 2015.

The Quartet was a temporary gathering of four central organizations that represented different sectors of Tunisian society and therefore were in a good position to negotiate. They invited 21 political parties into a national dialogue that allowed each party to have a say. Their national dialogue process shows what is possible when multiple parties are invited to the negotiating table. That the country's Islamist and secular forces could agree on common solutions shows how different voices can agree, even in situations that at first seem insoluble.

"Consensus requires well-planned preparation, genuine willingness for dialogue, pre-agreed controls of work and a framework in which ideas and viewpoints are shared by various political factions. In particular, a sponsor trusted and appreciated by all parties concerned should undertake the task of running and deepening the dialogue until it achieves its objectives."[3]

Image top f.l.: Houcine Abassi, Mohamed Fadhel Mahfoudh. Image bottom f.l.: Abdessattar Ben Moussa, Wided Bouchamaoui © Photo: Johannes Granseth / Nobel Peace Center

Principle 4

IN A DIALOGUE, YOU MUST LISTEN

Empathic listening requires you to listen to other people with kindness, so that they feel seen and heard during the dialogue. You listen with deep respect and humility to what is being said. Listening this way leads to increased understanding and empathy.

When people live in segregated societies, their opportunities to listen to each other are limited. There are fewer common arenas and safe spaces, which means that more conflicts can arise than necessary. Listening is more than merely hearing, listening requires focus and presence.

In conflict situations, it can be especially helpful to listen to different elements of a story – facts, feelings and needs.

Listening is a technique that must be practiced. You must remember to really listen and show that you are doing so. You will benefit from listening in meetings with your partner, your children and colleagues, and especially when you disagree with someone or find yourself in a conflict.

TIPS FOR GOOD LISTENING:

1. Listen to what is being said. Do not let your own thoughts and prejudices interfere with your ability to listen. Your perceptions can easily lead you to judge others long before they have finished speaking, and thereby limit your listening skills.

2. Do not give advice unless it is requested.

3. Do not interrupt. Let the other person finish talking.

4. Do not capture the conversation by drawing parallels to your own experiences, e.g., "I have experienced that too!" Allow the other person their time; you will get yours.

5. Be empathetic and show understanding for the other person's situation. Being empathetic means that you understand the other's feelings, without necessarily feeling them yourself.

6. Do not presume to know other people's opinions.

Nobel Peace Prize laureates and empathic listening

For many years, humankind has been practicing selective listening and using it consciously to oppress groups and individuals. Many Peace Prize laureates have experienced this for themselves. They have tried to find safe spaces for dialogue and non-violent action, but have not been met with respect and understanding. On the contrary, they have been met with violence. There are many reasons for the structural violence and racism that Black citizens have suffered in the United States, but in this context we will focus on the social consequences of a lack of listening and dialogue.

Martin Luther King Jr.

– The struggle for civil rights in the United States

Already as a child, Martin Luther King Jr. experienced how Black people lacked a voice. The racial divide was evident. Particularly in the southern states, Black people risked threats and violence if they spoke out. Nevertheless, King chose to devote himself to the non-violent struggle for civil rights in the United States. For this he was awarded the Nobel Peace Prize in 1964.

What can we do when those in power do not want to listen? King's life provides an answer to this. In 1955, he started a campaign to get the US government to make the policy of racial segregation in the southern states illegal. He remained a supporter of Gandhi's philosophy of non-violence, even when racists responded with violence against the peaceful protests of Black people. In 1963, 250,000 protesters marched on the Lincoln Memorial in Washington. There, King gave his famous "I have a dream" speech. It must have had an effect, because the following year, President Johnson passed a law banning all racial discrimination. Using non-violent protest, King made the situation of Black people more visible. His legacy inspires us to this day.

"People fail to get along with each other because they fear each other. They fear each other because they don't know each other. They don't know each other because they have not properly communicated with each other."[4]

Martin Luther King Jr.
Photo from the Nobel Foundation Archive

Principle 5

LET EVERYONE SHARE THEIR EXPERIENCES

Research can determine whether something is valid or not. But when in dialogue with one another, it is important that we recognise each other's experiences as equally as important as our own.

In a dialogue, everyone's statements and opinions are equal.
This implies that any statement will be valid, because it comes from the individual's own perspective. However, this does not mean accepting racist or sexist statements, for example. These can be questioned in order to understand their origins.

The recognition that everyone is in possession of parts of the truth allows us to get a more complete understanding of the situation.

One of the great dialogue theorists, David Bohm, believed that a fragmented understanding of the world is one of the main reasons for conflicts and war. When you divide up reality and analyse it from a particular point of view, you create a partial understanding rather than trying to understand the whole. Many people subscribe to one particular point of view, becoming totally engrossed in it and its minutiae.

Bohm believes that dialogue can help to change a fragmented way of thinking, and that this is the main reason why it is needed in all walks of life, relationships, organizations and professional disciplines. Dialogue contributes to a holistic worldview where we understand that everything is connected with everything, and that caring just about parts of the whole has consequences. He believed that dialogue was the method of creating peace.[5]

In any dialogue, we should speak from our perspective and use "I-messages". This reveals our truth and creates familiarity and empathy. By using neutral forms such as "people" or "one", you create a distance between you and the message. This becomes especially important when clarification is needed after conflicts or misunderstandings.

Speak from your perspective, explain how you felt when someone acted the way they did. Conclude by describing your need for reparation.

Nobel Peace Prize laureates show the way

One reason that conflicts get entrenched can be a lack of understanding of the other party's opinions. This will always be a challenge. An important strategy used by several Peace Prize laureates has been to create a process whereby differing parties can share their stories, experiences and insights. This can produce progression in a conflict that at first seemed insoluble. In order to move forward, it can be crucial to allow victims of violence or oppression to express themselves.

Juan Manuel Santos

– Dialogue and the peace process in Colombia

President Juan Manuel Santos was awarded the Nobel Peace Prize in 2016 for his efforts to end the 50-year-long armed conflict in Colombia. Santos took the initiative to start dialogue and peace talks between the government and the guerrilla group FARC. Santos' Prize was both recognition of his peace facilitation and an encouragement to continue the talks on peace and reconciliation. Santos was the recipient of the Prize, but the Norwegian Nobel Committee emphasized that it was also a tribute to the Colombian people, who never gave up hope of a just peace despite great trials and abuses, and to all parties who contributed to the peace process.

For many years, it was taboo to talk about the traumas and consequences of the civil war in Colombia. Inspired by the peace process in South Africa, the victims of the war were invited to share their experiences during the peace negotiations. In addition, the perpetrators were also given the opportunity to tell their stories. While the process was certainly painful and difficult, it also laid the foundation for the dialogues that followed. The victims' rights had to be safeguarded before the peace process could happen.

"Victims want justice, but most of all they want to know the truth, and they – in a spirit of generosity –desire that no new victims should suffer as they did."[6]

Juan Manuel Santos
© Photo: Mads Nissen/Politiken

Principle 6

ASK QUESTIONS

Asking open-ended and exploratory questions is helpful for understanding other people, especially when you disagree profoundly with someone. Dialogue does not try to force everyone to agree, but does involve everyone sharing their experiences. This allows you to question those you disagree with or do not understand properly. Well-formulated questions can be crucial.

Dialogue does not rule out constructive criticism; it requires that you take responsibility for how you express yourself and consider how to facilitate a safe, honest and open dialogue. Open-ended and exploratory questions help you to understand other people better. By opening up for deeper conversations, you get answers to your questions. You also give others the opportunity to clearly communicate their opinions and to explain their fears, hopes and experiences.

Dialogue is not the same as debate, but it is possible to arrange public dialogues and to invite dissidents into a dialogue process. This does not mean that you accept or legitimize radical, racist or offensive statements. You respect the person expressing the opinions, and acknowledge both their experiences and that their opinions are true to them.

HOW TO ASK GOOD QUESTIONS:

1. Ask open-ended questions (which do not allow for yes / no answers).
2. The questions should encourage more reflection and curiosity during the dialogue process. Therefore, formulate them carefully.
3. Ask questions in such a way that others want to clarify their views.
4. Ask questions that help you understand what you disagree with or do not understand.
5. Questions that start with *what* and *how* are less confrontational than those that start with *why*.
6. There are no stupid questions. Ask questions whenever you need to, so you don't later regret not asking them. Often, several people are wondering about the same thing.

Nobel Peace Prize laureates and the art of asking good questions

Many laureates have been involved in defending basic human rights. In countries that do not provide basic rights, laureates have challenged the authorities by asking questions that encourage them to take responsibility. In order to uncover human rights violations, it is important to involve a country's citizens. Questions that increase awareness and engagement also make it easier to create understanding between parties. It is crucial to trust that dialogue can change attitudes.

Shirin Ebadi

– The struggle for human rights

In 2003, Shirin Ebadi became the first Muslim woman and first woman from the Middle East to receive the Nobel Peace Prize. She had made a name for herself by promoting democratization and human rights in her home country of Iran. Ebadi was one of the first female judges in Iran, but was ousted after Khomeini came to power in 1979. She continued working as a lawyer to protect human rights, and regularly documented human rights violations committed by the authorities. In 2000, she was arrested for criticizing the Iranian regime.

Even after experiencing Khomeini's Islamist revolution, Ebadi kept her faith in dialogue, convinced that it was the key for achieving women's rights. She didn't believe that fundamental change could result from revolution, but rather from non-violent protests involving a dialogue that aims to create necessary changes in policy. Through dialogue, Ebadi presented a different way of relating to dissidents than that used by those in power. Dialogue proved to be particularly important in a country characterized by powerful disagreements.

"I maintain that nothing useful and lasting can emerge from violence" [7]

Shirin Ebadi
Photo from the Nobel Foundation Archive

Principle 7

TALK ABOUT THE DIFFICULT TOPICS

Dialogue is not a perfect interaction in which everyone must be kind and diplomatic. We must also dare to talk about what is difficult. Dialogue provides an opportunity to put a difficult topic on the agenda. It helps us to build bridges with others, both on an individual level and between nations.

Conflict-prevention work is just as important in peacetime. To talk about what is difficult is the first step in contributing to positive change and development.

There has been a noticeable polarization in public debate in recent years. An increasing number of topics have become controversial or risky to engage with. In particular, online hate speech has become more common. This has at least two effects: many people hesitate to share their opinions; others participate in "echo chambers" characterized by disregard for opinions or facts that challenge their own or the group's attitudes. These chambers avoid conflicting views and strengthen the group's belief in its own opinions.

Dialogue involves responding to differing opinions with open-ended questions to explore people's thoughts, attitudes and prejudices. Dialogue safeguards freedom of expression because it maintains respect for the people expressing statements and attitudes, while also holding them accountable for their opinions. It also allows us to respond to opinions with open criticism in the form of questions that everyone in the dialogue can engage with and express their opinions of.

Dialogue does not necessarily mean accepting the opinions expressed, but it does require respect for the person expressing the statements and attitudes.

There is a difference between acceptance and respect.

Nobel Peace Prize laureates address difficult topics

Many Peace Prize laureates have raised sensitive or controversial issues, sometimes based on their own experiences or those they have witnessed. This has not been welcomed by everyone, especially those with vested interests. Some issues can also be so painful and stigmatizing that many prefer to remain silent about them.

Nadia Murad

– Sexualized violence as a weapon of war

Talking about rape and sexual abuse is taboo in many societies. Nevertheless, Nadia Murad dared to speak out about what she and several thousand other Yazidi women experienced when they were attacked by Islamic State (IS) in 2014. In 2018, Murad and Denis Mukwege received the Nobel Peace Prize for their opposition to sexualized violence used as a weapon of war.

Nadia Murad belongs to the Yazidi minority and was born and raised in the village of Kocho, in northern Iraq. On August 3, 2014, Kocho was one of the first Yazidi villages in the area to be attacked by IS. While many in Murad's family were executed, she herself, along with around 6,800 other women and girls, were kidnapped and sold on as sex slaves. Murad was raped, beaten and tortured before she managed to escape three months later. When she then spoke out and told the world about the atrocities she and other Yazidi women were subjected to, it helped put sexualized violence in armed conflicts on the agenda. Murad herself did not want to enter into a dialogue with the abusers, but rather made a general appeal to us all and created space for a broader dialogue on this critical topic. By telling her story, she has placed the duty of responsibility on the abusers, as well as helping the Yazidi women and other victims of sexual violence.

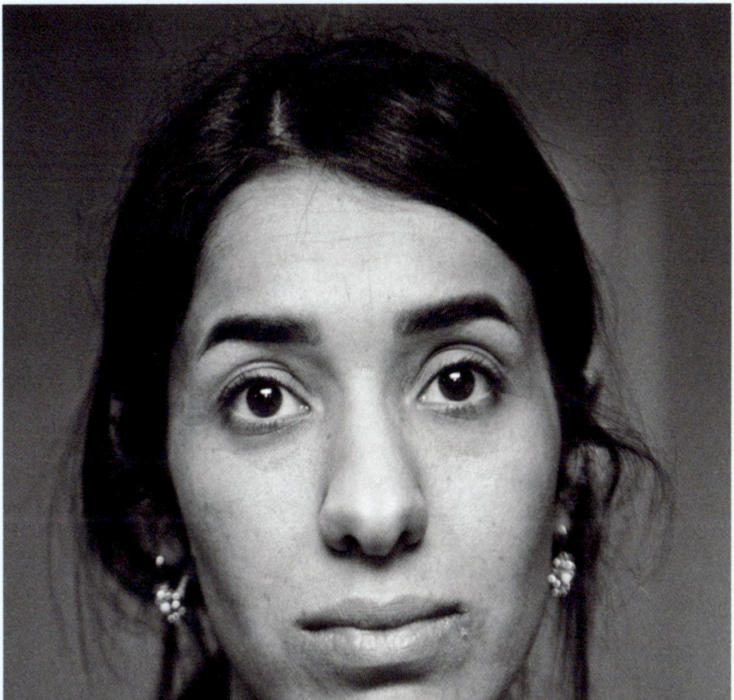

"Let us all unite to fight injustice and oppression; Let us raise our voices together and say: No to violence, yes to peace, no to slavery, yes to freedom, no to racial discrimination, yes to equality and to human rights for all."[8]

Nadia Murad
© Nobel Media AB. Photo: K. Opprann

Principle 8

CONTRIBUTE TO FORGIVENESS AND RECONCILIATION

Reconciliation means reconciling yourself with something that has happened in the past. We all have something we should forgive others or ourselves for. This may be misdeeds, but can also be something we failed to achieve or that didn't go the way we wished.

Dialogue provides an opportunity to overcome life's difficulties and face future challenges in a more constructive way. Dialogue can enrich your life and make you wiser and more resilient. To force solutions or compel parties to agree on something on the wrong basis will often result in conflicts flaring up again. Hurried decisions or incorrect solutions can, at worst, aggravate the situation or cause wounds and traumas to remain unprocessed with the parties involved.

Desmond Tutu was a master of forgiveness. In *The Book of Forgiving: The Fourfold Path for Healing Ourselves and Our World*, he presented four steps:

1. Tell the truth.
   Telling the truth will help give strength to the victim.

2. Express the pain.
   Shaming pain and pretending it does not exist means that it remains in your body and heart.

3. Forgive.
   Forgiveness is a conscious choice we make.
   We must acknowledge our compassion.

4. Renew or let go of the relationship.
   By telling the truth, expressing your feelings and finally forgiving, you will be able to decide whether to renew or let go of the relationship.[9]

Nobel Peace Prize laureates and forgiveness and reconciliation

Several Peace Prize laureates have been occupied with forgiveness and reconciliation. By ensuring that everyone explains their role in a course of events, those who have been wrongdoers in war are held accountable. For some, this is part of the healing process that follows the trauma inflicted by war. Several laureates have deep experience of this type of dialogue process.

Desmond Mpilo Tutu

– Forgiveness provides freedom and release from past wounds

A Nobel Peace Prize laureate who has worked ceaselessly for forgiveness and reconciliation is Desmond Mpilo Tutu. He was awarded the Nobel Peace Prize in 1984 for his role as a unifying leader in the non-violent struggle against the apartheid system in South Africa. Nevertheless, it is for the work he did after receiving the Prize, that Tutu is best known today.

His leadership of the Truth and Reconciliation Commission in 1995 has left its mark. Tutu's groundbreaking contribution was to show in practice how to enter into dialogues with the goal of forgiveness and reconciliation. His perspective was founded on a belief that forgiveness and reconciliation are natural and positive. The Commission's work certainly opened up a painful process, but Tutu was unwavering in his belief that we are capable of forgiveness and reconciliation. He also maintained that its work was necessary for South Africa to be able to completely liberate itself from oppression and apartheid.

"Forgiving is not forgetting; it's actually remembering - remembering and not using your right to hit back. It's a second chance for a new beginning. And the remembering part is particularly important. Especially if you don't want to repeat what happened."[10]

Desmond Mpilo Tutu
Photo from the Nobel Foundation Archive

WHAT GOOD DIALOGUE CAN CREATE

We must not accept everything that is said in a dialogue. Nor do we always have to agree. Nevertheless the process is still able to create change. When we talk to each other, we sometimes expand our perspectives and are able to understand one another better. Change does not have to happen overnight; it may be slow processes that take time. When we reach out to one another, we sometimes also change ourselves.

Dialogue creates change both within us as individuals and at group and community levels.[11]

INDIVIDUAL:

1. Increased self-reflection and insight about yourself, your own thoughts, attitudes and values.

2. Increased empathy for others. The traditional way of thinking about groups, which creates images of enemies, "us" and "them", is weakened.

3. Increased understanding of others, when you gain insight into their thoughts and life experiences.

GROUP AND COMMUNITY:

1. Dialogue ensures reflection on how history has influenced the development of social structures and conditions. Thus, we gain a common basis to speak from.

2. Increased sense of belonging in local communities by creating possibilities for dialogue and voluntary work. For example, when you actively share your experiences of life in the neighbourhood with each other and find similarities, this results in less division.

3. In the long run, improve society's structures and communication skills. More people will dare to take the initiative and use dialogue rather than other forms of communication and methods.

4. Opportunity for a collective analysis of reality and joint discovery of the causes and consequences of developments and events in society.

5. Collectively identify different ways to interact.

CONTINUE THE DIALOGUE

Dialogue requires time and patience and the absence of violence. The principle of non-violence applies to mental as well as physical violence. Safe spaces are necessary for people to be able to participate, be engaged, be honest and open, and share their experiences and perspectives with others.

It takes just one person to initiate a dialogue. Longer dialogue processes to bring about social change require broad participation and cooperation. Dialogue involves communication skills, but also develops an attitude to life. Dialogue resolves conflicts in a constructive way, prevents new conflicts and creates better interpersonal relationships. It is also an effective method for building bridges between peoples, groups and nations.

Of course, dialogue will not solve all our challenges. It takes effort and determination to create good relationships. Furthermore, to create a good and peaceful society and bring about sustainable change requires a range of initiatives. Though the state must do its part to contribute to increased welfare and development, each individual can also make a positive contribution to change. With the help of dialogue, you can put different topics on the agenda and enable more people to be able to participate. Together we can find creative solutions to our many challenges.

At the Nobel Peace Center, we hope that dialogue can help everyone find better ways to live in their community, despite disagreements. When values such as mutual respect and equality and methods like empathic listening are more common, nurturing relationships and friendships will become just as important as finding solutions to disagreements. The Nobel Peace Prize laureates have believed in, practiced and promoted this in their struggles for peace and justice.

Photo: Håkon Mosvold Larsen / Nobel Peace Center

"In my opinion, one of the most important things we can do today is to educate future generations about the need to use dialogue, understanding and a non-violent approach to resolving conflicts."

- Greeting from the Dalai Lama to the Nobel Peace Center's 10th anniversary in 2015.

MORE READING ABOUT DIALOGUE

Schirch, Lisa & Campt, David.
The Little Book of Dialogue for Difficult Subjects: A Practical, Hands-on Guide

Tutu, Desmond Mpilo & Tutu, Mpho.
The Book of Forgiving: The Fourfold Path for Healing Ourselves and Our World

Garrett, Peter.
A New Kind of Dialogue

Buber, Martin.
I and Thou

Isaacs, William.
Dialogue: The Art of Thinking Together

REFERENCES AND SOURCES

1. The 14th Dalai Lama (1997, March 10). *Statement of His Holiness the Dalai Lama on the Thirty-Eighth Anniversary of the Tibetan National Uprising Day.*

2. Williams, Betty (1977). *Nobel Lecture.*

3 Bohm, David (1996). *On Dialogue.*

4. Abdessattar Ben Mousa, The Tunisian National Dialogue Quartet (2015). *Nobel Lecture.*

5. King Jr., Martin Luther (1958, May). *Advice for Living, Ebony Magazine.*

6. Santos, Juan Manuel (2016). *Nobel Lecture.*

7. Ebadi, Shirin (2003, 19 October). *Al-Sharq Al-Awsat.*

8. Murad, Nadia (2018). *Nobel Lecture.*

9. Tutu, Desmond Mpilo & Tutu, Mpho (2014). *The Book of Forgiving: The Fourfold Path for Healing Ourselves and Our World.* HarperCollins Publishers.

10. Desmond Mpilo Tutu (2006) *The Optimist Daily.*

11. Schirch, L. & Campt, D. (2007). *The Little Book of Dialogue for Difficult Subjects: A Practical, Hands-on Guide.* Good Books; Skyhorse Publishing.

Stenersen, Øyvind, Libæk, Ivar & Sveen, Asle (2001). *Nobels Fredspris - Hundre År for Fred - Fredsprisvinnere 1901- 2000.* Cappelen.

Where nothing else is listed, all other quotations and texts about the Nobel Peace Prize laureates are taken from their Nobel Lectures and the Norwegian Nobel Committee's announcements. These are freely available on the Nobel Prize website, www.nobelprize.org.

NOTES